MW00390596

"In language that is both lyrical and exquisitely rendered, Sidney Morrison constructs a sweeping historical narrative about the life of the greatest orator of the 19th century and the most photographed man in America, Frederick Douglass. In this brilliantly constructed work, Morrison manages to achieve something remarkable—gift the reader with a gripping and absorbing story that manages to offer new insights into the complex life of an extraordinary human being who has been the subject of scholarly research for generations. Morrison's vivid imagination coupled with his thorough research and mastery of language works in seamless harmony to craft a stunning portrait of this prophet of freedom. It is a towering achievement."

—**MASUD OLUFANI**, multidisciplinary artist, writer, and actor, *No Cowards in Our Band*, based on the *Life and Work of Abolitionist Fredrick Douglass* (PBS TV)

"An engrossing and moving look at the complex figure of Frederick Douglass, the men—and women—who shaped his life, and his fight against injustice and search for self amid a nation's struggle to achieve its ideals."

—**SUSAN HIGGINBOTHAM**, author of *John Brown's Women*

"Morrison's portrayal of Douglass, a remarkable, complex man, will challenge, inspire, and deeply move you. Dramatic, immersive, brimming with insight, and entertaining, this is a must-read novel. Douglass was a leader in the struggle for equality and justice for all, and Morrison's life of Douglass is a timely reminder of our heroic past and our unfinished work."

—**SENTA GREENE**, CEO of Full Circle Consulting Systems and Co-author of *I Can't Come to School Today. . . Mom is in Prison and I Don't Have a Ride*

"Sidney Morrison's novel about Frederick Douglass is an important novel of epic sweep that I urge everyone to read. It is a great story about a great American."

—**JAY NEUGEBOREN**, author of *Imagining Robert*, *The Stolen Jew*, and *After Camus*

"We owe a debt of gratitude to Sidney Morrison for providing a fresh perspective on an iconic American figure. Morrison sheds new light on dimensions of Douglass' life rarely explored. In his riveting narrative Frederick Douglass emerges as a complex character, all the more worthy of our admiration and exceedingly relevant to our times."

—**BEN Z. ROSE**, author of *Mother of Freedom: Mumbet and the Roots of Abolition*

FREDERICK DOUGLASS

Hawthorne Books & Literary Arts
hawthornebooks.com

Library of Congress Cataloging-in-Publication Data is available

Library of Congress Control Number: 2023942521

First US Edition 2024
Printed in the United States of America
ISBN 978-0-9988257-9-3 (hardcover)
ISBN 979-8-2181942-2-2 (ebook)

FREDERICK DOUGLASS

A NOVEL

SIDNEY MORRISON

For Robert Ballenger,
and in memory of Lieutenant John W. Foreman

No part of the past is dead or indifferent.

—FREDERICK DOUGLASS

History is not the past. It is the present.
We carry our history with us.
We are our history.

—JAMES BALDWIN

TABLE OF CONTENTS

PROLOGUE: 1844

Frederick

"BOY, YOU'RE NO SLAVE," shouted the old white man who stood in the fifth row, interrupting Frederick with a voice so deep it should not have come from a slanted, withered body. "You're just another lying, big-headed nigger."

A few in the audience gasped, but no heads turned to investigate or condemn, as if the old man had been appointed to say what the others were thinking.

A young, wiry man with a bulbous nose stood. "Yes, prove it! You sure don't talk like one."

Frederick's neck veins throbbed against his crisp shirt collar and cravat; he didn't know what to say. He was usually quick to respond to verbal affronts with sarcastic remarks or pointed questions, but now he took a deep breath, lifted his wide chest, and glared at the hundreds who packed the town hall that Sunday afternoon in Massachusetts.

He waited.

Still wearing the dark coats and frocks required for the morning's church service, the people before him sat on benches with backs in rigid formation, a field of jutting rocks. Beyond the closed windows, the red, yellow, and gold leaves shimmered in the sunlight.

Rage reddened the face of the young man, and he looked around, agitated by the silence. "Prove it," he yelled. "Prove it!"

Now ignited, the audience began to chant, "Prove it." And as the chant swelled to a chorus of shouting and stomping feet, the customary reserve of New Englanders was unmasked to reveal the brutality of mobs, the faces of witch-burners, the crowd that chased William Lloyd Garrison in Boston.

Frederick smirked.

After three years as a lecturer, discovered by Garrison and other white abolitionists during an antislavery convention on Nantucket Island, Frederick had told his story countless times throughout New England, noticing surprise and suspicion in whites, overhearing the whispered comments about his yellow skin, his articulate speech. But before today he had never been confronted about his past with such raw effrontery.

He wanted to shout them all down with his bass–baritone voice. Frederick had learned to use this powerful instrument and could chastise like the best preachers or curse like a dockworker.

Frederick knew what he had to do. A shouted denunciation like the jeremiads of the Old Testament he quoted often, another story with more graphic details of his past, more revelations of the emotional pain he felt as a child—none of these would not satisfy the demands for proof. He needed to shock the audience, force their silence, destroy the last vestiges of doubt.

Frederick started to unbutton his overcoat. With every button, he recalled the snide remarks, the contemptuous questions, the mocking surprises: *Where did the abolitionists find him? His white father explains his intelligence. Who does he think he is, talking like a white man?* Even some of his white antislavery colleagues had suggested that he speak less formally and add plantation talk to his narratives for greater authenticity.

He unbuttoned his waistcoat and thought, *How dare you presume to judge me. I am your equal. No, I am better.*

Frederick deliberately folded his coats before he placed them on the chair behind him. He took the suspenders off his thick shoulders, leaving them as dangled hoops on his hips, and pulled at the tail of his shirt after releasing the lower buttons. Wanting no interference, he avoided the widening eyes and gripped hands of the meeting chairman, James Buffum, whose Quaker reserve was as tight as the cravat around his neck.

"Friend Douglass, what are you *doing*?" asked Buffum, motionless as he stared, at the nearby table.

"I'll *show* them," he said to Buffum. Frederick's face was hot. He was sure that the ridge across the top of his nose, scars from injuries long ago, bulged.

"No," said Buffum. "The ladies . . ."

"Let them *see*," said Frederick.

A few men pulled their female companions' arms, ushering them out. Most people remained transfixed as Frederick, gathering and lifting the folds of his shirt, turned around to show the work of the slave breaker Edward Covey, who was hired to crush his spirit and almost drove him to suicide. Frederick was fifteen, his lacerations the stories of an unforgettable year at a remote farm on the Eastern Shore of Maryland.

Exposing the gashes healed by thick lard, Frederick pulled his shirt as high as he could and held it there for what seemed an eternity. He counted the thirty seconds as he stared ahead, hearing the pounding of his heart, feeling the sweat of his brow, holding his breath as he clenched his teeth and felt the shocked silence.

The doubting old man then started to applaud. The singular clapping of his hands crackled like snapping wood in the silent hall. Another man clapped, and then another. Soon there was a standing ovation and shouted cheers.

"Hear, hear!"

"Yes, sir!"

Frederick turned his head to the right and grinned, enjoying Buffum's open-mouthed surprise as much as the deafening noise. He quickly tucked in his shirt and put on his coats before turning.

He waited for absolute silence, staring at three stone-faced men with folded, defiant arms at the back of the room. One of them lowered his arms, but still Frederick waited, demanding the capitulation of the other two.

The second man lowered his arms. Then the third. Only then did Frederick return to the exact place where he had stopped and continue his well-rehearsed speech. He concluded with his now famous parody of southern preachers defending slavery. "Oh, if you wish to be happy in time, happy in eternity, you must be obedient to your masters, their interest is yours," he intoned, enjoying his mastery of mimicry developed in childhood. "God made one portion of men to do the working, and another to do the thinking. Now you have no trouble or anxiety. But ah, you can't imagine how perplexing it is to your masters and mistresses to have so much thinking to do on your behalf. Oh, how grateful you are obedient to your masters! How beautiful are the arrangements of Providence! Look at your hard, horny hands—see how nicely they are adapted to the labor you have to perform. Look at our delicate fingers, so exactly fitted for our station, and see how manifest it is that God designed us to be this His thinkers, and you the workers—Oh, the wisdom of God."

Frederick knew his audiences. With laughter and applause, white Methodists, Baptists, and Congregationalists relished their superiorities. Southerners were the *true* Christian hypocrites.

Nevertheless, Frederick believed he had debased himself. The lifting of his shirt was vulgar and melodramatic, unworthy of a gentleman; it reminded him of the slave block where slaves were examined for physical assets and liabilities. He had successfully rebuked these New Englanders, but he knew he would never reveal his scars again. With no bill of sale, he had to find another way to prove himself. Legally, he was still a fugitive.

Frederick's credibility was now a matter of open discussion in *The Liberator*. One correspondent wrote, "Many persons in the audience seemed unable to credit the statements which he gave of himself and could not believe that he was actually a slave. How a man, only six years out of bondage, and who had never gone to school a day in his life, could speak with such eloquence, with such precision of language, and power of thought, they were utterly at a loss to devise."

After three years standing before the white public, Frederick could tolerate the whispered suspicions, the innuendo, the gossip shared by colleagues. But *printed* suspicion made his situation intolerable. He needed to respond in kind because he understood the power of the printed word, the fear it inspired, the hope it nurtured. As a youth, Frederick had dared to teach adult slaves how to read, creating a school in the forest of the Eastern Shore, and was almost lynched for it. Print mattered. A book could change the world.

Frederick knew what to do: write an autobiography and name family members, masters, and plantations. He would tell *everything* except the details of his escape and put the entire matter to rest. There was no other choice. All he had was his word. His career as a legitimate antislavery agent was at stake.

Frederick Augustus Washington Bailey Douglass had a book to write.

PART I: 1836–1845

Anna Murray Douglass and William Lloyd Garrison

1.

FREDERICK BAILEY WAS ACTIVE in his church choir and the debates of the East Baltimore Improvement Society. He loved to sing, and he loved to talk even more, always arguing. The women talked about him at the meetings, at church and the socials, noting his assets, making comparisons with the other men, and granting his superiority on several scales of value. There was no denying it. He was a tall, handsome man, and very smart. But his enslavement was an insurmountable barrier; no free woman in Baltimore was going to marry a slave.

But Anna Murray had different ideas.

She was an excellent cook and domestic servant at the house of Mr. Wells, the postmaster on South Caroline Street. A practical hard worker, she lived frugally and saved money for emergencies and the future, a possible life with a husband and children, like her parents, former slaves who raised twelve children on the Eastern Shore. She wanted at least four or five.

Anna had no suitors. They preferred younger, light-skinned girls. Now twenty-five, she was not pretty and fretted about her thick arms. Anna appreciated her black eyes, most of the time. Large and bright, they could detect foolishness in seconds, wither opposition with a glance, and see beauty in a pebble or a grain of rice. They also made men squirm. Then, at an Improvement Society social, she met Frederick Bailey.

Like most of the women attending the social, Anna had provided food, in her case the best fried chicken in the Point. She was one of the servers in the food line when Frederick came to the table. Quickly, she thanked him for comments made earlier. "Mr. Bailey, I liked what you said about those people wanting us all to leave."

"The colonization people?"

"Yes, them. This is *our* country, too."

"Yes," he replied before moving on.

Later, Anna saw an opportunity when she was talking in a small group of women. When Frederick began to approach them, they glanced over their shoulders, rolled their eyes, and quickly left. Anna did not go with them. Instead, she smiled and extended her hand, approaching him. "Mr. Bailey, I'm Anna Murray, and we all talk about you. You're hard to miss."

Her boldness clearly surprised him, but she was more taken by his cool acceptance of compliments. He was not shy.

"I've been the tallest since I can remember, or at least since I started to really grow," he replied.

"And you're good with words. You sure know how to talk and give speeches. I like the sound of them words, even though I can't read them."

"I have a hard time with many of them, too, in the Bible and in Mr. Shakespeare, especially in Mr. Shakespeare."

"I can't read none of them," she said.

"None?"

"I'm not ashamed. I never learned to read, too busy cooking and cleaning, and helping with raising white children. I keep thinking the time will come, and the time just gets away from me."

"It's never too late. I had a school on the Eastern Shore with grown men and women. They learned."

"I'm from the Eastern Shore, too," she said. "From Denton."

"Tuckahoe," Frederick replied. "Do you miss it?"

"I miss my brothers and sisters. I'm one of twelve. Do you miss your family?"

"What's left of it? No. My mama is dead. I don't know who my father is, and I barely know my brother and two sisters. Baltimore is what I know and want to know."

"I came here when I was seventeen. I had to get away from slavery, even though my mama and papa got their freedom papers just before I was born, a month before."

"And you're *free*," he said, unable to hide his bitterness about the singularity of his legal condition.

"And you'll be free someday," she said.

"I'm not counting on my master to do what that white man did for your family. You don't know Hugh Auld."

"Baltimore is too small a place for a man like you, Mr. Bailey. So, when are you leaving?"

Alarmed, Frederick looked around the room and came closer to Anna, whispering, "Miss Murray, we can't talk about this. This is dangerous, too dangerous. I could get arrested if someone heard."

She looked around, and then said with a casual lack of concern, "Nobody can hear us, and besides, my question could mean all kinds of things."

"Miss Murray, please."

"I can help."

"I hate to be rude, but we can't talk anymore." He turned away, obviously shaken.

When Anna saw Frederick next at church, she turned and smiled, nothing more. Then at midweek Bible study, she smiled at him and nodded her head before turning back around to listen to the explanation of Job. During a brief break, she said to Frederick, "Help me understand what makes the good Lord make children suffer?"

He answered, "I don't know either, and I'm tired of asking. I'm get tired of thinking, too. Sometimes, I just want to live."

Frederick turned away. They didn't talk anymore that evening. She saw him at another social and, from across the room, waved her hand. He waved back but didn't come to her.

At yet at another social in June, 1838, Anna again waved at Frederick, and this time he came to her, smiling and extending his hand. "Miss Murray, I must apologize for not coming sooner. I thought I should come with a better answer to your Job question. But I realized that if I had an answer as a condition for ever speaking with you again, that it might never happen, speaking to you again, that is, since the ways of the Lord may never be understood by me or anyone else for that matter."

Frederick sounded nervous, his words rushed. Anna took this as her cue to try boldness again. "Oh, don't worry, Mr. Bailey, since we are *not* courting, you haven't damaged your chances with me."

Frederick stepped back to protest, his words now more rushed and agitated. "Miss Murray, I don't think it proper to suggest *even* the possibility . . ."

Still smiling, Anna took a step toward him and gently said, "Mr. Bailey, I am only stating the obvious. These are places for people to see people and look them over, even at church. The good Lord might be at the front in the voice of the preacher, but everyone else in the pews is looking to the sides, measuring and planning and scheming."

"In church!"

"At socials, too, like this one."

"Are *you*?" Frederick asked, his eyes critical.

"Yes," she replied.

"Then good day, Miss Murray," Frederick said, starting to turn away.

"Wait, Mr. Bailey, I didn't mean to be rude. I was just telling the truth."

"I don't mean to be reminded again that I'm not good enough for *free* women."

"I said no such thing."

"You don't have to. I see the looks, the moving away. I know."

"I haven't looked away."

That comment disarmed Frederick, and he smiled again. "Only you have been willing to take the time. What should we talk about?" He paused, and then answered his own question. "Let's not talk about Job, though."

"Fine. Let's talk about family, then."

"Not that either."

Anna objected, "We all have them, and we all have stories about growing up."

"Some of them are not happy ones."

"Then let's talk about only the happy ones."

"They start happy, but they don't end that way."

"We all die, Mr. Bailey, even with a happy life before it."

"What about heaven?" Frederick asked.

"I hope for heaven," Anna replied.

"Hope, only hope?"

"Do you know anybody who came back to describe it?"

"No, but I have faith in the promises of Jesus."

"So do I." Anna was slightly irritated. She took a breath and replied, "Faith I understand. We all decide who to believe, who to trust, who to count on. We do it all the time, like I'm doing now."

"What do you mean?" Frederick's voice trembling slightly, as if it were the most important question of the afternoon.

"I believe in your future. I put my faith in you when I told you I would help you, and I meant it. *That's* faith."

He lowered his eyes, clearly moved, perhaps humbled. "Thank you, but what if I don't deserve your faith? What if you're wrong?"

"That not for *you* to decide. This is about *my* faith."

"And mine, too."

"Then do you have faith in *me*? Will you let me help you?"

He paused again and said, emphatically, "Yes."

"Good. Just let me know when the time comes."

"I don't want to go alone," Frederick said. "But I will have to. All my friends are free and will not leave their family and friends."

She almost asked, *Are we courting, Mr. Bailey?* But she refrained and said, "Maybe you will find someone to go with you."

"No, I will have to go alone because if I get caught, I don't want something to happen, an arrest, or worse. I can only take the risk for myself."

"Then that person can follow you, come later, after you reach freedom."

"They will still face so much risk, take so many chances."

"That's faith, Mr. Bailey."

"Could you leave Baltimore?" Frederick asked.

Anna took a deep breath. "Are we courting, Mr. Bailey?"

"No," he said. "It's too early for *that*."

Mortified, Anna could only say weakly, "I see."

"We're agreeing to get to know each other better for a future decision,"

Frederick elaborated, making the awkward situation worse.

"I see," she repeated.

"Total strangers get married, and even if they're not strangers they get married when they don't like each other. I've seen enough of that. He gets a cook; she gets a house. I don't want that."

She wanted to slap him, knock all this marriage talk out of his big mouth. What could *he* know about marriage? He was a man-boy, just twenty. He was in the habit of giving lectures, but he needed to approach some subjects with a measure of humility, at least a pinch of it.

But instead, she agreed. "I don't want that either." She tried boldness one last time that day. "When will you know?"

"Know what?" he frowned. He obviously knew she was asking about marriage. "On the day I decide to leave, you will know."

"Then what if you don't leave, then what?"

He hesitated, calculating to say the right thing.

Too late. "I see," Anna noted.

"See what?"

"What's more important."

Frederick had a confrontation with Hugh Auld on Monday, August 7, 1838, and the future was settled at last. When Frederick told Anna his story, his voice shook with the rage Hugh had ignited.

2.

FREDERICK HAD BEEN GRANTED permission to hire himself out and live in his own place, paying rent to the owner. This practice, common in Baltimore, New Orleans, and other cities, allowed slaves to find their own jobs, arrange salaries and length of service, and make predetermined payments to their masters. Cities needed armies of Blacks to pave and clean streets, build bridges, collect garbage, and dig sewers. Whites unable to afford a slave could rent one, and employers unwilling to house and feed scores of men could hire slaves to do a specific job and then let them go. There were countless opportunities for an enterprising slave and a willing master.

On the previous Saturday, Frederick didn't keep his usual appointment with Hugh to give away his earnings. That night he didn't have time to go to Hugh's house after work and also leave with his friends for a weekend camp meeting. He assumed that Hugh only cared about the money, not when he received it.

He enjoyed himself so much, singing hymn after hymn until late Sunday, he did not return to Hugh's house until Monday night with the expected three dollars.

When Frederick opened the back door, Hugh started yelling. "Where the hell have you been, you worthless nigger? Where? You're to be here every damn Saturday, every goddamn Saturday with my money, my money . . ."

Interrupting, Frederick tried to explain. This only made matters worse.

Stunned, Hugh stepped back, blinking with incomprehension. He started pacing the room. "You left the city without my permission?" He yelled louder. "How dare you leave the city without my permission? A slave can't leave without permission, and you know it. You expect me to believe you when you won't take a piss without calculating your advantage first."

Frederick persisted. "I didn't know I had to ask. Sir, I hired my time and paid you. I thought all I had to do was pay you."

"You had to be here on Saturday," insisted Hugh. "I'm the master, and I told you to be here *every* Saturday. Maybe I should whip a reminder into your Black hide. You're a slave, and you do what I tell you."

Frederick reached into his pocket and held out the bills, but Hugh scoffed, as if insulted by a bribe. "That will not change my mind. Your hire out days are over. Bring your tools and clothes home at once. I'll teach you to go off." Hugh revealed the fear behind his rage, the fear of all slave masters so close to Pennsylvania, the nearest free state.

One final appeal: "But, master . . ."

Hugh turned away to leave, *his* money still in Frederick's hand. "Just put the money on the table," he said and left.

Frederick stood there, unwilling to move for fear that he would rush through that door and grab Hugh by his narrow neck. His head ached with a pounding rage.

He threw the money at the door, needing to do something before feeling the full weight of disappointment and depression. The bills fell quietly to the floor. Frustrated by this feeble display, Frederick reached into his pockets for some coins and threw them with all the force he could muster. He had assumed wrongly that Hugh's greed mattered more than contracts, that avoiding daily contact with a troublesome slave mattered more than the rules of the system.

It was his own fault that this had happened. But Frederick was not yet ready to assume personal blame, so he decided to channel his energy into retaliation schemes. *So, you think I'm going to work on my own. Just wait and see. I'm not going to find one job, not one, and you won't get a penny. You want a shiftless, obedient nigger? I'll make your dreams come true.*

Frederick opened the door and felt the unusually cool night air coming in from the harbor on the Patapsco River. It soothed his face as he breathed it in. Closing his eyes, he thought of the North Star and stepped into the night, heading to his room on the Alley. The desire for freedom would grow in his heart, and soon, very soon, the desire would be so great that nothing, not Hugh or Thomas Auld, not the sounds of manacled slaves marching through Fells Point to waiting transport in the Inner Harbor, not the fear of slave patrollers roaming the fields and forests of Harford and Cecil counties between Baltimore and Philadelphia, not the fear of cotton and Alabama, not even the separation from friends, could keep him from crossing over into the promised land.

For a week, Frederick did only housework or stayed in his old room upstairs, reading, planning, and anticipating the delicious moment when finally comprehending Frederick's passive resistance, Hugh would rush into his room a flailing, drunken mess of anger and frustration.

Hugh summoned Frederick the next Saturday night and demanded his weekly payment as if nothing had changed except Frederick's return to the Fells Street house.

Again, Frederick didn't expect such a scene. *How could Hugh now believe that he had three dollars still coming to him? Was he that stupid?*

"But, sir, I don't have it," he said.

"You're a liar." Hugh didn't raise his voice. He didn't move in his chair. "You have it, even though you didn't work this week. Your savings."

Hugh didn't move in his chair. His eyes were wide pools of blue ice. He knew what was going on. "Miss Sophia gives me daily reports after I come home from work. I know what you're doing. You're a low-down, lying nigger. None of you can be trusted."

Frederick closed his eyes and heard a change in Hugh's voice. He went on. "I will find work for you, Freddy, work that will make your plantation days seem like heaven. You will work every day, Monday through Saturday, into the night, and you won't get a cent at the end of the week, not one damn cent. And when you're not working out there, you'll be working here, and you'll be so tired that you'll not want to see your free nigger friends."

Frederick opened his eyes, awakening from a spell. Hugh's voice, powerful in its serenity, shocked him. Behind that once handsome face now lined and gray was still the will to destroy Frederick's dreams. By trifling with it, Frederick had risked everything.

Hugh said softly, "I hate you, Frederick Bailey, and I will always hate you."

Frederick had to pick a specific day for his escape, make plans for it, and tell Anna. By openly declaring his hatred at last, Hugh had signaled that he surely was going to kill Frederick. Hugh would tell his brother Thomas, Frederick's legal owner, he'd just had to do it. And if Thomas would not accept his explanation, Hugh would ignore the inevitable threats about lawsuits and financial compensation. The brothers hated each other anyway.

On the day of Hugh's declaration, Frederick decided his day of escape had to be Monday, September 3. He would need two to three weeks to make all the arrangements, and the first Monday of the month, the day after the day of rest, made sense. The Sabbath made white folks lazy, and many of them had a hard time getting to work after church, time with family, and a late weekend whoring and drinking. Servants and slaves were up early, as usual. But many white people were not. Surely, Hugh would not be up that Monday.

He told Anna, "I'm going on the new train, the Baltimore/Susquehanna, on September 3, if I can find somebody who'll lend me his free papers."

"Yes, you'll need them, but there is not a Negro in these parts who will have papers that will fit what you look like. Do you know somebody who's big, tall, and yellow like you?"

"No," said Frederick grimly.

"Do you know some sailors?"

"No. Why?"

"Then you should dress like one of them, so you'll look like them, and people will see a red shirt with a knot around your neck, and a flat hat, and not *you*."

Frederick paused and agreed. "Yes, that's a good idea, dressing like a sailor."

"I'll work on that shirt and that kerchief, and I have a friend who was married to a sailor. He was away all the time, and she complained about him. But I know why she married him; he is some looker. And he has papers. I'll ask her for them, just to borrow."

"Will she do that for you? And don't those sailor papers have a date?"

"I don't know, but he just got out. But my friend will do this for me, if not for you. She might ask questions, but you should know that some of us free people want to help slaves. So, when I get them, you will need to see if the papers work for you. Or we just might have to come up with another plan."

He grabbed her hands and said, quickly, "And when I get to New York City, I'll send for you, and we'll get married there."

For the first time, he mentioned the word marriage and Anna went on as if this undeclared proposal was an assumed fact.

"New York?" she asked.

"It's the biggest city in the country. No one will know us."

"We'll raise a family," she added.

"A large family," Frederick added, anticipating the days when his wife and children would sit at a large dining room table and eat huge plates of meat, fish, and vegetables, or sit in the parlor and listen to him read, sing, and tell stories. A happy family.

"Mr. and Mrs. Bailey," Anna whispered, smiling. "Sounds good, sounds real good, even though you didn't ask me."

"But I did, I did," he protested.

Anna laughed. "I know you did, in your own Frederick Augustus Washington Bailey way."

"You like the sound of my name."

"Of course. It fits for a man with a heart and head as big as yours."

"Oh, Anna," was all he could say.

"And you'll need me from letting you get too big on your high horse."

"You won't knock me off that high horse," he said, grinning.

"Just a gentle pull, that's all, now and then."

When they arrived at the Wellses' house, she asked him to wait outside before he left to meet his friends. "I have something for you," she explained.

She returned quickly, holding out to him a small sack of cloth rapped with a thick string. When it touched his right hand, he could feel the coins.

Anna said, "You'll need this."

He started to protest, but she silenced him by taking his hand into hers and looking into his eyes. "You'll *need* this," she repeated. "Mr. Auld is not going to give you much, no matter how hard you work, and you have only a little time. I sold one of my featherbeds. I still have one, and I have a little savings . . ."

Her generosity moved him, and at that moment he wanted to say that he loved her, but he would not lie to her, not now when she was placing her life in his hands. She was his friend, but he did not desire her, did not sit up at night thinking of her, wanting her to be with him every night, like the passionate lovers in the plays and poems of Shakespeare. He had no Songs of Solomon to sing.

Not yet, he thought. Give it time. He listened to the talk. Some marriages don't start with love but can end with the deepest love imaginable. Wait. Be patient.

But he could see the love in her eyes, and he dropped to his knees. "Thank you," he said, offering marriage as her reward. "Will you marry me?"

"Now that's how it was *supposed* to happen earlier." She laughed lightly. "But this is good enough, and *our* money will help us through. Hold on to it. We're going to need it after we get married."

But now he didn't see a wedding ceremony before him. He saw all the potential pitfalls the weeks could bring him: white suspicion and a zealous train conductor scrutinizing every paper; Negro jealousy and a betraying friend needing a little reward; his own ignorance of geography; and Hugh Auld, dangerous because he was no longer predictable.

"Goodbye, Anna." He quickly turned away so he would not infect her with his dark misgivings. "We'll talk some more . . . soon."

Frederick joined his friends later that afternoon at Jim Mingo's, telling them the day of his escape. This was no surprise; they had talked about freedom many times before. The inevitable question came immediately: "How?"

Again, he hesitated, feeling that same cold fear that maybe, just maybe, one of them would tell. "I can't tell you," he said finally.

"What?" asked Mingo.

"I can't tell you, because someone might find out . . ."

Mingo, a large man with a voice to match, stood, slapping his big hand on the table. "Sir, you insult us!"

Frederick pressed on: "No, I trust that you would not betray me. You are my friends, and I know that you only want what I want. But the risks are greater when too many know."

"We are *not* the many." Mingo was proud to have risked his own liberty by teaching a slave.

"All it takes is one person, one slip of the tongue . . ."

"We are sworn to secrecy," said Mingo, relentless.

Frederick continued explaining, "You can't tell what you don't know. You won't have to lie."

Harris said, "You're right, Frederick. It's better that we don't know the details. If your way is found out, then that's one less way out for other slaves."

"That's right," said another, joining the change in attitude with nods of his head. "There can't be an Underground Railroad if everyone knows the stops."

"You'll need free papers," said John Chester, a man Frederick admired for his quick intelligence and knowledge. "You can use mine."

"Thank you, but no. If I'm caught, I don't want you to be accused of helping an escape."

"But you *must* have papers," said Mingo, now accepting the situation.

"None of you look like me," Frederick said.

Harris, always ready to amuse, commented, "Well, you're goin' to have some trouble finding a paper that describes a yellow Negro over six feet tall who weighs almost two hundred pounds."

Frederick revealed a small part of his plan to settle the argument. "I'll be a sailor. Sailor papers are general, and hopefully the conductor will be impressed by how I look, what I'm wearing." He didn't say more; he couldn't risk implicating Anna in his escape plan, not even to them. In the colored community, everyone talked.

"Yes, of course," said Harris, "struck dumb by your good looks."

"He'd better be, or I will be in deep trouble," replied Frederick. They all laughed.

At that moment, feeling a bond with them again, Frederick did not want to mention farewells or talk about his plans anymore. There would be time to say goodbye, and he did not look forward to it. Their farewells would have to be permanent. They had all talked of leaving Baltimore, of finding a place where they could be truly free, maybe California, or Canada, or even South America. Thousands of miles would separate them soon.

Frederick reached for a glass and lifted it up as a toast, saying, "To the United States Navy."

His friends replied, as one, "To the Navy."

★

For the next three weeks, Frederick worked as the obedient slave. He accepted without complaint the jobs Hugh assigned him and contracted for others when Hugh was out of things for him to do. On Saturdays, he relinquished his wages without a scowl, sneer, or comment.

The city now felt like a protective womb, its familiar landmarks sustaining him with memories as he walked the streets one last time. He would miss Baltimore. The last week came, and Frederick completed his arrangements. Needing the free time, he didn't work that last Thursday, Friday, and Saturday, and risked Hugh's suspicions when he presented him only six dollars that Saturday night in the kitchen.

Frederick saw the question in Hugh eyes: are you holding out on me? But Frederick offered no explanation, afraid to reveal that this was the last night he would ever have to give his earnings to another man.

Hugh smiled indulgently and said, "Now, Fred, I know you can have a better week next week. Right?"

A simple question was capable of eliciting insolence in a simple answer. From his early childhood, Frederick had learned the possibilities of inflection in a single word. But silence was equally dangerous, a void into which Hugh could dump hostility; and so, he answered with a delicate word reversal, deflecting power away from "yes" by giving it second place.

"Sir, yes."

Once, he enjoyed the game of irritation, finding just the word or gesture that would excite Hugh into spasms of invective, but no more. He wanted everything to be calm now, so he put on the courteous, grinning servant mask again. "Sir, anything more tonight?"

Pleased, too, Hugh smiled. "No, Fred. But check with Miss Sophia before you go to your room."

Frederick went into the parlor, where Sophia Auld always read Bible stories to three of her children. He felt a deep sadness seeing her there. He recalled the times when she had read to him and her son Tommy long ago, so determined to communicate the beauty of language and its moral power.

"Miss Sophia, anything else tonight?" he asked, never resorting to servile, plantation speech with her.

"No," was all she said, not bothering to look up at him.

He closed the door, still mystified that her love could change to hate.

Sunday night he could barely sleep, worrying about capture, anticipating everything that could possibly go wrong. He would miss the scheduled train. He would be betrayed, as he once was on the Eastern Shore. The conductor would doubt his papers and call for the police. Hugh would somehow find him and kill him on the spot, unconcerned what his brother Thomas thought.

On Sunday, he stayed away from the Auld house for most of the day. Hugh didn't care what Frederick did on Sundays anymore. He just had to be ready for work Monday morning in the house or at the shipyards.

That evening, he quietly knocked on the kitchen door at the Wellses' house. Looking around, he made sure no one could see him enter at the preplanned time. It was dark, and Anna opened the door without a candle.

After hugging her quickly, he tried to say what needed to be said, the words of comfort and assurance, the bright tokens of certainty offered by a calm voice. But fear gripped him.

"I'm afraid," he confessed.

"I would be more worried if you weren't."

"I stayed away from the house all day, and tomorrow morning I'll get up at daybreak, pretending I was going to work at Mr. Butler's yard again. Right now, he likes me going to yard for work without my telling him, and he gets his money at the end of the week, so he's not suspicious. This time I had only six dollars, but he didn't make much of it. But I was sure he could hear the beating of my heart."

"And the Pratt and Light Street Station tomorrow."

"And Wilmington, Philadelphia, and then New York."

"It's so far."

"But I'll be there, waiting for you to come."

"And when I come, we'll get married."

"The same day."

These declarations did not comfort them, but soon they were in each other arms, embracing in the dark after Anna had quietly closed the door to the alley.

"Frederick, be careful."

"I will, I promise. I will."

It was time to go. Now he had to be all business, or he would never leave her. "I will write to Mingo," he said. "He'll come and tell you the directions for where to find me. See you soon."

He saw tears in her eyes and looked away, fearing another delay. Without embracing her again, he ran down the street, and whispered again and again the name of their future home as if two words could somehow open the very air and place him on Manhattan's golden streets.

"New York," he whispered. *New York.*

3.

HUGH AULD CAME TO the Wells house three days later, pounding on the front door and yelling, "Where is he? Where is he? I know that black bitch knows where he went. She has to tell me!"

Mr. Wells opened the door and allowed Hugh to come inside. Hugh ranted. "It took some time to find out, but I've been asking around, and she's been seen with him at church and meetings. If anyone would know, *she* would know."

"Know what, sir?" asked Mr. Wells, maintaining his polite composure. "And are you talking about what Miss Murray knows?"

"I don't care what her name is," Hugh replied, his tone still hot but not as loud. "But if she helped my slave escape, there will be hell to pay. It's against the law to help a slave escape."

"And how do you know she helped him? And how do you know he escaped?"

"Of course I know," Hugh snapped. "He's not been back for three days. I demand to see her. I have questions to ask, and I will have answers."

"She is a free colored woman, sir," said Mr. Wells. "She doesn't have to answer your questions."

Hugh softened. He remained emphatic but was no longer belligerent. "Sir, you know we need slaves in Baltimore. And you know times are hard and getting harder. If all the slaves got away, we would be all ruined."

"We are not talking about all the slaves this morning, just one."

As if this was proof of his claims, Hugh declared with a triumphant rise of his chin, "Then you know what I'm talking about."

"I know Fred Bailey, if that's what you mean?"

"Then you know he's a slave, and you have to tell his master what you know."

"Sir, I am a free man, and I don't have to tell you anything. And if I did, the only way you could make me talk, if I knew anything, would be in court after I received a subpoena to testify before a judge. Good day, sir."

"Please, sir," Hugh pleaded, "you are a man of property. You should understand the impact of the loss of something valuable. I just need some help with getting my property returned. That is all."

Wells paused. "I will ask Miss Murray if she knows anything about where Mr. Bailey is."

"I need to ask her myself," said Hugh, stopping when Wells turned his back.

"No, you don't," Wells said, walking away. "This is my house."

He left the parlor and found Anna in the pantry. She had been listening, of course. How could she not hear so heated an exchange? Wells didn't offer any explanation or repeat Hugh's avowals. He only asked, "Well, Anna, what do you know?"

"Nothing, sir," she replied directly.

"Then you don't know about his escape?"

"No, sir," she lied, surprised that she was not at all nervous or feeling threatened.

"Were you not seeing each other? He's been here, I know."

"Yes, he sometimes called on me here, and we would see each other at church."

"He was friendly to you."

"Yes, we were friends."

"Was he courting?"

"Not yet."

"But you wanted him to," Wells said.

"Yes, but that can't happen if he's gone and decided I'm not that important."

"If he ran away," Wells asserted.

"*If* he ran away," Anna repeated.

"Slaves do that," said Mr. Wells, as if sympathizing with her loss.

"And if he did, I will miss him."

Her heart was beating rapidly, and she was already sick with worry. Nonetheless, she could see that her words had disarmed Mr. Wells. She could hear his thoughts: *Anna could not possibly take a burdensome and dangerous risk for a man who would leave her without saying goodbye, risking her safety and reputation for the kind of man the ladies of the house called a "cad."*

"Thank you, Anna. That is all," he said, smiling, and went back to the front parlor.

Unable to handle the disappointing news, Hugh started shouting again, incredulity in every syllable. "You actually believe that black bitch? You should know the niggers band together, free and slave together, working against us, making plans. They would kill us all if . . ."

Mr. Wells was not provoked, staying calm even in the face of an uncouth tirade. "Sir, you have said enough, and you will leave my house now, or you will be the one in jail."

"Are you threatening me?" cried Hugh. "Are you?"

"Yes," replied Wells. "And if you don't leave this very minute, I will send Miss Murray to summon the constable, and you will have not one but two coloreds adding to your troubles this morning."

"Damn you all to hell," said Hugh, turning toward the door. "Damn all you nigger-lovers to hell."

At that moment, it struck Anna that after five years working at the house, she had never heard Mr. Wells use the word "nigger." He was a very different kind of white man, thank goodness.

She would miss him when she left for New York.

Now Anna would have to wait to receive word that Frederick had arrived safely. Of course, she could leave right now if she wanted to. She was free. But how would she find Frederick? No, she would have to wait, work and wait, wait and pray. She hoped the Lord was listening.

The waiting was painful. Anna knew Frederick would have to take three trains and four boats to get to New York. Then, if he made it, he would have to send a letter to James Mingo telling him of his safe arrival, and that would take time. Mr. Wells always complained about the slow mail. Would it come by ship, by train, by coach? She didn't know.

In the meantime, she had to get ready: make sure she had her freedom papers ready for inspection at any time; pack her wedding dress, a new plum silk gown she made herself, simple, no frills, but accented with delicate, white buttons; wrap Frederick's three books of music carefully so they would not be damaged.

Anna recalled their visit to Mr. Knight's Bookstore, where Frederick bought his first book. He was excited about showing the store to her, still marveling at the piles of books, the smell, the dust, the promise of so much to read and know. When he revealed his interest in music books for violin and piano, she purchased them while he was distracted. When she presented the package to him on the street, he looked at her with a warmth she had never experienced before. She thought she saw a tear forming in his left eye.

"Oh, Anna," he whispered before taking her into his arms, his first show of public affection. They had not hugged, held hands, or kissed anywhere.

Nevertheless, she appreciated this heartfelt and spontaneous embrace because it was exceptional and she didn't know when it would happen again, if ever. Frederick could be hard and stubborn about his rules.

"Good," was her only reply, and then they walked back to Mr. Wells's house. Staying true to his character, Frederick talked all the way, describing the many books he saw and perused in Mr. Knight's store.

The memories of that day now comforted her, for they promised future books and a house filled with them and music for their family. But she needed more than promises; she wanted prophecy. One thing was certain: she had to tell Mr. Wells she was leaving.

Anna tried to be as brief as possible, fearing that revealing too much could ruin everything. "Sir, I'm leaving. I'm moving away." She almost gave her destination, but she stopped herself.

"When?" asked Mr. Wells, registering no surprise in his voice or eyes.

Again, Anna hesitated.

Mr. Wells explained, "I only need to know so I can hire a girl to replace you."

"I'm waiting to hear from Mr. Mingo. He'll come with a message."

Anna now felt she had said too much. She looked down to hide her fear.

She could hear the warmth in Wells's voice. "Anna, you are a free woman. You don't have to ask my permission to leave, and you don't have to tell me about where you are going either."

"Thank you, sir."

"And I know no one thinks slavery is good for *them*. It's for other people."

That was as close to an admission of his knowledge of the escape as Anna heard. But she needed nothing more to reaffirm that Mr. Wells was a good, decent man who had always treated her kindly.

With her free papers, Anna at least had some protections. The slaves in other houses were treated like dogs, slapped, kicked, and spat upon. Besides, Mr. Wells was a widow, and his children were older. He needed a cook and housekeeper, not a servant at the table, or a nurse for his children. Life was good under Mr. Wells's roof, but her days there were done.

Mr. Wells turned away, went out to the front of the house, and then returned, handing Anna ten folded one-dollar bank notes. "You'll need this," he said.

Standing in front of him, she exclaimed, "Sir, you can't do this!"

His involvement in a slave escape could bring all kinds of trouble for him and his family. People talked crazy these days when it came to escapes.

He pressed her hand, saying, "I can pay you whatever I want."

"But sir . . ."

"You'll need every cent," he insisted, stepping away to place the money on the sideboard. "There's no time for pride now."

He left the kitchen.

Anna whispered to the door, "Thank you, sir," and hoped that she would find another time to thank him face to face. He deserved that.

4.

THE NIGHT BEFORE HIS escape, Frederick could barely sleep. He was too worried about capture, anticipating everything that could go wrong. What sleep he did eventually get was due to the comfort that came from the simplicity of his plan.

After getting dressed at daybreak, he would pretend to leave for work and hide in the narrow alleys biding his time before going to the nearby Pratt Street Station for final boarding. He would not buy a ticket before boarding. The scrutiny of his face, body, and papers by the ticket agent could end everything. At the last minute, an acquaintance would rush to the platform and quickly give Frederick his bag. He would find a seat and hope the conductor would be too busy to notice the difference between the sailor before him and the man described in the papers.

In the alley, he sat behind some large containers, satisfied that he had cover for a few hours. But the hours gave him more time to worry. His mouth felt dry, and he felt sweat dripping under his arms and on his forehead. *Oh God. I can't look nervous. This will give me away.* He was about to lift his arm to wipe the sweat off, but he stopped, imagining a dirtied shirt sleeve sure to catch attention. He groaned, wearied by all the details that could entrap him.

Finally, it was time to get to the station five minutes before the train's scheduled departure. Frederick forced himself to keep his face turned away from the street, since some of the Negro workers, a small army of vendors, servants, and drivers might recognize him. He fingered his loosely knotted cravat as the first boarding whistle blew.

Frederick's stomach was sour with fear. *Where's Isaac?* Frederick frantically wondered, his thoughts a sudden, confused rush of insult and recrimination. *I knew he couldn't be trusted, the stupid fool!*

The whistle blew again.

Where is he?

Frederick hurried to the Negro-only car as the wood smoke, pouring out of the funnel shape stack of the engine, thickened the cool morning air.

"All aboard!" cried the conductor.

The train sputtered as it gathered steam. Frederick hesitated at the door of the crowded car, allowing everyone else to enter. Then he heard his shouted name: "Fred Bailey! Fred!"

Oh, my God, he used my name. He used my real name.

Frederick turned to Isaac, a thin young man with bulging arm muscles, and grabbed his two large duffel bags.

"Right on time," declared Isaac, grinning with pride.

Frederick said nothing and entered the crowded car. Quickly, he found a seat near the back at a window.

Now on his first train, feeling its rumble like a rolling thunder under his seat, Frederick understood the enthusiasm of journalists, who told stories of iron horses charging across the land. As he sat there preparing for the conductor's arrival and scrutiny of his forged papers, he was, for one fleeting moment, a soldier riding a chariot of fire through the parted Red Sea.

"Paper!" snapped the conductor entering the car. Frederick immediately pulled out the sailor's protection. He shuddered as he watched the conductor proceed down the aisle; the white man grumbled, sneered, and snatched tickets, as if everyone annoyed him.

The conductor examined the papers of every Negro passenger closely. Part of his job was to detect runaway slaves. He held each document with two fat fingers as he scanned it, inspected the face of the traveler, and then returned to a more intense reading, as if he suspected forgeries.

When done, he dropped the key document into the lap of the Negro and passed on, saying, "Humph!" Legitimacy seemed to surprise him every time.

Frederick felt a deep pounding in his chest.

But the conductor's demeanor changed completely when he came to him. As Frederick had hoped, the conductor saw his uniform more than skin color. Sailors were popular in Maryland, especially in Baltimore and Annapolis.

"Sailor," he said warmly, "I suppose you have free papers?"

"No, sir." Frederick smiled broadly. "I never carry my free papers to sea with me."

The conductor nodded his head. "Oh yes, of course." He leaned forward to speak confidentially. "But you do have *something* to show that you're a free man, don't you?" His tone was patronizing but still friendly. No doubt, he had to cross-examine hundreds of sailors in the area with similar stories.

"Yes, sir." Frederick lifted his chest proudly. "I have my protection papers with the American eagle on them. That will carry me around the world."

Struggling to keep his hands from trembling and praying that his face didn't sweat, he handed over the papers with their vague description of a Negro man. Frederick never looked away from the conductor's gray, inquisitive eyes, and never stopped smiling.

The conductor only glanced at the papers before handing them back.

"Where're you headed?" he asked nonchalantly.

"Wilmington," replied Frederick, looking for any change in the conductor's eyes. This city was the last slave city where city police officers, train conductors, and private citizens were especially vigilant. Here was their last chance to prevent an escape to freedom. Any Negro going to Wilmington was suspect.

"That will be three dollars." said the conductor, his eyes still kind, without suspicion.

He collected Frederick's money, gave him a ticket, and moved on, resuming his rude badgering of the other colored passengers.

"Paper! Let me see that paper, *boy.*"

Drained, Frederick, leaned back against the wood seat, closing his eyes for at least a few moments of rest, seeing Baltimore's harbor, its water bright and blue in the hot sun, the narrow cobblestone streets of Fells Point, the Auld house on Fells Street, his own room on Strawberry Alley, and the Great House of Wye Plantation on the Eastern Shore, its six tall chimneys rising above the thick maple and oak trees. A vision of great beauty still.

At Havre de Grace, all passengers had to disembark and cross the Susquehanna River by ferryboat before boarding another train. Frederick hurried to the boat's side railing to envision his first steps on the opposite shore. He heard a familiar voice.

"Fred Bailey, what you doin' in a sailor's suit? Man, where you goin'? When you comin' back? I didn't know you signed up . . . Mr. Hugh let you?"

The words were like rattling bullets in his back, and he turned to silence Nicholls, an acquaintance who worked as a hand on the ferryboat.

"Be quiet," Frederick whispered vehemently.

Oblivious, Nicholls went on and on. "It's good to see you, Fred. It's been a long time. You're lookin' good in dem clothes. You're going to the ocean; now that's a place I don't wanna see. I heard how dey treats sailors, though. Real hard. Are you sure you wanna do that?"

Frederick started to move away.

"I know it's hard to leave friends and places you know," continued Nicholls, a kind, handsome man with the brain of a peanut. "It wasn't easy fo' me to leave Baltimore an' work here. I know, yes, I know."

Frederick stopped to reply, hoping to dismiss him with brief civilities. He was surprised at how calm he was with this new danger.

"Yes, I'm goin' away, Nicholls. Thanks for understanding. It's hard to leave something close, so I need to be alone, if you don't mind. We'll see each other when I come back."

Nicholls smiled. "*Sure*, man . . . I know what you mean. It ain't easy, but you do what's you gotta do."

Frederick moved to another part of the boat, but this time he faced the passengers on the deck, preparing for anything as he leaned against the railing. He didn't want any more surprises. When at last he disembarked, and boarded the next train to Wilmington, he had another shock. The southbound train now waited at the station on the opposite side, and a former supervisor, Captain McGowan at Mr. Price's shipyard, sat at a window where he could see Frederick. He had worked under him just a few days ago. Unable to get out of his seat, Frederick quickly turned his head, hoping that the captain was distracted by the commotion of two waiting trains and would not notice him. The two trains moved on.

This was a mere moment, but the impact of that moment was long lasting. He felt like a caged falcon, trapped on all sides.

Then he heard a voice.

"Sailor," said a man with a nudge from behind. "That white man at the door is lookin' at you."

Frederick started at the touch and looked to the car door where Stein, a German blacksmith he knew at the shipyards, was staring at him. Frederick berated himself. *How could I be so stupid to believe that no one would know or recognize me? I knew this would happen, just knew it.*

His words to his neighbor were calm, however: "I never saw the man before. He probably thinks I'm someone else."

Stein turned away, and Frederick held his breath.

The conductor could immediately return with help to arrest him, or he could wait and arrest him just before the train reached the last station.

Frederick's hands tightened into fists, but he knew he would not fight if cornered. He had to survive. He had to live for another day to escape again.

There was nothing he could do until he saw the conductor again.

He felt drained, more tired than after a full day's work at the shipyards of Fells Point.

But nothing happened. Even so, he had to get through Wilmington. According to all accounts, Wilmington was full of kidnappers and bounty hunters eagerly waiting to take advantage of their last chance to grab fugitives before they crossed the Mason and Dixon line.

Frederick hurried from the train for the boat to Philadelphia, but he made sure to not run and call attention to himself. He ate a piece of bread and some cheese, taken from his bundle, to help slow his pace and naturally avert his eyes from the scrutiny of others. He didn't bother to note details of the city as he crossed it. He could have been in a tunnel focused only on the light at the end of it.

Finally, he arrived at the riverboat for Philadelphia. He showed his papers without any complications and boarded.

As the ferryboat pushed forward, he could feel the water's pull. The boat moved slowly on the Delaware, but soon the coast on the other side became visible, a blur at first, then distinct trees and buildings came into view. He wanted to celebrate, wishing for a cup to toast the fulfillment of his long-desired dream. But he checked himself. He would celebrate only when his feet touched the dirt of Pennsylvania. Even then his celebration could only be a quiet salute to freedom, simple and discreet. Again, he heard the thumping of his heart. He refrained from taking deep breaths because he wanted to hear every sound around him, the screeching birds, the shouting men at the docks of freedom.

Nothing dramatic happened when the boat landed—no checks of papers one final time, no questions or comments. He was now free to fly away leaving his cage behind. When Frederick stepped down the gangplank, he noted the exact moment when his right foot touched the hardened dirt.

Freedom's dirt.

He took deep breaths. At last, he was in Philadelphia, the City of Brotherly Love, the city where the Quakers insisted that slavery had no place. He knew some slaves still lived in Pennsylvania, but the low number only proved the state's refusal to support slavery or participate in the return of fugitives. He noticed that in Philadelphia there were not as many Negroes as there were in Baltimore, and they moved about without the habitual wariness and furtive glances of colored people under the constant threat of enslavement.

Frederick wanted to linger and savor the sights and sounds of new freedom, but he didn't have time. He needed to get to the next station for the train to New York. From everyone he knew and everything he had read, the city's message was clear: we want you; we need you. "New York, New York," he whispered as if chanting magic.

How could such a call be denied or resisted?

Consumed by the call of his new home, he could not sleep on the train as it rumbled through Pennsylvania and New Jersey. From the Jersey Shore, the great city shimmered in the morning light. The church spires and blocks of tall buildings made of brownstone and bricks, were a massive show of wealth and power, and scores of schooners, barges, and ferries were readying to leave or arrive in New York, their horns blaring as gulls hovered waiting to swoop on the refuse of thousands. Baltimore was a minor town in comparison. As he crossed the Hudson and approached one of the many Battery docks, his awe increased, but he was exhausted.

Walking the narrow streets, he could not resist the terrors of the vast unknown. He was lost in a maze of warehouses, taverns, shops closed for the night, brothels, and apartment buildings.

He had no plan, just the hope that a colored face would direct him to the Negro section of town, where he would quickly find a place to live. He cursed himself for planning his escape from Baltimore but ignoring the rest. Somehow, freedom would take care of the details, and New York would find room for one more refugee.

Frederick noticed a man walking toward him with a whitewash pail and brush, his step cautious, his body close to the wall. Frederick stopped, stunned that he recognized a familiar face. He rushed forward, calling out:

"Allendar's Jake! Allendar's Jake."

Instantly, he felt better. He was not alone. He knew somebody in New York, and one person was enough. Jake had worked with him in Allendar's shipyard in Baltimore before disappearing one day, leaving no word, and sharing no plans.

Jake started, looked around, drew Frederick aside into an alley, and whispered a warning: "Don't call me that, fool! It's Dixon now, Billy Dixon. What are you doing here? Man, I don't have no time for this. I need to get away."

Frederick couldn't understand the reason for the terror in Jake's narrow eyes, the hollow voice and cringing shoulders. He protested, "What are you afraid of, Jake. You're *free* now!"

"Damn it, don't call me that, I said. Those days are over, dead to me."

"All right, but . . ."

"And if you want yo' freedom to last, stay away from the waterfront."

"But that's where I'm goin' to work when . . ."

Jake's hand gripped Frederick's arm. "Stay away," he insisted. "The blackbirders will come and take you. Yards are the first place they'll go if you're a caulker. "

"Blackbirders?"

"Scum from the Five Points. They kidnap free Negroes and hustle them to boats and sell them south for sixty or seventy dollars a head."

Frederick struggled to take in this vital information. His disappointment muddled his mind. He thought Wilmington was the last place for kidnapping. *Not New York, no, not my* New York.

"And stay away from colored boarding houses, too. Niggers will tell for a price."

"But where . . ."

Jake cut him off. "Damn it, listen to me. You still won't shut up after all this time. The birds watch colored houses. They ain't safe. Don't trust nobody, they . . ."

His light brown eyes blazed, shocked by a revelation. Jake stepped back. "I don't know if you were paid to turn *me* in."

Dumbfounded, Frederick asked, "What are you talking about, Jake?"

Jake turned quickly. "Fuck this. I gotta go."

Frederick yelled after him. "Jake. Bill, Bill, come back!"

Jake didn't look back and disappeared in another alley, swallowed by rows of drab brick.

Frederick didn't know what to do. Jake had warned him not to depend on the very people with whom he hoped to build a new life. He had to go to the wharves. Where else could he work? He had to find rooms to rent in a boarding house nearby. Where else could he and Anna live?

Despite Jake's warning, Frederick drifted back to the wharves near the Battery. But now he suspected everyone, refusing to smile or connect with the eyes of others and risk starting a conversation. Hungry, he bought some bread from a street vendor. Many people packed the streets, rushing, yelling, selling. Frederick ate a few pieces of bread and, feeling tired, searched for a place to rest. He soon found some barrels to hide behind, and slept there, using one of his bags as a pillow.

Later, he found himself on Center Street across from a tenement near the city jail. A colored sailor watched Frederick from a window, and Frederick turned his back, afraid that any acknowledgment could lead to a meeting, questions, and inevitable exposure. He could trick train conductors, but not another colored sailor. Frederick looked down the street. He needed to flee.

He turned back to the window and started; the man was gone. *Where was he? Was this how the blackbirders did their work—watch and disappear, and then surround their prey on the street?*

Frederick fought the urge to run.

He looked around as if lost and needing directions. Then the sailor appeared. He opened the tenement door, came down the shallow steps, and crossed the street. He was trim but muscular in the chest and shoulders, with a long narrow nose, a constant smile, and bright, white teeth. The sailor's smile reminded him of a cat stalking a bird, sure of his kill, but Frederick took the offensive. Frederick knew that until he had legal freedom, he would always have to take risks. He held his head up and straightened his back. He would either make his first northern Black friend or meet a blackbirder. "Sir, I'm lost. Can you help me?"

"Sure, come with me," replied the man politely. "But don't think I can't see through you. You're no sailor, so don't waste my time with bullshit."

He started to cross Center Street. Frederick froze.

The man turned his head when Frederick didn't follow him. "I'm Stuart. Do you need a place to sleep?"

Frederick hesitated. Stuart continued walking, and finally Frederick made another crucial decision. "Yes, thanks," he replied, hurrying now.

As soon as the two men entered his unkempt and virtually empty room, Stuart asked, "Where did you escape from?"

Frederick's stomach constricted, and he held his breath. Helplessly, Frederick scanned the room, its stark condition obvious proof that no one lived there.

Stuart sat down and explained, "Colored men standing on streets and looking around like they don't know where to go usually are escaped slaves."

Frederick didn't reply.

"You can trust me," said Stuart warmly. "You'll have to trust me. You probably don't have nobody else."

Still nothing.

Stuart stood up. "Hungry?"

"Yes," Frederick answered, his voice soft and tentative.

"Here's some food."

Frederick ate the potatoes and bread eagerly. But he remained suspicious, casually checking the room for blackbirder hiding places. The room was too small for hiding anyone, but Frederick checked constantly.

Stuart explained more. "Look, my friend, if I wanted to get you arrested, I could have done it without bothering to meet you. I'd just get my money after they took you to the boats. Colored people get stopped, questioned, and arrested for anything around here."

"My name's Fred Stanley," Frederick said. "I'm from Baltimore."

"A *slave* from Baltimore."

Frederick paused. He could continue to lie and hope for the best or tell the truth, some of the truth, and hope for better. He then admitted the most important fact.

"I *was* a slave."

"How you goin' to make a living?" Stuart asked, not making a point of the key disclosure.

"I'm a caulker."

"Wrong job here," Stuart said immediately.

"But caulking is what I know."

"Forget it here. You'll get caught easy on the wharves. You won't last a day!"

"Then what should I do?" Frederick asked, disappointed, and irritated by the constant disillusionments.

"I don't know, but I know a man named David Ruggles. He can help you. He helps people like you."

"Do you work for him?"

"I help," Stuart said simply, as if that was all that had to be said.

Frederick reached out to shake Stuart's hand, touched by this stranger's generosity. "Thank you. Thank you very much."

Stuart nodded. "You'll have to change your name, whatever it is."

"It's Frederick Bailey. Not Stanley."

Stuart smiled. "You didn't have to tell me."

"I know, but I want to keep my first name."

"How about Johnson? With all the Johnsons around here, no one will find you."

"Then it's Frederick Johnson," Frederick said.

"And welcome to New York, where even a colored man can get rich." Stuart looked about his room, underscoring the irony. He spoke of men who, against all odds, now owned restaurants and taverns favored by bankers, merchants, and the city's wealthiest families. But his warmest words were for David Ruggles, director of the New York Committee of Vigilance, originally formed to halt the seizure of free Negroes, and now helping runaways as well.

"Just this year," marveled Stuart, "he opened a colored reading room 'cause the city won't allow coloreds into the city libraries."

Frederick frowned, struggling with obvious disappointment. *Why keep us out of libraries, too?*

Stuart explained, "White people hate us everywhere; they don't need slavery to hate us."

"But they can't take my wages, my hard-earned money." Frederick grew more anxious with every new revelation.

"You'll just make less for the same kind of work."

"Just like Baltimore. But it will be *my* less money."

"And Mr. Ruggles will help you find a job for that less money."

"When will I meet him?"

"Today, at 67 Lispenard Street."

"Thank you. I will not forget you."

"The Lord knows too."

Sailors were notorious for their immorality, so Frederick, genuinely surprised, asked, "You care?"

"We are all God's children, even sailors," Stuart replied.

"I'm sorry. I didn't mean to judge you."

"But you did. We all do, by skin color, uniform, by where we live, by what we do, by what we believe. I saw your fake sailor's uniform and decided to help you. If you didn't have it, I just might have ignored you. We somehow should get to know each other behind the uniform, behind the face, beyond the skin. Maybe we just don't want to know because then we'd all realize we're the same, just puffed-up little shitters and fuckers running from the truth about ourselves. And then just before we die, we beg the Lord to forgive our miserable, rotten lives."

That afternoon, after Frederick rested, Stuart took him to meet Ruggles, who was old and seriously ill. "I have an enlarged liver, dyspepsia, lung irritation, constant irritation of the bowels, and piles. Sir, I'm not going to sit around and wait for doctors to figure it all out. I'll be dead first. In the meantime, I have much to do."

His sparkling eyes and his soft but intense and confident voice matched the conviction in his words. The cane, the slow pace of his walk, and the knobby bones in his hands were the only proofs of his poor health.

When Ruggles learned that Frederick was a caulker, he immediately announced the need for another change: "You can't stay here in New York. You'll have a better chance to make a good living on the whaling ships out of New Bedford. Many are fitted there."

The fear of another new place unsettled Frederick. He was ready to accept New York, despite its terrors. The fear of another new place was too much. "I can't leave. I need to live here."

"Nobody *needs* to live here," Ruggles replied, indulgent kindness in his voice. He was not offended. "Some of us are born here, others come and stay. The city does that to people. But you can't stay. It's too risky with the kind of work you do."

"But I told Anna, the girl I'm going to marry, to come here."

"She'll come, and then you leave, together."

"Where's New Bedford?" Frederick asked, never having heard of the place.

"Farther north, in Massachusetts."

"I can't leave," Frederick said again, defeated but still trying to assert himself. *A free man should be able to choose where he wants to live.*

"You must leave if you want even half a chance. Trust me," Ruggles insisted gently.

Frederick hesitated. He felt weary. "When?"

"As soon as possible."

"After Anna comes and we get married."

"As soon as you're married, I'll make all the arrangements with Mr. Nathan Johnson in New Bedford. He is that town's most prominent, wealthiest colored man, a successful . . ."

"New Bedford," Frederick whispered. "How do we get there?"

"A steamer to Newport in Rhode Island, then coach."

Another new name and place raised more questions, but Frederick waited for Ruggles to continue. Obviously accustomed to giving orders, Ruggles said, "Write to Anna immediately. I'll make the wedding arrangements with the Reverend Pennington. He was a slave and ran away from Maryland on the Eastern Shore. He's an amazing man."

"Maryland, a slave from Maryland," Frederick marveled.

Ruggles briefly told Pennington's story. He escaped from slavery at the age of nineteen, coming from Maryland. He was trained as a carpenter and blacksmith before escaping to Pennsylvania, where Quakers taught him to read and write. He taught himself Greek and Latin. He was admitted to Yale, its first Black student, but he had to sit in the back and not ask questions. He never received a degree from the college, but after he completed his studies there, he was ordained a minister of the Congregational Church.

Astonished, Frederick took in every detail. He was going to meet and get married by a man who, once a slave, rose in the North as a learned, great preacher. If Pennington could rise from the Eastern Shore, so could he.

5.

FREDERICK REMAINED INDOORS FOR three days, preparing himself for his next encounter with the city by reading his two favorite books.

He now knew most of *The Columbian Orator*, the first book he ever bought in Baltimore, word for word, but he never tired of its speeches. Every day, he studied the editor's introduction with recommendations about hand gestures and tone of voice, preparing for the day when the world would be moved by the power of his words.

When he read the Bible, he always began with Proverbs or the letters of Paul to the Apostles, seeking advice, making resolutions, listing goals, always comparing his character to a divine standard, and falling short. Frederick then turned to the Psalms, singing silently with David and Solomon, his voice thrilled by the music of their words.

He had been baptized but he was all too painfully aware of the truth: the Lord was not at the center of his thoughts. He was. Still, Frederick had faith in the promises of the Lord. His Lord would one day fill him with the true spirit of faith, that grace-inspiring song and dance. And one day he would testify as a preacher to this gift and sing the praises of His Lord, establishing himself as a preacher who could inspire others to know the truth of Jesus's love and God's justice. The time was not his to determine. But he would preach one day. This was his future.

After three days, Frederick tired of reading. He wanted to see the great city he now had to leave, his imagination stirred by the tales David Ruggles told during and after dinner.

He recalled the warnings of that first day. Bounty hunters, white and colored, roamed the streets, and even free colored men were being grabbed and taken to waiting ships.

Regardless, Frederick needed to test his new freedom, go out and count on the large crowds to hide him. He couldn't stay in a room liked a caged animal. If he had walked the streets and alleys of Baltimore unmolested most of the time, he surely could walk the streets of New York in fresh clothes and be left alone when there were so many colored men around.

Ruggles raised no objections, only suggesting caution. After he closed the door, Frederick looked up and down the street before stepping down, took a deep breath, and began his walk through the colored neighborhood of row houses and apartments. After two blocks, one middle-aged woman, seeing him, turned away from her female companion, smiled at him for a moment, and returned to her conversation. Even on this first excursion, with all its potential for trouble, he liked the attention of women, but he recognized that in a city of thousands, he was just another tall, fair-skinned Negro man on the streets.

Frederick took note of the street names, making sure to get his bearings. The rows of buildings, all three or four stories high on street after similar street, made him worry about getting lost. He mouthed Ruggles's address just in case he had to ask someone for directions.

He eventually came to Broadway, where carts, wagons, coaches, barouches, omnibuses, and horses rumbled between mammoth hotels, restaurants, elegant stores, theaters, and offices. Thousands jammed the sidewalks, and traffic sometimes came to a complete halt. Yet Frederick was elated. He was swept away in the city's great artery, its blood rich and strong and very alive, so alive as to make him forget, for a time, the dirt and mud, the piles of garbage, the pigs allowed to roam and collect it, the deafening noise, and the occasional streetcar with the sign that read "No Colored People Allowed in this car."

New York did not have many colored citizens, but white New Yorkers seemed too busy to notice or care about those who walked nearby. Even when he stopped to stare, Frederick was ignored, as if he stood outside a wall too high to scale. He was invisible.

★

Anna arrived a week later with all that she could carry: pillows, bed linen, dishes, cutlery, a trunk of clothes that included a plum-colored silk wedding dress, Frederick's fiddle, and the three music books tucked within the clothes to protect them. Before departing, the driver had deposited the luggage on the sidewalk and knocked on the door.

"She's here," Mr. Ruggles said, hobbling with his cane as he came through the door to the back yard, where Frederick was raking leaves. When not exploring the city, he did chores. "Come help with the luggage."

Frederick dropped the rake and ran to the open front door. He found Anna standing at the bottom of the stairs of the shallow stoop and looking up to Frederick with those dark, sparkling eyes that could assess and comfort all at once. He paused for only a moment, taking in the sight of her, and then he whispered, "Anna" before quickly stepping down to take her into his arms. He kissed her on both cheeks, held her face in both hands, and kissed her lips before kissing her cheeks again. He repeated her name. "Anna."

"Frederick? Frederick?" Only his name could capture the wonder of this moment.

"I'm so glad I was home when you arrived. I'm out sometimes."

Ruggles stood at the door. "Frederick, please help with the luggage."

Frederick said, "Oh! Anna, this is Mr. Ruggles."

"Get the luggage, Frederick." Mr. Ruggles was a man used to directing others, but in a short time Frederick saw how his moral conviction inspired others to do what needed to be done. His was a different kind of leadership. Ruggles did not bark demands; he asked questions or declared simple, irrefutable truths.

"Of course." Frederick gathered one large bag, and took it up the stairs, all the while looking back at Anna, who followed him. He placed the bag in the foyer and quickly turned to retrieve the other.

After repeating the introductions, Frederick and Anna went into the front parlor, sat down, and started talking about their trips.

"Do you need something to eat or drink, Miss Murray?" asked Ruggles.

"Thank you, sir, but I'm too excited to eat now. But I could use a cup of coffee."

"I'll get that taken care of, and you two can talk. There's much to talk about."

Frederick insisted on Anna telling her story first, since it was the most recent. He also knew that he would take more time. He always talked longer, piling up details, explaining and elaborating with the joy of storytelling and a drive to dominate conversations.

As usual, Anna did not have that much to say. Planned with great care, her trip went smoothly, and she faced no serious problems. The train was uncomfortable with all the noise and shaking of the train car, and she had to sleep sitting in her chair when she could sleep at all. Anna also explained: "People now seem to keep the escapes quiet. Folks don't want slaves to know someone got away or get other masters all upset. Secrets, that's what folks want now, as if the white folks could keep all them escapes a secret. But I made sure nobody followed me to get to you."

"How do you know?"

"I know."

After they finished the stories of their journeys, Frederick had to tell her the truth. He had little money and no job, and now they would have to leave New York and go to an unknown city.

"It's fine. It don't matter so long as you're safe, and I'm there with you."

"Mr. Ruggles said we should get married on Friday night. Just him; the preacher, a Reverend Pennington; and another witness, his housekeeper, Mrs. Mitchell. A small ceremony."

"We don't need all the fuss. That will be just fine. I have my new dress and you."

He touched her hand that rested on the table and repeated tenderly, "And you."

Suddenly the enormity of the step struck him. He was getting married, and soon they would start a family, and he would have to provide for all of them. How was he going to find a job to support them?

On the morning of the wedding, Frederick took another walk, worrying about money, their future in a strange town, how he and Anna would spend their first night together, how he could please her, how she could please him. He was experienced and knew what to do. But she would be his wife! And what if they didn't enjoy their wedding night and future nights? What if they spent the rest of their married lives going to bed with only duty driving them to produce children? Then what?

When he returned to the house and saw Anna's calm and smiling face, he stopped worrying. Enjoy this day, this moment. *You are a lucky man*, he thought. *She wants to marry me. She didn't have to do this, and she certainly didn't have to leave everything and come here for me.*

You could be alone. How would that feel?

Be grateful; count your blessings, you damn fool!

He relaxed for a few hours, but just before and during the brief ceremony he fidgeted his fingers. Anna pressed his hand, trying to assure him. At the end of the ceremony, they quickly kissed, received congratulations from the three others, and stood together, whispering before sitting down for dinner.

"I'm so happy. I'm Mrs. Bailey now and always."

"I'm happy, too. I just don't want to disappoint you."

"Today's not the day for that. We have our whole lives to work through disappointments."

After a simple meal, Frederick and Anna retired for the night. Before Frederick followed Anna upstairs, Ruggles whispered mischievously, "Now don't you worry, Johnson. I can't hear too well, either."

As soon as he entered their small room and noticed its proximity to the other small rooms, Frederick declared, "We're not having our wedding night here, not in this room. We can wait."

Anna didn't protest, but Frederick continued as if he had to explain. "We'll find more private rooms in New Bedford. I don't know anything about the place. But the rooms will be our rooms, in a place we decide is good for us."

"Yes, Fred." She looked to him as she sat on the small and narrow bed. It was too short for his long body.

Frederick felt he needed to do something more appropriate to the occasion than what he was not going to do that night. He went to her, caressed her right cheek, held her face in both hands, and then gently kissed her on the lips. It was a light and speedy kiss because the soft luxuriousness of her lips immediately stirred his flesh.

He stepped back and said, "Congratulations, Mrs. Johnson."

"I can wait, Mr. Johnson."

6.

THE NEXT MORNING, FREDERICK and Anna boarded the *John W. Richmond* to cross the Long Island Sound to Newport, Rhode Island, arriving in New Bedford, a whaling town of 12,000 people on the Acushnet River near Buzzards Bay. Colored travelers were not allowed in the cabin, so Frederick and Anna spent the day on deck, sitting close together on a hard and narrow bench, holding hands. As a damp chill surrounded them, they placed a blanket on their legs without complaint, pressed closer, and waited to reach the distant shore. They disembarked quickly for the stagecoach to New Bedford and the house of

Nathan and Mary Page Johnson, who had responded to David Ruggles's request for help. Frederick planned to find work as a caulker. As they walked under a solid canopy of maples, he began to point to the large frame houses and beautiful gardens filled with chrysanthemums, asters, and dianthus.

"Negroes live *here*?" he asked, astonished when they arrived at 21 Seventh Street, once a Quaker meeting house, and now the home of the Johnsons.

Anna immediately thanked them for their hospitality, but Frederick, staring shamelessly, was more impressed by the size of the house and, once inside, the furnishings. The chairs and sofas, upholstered in rich damask, and a library filled with hundreds of volumes, suggested a wealth beyond nine-tenths of the slaveholders of Talbot County, and demonstrated clearly that a free colored man could be successful in New Bedford. Tales of rich New York Negroes were nothing compared to the tables, portraits, and books in the Johnson house. "I will live like this, someday," whispered Frederick to Anna, when they were alone for a moment before tea. "I will."

The Johnsons were the most successful merchants in New Bedford. In her early fifties and ten years older than her husband, Mary, called Polly, was the city's most desired caterer and ran a confectionary shop in part of the house. Nathan Johnson used this confection business to build commercial ties between the Negro and the white communities and was now the most prominent Negro in town.

As soon as they were seated, Nathan informed his guests of New Bedford's zeal for protecting fugitives. He named people and institutions, and described events, detailing the story of Black churchgoers who, using the pretext of a special meeting, lured an informer into their church and promised to kill him if he ever again participated in the return of fugitives.

Frederick thanked his gregarious host and reinforced that coming to New Bedford was the right decision. Johnson urged him to tour his "fair town," walk its few streets, and tour the wharves on the short but crowded waterfront. "Do it as soon as possible," he said.

Anna and Frederick turned to each other, hearing a short-term limit to his hospitality, but Nathan immediately corrected them. "Stay here as long as you need, especially since it is vital that you both take the time to find employment that matches your skills."

"Thank you, sir," Frederick replied.

"Thank you, sir," repeated Anna, now regretting her uncharitable assumption about the Johnsons' hospitality. It would take time, she concluded, to understand Yankees, Black and white. Unfamiliar places always made her uncomfortable, and Anna wouldn't relax until she found work and created her own space, even if that space was someone's kitchen or laundry room. She was determined to find work as a domestic as soon as possible.

When Polly learned that Anna was a domestic servant, she asked, "Did you cook?"

"Yes," Anna replied.

"Then we must talk about Maryland food, how it is prepared and served. I want to change some of the offerings in my catering business. Yes, folks are quite set in their ways around here, but I'm sure I can tempt them to eat different things. I love different kinds of food. Will you teach me?"

"Yes." Anna smiled.

Later, as his wife served tea, Nathan Johnson sat down with his guests and said, "You use Johnson as your name, but there's great confusion because so many newcomers take it. The older families here are not pleased by the number of Johnsons in town."

"Johnson is on our wedding certificate, sir," protested Frederick, looking to his host's face.

Johnson smiled, then replied warmly, "Another change will make it harder for you to be found. It will be a great honor to select a name for you."

"Thank you, sir," said Frederick as he glanced at Anna, who didn't smile as the men decided what her married name should be.

After dinner, everyone moved to the parlor, and Johnson, holding the book in both his hands, read a passage about Roderick Douglas of Alpine in Sir Walter Scott's *Lady of the Lake*:

Hail to the Chief who in triumph advances
Honored and blessed be the evergreen Pine
Long may the tree, his banner that glances
Flourish the shelter and grace of our line!

Johnson beamed. "What do you think? His Christian name sounds like yours: Roderick, Frederick."

"How does Mr. Scott spell the last name?" Frederick replied, an edge to his voice.

"D-o-u-g-l-a-s."

Frederick whispered the name five times and announced, "I'll take it with another *s* at the end."

Johnson frowned, puzzled by this amendment. "Why the added *s*, sir?"

"It's *my s*, sir," Frederick said, perhaps a bit too forcefully.

Johnson looked insulted, and Frederick made amends quickly. "Thank you, sir. I appreciate the generosity of your choice and hope to become worthy of it. Do you like it Anna, Mrs. Anna Douglass?"

Anna looked up from her needlework to say, "It's fine, fine. I hope we don't have to change it again."

"Douglass, it is," Frederick said. "From now on and always."

"Let thee hope," said Johnson, gently urging caution.

"Douglass, it is. Forever. I will not change it again."

After seeing their room in the Johnson house upstairs, Frederick told Anna that it was "perfect" for their wedding night. "Who knows when we'll find our own place, and it won't be as nice as this anyway."

Anna agreed, already used to his ways. About some things, he would make the decisions.

She prepared for the night, washing her face with cold water with her back to him. Frederick was reading in a corner of the bedroom, but she was nevertheless all nerves. She was relieved there was a changing screen nearby.

When she was done, she climbed into bed wearing her cotton nightgown, pulled up the bedding to cover her bosom, and waited.

When she first saw Frederick Bailey at the Society social, she shocked herself by desiring him. No other man had inspired so physical a reaction.

Anna had enjoyed watching him. He was a slave who tried to speak without an Eastern Shore accent, and he was comfortable in his Sunday coat, its cloth stretched by the muscles of his chest and back. The other women fluttered around him, but no one else had any serious interest in him. He was a slave with no future, they all said, dismissing him with regret.

But he had a future. He was a smart, ambitious man, sure to make his way in the world. He had dreams, and he could talk like the best preachers in town. Frederick Bailey was going to be a great man, some of kind of leader of men. That was certain.

Anna also wanted him to be a good husband and father to their children. But only time would tell. Years ago, her mama warned her that most boys don't grow up even though their bodies change; and if they wanted to become good, it would take time.

She knew she would be a good wife. She could do most everything needed: cook, clean, wash, iron, save money, help in any way.

That night, Anna knew what had to be done, the basic act, but she wanted to please Frederick, to do whatever had to be done. She just didn't know what that could be. Anna resolved to follow his lead. Frederick would know what she should do, having learned on the Eastern Shore and the Baltimore streets from girls who could not resist him. Who could resist such a good-looking man, especially if they didn't care about their reputations?

She watched Frederick, dressed in his nightshirt, dim the flame of the single oil lamp until the room was totally dark.

Frederick spoke first. "Anna, I'm happy. I don't deserve you," he whispered as he laid at her side.

Anna almost put her finger to his lips. She didn't want him to talk, not now. But she held back, keeping her resolve to follow his lead. While probing delicately, preparing Anna, Frederick kissed her, and Anna said simply, "Oh, Frederick, oh!" when, at last, their bodies became one.

They lay in each other's arms, silent and serene, for about ten minutes. Then they began again, taking off their night clothes, drawing on what they had learned, trying to get closer before they had to face the new terrors of the unknown land. For the first time, Anna tenderly touched the long scars on his back. In his nakedness, Frederick allowed her to touch that vulnerable part of him. Her knowledge of him seemed complete.

They didn't speak of love that night, but she didn't mind. Anna now understood the meaning of the whispered, forbidden phrase "making love." It captured what she had experienced, without guilt, shame, or fear. She had become a desirable woman who helped her man escape slavery and start a new life. This had to be love. What else could it be?

7.

THE VICIOUS WIND FROM Buzzards Bay chilled the two rooms of their small house behind 157 Elm Street, forcing Frederick and Anna to wear coats and scarves as they huddled away from the window. They never had enough oil or wood and ate broth, potatoes, and bread morning, noon, and night. After living with the Johnsons for almost a month, they now had their own place, but that winter Anna stopped working, and Frederick had been laid off from another day-labor job.

Following Mr. Johnson's advice, Frederick first toured the town and marveled at the wealth concentrated in New Bedford. Even the houses of Negroes were better than the houses of most whites in Baltimore. He assumed that with all the money in town, jobs would be easy to find. He went first to the wharves. Unfortunately, jobs did not come easily.

He earned his first *free* dollar—two silver half dollars—by shoveling a pile of coal into a minister's cellar. He ran home to show Anna, who understood his triumphant pride. "The first will always be the best," she said.

He borrowed a saw from Mr. Johnson and searched for woodcutting jobs. Whalers needed wood for the fires they used to boil down whale fat in huge pots. Frederick was not discouraged when he went into a store to buy cord to brace the saw and the clerk declared with gruff certainty, "You don't belong here." Smarting, Frederick glowered at the man, handed over his money, and departed. He found work that day.

But he wanted to be more than a day laborer. He wanted to earn a salary for using the caulking skills he learned in Baltimore. Instead, he took various day jobs, sawing wood, shoveling coal, digging cellars, moving rubbish from back yards, loading and unloading cargo, and scouring cabins until most work disappeared that winter.

Anna was pregnant, and her mornings that February began with a rush to the bucket in the other room where she would vomit with violent spasms until she fell back, exhausted, and returned to bed and worry. With beef at twenty-five cents a pound and small turkeys for a dollar fifty each, food prices were high and going up. Anna wanted to work, believing that a good wife helped her husband make ends meet, but she was too weak to do more than wash and clean and cook at home.

Anna's illness worried Frederick, even though Anna discounted it with talk about all the "good changes" that come with babies.

"If you think I'm big now, you just wait and see," she said lightly, after groaning again.

He couldn't smile, knowing that women died from pregnancy or childbirth. The possibility of a life without Anna was almost unbearable, and at night he paced the room, struggling with memories of other losses, resisting the urge to blame the baby, as he watched Anna toss and turn in bed. He felt betrayed, as if Anna was a conspirator against his need for order and control.

Their first, happy days in their new home seemed so long ago, but a glance at the door brought that day all back to him, and he smiled again.

After bringing in their belongings on the day of their move to Elm Street, Frederick had said, "Anna, please step out the door."

Dubious, Anna said, "Now why should I do that? I'm already here."

"Now, Anna," he pleaded.

She puffed her cheeks and narrowed her black eyes; that look could freeze hot oil, but Frederick persisted. "Anna, a simple request as your husband."

He put out his hand to lead her. Anna resisted for a final moment, looking down at Frederick's hand as if it was dirty before supper. Then she put her hand into his, and he led her to the door.

Outside on the landing, he said tenderly, "Our first home, and I need to *carry* you inside."

Before Anna could protest, he quickly put one arm behind her back and another below the seat of her dress and lifted her up.

"Fred, put me down! Frederick . . ."

Frederick laughed uproariously, enjoying Anna's surprise and loss of control, the unexpected play.

Anna then started to laugh, even as she continued pleading with him to put her down. "Put me down, now," she commanded. "I'm too heavy."

Finally, Frederick consented and lowered her legs to the floor. He said, "Now we're married, *really* married."

"You didn't have to do that," said Anna. "We had the ceremony, the wedding night."

They had never mentioned or discussed these events.

"I know, but this is our first home, where so much can happen."

"Yes, so much," she said with gentle sarcasm. "The place where Frederick Augustus Washington Bailey Johnson Douglass went out of his living mind."

He took her into his arms. "Welcome, where wonderful things *will* happen."

"We'll be happy here," Anna replied, her truth as incontestable as the light and air of the room surrounding them.

And now, four months later, he quietly reaffirmed the blessing of his new life. Freedom still excited him, its power undiminished by cold wind, illness, bills, and paltry meals. Even though libraries, theaters, lecture halls, hotels, and most stores were closed to him, New Bedford was home.

He found salaried work at Mr. Richmond's brass foundry that spring. He pumped bellows and emptied large flasks six days and two nights a week. But the thrill of working in the brass foundry passed. The work was hard, uncomfortable, monotonous. The heat from the furnace suffocated the room, where Frederick would have to stand for hours pumping the bellows. And smoke and grime dirtied his skin and clothes, forcing him to bathe every night. The noise prevented any talk among the men.

He occupied his time with thoughts of the future. Although he appreciated the opportunity to work regularly for Mr. Richmond, Frederick wanted to ply his own trade, feel the wood and tar on his hand, and witness the slow creation of a work of beauty, a grand schooner or sloop, a ship tall with masts touching the spacious sky, its unfurled sails like flapping wings.

Yet he remained restless and unsure, bothered by the absence of certainty. *What is my calling*? he wondered, fearful that he was already adrift in his new life.

Who am I?

He didn't know his birthdate. He didn't know the name of his father. He didn't own legal freedom papers.

Frederick felt like an impostor, and he needed something true and permanent, a rock that nothing could shake or erase by wind or tide. He still believed that he could be a preacher someday and he thought it proper for him to join an integrated church after arriving in New Bedford. He went to nearby Elm Street Baptist and applied for membership.

The minister, a young man with kind blue eyes and an open smile, received

Frederick with a strong handshake, asked him to sit down before his desk, and immediately assured Frederick that he and all his people were welcome. "We harbor no misgivings," said the Reverend Bonney, looking directly at Frederick, who maintained a slight smile.

Then Bonney leaned forward and said softly, "But . . ."

Frederick hands were fists as they rested on his thighs. "Yes, but?"

Bonney leaned forward with his own fists on the desk and explained, smiling continuously, "We require separate accommodations to *accommodate* those unconverted members who have not yet been won to Christ and his brotherhood. You do understand, don't you?"

"But, sir . . ."

Make the unconverted, white and Black, take the second-class pews, upstairs. Frederick's pride more than his Christianity demanded his seat on the main floor of Elm Street Methodist.

Bonney leaned forward even more and arched his eyes. He said evenly, "Our Lord never forgot the sinner, and we should not."

There was a long pause. Bonney never stopped smiling, his composure like a shield.

Frederick took a deep breath. "Very well," he replied, convincing himself that the whites of Elm Street Baptist would eventually see the errors of their ways and receive its Negro members into true Christian brotherhood, and stop the practice of segregated pews.

The Reverend Bonney proved to be an effective and insightful preacher. He told stories, using short quotations to illustrate and emphasize his lessons, and revealed an affinity for family conflicts in the Old Testament.

Frederick was impressed.

At the end of the Sunday sermon, Bonney, sang "Salvation 'tis a joyful sound" with mellifluous tenderness in his tenor, and invited members to come forward and taste the bread and wine of the Lord's Supper.

The colored members of the church, followed by Frederick and Anna, came down from the gallery and stood against the back wall. As the white celebrants emptied their rows, the others waited, their eyes riveted to the ground. Frederick watched closely, wondering why they were unsmiling and nervous, their heads bowed as if the altar was now too sacred to approach. Why were they not moving forward after the last row had entered the center aisle?

Bonney waited for several minutes after the last white member returned to his seat. Then as he waved his hand, he announced in that high- pitched voice, "Come forward, colored friends! Come forward. You, too, have an interest in the blood of Christ. God is no respecter of persons. Come forward and take this holy sacrament to your comfort."

Now that separate pieces of bread and different cups were ready for them, the colored members went forward, their heads still bowed, arms limp. Frederick closed his eyes, seeing Thomas Auld mouth similar pieties, that white skin oily with rancid hypocrisy.

In Baltimore, there was no pretense of equality, either, but slaves still shared the bread and wine. Frederick turned quickly. He had to leave before a curse spit out of his mouth to dirty the white walls. There had to be a solid barrier between him and the Reverend Bonney, who now represented every southern minister he despised. He pulled at Anna's hand.

She didn't resist, understanding the reason for their hasty departure. Frederick slammed the door behind him, angry that he had been such a fool. He would not be duped again. He would try other integrated churches, but he would ask detailed, pointed questions during the initial interview *before* he attended another humiliating service. But he was not successful. All the churches he investigated had the same practices, separate seats in the gallery, and separate sacraments. He would have to join a Black church.

He found Zion Chapel, a congregation of the African Methodist Episcopal Zion denomination that met in a schoolhouse on Second Street. Its minister, the Reverend William Serrington, was a pious and intelligent preacher who lacked eloquence but had no illusions about the purpose of his church. "Mr. Douglass, we can be ourselves here," he said, repeating the argument made for separate Negro Methodists churches since the turn of the century. "We cannot be humiliated, and we don't have to wait until *they* overcome before we do for ourselves what needs to be done."

"I understand," Frederick agreed.

Frederick soon served as steward, sexton, class leader, clerk, and exhorter.

He went with Anna every Sunday, and they attended church meetings during the week. At one such meeting, Frederick spoke against the idea that the "Negro problem" could be solved if only Negroes emmigrated to Africa or anywhere else. He wanted to escape his past and leave the details of his story behind, but Frederick had to denounce colonization. "No, we are *not* leaving," he asserted. "This is *our* land, and we will not leave so we can make it convenient for slavers to continue their odious enslavement as we board ships back to where they captured us. No, they have to live with us, as we have learned to live with them."

In January, a Negro man, a few years older than Frederick, came to his door and asked him to buy a subscription to the *Liberator.*

Frederick immediately declined. He had no money.

The man, Mr. Seneca Morris, gently persisted as he lifted the four-page sheet, nine by fourteen inches, four columns to the page, closer to Frederick's face. Frederick scanned it again, intrigued that a white man named William Lloyd Garrison printed an antislavery paper and sold it to coloreds.

"The rate is only two dollars a year," Mr. Morris continued, "and if you can't pay now, we still would like you on our lists. And when times are better, Mr. Garrison will gladly accept payment."

"You'll give it to me free for now?"

"Yes."

Frederick remained unimpressed by the paper's appearance. There were no illustrations, and the letters were cramped, making it hard to read. But he liked the inscription below the title: "Our country is the world—our countrymen are mankind."

Nevertheless, Frederick declined the offer. He had enough to read, just finishing Scott's *Quentin Durwood*, and was about to begin Gibbon's *The Decline and Fall of the Roman Empire*, both loans from Nathan Johnson.

But he glanced at a line that forced him to read further. He put his hand under the paper for support as he read with growing excitement Garrison's manifesto, reprinted from the first issue: "I will be as harsh as truth, and as uncompromising as justice. On this subject I do not wish to think, or speak, or write, with moderation."

He looked up and asked, "Who is he?"

But he didn't wait for an answer and continued reading: "Tell a man whose house is on fire, to give a moderate alarm; tell him to moderately rescue his wife from the hands of the ravisher; tell the mother to gradually extricate her babe from the fire into which it has fallen—but urge me not to use moderation in a cause like the present. I am in earnest—I will not equivocate—will not excuse—I will not retreat a single inch—And I Will Be heard."

"He's a great man," said Morris, raising his voice. "He says what no one else dares to say. He's the colored man's best friend."

Frederick looked up, realizing that they were still standing near the closed door on a cold, early evening. He stepped back with a sweeping gesture of his left arm and invited Mr. Morris to sit. "Please, tell me more about Mr. Garrison, and accept my apologies for not inviting you sooner."

Mr. Morris, a thin, owlish man dressed in clothes too large for him, knew few personal details, not even Garrison's age. But Morris had some facts. Born in Massachusetts, Garrison went to Baltimore about ten years ago to become the editor of *The Genius of Universal Emancipation*, the antislavery paper of the Quaker Benjamin Lundy.

"Baltimore!" said Frederick, amazed. "I was there then, I think, but I don't remember his name. I was a boy."

Morris explained that Garrison first supported the movement for gradual emancipation through colonizing freed Negroes abroad, but he concluded that the only just antislavery position was immediate emancipation without colonization. "They put him in jail," said Morris, closing his eyes and nodding his head.

Garrison must have been the abolitionist that Hugh Auld talked about! A part of Frederick's past was now making sense. There was a mysterious confluence between two disparate lives, as if part of a divine plan. Morris shared more information.

Upon his release from jail, Garrison returned to Boston and began publishing his own antislavery journal in 1831, just months before Nat Turner's ill-fated revolt. "A mob tried to kill him in Boston," continued Morris, obviously proud of Garrison's near martyrdom. "He tells the truth about white people, and they don't like it, not one bit."

Frederick needed no further proof. Here was a man willing to die for Black freedom, a white man stirring up trouble, a man with a clear mission worthy of serious study. "Send it to me, and I promise to pay when I get the money. You won't regret this, nor will Mr. Garrison."

"Welcome," said Mr. Morris, extending his hand to a new convert.

Frederick took it but objected to the inference. "But I didn't *join*."

"We're all students in Mr. Garrison's school," concluded Mr. Morris solemnly as he leaned back in the chair. "I suggest that you join our colored antislavery society here in town. You will learn much, I can assure you."

"That is perhaps true," said Frederick. "But I want to read more of the *Liberator* before I join anything. I need to know what I'm talking about."

"Very well," Morris agreed, relaxing into his chair, his work done. "I'll have tea," he added before the offer of any.

As promised, the *Liberator* came every week. An impatient Frederick eagerly read every column, every word. He read the columns, editorials, and letters two and three times at first sitting, absorbing ideas, memorizing passages. He also took the paper to the foundry and posted it near the bellows for further study when bored.

Frederick found much of the *Liberator* confounding, and sometimes confusing. It was a knot of invective and biblical allusions in paragraphs crammed with asides and hyphenated phrases with exclamations marks. The editor was waging a complex doctrinal battle to extend the range of antislavery thought, and in article after article Garrison demanded that all "*true abolitionists* embrace peace, the rights of women, and the doctrine of 'nonresistance,'" which denied the legitimacy of all human law and government.

It was apparent that not all abolitionists in America agreed about the best way to end slavery; but Garrison was indubitably clear, having drafted a

Declaration of Sentiments of the American Anti-Slavery Society that delegates at a convention in 1833 unanimously signed.

Antislavery was a Christian movement, and its methods were moral, not political. Frederick wasn't sure these issues mattered to the enslaved. Nevertheless, Frederick began to love the *Liberator*. It denounced slavery and racial prejudice, exposed hypocrisy, and demanded immediate freedom and equality with burning intensity. Its opposition to authority especially appealed to Frederick, who spent his entire life struggling against it. He also celebrated Garrison's attack on the clergy.

Often, Frederick would lower the sheets to his lap and close his eyes, trying to recover from the shock of seeing such brutal truths in print. This white man had impudence, pounds of it. And he certainly had courage.

To Anna, he read a favorite passage, needing to share his discoveries.

"Just listen, just listen," he insisted one evening, and Anna put down her darning as a signal to begin. Frederick read from a "Short Catechism:"

Why is immediate emancipation wrong and dangerous?
Because the slaves are Black.
Why are our slaves not fit for freedom?
Because they are Black.
Why are abolitionists fanatics and madmen?
Because those for whom they plead are Black.
Why are the slaves contented and happy?
Because they are Black.
Why don't they want to be free?
Because they are Black.
Why is slavery the cornerstone of our republic?
Because its victims are Black.

With each refrain, Frederick's voice became more impassioned and more mocking. The racist argument, heard since childhood at the dinner table and in the parlor and church, was now reduced to the absurdity of mere color, and Frederick chortled, enjoying what was now a silent duet with an intellectual and emotional partner.

Frederick now leaned forward in his chair and waited for muted but enthusiastic agreement. Anna was never effusive, but she was direct and to the point.

Anna smiled but said nothing.

Frederick snapped the thin paper shut. "Well, Anna, what do you think?"

"He does go on," she observed, still sewing.

"Is that all?" he asked, his eyes focused on the rise of that needle.

Anna continued, "You read good, real good."

"No, not my reading. The words—*his* words."

"We've all heard them lies before."

"There in print, Anna. It's . . ." Frederick stopped as he watched another pull of the needle through a pair of his trousers. There was no point in continuing. Unable to read, how could she fathom the power and significance of the published word?

She observed with quiet force, "Be careful, Frederick."

"What do you mean?"

"Be careful. You'll trust that man, and he will let you down like all the other white men."

"What men?" he asked, knowing the answer, and yet still irritated with Anna's insistence on telling the truth.

"There are good white men, but the ones you knew, the ones you told me about, and thought would do right by you, *those* men . . ."

Incensed, he interrupted her. "There is no comparison, and you should know that."

"You hated them for not being who you thought they were."

"That's not true, not true at all. I hated them because they beat me, beat my Aunt Hester, my cousin Henny."

"Just be careful, that's all," Anna insisted gently.

"Mr. Garrison is our friend. He was willing to die for telling the truth about us. How can you put him and those others together? I never thought you feared all white people."

"That's not true. But they all have to prove . . ."

"That's enough," Frederick insisted, and he added the word "please" when Anna's wide eyes and lifted eyebrows told him he had gone too far.

But Anna smiled. "Just wait until you get into that paper."

"What?" Frederick asked, searching for a clue to this irrelevant reply. It exasperated him, these sudden shifts in conversation, as if Anna were listening to someone else.

"I'll be so proud when your name is in there. It'll happen, that's for sure. You'll see."

Frederick leaned back into his chair. "I can't risk getting in the papers, you know that."

"Frederick Bailey can't, but Frederick Douglass can. You do want to, don't you?"

He didn't reply, knowing the answer.

8.

EVEN THOUGH IT WAS only a line in the *Liberator* declaring that Frederick Douglass had spoken against colonization on March 12, 1839, he gasped before muttering, "My god, my god." Frederick stared at the issue of the *Liberator,* his eyes blinking as he tried to focus on the small print.

"What is it?" asked Anna, her voice rising. She was now feeling much better. The nausea and vomiting had passed. She was eating more, fattening her face and arms, and cooking and cleaning with alacrity. The coming of spring in Massachusetts, she told Frederick, also lifted her soul. Finally, she could look out to Buzzards Bay and not see the thick, endless gray foam push against the blackening sky.

"Look, Anna!" Frederick exclaimed. "My name, there. It's in the paper."

"Oh, Frederick," she said proudly, as he pointed to the lower corner of the third page. Anna touched his arm. "It's good."

"It will be so much better when you can actually read the words, when I get the time to teach you."

Anna's smile faded. "It's too late for me."

"No, it isn't. Besides, my name isn't too long."

"It's too late."

"Why?" He was baffled by her resistance to learning how to read even his name or hers.

"There's no need, and I'm too old for lessons."

"We all need . . ."

"I don't."

"But . . ." He stopped; he didn't want an argument to ruin the pleasure of seeing his name in the *Liberator* that day.

He saw his name again in the March 29 issue of the *Liberator*. He had signed a petition against colonization after joining the New Bedford Antislavery Society just a few weeks before. Three Zion church members had urged him to join the interracial organization.

His name was listed in alphabetical order among the other Black and white petitioners. The thrill of seeing his name again had not diminished, and now he silently relived that moment when he spoke to an integrated audience for the very first time, urged by Reverend Thomas James, an ordained minister for the African Methodist Episcopal church who was born a slave and witnessed his mother being dragged away, never to be seen again. "Tell your story," James insisted. "Attacking slavery is a religious act."

Even so, Frederick felt out of place. He froze, unable to respond, despite his fantasies about subduing white crowds.

Yankees were strange, Frederick had decided soon after arriving in New Bedford. On the docks they worked hard, accomplishing with four men what a squad of ten would do in Baltimore. But they didn't sing or tell jokes during the workday, and they rarely raised their voices. They held their heads high, convinced that their way of life, simple, stern, and godly, was superior to all others. They hated with a purity unknown to Maryland, and their prejudice hung around Frederick's neck like a heavy stone.

Everything strange, unusual, different, or new was feared, and Yankee whites never let an opportunity pass for declaring that strangers didn't belong. Frederick could not ignore the wide-eyed malevolence and pinched noses, the inhalation of breaths, the clenched teeth and fists whenever he walked the streets away from the wharves.

Some women crossed the street rather than pass near him. Those who did come close invariably clutched their bags to their chests and looked away. The men glared, demanding that he avert his eyes, or pretend that he did not exist. A few spat after Frederick had passed. Others merely gawked as if a six-foot creature dressed in coat and trousers had pranced by with a bright red ball bouncing off his nose.

They seemed afraid of him, and at times their fear pleased him. But this constant self-assessment of his own value often overwhelmed him, making him want to cover his ears and no longer hear their curses: Nigger, low down, ignorant, good-for-nothing, big-lipped, foul-mouthed, stinking ape from Africa, heathen, devil worshipper, blood drinker, flesh eater, sexual monster. Savage. Child. Nigger, who do you think you are?

That night at the New Bedford Antislavery meeting he wanted to flee. The moment he had dreamed of had come at last, but there was no joy in it. Frederick turned his head to verify his escape door.

He couldn't move. This was his moment.

Frederick took a deep breath and returned his eyes to the sight of the expectant and smiling faces of the mostly white members of the New Bedford Society, men and women who had faced opprobrium and danger on his behalf and of slaves and free men and women everywhere. These were his people now. He had to trust them.

He told his story. It came in phrases and pauses, a sputtering of reminiscences that didn't flow like the great sermons of the preachers he admired, but he persisted with grim determination, as he avoided incriminating details. "I was born in . . . a slave state. I don't know my exact age. I've seen no records. I wanted to know my birthday. The white children knew theirs, but I didn't. This made me sad. My father was a white man. That's what everybody said, but I can't be sure. I didn't know my mother. I saw her at night, five or six times, maybe.

I've had two masters. They owned me, but I can't tell you their names. One of them sent me away to be beaten."

At the end of his talk, he received warm applause from everyone in the audience. Anna was there, and she applauded too, but he didn't describe his fears to her later that night, and he didn't refer to them when again he saw his name in the March 29 *Liberator*. He had even more exciting news to tell her. Mr. Garrison was coming to New Bedford to speak on April 16.

"That's nice," was all she had to say at first.

Frederick clenched his teeth and inhaled deeply through his nose, remaining calm and giving himself a moment before a reply. The midwife had said that nothing should upset her.

Didn't Anna understand?

"I see," he said coldly.

"Since I can't go, you'll be my eyes and ears," said Anna, as if she had heard nothing to concern or alarm her, "and I know you'll tell me everything about it."

"More than you'll want to know," he noted sarcastically.

"Oh, Frederick," she said without offense, shifting in her chair. She was heavy, fat in the face, neck, and arms, and uncomfortable all the time, "You're so serious all the time, about everything."

"All I want is for you to understand."

"I do," she insisted with fierce pride, her eyes declaring the end of their conversation.

The day came, and William Lloyd Garrison spoke in Mechanics Hall before men and women who faced criticism and possible risk by coming out to hear the "dangerous" Garrison and sit in an integrated audience.

It rained that night, and Frederick sat uncomfortably in his wet clothes, thrilled and, to his dismay, a little disappointed. Garrison was a short, thin, balding man who wore steel rimmed spectacles on a narrow but prominent nose. His tight, black overcoat and loose cravat made him seem small and distracted, like a mortician at the wrong funeral. But his voice was strong, earnest, and unforgettable. It projected an absolute and passionate conviction impossible to ignore.

Garrison proudly proclaimed, "The ungodly and the violent, the proud and pharisaical, the ambitious and tyrannical, principalities and powers, and spiritual wickedness in high places, may combine to crush us. We shall not be afraid of their terror, nor be troubled. Our confidence is in the Lord Almighty, not in man. What can sustain us but that faith which overcomes the world?"

Frederick had never heard such words. There was a profound difference between hearing them and reading them, and their utterance was made more stirring by the calm of Garrison's moral outrage. He was direct and to the point, but he never raised his voice, as if he knew that ideas could burn without the wind.

At the end of his long speech for universal reforms, Garrison concluded, "Together, hand in hand, we will rise above the dung heap of this mortal world and achieve ultimate moral victory."

Frederick saw and heard the qualities of the true abolitionist. Garrison denounced slavery and prejudice with a reckless courage that made some people blink and cover their eyes and others stare into the bright light he would thrust into their faces. He needed converts to inspire and enemies to expose. In the battle between good and evil, only unconditional surrender was possible. Garrison was a holy warrior. "I have need to be all on fire, for I have mountains of ice about me to melt," he concluded.

Frederick decided what he would do. He would preach about slavery using every tool learned in *The Columbian Orator,* and he would take every opportunity at the meetings of the New Bedford Antislavery Society to become like Garrison, an honest and courageous man in a land of hypocrites, knaves, and fools.

After the ovation ended, Mr. Garrison explained that he had another meeting to go to and left the hall surrounded by his white New Bedford supporters. Frederick felt abandoned, almost desperate, struggling to remember everything he saw and heard, wanting a lasting impression since he did not know when he would ever see the great man again. *I must see him again. Be with him, near him.*

Frederick turned to his associate, Dalton Price, a cabinet maker who was one of the most cultivated men in the Society, "He is everything I want to be."

Frederick swore to himself, *Garrison's words are my words, and I will be heard!*

9.

TWO YEARS PASSED BEFORE Frederick saw Garrison again.

In the meantime, on June 24, Frederick and Anna's first child was born. He rushed home from the foundry when he received the news that Anna was about to deliver.

Mrs. Cannon, the stout, middle-aged midwife, assured him Anna was doing fine. But Anna's deep moans from the bedroom told him otherwise. He tried to go in, but Mrs. Cannon blocked the doorway, using both hands to restrain Frederick.

"Sir, you can't go in."

"Mrs. Cannon, I've seen . . ."

"But this is your wife!" Mrs. Cannon exclaimed.

"And this is my home," he shouted, putting his arm on her shoulder, ready to push her aside. He had to make sure that Anna was well, that everything was fine, that nothing would go wrong. He needed assurances from Anna herself. He narrowed his eyes, flared his nostrils, and said, "Now do what I tell you."

Mrs. Cannon reluctantly stepped aside, but followed him into the room, keeping a safe distance. The room was dark, the curtains drawn even though it was hot and humid. Anna's bed sheets were drenched with sweat, and her covers pulled toward her chest in tight knots.

"Anna, Anna. I'm here," he whispered. He put his hand on hers. "I love you, Anna."

Anna did not open her eyes, but she smiled before she shuddered with the next contraction.

"Say something, Anna. Are you alright?"

She nodded her head, then shuddered again.

Mrs. Cannon intervened. "Mr. Douglass, it's time. You'll have to leave now. She's ready, and you'll just be in the way. I can't work with you here. I'll have you come in as soon as the baby is here."

She gently pulled at his arm when he did not immediately respond. He looked at her hand, offended by her touch, but Mrs. Cannon ignored him and led him to the door. "It will be soon," she said sympathetically. "Now don't you worry."

He was out the door, then heard the key turn. "You can't shut me out!" He pounded the door with his fist.

The door opened immediately, and Mrs. Cannon pleaded, "Mr. Douglass, Mrs. Douglass don't want you rushing in here when the baby comes out. No wife wants that!"

The door closed again.

He crossed the room and sat down. He didn't know what to do next as his mind filled with images of legs, screaming babies, bloody sheets, and hot water. He jumped up and started to pace, hoping to break his obsessive thinking about death and childbirth. Too many mothers and babies had already died, making it all too common, ordinary, and expected.

Soon he heard a baby's loud cry, a hearty cry for someone so new. He rushed to the door to go in and then stopped when he remembered that it was locked. He stepped back, anticipating Mrs. Cannon's appearance.

She came out smiling and nodding her head. "Mr. Douglass, everybody is fine. Anna is a strong woman, and you have a daughter."

"A daughter," Frederick whispered.

Mrs. Cannon heard a hint of disappointment. "Now Mr. Douglass. I know you men all want sons first, but you don't decide these things. And if your daughter is like Mrs. Douglass, she'll make you proud."

He went inside. Anna was sitting up in her bed, pillows propped behind her. The tension in her face was gone.

"Anna," he whispered.

He saw the little one cradled in her arms and wrapped in large towels. She was so small, so fragile, and her face was a deep red ball of furrows, like a rose.

He kissed Anna on the forehead and then stepped back to look at his family. He trembled with the love and joy he felt. Anna held out the child to him with a small, gentle lift of her arms. "Oh, Fred, she is ours, not Thomas Auld's, not Hugh Auld's, not nobody else's. She's *ours*."

"Yes, ours." For this child, forever free on northern soil, he had to make her proud. Pride, fierce ambition, gratitude, and sheer joy stirred within him all at once, and visions of himself as a gentleman of color and a pillar of the community raising a family whose future was brighter than his own appeared in his mind's eye. He whispered tenderly, "Oh, Rosetta, *our* Rosetta."

Then Lewis Henry came on October 9, 1840, sixteen months after Rosetta. Frederick made sure to list their birth dates in his own ledger of important events; he would no longer leave important dates scattered in church baptism records and court files, difficult to find, easy to lose from fire or neglect.

And a third child was on the way.

The family also moved to a larger house at 111 Ray Street. Frederick now had steady work. Money was still tight, but more importantly, everyone was safe and healthy, and Frederick continued his self-education, studying scripture, reading every issue of the *Liberator*, and attending antislavery meetings weekly.

He followed the career of Garrison closely, absorbed by the *Liberator's* accounts of how he wrestled control of the American Anti-Slavery Society when its leaders refused to allow women on the executive committee. Garrison, insisting on the equal status of women delegates, went to the World Antislavery Convention in London and refused to participate when the London committee would not allow female delegates to vote.

Now Garrison was back in New Bedford preparing for a major midsummer antislavery convention on the island of Nantucket, sixty miles to the south. Many of the great luminaries of the abolition cause would be there: Garrison, Wendell Phillips, Parker Pillsbury, Edmund Quincy, Lucretia Mott, and others.

Garrison didn't give a speech at the Bristol meeting, but Frederick wanted to follow him to Nantucket, even though it would mark the very first time he would be away from his family. The meeting in Nantucket promised to be the most exciting and important antislavery meeting in his life.

William Coffin, a white Quaker and bookkeeper in the Merchants Bank who had heard Frederick speak at an antislavery meeting at Zion Chapel, urged him to go. An ardent abolitionist, Coffin told Frederick his story must be heard by far more people. "A multitude awaits thee," he said during the Bristol Meeting. "I'm going immediately to help with the preparations, and I'm going to ask thee to speak there, when the right moment comes. Do it."

This confession made Frederick even more nervous. He wanted to attend the meeting, but now he had the added pressure of speaking before a distinguished interracial audience.

Nevertheless, he agreed.

But he wondered if the thirty-five white men and women, gathered with six Negroes to board the steam ferry to Nantucket, would do more than pass resolutions against discrimination. He found out almost immediately.

When they boarded, entering the main cabin with other white passengers, the white passengers huddled in small groups, whispered unheard curses on contemptuous lips, and kept their distance as if the abolitionists were lepers.

The ferry's captain, Lot Phinney, entered the cabin. "Ladies and gentlemen, the company rules forbid colored people in the cabin. They can be accommodated on the upper deck."

"This is a disgrace!" cried a young white delegate.

"Yes, an outrage!" said another.

A burly man, whose red hair accentuated his flaming face, shouted from the rear, "Look at the apes and their keepers. Nigger lovers!"

Another protested: "We're not sitting in the same room with dirty niggers! Get them outa here!"

The captain raised his arms to silence the threatening crowd. "The *Telegraph* will not leave until the Negro passengers occupy separate quarters."

Frederick would not move.

When three other Negro delegates started to leave, Mr. Garrison pointed to the captain and declared as if he were on stage before hundreds, "See, ladies and gentlemen, how the long arm of the slave power reaches into the free, clean air of our North, polluting the hearts of men!"

Phinney didn't flinch. He even smiled. "Mr. Garrison, you are aboard *my* vessel, not in Boston trying to shame a mob. I have my orders. We will not leave until your colored friends leave. You and the other ladies and gentlemen may stay, of course, to enjoy our accommodations."

Garrison countered, "Are not our colored brethren entitled to the benefits of the cabin, since they paid the same as did the rest?"

A very tall man, Captain Phinney stepped forward and looked down at Garrison. "I have my orders."

"We shall not leave until our colored friends are properly accommodated!" insisted Garrison, his tone strong but still polite.

Phinney changed tactics. He softened his voice and lowered his head to confer with Garrison. "Sir, you must stop this protest."

Garrison softened also. "Sir, you must give me what I want."

"I cannot have Negroes in . . ."

"Let us have all the upper deck for a meeting," said Garrison.

Phinney grinned. "Sir, a compromise. You?"

"Repeat not that word," said Garrison with a smile, looking up to heaven. He announced to everyone, "Let us all leave this cabin as our moral protest against bigotry, and on the upper deck, under the pure blue sky of heaven, proclaim the righteousness of our cause. May those who wish join us."

He marched through the crowd and climbed the stairs to the upper deck, with cheering all about him. The delegates followed.

Garrison's stand was proof to Frederick that his new associates were true to their printed word. They would share discrimination with their colored friends rather then watch them face it alone. His respect for Garrison deepened.

Despite the integrated meeting aboard the *Telegraph*, Frederick and the five Negroes distanced themselves from the white passengers when they disembarked on the island. The mere sight of an integrated group created consternation. People pointed, clustered in small groups, and murmured quiet insults. The Negro men didn't want a confrontation on the streets.

The port was filled with whalers, and Nantucket's Main Street was packed with people rushing into the Custom House, the Pacific Bank, and shops. Above it all on the hill sat large brick mansions built by whale oil.

Then Frederick saw Coffin, who approached him with complete indifference to the conventions of public intercourse, greeting him warmly, shaking his hand, and welcoming him to "this most beautiful isle." He was equally warm and gracious with the other men.

Coffin quickly told them about the changes to that night's meeting. The meeting was originally scheduled for the Athenaeum, the town's elegant cultural center. But the Athenaeum's trustees revoked permission for use of the hall when they learned many unacceptable facts: hundreds of Black and white outsiders were coming to town, outsiders who by practicing racial and women's equality could invite violence; and the Antislavery Society had invited 200 residents of Guinea, the Black section of town, promising them exposure to an important Black speaker. The meeting had to be moved to the Big Shop, a large building for making harpooners' boats at the end of town, just below the Quaker cemetery. A large crowd was expected.

That night the Big Shop was so packed that many had to look through the windows from the outside. Others had found space in the loft, their legs dangling from the rafters. Workers patrolled the perimeter to discourage rowdies.

Inside, the prominent leaders and speakers of the Massachusetts Antislavery Society sat in chairs with tables at the front—Garrison, Wendell Phillips, Lucretia Mott, Parker Pillsbury, Edmund Quincy, and John A. Collins, the society's general agent who hired antislavery speakers and arranged their schedules. Frederick sat in the third row of the audience, Coffin at his left side.

Garrison was subdued, and the speeches that followed supporting the resolution were prosaic and dull. Even the oratory of the fiery Wendell Phillips was restrained. The Quakers were solemn and still, but the Negro boys and men in the rafters, now restless, began to grumble.

The speeches supporting the resolution had ended. Coffin turned in his chair and whispered to Frederick, "Now is thy time."

Without hesitating, Frederick stood, and asked, "Mr. Chairman, may I speak?"

"Yes," replied the chair, registering no surprise. Frederick turned to face the people behind him. He knew that this was his hour, this was the defining moment of his future life as a free man. There could be no more denial or even hesitation. This was destiny.

He stammered. He apologized for being a novice. His sentences were fragmentary, disconnected, and random as he struggled to frame a compelling narrative. But he told his story.

"I feel greatly embarrassed when I attempt to address an audience of white people. I am not used to speaking to them, and it makes me tremble when I do so, because I have always looked up to them in fear. My friends, I have come to tell you about slavery. What I know of it, as I have felt it. When I came north, I was astonished to find that abolitionists knew so much about it, that they were acquainted with its deadly effects as well as if they had lived in its midst. But though they give you its history—though they can depict its horrors, they cannot speak as I can from experience; they cannot refer you to a back covered with scars, as I can; for I have felt these wounds. I have suffered under the lash without the power of resisting. Yes, my blood has sprung out as the lash embedded itself in my flesh. I can tell you what I have seen with my own eyes, felt on my own person. I have the gratification to know that if I fall by the utterance of truth in this matter, that if I shall be hurled back into bondage to gratify the slaveholder—to be killed by inches—that every drop of blood which I shall shed, every groan which I shall utter, every pain which shall rack my frame, every sob in which I shall indulge, shall be the instrument, under God, of tearing down the bloody pillar of slavery, and of hastening the day of deliverance for the three million of my brethren in bondage."

An outburst of applause struck his entire body as a roar filled the hall. His feet shook with the rattle of the floorboards from pounding feet.

Garrison jumped to his feet and came to Frederick, taking his hand and leading him to the front of the assembly, where he raised his own arm and shouted to the crowd: "Have we been listening to a piece of property, a beast of burden, a chattel person, or a *man*?"

"A man! A man!" answered the audience. "A man!"

Garrison went on: "Shall we ever allow him to be carried back to slavery—law or no law, constitution or no constitution?"

"No! No!" screamed the crowd, now standing, galvanized by Garrison's rhetorical questions.

"Will you succor and protect him as a brother man—a resident of the old Bay state?"

"Yes, yes, yes!" all answered. Many still applauded, and a crowd of men pressed forward.

Garrison released Frederick's hand, stepped back, and personally applauded Frederick. This tribute touched Frederick deeply. He tried to find adequate words, but all he could say was, "Thank you, sir. Thank you. Thank you."

Then came another shock after he was surrounded by the congratulating leaders of the Massachusetts Society. John Collins, the general agent of the Society, asked him to become a full-time employee. "Join us, Mr. Douglass," Collins said. "We need you."

At thirty years of age, with large, soft hands and a determined glint in his gray eyes, Collins did not wait for Frederick to answer. He went on, "You have a gift, and as a former slave you will give us great credibility."

Frederick shook his head and gently protested, "Sir, I can't do this. I'm not able. I don't have the experience, the education."

Collins waved his right hand. "Sir, you have proven yourself. Just tell your story."

Frederick tried another tactic. "I have a wife and two children to take care of."

"We'll pay you four hundred and fifty dollars a year."

This was a good wage, a reliable wage, even if it meant being away from home. And yet, still reluctant, Frederick countered with another argument. "The publicity might bring recapture. I can't risk losing everything."

Collins's eyes softened, and he spoke gently, "We'll do everything we can to protect you. Just tell your story, as I have suggested, no names, no specific places. No one will be able to know; there are other slave speakers."

"But why should I then?"

Collins said what Frederick wanted and needed to hear, "But there is no one like *you*. You can talk to us, unlike those other fugitives. You can make white audiences *see*."

Frederick finally agreed, but with a condition. "I can't leave my family off and on for a year, and I don't have that much to tell. I'll do it for three months. I'm sure that by then I'll have done what I can to be useful."

Collins didn't hesitate. "Good, good, Mr. Douglass. Go home, tell your wife, and meet me in Boston on the twentieth. Here is my address. We'll discuss your job, and what I plan for you, in greater detail. When you arrive, I'll have a place where you can stay. Our colored friends have been most gracious."

"Thank you, sir."

"No," Collins said. "I should thank *you*. Welcome to the ranks of freedom's friends."

Later, after all the speeches were said and the resolutions passed, Frederick returned to Guinea a hero. The colored citizens of Nantucket and their colored guests from New Bedford surrounded him, patting his back, shaking his hand, and marveling at his ability to move the white folks.

★

In bed at his host's home that night, Frederick reflected on how his life was going to change, and he would have to tell Anna. He looked to the ceiling *What have I done? What have I done to Anna and the children? How can I leave them for three whole months? How will Anna manage?*

On the trip back to New Bedford, he tried to not brood. After all, he now had a well-paying job, enough to cover the bills. Nevertheless, he was keenly aware of the sacrifices Anna had made on his behalf. Now she had to sacrifice even more. He also could not avoid the potential future. If successful, he could be offered a permanent position with the Massachusetts Society, a position that would entail even more time away from home.

But he was not seeking her permission. As the man of the house, he had the final word on most matters. Anna understood that. However, her approval and support still mattered. He wanted even more; he wanted her blessing.

When he reached home and told her about the job offer, she sat there as inscrutable as a statue, rocking Lewis in her arms gently, her eyes on her son born on October 9, 1840.

Anna looked up and smiled. "He'll be so proud of his Daddy. This is what's *supposed* to happen."

"Then you don't mind, my being away and all?"

"I can manage. It's only three months."

Frederick could not promise her this. He hoped that his contract would be extended. This was the work he wanted to do more than anything else. "It could go longer, if I'm successful, if I satisfy my new employers."

Anna's eyes widened. "If?" she sniffed. "There'll be no *if*. They'll have to give you more time, so good you'll be. And if they don't, they'll have *me* to answer to."

"Oh, Anna." Frederick rushed to embrace her in the chair across from him. "I will make you proud, too."

"Already am."

10.

INTRODUCED IN 1841 TO audiences as "a recent graduate of the peculiar institution with his diploma written on his back," Frederick garnered reviews that extolled his virtues and qualifications.

Douglass's appearance, reported the *Liberator*, "gave a fresh impulse to anti-slavery." And the editor of the *Higham Patriot* said Frederick reminded him of Spartacus, the Gladiator: "He is very fluent in the use of language, and appropriate language too; and talks as well, for all we could see, as men who spent all their lives over books. He is forcible, keen, and very sarcastic; and considering the poor advantages he must have had as a slave, he is certainly a remarkable man."

Frederick prepared his speeches by scrawling about two dozen words on a sheet of paper. When Collins first saw this, he asked, "What's this?" and Frederick laughed. "This is my speech!"

Using these words as his rhetorical outline, Frederick always began deliberately and calmly with a soft voice that at first could barely be heard; he often admitted that he was nervous speaking before white audiences. Then his voice would become louder, deeper, and clearer, a crescendo accompanied by hand gestures and movement on the platform, as if preparing for extended exercise. Then he would assail his target, usually the narrow and vacuous mind of the bigot and the enormous iniquity of the system which he claimed as its cause.

"People in general will say they like colored men as any other, but in their proper place," he said at one point. "Who is to decide what is their *proper* place? They assign us that place; they don't let us do it for ourselves, nor will they allow us a voice in the decision. You degrade us, and then ask us why we are degraded—you shut our mouths, and then ask why we don't speak—you close your colleges and seminaries against us, and then ask us *why* we don't know more!"

Frederick enjoyed exposing the absurdities of slavery's defense through exaggeration. His parodies of white preacher sermons justifying slavery to slaves delighted Collins and many others. Hoots, hollers, and enthusiastic applause interrupted Frederick repeatedly. Abolition was serious business, and laughter was a deadly weapon.

But there was also seething anger, the anger that fueled his desire for freedom. Even when Frederick began his lectures with the admission that he was embarrassed and inexperienced before white people, he would not ignore the potential dangers slavery posed for everyone. He issued a warning: "On the agitation of this subject the slave has built his highest hopes. My friends, let it not be quieted, for upon you the slaves look for help. There will be no outbreaks, no insurrections, whilst you continue this excitement: let it cease, and the crimes that would follow cannot be told."

"That is not *our* way," warned Collins, reproving but not angry. "We are peaceful, seeking moral change."

"It is my hope too that they can be persuaded, but if we cannot, then there might be blood."

"Don't say this," said Collins, still gentle, like a teacher with a resistant, but favored student. "We are moral resistors, *peaceful* resistors. This is the Garrison way."

"He is not a Quaker, nor are you," Frederick observed.

"But his mentor—Benjamin Lundy—and many of our followers are Quakers. Garrison believes that by using their tactics, we can prevent a conflagration."

"That is what I meant."

"Be careful. You should tell your story; just tell your story."

But he would not just tell his story.

He did more.

He denounced.

He resisted.

Collins had organized a campaign against segregation on the Eastern Railroad between Boston and Portsmouth, New Hampshire, calling for ride-ins, boycotts, court action, and legislative action. Earlier in the year, the New Hampshire radicals Parker Pillsbury and Stephen S. Foster had urged that all white abolitionists take their seats in the "Negro pew," wherever it may be found, whether in a church, a railroad car, a steamboat, or a stagecoach.

They wanted the official endorsement of the Massachusetts Society, but Garrison and the majority considered such a resolution morally coercive and contrary to the moral spirit of nonresistance. Garrison would join Negroes in the Negro car, making the point of equality that way, but he would not demand that whites go the Negro car, or insist that Negroes sit in the white cars. He would leave it to the individual to act according to his conscience about how to protest peacefully against discrimination on the train or elsewhere.

Collins began in September a campaign to board the white cars with Frederick.

In Newburyport, he and Frederick boarded a white car of the Eastern Railroad and, as expected, the conductor asked Frederick to go to the Jim Crow car, as it was now derisively called, closest to the soot spewing out of the engine.

Frederick refused, civil in his tone. "No, sir, I have a right to be here."

The conductor turned away, snarling, "Very well. I will get some people to *help* you."

When the conductor, red faced and puffed up in the chest, returned with five men, he asked Collins, who was sitting next to Douglass, to move so he could drag the "nigger" out more easily.

"And why should I make it *easier* for you, sir, to violate the state constitution?" Collins asked. "If you do so, it will be *over* my person."

The conductors and his henchmen, other railroad employees, grabbed Frederick, who did not resist, and carried him to the forward car.

Collins's campaign was getting attention. The newspapers were already filled with the exploits of whites and Negroes protesting the segregated cars at stops throughout the line.

When Collins, Frederick, and James Buffum, a white Quaker, boarded the train at Lynn outside of Boston with Frederick and Collins in adjoining seats in a white car and Buffum behind them, a few passengers stared, but no one said anything, perhaps hoping that a scene could be avoided.

But then that same conductor who had accosted them days before came into the car. Frederick and Collins turned to each other, smiling but saying nothing.

With a high, pinched voice, the conductor pounded his right fist into palm of his open left hand. "Get out, *now*!"

Buffum, already known for buying tickets on a steamship for two colored women so they could sleep in a cabin, intervened with mocking civility. "Sir, can I ride with him, if he goes into the forward car? I want to have some conversations with him, and I fear I shall not have so favorable an opportunity again."

The conductor pounded his fist into the palm again. "No! I'd as soon haul you out of his car as I'd haul him from this."

Frederick said calmly, "There are very few in this car. Why do you order me out since no objection has been made?"

Suddenly, an unanticipated white supporter added, "I've no objection to riding with this colored gentleman."

The conductor turned his head sharply, but the man continued, "Let's take a vote on this controversial question."

"That's just what I want," agreed Buffum. "Let's vote."

A second passenger joined them, saying, "And I have no objection, either."

"Absolutely not!" roared the conductor.

Frederick turned to Collins, who also smiled at this turn of events, and then said to the conductor, "Sir, if you will give me any good reason why I should leave this car, I'll go willingly. But without such reason, I do not feel at liberty to leave. You can do with me as you please."

"You know the reason."

"I want to know the real reason, and I mean to continue asking for the real reason again and again, as long as you continue to assault me in this manner."

The two white supporters then called out, "Yes, give him one *good* reason."

The conductor turned to Frederick and said with cold vehemence, "Because you are B*lack*."

"Well, well, well. Honest at last," said Collins.

The conductor immediately turned with a huff and left the car.

"There he goes again, getting help. Are you ready, Frederick?"

Frederick nodded. He noticed the crowd of men at the door, ten of them with upturned sleeves, mouthing profanities.

"Snake out the damned nigger!" cried the point man of the gang.

"Take him out," ordered the captain, safe in the rear.

Six men reached over Collins and grabbed for Frederick, but Collins would not get out of the way.

"Damn this nigger lover," said one man.

Someone punched Collins in the back of the head, and another plowed his hand into his face and cut his lip. Blood splattered his shirt and trousers. Frederick's large hands gripped the seat. He was resisting their attempt to remove him, even as the white men pounded his back.

Enraged and amazed at Frederick's strength, the crowd of men now pulled at the entire seat, tearing the boards below. They were going to deposit it and the two protestors on the platform.

Buffum objected vigorously, repeating the phrase, "this is not right," but he did not intervene. The other passengers retreated to the far corners of the car and watched silently, mouths agape.

With one powerful collective lunge, the men grabbed Frederick, still gripping his seat, and carried him out to the platform. They then tossed Collins headfirst to the floor.

"Keep your nigger asses out of this car," someone scoffed as the entire group laughed and cheered.

But this was not enough. One man kicked Collins in the back as he lay on his side on the platform, the sickening thud making him curl up and cover his head. "Nigger lover!" Buffum rushed to Collins. "John, are you alright? John?"

He knelt beside his friend and yelled out to everyone on the platform, "This is an outrage! Have you no decency? He was on the ground! This is . . ."

Douglass's luggage came flying out of the car and opened when it hit the ground. More raucous laughter followed as Frederick's linen rolled in the light wind. The smug conductor stepped out from behind his henchmen. "Mr. Collins, you are free to return to the car you paid for."

Buffum declared, "This is something that the authorities will hear about. And the public will learn of the barbarities of this railroad company."

The thugs returned to the train, and the conductor sniffed. "Mr. Collins, you have a moment." Rising, Collins held on to Buffum. Before returning to the car to continue to the next town, he hobbled over to Frederick and said sternly, as he winced from his pain, "Mr. Douglass, you resisted."

"Yes," Frederick agreed, baffled by the reproach as he rubbed his sore backsides.

"You were not to resist. You dared to resist. You had your instructions. We are peaceful protesters. That is the Garrison way."

"But sir, we can't allow thugs . . ."

The train whistle blew.

"I'll speak to you later," said Collins ominously, and boarded the train.

Frederick looked to Buffum. "Is he going to fire me?"

"Friend Douglass, Mr. Collins will not fire you. You are a prize we cannot do without. He has great plans for you, but you must do things his way!"

"Must I?"

"Yes, of course. Now let's find a way to meet him in Newburyport."

Collins waited to speak to Frederick about his behavior, and when he found a private moment in Newburyport he explained his philosophy of radical resistance. It was essential, and it had to be peaceful to maintain the moral high ground. Because abolition inspired such fierce passions, abolitionists had to create a stark, peaceful contrast to their opponents in an effort to shame them.

After Elijah Lovejoy had used guns to defend his fourth antislavery press—the first three having been destroyed by mobs—in Alton, Illinois, four years before and lost his life, a protracted debate about resistance and violence had ensued. Most abolitionists were committed to nonresistance even after a series of riots roiled American cities throughout the 1830s. But there was growing fear that if abolitionists were not careful, they would "return evil for evil" after gradual slips on a slope of rationalizations and excuses.

There could be no compromise with slavery. But there also could be no compromise with physical resistance or violence.

Collins said, "I need you to tell me more about your reaction to northern prejudice. You refer to it several times in your speeches as a weight around your neck."

The observation surprised Frederick. He thought that Collins's words were preparation for a direct challenge: Why did you resist?

Frederick paused, and then carefully replied, "Back home, we're around white people all the time, everywhere. They know us. We know them even more because we must know how to survive. Here we're deliberately kept apart, and so we are strangers, feared like invisible monsters. I thought with slavery gone in the North hate would be less strong. But I was wrong, so wrong, even foolish."

"What blinded you?"

"Hope."

"Hope is not a strategy. We must break down the barriers. Peacefully."

"You already know how hard that will be."

"Justice and equality are never easy. But you must understand power is the cause of injustice and inequality. Race is the excuse."

"Then there will be a struggle. Power is never given up freely."

"Peaceful struggle only," Collins insisted.

Collins never mentioned any concerns about the Eastern Railroad incident in his final report to the Massachusetts Society and heaped only praise on his new charge. "His descriptions of slavery are most graphic," he wrote, "and his arguments so lucid, and occasionally so spiced with pleasantry, and sometimes with a little satire. He is capable of performing a vast amount of good for his oppressed race." He reported that Frederick earned $170.34 for his three months of service and urged the Society to accept his recommendation to hire him full time.

Collins had earned Frederick's gratitude and respect as well.

During their tour, if there were free Negro residents in town, they would gladly take the two men in. But often there were no volunteers, and Frederick and Collins would have to sleep in a barn or under a tree. Collins would not accept accommodations for himself if they excluded Frederick. Surprised, Frederick urged Collins to accept whatever offers came his way, but Collins was adamant. "We are together."

"I will never forget this."

"We are brothers in the work. True warriors."

"Peaceful warriors," reinforced Frederick.

"Indeed."

11.

FREDERICK ALWAYS CARRIED HIS favorite review in his coat pocket. Nathaniel Rogers, editor of the abolitionist *Herald of Freedom*, wrote, "This is an extraordinary man. He was cut out for a hero. A commanding person over six feet in height, and of most manly proportions. His head would strike a phrenologist amid a sea of them in Exeter Hall, and his voice would ring like a trumpet in the field. Let the South congratulate herself that he is a fugitive. It would not have been safe for her if he had remained about the plantation a year or two longer. As a speaker, he has few equals."

Occasionally, this tone of amazement and wonder annoyed Frederick. He was no miracle of nature, some rare bird suddenly able to talk like a lawyer making a case. He was the creation of his own ambition, the result of constant reading and study, unrelenting hard work, and persistent striving for improvement. If perfection was unattainable, excellence was not negotiable. He had to be the best.

Even Collins had misgivings, saying to Frederick at one point, "Better have a little plantation speech than not; it is not best that you seemed too learned. Give us the facts, and we will take care of the philosophy."

Another antislavery agent went so far as to warn him, "People won't believe that you were ever a slave, Frederick, if you keep on in this way."

Keep on in this way.

Trying to be charitable, Frederick silently acknowledged their good intentions, but he could not ignore the patronizing demarcation of limits they would most assuredly not apply to white men. After all, self-improvement was the American way celebrated in song, posters, speeches, and stories. But apparently, the cultural suggestion of limitless possibility didn't apply to him. Frederick took note, wondering when he would have to openly challenge the stereotypical assumptions of his white friends and colleagues.

In the meantime, he went along, even when Collins insisted that he and his family leave New Bedford and live in or near Boston. In fact, Collins found a house in Lynn near the railroad tracks and told Frederick in late October that he and abolitionists in town had paid the lease and the house was ready for Frederick and his family to move into it.

Done. No warning, no inquiries, no suggestion, no invitation.

Frederick could only stare at Collins when he announced his "good news" on the lecture circuit.

Anna and the children would have to go north to another strange place, leaving neighbors, friends, and their church. Frederick could see Anna's stone face and burning black eyes when told the news, and he dreaded that moment.

Collins was so caught up by the convenience of the move he didn't seem to notice Frederick's concern. "Since we must travel so much by train, it will be perfect for you to live near the station, and you can get to Boston for meetings, and to other towns so much faster. And Lynn is a good antislavery town, full of

Quakers. New Bedford is just too far away for someone of your prominence."

"But Anna."

"The Ladies of Lynn will be of great help. Don't you worry. We have thought of everything."

"But . . ."

Collins waved his hand. "Take a break for a few days, make final arrangements, and meet me in Providence. We have work to do."

His enthusiasm muted by the prospect of what could be his most intense domestic conflict since his wedding, Frederick could only manage to say, "Of course."

Collins wanted Frederick to be a *permanent* employee of the Massachusetts Society, and living in Lynn was, indeed, far more convenient for the Massachusetts Society in nearby Boston.

In the stagecoach back to New Bedford, avoiding and boycotting the Eastern Railroad from Boston for good reasons, Frederick rehearsed all the possible ways he could announce the news to Anna, all the possible ways he could counter objections. He stewed about this for hours, barely noticing the usual bumps in the road, the rank smell of cramped men.

Finally, he was home. He had come without warning, and Anna was happy to see him. "I thought it would be weeks before I saw you again. I could have cooked a good, hot meal for you."

It was late, and the children were already asleep.

"How are you feeling?" he asked.

"Fine," she said quickly. "Not sick like the other times. What's wrong?"

Knowing him all too well, Anna could see the preoccupation in his eyes, and hear it in his voice. Embarrassed, Frederick almost turned away, thinking, *How did I think I could fool Anna?*

He came to the point. "We are moving in November to Lynn, near Boston. The Antislavery Society there has secured a house. It will be safer for me, and I will be able to get to you and the children faster. This is a good thing, a larger house." The words flowed in a rush as he looked to Anna's eyes, refusing to avert his own.

Frederick stopped and waited. The room seemed hot in the cool, autumn night, and he felt the sweat under his cravat.

They both were still standing when Anna asked, "When will white people stop telling us what to do?" She seemed astonished rather than angry.

"We are free to say no."

"And give them a reason to not keep you?"

"They won't do that."

"You're *that* good," she teased.

"That's not what I meant."

"That is what you meant. Besides, they must really want you if they will go to so much trouble."

"I was surprised."

"Our next one is goin' to be born in a bigger place, better than these rooms. I hope it's not so cold there. The white folks sure got the name right for the water out here. Buzzards Bay, it makes roots hard to grow. I'll have a better garden now."

The crisis had passed more quickly than he had anticipated. Grateful that he didn't have to resort to authority, Frederick thanked her, reaching out with his hands to hers. "Thank you. You will not regret this."

Anna responded by quoting from the Book of Ruth, "For where you go, I will go, and where you lodge, I will lodge."

He gently touched her cheek, and then he kissed her lightly there. "Thank you."

She stepped back and said with that combination of seriousness and mockery that was uniquely hers, "Now I'm *not* going to ask you to never have me move again. That's too much to expect as the wife of Frederick Douglass, a man on his way. But, please, give me at least a few years where I can put down some roots, some *real* roots, so my garden can really grow."

"I want a home, too. I promise."

"You promise to keep us in Lynn for at least a few years."

"Yes."

"Let's go to bed. I feel fine."

Frederick immediately recognized that subtle smile, an invitation to make love before sleep. "Are you *sure*?"

"There are other ways for not hurting me or the baby."

"Anna!"

"Who says we aren't supposed to talk about such things?"

★

As anticipated, when Collins recommended Frederick as a permanent agent of the Massachusetts Antislavery Society, the Executive Committee unanimously agreed.

Two days later, four thousand people gathered in Faneuil Hall in Boston for a public meeting calling for the abolition of slavery in the District of Columbia. It was the largest gathering of abolitionists Frederick had ever attended, and now formally legitimized as an antislavery speaker, he was even more excited to be in the collective presence of such antislavery luminaries as Garrison; Wendell Phillips, the movement's greatest orator; Maria Weston Chapman, the executive secretary of the Society and its executive director; Abby Kelley, the

Society's most active female speaker, who just the day before had branded the clergy "thieves, robbers, adulterers, pirates, and murderers"; and Charles Lenox Remond, the most renowned Black member of the Society, who had returned from Ireland in December.

Such large gatherings had great potential for disruption, for they attracted whites bent on demonstrating their hostility to Black people and white supporters of racial equality. Boston's Irish are not our friends, Garrison grimly warned Frederick.

Even so, Garrison did not hold back his enthusiasm for Frederick, taking him by his hand and declaring before the crowd, "It is recorded in holy writ that a beast once spoke. A greater miracle is here tonight. A chattel becomes a man."

Emboldened by such an introduction, Frederick stepped to the edge of the platform and declared with a passion that swept him up to a height of conviction and eloquence that surprised him, "It is a slave by the laws of the South who now addresses you. Thank God that I have the opportunity to do it. Those bondsmen, whose cause you are called to espouse, are entirely deprived of the privilege of speaking for themselves. They are denied the privileges of the Christian—they are denied the rights of citizens. They are not allowed the rights of the husband and the father. It is to save them from all this, that you are called. Do it!—and they who are ready to perish shall bless you. Do it! And all good men will cheer you onward. Do it! And God will reward you for the deed. Do it!"

The hall resounded with the chant of "Do it!"

Frederick now understood, down to the core of his being, Reverend James's insight that antislavery speech could be a religious act. Recalling the sermons of Negro preachers on the Eastern Shore and in Baltimore, and using them as models for his own work, Frederick was his own kind of preacher now. He was not calling men and women to salvation and heavenly peace, but he was summoning them to a high purpose. By responding to that call, they would find the true meaning of brotherhood and the American dream and save their own souls. They were his flock, and his church was every lecture hall in America where they could hear his voice.

The laughter, the shouts of "Hear, hear," and applause were constant, but nothing could match the calm and inner peace he felt before the four thousand. The representative escaped slave, he was home.

12.

HE REMEMBERED VIVIDLY WHEN, as a new reader of the *Liberator*, he first encountered her words and asked himself: *Who is this woman*? He kept piles of the newspaper, but some editions he set aside after circling provocative letters or reports with a pencil.

Defending her right, as a woman, to speak to mixed audiences and to men alone if she so desired, Abby Kelley had declared that "I have well counted the costs and have decided to obey the dictates of my conscience even if all my friends should turn against me. She signed her letter, "For the truth at whatever cost."

At whatever cost.

Always attracted to strong, intelligent women, Frederick had hoped to meet her one day and spend time in her company. His eagerness increased when the *Liberator* reported her denunciation by a minister who publicly called her "Jezebel." Again, Frederick circled the report with pencil and put it aside to reread. Frederick wondered how any woman could survive such an attack on her character and reputation. Frederick also wondered about the allure that so rattled men.

Of course, the broad characterizations were utter nonsense. They suggested men were highly susceptible, weak, and silly, all lust ignited by the slightest provocation. Abby Kelley's public response to the incident when she was called a Jezebel hit the mark. She only noted in the *Liberator*, "Those who rail most loudly against evil are themselves most consumed by it."

Frederick was enthralled.

After spending time with her in Massachusetts in countless meetings, sitting across from her in crowded coaches and trains, and talking with her and Dr. Erasmus Hudson, an old friend, about the cause and the best strategies for bringing about change, Frederick now enjoyed her company and appreciated her notoriety.

Still grieving the death of her mother in February, Abby wore a plain black dress and a gray shawl. She was the model of Quaker modesty, luxurious chestnut hair; clear, almost luminous white skin; and the absence of "thee" and "thou" and the other expressions of "plain speech" for which Quakers were famous. She had officially withdrawn from the Society of Friends two years before, citing its refusal to denounce slavery and segregated pews at Friends meetings.

Frederick surmised that it was this combination of beauty, modesty, and sheer will that so provoked her opponents. Even when his group, including Dr. Hudson, who gave up his successful practice to become an antislavery lecturer, walked the streets to meetings arranged by Collins for a receptive audience, most of them small, it was clear that men despised her most of all.

Invariably, Abby forged ahead, never looking toward her accusers, always holding her head up. She was a warrior in a petticoat, peaceful, nonresistant, unflinching. Her walks in the streets with two men especially rankled others.

Women sneered, cringed, and sometimes pointed. But men, rowdies or gentlemen, hurled insults:

"Whore!"

"Nigger lover!"

"Bitch!"

One man ran up to them cupping his genitals. "So, you think Black dick is better than mine? Just give me a chance and I'll show you I'm better than some nigger."

Even this outrage did not provoke Abby and her colleagues, for they had agreed from the very beginning that their refusal to respond in public to verbal attacks was proof of their moral superiority. Abby's position was clear. "I don't need your help," she admonished Frederick and Hudson. She insisted that as long as she was not physically assaulted they must accept her position.

The three were constant companions.

Frederick listened carefully to every anecdote and detail revealed at meals, on trains, on the platforms after lectures and meetings, when they reviewed the antislavery argument and the heightened emotions of the day.

Abby's stories revealed much about the rise of abolition after Garrison started the *Liberator*, filling in details not mentioned there or referenced only indirectly. During those early months of 1842, Garrison traveled only intermittently, but his own stories in personal conversation and in the *Liberator* always had him at the center of events.

Without ever boasting or implying any criticism, Abby Kelley was more central to the development of the cause than Garrison was willing to acknowledge. It was her election to the executive committee that led to the breakup of the American Anti-Slavery Society. It was her insistence on speaking at the World Anti-Slavery Convention in London that forced the English to ban women from the floor.

Garrison's omissions bothered Frederick. They seemed to explain Collins's intemperate outbursts and snide aspersions against Garrison. Collins wanted more recognition for his work in the field, claiming he was most responsible for the movement's success, since he hired and mentored "the best people," like Frederick.

But Frederick had never encountered such a band of people, and never regretted the time with Abby and Erasmus Hudson. He concluded that these were the best people he had ever met, that now he was living the best days of his life.

He was so busy with his associates he missed the birth of his third child, a son named Frederick, Junior. Anna chose the name. Both touched and honored, Frederick could have not been more pleased by the selection and made sure to tell Anna.

Like the others, the new baby looked like Anna, dark-skinned and round in the face with huge eyes that suggested that nothing could pass their notice. Anna and the children were all reserved and didn't reveal emotion except through orbs as black and bright as coal. Rosetta and Lewis didn't say much, and even baby Frederick rarely cried.

Unsolicited, Anna assured Frederick that she managed well in his absence, growing seasonal vegetables, taking in laundry, and repairing shoes.

"Repairing shoes? When did you learn this?"

"It's no matter. The money is good, that's what's important. Now tell me about your travels. There's sure more to talk about than having babies, cleaning the house, and binding leather."

He told her about his tour and made light of his assaults on the railroad. He was "fine, just fine," he told her, and didn't elaborate because he knew the sit-in and boycotts were the talk of the town, especially after the Eastern Railroad declared that it would no longer stop at Lynn because too many protests had occurred there.

But the order backfired. White people came to the station and became angry when they discovered they couldn't take the train. Citizens also organized meetings supporting the protests. The superintendent of the railroad then backed down and ordered the trains to stop at Lynn again.

"You all sure know how to get them white folk hoppin' mad," Anna said.

"That's the point," replied Frederick. "Make their laws, rules, and ways of doing things so inconvenient they will give them up."

"What about all that talk about loving the enemy, bringing souls to salvation?"

Frederick paused. She had indeed been listening to his extended talks about the way to end slavery. "That too," he said defensively, as if he had been found wanting in his commitment to moral suasion as the one, true way.

"Tell me about that white man who goes into those churches and calls them whorehouses because of what slavery do to the women." Anna chortled, "Lord, lord, lord, I know them people sure didn't like hearing *that* truth."

He almost asked, how do you know about Stephen Foster? But he only said, "No, they don't like what he has to say. He's been thrown out, even out of a two-story window."

"Do that man really believe that making them folks mad is going to make them let us in?"

"He believes that shaming them can work."

"So, there are fools in the cause, too," she said. "When people are shamed, they don't act right. They just get even."

He agreed that church invasions were provocative but ultimately ineffective. The invasion of sacred spaces always antagonized and never convinced insulted ministers and their congregations. But Frederick secretly enjoyed the spectacle.

Foster was one of those men easier to admire than love, a smug, self-righteous crank with boundless courage. But Frederick continued to review his schedule and describe key players on the lecture circuit until Anna rolled her eyes, silently declaring she had heard enough. The roll was subtle with the slightest lift of her chin. It was not curt or rudely dismissive, but by exposure to Anna's expressive eyes Frederick could easily interpret the range and gradations of her visual messaging, as if she were a director in the audience giving the signal for the curtain to come down. And for the sake of domestic peace during a brief visit, he would not insist on its rise again.

After three days, Frederick was back on the road, his duties as a parent sufficiently met as far as he was concerned. He made sure there was enough money for provisions, read selections from the Bible for Anna, and permitted Rosetta, now three, to sit in his lap for a few minutes. He was reluctant to admit it, but he didn't like being around small children. Their constant need for attention and instant gratification annoyed rather than charmed him. Perhaps his years of watching the Auld brood had soured him.

Unlike the Auld children, Rosetta and Lewis were not loud and raucous, and Anna would not have allowed unruly demonstrations of joy or affection in any case. Even so, they bored him, and he eagerly counted the hours for his return to the road, where he remained fascinated by his new companions.

Of all the people Frederick met and traveled with that spring, Abby Kelley fascinated him most of all. She didn't reveal her past in one narrative rush, dominating a conversation with the autobiographical details that Frederick was eager to hear. Abby's modesty and reserve precluded this, but she was willing to answer questions about her past, the path that brought her from a Massachusetts farm to platforms and halls through the northeast.

Frederick had a keen need to understand how a young white woman, now thirty-one, would challenge almost every imaginable convention to embrace racial equality and immediate emancipation, and publicly advocate for them despite censure and physical threats. Instinctively, he sensed that if he could penetrate the mystery of her development, he could succeed more successively with the hesitant, the reluctant, and the fearful.

For some, a conversion to abolition could come as swiftly and dramatically as Paul's conversion on the road to Tarsus; and as a believer in the power of eloquence, Frederick still hoped that he could formulate a line or a speech that would have the same impact: immediate, soul stirring, life changing.

But the path for most people was neither simple or singular. Like his own, there were side roads, detours, and obstructions along the way. Frederick hoped that by understanding Abby Kelley's journey, he could become a more successful agent and, one day, a leader.

Unfortunately, he was more than curious. He had worshipped Abby from a distance, constrained by convention, propriety, and marriage vows. Now he was infatuated.

He remembered the exact moment when his admiration shifted to deeper feelings, exhilarating, and disturbing all at once. They were having dinner, and their hosts and Dr. Rogers had stepped out for a walk, leaving them alone. It didn't seem awkward or unusual at the time. They were trusted.

Perhaps too boldly, he suddenly asked her, "Are you afraid? With all the criticism, with all the aspersions and worse, are you?"

"Yes, and if we are not, then we are fools."

"When were you the most afraid?"

"Most people, I suspect, would expect me to name the attack on Philadelphia Hall in 1838. But those jeering boys and men waited until we adjourned, allowed us to leave arm-in-arm through the mob, and then burned the place down. That wasn't personal. An angry man coming toward me with a bat in a schoolroom was personal."

She described the incident dispassionately, her voice even and unwavering, and her eyes direct and unapologetic. Prepared to speak in a crowded village classroom, she stood at the front and watched in horror as a burly man, his faced reddened by rage, came forward, swinging a club in the aisle. She tried to stay calm, hoping to not reveal terror in her eyes. "Then he said something absolutely vile. I've heard it all before."

"Where's the damned nigger bitch that's going to lecture here tonight. Where is she? Tell me where she is?" the man shouted, according to Erasmus, who later told Frederick the exact words that Abby refused to repeat.

Some women screamed, she continued, and then the man pounded the oil lamp on the front desk, shattering it, propelling nearby candles, darkening the room. A single candle flickered on a side table as more screamed and rushed to walls, windows, and doors. A few in the audience of mostly women protested, crying out, "No."

A gentleman took Abby's hand and led her through a side door, taking advantage of the confusion and apologizing for what she had to endure. Never had she confronted this kind of close, physical assault, but she consoled the almost distraught male organizer of the event, "We're here to shake the spirit."

She paused at the end of her account. "I was also a shaken spirit, but I hid it with a fierce anger."

"Anger is a needed driver."

"Only if our eyes are open."

Frederick was so filled with admiration of her at that moment, he wanted to praise her, to testify to her unconquerable will, offer some measure of a deeper devotion. But he held back, fearing that he would make an absolute fool of himself.

Fortunately, she excused herself, rising from her chair. "I have said too much. Please accept my apology. Good night. Offer my apologies to our hosts. I will see you all in the morning."

"Good night," was all he could say. And then she was gone.

He retired to his own room and, as if compelled, retrieved his copy of the February 18 *Liberator* that included that almost ecstatic description of Abby Kelley's appearance at the January meeting of the Massachusetts Society.

Later, he decided to never read it again or carry it in his satchel at all, for it exposed him as a muddled, dishonorable fool who, as a married man, had no business holding on to such a document.

That night, he awakened covered with sweat.

Abby had become an object of desire.

Frederick was horrified.

13.

HE THOUGHT HE WAS a good man, better than almost everyone around him, white or Black. But now he could feel the bitter reality: he was just another man with a consuming need to taste forbidden fruit. He could hear the question from the past: *So, who do you think you are?* And he could also hear the answer, loud and clear: *Now you know, boy. You are just an animal.*

He knew he would not be able to sleep. Instead, he would brood about his discoveries and next steps. He had to plan carefully. Abby could never know he had any impure thoughts. He could never be alone with her again, even for a moment. He would not sit beside her on the train or on stagecoaches, even across from her. He would not look to her eyes. Their conversations now would have to be curtailed, reduced to brief exchanges, careful, free of emotion, impersonal at best.

Quickly, he realized the folly of this plan. An astute observer, she would immediately detect the changes in his demeanor and conversation and ask about them, a concerned friend always eager to support the distressed or preoccupied.

No, he would not distance himself and call attention to himself. But he made a vow: he would be a true gentleman, the very model of rectitude and honor. He would carry the burden of his race proudly, without any possible recrimination.

By dawn, Frederick had his new plan. He would be more formal in speech and bearing, making sure his collars were stiff and pure white and tied with a perfect knot. He would smile less and frown more, taking advantage of the furrow at the top of his nose and the deep lines in his cheeks, already noted by observers, as expressions of deep thought and serious intent.

At breakfast, he sat with Dr. Hudson, Abby, and their hosts, Mr. and Mrs. Campbell, and said, "Good morning" with a nod toward each of them.

"Did you sleep well?" asked Dr. Hudson.

"No, sir. I'm afraid I was preoccupied by many things."

Abby turned to Dr. Hudson and confessed, "Last night I told him about Philadelphia and the burning of the hall."

"A terrible night, indeed," said Dr. Hudson. "But you and Mrs. Grimke were victorious."

"You give me too much credit."

"You are too modest, as usual. You went back to the hall after the mayor allowed the mob to burn it down, and then crossed town linked arm to arm with a Negro woman to a Negro schoolhouse."

"I was not the only one."

"No, but you were the one who strongly favored a resolution against prejudice, urging whites and Blacks to visit each other in their homes."

"Not everyone was happy with the wording. Some said that it would give credence to charges of *amalgamation*."

At the mention of that word, Frederick immediately stood, gripping his napkin. "Excuse me, I have more to do." He struggled to control the tremor in his voice.

"Have I offended, you again, Frederick?" Abby asked, her entire face the image of remorse and regret.

"Again?" asked Hudson, turning to her. "What happened?"

She looked down to her plate, surprising Frederick. Abby was never perturbed, until now.

Frederick said emphatically, "I should not have asked about Philadelphia."

Abby looked up, her face the very image of calm poise, as usual. "It was history, not a confession."

He returned to his room and heard a knock at the door.

"Yes?" he asked, rising from his chair.

"It's Erasmus. May I speak with you?"

Frederick hesitated, but then answered, "Come in."

Dr. Hudson entered. A tall physician of wealth and prominence, practicing surgery before relinquishing his practice for the antislavery work, he retained the presence of a successful gentleman, his bearing, well cut clothes, a well-modulated voice, and his age at thirty-seven all reinforcing the esteem he universally received in abolitionist circles. To a new generation of agents, he was more a father than a brother in the crusade.

"You are both my friends," Hudson said, "but something happened last night."

There was not even a hint of accusation in the inquiry. He was that kind of man. Frederick relaxed somewhat, lowering defenses he had nurtured over the years before older white men. Now ashamed that he had to remind himself, for even that one moment, that Dr. Erasmus Darwin Hudson, was not like other white men, he answered quickly, "I should have never asked about her fears. It was presumptuous, rude, unseemly."

"We all have them, and I'm sure she never denied them."

"No, she didn't, and then she told me about Philadelphia and an incident in Cornwell Bridge."

"A terrible, terrible incident," Hudson said sadly.

"Were you there?"

"My wife and I were there. We had arranged the meeting; it was in just another small Connecticut village. We blamed ourselves for exposing her to such brutality, to such vile language."

He described that night and repeated the exact words that Abby could not.

Frederick's admiration was quickened again, and as quickly as it emerged, he suppressed it. "My tactless interest forced her to return to a wretched scene, reawakening memories that should be forgotten."

"You did no such thing, my friend," Hudson said. "She chose to tell you. She cannot be forced in any way. She is remarkable. Extraordinary, actually."

"How can I make amends?"

"Remain her friend. She has the gift of friendship, with women and men, married and unmarried. Not for one instant does she doubt her equality. Most men fear that and can't abide her honesty. I hope you can. She greatly admires you and was most impressed with your eloquent plea that the word "white" be removed from the Rhode Island constitution last fall."

"She admires *me*?"

"We all do," Hudson replied.

"Sir, I don't know what to say."

"You can return to breakfast and help finalize plans for our next engagement. That's what you can do. You will not need to apologize. You did nothing that requires one. Believe me, if you did something that required it, she would inform you. After all she has been through, she is committed to the honesty of her position and will not be intimidated. Fear is natural; intimidation is learned."

They returned to breakfast, and Abby received her friends at the table with bright, delighted eyes and a soft, dazzling smile.

Yes, she was beautiful.

Frederick could not deny this fact, convinced that denial would only give it greater power over him. But he kept his resolve to maintain a studied detachment and social distance, avoiding personal questions or disclosures, focusing exclusively on professional matters.

"Are you not feeling, well, Frederick?" Abby asked.

"I'm just tired," he lied. "This campaign is grueling, and I have to admit to your superiority in this too. You have amazing stamina. You're unflagging. I can barely keep up. This scheduling is almost too much."

"It was those years on the farm. Morning, noon, and sometimes into the night, milking, lifting, helping my father. He had only one son. He had to use his seven daughters."

"I appreciate your concern, but I will persevere, inspired by you." And he added quickly, "And the others."

"I'm living in the school of Frederick Douglass. I can think of nothing better, for you have brought me closer to the slaves than anyone else. We will now pour vinegar and no more honey on the wounds of slave masters and their supporters *everywhere*."

Frederick almost gasped. Once a Quaker, she was now a warrior.

They ended the tour triumphantly in Boston that May. The press was laudatory, and Frederick basked in the effusive praise. A correspondent in the *Liberator* reported, "It has been my fortune to hear a great many anti-slavery lecturers, and many distinguished speakers on their subjects; but it has rarely been my lot to listen to one whose power over me was greater than Douglass, and not over me only, but *over all* who heard him."

There was the key word: *power*. It would be his, not by the gun or the sword, not by the muscle of his arms and back, not by the money he could earn. It would be his through the power of his words.

After the tour Frederick found a terrorized Negro community. Hundreds of colored people in and around Boston had fled to western Massachusetts, Vermont, and even Canada. Those remaining disappeared from public life, choosing to huddle in churches and basements and wait for the danger to pass.

The community once believed that it had the protection of Massachusetts law, but the complicity of city and state officials in the arrest of George Latimer shattered its faith.

A newcomer to Boston, Latimer had been suddenly arrested after a Virginia planter applied to the federal courts for a certificate of removal, as the Fugitive Slave Law of 1793 required. Freed by his late mistress's will, Latimer appealed to Massachusetts for release from jail and a jury trial to settle his case. Declaring that Latimer's case was a federal matter, a local judge refused to release Latimer or grant him a jury trial.

These developments stirred hundreds to post handbills, carry placards, circulate petitions, and organize mass meetings. The abolitionist community united behind William Lloyd Garrison to rally support for Negro citizens now threatened by a law never before enforced in Massachusetts.

Latimer's case was appealed to the State Supreme Court, and its chief justice heard arguments while crowds gathered outside the jail. The chief justice ruled against Latimer.

Now bounty hunters had the right to kidnap off the streets, leading more Negroes to flee. Many whites in Boston, even those who objected to Garrison, were outraged. Their "cradle of freedom," the birthplace of the American Revolution, had been violated by enslavers aided and abetted by Massachusetts. If they could control judges, then who, indeed, would be next?

Emboldened, Frederick went on tour again, this time with Abby and Collins to western New York, urged by the American Anti-Slavery Society to revive antislavery there through a series of One Hundred Conventions, as Collins had named the newest lecture meetings throughout the East.

He saw Rochester, a beautiful city, for the first time, but he could not stay.

Frederick drove himself relentlessly, determined to prove his worth and allegiance.

Latimer had to be freed.

Massachusetts had to stand up to slave power.

Abolition had to win.

No Negro was safe.

He was not safe.

Speech after speech, morning, noon, and night, day after day.

Then he got sick.

At first the cough was dry and shallow, and Frederick tried to suppress it by will alone. He hated when others coughed in public halls, and believed offenders deserved immediate expulsion. But his cough would not stop. It deepened and began to hurt his chest.

In New Bedford, he gave another speech, then sat down and started to cough again. He became dizzy and leaned back to prevent a fall.

The cough became an ugly rattle, and the sound frightened him. He wordlessly turned to Remond, the other Black speaker on the lecture circuit, and rushed from the stage. Remond followed him, asking desperately, "Douglass, Douglass, what's wrong?"

Paralyzed by the thought that he was about to die, Frederick couldn't answer.

"Let me help you," Remond pleaded, reaching for his arm. "Do you need a doctor?"

Remond managed to get a carriage and took Frederick to the house of Nathan Johnson. It was decided by the Johnsons that Frederick's illness would be too upsetting to Anna and the children, and the trip back to Lynn too hazardous.

In bed, Frederick started to cough up blood, but the doctor said there was no serious cause for alarm. Frederick moaned at this proof of the incompetence of doctors. But after two hours, the bleeding stopped. Dr. Morgan announced that there was now no need for him to stay, prescribed rest, and departed with assurances.

Throughout the night, Remond sat beside him, putting wet cloths on Frederick's forehead, wiping his face, lips, neck, and chest. He also helped Frederick, too weak to leave the bed, with the chamber pot.

By the next morning, Frederick was feeling better, but Remond insisted on accompanying him back to Lynn and staying for as long as was needed.

Frederick protested, "You don't need to do this. Latimer needs you."

"*We* need you."

Surprised by this remark, Frederick arched his eyebrows.

"I know," said Remond, amused. "Our beginning was not auspicious."

Frederick vividly remembered their first encounter at a reception in Boston the previous December. This ugly, frail, thirty-year-old man with ebony skin and a long nose like a beak pointedly scanned Frederick's outfit from top to bottom, his jacket and trousers in stark contrast to Redmond's elegant and expensive attire, and said to Garrison, who introduced them, "So, this is my competition."

"No, sir. Your associate, your student," Frederick replied, tightening his grip on Remond's small, spindly hand.

"You have much to learn, I hear, having just escaped from the house of bondage," Remond continued.

"Three years of freedom is a lifetime to . . ."

Remond interrupted, raising his right hand as if swearing before a jury. "A metaphor? How poetic, how liberating for one who couldn't know the richer elements of the language on a plantation."

"Sir, how could you know anything about . . ."

"Friend Garrison, I understand that some people recently have protested against the segregated cars in a flamboyant manner."

"But Mr. Remond," challenged Frederick, "do *you* object to our method of protest?"

"Mr. Douglass, I am unwilling to descend so low as to bandy words with superintendents or contest my rights with conductors."

"Then how do you travel to Salem, since the Eastern line is the only way?"

"I can afford to hire private conveyances, sir. I come from wealth."

A mortified and addled Garrsion sputtered, "I too come from humble beginnings, but the cause has room for all good men and women. I know you both will make a grand contribution."

"I have already, sir," Remond insisted.

Now sitting at Frederick's bedside, Remond grinned. "Indeed, our beginning was *not* auspicious. I hated you once, hated you so deeply that I prayed to God for relief from it. Envy can kill the soul."

"We're friends now."

"But all men are not created equal. You are the better speaker. You can't imagine the strain I felt when you came along. I was somehow diminished by another Negro before the entire free colored community, by a *slave*."

"There it is again, my being born a slave and you free."

"It *is* exhausting being the perfect Negro, whose fate the entire race depends on. Fail and, in the eyes of whites, the entire race falls. Believing this, I almost drove myself crazy."

"There's room for two perfect Negroes."

Remond laughed. "You are impertinent."

"I'm sorry."

"No, you're not."

His throat was sore, but Frederick was glad to have a voice again. "I was born insolent. I will always be insolent."

"Yes, Frederick, you are the better speaker, and I'm the better *man*."

"What!"

"We can make a joke now and then, you and me, the ones everyone watches."

"Now that there are two sly foxes working together, it will be easier for both of us."

"Indeed."

14.

FREDERICK REMAINED SKEPTICAL ABOUT racially separate organizations, but now he recognized the need for colored men to gather and discuss how they could improve Negro life. Most whites believed that Negroes could do nothing without their help and supervision, and Frederick sensed that too many white abolitionists shared this belief. They openly dismissed the Negro convention movement as pretentious and divisive, even dangerous. There had not been such a convention since the mid-1830s. But the emergence of the Liberty Party—which called for radical political action—renewed interest in the

Negro Convention movement, and Negro leaders were gathering in Buffalo to proclaim the movement's support.

It was the perfect opportunity, Frederick thought. He could persuade the other Negro men that only Garrisonian principles could end slavery. He could emerge, at last, as a national leader, someone to be reckoned with, maybe a man to fear.

About sixty men gathered at the National Convention of Colored Citizens, most of them from western New York, Michigan, and Ohio. Only two, Remond and Frederick, came from Massachusetts, and they were received with cordial suspicion, like delegates from the enemy camp bearing a white flag. The president, Samuel Davis of Buffalo, noted at the end of a long list of names Remond's illustrious career and Frederick's emerging one, and then declared that the Constitution of the United States guaranteed freedom and equality to all citizens.

"All *white* males," jeered Frederick softly, ready to defend the Garrisonian standard with an argument even after a compliment.

Remond turned his head sharply. "Not now," he commanded before nodding and smiling to those who sat nearest.

Frederick took a deep breath and waited.

The opportunity to argue came later that afternoon when, after several hours of earnest but pleasant discussion about the establishment of a national Negro press, the development of a frontier agricultural community, and education, Reverend Henry Highland Garnet offered a resolution advocating political action as the best way to end slavery.

The resolution was immediately referred to a committee to avoid a rancorous floor fight.

The tall and dignified minister from Troy, New York, ordained earlier in the year after studies at the Oneida Institute, impressed Frederick. He hobbled on one leg and crutches after his other leg had been amputated in 1840, following a sports injury. His skin was dark brown, and he carried it without apology. The son of slaves, he was born in Kent County on the Eastern Shore of Maryland, north of Frederick's birthplace, and escaped with his family to Pennsylvania before settling in New York City. Philosophically, Henry Highland Garnet represented everything Frederick opposed, and Frederick knew that a fight with him was inevitable.

Garnet devoted most of his time to making his case for a political solution to slavery at committee meetings, while Frederick vigorously argued that party affiliation was affiliation with corruption, citing example after example from state politics and the administrations of Andrew Jackson, Martin Van Buren, and John Tyler. But the majority sided with Garnet, who received only seven dissenting votes when his resolution came to the floor.

But on that August 16, Garnet quietly rose to make a speech that broke the relative peace of the convention. It was like no speech Frederick had ever heard.

"Brethren," Garnet declared, addressing his remarks not to delegates but to slaves everywhere, "it is wrong for your lordly oppressors to keep you in slavery as it was for the man thief to steal our ancestors from the coast of Africa. You should therefore now use the same manner of resistance as would have been just in our ancestors when the bloody footprints of the first remorseless soul-thief was placed upon the shores of our fatherland."

Africa: never had Frederick heard references to the unknown and uncivilized continent suffused with such wonder. The warmth of sunlight, the rustling of leaves on the wind, and images of ancestral homes came through even as Garnet spoke of brutal abductions.

"Brethren, the time has come when you must act for yourselves. It is an old and true saying that, if the hereditary bondsmen would be free, they must themselves strike the first blow. You can plead your own case and do the work of emancipation better than any others."

Frederick leaned forward, straining to take in the meaning of these words as they washed over him like waves; he breathed deeply. *He can't be saying what I think he's saying.*

"Think of the undying glory that hangs around the ancient of Africa and forget not that you are native born American citizens, and as such, you are justly entitled to all the rights that are granted to the freest. Think how many tears you have poured out upon the soil which you have cultivated with unrequited toil and enriched with your blood; and then go to your lordly enslavers and tell them plainly, that you are determined to be free. Appeal to their sense of justice and tell them that they no more have the right to oppress you than you have to enslave them."

Frederick closed his eyes and relaxed the muscles of his back and neck. He was pulled back from the cliff, hearing the words of moral suasion, the appeal to a sense of justice. The threat of violence, heard in that reference to an old saying about hereditary bondsmen, had been checked for the moment.

Garnet went on, "Inform them that all you desire is freedom and that nothing else will suffice. Do this, and forever after cease to toil for the heartless tyrants, who give you no other reward but stripes and abuse. If they then commence the work of death, they, and not you will be responsible for the consequences. You had far better all die—die immediately than live slaves and entail your wretchedness upon your posterity."

Frederick's eyes shot open. The call for a boycott was radical, but not disturbing. Slaves had refused work in any number of ways. But the call to suicide was unnerving, absurd, outrageous. To kill oneself and end the possibility of freedom? No, never.

But Garnet was not talking about suicide. He was making a call to arms: "If you would be free in this generation, here is your only hope. However much you and all of us may desire it, there is not much hope of redemption without the shedding of blood, let it all come at once—rather die freedmen than to live as slaves. Brethren, arise, arise! Strike for your lives and liberties. Now is the day and hour."

The verbs penetrated Frederick's chest and skull, making him fall back into his chair. The final peroration was an immobilizing blast of bullets: "Now let every slave throughout the land do this, and the days of slavery are numbered. You cannot be more oppressed than you have been—you cannot suffer greater cruelties than you have already. Rather die freemen than live to be slaves. Remember that you are four million!"

There was stunned silence for just a moment; then waves of thunderous applause and shouts filled the room. Garnet stood still, his eyes closed and head bowed, as if absorbing the sounds before him. He then lifted his chin and smiled, acknowledging the ovation. He said repeatedly, "Thank you, thank you."

To Frederick, Garnet had the courage for saying the unmentionable, articulating in public what slaves only dared dream or whispered late at night. His words gave form to the pent-up rage that Frederick felt when thinking of the floggings, beatings, and killings by overseers on the vast Wye Plantation, where he had lived, the constant abuse he had endured when he was rented out to Edward Covey, the attack he had suffered in the Baltimore shipyards, and much more. These white men deserved a sound thrashing, a fist in the face. He could see the terror in their blue eyes as he leaped to grab their necks, tightened his grip, and watched the life drain out of their bodies. Death to all slaveholders, that was what he wanted when he allowed his heart to be free of all restraint, all rules. When tired of talking, when he no longer wanted to persuade hostile fools and bigots on the antislavery lecture circuit, he also thought that only insurrection could stir the nation to end slavery.

But beyond any hopes for glory was a despair so deep that only a sudden, cataclysmic event could assuage it. In that emotional realm, he knew that principals and beliefs could not persuade, that thousands would have to die. Suicide or murder: thousands would have to die.

It was the greatest speech he had ever heard. It was far greater than anything he had ever uttered. Frederick opened his eyes, suddenly afraid. He was about to succumb to emotions that could destroy his career and family and the entire nation. He had to restore order to his own unsettled equilibrium and, more importantly, not allow Henry Highland Garnet to unleash forces that would surely end any chance for a peaceful end to slavery. No one should hope for Armageddon, fire, and blood, or pray for the desolation invoked by the bloodthirsty prophets of Zion.

Frederick stood, his hand up for acknowledgment from the convention president.

"Yes, Mr. Douglass," asked a baffled Samuel Davis, the convention chair.

"I move that Mr. Garnet's speech, eloquent though it is, not be accepted as the opinion of this convention. The rebellion which he calls for frees the master of his responsibility to free his own slaves."

A few gasped, but then a suffocating silence filled the room as all turned to Frederick with astonishment, resentment, anger, and disappointment. Frederick could hear the unspoken questions: *How dare you? Have you no tact or manners? How can you be so rude?*

Garnet stared at Frederick, his silence chilling the room like a curse at a wedding.

Frederick turned to Remond for support, but Remond, who had joined in the ovation, was also appalled, pushing his back into the side of the chair as he tried to distance himself in a small space, his uncomprehending eyes the final judgment of a friend's absolute folly. Frederick could see Remond's intention: he was not ready to return to earth and debate the issue.

Garnet's speech was indeed exhilarating.

An apologetic but strong voice from the back of the room shouted out, "Reverend Garnet, I too am opposed to your speech, for violence is *not* the answer. Innocent blood will be shed."

Suddenly there was a barrage of calls to the president for motions and resolutions. Reverend Garnet sat down, and a heated debate over the merits of insurrection ensued. Neither he nor Frederick said anything more to the general audience, leaving it to the others to articulate the opposing views. Garnet never turned in his chair to acknowledge Frederick, and Frederick didn't try to make amends.

Reaching no satisfactory conclusion to the floor debate, the delegates voted to give the speech to a committee for possible revisions. The meeting was tense, as Frederick and three others sat around a table that afternoon going over Garnet's lines word for word for possible excision.

Sullen, Garnet refused to say more than, "No, don't change it . . . No . . . I won't have it . . . No."

Frederick was not reticent, arguing for the deletion of several passages, especially lines about dying. He believed that the publication of such comments would do unparalleled damage to the abolitionist cause, especially alienating those who might be inclined to support freedom. But with a will as powerful as his upper body, Garnet managed to keep the editing pencil away from almost all his lines.

On the floor again, Frederick repeated his motion: no endorsement or publication of Garnet's speech. Free Negroes had reached a new level of frustration and anger, he argued, but Garnet, a formidable opponent, had deliberately shattered the peace of their gathering and unleashed disagreements that could give comfort to those who claimed that Negroes could never unite and agree on anything. He had to be stopped.

Frederick's motion passed by one vote.

Using a cane to stand, Garnet declared to the delegates, each word precise and filled with disgust, "I promise you that I will have my speech published somehow, somewhere. Sirs, your abolitionism is abject *slavery*."

Holding his head high, he limped out of the room, silence surrounding him. When Garnet went through the door, Remond whispered to Frederick, "You have made an enemy."

"We are right," Frederick replied, startled at first by Remond's unequivocal assertion.

"But don't celebrate this as a personal victory," Remond added. "People still remember Nat Turner. Calling for armed resistance in 1843 is unwise. It could set us back for years."

"I won," Frederick asserted.

"You have a gift, Frederick, for making enemies."

"Enemies are the measure of a man."

"Mr. Garrison will be proud. You've made an enemy for life."

"We won."

"Too late, Douglass. You were more honest the first time. You said *I*."

"There were other votes."

"It was *your* resolution. He won't forget that."

"Someone had to break the spell."

"The very substance of the ambitious is merely the shadow of a dream," replied Remond.

Frederick frowned, feeling judged by an unfamiliar reference that sounded like so many of the quotations in *The Columbian Orator*.

"Shakespeare," Remond said. "You do read Shakespeare, don't you?"

"Yes, of course, but not everything yet. And what, sir, do you mean to suggest?"

"We're all ambitious men, and we all want something because we have a dream for ourselves, that's all."

"And what is wrong with that? We all have dreams."

"But do we admit to the shadow, that it might come from a dark place?"

"Hope is not dark."

"What are *we* trying to prove, and to whom?"

"That we have the right to define ourselves, and our place in the world."

"A worthy sentiment, my friend, but you made sure that Mr. Garnet could not have his place over you."

"I disagree with Mr. Garnet, that is all, and I said so."

"I doubt that he feels that way."

"I can't be responsible for his feelings."

"You have an enemy even so. Are you proud of that?"

Frederick hesitated for a moment before answering. "Yes, I am."

Remond grinned. "Honesty can be bracing, almost refreshing. Thank you, Frederick. I look forward to your future battles with Henry Highland Garnet."

"I'll be ready."

"And he will be, too."

15.

FREDERICK WENT ON TO Pendleton, Indiana, with two white agents, George Bradburn and William White. The three men learned from their host, a physician, that a mob might come down from a rum-drinking dive and drive them away. "Folks 'round here don't like race mixing," said Dr. Russell. Nevertheless, they went to the designated meeting spot, where 130 men and women were gathered.

"This is as good as a camp meeting," Dr. Russell said, and gestured Bradburn to come forward. "Build on it!"

When Bradburn began his stock speech, Frederick and White noticed a group men starting to appear at the periphery of the crowd. They said nothing but turned their heads to keep track of the growing numbers. Bradburn continued, his voice staying calm as the new arrivals sat in the available chairs at the rear.

White whispered to Frederick beside him, "To the right there. But I can't point."

Frederick heard the terror in White's voice and immediately turned, finding a young man standing barefoot in a pair of homespun pants hanging low on his hips and a loose, slouching shirt that exposed his left shoulder. He was staring with raw, open insolence.

The young man raised his hand, as if making a signal, and all the men who had gathered stood and walked out, silently retreating to the trees.

Bradburn stopped when he heard the collective shouts of thirty men. Two by two, armed with eggs and stones and led by a man wearing a coonskin cap, they came rushing toward the meeting circle.

The audience jumped up, but White begged everyone to stay. "Please sit down. Please be seated."

"Surround them!" ordered the mob leader. Some of his followers circled the audience while others stationed themselves at the foot of the speaker's stand.

Rocks started to fly, then rotten eggs. The rocks missed, but the eggs splattered all three men, who stood perfectly still, letting the stinking mess drip without a word. They had learned that the sight of stoic, unflinching men and women covered in rotten filth sometimes shamed audiences. It was quiet. The hecklers seemed confused, disoriented by the eerie silence and the sudden loss of energy.

A man jumped up on the platform and overturned the table and began pulling the lecture stand to pieces. That was the signal his friends needed. They pushed protesting members of the audience out of the way and started wrenching and pulling whatever wood pieces they could get their hands on.

Someone took a swing at White with a piece of timber, but Frederick grabbed a club to protect him. He pounded White's attacker on the head. The man collapsed to his knees, unconscious.

At that instant, the fight changed. A Negro had struck a white, violating the laws of God and country, and someone in the crowd shouted, his voice garbled with disgust, rage, incredulity, "Kill the nigger! Kill that *damn* nigger!"

Frederick bolted. His run was wild and blind. He didn't know where he was going and didn't care. He knew that if the enraged men caught him, they would murder him. He jumped over rocks, tore through bushes, his heart pounding so loudly that he could no longer hear the cursing behind him.

But he did not run fast enough. Almost beside him, a man swung a heavy club against Frederick's right hand. Frederick screamed and fell to the ground. He held it with his other hand, and was about to be clubbed again when White, who had run after him, deflected the club with his own. A stone hit White on the head, opening a gash that covered his face with blood. He fell to the ground near Frederick and was kicked in the mouth. The sound of the blow that shattered teeth, and the low, agony-filled moan coming from White, deflated Frederick's spirit. At the same time, his concern for White deepened when he saw his blood-filled mouth. Frederick wondered why they were not killed.

Finally, the attackers mounted their horses and rode away, leaving Frederick and White moaning on the ground. Someone helped them up and led them, one at a time, to the carriage of a Quaker who had volunteered to take them home.

Through his pain, Frederick kept on saying, "Is he alright? Is William all right?"

"He's lost some teeth, but he'll be fine, Mr. Douglass," said the consoling Quaker. "My wife will dress thy wounds, and everything will be new again, and the other young man will be up in no time. Have no fear."

Frederick promised himself to never forget William White and the day he saved his life. But on that day he never thought about the upraised club that would have everyone in Boston talking.

He had resisted.

Again.

After five days, Frederick's entire body still ached from the blows to his head, back, and hand. The pain throbbed in his right hand and seemed to course through every tissue of his right side, making him stiff and sick to the stomach. And now George Bradburn, the oldest of the three antislavery agents, was challenging him on philosophical grounds while he was still recuperating.

"Where's your consistency, Douglass?" demanded Bradburn, with no trace of sympathy for the injured man sitting up in bed. "Why did you fight?"

"And where were you, and why didn't you?"

Bradburn glared for a moment, then said coldly, "We prove our moral superiority by refusing to resort to the tactics used by our enemies. If we fight, sir, how are we any different?"

"Nothing has changed. We're for freedom; they are not."

Unappeased, Bradburn pressed on, "And what of the cause? Did you not consider for one moment the disastrous consequence your resistance may have? Did you think of anyone but yourself?"

Frederick almost laughed, but checked himself, fearing the pain. "Mr. White knows the answer to that question."

Frederick smiled at White, who was standing with a bandage around his chin, a restorer of Frederick's sagging faith in his white colleagues. Some people could and would do more than vote for resolutions, sign petitions, and boycott railroads.

"Gentlemen, please," White pleaded, his pale blue eyes widened by confusion and divided loyalty, shifting quickly between the two other men.

"And why don't you ask him the same question that you asked me? He fought, too, or are you holding Negroes to a higher standard?"

"Mrs. Chapman will hear of this." Bradburn's threat was clear. Maria Chapman, as the secretary of the American Anti-Slavery Society, demanded absolute allegiance and refused to tolerate heresy, dissent, disobedience, or confusion. Maria Chapman, a widow, ran the Society, raising money, organizing bazaars and tours, consolidating support, settling disputes, always behind the scenes, an indefatigable writer of appeals, agendas, minutes, resolutions, and countless letters.

Unable to write his own defense, Frederick said to White, "Make sure that you also tell her our version of what happened, and don't wait. John Collins has already attacked me."

16.

PREPARING FOR AN URGENT meeting with Garrison about Frederick and his misadventures, Maria Chapman read again Garrison's assessment of

Frederick: "Our new friend Douglass, that splendid young man recently escaped from slavery, displays an independence which, if not checked, can bode trouble. He alluded to violence as a possible outcome when whites fail. . . . This is dangerous talk. We have made great effort to dissociate ourselves from Nat Turner and other killers. Ours is a peaceful movement, dedicated to arousing a slumbering nation from moral death. But this young man, once educated, will serve us well. It is important that he have as many opportunities as possible to talk and dine with you and others and learn *true* antislavery principles. He has a magnificent voice, and when it becomes a pure vehicle for our enterprise, purged of self and clannish concerns, it will rattle the very foundations of oppression. Mr. Phillips says that a gift like Douglass's is rare. Indeed, Mr. Douglass is our prize exhibit."

But managing Frederick Douglass was proving to be difficult. Douglass was now openly challenging John Collins, who was giving anti-property talks at abolitionist meetings, and threatened to resign if Collins continued making his case for the elimination of all property as the solution to ending slavery. A true disciple of Garrison, Frederick insisted the abolition of slavery was a moral problem, not an economic problem.

Now Maria Chapman had to unravel the controversies swirling around the young man. Besides challenging Collins, Frederick had attended a Black men's convention in Buffalo and exacerbated tensions in the colored community, undermining the Society's commitment to colored harmony. Worst of all, he had behaved like a pugilist in the forests of Indiana.

Frederick was indeed correct in his assessment of Collins. Collins was no longer a true abolitionist. Convinced that Collins was disloyal, Maria Chapman demanded Collins's resignation, which he provided. "I can do more for humanity outside your narrow cause," he replied. She never heard from him again.

Nevertheless, a novice in the movement like Frederick had no business casting judgments against his superiors, especially the man who discovered and offered him a position. Frederick was an intelligent man, to be sure, an astonishing speaker, an impressive specimen of Black manhood, but he had to stay in his assigned place. For the good of the cause, of course.

The clock struck two. Mr. Garrison would arrive at 2:30 sharp, knowing that he could never be late at 39 Summer Street. He would find Maria Chapman waiting for him in the drawing room, standing there ready to receive him with the bearing her friend Wendell Phillips said "befit a line of duchesses."

Her relationship to Garrison remained ambivalent. William Lloyd Garrison had a moral force that she found in no other, and she marveled at his ability to attract the rich and poor, the educated and ignorant, ministers and farmers.

But Garrison was a small, clumsy, fussy, graceless man who was socially, financially, and physically inept. The *Liberator* was a mess, put together with obvious haste and carelessness, its layout chaotic, without reason. He seemed intellectually distracted, unfocused, at times more interested in herbal remedies than justice. *Conundrums abound, and mystery surrounds us all,* Maria Chapman mused. *After all, God chooses as His instruments people she would not touch with a pair of tongs.*

★

Standing in the drawing room surrounded by her circle of antislavery intimates, she was ready to pass judgment on the behavior of her unruly agents after receiving letters from Frederick and others, pages of explanation, description, justification, criticism, and defenses covering the events of the summer and early fall.

"Gentlemen, by all accounts, the One Hundred Conventions has been a resounding success, even though our agents have raised only four hundred dollars."

Garrison, Wendell, and Samuel May, her favorite minister, all nodded their heads, and echoed, "Yes."

"But, our glorious specimen of fallen humanity is *unregenerate*."

Wendell immediately began a defense: "He is proud, but . . ."

"Humility is more appropriate. And he is having a negative influence on Charles Remond, who never used vulgar language in public before traveling west with him."

She slowly sat down and reviewed the epistolary evidence.

After witnessing another public argument between Frederick and another agent, an unnamed correspondent concluded, "These men, talented and glorious specimen of 'fallen' humanity as they are, are still unregenerate men who beget pride when humility is needed."

If the essential problem could be so obvious to total strangers in the western wilderness, Maria Chapman surmised, then surely something had to be done.

"It is difficult for us to imagine ourselves in the position of colored persons in this nation," explained Reverend May, a stooped but tall, gentle man who had managed to remain a friend of Maria Chapman's and all her enemies. He gave generously of his time and energy, loved unconditionally, and tried to make peace always. "If we did, then we would not wonder that their manners are sometimes cold and repulsive. They are apt to be so, unless they are servile and cringing."

With delicate condescension, Maria Chapman turned slightly in her chair and patted his hand on the armchair rest beside her. "But even a slave knows when to be quiet. And John Collins, though not his master, was still his superior."

"Are you suggesting Frederick's dismissal?" asked Wendell delicately.

"No, of course not. He is too valuable. Hundreds come to hear him speak. No, only John Collins needed to be dismissed for poisoning our efforts with his anti-property ideology."

"Who will replace him?" asked Wendell. "Miss Kelley could do the job. It's time for a woman."

Maria Chapman started and then smiled, collecting her thoughts. Of the superiority of women, she had no doubt. She condemned traditional females as victims of "domestic tyranny" and "toys to gratify the perverted tastes of men."

But she still found Abby Kelley too outrageous: she traveled alone and with unmarried men and Negroes; and she said unseemly things on stage. Having failed miserably as a public speaker herself, Maria concluded that no woman should abase herself before rabble. That Abby was willing to do this again and again was no recommendation in Maria's eyes. And rumor had it that Abby was developing far too close a relationship with Stephen Foster, that uncouth crank from New Hampshire who interrupted church services and dared to compare himself to St. Paul and even Jesus. Some also whispered that Abby had to resist the advances of Frederick, who allegedly yearned for white flesh.

Maria Chapman demurred. "Gentlemen, Miss Kelley, with all her talents, would make our cause that more difficult in the west, where men have a horror of gynocracy. With me as secretary of the executive board, her appointment would be too much. Strategy must always be considered."

"Then what about Frederick?" insisted Wendell. "As the most gifted speaker in the field, his elevation as general agent would demonstrate to a doubting nation our commitment to equality."

"Some are saying that he was not a slave, that he speaks too well for one to have just been a slave less than five years ago."

"A genius can be born a slave," observed Wendell dryly.

Tiring of such praise, Maria Chapman asked coldly, "Can he prove it?"

"He can write a book, his autobiography."

"Can he write?"

"You have letters from him."

"Yes, but they are awkward in style, full of sentences burdened with bungled metaphors, dangling clauses, and lost modifiers, so unlike his speeches. Literature may not be one of his gifts."

"He will write as he speaks. An autobiography is not the same as a business report to the Society secretary."

Reverend May intervened. "It will be an important book because Mr. Douglass will write it himself."

"And he will not have to dictate like other ex-slave narrators," continued Wendell, keeping his eyes on Maria, who was unusually silent, almost withdrawn.

She brightened, saying grandly, "It will be a glorious source of revenue for the Society. If it is good, it will sell by the thousands! You should urge Mr. Douglass to write his book."

"Don't you fear that such encouragement will increase a dangerous arrogance?" asked Wendell with gentle irony.

Maria Chapman lifted her chin and declared, "There is no one who has been obliged to wrestle and prevail who has not been accused of it, as if it were a crime, instead of being, as it is, a momentary necessity upon those who are born to set right a time that's out of joint."

Wendell smiled and added, "You are wise to see that."

"When one is perfectly right, one neither asks for nor needs sympathy or approval."

Wendell was her dear friend, her best friend, but even he could be, at times, presumptuous. Only her dearly departed husband understood. He never dared to disagree, let alone challenge her. He knew her enemies called her "the Contessa."

Maria Chapman rose from her chair. "Gentlemen, please join me at the table. We have so much more to discuss. I'm eager to share with you my reading of Mr. Emerson's latest collection of essays. And have you read Mr. Hawthorne's tales? My sisters declare them splendid, although I don't see why they waste their time reading stories when philosophy is what the world needs."

And she was off to the dining room, followed by her court.

★

With his hand wrapped in bandages and his arm in a sling, Frederick continued traveling, back to Ohio and then on to Pennsylvania. He had some restless nights, reliving the Pendleton attack and dreaming about mutilation and death. He eventually fell asleep, knowing that he could not stay off the road, that it was his destiny to speak out and never be silent. And with this recognition came an understanding that he was not ready to declare to anyone. He knew that violence was essentially a part of his life, that it was in his bones and blood, a part of his heritage and citizenship as an American. He had principles that he hoped could suppress its inexorable sway, but violence was there, ready and waiting to destroy slavery or himself. An angry man, he was not a pacifist, and his commitment to Garrison had limits.

He was always angry.

And he could not keep his roiling emotions to the stage.

Before retiring one night, Anna said as she sat in bed, “I’ve tried to not say nothin’ about it. I’ve fought the feelin’ hour after hour, saying to myself, No, don’t say nothin.’ He has enough trouble. Home is where he don’t need no problems. But you don’t sleep right. You toss and turn, and you sometimes cry out in your sleep, almost crying like you’ve seen somethin’ terrible, something that hurts your soul.”

Anna paused, struggling to control the tremor in her voice. “Now I can’t be sure what’s goin’ to happen, but I don’t want to open that door one night and find groups of men there to tell me that somebody threw you down the stairs or off the stage and broke your neck, that you’ve been killed at some meeting. I’m used to you being gone, and we’re managing. But I can’t get used to, and I’ll never get used to, waitin’ to hear about you getting’ killed.”

Beside her, he started to reassure her, but she interrupted him with an intense emphasis, “And I don’t want our children getting used to having no father.”

She turned to him, a silent reproach in her eyes. For all her words of acceptance of his career, he knew that his absence as a father, now that he had sons, was just not right.

“I’m doing the best I can, Anna.”

“Frederick and Lewis *need* you.”

“Tell them that I love them, over and over, tell . . .”

“You should, too. Rosetta asked me if you love her. She should not have to ask that, Fred.”

They said nothing for a few minutes, each looking straight ahead, immobile, almost breathless.

Finally, he asked, “What should I do?”

“Spend more time at home.”

“I can’t stop now. More and more people are saying I wasn’t a slave. People are not believing me.”

“Frederick. I’m not asking that you stop. I know better. Just take a rest. Don’t do so much. Let’s see you for a time. They don’t treat you right.”

“Only Mrs. Chapman.”

“They treat you like some plantation boy.”

“She is like that with everyone.”

“I’m sure she don’t use them words with the white men.”

“Anna, Mrs. Chapman is not the issue. I’m on the road most the time, away from her.”

“When do you leave again for more than a few days?” she asked, her words both weary and accepting.

“Around the twentieth, the annual meeting in Boston . . .”

"And then?"

"I don't know. It will all depend on what the executive board decides about the success of the One Hundred Conventions."

"Will you be here for Rosetta's birthday?"

"I don't know. I hope so, but June is far away and . . ."

"Promise me."

"I can't."

"For her."

"I'll be here," he said, touching her right hand with his left.

Anna kissed Frederick on the cheek and then lay her head on his shoulder, waiting.

Without a word, he shifted his body toward her and kissed her lips, suddenly taking pride in his refusal to visit brothels to relieve himself when he could not be with Anna. There were few brothels outside of urban centers that would accept his business in any case, but he had a moral standard to uphold as well. He was a gentleman, not some randy, rutting buck with only sex on his mind. White men could be excused for succumbing to the attractions of the flesh, but not a Negro abolitionist. A compromising position could damage the cause for months, if not years. No, he had to be stalwart, steadfast, and chaste. A good husband.

Frederick reached for Anna, forgetting caution, ignoring the awkwardness of his bandaged right hand.

"Oh," Anna said, sounding pleased.

Afterward, Frederick waited for her to initiate the usual exchange. She always said first, "I love you," and then he would reply, "I love you, too."

But this time she didn't say the expected words. He could hear her think, *Say it, please. Say it now. For once, be first.*

The rest was only silence.

17.

ANNA WAS PREGNANT AGAIN, and Frederick informed her that the next child, if a boy, would be named Charles Remond. She didn't ask for an explanation, given the warmth that had developed between the two men as they traveled together.

He was traveling more than ever, so the opportunities for making babies were few. Frederick constantly talked about the movement as if nothing else mattered. She had accepted the move to Lynn without much fuss. She didn't like the idea, but she gave in soon enough. Sending Rosetta away was another matter.

Frederick had his reasons, good reasons, he claimed. Rosetta had to go to school, of course, but Lynn didn't have enough children for a separate Black school, and Lynn city officials had no desire to integrate their schools even in a town full of Quakers and abolitionists. Frederick considered Salem and New Bedford, the only towns in that state that had integrated schools, but the daily trip was too long for a little girl. She could stay with the Remond family in Salem, but Frederick concluded that Rosetta had the best chance for a fine education in the hands of private tutoring from the Quaker sisters, Abigail and Lydia Mott.

Frederick met the Motts, friends of Abby Kelley's, in 1842, while on tour, and the sisters were well known for harboring fugitives on the Underground Railroad and spoke against slavery at countless meetings and conventions. Abigail was a former teacher in the Albany schools and openly declared that it was her life's mission to educate girls, especially Negro girls, as thinkers and writers and future wives trained in the classics and the domestic arts. Abigail said that she would be honored to tutor his daughter.

Frederick spoke to Anna as if offering a prepared statement, "The arrangements for Rosetta have been finalized, and the Motts are prepared to receive her when I take her to Albany. When time and circumstances permit, we can travel there to see her. I have no more to say."

Anna was left to give Rosetta the news.

Frederick tested Anna again, a month after Rosetta's departure, when he told her that he had had a reunion with his youngest sister while on tour in Pennsylvania, where she was introduced to him by Quaker family who helped her escape.

Even though Anna had accepted long ago that she would never see her own brothers and sisters again, she missed them. Still, she was happy about Frederick's reunion with his sister, even if he barely knew her. As children, Frederick and Harriet did not live together, and he saw her only on a few occasions. He had no detailed memories of her, but he was excited anyway. Harriet was a tangible link to his past, to the Eastern Shore, to his other sister, Eliza, and most importantly, to his grandmother, now a guardian angel in his memories.

He said his days with his grandmother were the happiest days of his life. Anna wanted to hear that the happiest days of his life were the first years of his marriage and the birth of his children, but she understood the power of those Shore days when he was a boy playing and having adventures, carefree, blissfully ignorant, without responsibilities of any kind. Anna had never seen Frederick as happy as he was on the day Rosetta was born, but the weight of responsibility as a provider fell upon his shoulders, and the long, grinding hours in the foundry and on the wharves made him sullen and distant. Now his bright eyes on that day and the broad smile had returned, and Anna was truly happy for him.

Later he revealed his plan to meet Harriet in New York during a convention and bring her to Lynn to live with them. There was no warning, no consideration of the necessary preparations or her feelings about how this new member of the household could impact their lives. Asking Anna's permission was out of the question, of course. Family was family, and families lived together even in cramped quarters. That was the way it was with white and Black folks.

Nevertheless, Anna raised objections.

"But you don't know her. You never talked about her. How did she find you?"

"She was living in Baltimore and learned about me there."

"How could she? You're not Frederick Bailey no more, not for a long time. How could she know that Frederick Douglass is her brother?"

"Can't you be happy for me? Your suspicions can be as cold as winter."

"I'm just trying to protect you, protect this family."

"Why would anyone try to pretend to be my sister, for heaven's sake? We don't have money."

"Whatever we have, we have more. She was a slave."

"We all need family," Frederick said.

Anna relented. "It will be good having another woman in the house, and hearing the Shore in her voice, and seeing it in her ways. It will be like going home."

"Yes, she will be good for the family. She can help in all kinds of ways, surely."

Like Anna, Harriet was plain and dark, and she stood at the same height. But she was also thin without flesh in her cheeks or on her chest, as if she had no breasts. She had puffs under her eyes and full lips larger than even Anna's. Only Harriet's dark, penetrating eyes and knitted eyebrows, with the merest hint of a furrow at the top of the nose, suggested a resemblance to Frederick. Anna thought she looked more like her own sister Lottie, five years her junior. Harriet certainly spoke with the accent of home.

Anna kept her assessments to herself as Harriet became an active member of the household. She enthusiastically volunteered to help in any way with the cooking, the cleaning, and the care of the children. She also offered to help with binding shoes and other ways to raise income, cleaning other houses, taking in laundry, and cooking meals for sale at church bazaars and antislavery meetings. From the beginning, Harriet openly acknowledged and accepted Anna's domestic authority, always asked for permission from Anna, and thus never overstepped any possible boundaries. Harriet was always pleasant, smiled without simpering, and never complained or gossiped. She always had good things to say about people. Anna could not think of an instance when Harriet criticized, condemned, or disparaged anyone. Anna concluded, *That girl don't have a mean bone in her body.*

One day, Harriet said, "Anna, why don't you do whatever you want to, take a walk, putter in the garden, and I just take care of the children, play with them, feed them, do whatever. Just take your time all for yourself. You deserve time all for yourself. I don't have much, poor as I am, but I can certainly give the gift of time. Now what you think? How about it?"

Always taking her domestic duties seriously, Anna was immediately inclined to reject the offer, but she could see in Harriet a natural, authentic desire to please, and she agreed, "Sister, I'll take up that offer."

"Good! You deserve this. And take as long as you need."

"Thank you," Anna replied, now imagining the list of things she wanted to get done, things she would enjoy without worry. She was about to have a little vacation. "I can't do much, you know," she added, touching her large belly.

"Even more reason to have it," said Harriet. "Once the baby comes, time will not be so free with nursing and all the rest."

Anna liked her, whatever her doubts. She was kind and generous, and great company because she never tried to compete with Anna, even when Frederick was in the room, as some sisters and sisters-in-law are prone to do. It was clear that Harriet's primary allegiance was to Anna. Furthermore, Harriet had a positive influence on Frederick. Around her, he was more relaxed, more willing to admit his faults, especially his tendency for self-pity. He observed once, "You just have to give me a look, and I get less snapping, and my under lip, hanging' like the lip of a motherless colt, will hang just not so low for all that."

Around Harriet, Frederick would casually return to his Eastern Shore accent without self-consciousness or explanation. It then came naturally, and he obviously enjoyed a banter that he had abandoned in the drawing rooms of Boston and New York, for obvious reasons.

Anna smiled. For all his talk against slavery, Frederick still loved the Eastern Shore, just as she did. Far more verbal than Anna could ever be, Harriet could powerfully evoke the Eastern Shore by just describing how she could make crab cakes.

One day, two months later when the two were alone while the children napped, and Frederick was away on tour, Anna said lightly, as they were tying up some leather shoes, "So what is your real name?"

Harriet paused, holding her needle and thread in midair. Then she slowly lowered it. Harriet looked to her lap and replied, "My mama named me Ruth, and my last name is Cox. Ruth Cox. I'm sorry."

"The Lord must have a hand in this, you being named. You know the story, don't you?"

"Yes," said Harriet before quoting the famous passage from the Old Testament: "Where you go, I will go, and where you stay I will stay . . ."

Anna finished it: "Your people will be my people."

"You *are* my people," said Harriet, her eyes moist with tears. "I wanted you to be my family, and so I lied. I'm so ashamed."

"Don't be. It says something about them Baileys."

"Everybody knows about them around Easton, even when they were scattered. Betsey is still living in St. Michaels."

"Did you tell Frederick about Betsey?"

"Of course."

"But your life is built on a lie."

"I know, and I'm sorry if I have hurt you or Frederick, but the time here has been wonderful, and he was so happy when I told him I was his sister. When I heard him in Pennsylvania, he was so wonderful on stage, and when he mentioned he had sisters, one of them he barely knew, I saw my chance. He asked me lots of questions, and I knew most of the answers."

"*Most* of the answers? Do you think he still doubts you?"

"Sometimes. He looks at me, wondering."

"But he is happy, and so am I. I have a friend, a real friend, and a helper, so let's just keep it as it is. You're Harriet, and to the children you will always be Aunty. You know that families have close friends who are so close, they might as well be brothers and sisters, aunts, and uncles. This won't be the first time or the last. Harriet Bailey, that's you from now on."

Harriet stood up and embraced Anna. "Oh, Anna. I love you."

"I love you, too, Harriet."

They stood in their embrace for a few moments, then Harriet disengaged and asked, standing away, "Will you tell Frederick?"

"No. But one day you might need to."

"I can't, I just can't. It will be our secret. You know how he can be when he gets angered. When someone said his wrath is like a lion, I know exactly what that means, as surely you know, being his wife."

That was as close to a criticism of her "brother" as she had ever offered, and she immediately self-corrected her conclusion in an uncharacteristic bumble. "I—you know what I mean—I didn't mean by—that's not what I wanted to say—and the public sees that lion . . . And . . ."

"Don't worry about me, but you're right, and you might be able to tame the lion at least for that moment by finding some way to tell him."

"No, I can't. I'm afraid to lose everything."

"I will leave it to you."

"Thank you so much, for everything."

On October 21, 1844, Anna gave birth to a healthy son. The midwife and Harriet had made the delivery seamless and uncomplicated. The boy was named Charles Remond, as expected.

Now feeling more grateful and inclusive about his growing family, Frederick admitted to Anna that he knew that Harriet was not a sister, and he didn't care. "She's our sister now, and I love her too."

"Will you tell her? She's worried about you finding out."

"Yes, I will. I don't want her to worry, and I don't want you to worry about her, either. We'll all be happier without that hanging over our heads. I will need peace, too."

Frederick was home to write his book.

PART II: 1824-1836

The Baileys, the Anthonys, the Aulds, and the Lloyds of Maryland

18.

"TELL YOUR STORY," JOHN Collins told Frederick at the beginning of his career. This simple injunction helped Frederick to overcome his fear of speaking before white audiences. Now, six years later, he had the same story to tell, but the written words would not come. After three days of effort, he could not think of how to write his story. The paper in front of him remained blank. For inspiration, he returned to *The Columbian Orator* and read favorite passages from the Old Testament. He wanted to capture in his own book the cadences and the direct simplicity of the Lord's call to the people: "Declare ye in Judah, and publish in Jerusalem," he read, savoring every word, "and say, Blow ye the trumpet in the land: cry, gather together, and say, Assemble yourselves, and let us go into the defended cities."

But he had no documents, no proofs for dates or a true chronology. When was he born? When did he go to Baltimore?

All he had was memory and imagination, and his need to write the most powerful indictment against slavery ever written. *If only I could preach this book*, he thought desperately as he lifted the pen once more. If only.

He saw the first word of his story on the sheet of paper before him and poised his pen. The beginning was simple: the facts of personality and geography, one forged out of the other. He wrote without pause: "I was born in Tuckahoe, near Hillsborough, and about twelve miles from Easton, in Talbot County, Maryland."

Frederick then delineated his world, its roles defined and characterized by skin color, and mentioned his mother by name first: "My mother was named Harriet Bailey. She was the daughter of Isaac and Betsey Bailey, both colored, and quite dark. My mother was of a darker complexion than either my grandmother or grandfather. My father was a white man."

He reread these opening paragraphs, and instinctively stayed with the story, continuing with the few details he knew about his mother. After another paragraph, he admitted, "I received the tidings of her death with much the same emotion I should have probably received at the death of a stranger."

His honesty surprised him. He could have announced her death with all the usual trappings of sentimentality, popular in novels, but the starkness of his words suggested the utter desolation of his loss and slavery's power to kill love. *This is what it does to children. This is slavery.*

He rose from his desk. He had to take a break. He could not sit still. The memories made his neck and back ache. Frederick left the room and went out to the kitchen. But as he walked away, he could see the indictment against his father forming in his mind: "Slaveholders have ordained, and by law established, that the children of slave women shall in all cases follow the condition of their mothers, and this is done to administer to their own lusts and make a gratification of their wicked desires."

As much as he would like to deny his influence, Frederick knew that his father, mysterious and powerful, would stalk the pages of his narrative, defining the character of slavery through violence and sexual frustration, and forming a young boy's character by providing a model to despise.

He left his desk now and then to toss a ball to Lewis and Frederick, but his narrative plan, now forming in his mind, demanded long hours in his chair.

At times, he could not bear staring at the blank page and the stark truth that seemed to lie there waiting to emerge through the thin sheets and ink. It was thoughts of his grandmother, the first important figure in his life, that made him stop writing for a day. Feelings long denied, the terrible loss, the abiding sense of betrayal and abandonment, the unanswered questions, the rage that comes when unfinished business makes hope hollow and the future forever insecure, all this and more swelled up, like dark bile, to sicken his heart and make him pause.

For the first time in years, alone in the dark of his room, and too ashamed to reveal that he was still essentially a child, he wept, feeling a guilt lodged within the most secret corners of his heart and so thick that no vessel could contain it.

He had given up on ever seeing her again, and he never tried, once he was in Baltimore. He suppressed his feelings for his family over the years and refused to discuss his reluctance to find them even with Anna, who did not comprehend his indifference. He spoke of the Baileys often in his speeches, and he damned slave owners for destroying families, but his outrage was hollow, for it never touched his deepest fear—that slavery had succeeded in freezing his heart.

Now he cried, afraid and yet relieved that he could still feel his childhood pain and the solace of unconditional love. He cried for Betsey Bailey, not because she needed pity. She was proud, unflinching in her acceptance of the truths of her situation and her life. But she deserved some measure of thanks from him, some token of his esteem after all these years. At last, he was ready to fully think about her, and thank her through the words he needed to write. Her fate defined the character of slavery, and her existence made his character possible. His confidence was born in her cabin.

Suddenly, the words came, and his pen moved quickly:

"If any one thing in my experience, more than another, served to deepen my conviction of the infernal character of slavery, and to fill me with unutterable loathing of slaveholders, it was their base ingratitude to my poor old grandmother. She had served my old master faithfully from youth to old age. She had been the source of all his wealth; she had peopled his plantation with slaves, she had become a great grandmother in his service. She had rocked him in infancy, attended him in childhood, served him through life, and at his death wiped from his icy brow the cold death-sweat, and closed his eyes forever. She was nevertheless left a slave—a slave for life—a slave in the hands of strangers; and in their hands she saw her children, her grandchildren, and her great-grandchildren, divided, like so many sheep, without being gratified with the small privilege of a single word, as to their or her own destiny. If my poor old grandmother now lives, she lives to suffer in utter loneliness, she lives to remember and mourn over the loss of children, the loss of grandchildren, and the loss of great-grandchildren. The heart is desolate. The children, the unconscious children, who once sang and danced in her presence, are gone."

The pen fell from his hand, as if the strength in every muscle of his body had drained away. Frederick stared at the wild scribbling on the page, afraid to reread what he had written in a rush of anger and grief, this fantasy of ingratitude and abandonment. Frederick's version of events reflected what he thought should have happened, given the character of the men and the system they supported and that protected them.

He stood and looked out the window. It was snowing. Already the snow had covered the window and trees, leaving strips of a soft, white blanket. The fire had been burning for hours, and the house was warm.

"Gram' Betty," he whispered, saying that intimate name for the first time since he was ten. "We're here: Rosetta and Frederick, Jr., and Lewis and Charlie and me. We're here." These were his private feelings, ones he would not share with his readers. Frederick steeled himself and went back to work.

He was determined to not give his readers a sweet, docile Negro, grateful and emasculated, to pity. If this was what Northern readers demanded, then he would disappoint them. He had to speak with a strong, clear voice and say unequivocally: Here I am, a *man*, like you.

Memories flooded Frederick's mind, characters marched before his eyes with insistent voices, demanding his attention. There was so much to tell.

19.

IT WAS EARLY AUGUST, and Betsey Bailey climbed the ladder to the loft of her windowless cabin near Tuckahoe Creek, awakened Frederick with a gentle nudge, and whispered as the other children slept, "Fred, come on down. We're going on a trip."

It was dark with just a hint of light on the horizon. She could hear the rustling leaves of the sweet gum trees. Soon the air would be thick with moisture, and walking twelve miles would be difficult for a boy. But she was prepared, stuffing one pocket with cornbread, a ripe peach and pear in the other. She was sure that her grandson would pass the time by talking every minute. That was his way, asking questions, answering them, too, even if he didn't know what he was talking about. He always told stories. He liked hearing them, but he liked telling them even more.

"Where we going?" he asked, rising immediately, excited and curious. "It must be some place important if you got a clean bandana on your head," he noted.

She had washed, dried, and ironed her best bandana for the trip to Wye Plantation, but she was not going to tell him about their destination. He had nightmares about "old massa" ever since he learned about him. She tried to hide the truth from Frederick for as long as possible. He would know eventually what it meant to be a slave, that she was owned by another, that he would eventually have to leave her, as did all her children and grandchildren.

What Frederick would later learn was that "old massa" was Captain Aaron Anthony and that after working as a captain on a schooner owned and operated by Edward Lloyd, he had taken a job as Lloyd's general manager of Wye Plantation, which included thirteen farms, 500 slaves, and nearly 10,000 acres. As Lloyd's chief overseer, Anthony lived rent free in a separate house on the main Lloyd estate.

For now, Betsey would keep Frederick ignorant and happy as best she could. He would have a kind of freedom. It would be her way of saying no to slavery, at least for a while.

She had succeeded for the most part, and Frederick would run through the fields, roll in the dust, play in the mud, dive into the stream, and always come back with stories to tell or more questions to ask, thrilled by discovery and adventure while protected within the limits she set. When a cousin was no longer there, he would either not ask about it or easily accept her answer, "On a visit."

Despite her efforts, there were times when he would sob and she would immediately know the cause. Even when overcome by despair, Frederick would ask crucial questions: Who is the old massa? What is a slave? Will he take me away?

Once, he told her a nightmare he'd had about the Master that she would never forget. The unknown master had become a monster, and his teeth, bloody and sharp, tore off arms and legs and crushed bones with a loud snap. His huge eyes bulged as he searched the fields for more prey, and the children, screaming as loud as they could, ran from him as a long tongue, darkened by blood and the mud of the field, rolled out to scoop them up.

"Now, now," she said, rubbing his head with one hand and holding him close to her chest with the other, "the old massa is no such thing. He's a man, just like Grandpa Ike, just a man."

"A *white* man," Frederick said, "like a ghost, a monster ghost."

"No, child," Betsey said, "no ghost, just a white man who has some land and some houses."

"And us," added Frederick.

"We work for him, yes."

"Do you get money, and how much?"

"That's something you and no child need to know," Betsey replied. "There are childish things and adult things. That's one of the adult things. So, don't worry about it. We have a roof over our heads, and food on the table. We have enough money for that, and that's all you need to know, you hear?"

"Yes, Grammy," he replied, and that was that, until the next time doubt and suspicion crossed his mind and more questions needed answers. Fortunately, these episodes would pass quickly, and he would return to his games and adventures, a happy and confident boy who knew, just knew, that he was her favorite, smart, curious about everything, as if the world was created to entertain him.

Of all her grandchildren, he stayed with her the longest. But she always knew she would lose Fred eventually. Her children and grandchildren were not hers to keep. They were travelers on the roads to the Anthony properties, Wye Plantation, or farms where they worked as rented slaves. Her cabin was only a waystation for short visits, usually at night, when her daughters would hurry in to hug their sleeping children or leave a new one for her care, before rushing out to return to their quarters undetected. Sometimes they were gone for a year or more, unable to get away or travel the great distances. And sometimes she would hear about new babies and not see them for months.

Even so, she loved having a big family, and swelled with pride when she had twelve babies of her own, nine daughters—Milly, Harriet, Jenny, Betty, Sarah, Maryann, Hester, Cate, and Prissy—and three sons—Stephen, Augustus, and Henry, her last born just four years ago, when she was still strong and able at forty-six. Three of them were dead: Stephen at eight, Augustus at four, and Cate, just a babe. But she had a slew of grandchildren. Milly had seven, Harriet six, Jenny three, and Betty three. Hester would have her own soon enough.

Frederick was Harriet's, but Harriet worked on other farms and couldn't get away to see him much. And when she did come, he was asleep with other children crowded together on straw mats in the loft.

Unlike Frederick, Harriet was not much of a talker. She was like all Betsey's other girls, pretty, smart, stubborn, with a mind of her own. About Frederick's father, his mother had little to say. "He's a white man," Harriet said casually before Frederick was born. "We all can tell when the baby comes."

"Is it the Master's?" asked Betsey.

Harriet didn't flinch, answering the question casually. "It don't matter. With all them white men takin' us for the takin', who knows which one is the one?"

"He'll look like somebody," Betsey countered.

"And what difference will that make?" Harriet said. "A yellow nigger is still a nigger, and a yellow slave is still a slave."

Even with rumors flying around that Captain Anthony was Frederick's actual father, Harriet never confirmed or denied it. Betsey was now sure Harriet really didn't know.

But on this August morning there was one fact that could not be denied: Betsey had to take Frederick to Captain Anthony's house on Wye Plantation.

Unconcerned about waking up the others, Frederick rolled over two cousins and scrambled down the hemp ladder to the clay floor.

"Where? Where? Where?" he sang, happy about another adventure.

"Hush now," she said, "and wash your face and put on this clean shirt."

He stared at it, shocked. "But it's not Sunday. Why?"

She turned away to speak to Isaac, who sat in front of the fireplace staring at the early-morning fire and pressing his lips.

Frederick pulled his grandmother's skirt. "I didn't do nothing. I didn't," he protested. Isaac was a man of few words who brooded most of the time when he was not out working. All the children were afraid of him. Their fears of her were nothing by comparison.

"Hurry," Betsey admonished him. "Get dressed."

"What about something to eat?"

"We'll eat on the way. It's a long way."

Frederick shook his head. "No. I'm not going. No, I can't."

Betsey gripped Frederick's shoulder, making him buckle. "No more foolishness. Now git ready. We're going."

And that was that. He dressed, patted some water on his face, and took the wrapped biscuits she gave him.

"Bye, Grandpappy," Frederick said, waving his hand from a safe distance.

Isaac didn't respond, and Betsey gently pushed Frederick out the open door. They passed by the heavily fruited peach and pear trees and started west on the rutted, dusty road across Talbot County.

When Betsey first came to Tuckahoe from Skinner Plantation on the great Bay with Miss Ann, who had married the Master, she had hated everything about it, the long marshes, the hard, almost barren dirt, the run-down farms and fences, the bugs, and the white-trash renters. But then she jumped the broom with Isaac, found a cabin, started a family, and worked hard, taking advantage of the virtual freedom the Master gave her.

He left her alone most of the time, and she would cross on foot the counties of the Eastern Shore determined to make money. She was a midwife and nurse. She made the best skein nets, caught buckets of shad and herring, grew sweet potatoes in gardens all over because she had more than "the good luck" of slave talk. She didn't use seed potatoes bruised in digging. She made sure they were not planted in shallow ground after burying them deep in the floor of her cabin during winter. Hauling everything on her strong back, she sold what she didn't use at home, and made enough money to seem free. She was never rented out.

Betsey was respected in the colored community and admired for her skills by white people. She raised a large family that the Master promised to never break up. And now she had come to love the lands around her as she roamed beyond the fences and walls that confined most people, Black or white, to just one farm house or one plantation or one town. She knew the beauty of the Eastern Shore, the Lord's good acres.

After twelve miles, Betsey and Frederick came to a partial clearing were two parallel lanes led to a magnificent white house with six brick chimneys that could barely be seen above the oak trees. One of these lanes, covered with white pebbles, had an ornamental iron gate through which Betsey and Frederick did not pass. They took the other lane, the service road that ran eastward behind the Great House bordering a twenty-acre meadow. Along this road were many smaller brick houses, the quarters of the hundreds of slaves who lived and worked at Wye Plantation. The noise, a combination of song, laughter, yells, shouts, curses, bangs, clatter, and booms, made Frederick cover his ears.

At the end of the meadow, where sheep by the hundreds grazed, stood the ancestral home of the Lloyds of Wye, a late Georgian-style mansion built in 1787. Frederick was stunned. "It's so big," he said. "Bigger than our house."

It always impressed Betsey when she saw Wye House. It seemed to shimmer like another sun come down from the skies.

Betsey pulled at his arm and soon they arrived at a brick house behind the bigger one, where the Anthonys lived.

"This is the Master's house," she explained, taking Frederick's hand and pulling him gently to the back, where the kitchen house stood. In the yard Brown, Black, red, yellow, and almost-white children, ran about playing games.

Frederick drew closer to his grandmother as the children surrounded them and asked questions whose answers they did not wait for.

"Who you?"

"Where you from?"

"We're goin' to play whip, wanna play?"

Before entering the door of the kitchen house, Betsey turned to Frederick and said, "Fred, go and play. Be good. They is kin."

He shook his head and looked to the ground. Pointing, Betsey continued, "They're other cousins. That's Phil and Steve and Jerry and Nance and Betty, and that's your brother Perry and your sisters Sarah and Eliza."

"So?" he said, shrugging his shoulders.

Betsey sighed, tapping him in the rear, and said, "Be good, so I say, and go on and play."

After a few words to the captain, she was on the road again, back to Tuckahoe Creek. She cried and cried until she could not spill another drop. After the tears, she knew she did the right thing. Her Frederick would have a better life on Wye Plantation.

20.

LISTEN AND STAY PUT.

Betsey told him to wait outside a large, unfamiliar house after a long, tiring walk across large fields and dark forests. And as he watched her enter the back door and disappear, Frederick resisted the urge to follow her, despite the dread that gripped his stomach. Betsey had to be obeyed, and so he waited, leaning against the wall of the house, and watched a new game on the yard.

Children ran to form a single line, each child holding the hands of the person in front and behind.

"Hold tight," his brother Perry shouted at the front of the line, "real tight or it ain't no fun."

At eleven, Perry was the tallest and strongest, and as he started to run, everyone followed, clenching teeth, and moaning as "the whip" twisted and turned in tight hands.

"Don't break it," someone said, giggling.

Soon children at the whip's end, too slow or small to line up at the front, were hurled across the yard, separated by the force of the line's motion. A small boy with golden hair lost his connection and tumbled to the ground, then another fell, and then another. Soon the speed of the whip was too fast, and boys and girls flew in all directions, groaning, hooting, and hollering, and laughing too as they fell. The remaining line continued on.

Frederick laughed too.

One of the children ran out of the house, shouting as if she enjoyed delivering the news, "Freddy, Freddy. Gram Bettys gone. Gram Bettys gone, gone, gone!"

Frederick screamed, then pushed the girl aside and ran into the cook house. "Grammy," he cried out repeatedly as he ran around the large room. With her since the day he was born six years ago, he could not believe his eyes and ears. When she had to leave their cabin for even short trips, she always told him why she was leaving, where she was going, and when she was coming back.

The other adults, three women he didn't know, stood against the wall, watching with blank faces, saying nothing, as if they didn't care about him.

When it was clear that his grandmother was not there, he threw himself to the hard ground, pounding it with his fists.

His brother and sisters had followed him into the house and now tried to comfort him, patting his head and shoulder.

"Don't cry," said Eliza, two years older. "Here, have a peach. Don't cry."

Frederick looked up and knocked the golden ball out of her hand. It rolled across the ground.

His other sister, Sara, who was ten, offered a pear. He hit the second gift even harder. Eliza commented, "He'll get over it," and turned to leave. Perry and Sarah followed their leader into the yard.

Frederick continued crying on the ground but eventually fell asleep there. The noise of a busy kitchen did not disturb him, and he did not wake up when he was moved to a nearby closet and placed on a straw bed.

But in the morning, he had another shock, receiving a kick to his side.

"Get up, nigger!" shouted the thin, Black woman with a high, shrill voice, a distant cousin called Aunt Katy. "You ain't sleeping all day!"

Frederick jumped up, stood at attention, his arms at his sides.

Grinning, Katy said, "You didn't get up when I told you to, so you're getting nothing to eat. I'm the master here. You do what I say, or you'll wish you dropped dead, and you can forget Bets. You won't see her again. Never!"

Frederick cried out, "No!" He knew this mean woman was telling the truth.

She lifted her hand to strike him, and, after taking a step, said, "Shut your mouth, damn you."

Captain Aaron Anthony entered the kitchen, saying casually, "Good morning, Katy. The usual."

As if by magic, her tone softened, and she said, moving toward him. "Yes, Massa."

Frederick stared at his first sight of the "old massa." His grandmother had told him that he owned the farm where they lived but worked somewhere else. Since the master never came to their cabin, Frederick would think of him only now and then. Now here he was.

"Is this the new boy?" asked Captain Anthony, coming up to Frederick and lightly placing his hand on Frederick's head. "Are you?" he asked Frederick.

"Yes, Massa," he replied, his lip trembling.

"Now, Katy, you haven't been scaring this boy, have you?"

"No, Massa," replied Katy.

He took Frederick's hand, leading him away from the closet to the center of the kitchen. "How's my little Indian boy?" he asked gently.

Frederick said nothing.

Katy snapped, "You say something when the massa's talking to you, boy!"

"Now, Katy, don't scare the boy. He's new and doesn't know better."

Katy went on, her voice hardened. "In my kitchen, every child knows, or else."

Captain Anthony, dismissing her warning, said to Frederick, "Be a good boy, and everything will be just fine."

He patted him on the head and started to go, but he stopped when he saw an orange on the counter. "Do you want this?"

Hungry, Frederick grabbed it and clutched it to his chest.

Katy started to protest, her mouth opening wide, but Captain Anthony interrupted her with a raised hand. "Now, Katy, don't. I'll be waiting in the dining room. Miss Lucretia will be joining me this morning."

Katy said nothing until Captain Anthony was out the door and across the small yard separating the kitchen house from the main house. Then she pounced, snatching the orange from Frederick and pushing him away.

"You dirty little bastard!" she screamed, slapping him across the face. "Don't you *ever* shame me in front of the massa."

Frederick fell back as he cried out. Now against the wall, he rubbed his cheeks, and fixed his eyes on Katy as he cried.

"After I'm finished with you, you'll wish you were dead. I'll kick the shit out of your high-horse little ass. I can do whatsoever I want. I'm the massa here."

Katy turned his shoulders and pushed him forcibly toward the door, chanting as she went: "I'm the massa here, the massa." She gave him one final shove, almost making him fall into the large, empty trough outside the kitchen door, and announced, "And stay out until I call you back!"

A short while later, Katy appeared with a large bucket and poured mush into the large trough. When done, she raised her hand, held it there for a second, and then lowered it. The children rushed forward as Katy turned away. The older and bigger children went first, getting on their knees and, in a tight circle, thrusting their faces and hands into the mush. Behind them, the younger ones, waiting impatiently, leaned over the hunched backs to make sure some food remained, squealing like pigs.

When the older boys and girl had their fill, the young ones scooped up the rest, emptying the trough. Not a grain remained.

Frederick stared at the trough so stunned by the sight he only looked up when Katy appeared again.

"Now, boy, you never going to get food that way, now will you?" she asked. "I guess you're goin' to starve. Well, that'll be just one less mouth to feed."

Frederick said nothing, but Eliza had something to say after Katy went back inside: "Steal or die," she said, starting off.

"Where you going?" Frederick asked, following her.

"I'm going to get some better food from the Lloyd niggers," she replied, before reaching the gate. "Want to come?" Earlier she had explained that Captain Anthony worked for Colonel Lloyd, a very rich man who gave his workers more food than they could eat.

He looked back to the cooking house. "No," he replied, horrified and frightened. "I can't. She'll beat me if she finds out."

"Suit yourself," Eliza replied, leaving him.

For the next few days, he stood away from the others, sulking or crying. And when he bothered to interact, he bothered them with questions: Where's Grammy? When is she coming back? Why did she leave? He stayed away from the trough, too, explaining to Eliza when she brought him a handful of corn meal. "I'm not a pig."

"You'll be a pig soon," she predicted, laughing. "You'll get hungry. So, you better watch and learn."

"No spoons?"

Eliza laughed harder. "Nigger, are you dumb?"

Before he learned how to fight for food at the trough, he grabbed at crumbs that fell from the kitchen table, pushing away the dog Old Nep, or followed his Aunt Milly to scoop up crusts, bones, and other scraps when she shook the tablecloths after Anthony family meals, making the cats hate him, too.

But eventually, he approached the trough, and when the bigger children, including Eliza, had their fill he jumped in with the younger ones, scooping mush with his hands, and licking his fingers to get every wet kernel.

"I want more," Frederick said plaintively.

"Try harder" was all Eliza had to say.

He did, and he ate more. But he was always hungry.

One day after another complaint about food, Eliza said, "Tomorrow we'll go to the Long Quarter. There's plenty of potatoes and corn and oysters and chicken. Niggers steal so much chicken they run the other way when they see us comin'."

Frederick laughed with her, but then Eliza became serious, stooping to face him eye to eye. "You have to do what I tells you, you hear?"

"Yes," he agreed. "But will Aunt Katy know?"

"If she don't say nothing about staying 'round, then we leave."

"But what if she wants us to do something, or . . ."

"Do you want to go or not?" Eliza asked, taking a step toward him.

He relented immediately. "Yes."

"Just us two. Them Lloyd niggers don't like packs of Anthony niggers grabbing after their food. We might have to take something."

Frederick froze.

Incredulous, Eliza asked, "You never took something before?"

"No need," he replied.

Eliza then shoved her brother at the chest with both hands. "Don't tell me about all the good food you had with Grammy Bets, you hear?" she yelled. "Don't tell me about all the good times. I don't want to hear one peep about it!"

Taken aback, Frederick didn't reply, but his sudden tears made her look down.

"I'm sorry," she mumbled. "Don't mind me. I say mean things sometimes, but I don't mean it. It's just . . ." The words trailed off.

Taking her hand, Frederick comforted his sister now. "I get mean and mad, too."

Eliza grinned, looking at Frederick again, and said, "Like since you came."

"Yeah," he agreed, "and tomorrow, we won't be mean. I want them Lloyd niggers to like us."

"They'll like us so much we'll get hills of bread and potatoes and oysters. Heaps!"

"So, we don't have to steal?" Frederick suggested carefully.

"We *might* not have to," Eliza replied. "We'll ask. But we have to be careful. Some of them don't think too much of us."

The next day, Frederick and Eliza left through the back gate and ran down the road toward Frederick's new world. He listened carefully to his guide, who at first described the wonders of Wye Plantation with indifference. But as she described more, she became excited, sharing countless details about the Long Quarter, a rough, low building that housed hundreds of slaves; the barns, stables, storehouses, sheds, and shops, where artisans and mechanics created and repaired incredible tools and equipment for the Lloyd farms; the parks, where rabbits, deer, and other wild game roamed freely, and where red-winged black birds covered the tops of poplar trees; the gardens, filled with roses, black-eyed Susans, golden aster, and other flowers; and the Great House, which stood in a separate meadow, its surrounding trees like another gate.

By midday, Frederick was no longer hungry, having received a large piece of bread from the blacksmith, Uncle Tony. But Eliza made it clear that success today did not mean success tomorrow.

"Things change all de time," she explained. "He might get whipped, or he might have to fight his wife or somebody else, or he might be gone tomorrow, sold to some white man. It's best to move around, so not to push nobody. But remember this—everybody is aunt and uncle 'round here. No respect, no nothing."

"Do you know who your daddy is?" he asked.

Walking beside him on the road back to Captain Anthony's, she did not pause or look toward him when she answered. "No," Eliza said, unsurprised by the question. "Everybody wants to know who their daddy is. They aren't around much, or never come around."

"Is he the same as mine?" Frederick continued.

She stopped, her taunting eyes making him wince, as if they had burned holes in his flesh. "Look at me, and look at you," she replied. "We have the same mama, but your daddy's a white man."

"A white man!" Frederick exclaimed, stepping back.

"Don't act dumb," she said, now pushing him again. "Your skin is yella, almost white. Haven't you seen? But don't you think you're better 'cause of it, yella boy. You have nigger hair, nigger nose, and nigger lips, and you're no better than nobody."

He pushed back. "No, I'm not!"

Eliza pushed harder. "So you think you're better than me?"

"No, that's not what I said."

"White don't make you better. We're all the same, all the same, you hear, even if what some say is true, even if your daddy is the old massa."

"What!"

"I don't believe that talk, and you better not, 'cause I'll hate you. I'll hate you!"

"No, I'm not better," he pleaded. "It's just a story, a lyin' story. I don't believe it."

Eliza stopped, her voice warming again. "All right. Sorry."

"Sorry, too," he said. "Don't be mad at me."

Eliza took his hand in hers and said, "Let's run home."

Pulling her brother behind her, Eliza boldly entered the kitchen house to ask Katy what she should do for the rest of the day, as if their long absence mattered not at all. Katy was preparing the midday meal, the aroma of molasses and roasting pig thickening the humid air. She answered as she cut the potatoes, "I'll call you if I need you. Phil, take them peelings out."

Leaning against a wall, her sullen son demanded, "Why do you have to ask *me*? Eliza just asked to do something. Ask her or ask the new boy."

Still cutting, Katy did not turn from her work. "Don't you talk back," she said, gritting her teeth. "Do you hear me?"

Tall and muscular at eleven, Phil stood straight, his chin out, ready to fight. "Yeah, I heard you," he answered. "Ask somebody else."

Katy quickly turned around, holding up a huge butcher knife, its blade a silent warning to Phil to shut his mouth *now*.

Frederick shuddered.

"Nigger," said Katy, her voice dark with menace.

"No," said Phil, uttering the forbidden word.

Katy lunged at him, holding the knife ready to stab him. Eliza and Frederick screamed as they fell against the walls, getting out of the way. Phil ran to the other side of the room and crouched like a dog. "No," he said again, his voice weaker but still defiant.

Katy rushed across the room, but Phil, sweating and breathing heavily, was swift enough to stay out of her hands. He ran to the other side of the room, ignoring Frederick and Eliza.

She's going to kill her own boy, thought Frederick, *and I'm next.*

Within seconds, Katy caught her son, grabbed his arm and said, "I told you to not sass me. Don't you *ever*."

He struggled to free himself, yelling, twisting, and now pleading. "Please, don't, please."

"This will teach you," she said. Suddenly, she cut his arm near the wrist, leaving a large, open gash like a thick red worm.

Stunned, Phil fell to his knees, screaming. Katy released him and dropped the knife to the floor. Phil held his arm to his shirt, darkening it and his trousers with blood. He screamed hysterically as his mother tried to comfort him.

"I told you not to sass me," she said, "but you'll be all right."

Katy dressed Phil's wound, wrapping it in thick folds of cloth. At first, the blood soaked through, but as the dressing thickened, less and less blood could be seen. When she finished, she said, as if nothing had ever happened, "Now Phil, take out them peelings."

"Yes, Mama," he whispered, humbled at last.

"You know I loves you," she continued, turning to retrieve her knife, "and this was for your own good."

"Yes, Mama," Phil said again, louder as if to convince himself. "Yes."

"And everybody else git outa here if you know what's good for you."

They ran out, telling their story as soon as they passed through the door. Frederick recalled every detail, repeated every word, and Eliza repeated his lines like a chorus. Surrounded, they enjoyed the attention even as they shuddered at the details.

When Captain Anthony heard about what happened, he hurried into the kitchen calling out Katy's name. Eliza and Frederick dared to go inside again while the other children remained outside. Excited and reckless, they didn't think until later about the possible repercussions of being witnesses. Having seen a terrible thing, they now believed they had a right to see the result.

Katy turned from her work with a smile, ignoring his angry voice.

"Yes, Massa?" she asked, as if she had no blood-spotted skirt.

"Where's the boy?" he demanded, looking to the corners.

"What boy?"

"You know what I'm talking about, Katy. Don't act like some stupid nigger."

Katy waited.

"Did you cut him?" demanded the captain.

"Yes," replied Katy without hesitation, never looking down or away. "He sassed me."

Captain Anthony started to pace, unable to fathom her confession. "This is not acceptable," he shouted, shaking his head, and pointing at her. "Have you no feelings for your own flesh and blood? You're his mother, his mother, for God's sake! Don't you feel *anything*? I can't believe you; I just can't believe that you would do something like this."

Katy stood still, but her eyes followed the master about the room; there was no fear, only a bemused tolerance of his outrage.

He continued: "I will not have this, and I am warning you that if you ever do something like this again, I—" Captain Anthony stopped to emphasize the importance of his words: "If you do, I will take the skin off *your* back. Do you understand me? Do you?"

"Yes, Massa," she said evenly.

"These children are in your care," he concluded. "Take care of them. I expect them to grow up unhurt." He hurried out, muttering words and phrases: "Her own boy. I can't believe this. Damn . . . won't have it, won't have it."

Frederick started toward the door.

"Stop right there," Katy calmly ordered.

He stopped but did not look up.

"Look at me, and remember what I tell you. He will never touch me. Never! I'm his favorite, and I'm the best cook there is. I'm the one that takes care of this house and this here kitchen, and all his affairs. He needs me, and he knows it, and he lets me have my own babies stay with me when nobody else can, not your mama, wherever she is, and all those other worthless aunts of yours, and so if you have ideas that now I'm going to be some mealymouthed nigger shaking in some corner, you don't know Aunt Katy, boy. You don't know me at all."

Then she taunted him, her tone more cutting than ever. "Who's the massa here? Who?"

He didn't hesitate. "You're the massa."

"Say it: 'Aunt Katy is the massa here.'"

Frederick repeated the crucial phrase, loud and clear.

"Good," she said, grinning. "Now go outside and don't go anywhere like you did this morning. No supper for you tonight, boy."

Outside, Eliza declared the obvious, "She hates your guts."

"But why?" Frederick asked, tears flowing.

"She thinks you his boy, the massa's boy."

"But you said I'm not, and I had better not even think . . ."

"I can't tell her what to think, just you. And you have to listen to me now and do everything I tell you, no matter what, or else."

Frederick relished the attention and enjoyed the lessons she taught, even when they bewildered him at first. There was so much to learn about who was who and what was what. He was an eager student, absorbing the names of kin, the identities of the Anthonys, the Lloyds, and all the important colored folks on the plantation.

Aunt Katy ruled the kitchen, and two of his real aunts, Milly and Hester, helped her. Besides Phil, Katy had three other children, Jerry, Billy, and the infant Caroline. Milly had children, too: Betty, Tom, Henny, and Nancy.

Although Frederick learned the names quickly, he didn't try to get close to cousins or his brother Perry or other sister. Frederick was only interested in the way things worked, knowing the rules needed for survival, and a possible rise in the slave ranks. "Some of us become house niggers," Eliza observed.

Even so, Eliza hated all the Lloyd slaves, house and field. They felt superior just because they belonged to Colonel Lloyd, proudly announcing at every opportunity, "I'm a Lloyd nigger, and you just a Anthony nigger."

But there was one Lloyd slave everybody had to know, and whose authority everybody had to accept and respect: Uncle Isaac Cooper, the crippled doctor of religion and medicine in the slave quarters. He was old and permanently maimed from a fallen tree, but hundreds came to see him for help, and he could still draw blood as quick as lightening.

Once a breeder of fighting cocks for the colonel and a house servant of Colonel Lloyd's father, Uncle now propped himself on a three-legged stool while leaning on crutches in his cabin. Sent by Captain Anthony to learn the Lord's

Prayer, all the children sat before him as he declared his faith while swinging four large hickory switches above their heads. "There are only four medicines you need in this here world," he said, "epsom salt and castor oil for your body, and the Lord's Prayer and the whip for your soul."

Standing still, they waited, cowed into absolute silence by the lingering sounds of the brandished whips, long and shining in the dim light of the cabin.

"Now, you're all goin' to say the prayer of Lord Jesus, our Savior," he continued. "And you will repeat what I say."

He paused and closed his eyes, as if in silent prayer. Then with his eyes still closed, he yelled, "Kneel!"

Everyone jumped before scrambling to his or her knees. They pushed, shoved, and complained about space, making so much irreverent noise that Uncle Isaac inhaled deeply, and shouted, as if proclaiming before a Sunday multitude in the open field, "Quiet! Quiet in this place. This is the Lord's holy time."

When there was absolute silence, he leaned forward and said, "Say after me, 'Our Father.'"

Promptly, they all replied as one, "Our father."

Uncle Isaac continued, "Who art in heaven."

Two response groups had immediately formed, entering at different intervals.

Uncle Isaac inhaled deeply, the stink of the mistake forcing him to issue a warning: "Hear this and hear this good. You'll feel this whip if you don't mind me and listen. Listen!"

He tried again: "Our father."

"Our father," they said again in perfect unison.

"Who art in heaven."

They repeated it perfectly, and proudly nudged each other, grinning at their accomplishment.

Uncle Isaac pressed on: "Hallowed be thy name."

Confusion again.

Frederick held his breath, waiting for a sudden flash of the whip. *The dumb fools! Can't they hear?*

He glanced at Eliza, who seemed to agree.

Uncle Isaac went on, but mumbled chaos ensued, and without warning, Uncle Isaac struck the neck and shoulders of Aunt Katy's second son, Billy. Billy yelled out before cowering below the old man, his hand to the bloodless welt on his neck.

Everyone except Frederick crouched their heads and tried to press their bodies even lower into the ground. He stared at the sight, never having seen anyone hit by a whip.

Uncle Isaac asked, menace thickening an already deep voice, "Boy, what you lookin' at?"

Frederick was quick enough to reply respectfully, "Nothing, sir."

Uncle Isaac leaned forward again, and said, "All right. You're going to say this here prayer, and if you makes just one mistake, I'm gong to stomp you into a mud hole."

No one laughed at the obvious absurdity of such a threat. His legs couldn't stomp a cockroach. But one fact could not be denied: if Frederick failed, he would get the worst kind of whipping.

"I'm going to say this just one time. I'll say a line, give you just a moment to repeat it, and then I move on, and you had better not make a mistake, not one. But I'll give you time, a little time." He grinned and winked his eye, as if signaling to the rest of the children he was going to be patient before disaster.

Slow and deliberate, Uncle Isaac began again. With each line came a pause before Frederick repeated it. As the lines became more complicated, Uncle paused more. But the lines didn't defeat Frederick, who repeated every word exactly.

Carried away by his success, Frederick now pompously stated the final cadence, "For thine is the kingdom, *and* the power, *and* the glory forever. AAAAmen!"

Uncle gaped at Frederick, his eyes black pools of disbelief. Confused, everyone else turned to each other for signals for what to do next. They wanted to celebrate Frederick's success, but they also knew Frederick had made a fool of the old man and made a fool of himself. By showing off, Frederick had violated a fundamental rule of the quarter: respect your elders.

But Uncle Isaac didn't raise his whip to strike Frederick down. Instead, he said with a quiver in his voice, "Just git out of here. All of you children, get out of here now."

Everyone rushed from the cabin. Outside, they surrounded Frederick, hooting and patting him on the shoulders. "You really showed him," said Billy. "You showed him good."

Eliza stood away from the group, waiting. While talking to the others, Frederick could see the scornful eyes meant to wither him.

He came up to her. "What did I do? What did I do now?"

"You know what you did, you dumb nigger."

"I did what he told me. I didn't want no whipping."

"Stupid, that's all. I can't help you with this one, no sir. The word will get around here, and nobody, especially around here is going to help some Anthony nigger showing off to a Lloyd nigger, especially to Uncle Isaac. So, you think you're better? Well, if Uncle Isaac don't like you, nobody's going to like you, just nobody. His word is strong around here, mighty strong. There will be no help for you. There are just some folks you just don't fool around with. Couldn't you just stop? Couldn't you just help yourself?"

He repeated his defense. "No whipping."

Eliza rolled her eyes. "So? Everybody gets a whipping now and then. There's whipping, and then there's a real whipping. He couldn't hurt you that way, not him. It's like a game: show respect and you win. When are you going to play right?"

Eliza walked away.

"I'll learn. I'll do better. Promise. Don't be mad. Please. I'll be good," Frederick pleaded.

She turned around, unmoved. "You're smart and stupid, real stupid, and now it's going to be hard for the rest of us. Just you wait and see. We're all going to be in trouble now."

They waited for retribution, but it didn't come. For the first time, Eliza was wrong, and, knowing better, Frederick did not tell her.

But he enjoyed his little victory, especially when he heard how his lesson got back to the master and Colonel Lloyd himself. They were impressed.

"Who is that boy?" the colonel was heard asking.

21.

AFTER AARON ANTHONY DRESSED in the usual black overcoat, gray trousers, white shirt, and brown cravat, he always turned to his Bible for guidance or consolation. But on this surprisingly cool morning in a cramped room illumined by a single candle, Anthony avoided it, fearing damnation. He knew scripture would condemn his dreams of Hester Bailey, her amber skin, large breasts, wide hips, and long legs still irresistible snares to a righteous man trying to save his soul after what he had done to her two days before.

Hell is never full.

He wished Katy had not told him the truth about Hester and Ned Roberts. "I warned her to stay away from that Ned Roberts," she noted, the solemnity of her disclosure undercut by her grin and sparkling eyes. "Didn't you tell her? Why didn't she listen? But no, she had to do what she wanted to do, and . . ."

"Shut up," he shouted, irked by her enjoyment of the disclosure, and then jealous rage coursed through his body with a light that seemed to blind him. He bolted from the kitchen, charging into the still dark, early morning toward the Lloyd slave quarters like a snorting bull. He found her half naked in Ned's bed, and he grabbed her arm and pulled her away, ignoring her shocked protests, and knowing no one, including Ned, would stop him.

Hester had to be punished, made an example to all the other Bailey slaves he owned, even the children now hiding in the cook house closets and side rooms, suddenly awakened by the uproar.

"I told you to stay away from that Lloyd nigger," shouted Anthony. "I told you to stop seeing Ned, but you wouldn't listen." Ned was a tall and very handsome young man, a favorite of Colonel Lloyd's, who bestowed on him supplies and privileges granted to few others.

Moving swiftly, Anthony made her stand on a low bench naked to her waist. Her wrists were tied to a twisted rope that stretched her arms toward the large iron staple on the ceiling beam. Anthony then stood behind her, brandishing a three-foot cowskin whip painted blue and tapered at the tip. It quivered when he raised it.

"No, Massa, no," Hester whimpered, jumping lightly on the bench. "Please, please."

Anthony continued yelling, "So you think I'm not good enough, you damn bitch! Well, you'll remember this, long after fucking Ned Roberts!"

Looking over her bloodied shoulder, she begged, "I won't do it no more. Please."

"I bet that's what you said," Anthony said, mocking her. "Please give me more, and more, and more, all you got!"

He twisted his body, flung his arm back, and thrusted his right arm forward with the weight of his body. The whip cracked on Hester's shoulder, and she screamed again. The blood dripped from the open wound to the floor.

"No, no, no," she continued, jumping and twisting.

Anthony wiped the blood off the cowskin with his left hand, smearing it before saying, "You damn, Black bitch . . . fucking a nigger over me, over *me*. This will teach you!"

Again, he struck her with great force, finding a fresh spot on her skin. "Bitch," he shouted.

"I promise . . ."

Anthony accelerated his pace, striking again and again. With each blow, he called her a name, listing every possible insult.

"Your promises mean nothing," he continued. "After favoring you, after letting you work here, you go off and fuck that nigger, that *Lloyd* nigger."

"I forgot," she told Anthony.

"Forgot?" he asked. "You damn lying whore, you didn't forget, and you won't ever forget what I tell you from now on!"

He continued striking.

Finally, he slumped down on a chair and put the stained whip on the table. Anthony wiped the sweat from his forehead with his hand. "Whore. Whore. Whore," he intoned.

Hester was exhausted, too, no longer screaming. She moaned on the bench, a wounded animal unable to get away.

Anthony sobbed as he untied Hester's arm. His voice was full of regret and jealous love. "You're mine. Don't let me see you with him again. You can't stay here, not anywhere near that boy you fucked. Leave for the Kentucky farm before the sun comes up," he said, and left, rushing back to his house and bed, knowing that Katy and Hester's sister would administer ointments that would heal her wounds, and confident that every slave on Wye Plantation would hear about the beating and share the moral of the story: disobey and you will be next.

Anthony eventually fell asleep, but it was a restless, troubled sleep, for he knew that the lessons learned were not simple at all. Even as a married man he had coupled with Hester's mother and sisters without messy scruples. Slavery was its own world with separate, independent rules. But now, at fifty-seven, he was old. His wife, Ann, and three of his six children were dead, and time with its inexorable rush to decayed distinctions had left him anxious and confused. His sudden shifts in mood, from jubilation to despair, from serenity to cruel belligerence, disturbed and frightened him. He was no longer a man in control of his life.

For a few moments, he pretended that if he could not recall the words that sealed his fate he could escape it. But with constant reading of scripture, he remembered entire passages. He shuddered, seeing in his mind's eye St. Paul's warning to the Christian Romans: "Let no sin reign in your mortal body, that ye should obey it in the lusts thereof. Neither yield your members as instruments of unrighteousness unto sin. The wages of sin is death."

The word of God was indisputable proof. After yielding to Bailey flesh, Anthony was going to burn. The Lord would surely make room in hell for him.

Anthony shook his head. *No, no, no*, he objected in silent, desperate prayer, hoping that the Almighty could be appeased by a long life of success and good works. To restore his self-confidence, Anthony turned to the only other books that mattered to him, his ledgers with lists of purchases and donations.

Anthony opened the pages of his most important inventory, "My Black family," and immediately found Hester Bailey's name and birth year, 1810. For a moment, the notation confirmed his absolute power, but then he saw her mother's name, and his will capitulated to vivid memories of infatuation and desire. A remarkable girl, that Betsey Bailey, tall and beautiful, her black eyes suggesting a disdain for anyone who didn't recognize her gifts and place in the world. She was alluring with soft, chestnut brown skin, a dazzling smile, and a slender waist and hips that refuted her many pregnancies. Though married to Isaac Bailey, a free Negro who cut and dressed timber from pine, walnut, maple, and oak trees, she did not resist her master's advances. She seemed to enjoy her favored position, her fertility Anthony's guarantee against unnecessary expenditures. He didn't need to purchase any slaves.

By 1824 Anthony had three farms of 600 acres and thirty-six slaves, all descendants of Betsey, who had produced nine daughters, three sons, and twenty-five grandchildren. For years, this genealogy represented to Anthony a triumph of will, the successful conquest of history, and documentary proof of his new status: a true master.

Anthony recorded the birthdates of as many slaves as he could, including those who died in infancy. Now, he glanced at the birthdates of some of the more recent members of the clan: Arianna, October 1822; Kitty, March 7, 1820; Stephen, July 1819; Frederick, February 1818.

Frederick Augustus Washington Bailey.

Anthony grimaced. Masters often gave slaves Latin names, filling plantations with modern day Black Romans, mocking slave ignorance and the irony of naming slaves after nobles and emperors of an advanced civilization that never questioned slavery.

Anthony had nothing to do with Frederick Bailey's middle name, Augustus, which had been given in memory of Betsey's son who died as a child, yet another example of that maddening combination of family honor and nigger presumption in a close-knit family repeating surnames year after year through generations: Hester, Phil, Harriet, Betsey, Jenny.

But Frederick was new, distinctive.

Why had his mother chosen it?

No, matter. The yellow boy could be useful. And now that his wife Ann was dead, Anthony no longer worried about upsetting a woman who could accept a Black mistress but not a yellow bastard.

Colonel Lloyd had told Anthony that his youngest son, Daniel, needed a companion, one of the boys, who could live in the house and play with him.

Freddy could be that boy. Anthony had heard stories: Frederick was smart, maybe too smart, loved to talk, and asked perhaps too many questions. That could be a real problem for any nigger on Wye Plantation or anywhere in Maryland.

Nevertheless, a grateful Colonel, pleased by Freddy's service, might show his appreciation by inviting Anthony into the parlor of Wye House through the front door. Anthony was more than just hired help. He deserved an invitation as another wealthy slave owner.

At last, he turned to the family Bible and read the dedication that reflected his once righteous confidence in the ways of the Lord. Using a heavy quill and thick black ink, he had written, years before, "Violate not the sacred commands of God. Through Faith I am determined to conquer tho I die. All of you, my children, violate not the sacred commands of God ritten in this Book." He had paused, unsure of his spelling, but had pressed on, scribbling with renewed vigor, "Read and keep them holy. Walk upright and honorably before God and man that you may be heirs to the kingdom of heaven and meet me on the Banks of Deliverance and long Dwell together."

The path to salvation was now clear: have faith, avoid evil, and do good.

For Frederick.

22.

LUCRETIA ANTHONY AULD KNEW the rumors, heard the whispers. Her father had a yellow son, and the boy Frederick might be her half-brother.

Anthony did not tell her Frederick was coming to their house, but when he arrived she decided to watch him closely, listen and learn more.

One afternoon she heard a commotion.

"We're better!" shouted Ike Cooper, the son of a Lloyd blacksmith, a year older than Frederick, maybe two, but no relation to Uncle Issac Cooper.

"No, you're not," Frederick replied. "You won the game. That's all!"

"We de Lloyds!" Ike countered, now almost nose to nose. "We de *Lloyds*!"

Frederick laughed and said, "You're not! You're just a nigger." All the other children surrounded them, cheering, and calling for a fight.

"Fuck yo' ass!" cried Ike. He pushed Frederick in the chest.

Frederick pushed back, saying, "You too!"

Ike pushed again, now harder, and chanted, "Tuckahoe nigger, nobody from nowhere. Tuckahoe nigger!"

Frederick shoved Ike with such force he fell on his back, his arms and legs quivering slightly like an overturned roach in the dust. For a moment Ike said nothing, only staring at his enemy. He probed the dirt with his long fingers. When he found a large cinder, he hurled it at Frederick's head. Frederick screamed, and he screamed even louder when the blood flowed between the fingers of both hands pressed against the wound. He howled and jumped before running into the cook house.

Katy met him at the door of the cook house and said, "Serves you right. I told you to stay away from them Lloyd niggers."

Lucretia emerged from the opposite door facing the main house. "What's happening?" she inquired. "I heard . . ."

She noticed Frederick and, assuming Katy's guilt, said, "Oh my God, Katy, you didn't?"

"Not me," Katy replied, no concern in her voice.

"The master will hear of this," Lucretia said, looking around the room for a cloth to stop the bleeding. "Get me something," she implored. "Anything."

"Yes, Miss Lucretia," Katy replied, and then insisted, "Not me, not me."

"Everything will be all right," said Lucretia as she applied the cloth to the wound and led Frederick out of the room, taking him around his shoulder, unconcerned about staining her midday frock.

"Bring some water," Lucretia ordered in a soft voice, her back to Katy, "and everything else I may need."

In the parlor of the main house, a small but well-appointed room with large, upholstered chairs, an area carpet, heavy draperies, and a gilded clock on the white mantle of the fireplace, Lucretia washed the blood from Frederick's face, dressed the wound with herbed balsam, and before she bandaged his head, said, "Now there. It's not so bad. You will have a scar for a while. It looks like a cross."

Frederick remained silent, his head down.

"Now tell me what happened?" Lucretia asked. She looked to the floor and saw his dirty feet.

Animated by her request, he told his story, surprising her with its vivid and dramatic details, the colors, the sounds, the words exchanged. But he continued staring at his feet.

Lucretia went to the table between the two front windows. "I have something for you," she said, coming back to open her hand and reveal a piece of peppermint candy.

He hesitated and stared.

"Do you know what this is?" she asked.

Lucretia's husband, Thomas Auld, entered the room. Frederick took a step back, fear in his eyes. Before she could assure him, Thomas winced, snorted his disgust, and said, "Why do you bother with the niggers? And why is he here?"

Approaching him, she said with the sweetest and lightest tone she could manage, "Now, Thomas, he's part of our Black family now, the new boy from Tuckahoe."

"I'll be damned if this yellow nigger is anything to me."

"Thomas, your language," implored Lucretia, looking back to Frederick.

"Get him out of here before he smells up the place," Thomas replied before he turned to leave, holding his nose to accentuate his repulsion. Thomas slammed the door behind him.

Lucretia was amazed how Thomas had become ugly, a contrast to the first time she saw his chiseled cheek bones, dimpled chin, thick golden hair brushed high and back, and those incredible eyes so large, so clear, so blue and bright they seemed like orbs granted from heaven to highlight a perfect face. The fact that he was not a slave owner and did not want to be one also made him more attractive to her then, a man determined to avoid slavery's tangled web.

But he could not escape it, hating a starving little boy.

Dismayed, Lucretia stood still, staring at the door. She faced Frederick again, and said, "Now, Freddy, you go outside and play. Do as I say and try not to get into trouble." She didn't like the sound of her voice, trembling with false cheer, embarrassment, and chagrin.

Frederick put out his right hand.

"Oh, of course," Lucretia said, remembering the piece of candy held in her hand. She was still agitated but relieved. Today's business could now come to an end. She dropped the candy into the palm of Frederick's hand.

"Thank you, Miss Lucretia," he said, grinning.

Surprised by the clarity of his words and the absence of slave intonation, and moved by his pride, she almost asked, "Now how did you learn to talk like that?" But instead, she returned to a more urgent matter. "You may go, and I know what Katy's doing. If you ever need something to eat, just come to me, you understand?"

"Yes, ma'am," he replied, surprised at what she knew.

She explained, "There's no secrets here. This is not Wye House, just a small house, and I can hear you singing sometimes. You have a sweet, beautiful voice. Just come to the window on the other side, away from the cook house, and sing, and when I hear you, I'll have some bread and butter for you. Now go."

Frederick departed, and Lucretia leaned against the closed door. She wished she could spit out the bitter taste of irony, secrets that grinded her teeth and twisted her heart. She wished she could forget the distant and desperate cries, the shouts and screams heard that terrible night when her father punished Hester.

She couldn't hear specific words, but she knew what was happening. She knew she would do nothing to stop the beating, and she knew that no one would say anything about it the next morning. Silence made living with slavery possible in polite homes.

Now twenty, almost twenty-one, Lucretia had lived on the Eastern Shore in Maryland her entire life, the daughter of slave owners who accepted slavery's conditions in exchange for a comfortable life. They protected an inferior race; gave it shelter, food, and true religion; and expected to receive from their slaves comfort, wealth, and, if not wealth, at least financial security, eternal gratitude, and even love. It seemed simple, especially when her mother, a tyrant of fantasy even as an invalid, was alive to sustain these illusions. But when Ann Skinner Anthony died in 1818, Lucretia had to face ugly truths about her father and slavery.

There was talk, mere whispers really, that Anthony was involved with Betsey Bailey. But Lucretia had no proof and didn't want any. It was enough that her father was married for twenty years, seemed to love her mother, was gracious with gifts and compliments, solicitous about her wishes and needs, and attentive but gruff in the way of the unschooled and unpolished.

Lucretia remained horrified by the stories about her father and the Baileys, what he had done with Betsey and now was doing with Hester and maybe the others, too, including Milly and Harriet. The yellow children in the yards could be his, but they were probably not.

But of all of them, Black, Brown, and almost white, Frederick was the only one allowed to stay with Betsey for all six years of his young life. And he was the only one Anthony asked about or whose treatment and lessons he expressed any interest in. Frederick resembled him in the shape of his face, the lips, the intense eyes, that ridge between them. There were Bailey features, too, the wide nose, the prominent cheek bones, and the high forehead. Lucretia had not seen Harriet, Frederick's mother, that often, and was told that Harriet came only at night when the boy was asleep and left at dawn before he awakened. Even so, Lucretia could tell that Frederick had the intelligence, grace, and pride of all the Bailey women.

Frederick Augustus Washington Bailey, listed in the ledgers, was her half-brother, and she felt a duty to protect him.

23.

THE DAY CAME WHEN Frederick was finally summoned to Wye House. He rode behind his master in the carriage. Frederick was excited and scared, too. Of all the children, he was the one selected to go the Great House; he was the one to see the things inside and learn what was true about the Lloyds, mysterious white folks to most people. He could make Captain Anthony proud, and maybe, just maybe, he would tell everybody he was Frederick's father, and make them all, including Aunt Katy, afraid to hurt him.

But Frederick worried, too. What if Daniel Lloyd and his family didn't like him because he was not clean enough or smart enough? What if he disappointed the captain, who would then allow Aunt Katy to do whatever she wanted? The what-ifs like heavy rocks on his head, sinking his shoulders, and the Great House, though impressive, seemed less bright, less grand.

The ride didn't take long. Anthony brought the carriage to the large cook house behind the mansion. It was the size of Captain Anthony's entire place. Frederick wondered, *How could white people eat that much food?*

Anthony stepped down first and told Frederick to get out of the carriage. He didn't wait for Frederick to follow him.

When Frederick entered the house, he didn't see his master. He saw only the back of a cook at a large table and a tall white boy standing beside her. The boy took a step and protested loudly, "But, he's just a little boy, Aunt Livy!"

Olivia's head was wrapped in a bandana. She stopped cutting potatoes and said warmly, "Now, Master Daniel, honey, he can't help himself for being what he is. And your daddy wants only the best of all them nigger boys out there. He's the smartest, so I've heard."

"So?" replied Daniel, defeat in a single word.

"It's done, honey, so just come over here and meet the boy and take him with you. He's all cleaned up, fresh shirt, washed feet. Now stop wasting my time and get on."

"Aunt Livy."

"Now," she ordered.

Daniel crossed the large room. "What's yo' name?"

Olivia said, "You know it already. I'm sure Colonel Lloyd told you."

"I want to hear him say it," Daniel explained.

"Fred," Frederick whispered, keeping his head down.

"It's a good name," declared Daniel, "so you don't have to look down when you say it. And we're going to be friends."

Daniel gently pulled Frederick by the hand. But Frederick resisted, taking only a step with his head still down.

"Don't be scared," said Daniel kindly, stopping to make his point. "Just come with me and do what I tells you, and go where I go, and you'll see all kinds of things, wonderful things. . . ."

Frederick looked up, surprised. Daniel immediately explained, "Yeah, I can talk like all you niggers. Been 'round you all my life. Maybe, if you're real smart, you'll learn somethings from me and become a real house nigger." He giggled and pulled Frederick again. "Come on," he said, offering an invitation more than a command.

Daniel became Frederick's teacher, answered his every question, named for him every object of interest, introducing Frederick to unknown, magical sights and sounds.

"What's that?" became the constant call, and Frederick solemnly repeated the perfectly enunciated names as if they were magic: cantaloupe, eggplant, asparagus, celery, French beans, parsnips, radishes, all in Mr. Dermott's huge garden. Daniel took Frederick to the poultry pens, the smokehouses, and the dairy, where Frederick mentally gorged himself on venison, veal, mutton, capons, guinea fowl, pheasant, and partridge.

On several occasions, after eating in the Great House, Daniel would share cake and pieces of unfinished roasted chicken gathered secretly and hidden in his pockets. He enjoyed watching Frederick eat. Frederick would stare at a morsel as if it were silver, then roll it in his mouth to savor its juice, chew with constant pauses, and then finally swallow. "You really like eating this stuff," observe Daniel. "It's just food to me. Fills my stomach, keeps me going, that's all."

Astounded, Frederick kept on eating, afraid to show his honest reaction. *That's crazy. Have you ever been hungry?*

Even so, questions continued. Frederick had just eaten grapes from Spain.

"Where's Spain?" Frederick asked.

"Far away."

"Farer than Baltimore?"

"You know about Baltimore?"

"My cousin, stuttering Tom, he said it's a bright, golden place across the bay."

"Spain is really far, across the ocean."

"What's the ocean?"

"A big, big water."

"Bigger than the bay?" asked Frederick, incredulous.

"Much bigger, bigger than America."

"What's America?"

"This whole place."

Frederick proudly declared, "This here is Maryland."

Daniel laughed, shaking his head. "My sisters would just die if they heard the likes of you, just die. A nigger correcting his master."

Frederick immediately protested. "No, Massa, no, but this here is Maryland, isn't it?"

"Yes," said Daniel. "I just wish you didn't tire me out with all the questions."

With Frederick following, Daniel approached the rear of the house as if he intended to enter it, and then tipped around the right side of the house to the long veranda and its expansive shrubs. The leaves were so thick no one could see them. Daniel stepped up on a pile of rocks already in place. Looking back to Frederick, he put his finger to his lips, signaling to Frederick for absolute silence.

Colonel Lloyd and his neighbors, Mr. Jepson, Mr. Peake, Mr. Skinner, and Mr. Lockerman, were sitting with glasses of brandy or whiskey in hand, sipping their drinks as they leaned back in their chairs.

"There's too much killing of the niggers going on," said Mr. Jepson, a fat gentleman with a cigar permanently attached to his face. "Things are getting out of hand, just out of hand. Why, it was completely uncalled for that stupid Mrs. Hicks to kill that girl for falling asleep while she was watching her baby."

Mr. Lockerman, a thin man who shifted constantly in his chair, protested: "But she stayed asleep after Mrs. Hicks called her several times. I would be upset if I found a baby crying and some nigger just sleepin' away."

"But to go in there and get a piece of firewood and pound her head in. That's expensive."

Lockerman stopped moving to make a joke. "Well," he said for emphasis, "you know what they say: it's worth but a cent to kill a nigger, and half a cent to bury him."

No one laughed, and Jepson said, as if to shame his neighbor and longtime friend, "Sir, we cannot have niggers always afraid. Yes, they need to know their place, but a happy nigger is a good slave."

Colonel Lloyd finally spoke. His voice was soft yet deep. It reflected the quiet confidence of a man who was the richest in Maryland, the fifth in a line of Lloyds going back to 1660, and had served in Annapolis as a governor and state senator. At fifty, he was handsome with premature white hair, brilliant blue eyes, and ruddy skin. He wore a formal waistcoat and cravat even in summer, but impeccable tailoring could not hide the fact that he ate too well and drank too much. He had puffy cheeks and fat thickened his waist.

"Yes, gentlemen." said the colonel, leaning back in his chair. "There is a limit. Consider John Beal Bordley. What's the point of his going down and shooting an old man for fishing on his property? Negroes all over go down to his place and fish for oysters every Sunday night. They enjoy it. So, on one night, Bondy insists on his property rights and kills a man. This is contemptible behavior for a slave owner. Such a man will never be welcome in this house."

His guests nodded, accepting this exclusion without comment.

Colonel Lloyd added pompously, "We must be good to our Negroes."

Daniel stepped down and gestured with his head for Frederick to leave. Below the landing on which the gentlemen sat, the boys moved cautiously, trying not to rustle the leaves. When they were at a safe distance, Daniel looked back toward the house and said venomously, "He should know. He goes over to see that Sally Wilkes and treats their nigger boy better than me."

Frederick's mouth dropped open and Daniel rushed to explain. "I know sleeping with slaves is what you do to become a man and all, but Daddy shouldn't treat us like we're nothing. He cares more about that Bill, and it just isn't right, not right at all."

His voice trailed off. Daniel had spoken about Colonel Lloyd without the customary respect, the usual deference. Frederick was confused, and Daniel said with jeering irritation, "How can you understand? What do niggers know about family? You don't have a daddy, anyway."

"I want a daddy," Frederick said, his eyes blinking.

"It's better not having one," replied Daniel.

★

For weeks, Frederick was not allowed to enter Wye House and returned to the Anthony's at the end of every day. Olivia explained to both boys, "Honey, you know them Anthonys and their niggers don't come in the house, and the master's word is final."

Daniel stepped closer, smiling sweetly. His voice stayed calm and even. "Aunt Livy, the captain comes here most every day before going with Daddy to ride around."

"That's business, child."

"I want Fred to sleep in my room," he replied, insistent but still pleasant. "Fred needs to be there when I wake up."

"He's no house nigger."

"We'll make him one."

Olivia arched her eyes. No longer smiling, she replied coldly, "The guv'ner won't have it."

Daniel conceded, his eyes averting hers.

When they were outside, he said to Frederick, "She's hard sometimes. But I love her. And she loves me. But don't worry. It will happen, just you wait and see. I'm sure of it. Until then, let me tell you about what's inside."

Daniel described the white walls, the spiral staircase, the paintings, the silver in cabinets and on the tables, and Frederick, out of sheer excitement, relentlessly peppered him with questions, demanding specific details.

Finally, the day came. Colonel Lloyd had granted permission after consulting with Captain Anthony. Olivia reported with the good news. "Now you boys just stay out of the way when we all has things to do, you hear? And don't you wake nobody in the mornings. And wash them feet before you go inside, both of you!"

Frederick grinned, and Daniel shouted only, "Yes!" before grabbing Frederick's hand to take him out for the needed washing.

Afterward, they went inside. Daniel grinned, enjoying Frederick's awe. Daniel named and described everything for him: the light shimmering through the windows; the bright polish on the wood; the height of the ceilings; the paintings, family portraits by Benjamin West and Charles Wilson Peale of generations of Lloyds; antique furniture imported from Europe; French crystal; Irish linen; pounds of silver plates displayed on sideboards, tables, and chests; hundreds of books; and the house servants, all beautiful and handsome, mulatto and well dressed, who cleaned, dusted, brushed, and polished what seemed to need no improvement.

"Now Freddy, let me show you my room, and where you're going to sleep when you stay here. You'll be on the floor at the foot of my bed. Come."

Daniel's bedroom had a bed, a chest at the foot of it, a chair near one of the two large windows, and another chest with a washbowl on top of it. The mantle over the fireplace was empty, and not a single toy cluttered the carpeted floor. There were two portraits on the walls, more Lloyd ancestors.

Daniel plopped on the bed and said, "You'll be sleepin' in here, and your spot will be at the foot of my bed on the floor between the posts and that chest. It will be moved a little way, and I'll have some blankets put there. And you won't have to hear that Aunt Katy all day and night and scrap for food." Frederick had told him everything about her treatment of him.

"Thank you, Mas' Daniel."

As if not hearing this acknowledgment, or caring, Daniel immediately changed the subject. "Now let me tell you about my brother Murray."

James Murray Lloyd was Daniel's hero, and Daniel judged everything through his brother's eyes. Murray looked like his father, tall, handsome, and impeccably dressed. And like his father, he hunted, raced, gambled, and drank with the best.

Colonel Lloyd favored his second son, seeing in him so much of himself, but tradition required that the first son, also named Edward, inherit the wealth and control of Wye Plantation.

Daniel became Murray's imaginary lawyer and appointed Frederick the jury, acting as if relentless repetition of his argument would somehow change the final verdict. Frederick dutifully listened and asked no questions. "It's so unfair," whined Daniel. "Edward doesn't ride. He doesn't hunt. He doesn't sleep with the slave girls. He likes music and plays the piano and grows flowers. A real man needs to own this place."

But Daniel reserved most of his hatred for Bill Wilkes, the almost-white coach driver who looked so much like Murray.

Colonel Lloyd never openly admitted that Wilkes was his son, but he favored him in important, noteworthy ways. He had his personal tailor, Mr. Charles Eckhoff, make Bill's coats and pants, which cost four times as much as the garments he made for other house servants. And Bill's boots and shoes were made by William White, the shoemaker who charged the same price for the shoes and boots of Colonel Lloyd and his white children. Bill Wilkes wore his clothes and heritage with pride, and Murray Lloyd openly swore that he would strip him of everything.

A few weeks after Frederick could sleep over in Wye House, Murray demanded that his father prove that Wilkes got no preferential treatment, that he was just "another impudent nigger." The confrontation began at the dining room table when Murray's oldest sister, Elizabeth, who enjoyed irritating him, casually praised Bill Wilke's superiority as a driver. Colonel Lloyd, Murray, Daniel, Elizabeth, and their other sister, Sally, had gathered for the afternoon meal. Frederick was told to wait outside the room, but the door remained open.

Colonel Lloyd responded to Elizabeth, "Yes, my dear, he's a good driver," and continued eating, as if the subject was closed.

But Murray said, "That's more than you ever say about what I can do." He smiled and leaned forward to punctuate the impact of his words. Everyone stopped eating.

Colonel Lloyd stood up slowly, after carefully placing his napkin on the table beside a plate still full of ham, chicken, and vegetables. He said solemnly, "James, we will continue this in my study."

He rarely used Murray's first name, a sign that serious consequences would follow, but his face revealed neither anger nor distress. He only said, "Excuse us," before leaving the room.

Murray followed, and everyone else remained seated, staring at the door. The servants in the room stared ahead like blocks of salt as if they heard and saw nothing, waiting silently for instructions. Daniel bolted toward the door. Always the defender of protocol, Sally, thin, dour, and without any of the physical attractions granted by nature to the others, protested ineffectually, "Daniel, you must . . ."

Amused by the turn of events, Elizabeth said dismissively, "Oh, men are such boys!"

Daniel raced to the other side of the house, signaling Frederick to follow him.

The two boys crouched below an open window and listened. Murray's voice was loud, insistent. "You're saying, Papa, that you prefer that Wilkes nigger to me?"

Daniel pressed his ear to the study. His father replied, "No, son, I didn't mean—"

"Then prove it to me, prove it to me that he's just another nigger," Murray shouted like a spoiled child.

"How?" asked Colonel Lloyd, already seeming defeated.

"Sell him."

Colonel Lloyd regained his strength momentarily. "No, I can't!"

"Why can't you?"

"I won't."

"Then beat him, and beat him in front of me and everyone else who's there to watch. That will be enough."

"He's done nothing. I can't."

"If you care at all about me, you will do this."

"I've done everything for you."

"It's not enough, this is what I want . . . now."

With great sadness, the colonel said, "Very well." A moment passed. Then he added, vehemently, as if passing a sentence, "And once I give this, you will never get anything else about Bill Wilkes from me. Do you understand?"

Murray did not answer. Colonel Lloyd shouted, "Do you understand. Do you?"

"Yes, sir."

"Now bring me that whip. Tell everyone to come and see a father's love."

Colonel Lloyd walked out the back door toward the carriage house, ignoring the group of slaves who gathered to follow him. When the carriage door opened, Wilkes stared silently, amazed as Colonel Lloyd approached him with the whip in his upraised arm. Only his footsteps could be heard.

Colonel Lloyd said in a hollow voice, as he lowered his whip, "This is for your impudence today when . . ."

Without further explanation, he struck Wilkes on the shoulders. Wilkes fell gracefully to his knees, offering no resistance or protest.

Unsatisfied, Murray snapped: "Harder, harder. More, more!"

Murray grabbed for the whip. "Give it to me. I'll show you how to beat a nigger!"

Colonel Lloyd dropped the whip and powerfully slapped Murray in the face with the back of his right hand. The force propelled Murray backward to the ground.

"I gave you your proof!" the colonel yelled, breathing heavily.

"I'll . . . I'll," mumbled Murray, stunned. He rubbed his reddened face.

"You'll do what?" demanded the colonel. He retrieved his whip and flung his whip into Murray's lap. "Do it, then. Use it!"

Murray looked around, disoriented. He ran out of the carriage house, rushing through the group of slaves who watched the episode in silent shock. The colonel turned to Wilkes, who remained on his knees, his head bowed, and reached under his arm to lift him up. He apologized, saying softly, "I'm sorry. I had to."

Bill Wilkes said nothing and kept his head down. Colonel Lloyd pulled from his waistcoat a gold watch and chain. "Here," he said, trying to disengage it with a trembling hand. "Have this. Take it, please. Please."

With tears in his eyes now, he put his arm around the young man, and started toward the gate with him, saying again and again, "I'm sorry."

Wilkes said, "I'm all right, sir," and palmed his new, prized possession as they walked past the slaves, including Frederick, who all looked away to avoid acknowledging the unbelievable sight.

One week later, Colonel Lloyd sold William Wilkes to Austin Woolfolk, the Baltimore slave trader.

The Lloyd family insisted Wilkes had to go. Nothing less, everyone argued, could restore order to a plantation shaken and disrupted by the sight of Edward Lloyd striking his own son before slaves and, most deplorably, giving Wilkes his watch and chain after a whipping. Harassed by even the oldest son Edward, who rarely intervened, Colonel Lloyd eventually capitulated to family pressure and arranged for Wilkes be taken to Baltimore in chains during daylight hours. Every slave not already in the fields, said Elizabeth, had to see Wilkes's removal, including Frederick.

Unwilling to watch, Colonel Lloyd left for Easton before dawn. The slaves not assigned to the fields were assembled at seven in the morning. The air was cool and brisk, the sky like a gray, dirty sheet.

Austin Woolfolk had sent two agents to get Wilkes, who, displaying no emotion, said nothing when his wrists were handcuffed. Murray and Daniel Lloyd, the only family members present, stood in front of the Long Quarter slaves with arms folded and legs apart like guards posted to prevent a sudden rush to free the prisoner, an unnecessary precaution.

At first, no one said a word. Men, women, and children huddled in small groups, their arms around one another, their eyes staring ahead. Their worst fear, the fear of separation, was happening before them, claiming even Bill Wilkes, almost white, good looking, smart, and well trained. If he could go, no one was safe. If flesh and blood could go to "Woolfolk," a name representing all slave traders, then even loyal, submissive slaves had no protection.

Eastern Shore slave families feared being sold down to "Georgia," their name for life on the rice and cotton plantations of the deep South, the heat, the rotting wet, the bugs, the sickness, the never-ending work. They knew that if loved ones went there, hundreds of miles away, they would be lost forever, never to be seen or heard from again.

For generations, slave families remained intact. In fact, Talbot County planters took pride in saying, "We don't deal with slave traders." But now economic conditions had forced a change. Cotton plantations in Georgia, Alabama, and Mississippi needed more slaves, and slave traders, flooding the Eastern Shore with advertisements saying, "Cash! Cash! Cash! for Negroes," rushed to Maryland with offers too good to resist. Austin Woolfolk had set up his field headquarters at Solomon Lowe's Tavern, owned by Colonel Lloyd, in Easton, and offered up to $400—far more money than most white people earned in a year—for prime young males.

Now from an undeniable painful and raw reality came a low, deep hum from the huddled slaves. The stifled and angry sound of broken hearts made Murray snap his head and stare his demand for silence. Daniel knew what was coming. There was no way the slaves could remain silent, not on a day such as this. Song was their way.

No one sang the opening line, no doubt afraid that Murray would order the guilty man or woman to climb into the wagon with Wilkes. But the hum continued, and tears filled many eyes, including Frederick's.

Wilkes kept his head bowed, even when the wagon started to depart, its wheels crunching rocks in the mud. His shoulders drooped, and his manacled legs were pressed together. Though tall and large-framed, he now seemed like a frightened boy, stripped of his finery.

Despite the defense his family offered to excuse this day and his father's allegiance to Murray, Daniel could feel a sob churning in his gut. He saw himself in that cart, separated and alone too. He could not be sold, of course, but he would soon be sent away to a school in Easton or Baltimore, separated from Olivia and Frederick, and all the things he loved.

He saw Frederick standing across from him with those eyes mirroring the slaves' pain and judgment. Thinking of his true and lasting allegiance, Daniel turned away from Frederick, suppressed all remorse and pity, and looked instead to Murray. He then followed him up to the house when the wagon started its roll toward the main gate.

Daniel heard the slaves' lament when he neared the house. It began slowly with an anonymous bass voice. Soon the melody, at first lilting and languid, a message of deliverance and rest, was now a thunderous strike hurled into the skies, taken up by all against the Great House and the everlasting shame and dishonor that darkened the morning sun:

I don't feel weary and no ways tired
O glory hallelujah
Jest let me in the kingdom
While the world is on fire
O glory hallelujah
I don't feel weary and no ways tired
O glory hallelujah
Goin' to live with God forever
While the world is on fire
O glory hallelujah
I don't feel weary and no ways tired
O glory Hallelujah
And keep the ark a-moving,
While the world is on fire
O glory hallelujah.

Although Daniel could not see from the house whether Frederick was singing, he was sure that the boy was joining his own to ask the Lord to judge the Lloyds and all their kind. Daniel vowed to never mention this day to Frederick, but he was sure that Frederick would never forget it. He never forgot anything.

24.

AT CHRISTMAS, FREDERICK WAS sent back to the Anthony house, and Katy was determined to put him back in his place. She resumed her campaign of starvation with renewed vigor. Katy made sure that no one helped Frederick with pieces of cornmeal ball or pickled pork, warning each child that if they did they too would eat nothing. No one was willing to risk her anger. It was too cold that winter, and every morsel counted.

Katy continued to belittle and unnerve Frederick.

"Your mama was here," she announced without warning one morning in late January, her voice light, malicious, teasing. She smiled, enjoying his shock to this news.

Frederick gaped, trying to understand. He knew he had a mama who worked at a white man's farm near Tuckahoe Creek, twelve miles east. But he never saw or heard from her. Harriet Bailey was just a name to him.

Katy elaborated, "She comes at night after workin' all day, but you're sleepin by then, and she has to leave before you wakes. It's a long way back to Hillsboro on two feet."

"She came to see me? My mamma came to see me? She is coming back, ain't that right? When?" Doubt thickened the voice rising from his breathless, weak chest.

"I don't know when the bitch is comin' back. But you won't know either 'cause you'll be asleep. Since you got here, she's been here about three times."

"Three times! Why didn't you tell me."

Aunt Katy giggled, enjoying Frederick's anguish. She took a step toward him and said simply, "I hate her, that's why."

A week later, offended again for an unexplained reason, Katy declared, "I'm goin' to starve the life out of you."

On some days, and again for no apparent reason, she relented, and he was always grateful, as any hungry child would be, for any offering. Her withholdings, however, were now received without protest. He would just turn away with a resigned, "Oh."

But when she sliced apples for the children one night and withheld a slice from him, he ran out, crying. He returned and sat by the fire for a long time, staring at it. Katy ignored him, and eventually left the room, leaving an ear of corn high above a shelf, a test to see if Frederick would climb up to get it, shell off some of the grains for roasting in the ashes, and give her another reason to punish him, even though she didn't need one. When she returned, she noticed the husk was back on the shelf, the empty half turned around close to the same spot, but not the exact same spot, and a few kernels were still on the little stool near the embers.

Frederick's mouth was full, and he swallowed quickly when Katy came into the room. She was just about to say something when Harriet Bailey entered the kitchen.

Katy identified her, saying only, "Harriet" and Frederick immediately ran to her, his arms out, crying "Mamma! Mamma!"

"You're early," Katy said. "How were you able to get here so soon?"

Harriet didn't answer, listening instead to Frederick's detailed descriptions of starvation, deprivation, and cruelty. Katy didn't bother to intervene, watching and listening as if stone.

Harriet sighed deeply as she listened. When some detail particularly upset her, she would look over her child's head to glare at Katy, who glared back, irritated by Frederick's sobs more than anything else.

Harriet said to Frederick, "There, there. I brought a ginger cake, just for you today." She presented him a cake in the shape of a heart. "Here, my valentine."

Frederick gently cupped the treasure in his hand, a sweet cake with a rich, dark ring glaze on the edge. He touched the cake's surface, then put the cake to his nose, luxuriating in the aroma. He took a quick bite and closed his eyes, savoring the taste.

Harriet stood up, leaving him in the corner, and approached Katy. "Don't you ever starve my child again. Don't ever!"

Katy didn't flinch. "I'm not afraid of you," she replied, now disgusted. "You're just a rent nigger who gets away now and then. You're nothin'."

"You'll see I'm more than nothing when I tell the massa about how you've been treating' Fred and all the others. He won't stand for this. You're mean and not fair, and I know he wants better for his own."

Katy mocked her words. "His own?"

Harriet continued: "You can't stand it that the master wants my children here. But he does, and you can't do nothing to change it, but you're trying to hurt them, and especially my Frederick, and if you hurt him again, you'll wish you and me never knew the other."

Katy laughed derisively. "I hate you and all you Baileys. You think you're so damn high and mighty. I don't see what anybody sees in any of you. My brother Noah is a damn fool for livin' with your sister, another no count. You all ain't nothin' cause you're out there on the rent, and I'm here at the Great House Farm doin' what needs to be done to keep this house clean and the food good. I do all the work for the massa, *all* the work."

"But he chose me," Harriet said proudly, lifting her chin.

"Like he chose Hester," Katy said, her contempt now fully exposed. "And he kicked you to the side, just like he did her. But I'm still here."

"Then why are you afraid, of me and my boy?"

Katy rolled her eyes, the idea was so ridiculous. "I'm not afraid of you."

"And jealous. You're dried up and jealous. You're just his cook, and he don't care about you, and if he don't care about me now, I still has more than you ever did. And you don't have nothing like mine, nothing." She seemed tired and sad, her last words trailing off to a whisper. She returned to Frederick, who stood there smiling, basking in the power of her love and praise.

Unimpressed, Katy said with threatening finality, "You'll be gone soon, but I'll still be here, as always. Here!"

Katy left the kitchen, leaving Harriet to cradle Frederick in her arms and hum a song that lulled him to sleep:

Don't be weary, traveler.
Come along home to Jesus;
Don't be weary, traveler,
Come along home to Jesus.
My head got wet with the midnight dew,
Come along home to Jesus;
Angels bear me witness too,
Come along home to Jesus.

A few months later, Frederick was still not back at Wye, and Katy received word that Harriet Bailey had died. She called Frederick to tell him the news with a malicious glee she did not bother to hide. She could have summoned Harriet's other children, but she would leave it to Frederick's big mouth to spread the news.

"She's dead. Your mamma's dead."

Frederick didn't react, saying nothing, revealing nothing. This surprised Katy at first, but then she realized that Harriet was essentially a stranger to him, just a name. He had seen her only once, months ago. For an eight-year-old child, this was time without end. Frederick only waited.

Katy said, her voice light but still cold, "I told you, boy, that I would win. I'm still here; she ain't. She be sick for a long time. Now you just has me, and when them Lloyds are through with you and they toss you out like tomorrow's slop, you'll be mine, all mine, and I won't care about you no more, just like all the rest."

Frederick didn't look away and, using the clearest diction learned from Daniel, asked, "Ma'am, may I go now?"

Katy flinched for a second, hoping that he didn't notice her surprise, hear any hint of admiration, or feel her dark recognition that he was more uppity now than ever. This yellow boy was something else, and she would have to work a lot harder to crush him.

Katy lowered her head, took his by the chin into her hand, and said sweetly, "Yes, child. You're such a good nigger."

With the coming of the new year, her entire world collapsed.

Colonel Lloyd retired Captain Anthony, feeble and sick, from his job at the start of the year. The new chief overseer, a Mr. James McKeel, was soon to move into the house. And Lucretia and Thomas Auld were leaving for their new house in Hillsboro. Acting on her father's behalf, Lucretia told Katy that she would be rented out for the rest of the year, and all the children, including Katy's, would return to Tuckahoe.

All the children, except Frederick.

He was going to Baltimore.

25.

THE CITY BEGAN AT the sea, spreading out from Fells Point on the Pataspco River to the northern hills. At Baltimore's docks, the masts and sails of countless clipper ships dominated the skyline, while others still under construction were mounted on blocks like the massive skeletons of prehistoric mammals, waiting for their first slip into the rolling, bright water. Beside the shipyards were wharves piled high with wheat, sugar, rum, molasses, and coffee, its aroma rich and bittersweet, overpowering all the others. The noise of mauls, saws, sledgehammers, and handspikes was loud and constant, as were the curses and songs of carpenters and caulkers. Determined to meet the demand for the swift and sleek schooners that made Baltimore famous and prosperous, foremen shouted orders morning, noon, and night.

Jutting into Baltimore's inner harbor at the tip of Fells Point was the "Hook," a narrow peninsula of twisted, cobblestone streets, muddy alleys, taverns, bordellos, and the low, monotonous row houses that sheltered the fitters, carpenters, chandlers, caulkers, and sail makers who worked in the yards. Fells Point and its Hook were the source of the city's wealth, but the successful abandoned it at night, finding comfort in the more spacious homes on Monument Square, in Howard's Park, near the spires, copulas, domes, and towers overlooking the city and Fort McHenry below.

Hugh Auld lived in the Hook, at the corner of Aliceanna Street and Happy Alley, in a small and drab two-story frame house, its walls covered in dirt and corroded paint. He was a ship's carpenter, working at James Beacham's shipyard at the foot of Lancaster Street nearby, just another in the vast army building the largest ship ever commissioned for Baltimore.

Hugh planned to have his own shipyard someday, where, as master builder, he would supervise the construction of ships grander than the *Sally Lloyd* or *Republican Star*. Successful, he would move from Fells Point to a mansion of red brick and white marble. Or perhaps his would be an all-white house surpassing the splendor of Belvedere near Mount Vernon Place.

His dreams were powerful but unstable, undermined by the burden of a wife and son, with more children to come. He struggled to save money, but food, clothes, and rent took most of it, and he had to set aside just a little each day for a bottle or two of brandy. He needed his liquor after a hard day's work.

Hugh was sure of one thing. He was not going to make his way in the world by marrying some slave owner's daughter, as his brother Thomas did when he married Lucretia. He would rise to the top of Hampstead Hill on his own, through grit, sweat, and raw ambition, without having to support a bunch of needy niggers.

He hated Black people, their size, muscle, and capacity for work even on hot, blazing days. Slave or free, they were his competition, and jobs were not always easy to find. He hated their love of song, which made them pound, saw, and beat harder and faster, setting standards by which white men were judged. Even so, their melodies could make these same white men cry and laugh with them, as if they were all equal before the power of music, changed somehow by undulating harmonies and propulsive rhythm. And he hated their faith, its God always just and good, its heaven open to all who believed in Him, a positive, always hopeful faith firmly grounded in the love of Jesus.

Hugh Auld knew better. His God had created the world, a snare of corruption, to test his creatures, knowing that most would fail. And for these failures He created a vast pit, a hell of endless flame, endless torture, endless pain. Nothing could be done to appease His wrath. Nothing could be done to change the ultimate, preordained decision.

For Hugh, the lesson was clear: make money, be comfortable, enjoy good food, good whiskey, and good women, and don't worry about damnation. A true failure was not a damned soul. A true failure was a damn fool who wasted his time on salvation. We live in a shit house, he concluded. Don't pray about it. Paint it.

The piety of his wife Sophia annoyed him, like a persistent, buzzing fly in a closed room. Most of the time, he ignored her, his proof that her muted hymns, readings from the Bible, and prayers at the dinner table could not touch him.

He even allowed her to receive her minister and itinerant preachers on Sunday afternoons and Tuesday evenings, when they would gather in the parlor and study the scriptures, clucking like hens over delicate morsels. It amused him to see their pinched faces and squinting eyes struggle to understand what was clear to anyone without illusions.

But sometimes he lost his self-control and struck out with a volley of profanity and blasphemy, making Sophia cringe, forcing her to redouble her efforts to please him.

He loved that about Sophia, this eagerness to please, and with her beauty, flowing blond hair, large blue eyes, soft unblemished skin, small waist, and firm, small breasts, she made a good wife. She cooked and cleaned without complaint, and at night, when he wanted her, she did everything he required.

Now she had another mission: take a plantation nigger from the Eastern Shore and make him a city slave and companion for their son. Lucretia Auld's letter could not say enough about this boy, Frederick, how intelligent, courteous, cooperative, and well-spoken he was, far superior to most Black children. But Hugh didn't like slavery, and not because he cared about the freedom and treatment of Negroes. All he could see was the financial and emotional drain they were on those who owned them. They were children, needing constant supervision, food, clothes, and shelter. Hugh had one son and expected more children. He didn't want a nigger kid too.

But Sophia had a point. It would be good for Tommy, only three, to have a protector on the streets when playing outside. Wagon drivers were reckless, and bigger boys, as usual, would try to beat him. Besides, the slave boy could help with the household chores until Tommy could work. Hugh's sons were not going to become fat and lazy, weakened by slaves doing everything. They were going to wipe their own asses and work twelve-hour days, just like he did. And Hugh promised himself that when he got rich he wouldn't give his first son a big house to live in. The boy would have to build it with his own money.

Hugh reluctantly agreed to accept the newest member of the household but only with severe detachment, determined to not give this slave, a bigger boy than he expected, the slightest hint that he would ever care about him. He had seen too many niggers insinuate themselves into white families, make themselves indispensable, turn the tables, having whites become their slaves.

Hugh didn't smile that Sunday morning in March of 1826 when a deckhand from the *Sally Lloyd* knocked on the door and presented Frederick to the Auld family. For a moment, he wanted to slap Sophia for smiling with too much delight at the sight of the boy, and saying with great warmth, as she gently pulled Tommy from behind the folds of her dress, "Tommy, this is *your* Freddy. He is going to take care of you."

26.

"HOW WAS THE TRIP?" Sophia asked in the parlor, sitting down with Tommy beside her. "And how are Miss Lucretia and Master Thomas? Do you like Baltimore?"

Frederick bowed his head, looking down to his dirty feet.

She said tenderly, "You must be kind to little Tommy." It was not a demand. It was a gentle invitation to join her in the raising of her little son.

"Yes, Miss Sopha," Frederick replied, his head still down.

"Oh, Hugh," she said, clapping her hands. "Did you hear that? He called me *Miss Sopha*."

Hugh stood behind him, his arms folded, and only grunted.

Sophia's voice rose in pitch, becoming more tense and shrill, as she turned from Hugh's cold stare to Frederick. "Come, I'll show you your room. It's above the kitchen, and then we'll talk some more later. I need to tell you about your chores, and I want to hear all the news from the Eastern Shore."

She stood up and took Frederick by the hand. Then she said to Tommy, who sat still in the parlor under his father's stern gaze, "You come, too, and take Freddy's hand so you won't get into trouble."

Without hesitation, Tommy took it, and the three of them went to Frederick's new room under the rafters. Stroking the straw bed covered with blankets and a quilt, he marveled, "Mine, all mine," while looking at the ceiling.

"I hope it's comfortable," Sophia replied. "Sit on it and see, and then tell me all about what's happened with the Anthonys and the Lloyds. Lucretia tells me you love to talk."

Frederick sat but kept his head down, and Sophia insisted warmly, "Now, look up, and don't be afraid. Please, don't be afraid."

He raised his head, and Sophia dropped to her knees in front of him, leaned forward, delicately touching his knees with one hand, and said seriously, "I know this is hard for you, coming this far, far from everything that you once knew, but I will take care of you. I promise. You are a part of my family now, and this is your home."

Encouraged daily, Frederick began to venture out and explore his new neighborhood. He always returned with detailed, exuberant accounts of his adventures, finding the town pump on the corner at Washington Street for pails of water, taking Tommy for walks after his afternoon nap, running to the market for meat and vegetables.

Fells Point was exciting, and the dangers of careening wagons, gangs of boys chasing him down the street with shouts of "Eastern Shore man," and the large crowds at the docks were surpassed by the sounds and sights of constant shipbuilding at the end of Lancaster Street, not far from the Auld house: the tightening stays and shrouds; the clang of the caulking mallet closing seams with oakum; the thunder of the maul driving the spikes; the grate of the whip riving the oak timbers; the ring of the broad ax shaping the ship's knees; the yell of children picking up chips for fires. Hugh worked at James Beachem's shipyard that spring, where hundreds rushed to finish building a sixty-four gun 1,800-ton frigate for Brazil.

★

Sophia could not have been more pleased. Frederick was everything Lucretia had promised and more. A handsome, light-skinned boy with strong cheeks and an easy smile, he was intelligent, well mannered, cooperative, eager to please, hard working, gentle and patient with Tommy, and surprisingly well spoken for a slave from Talbot County.

She too was from Talbot County, born to Richard and Hester Keithly, poor but strict country Methodists who taught her that slavery was a moral crime, indefensible, and repugnant. It debased the owner. Sophia was eternally grateful for the moral education her humble parents provided. They believed that hard work deserved respect and honest dollars and that every man and woman's work should receive a just recompense. So, as a dutiful daughter, Sophia became a weaver, sitting at looms with raw, bloody hand, and receiving almost nothing for wages. But at least she was paid something.

The arrangement for Frederick made her uncomfortable, but she consoled herself with the knowledge that legally Frederick was not hers and that she would treat him as a member of her family. He would eat at her table and receive a religious education. What she did for Tommy, she would do for him. After all, Tommy adored him, and made no issue of Frederick's color.

Sophia wished that Hugh would be more accepting of the boy. He was not impressed with Frederick's qualities, and when she extolled them at the dinner table, he snapped, "He's just a nigger."

Sitting there, Frederick didn't react. He continued eating as if he were deaf. Tommy started, then turned to his mother for an explanation, delicate tears in his eyes. Sophia was sure that Tommy didn't understand the conversation, but he was sensitive to the sudden changes in his father's moods. They frightened him.

One Monday morning, several months after Frederick's arrival, she found her path. The boy asked her to teach him to read.

"I want to read the Bible," he explained.

That was all she needed to hear, and quickly Sophia gathered paper, pencil, and her Bible at the kitchen table to begin instruction, starting with the alphabet. The prospect of Frederick learning letters, then words and sentences, and entire verses of scripture excited her. She could vindicate them both, proving that Frederick was a special child, and she a special wife, a resourceful woman capable of inspiring great achievement, the salvation of another soul, and a valuable contributor to the family. Their success would be a wonderful surprise, and she would teach Frederick while Hugh was at work and Tommy took his daily nap.

She drew a letter on a sheet of paper, held it up, and said," Freddy, this is the letter A. Say A. . . ."

He quickly replied, "A."

Weeks passed before she was ready to reveal her triumph to Hugh. By then Frederick knew the alphabet and could read words of three or four letters.

Sophia proudly revealed her news on Sunday morning, after breakfast and before church, when Hugh was usually in his best mood because he would be alone for most of the day. At the table, Sophia stood and clutched her Bible in her arms, smiling sweetly.

Looking up, Hugh dismissed her with light sarcasm, "I don't want to hear a sermon, not today."

Unnerved for just a moment, she looked at Frederick and said, "Oh, no, my dear. But I have some wonderful news, which will please you . . ."

Hugh knitted his eyebrows. "What is it?" he asked, now trying patience.

"Freddy has been a wonderful student. He is smart, and I intend to stay with him until he has mastered everything he needs for reading the Bible. It's his Christian duty to learn, as it is my Christian duty to teach him."

Leaning forward, Hugh shouted, "What did you just say?"

Although her voice trembled, Sophia pressed on, almost incoherent. "My duty . . . Christian . . . the Bible . . . salvation for me, for him . . . a good student . . . teaching is . . ."

Hugh leaned back in his chair. "You simple fool, you stupid, simple fool."

Sophia continued, sure that he misunderstood: "He wants to read because he heard the words. Lucretia was right when she said . . ."

Hugh's patience snapped like a brittle twig. He pounded his fist on the arms of the chair before rising. Sophia stepped back, her Bible a small, thick shield pressed against her chest. Tommy began to cry. "Don't you know it's against the law to teach a nigger to read?" Hugh continued, berating her with a rigid, wagging finger. "It's not only illegal, it's unsafe. You teach a slave to read and soon you're asking for all kinds of trouble. Eventually they'll get ideas in their damn heads, and before you know it, they're good for nothing. Learning spoils the best nigger in the world. Don't you know that? Ignorant, he is happy and content, but give him some learning and he'll be unhappy and do a great deal of harm. He certainly won't obey his master. Don't give niggers an inch of reading, or they'll want a mile of freedom. Even reading God's word is dangerous. He might get some ideas in his head. You fool, you stupid fool."

She was sure that he was going to slap and punch her, disregarding her condition. Another child was due in November.

"I'm sorry," she whispered, now realizing that Tommy was beside her, pressed against her legs, whimpering. Frederick had retreated to the door, stepping out of Hugh's way as he approached Sophia.

"You're sorry. You're damn well lucky that you only have to be sorry."

He returned to his chair, picked up the paper, and started to read. From behind the sheets, he said, "The lessons will stop as of this moment. Right now!"

Sophia managed to say, "Yes, dear."

"And, Freddy," he added, putting his paper in his lap, "you will forget this reading stuff the missus taught you. It's not for you, you understand. Miss Sophia made a mistake, a very bad mistake."

There would be no more lessons. Sophia would read the Bible to Frederick, as any responsible religious woman should, but she would not leave it or any other book around for him to try reading. Newspapers had to be tossed out or burned, and letters and important documents had to be stored away under lock and key. She now recognized the deep gravity of her error, and realized that only absolute, relentless vigilance could restore peace to her family, and win back Hugh's approval. Her marriage was more important than teaching a slave how to read.

A year passed. Hugh and Sophia learned that Aaron Anthony had died in November of 1826 and Lucretia the following summer. There was no will, but when the estate was settled, the heirs, Richard and Andrew Anthony and Lucretia's husband, Thomas Auld, decided to divide the family property, including all the slaves, and demanded Frederick's return to the family farm near Tuckahoe Creek for the final sale.

Hugh explained the standard practice: when a slave master died intestate, his slaves were lined up on a pre-named date and evaluated by outside appraisers appointed by the Orphans' Court. The slaves were divided into lots of equal value, and each heir was assigned his share of the inheritance. Frederick could become the property of Richard, Andrew, or Thomas Auld in this unpredictable lottery.

Sophia cried out, "Oh no! Oh no, he'll never come back!" She paced the room, gripping the letter against the folds of her skirt, struggling to find a way to beat the odds. Andrew and Richard Anthony were strangers, and so she put her hopes on her brother-in-law, now a widower.

"Hugh, do something," she demanded, desperate. "Write to Thomas. Tell him . . ."

Frederick had become an even greater help now that Sophia was also the mother of Ann Elizabeth, born in November. With Frederick watching Tommy and Beth, and running errands, life was easier. Even Hugh had admitted reluctantly, when whiskey had softened him, making him sentimental, that Freddy was a model boy, tall and athletic, obedient and respectful, unlike Tommy, who cried and cringed too much.

Hugh was philosophical, saying, "Sophia, there's nothing we can do. It's all luck. Thomas might not even get the lot that will include Freddy. We'll just have to wait."

"They might sell him, and he'll disappear on some farm. We can't let that happen, Hugh. It will be too hard on him, Hugh. Make an offer, Hugh. Buy him."

Hugh exploded, "I'm not spending my hard-earned money on some nigger, even if it's Freddy. And where is this money going to come from? Do you know how much a slave costs, and especially a smart, good-looking one like Freddy? He won't be cheap, and Thomas, cheaper than most, won't just give him away, even if he gets him. Now, be quiet and bring him to me. I'll tell him."

"I should tell him," Sophia said.

"No! I'm the head of this house, and Thomas is my brother, not yours. Bring him."

Sophia went to get Frederick from his room, and whispered only, "Master Hugh has something to tell you."

Frederick immediately asked, "What?"

She took his hand and said nothing more. She almost said, "Don't worry," but she was sure that Frederick, as sensitive and intelligent as he was, would know that a suggestion to not worry meant that he should.

With Sophia still holding Frederick's hand, they entered the parlor. Hugh was standing with his back to them, his arms folded as he looked through the window.

Sophia said, "Hugh."

He didn't turn around.

"Hugh?"

She hoped that he was considering how to break the news gently, how to speak the truth but not shatter Frederick's heart.

Hugh turned around. His face was stern, without a trace of empathy. "Your new master is my brother, and he wants you back on the Eastern Shore," said Hugh with chilling calm, "and so you have to go, and there's nothing we can do about it, and I don't need to see tears or hear your damn questions. I have nothing more to say."

He returned to the window. "He leaves on the next boat to St. Michaels in two days."

"Two days!" protested Sophia.

"Shut up, and just get him ready. And don't fill his nigger head with what he doesn't need to know."

Sophia pulled at Frederick's hand, and they left the room. Tears flowed from Frederick's eyes, and after pulling far enough away so Hugh could not hear her, she whispered, "Don't worry, but no questions. You'll be back. God will send you back to us."

Sophia said nothing more about it, but when it was time for Hugh to take Frederick, scrubbed clean and dressed in his Sunday church clothes, to the wharf for his departure aboard the schooner *Wildcat*, she cried uncontrollably as she hugged Frederick at the door. Frederick and Tommy cried too.

"Damn it," Hugh snapped. "That's enough!"

Immediately, everyone obeyed, wiping their tears. Tommy hid behind his mother, and Sophia spoke with a tenderness that even in that moment she knew would arouse resentment in Hugh and lead to retaliation. She didn't care. "We love you," she said, taking Frederick's hands, "and we always will, and remember us till you get back."

Hugh yanked Frederick's hands away and said, "We're going now."

Sophia said tentatively, "Maybe I should go with . . ."

"No, you're not."

Hugh and Frederick went outside, and Sophia watched them step into the brick pavement street, Hugh holding Frederick's left hand until he pushed it roughly aside, repulsed by any gesture of gentleness and kindness. "Come on, and stay beside me."

27.

TRAVELING ON A BOAT all alone, he cried that first night until he fell asleep, exhausted by fear and a terrible sense of loss. He didn't know if he would ever return to Baltimore and the Aulds. He might be sold and sent far away, even away from the Baileys, now strangers.

The next morning, dread still roiled in the bottom of his stomach, but he was also curious. How would the Baileys treat him? Should he talk to Gram Betty after what she did at Wye Plantation? What should he say, if anything, to the others? Would he get into more trouble because he knew more, had seen more? Returning from a magical city, Frederick wanted to impress his Black family with stories about the great city, his mouth flapping all day and late into the night.

When his boat approached the St. Michaels Harbour, Frederick decided to hate everything he saw and heard, the small, dirty houses, the absence of crowds. And from the moment he was greeted by a distant cousin sent to take him to Gram Betty's house and smelling like a pig, Frederick curled his lip, raised his eyebrows, and flared his nostrils. He was sure his eyes were ready to pop out of his head he was so disgusted.

When he arrived at Betsey's cabin, a shack that now seemed smaller than it was when he was a little boy, Betsey immediately hugged and kissed him, and with tears in her eyes, she observed, "How you've grown. You're my little yellow cake no more. You're a big boy now. Just look at you, all dressed up." He wore a clean, white shirt, and brown trousers, but no shoes.

Frederick leaned into her arms, forgiving what had happened at the captain's house at Wye Plantation, surprised by the gray hairs and wrinkles under her eyes.

Betsey continued, "I thought I would see you no more, but praise the Lord, I was wrong. Sweet Jesus, I was wrong."

Then came the introductions and reunions, three young sisters—Kitty, Arianna, and Harriet—Frederick had never met, Aunt Prissy and Aunt Hester, cousins, old playmates, and old enemies.

He clung to Betsey when he saw Katy and her four, including Phil, but Katy stayed away. Everyone knew about what she had done to Frederick and how Betsey confronted her once she found out. Their fight was the talk of the county, witnesses and gossips wagging their tongues about the slapping and cursing, the pushing, the rolling on the ground, the hair pulling. It was "something else," they repeated, glee and wonder in their voices. Betsey had "kicked the shit out of her ass."

Now Katy sat in a corner, her children trying to comfort her as she wailed about what was to come. She was different, broken, no longer the all-powerful, frightening cook in Captain Anthony's kitchen.

Except for Katy, everyone was happy to see Frederick, the prodigal son returning from the magical city he now described with more details than Cousin Tom could ever give. Even Tom listened with rapt attention, showing no jealousy, and making no effort to compete with or downplay Frederick's incredible stories.

Betsey was also impressed. "Just hear that boy," she said to her daughters gathered in the log cabin. "Talks up a storm still, just hear 'im."

There was all the talk about the family slave sale. No one tried to hide the fact of the sale, and everyone seemed resigned to it. But the adults repeatedly expressed their greatest fear, the fear of separation. They couldn't bear the idea of a wife being taken from a husband, children from parents, brothers from sisters.

Men and women huddled in corners and shared the smallest shreds of good news, rumors to support the wildest and most impossible hopes. They tried to find comfort through endless repetition of the Eastern Shore saying, "On de Eastern Shore, we keep our Black families together."

But no one could escape the brutal equation. There were three Anthony heirs, and at least one third of the slaves would go to Andrew Anthony, already known as a "drunken sot," a wastrel who gambled away his money as soon as he earned it. His wife, Ann Wingate, entered rooms cautiously, her eyes darting from corner to corner, her shoulders arched as if she expected to be kicked like an old dog at any moment. All the adult slaves agreed that life with Andrew would be terrible and put all their hopes in Richard and Thomas, ignoring the fact of equal division. At least there were no bad stories about Richard, and Thomas was married to a good white woman, they heard. That should mean *something*. A good woman could make a better man.

A few days later, Eliza lashed out at Frederick: "You talk like 'em, dress like 'em, smell like 'em, act like 'em, and shit like 'em, too," she said, suddenly provoked. "The white boy's nigger, that's what you are. I knew it! I knew it!"

Frederick challenged her: "Why you mad? What did I do?"

Eliza rolled her eyes. "Nigger, are you that dumb?"

Frederick said, "Kiss my ass, Aunt Katy, the *new* Aunt Katy."

She raised her hand, but Frederick didn't flinch.

"Do it," he said. "Just do it."

Eliza suddenly turned away and ran toward the cabin.

Two days later, Eliza apologized, and Frederick apologized, too. Their bond had been deepened by witnessing what happened to their brother Perry the day before. The fight between the two of them had been all but forgotten.

Unusually sober that afternoon, Andrew Anthony had ordered Perry to bring him a tool. Perry had brought the wrong one, and Andrew had grabbed him by the throat with both hands, throttling him until his eyes seemed ready to burst, then thrown him to the ground.

"You stupid-ass nigger!" he screamed. "You've got the brain of a goddamn roach."

Back against the wall, and too terrified to protest, Eliza and Frederick watched in horror as Andrew lifted his boot and stamped Perry in the head. Perry screamed.

"*Roach*," sneered Andrew as he stamped Perry's head until the blood, bright and thick, gushed from his ears and nose. Almost fifteen, and with the body of an adult field hand, Perry didn't try to get up from under Andrew's heel. He lay there, later explaining that he knew better than to get up. He wanted to live.

Andrew turned to Eliza and Frederick, who had not moved or said a word as they pressed against the wall, and said calmly, like a parent or teacher giving final instructions. "That is the way I will teach you, one of these days."

He left.

Eliza and Frederick turned to each other, looked down at their brother, who rolled on the floor, groaning while holding his head in his hands, and left Perry there, running to get help.

Prayers for deliverance went up day and night.

But no prayers could stop the coming of the appraisal day, Thursday, October 18, 1827, a bright and clear but cool morning. Fall had come, turning the hills to red and golden mounds.

The court-appointed appraisers, James Chambers and William A. Leonard, friends of the old master, had all twenty-nine slaves—men, women, and children—line up in a row in front of the log cabin. There was no assigned order. Everyone clustered with those whose nearness comforted them. Frederick stood beside Betsey, who held his hand. On the other side, Eliza took Betsey's other hand, while standing with Perry and her other sisters.

Chambers and Leonard moved slowly down the line, asking for names, stopping to make a physical inspection. They spoke softly, with the quiet efficiency of professionals. Their commands were impersonal, unthreatening.

"Open your mouth."

"Take off your shirt."

"Show me your legs."

They made no comments about the quality of what they examined. The only noise came from the animals in the yard, some feet away. The slaves stood silently, their heads bowed, waiting for the Anthony family decision that would fix their futures for life.

Frederick tried to see the reaction of every adult, gauging what he should do and say later. He noticed the tears that rolled down Aunt Hester's cheeks when she had to open her blouse and show the scars on her back, the scars left by the whip of Aaron Anthony, scars that crossed her back like a thick, disheveled spider web. But Hester said nothing.

Frederick and Eliza could not look away. This was the first time they had ever seen the scars from that terrible night.

When the appraiser's work was done, they dismissed the assembled slaves, saying that later that day they would be called again and told their new owners.

Inside the log cabin, the public and silent resignation exploded. His grandmother and aunts vehemently protested their treatment.

"We ain't sheep, we ain't cattle, we ain't hogs!"

The process was new to them all. They had been Anthony slaves for all their lives, and never had to stand before white men who decided the worth of their bodies. Furious, Hester pointed her finger into her chest, "This belongs to me! This belongs to me, and I has the right to say how much it is, and it's worth more than whatever they say it is, much, much more, and my scars has the worth of anything, anything they got!"

But her anger suddenly dissolved, and she crumbled to the floor, her head in her hands, as she sobbed and rolled her body back and forth.

She mumbled repeatedly, "I ain't a sheep, a hog. . ."

Betsey watched her daughter cry but did not move, allowing her the time to say and do what she needed to do, and then she crossed the room and knelt beside her with her arms across Hester's back.

"We're human beings," said Betsey with fierce but quiet dignity. "They is the animals."

Within the hour, the verdict came.

Chambers and Leonard, determining that the Anthony Negroes were worth $2,800, divided them into three lots valued at approximately $935. By law, family ties did not have to be considered, they said. But the appraisers tried to keep families together.

They assigned Betsey, Perry, Eliza, and Frederick's other sisters to Andrew Anthony, who also received Betsey's daughter Betty and her small children. Richard Anthony was awarded Aunt Katy and her two youngest. Frederick's Aunt Milly and cousins Tom, Henny, Nancy, Prissy, and a baby went to Thomas Auld.

Chambers and Leonard did not try to keep Frederick with his brother and sisters. They awarded him to Thomas Auld. Then his grandmother told Frederick even better news: Master Thomas was sending him back to Baltimore to live with his brother's family.

Frederick couldn't restrain himself and started jumping around the room. "Yeah, yeah, yeah!" he cried. That's what he wanted, never hiding the fact from the very beginning he wanted to go back to Baltimore.

Betsey's eyes narrowed, and her nostrils flared. The entire room seemed to freeze at that moment, and Frederick stopped jumping.

"You still haven't learned, has you?" she asked sadly. "The winner ain't got no right to strut." She repeated more forcefully, "No right."

He crouched, ready to receive a blow. But her arms encircled him, pulling Frederick to her chest, then holding and cradling him tight.

Betsey was crying, but as she wept, Frederick could hear joy and great relief in her voice, as if a terrible burden had been lifted. "Oh Harriet, Harriet, Harriet. I knows you're watching over him, this special one, 'cause he's going back. No plantation life for this boy, no pickin' and cleanin' till dark, no whippin's, nothing like what we might be getting' in Mr. Andrew's house. I always knew he was different, and I prayed to you to talk to Lord Jesus and have him step in with the Lord, and the Lord God Almighty has come to this house and this place and put his hand on my Frederick again. He ain't goin' down, he ain't goin' down, but up to bright glory, he ain't goin' down."

28.

FREDERICK WAS ALMOST NINE years old and had his own room, a small attic room on the third floor of the Auld's rented house on Philpot Street. From there he could hear the noises of the yards and see the tops of masts of the many ships waiting to sail down the river to the Chesapeake. But few above the street could escape the sound of muffled cries and rattling chains heard late at night when the slave traders marched slaves in two rows to the ships at the yards.

Awakened on the first night of his return to Baltimore by the sounds of rattling, whips, shuffling feet on cobblestone, and the low moans of men and women, Frederick went to the window and began to sob, tears falling to his face, his entire body shaking uncontrollably.

He didn't hear when Sophia entered, nor did he start when she took him into her arms as he continued to cry and tremble.

"Hush, child, hush," she said tenderly. "Everything's all right. They won't come to get you. I promise. They'll never come to get you. You were taken once, but not again."

Eventually, Frederick fell asleep. Months would pass before he was able to sleep through the forced marches from Mr. Woolfolk's slave pen, screened behind a white house and tree-lined drive, on nearby Pratt Street. But he learned how.

As he grew older, he struggled to understand the changes in his body and soul, the frequent shifts in mood, extreme sensitivity to common sights and sounds, constant irritation with everybody, and a ceaseless urge to have sex with girls or masturbate.

Frederick longed for certainty, a guarantee of freedom and salvation, a conviction that his life would add up to more than sweeping floors and listening to white foolishness with a blank grin. Most importantly, he wanted to be free, but if he could not be free, at the very least he wanted to know why. Maybe with God's saving grace, he could find peace.

He decided to talk to Charles Johnson, a Black lay preacher he met at the Bethel African Methodist Church. The Aulds did not object to his attending, assuring him that Black Christianity was good for slaves.

Johnson, a tall middle-aged man with kind eyes and a gentle smile who didn't treat him like a teenage, ignorant fool, declared, "You must seek the Lord through prayer. *Seek* him." He recommended no passive waiting for God's grace. He gave it to those who hungered for righteousness.

"Give up yourself. Give it up," Johnson urged Frederick.

Frederick tried night after night to give himself to God. His prayers started as resounding invocations and ended with impotent, garbled mumblings. On his knees, he sometimes pounded the floor with his fists, frustrated by the bitter truth. His pride could not accept this surrender.

Trust in the Lord?

Why should he trust Him? The Lord did nothing.

At Bethel Church Frederick, surrounded by the chosen, Frederick felt intense isolation, relieved only by his participation in the music. Otherwise, his struggle was a private struggle.

But one Sunday morning, when the air was cold and crisp, and the cloudless sky was bright like hardened blue glass, Frederick heard a voice behind him shout, "People, let us bring him in. With the Lord's help, let us bring him in."

Frederick turned around to find an old, thin Black man smiling serenely at him, as if he had known Frederick for many years.

Before Frederick could ask, "Who are you?" the entire congregation started to sing, its voice rich and deep, its longing irresistible:

Deep river,
My home is over Jordan.
Deep river, Lord.
I want to cross over into campground.

Deep River,
My home is over Jordan.
Deep river, Lord,
I want to cross over into campground.

Oh, don't you want to go,
To the Gospel feast;
That Promised Land,
Where all is peace?

Oh, deep river, Lord,
I want to cross over into campground.

The guest preacher that day was Father Waters, famous in Black Baltimore for his fiery oratorical skill. Everybody there now gave their complete attention, loving eyes, and inviting arms to Frederick, ready to enfold him.

"Accept us, boy," said Father Waters, holding Frederick's gaze. "As we accept you, as the Lord accepts you."

"I'm a sinner," mumbled Frederick, not knowing whether Waters heard him over the congregation's singing.

"That's why there's love," the old man replied. "The Lord loves you, boy. Jesus loves you, *your* Jesus."

For the first time, looking into the old man's eyes, Frederick believed, and he believed because he knew this man could not be lying.

Frederick saw what he had never seen before, a man who accepted him without judgment, without proof of his worthiness, without control between master and slave. He had what he always wanted: love without boundaries and a pure trust he had lost long ago.

"Yes," said Frederick, happy for the first time in months. His voice became louder, as he repeated this one, affirming word, and soon it seemed to rise above the song of the entire congregation as it shouted its praise of God: "My Lord calls me. He calls me by the thunder: The trumpet sounds within my soul."

"Yes," said Frederick one more time, and he fell into the old man's outstretched arms.

★

Charles Lawson heard about Frederick from the preacher Charles Johnson, and he had a dream, a mystic vision, which revealed Frederick's future to him. Lawson could barely read, recognizing his name and a few brief passages from the Bible, but he was free. He worked as a drayman on Fells Point, and prayed every day, everywhere, as he walked, as he worked, as he ate, as he rested. Folks said he lived more in heaven then any shack in Happy Alley. His life was a prayer, and colored boys and young men needing guidance turned to him, the "uncle" who didn't drink, gamble, smoke, whore, curse, or punch sons for no reason.

"You're destined to become a mighty preacher," said Lawson solemnly to Frederick, who sat on the floor, enthralled. "You're goin' to do a great work for the Lord, a great work, and you must prepare for it by reading and studying the scripture day and night, no matter what."

"Day and night?" asked Frederick. The intensity of his experience at church had passed. He did not doubt Uncle Lawson's love; it was true, and it was constant, but Frederick could not admit to Lawson that his conversion was a performance. He did what was expected, crying, and shouting, singing, and falling into waiting arms. But there was no true surrender, no complete and passionate giving of himself. Even as he sang and prayed that memorable day, surrounded by the exultation of an entire church community's love, he saw himself acting a part, living a lie.

Everyone was so happy for him, watching him fall into the arms of Uncle Lawson. But it was an act. He couldn't disappoint Lawson or the congregation, so he played his part, accepting the love all around him. However, he felt no closer to God. God remained a mysterious, distant power, and every fiber of Frederick's being refused to submit to that power, any power.

At the threshold of manhood, Frederick was more attuned to the needs of the flesh than the demands of the Holy Spirit. His body ached with desire; arousal came suddenly, even at church, demanding satisfaction in night dreams. Nothing else mattered but relief.

Frederick begged for release from the guilt and shame, saying again and again, "I'm a sinner. Please help me."

"I understand, my son. I traveled this path too when I was young," Lawson said after Frederick told him that he had evil, unspecified thoughts.

"No, you don't understand. I'm bad, I'm really bad," Frederick insisted.

"Son, I do know. I have a dick, too, and it got me into so much trouble back in the day."

Frederick's mouth opened. Uncle Lawson was the purest Christian he had ever met, and his words seemed to have come out of the mouth of another, as if a demon had suddenly possessed him.

Lawson smiled and looked down with radiant pride. "I was a sinner, too. We are sinners until we give ourselves to the Lord. Trust in Him, and he will provide, make you free. All things are possible with him. Only have faith in God. I will lead you to the way, the path of his righteousness for his name's sake."

"Teach me to pray as you pray," asked Frederick, eager to please his mentor, whose spiritual strength seemed to make him younger and more vigorous. People said he was seventy years old, or more.

"Read the word of God, read, read. And when you've read it all again and again, then the words will come to you, your words built on His words. I know you are selfish, boy, like all children, and I know the Lord has second place in your heart, still."

Frederick protested, shaking his head, perpetuating the lie. "No, that's not true."

Lawson's smile never left him. He put his hand on Frederick's shoulder and said, "If you need right now to lie, I understand, but you don't need to, especially to me. The Lord is victorious when honest sinners change. He don't need to celebrate the saints. Just remember, you're going to be a great preacher someday, and some will hate you. But remember, you are Joseph, and in the Lord's book. Remember, Joseph had a coat of many colors, and his brothers hated him."

"And he dreamed a dream, and told it, and they hated him yet the more," replied Frederick, quoting Genesis.

"Some will hate you, my child, for the coat you'll wear, and for what you'll say."

"And he was sold into Egypt, as I was sold . . ."

"But from it you will rise and rule with the power of your dreams. And the Lord said, 'I am God, the God of thy Father. Fear not to go down into Egypt. I will go down with thee into Egypt, and I will surely bring thee up again.'"

"When?" Frederick demanded.

Undisturbed, Lawson continued to quote scripture: "Trust in the Lord and do good; so shalt thou dwell in the land, and verily thou shalt be fed. Delight thyself also in the Lord, and he shall give thee the desires of thine heart. Commit the way unto the Lord; trust also in Him, and he shall bring it to pass."

"How?" Frederick insisted.

"If you do what the Lord says: cease from anger, forsake wrath. Boy, you are angry all the time, *all* the time. You've got to stop."

"I have reasons," Frederick replied, undeterred.

"We all have reasons to do evil, boy," said Lawson, still patient, his voice still warm and indulgent. "But the Lord is clear: fret not in any way to do evil, for evil doers shall be cut off, but those that wait upon the Lord shall inherit the earth."

"I'll try."

"No," Lawson replied with unusual vehemence. "Do it. You must do it. Don't wait until you feel it. Do it, and then the Lord comes into your heart."

"If it isn't in my heart, am I not a hypocrite?"

Lawson shook his head. "Boy, you are so hardheaded, but you had better listen to me because I love you. Goodness is a habit like everything else. First, goodness feels funny, like walking for the first time, like talking, too. You stumble, you fall, you make mistakes, you fail. But you get better, and soon it becomes so easy you'll think you've always done it. Then it sinks deep into your heart, deep."

"Then accepting the Lord doesn't change everything," said Frederick, deflated. "Then what's salvation?"

Lawson touched Frederick on the arm, a rare moment of physical affection. "What changed was what you were looking at. You changed from looking inside to looking outside, to something higher, to something so much bigger than you. Where we turn our eyes is the biggest step of all."

Frederick knew he should turn to the Lord, trust in him, even though he could not see him, touch him, even know him.

That was true faith.

But he didn't have it.

Deep down, he knew he didn't have it.

He wanted it, but he trusted himself more.

He knew himself.

"Then what should I do now, before I become a preacher?" he asked, more comfortable with seeking advice. "What should I do now to bring the Lord into my heart?"

"Teach our boys to read, the ones at our church," Lawson replied. "Great preachers are great teachers. Start with letters. You can meet here. They will be your new friends if you give freely what you know."

"Yes," Frederick agreed. "Some white boys taught me. I'll do the same."

"Praise the Lord," said Lawson. "Let's pray."

And the prayers continued into the afternoon with Frederick hoping that the Lord was listening and remaining unsure that He was.

But miracles began to happen.

Walking on Patterson Street, not far from the center of the city, where he was exploring more and more these days, he found scattered, wet pages from a Bible lying in the gutter. Immediately, his eager eyes, always looking for literary scraps, advertisements, discarded newspapers, could see the numbered, short paragraphs that indicated sheets of scripture. Excited, he bent down to gather them up, forgetting to look around for witnesses. He wasn't supposed to read anything, Master Hugh and Miss Sophia declared, and their supporters were everywhere, they warned. Every white was a spy.

Frederick put the pages into his front pocket and hurried home, cutting his expedition short. He had to wash and dry the pages before adding them to his small but growing collection of reading material that was now his most prized possession.

29.

FREDERICK JOINED THE PHILPOT Street Gang, becoming friends with the sons of the white carpenters and shipfitters who worked and lived nearby on Fells Point. At first, they chased Frederick in a pack, calling him "Eastern Shore Man." Fells Point was their territory. But when "the town boys" from the central city crossed the drawbridge to Fells Point looking for a fight, Frederick spontaneously joined his neighbors to repel them, throwing rocks and garbage while yelling curses. The town boys surrendered, and the Philpot boys celebrated, hooping, hugging, slapping hands, jumping, inviting the colored boy into the group.

"You're a crazy nigger," said Gus, the leader, an older, more experienced boy.

Frederick proved he was just as good at pitching coppers, running from Constables North and Bangs, grabbing food from street carts.

As the boys ran the streets or played games, Frederick would point to posters and signs and ask, "What does it say?"

And they would answer, "What word?"

And he would point. "That word!"

The call and response game, called "What word?" happened all day and was played between games of war, tag, and penny pitching. When enthusiasm slackened sometimes, Frederick would pay for lessons with biscuits Sophia made. The word game always filled their time. Several months later, he could write his name and some words, and he could read more.

Frederick resorted to other measures to gain knowledge of language. Alone in his attic room, as the candlelight flickered at night and cast shadows on the low ceiling and beams, he copied the italic letters from a copy of Webster's *American Spelling Book*, using a flour barrel as his writing desk, until he could write all the letters without referring to it. He secretly borrowed Tommy's copy books, stored by Miss Sophia in a cupboard after Tommy brought them home from school, and recopied each letter in the spaces between the lines or on pieces of pine blank stolen from the shipyard. Whenever Miss Sophia left him alone to watch Benjamin, the newest Auld, he would take out the books to work.

Then came the discovery of speeches recited by the other boys from school, speeches about freedom in a book Frederick wanted more than a pile of biscuits.

Frederick asked them for the name of the book of speeches.

"*The Columbian Orator*," said Gus pompously. "By Mr. Caleb Bingham."

"Where can I get it?"

Gus snapped, "How the fuck are you goin' to get fifty cents, you tell me?"

"I'll get it," Frederick replied, frowning as he looked to the others.

"And where are you going to get it?"

"A bookstore, where else?" Frederick replied.

No one laughed.

But Gus smiled when Frederick eventually showed him his copy of *The Columbian Orator*. "You are a crazy and *stubborn* nigger," he said. "I bet you just walked in there like some white boy."

"I didn't steal it."

Gus pointed out, "You can't read those speeches. I mean you don't know how to read those speeches. I can barely read them myself."

"But one day I'll be able to read my first book from cover to cover," Frederick replied, still excited. The Bible first, then this one."

"You're not becoming a limp dick, are you?" Gus asked, referring to religious boys whom they chased on the streets, throwing rocks, and calling names. Holding their Bibles to their chests like holy shields, the "limp dicks" easily identified themselves.

"Oh, no," Frederick said, shaking his head. "I'm going to use whatever I can find, the Bible, the newspapers, anything."

Gus smiled again. Fred was big now, but when excited about learning, he was like a boy receiving a long-desired toy at Christmas.

Frederick continued to brood about slavery, now a constant topic of talk after *The Columbian Orator*.

"I wish I could be free. I'm a slave for life," he said, sitting in an alley.

"Some of you become free, freed by their masters," said Jim Cordery, the fat one.

"Master Hugh? That will never happen. I'm a slave forever."

He repeated the phrase "a slave forever" so many times Gus finally limited him to saying it once a day. Gus was losing what little patience he had left. He understood Frederick's hope, even if none of them understood all the words about freedom in those speeches. Most people, Black and white, yellow, Brown, and red wanted freedom.

But there were basic facts.

Not everyone could be free. All white people were free, and Frederick wasn't. And from everything he heard and knew, God created slavery too. It was in the Bible.

At thirteen, Frederick, tall and gangly, with wide shoulders and long, wide feet, towered over all his friends, even Gus. Frederick now had a deep bass voice, some hair on his face and chest, thick, powerful hands, some money in his pocket from jobs in the yards, and he learned most things faster than anybody.

He also could feel the change in the way white people looked at him and talked to him. Gone were the usual smiles, the pat on the head, the elaborate courtesies, indulgences, and excuses granted to children on the streets. He saw darting eyes of suspicion, that sneer whites wore as comfortably as a jacket or skirt.

"See what I mean," Frederick would say, needlessly pointing to the obvious. His friends knew all the signs, learned at home.

As Gus explained, "Hating niggers comes in the milk. My mamma's tits were full!" And as Gus expected, Frederick wanted to know how he and their other friends escaped its bitter taste, how he could be accepted by them despite the early lessons.

"I don't know," Gus replied, "and besides, you're almost white!"

Gang membership could not stop the changes happening to them all. They were growing up and drifting part. Some had apprenticeships and jobs; others had girlfriends. They weren't kids anymore. Gus and the others had heard about Frederick's religious conversion with his new friend, Charles Lawson. The Hook was a small neighborhood, and gossip traveled quickly. At first, no one challenged his new plans for the afternoons or the weekends. His time was not really his own, anyway, with another baby in the Auld household.

Gus ran into Frederick at the corner of Storm and Market streets, a coincidence that made a hasty crossing of the street to avoid each other impossible. They had not talked in months.

"So, Freddy, you been too busy to see your old friends?"

"I'm studying to be a preacher."

Gus paused and said evenly, "So, you are a limp dick. But you'll be a good one, that's for sure, a damn good one. You always liked words."

Frederick smiled, and said only, "Thanks."

Gus's face burned as he stepped forward and grabbed Frederick by his coat lapels with both hands. Frederick kept his arms to his sides, surprised but clearly not afraid. "I was your friend, but when you had no more use for me, you dropped me and all the rest of us like rocks. We treated you like one of us. We didn't really care what you were, where you came from. So, what if you was a slave, so what if you was a nigger? We didn't care, and we didn't let nobody throw that shit into your face, either, or they paid if they did, but as soon as you got your Black God and your Black religion and your Black friends, we didn't matter no more. Now Black is everything, more important than true friends. You don't forget your friends. You don't use them up and spit them out, like you did. You're a traitor, that's what you are, a limp-dick traitor. You'll probably lie to yourself about this too. But nothing's going to change what I know: you don't know how to be a friend. You use people, that's all. Yeah, you use people, and you probably use God too. Fuck you! You're a traitor."

He turned away and repeated: "Traitor."

30.

FROM VIRGINIA CAME THE shocking news of a slave revolt led by a Nat Turner, who organized a band that killed over sixty white men, women, and children in August, and was still at large. Sophia and the entire South were terrified. She listened carefully to every bit of news as she pretended to be indifferent, her attempt to prevent fear from overwhelming her.

Rumor had it that a thousand, armed Negroes were on a rampage in Virginia, killing and looting, and that Maryland, right next door, would be next. The South's worst nightmare realized, stalking the countryside, butchering innocent women and children. What if all the Negroes, outnumbering whites in some counties three to one, armed themselves with pikes and clubs, and killed whites?

At church, almost everyone told stories about Blacks being killed in cold blood, some by decapitation without trial, sudden arrests, kidnappings, arson, disappearances, loss of jobs, riots, and more restrictive laws.

Hugh ranted about Negroes as ungrateful, uncivilized beasts who needed to be killed or sent back to Africa immediately. "We need to get rid of them all," he said to a group of shippers in the parlor one late September evening "before them damn abolitionists rile them all up."

Others throughout the South joined in a chorus of abuse against abolitionists, blaming them for everything wrong with the nation, charging them with treason now that they had their own scurrilous newspaper, the *Liberator*, published for the first time that January of 1831.

As news filtered in from Virginia, Sophia no longer allowed Frederick to hold her three young children: Ann, now five; Ben, three; and Hugh Wilson, nine months. She needed Frederick's help managing the house, but she resisted affection between Frederick and her children, explaining nothing and moving swiftly to take them from him whenever he intervened, only saying, "I'll take care of it."

One October night, after Turner's arrest and more lurid details of the revolt came to light, Frederick reached for baby Hugh when Ben, irritated by some offense, grabbed at his new brother on the floor of the kitchen.

Sophia cried out, "Don't you touch my baby! Don't you dare touch my baby!"

Startled and confused, the baby started to cry. Frederick froze, turning to Sophia for an explanation as the baby's cry became louder.

"Don't you touch . . ." she insisted.

Frederick blurted out, "But he needs . . ."

Sophia quickly swept up both Ben and Hugh and stepped away, holding the children close, protecting them from danger. "He was a house slave, too, and those ten children, those poor children."

"What?" asked Frederick, confused. "Who?"

"Don't you come near us. That Nat Turner . . ."

Frederick groaned as if he had been kicked in the groin. "Oh, my God. Oh, my God. I couldn't . . ."

"Stay away from me, from us."

The children now started to wail, and Hugh pounded on the door as he came in, asking, "What in hell is going on?"

She said, "Nat Turner," as if those two words explained everything.

Hugh looked at Sophia and then at Frederick, who stood stunned. His laugh was loud and mocking as he crossed the room and put one arm around

Frederick's slack shoulder. "Are you mad? Not Freddy, not this boy. He couldn't hurt nobody, not even me."

Flustered, Sophia insisted, "But you said. The stories. Nobody can be trusted, not even Fred."

Hugh waved his hand, dismissing her fear. "Don't be ridiculous. Freddy's not some farm nigger nursing a grudge. Besides, he's just a big boy."

Humiliated by Hugh's rebuke, she lowered her head and put Ben down beside her. She started to leave the room with the baby in her arm when Hugh gave an order.

"Give him to Freddy."

Sophia hesitated, and Hugh snapped, "Give him now!"

Hugh pushed Frederick forward to receive the baby, and Sophia stepped forward, her tears almost blinding her.

When Frederick had the baby in his arms, the baby giggled, and Hugh noted triumphantly, "Now see what I told you. Freddy's different, and he's no fool. We're the best he's got."

★

By December Nat Turner was dead, hanged after a speedy trial.

Hugh remained agitated. Money was tight, sales were down, and he needed to blame somebody for what was happening to him. The abolitionists became his scapegoat, and in his eagerness to see them behind everything going wrong in his life, he poured over the *Baltimore American* for any references to the dangerous group. He also read the *Liberator*, arming himself with their own words for rationalizations, excuses, and self-justifications. The *Liberator* wasn't banned in Maryland yet. But with his usual carelessness, he left copies lying around that Frederick found and secretly read.

Hugh received a letter from his brother Thomas, who offered another slave as a support for Sophia and the children. "Accept Henny, Frederick's older cousin and a good girl, as a token of our good wishes," Thomas wrote, "and we thank the good Lord that we have the means to assist you and yours in times of peril."

"We don't need another nigger in this house. Thomas married that Hambleton bitch after Lucretia died, so he can afford to take care of all of them."

Sophia gently pleaded with him to reconsider, pointing out that now that Tommy was in school, and Frederick was working at the yards, she needed another set of hands in the house to help her with the chores. Winter was coming on. Sausages, candles, mince pies, and winter clothes had to be made. The house had to be outfitted, doors blocked up with leaves or seaweed, and windows sealed by pasting. And the children could benefit from a young woman in the house.

"Very well," said Hugh.

But when he first saw Henny, his rage exploded. The girl, about sixteen, just stood there at the door holding her bag with arms severely damaged by fire. She had no fingers on either hand. Hugh shouted, "Damn Thomas to holy hell for dumping on me some cripple. So, this is his good will, getting rid of some useless nigger that he won't feed anymore. He was cheap then. He's cheap now. What are we going to do with a useless nigger? She can't even hold a goddamn bucket! I can't believe his sickening, self-righteous nerve."

When Hugh's rant was done, Sophia said sweetly, "Please give her a chance. I need the help. Please, and if she doesn't work out, we'll write to Thomas, thank him, and express our regrets."

"Two weeks. I'll give her two weeks, and she had better perform."

"Thank you, Hugh," she said, turning to Henny. "Welcome to our house."

For the next two weeks, Henny tried helping Sophia and the children, always offering her support, always smiling, even when the children ran from her, calling her "Monster" or "Stumps."

But Henny could carry only gross burdens, large packages in her arms, or wash floors with rags wrapped at the ends of her hands. She dropped plates, buckets, boxes. She couldn't do any cooking, or canning, or sweeping.

At the end of the two weeks, Sophia had to admit to Hugh that Henny was not working out.

"She's useless, then," said Hugh.

"Yes, I'm afraid so."

Triumphant, Hugh clapped his hand once. "We will send her back immediately. We'll show Thomas that we're not *that* desperate, like poor relatives who'll take any scraps that roll off his table."

Thomas's response to Henny's return was quick and curt. His note to the Aulds, scribbled in broad, thick strokes, declared, "For your base ingratitude, you will send Fred back to the Eastern Shore on the next ship to St Michaels. Since you couldn't keep Henny, you shall not have Fred."

31.

UNTIL HE BOARDED THE *Amanda* for the Eastern Shore, Frederick hoped the Lord would intervene and change Thomas Auld's heart, and every day Frederick looked out of his room window expecting to see a sailor rush down Philpot Street with the white message paper announcing the truce between two waring brothers.

Frederick hid his tears from Hugh and Sophia and made desperate bargains with God, making commitments he could not keep. *I'll never lie or steal again. I won't fight, curse, or fornicate. I won't even think about girls*, he said to heaven, and reached for the Bible. But his body failed to cooperate.

As he sailed into St. Michaels Harbour, he could see the rotting, scattered, unpainted houses; the sagging shacks blackened by the salt air and cowered by the constant, chilling wind; the plantations on the heights that seemed to mock the sagging dwellings below. He could not hear the pounding sounds of financial success. There was only the silence of a graveyard by the sea. No one seemed to move about.

As he was about to land, Frederick impulsively stroked his canvas bag holding *The Columbian Orator*. He had carefully hidden it in his packed clothes and wondered where he could hide it in the house of Thomas Auld.

After he crossed the narrow footbridge to the unpaved and deserted main street of the village, Frederick's first view of Thomas's store on the corner of Cherry and Talbot streets confirmed his worst fears. The building seemed to wilt under the weight of humidity and defeat. There were no customers going in or out. Frederick decided that Thomas Auld was a failed businessman and should have stayed a sloop captain.

Frederick made a silent, bitter vow: *This hole will never be my home. Never.*

He had only vague memories of Thomas Auld, once a merchant seaman who travelled most of the year. But Frederick could never forget Thomas's remark to Miss Lucretia, when she treated a severe wound to his head: "What is it with you Anthonys? You would think all these niggers were family for God's sake! When I'm here, I don't want this nigger around me."

Frederick looked to the street one last time, noted two white men strolling with jugs on their shoulders, and walked to the back of the main house behind the store. He found the kitchen, a separate building, and knocked on the door.

A young woman opened it, and Frederick recognized his sister Eliza at once. Tall, dark, beautiful, and thin, she was surely Grandma Betty as a girl. But Eliza's eyes, more than anything else, identified her as a different Bailey. Betsey's eyes were black, gentle pools. Eliza's were hard like black ice. She had no time for sentiment.

"Well, well, what do we see here? My brother is a young buck, all tall and big. What have they been feeding you in Baltimore? Well, you won't get to eat that much here, I tell you, but don't you worry, we'll take good care of you."

She embraced him, but Frederick kept his arms to his sides, his body stiff, his face unsmiling.

Eliza stepped away and observed with unwavering eyes, "I see you're not ready for us. Well, we're all you've got, and Baltimore might as well be on the other side of the moon."

"What do *you* know about the moon?"

"Now *that's* the Freddy I remember."

Cousin Henny, standing near the fireplace, said softly and sweetly, "Hi, Freddy. It's good to see ya." He didn't respond, and she added, "I knows it's all my fault for why you're here. I didn't work out with Master Hugh. I'm sorry."

"Hi, Henny. Don't worry about that. We got caught up between two brothers, that's all."

Eliza announced, "Captain Auld's been waitin' for you. He's been struttin' around like a cock, knowin' he beat out his brother. You're a prize."

"No, I'm not."

"Yes, you are. Just look. He could get good money out of you, or for you. As cheap as he is, you can count on it."

He trembled, and Eliza, noticing, said, "But don't you worry. I'll give you all de help I can to prevent that from happening, a sale I mean. There are ways, but nothin's perfect, as you'll find out. But I'm still here, and if you remember, I'm not the easiest person to get along with. Now let's go to the captain and Miss Rowena. They can't wait to see you."

"I'm not the same. I've changed."

"The Shore ain't changed a bit. Get used to *that.*"

They were at the back door of the main house within seconds, and before they entered Eliza named the members of his new white family: Captain Thomas; Miss Rowena, his second wife; Amanda, the daughter of Thomas and his first wife, Lucretia; and Thomas's younger brother, Haddaway.

"The one to watch is Miss Rowena," Eliza warned. "She married beneath herself."

They went inside without knocking. Eliza left him alone in the rear of the house for a few moments, and then returned to lead him to the front parlor, where Thomas and his wife were waiting. The chairs, the tables, the clock on the mantlepiece, the portrait of a stranger above it, and the striped wallpaper suggested a wealth contradicted by the storefront.

"Ah, Freddy," Captain Auld said smugly, "Welcome to your home."

Frederick winced. Thomas looked like his brother, even though Hugh was not as tall or thin. Thomas had the same clear, blue eyes, thick blond hair, thin lips, and thick lines that divided his cheeks and created huge dimples. He too was extraordinarily handsome.

Beside him sat Rowena, twenty-one, thin, plain, and dressed in black since the death of her last baby. She had a persistent cough, and with each cough, she held a napkin to her mouth, demurely lowering her green eyes, and then lifting them, daring anyone to object to the sounds she had made.

Amanda, her stepdaughter, stood to the side. She was a pretty little girl with clear blue eyes like her father's. She stared at Frederick. A remarkable creature, prepared to delight, had just come into her midst. Without looking at her, Rowena said coldly, "Stand straight, Amanda, even when receiving a nigger."

The seven-year-old child obeyed at once, still smiling at Frederick. Rowena said, "There is no need to smile and give him ideas."

Amanda's eyebrows knitted. *What ideas*?

"Although we all live in this small house, he will not be a friend," Rowena told Amanda. "Niggers cannot be your friends."

That lesson completed, she turned to Frederick. "I am Miss Rowena, and my husband is Master Thomas, or just "master." He is not to be called captain under any circumstances. His daughter is Miss Amanda, but because she is a child, she can only make requests of you through me. Is all this clear?"

"Yes, ma'am," said Frederick, perhaps too loudly and clearly, but loudly enough for Eliza, who was listening to everything on the side of the parlor door that remained ajar.

"As the mistress of this house, you will receive direction from me, and I will not tolerate any ideas, behaviors, or attitudes that you may have learned in Baltimore. You will eat when I tell you to and dare not think for one moment that you can eat us out of everything because you're growing like some field horse."

Her cough returned, and Frederick occasionally looked to Thomas for some indication of his views on all this.

Rowena turned to her husband and said sweetly, "Now, Thomas, do you have anything to add? I've tried to be thorough, since you're not as experienced with slaves."

"No, my dear, you've covered the essentials to my satisfaction."

"You will find that your master will compare most favorably to his brother," continued Rowena, returning to Frederick. "Master Thomas does not swear or drink, and we attend church every Sunday. This is a religious household, and I will have no violations of the commandments in this house."

Frederick slightly turned his head to hide his contempt, but it was too late. Rowena understood the subtlest forms of slave protest. She frowned, placed her napkin to the side of her skirt, rose with great dignity from her seat, and stepped up to Frederick, who looked down on her with serene acceptance of what was coming. He tightened the muscles in his neck.

With a wide swing of her hand from behind her skirt, she slapped him in the face. The force of the blow made his head jerk for a moment. He closed his eyes and reopened them to see a shocked Thomas and Amanda Auld.

"You stink of Baltimore. Take a bath in the kitchen and wash it off your nigger skin."

She returned to her seat, coughed, and put her napkin to her lips. "Now, go," she said.

Eliza had retreated from the door to wait for Frederick in the pantry. She was shaking her head when he entered. "This won't work," she said with light mockery. "If you're goin' to survive this house, boy, you'll need to do better than put on airs before a bitch who knows every inch of puttin' on airs. She's a Hambleton, and in these parts, that's almost like the Lloyds. Even her shit don't stink."

"I'm not a boy who doesn't know how to deal with white folks. There were more white folks in Baltimore than you'll ever see here."

She laughed. "You're still as uppity as ever. But Freddy, you're here, and there are four people in this little place you had better learn to get along with 'cause this is all you've got. The captain, Miss Rowena, Henny, and me. And I'm easy 'cause I don't believe I'm good, prayin' all the time, and going to church every Sunday, and all that. I'm sure that if my judge is their Lord, then I'm goin' to burn in hell for sure, and so I think I just as well try to get on the best I can."

"Don't you believe in the commandments?"

She rolled her eyes and asked, "Boy, did you get religion in Baltimore, too? Now what am I going to do with you? I see I have a lot a work to do."

"You can't take that from me. They took Baltimore from me. Nobody, not even you, is going to take my Lord from me."

She dropped her smile. "I don't, *can't* do that, Freddy, nobody can, although some white folks will try. But you'll have to change some ideas if you're going to make it around here. You'll have to, or they will sell you and send you south. We're living with mean and cheap people, and they don't care for us, not since the great dividing."

"Where's Gram Betty?"

The question surprised them both, especially Frederick. Before today his silence about her had been his way of protecting himself from the pain of loss. And he was afraid to admit openly that he had never forgiven her for what she had done to him so long ago.

"I should have seen that coming somehow. You asked about her enough times at Wye Plantation, until you realized that she was not coming to get you. And then you stopped talking about her all together. She's still at de farm. Master Andrew let her stay there. She's fine, but she's gettin' old, and Grandpa Isaac is gone. But Master Andrew sold our sister, Sarah, and Aunt Betty and all her children to a man in Mississippi last summer. And when Andrew goes, there'll be another upset. Death always shakes things up."

"Do you see her?"

"No. It's hard to get away. I usually can only get as far as Martingham, the plantation of Miss Rowena's folks. Uncle Henry, Gram Betty's brother, is there, and Cousin Tom. You remember Stuterrin' Tom, don't you?"

"Does she ask about me, say anything about me?"

Eliza readied herself to attack his bottomless selfishness. She waited, and he insisted, "Does she? Does she?"

"Yes," she replied.

"How much?"

"I can't count the times! Does it matter? She told all of us how leaving you at Wye Plantation broke her heart. You were her favorite. We all knew that. But even after all that's happened, you still have family. You have me, and I never forgot you either. You can cry all you want, but when you're all dried up, you will need to listen to me and make the most of what we got here. I ain't just sitting around. I'm making the most of the situation. So can you."

"I'm not crying. I'm too big for that."

"There's inside crying, and it can go on for years."

★

For a while, Thomas had little to do or say about Frederick until a lamp from Thomas's carriage disappeared.

He stormed into the kitchen one summer night, looking for Frederick.

"You know what happened to my lamp? Where is it?"

The stupidity of the accusation incensed Frederick. *What in the hell would he do with a carriage lamp? Walk around with it?* Before he could stop, he heard himself deny the charge, declaring, "How should I know?"

Thomas's entire body stiffened. He recovered, and before rushing from the room, he said, "Damn you!"

Frederick looked to his sister. She said nothing. Thomas would be back, and there was going to be hell to pay.

Thomas, followed by his brother Haddaway, returned with the cart whip, a thin leather snake that seemed to undulate in the air, and without a word, his arm swinging in one grand arc, he gave Frederick a steady flow of blows to the shoulders and head.

The cart whip was light, but Frederick covered his head with his arms and dropped to his knees, exposing his wide back to the weight of his very first lashing, a steady barrage of stinging bites.

"Get up, damn you!" Thomas yelled. "Get up!"

Frederick would not move, and the blows intensified, a storm having been unleashed. Thomas inhaled deeply as he lifted his arm and jumbled words filled the sweaty air.

Haddaway begged Thomas to stop, but he kept a safe distance and stayed at the door as he witnessed his brother beat a slave for the first time.

Thomas stopped. Exhausted, he fell back clutching his sides and heaving, ready to vomit. He tried to speak. Words sputtered like weak, scattering bullets. "Don't you ever . . . damn you . . . nigger ass . . . disrespect . . . master . . ."

Haddaway now approached Thomas and softly pleaded with him to walk away. "You can't kill yourself like this. What's gotten into you?"

Frederick did not lift his head until the Aulds were gone.

"It didn't hurt," he assured Eliza.

He looked to her. She stood near the fireplace with folded arms and a nasty, critical grimace on her face. "I told you. You just couldn't keep your big mouth shut. Don't expect me to feel sorry for you, because I can't feel sorry for a stupid nigger."

"I didn't do anything."

"You didn't lie, fool. You didn't lie."

"It didn't matter. He was just waiting for an excuse. He hates me."

"He sure does, and you know what? He hates you because you're bigger and smarter than he could ever be. Now you better take off that shirt. We can't let those burns and scratches set in." She paused, and then added with a fierce determination, "And don't you show them they hurt you. Don't you dare make them think you're afraid. Act dumb, but not afraid."

32.

THOMAS AULD PRAYED MORNING, noon, and night, hounding heaven for a saving experience. The lashing of Frederick two days ago now made him desperate. He was surely a man out of control, an evil degenerate offended by a mere boy who had every reason to be sullen and uncooperative.

Following Lucretia's instructions to take care of him seven years ago, Thomas had sent Frederick to Baltimore, where he was spared the rigors of plantation slavery, having opportunities few Eastern Shore Negroes ever dreamed of. Now he was back, made to return out of spite, a city slave in a strange place, an intelligent boy taller than Thomas and every other white man in St. Michaels, and a constant reminder that Thomas had failed to keep his promise to his beloved wife. Protect Frederick, she pleaded, as she lay dying.

Thomas believed that salvation would resolve the conflicts of his character and the hatred and insecurity of his frightened heart. He hated Rowena, who could never be Lucretia. He hated his brother and constantly worried he would match or surpass Hugh's failures. He hated the Baileys for witnessing his inadequacies as a master and a man.

The Lord had come to Thomas at the great camp meeting in Haddaway's Woods on the Bayside. From that moment on, Thomas was a zealot, now praying daily with uncompromising vigor to a God who was hard of hearing; reciting verses of the Bible in almost every conversation; and providing food and shelter for every traveling preacher who came to St. Michaels on the Methodist circuit. He demanded that Frederick, Eliza, and Henny join his family in prayer in the parlor on Sundays, with the Baileys standing at the door of the room, as Rowena stipulated.

But on one Sunday evening this invitation backfired.

The visiting preacher, the Reverend Cookman, started playing the opening chords of "God, Most Holy, Most Wonderful" on the fortepiano and turned to the assembled Aulds and Baileys and announced, "Now let us all sing."

Perturbed, Rowena turned to look at the slaves, and the preacher began without them, filling the room with a booming if ragged bass noise. The Baileys in turn looked to Rowena for permission to participate and she nodded once. Henny then began, followed by Eliza, their voices soft and low and quite beautiful. Frederick entered the refrain, asserting his voice above the Aulds' enthusiastic atonality.

Beaming at the sound of Frederick's mellow and flexible bass-baritone, the preacher increased the volume of his light tenor voice, as if trying to create a duet amid the rumbling, chaotic accompaniment of the other singers. The women began to drop out, first Eliza and Henny, then Rowena, who stared at Frederick, her eyes cold, her jaw tight.

The vocal line thinned as the preacher stopped singing to listen to Frederick, who sang with his head high, his face beaming with religious fervor and pride. When he was done, the preacher clapped vigorously and exclaimed, "That was wonderful, Frederick. Sing another hymn for us."

Immediately, Frederick declined. "Oh, no, sir. I can't."

The preacher turned to Thomas. "Captain Auld, will you be so gracious as to allow Frederick, an ardent Christian like yourself, to sing again?"

Rowena had flinched at the offending title, but he only smiled dimly, leaned forward in his chair, and said sanctimoniously, "Oh, of course, he is free to sing praise to the Lord."

Frederick sang a solo this time with even greater fervor and skill, his voice caressing the melody with delicate variations in the second verse of "My Lord Is Near to Me."

At its conclusion, the preacher said, "Thank you, *Frederick*." As if to underscore the use of the formal name, he turned to the Aulds and noted, "Further proof that slaves have equal souls before God."

"Praise be to the Lord," Thomas replied, now planning to file a complaint to the elders with a demand for the Reverend's dismissal. "Fred, you may leave us now."

Frederick waited in the kitchen for Captain Thomas. He knew some kind of punishment was coming.

"I should have mumbled," he declared to Eliza.

"Liar! You knew exactly what you were doing."

Thomas then suddenly came in with an upraised whip, followed by Rowena, who tried reaching for it. "Stop, Thomas, stop. What will our Christian brothers and sisters think and say when they hear you whipped a slave because he sang in your house during a prayer meeting? What will people *say*?"

Thomas lowered his arm, but his face was full of rage. "In this house no one will ask him to sing again. Is that clear?"

She protested tentatively, "We have a duty . . ."

"We will teach, but he will not sing in this house again, ever . . ."

"Christians sing, Thomas."

He turned on her with such force that Rowena flinched. "*Never* in this house. He can sing his head off in Haddaway Woods, but not here!"

Thomas pounded his fist against the door to accentuate the point, and left the room, leaving everyone, including Rowena, speechless. She took a step back and placed her hand on the table for balance. When she turned to Frederick and Eliza, she was grinning. "This is the master as he truly is, and don't you ever forget it."

She hurried out the room.

Eliza then said sweetly, "She just loves it when he's like this, trying to prove himself, pretending something he's not. He's a weak man and tries to please her. Rowena loves the show, though. It proves her power over him. She's something else, something else for sure."

A month later, before breakfast one morning, Captain Thomas tied Henny by her wrists to a bolt in the joist above and beat her with a cowskin. He moved quickly, ignoring her desperate protests, her need for an explanation.

"What did I do? I'm sorry, massa, for what I did, for what it was. I'm sorry."

Thomas had only one thing to say, and he repeated a passage from Luke 12:47 when Henny repeatedly asked why. He answered her with: "That servant which knew his lord's will, and prepared not himself, neither did according to his will, shall be beaten with many stripes."

Frederick and Eliza were appalled. Tears flowed from their eyes as they watched each time the cowskin struck Henny's back. They turned away, unable to watch any more as Henny cried.

At last, Thomas was done and stepped away from the girl hanging above him. He said softly, "I'll be back," and he left her there with a command to Frederick and Eliza. "Don't you dare to bring her down, or else!"

As soon as he was gone, Frederick and Eliza rushed to Henny with water and rags to soothe her wounds.

"I don't know what I did, Freddy, I don't know what I did? Why, why, if only I knew why."

"No reason is good 'nough," said Eliza bitterly. "No reason in the world."

"I try to do right. I know I'm not smart, but I try," Henny insisted. A single word captured the incomprehensibility of the world: "Why?"

"I hate his white, Christian ass. I hate him," Frederick said, seething as he took deep breaths. "I hate him and all his fuckin' kind. He can pray all he wants, but he's goin' to burn in hell. God ain't fooled. Thomas Auld is going to burn!"

Three hours later, Thomas returned from the store and beat Henny again, opening her old wounds with the same cowskin, repeating the same passage from holy scripture. Then he had his midday meal.

Thomas finally ordered Frederick to untie Henny. She fell into Frederick's arms like a rag doll, her skin raw from the repeated blows to her shoulders and back. Henny didn't open her eyes but cried softly as her blood soaked Frederick's shirt.

"I'm sending her to Martingham to see Uncle Jacob Taylor," said Thomas, annoyed by the anguish before him. "He's the best in Talbot County for treating injured slaves. She's good for nothing here anyway. I'm sick of her total uselessness. She not worth a *damn* thing."

"Yes, captain."

"Get her ready."

"Yes, captain."

When he was gone, Frederick and Eliza tried to console Henny, gently stroking her hands, delicately covering her wounds with larded linen. But she said nothing and kept her eyes shut, having withdrawn into a private, safe place beyond pain, where they all had to go, now and then, to stay sane and alive.

Henny was cleaned and given food and sent away with a note tied to a rope around her neck. She would have to find her way to the Hambleton Plantation alone, since Thomas did not have another household slave to spare.

That night, a young man came to the kitchen door, introduced himself as Wilson and, holding his head down, said that he heard that Frederick could read and write.

"Who told you that?" demanded Frederick, hiding his terror.

Before Wilson could answer, Eliza behind him said, "I did."

"Are you crazy? Look what happened over nothing, and now you go 'round telling about me. Do you want me to get what Henny got?"

"He won't," replied Eliza casually.

"How do you know that?"

"He's afraid of you," she answered, smiling.

Frederick laughed at the absurdity, throwing his head back in a melodramatic gesture of contempt. "He gave me my first whipping, remember?"

"I've been watchin' him for years, and it's just like you to think you know what's goin' on 'cause you're you. Lord, someone is going to have to knock you off your high horse."

"Well, it won't be you."

"You'll make a good teacher," Eliza countered before turning to Wilson, who was looking down, embarrassed by the exchange. She noted with soft, almost seductive charm, "Well, what do you have in mind for my brother?"

"Miss, we, a group of us men, want to learn our letters, and our boys need this, too."

"How many?" asked Frederick, stepping toward him.

"About twenty."

"Twenty *boys,*" said Eliza, a cutting edge to her voice once again.

"We can't have girls there," Frederick objected. "That won't be right or proper."

"Your nigger school one day better have girls 'cause the mamas teach first, even as the babies suck." She turned to Wilson for a response.

"Yes, miss," was all Wilson could say, bewildered and enthralled.

"Where will it be, and when?" asked Frederick.

"At the house of James Mitchell. He's free. We wants to start next Sunday."

"A week from now!" exclaimed Frederick.

"Do you need more time? I have some spellers and some testaments. I collected them from de garbage, but they of still some use."

"Oh no, a week's fine. Tell me how to get there."

Eliza said tenderly, "I'm proud of you, Fred."

He started, "What?"

"I'm proud of you 'cause you're going to change people, make them better, even if your head gets big like a pumpkin."

"But I couldn't help Henny."

"We do what we can," Eliza answered, touching him lightly on the face.

"I'll teach her, and you, too!"

"We'll see if we'll hire you into service. We Bailey girls don't just take any boy that comes along. We'll have to see what you do out there before . . ."

"There you go, knockin' me off my high horse," Frederick said, embracing her.

"Somebody has to do it, but only somebody that loves you."

"I love you," he whispered, saying these three words for the very first time. He could now admit his good fortune: he had a sister.

★

Frederick was a zealous and yet patient teacher, careful in his application of his own experiences, and tactful with a group of men and boys whose ignorance was his not too long ago. In return, they gave their devotion, born of a respect for what Frederick had achieved in so short a time. His students treated his literacy as a sign of the Lord's favor. He sent this boy to teach and deliver them, they said. They called him "teacher" and listened to every word as if he held the key to every mystery. Frederick loved the attention.

After two Sunday sessions, the school's existence was no longer a secret. Wilson and Mitchell were told that outraged whites in the community held meetings and planned to disrupt the next Sunday session. Wilson pleaded with Frederick to continue, assuring him that although Sabbath schools were unpopular, they were not illegal.

Interrupting a lesson with Frederick and his students, a small mob of white men, armed with sticks, rocks, and clubs, stormed Mitchell's house, pushing in the door, turning over chairs, grabbing books, and shoving the frightened men and boys against the walls. Crying, one boy begged for his life.

Frederick recognized most of the white men. The last man to step inside the room was Captain Thomas. Frederick strategically bowed his head while Thomas ranted about the station of the Negro, the great chain of being with the lowly Negro at the bottom just above the apes, the need for slaves—docile, ignorant slaves. Thomas flayed his arms, moved about like a caged animal, panic in his wide eyes, as if facing a bloody spike.

But calm returned to Thomas just before he mounted his carriage when he told Frederick, "City life has ruined you for every good purpose and fitted you for everything that is bad. You will pay dearly for embarrassing me, making me the laughingstock of my town."

Later that week, after Henny had returned, Thomas came into the kitchen brandishing a piece of paper. "I don't know why I didn't think of this before," he said. "Henny, you're free. You're your own person now. I don't have to be bothered with you. You're off my hands at last. You're free."

He was grinning, pleased by his cleverness. He looked to the three slaves, who received the news stupefied. "Well, well, well. I've shut up your big Bailey mouths at last."

"You can't set her adrift to take care of herself. She'll starve and die," objected Frederick, as if speaking to an equal.

"It's done," Thomas said, "Gather up your things, Henny, and get out by noon. You'll have to find some place to live."

He turned on his heels and left the room.

Too shocked and angry to move, Eliza mumbled her rage: "He can't do this! He can't! I bet Rowena gave him the idea. I just never thought they could sink so low."

Frederick kept on repeating, "She'll starve and die, starve and die . . ."

They were too absorbed with their own reactions to hear Henny's soft, excited words at first: "I'm free! I'm free. I'm free. . ."

When they finally heard her, they noticed the impish smile and the embrace she gave herself with those damaged arms.

"He can't beat me no more. I don't has to listen to him and to Miss Rowena ever agin. I can do what I wants to do, and if I starve my body; it's my own. I'm free, free, free."

Eliza rushed to Henny and took her into her arms, crying. "Oh, Henny."

"Don't cry for me. I'll take care of myself. Don't fret. I will. I'll stay in town, or maybe live with Gram Betty. She's gettin' old and needs some help now. Don't worry. I'm not dead yet."

"But," said Frederick helplessly.

"No buts about it. Don't fret. If I can stand the kinds of whippins' I got from Captain Thomas, then bein' on my own can't be half as bad. I'm strong, real strong, don't you know?"

"You're stronger than all of us," Frederick confessed.

"Before I go, Fred, you need to do somethin' for me. You needs to read that paper for me and makes sure it say what he says it say. I'm goin' to need it if dem patrollers start huntin' for runaways."

He read the paper quickly. "Yes, it's real."

"Good. Now, let's celebrate before we say goodbye. Let's have a party and eat something real good."

"What should we have?"

"I picked somethin' up just this mornin' when Miss Rowena was snorin' in her bed, a pick of dem biscuits and some jam I put in this here tin." Henny then turned to pull out a bundle rapped in cloth from behind a large basket. She giggled and said, presenting the basket to Frederick and Eliza, "Now you didn't think Miss Rowena could be so nice in her goin' away presents, now did you?"

In December, when the wind from the Bay seemed to penetrate every wood plank in the Auld house, and when no amount of fire could warm it, Thomas announced his final surprise of 1833. He came into the kitchen, sat at the table, and said to Frederick, who was sweeping the floor, "I've decided that you are incorrigible, and that only the rigors of work on the Bayside will break you."

Frederick gripped the handle of the unmoving broom but said nothing, as he stared at Thomas.

Eliza also said nothing, sitting at the table across from him, her face frozen.

Thomas went on: "He's a poor farmer, a renter, who needs a helping hand, so he hires a slave or two to work the worst land in Talbot County for wheat crops. He's willing to pay, but I've reduced his rates for two excellent reasons. He's a religious man, I understand, very strict in the cultivation of Christian piety. And, more importantly, he has a reputation for breaking the spirits of the most obnoxious niggers in these parts."

"Covey," said Eliza solemnly.

"Yes, Covey, the very one, Mr. Edward Covey. He'll be your master for at least one year, Fred, with the contract renewable at the end of it. You're big and strong. I'm sure that he will find great use for you."

Thomas stood, completing his announcement: "You will leave this house on the first day of January, and you will return the best nigger in Talbot County. I look forward to the blessed day. Good night."

33.

EDWARD COVEY'S SMALL, UNPAINTED house stood at a low cliff overlooking the Chesapeake at the end of a narrow lane seven miles from St. Michaels. Frederick knocked at the door and entered before anyone answered. He found Caroline, Covey's pregnant cook, standing by a table near the fireplace. Edward Covey entered the room. He was a small, wiry man, twenty-eight and about five foot seven, with a short neck and rounded shoulders. His green-gray eyes were set far back in his head and constantly moved, restlessly inspecting, never relaxing.

"You look strong and healthy," he said to Frederick, speaking from the corner of his mouth like a growling dog about to lose a bone. "We begin in the morning. Caroline, give him some hot food, and show him where he's going to sleep."

Covey lightly pushed Frederick's shoulder and said, "Turn 'round."

Frederick obeyed, turning once.

"Keep on till I tell you to stop," said Covey, his voice more menacing.

Frederick turned another three times before Covey touched his shoulder again.

"That's fine," he said, putting up his hand. "You're too big for Freddy. You'll be Fred 'round here."

He left. Caroline could see confusion in Frederick's face, and she explained Covey's apparent sensitivity. "Don't you think he cares about your feelings. You're not a boy no more. That's as clear as can be, but you're still a nigger." She told Frederick what she knew about Covey and his family.

Covey rented 150 acres from the family of Thomas Kemp, the famous shipbuilder, after first working as an overseer. He married Susan Caulk less than two years ago and now had an infant son. Also in the household were Covey's cousin Jimmy Hughes and Mrs. Covey's sister, Emma Caulk, a hunchback. So far, Covey was a failure as a tenant farmer, even with the help of hired slaves like Bill, who had been working for Covey for three years. Covey didn't have much money despite all the work, but there was one good thing about Covey. He worked as hard as everyone else, sometimes along with them. Caroline was Covey's only slave, bought to breed for him. She also warned Frederick about Covey's deceiving ways. He would crawl in ditches and gullies, hide behind fences, bushes, and stumps, watching, listening, trying to convince his workers that he was everywhere, and knew everything.

"He's the snake. Nothin' gets pass 'im, nothing. I always speak de truth. No lies, I say. It's de best way, though I knows some women, including my mama, say that all de men wants is de lies. Build them up 'cause de white man is always tearin' them down. So, tell dem how big and important they is, tell them they is de *whole* world. But I guess I'm *not* what she wanted. I can't help myself. I have to tell de truth to you niggers 'cause de lies make you crazy, and you don't need crazy when you're dealing with Mr. Covey. You need to see what is. The dead and the stupid are close friends. Just do what he says. Just do it. That's all. Keep your body strong, real strong, and don't let him gets into your head. Don't let him get there. Think of de Lord or think of me when he starts beatin' you. That's why he called the breaker. He going to beat you day and night, boy. Day and night."

★

Frederick had never worked on a farm, but the next two days were not difficult. He spent them chopping wood in the forest two miles from the house and returned exhausted. But at least he knew how to use an ax, having acquired this skill in Hugh Auld's shipyard.

And then everything changed.

At dawn on January 4, when the cold morning seemed ready to freeze the eyes and brain, Covey roused him from bed and told him to take out the team of oxen and return with a cartload of wood.

"Sir, I don't know how."

"To the barn," Covey said, and turned to go without waiting for Frederick to follow.

In the barn, Frederick was introduced to the oxen, Buck and Darby, their huge horns twisted crowns of alien power. He stared at the pair of animals.

Buck was the "in-hand" ox, and Darby the "off-hand," said Covey, who didn't explain these terms, He continued with the vocabulary of control: whoa, back, gee, and hither, which he defined only once, never checking to make sure that Frederick understood.

Covey asked, "See this rope?"

Without waiting for an answer, he took the end of the ten-foot rope that was wrapped around the leader, Buck, and gave it to Frederick. "You gotta hold on to this so they won't run away with ya," said Covey.

Buck and Darby just stared back at Frederick. He was sure they could smell his fear.

"Pull to stop 'em, but you get that wood, you understand me, boy?"

"What if . . ."

"Git that chopped wood," Covey commanded.

"Yes, sir."

"Slap his rump," snapped Covey.

Frederick obeyed, and they were off, three thousand pounds of beef pulling an empty cart and a thick-boned boy. Frederick tugged at the ropes, and the cart bounced neatly in the lane up to the main road.

When he saw trees where the chopped wood was on the far side of the field, Frederick thought he could control the wagon. But when they crossed the main road, he noticed that his tugs on the rope were not slowing the oxen down. Breathing heavily, they seemed determined to dash toward the trees.

Within seconds, they made their run, and the cart bounced against tree stumps and tilted on its wheels from side to side. Frederick pulled the ropes and ordered the oxen to stop, but his commands were ignored. He realized that he could be crushed by the bouncing cart. Yet he would not let go even as the rope burned the palms of his hands and made them bleed.

Finally, the cart hit a tree. The frightened animals were now entangled in the underbrush and saplings, their blazing eyes blaming him for the accident.

He started to walk in a small circle, assessing the situation and repeating the phrase, "It's not my fault, it's not my fault," as if this chant could prevent the inevitable punishment.

Frederick set out to clean up the mess as best he could, putting the cart back on its wheels, using the ax to cut the vines and free the oxen, who cooperated now, quietly pulling Frederick and the cart to the wood he had cut by hand and left in a pile the day before. The oxen remained still as Frederick filled the cart and returned to the lane at the Covey house.

At the gate, a heavy board sagged between two huge oak posts, and Frederick released the rope on the horns of Darby to push the gate open. As soon as he pushed it, he heard the charge of the oxen. He pressed himself against the post as they dashed through, catching the gate between the wheels and overturning the cart body.

He saw Mr. Covey waiting in the barn lot, his arms crossed at the chest, his legs wide apart. Frederick hurried over to explain his day. Covey scowled but allowed Frederick to tell his tale. Uninterrupted, Frederick blamed the oxen for everything.

Then came the order: "Go back to the woods again."

"Sir?"

"Connect the oxen and take them to the woods again."

The oxen looked at Frederick with trusting eyes as if nothing had ever happened. And when he took the ropes as per his earlier instructions, the oxen obeyed immediately after being rehitched. Covey followed behind them.

When Frederick found the earlier spot, Covey ordered Frederick to stop the cart. Frederick obeyed, then heard Covey mutter, as he started toward the trees, "I'll teach you how not to break my gate and waste my time."

Frederick watched Covey march over to a black gum tree, cut off three shoots, from four to six feet long, and shape them into ox goads with a large jack knife.

He returned with an order, "Take off your clothes."

Frederick didn't move or say a word.

"Take 'em off."

Frederick continued to refuse.

"I'm warning you. Damn you to hell, take them off now!"

Nothing.

Covey leaped like a dog and knocked Frederick to the ground, where he tore his shirt and pants in large, ragged strips. Frederick curled into a ball against the hard, freezing ground. Covey struck the back of his head with the goads, and Frederick covered it with his hands. Covey could now pull off the last remnants of his trousers.

"I'll teach you, nigger."

Covey jumped up and thrashed Frederick's back with wide, powerful swings. The blows split his skin, and blood flowed.

Covey gathered up the pieces of Frederick's clothes and made a bundle to carry back to the house, leaving him naked. "Just get your ass home with that wood."

Frederick waited until he was convinced that Covey was out of sight, and then struggled to stand. Every muscle was sore, and his skin seemed to burn as blood clots cracked open. He prayed for escape from the cold and humiliation and the memory of his first thrashing. He hurried back, crouching in the cold wind as he covered his private parts.

The next morning, Covey made him rise at dawn, marched him out to the fields and kept him there until sundown, driving him until he was ready to drop, flogging his back when his work slackened, kicking him when he mishandled a tool, cursing his incompetence. The city ruins niggers, he said.

Day after day Frederick received this treatment, and every night he cried himself to sleep after working in the fields until eleven or twelve at night. His sleep was fitful because the time of Covey's early morning calls changed from day to day, and there was hell to pay if he didn't rise at once: a slap across the face, a volley of blows with a long, sharp stick across his back, a kick in the rear. Some nights he didn't sleep at all, for fear of missing the sound of Covey's voice in the early morning. Frederick now flinched when hearing it, and the sound of Covey's footsteps made his stomach turn. Frederick was always tired, and the infinite depths of exhaustion continued to astonish him.

Covey didn't starve Frederick; there was always enough food to eat, and for that Frederick was grateful. He needed large hunks of bread and meat to work the long days, and Covey insisted that Caroline give Frederick as much as he wanted.

Another consolation was Covey's commitment to Sunday as the day of rest. He would rise with a smile, dress in his best clothes, and join his wife for the weekly trip to church. On Sundays he required nothing of Frederick, Caroline, and Bill Smith, another slave rented to him, giving them the entire day, until sundown, to do as they wished.

Frederick would lie under a tree too exhausted to cry and think about murder or suicide. January 1, 1835, when his contract ended was an eternity away, and he could not imagine how much more he could take. His back was a web of cuts and gashes, and he was tired down to the bone. He could barely move sometimes, and his pain was now as familiar as his skin, impossible to shed.

Frederick had never encountered a man who took such pleasure in giving pain. The religious hypocrisy he could tolerate, but the grin on Covey's face when catching Frederick at rest, the piercing green eyes that sparkled when he struck a blow, and the low moan that always followed the floggings, a kind of physical relief, he could not stomach.

Frederick hated the inspections. Sometimes Covey came out to the fields at midday and ordered Frederick, when alone, to stop working. At once, Frederick knew he had to stand straight like the most formal butler in a plantation house, legs slightly apart, chest out, head up with the chin lifted, eyes straight ahead without a touch of arrogance. It was a performance that had improved with practice.

"Stand tall," Covey always said.

"Turn around," Covey would say, his voice strange and heavy, almost hoarse.

Frederick had to turn slowly with even steps at least three times, until the turns were satisfactory. When he faced Covey, he could see hungry eyes examining him from head to foot even as his own head did not move at all.

"Good, very good," Covey always whispered.

Then came the order that was now too common to be strange anymore: "Now take your clothes off, all of them."

Frederick now always closed his eyes as he lowered the trousers over hips and thighs, crouching slightly before stepping out of them. He didn't want to see the sudden delight of those incredibly green eyes.

Covey would then come forward and stand directly in front of Frederick, his legs just an inch or two from Frederick's genitals, his head at Frederick's chest. Every muscle in Frederick's body tightened. This was the crucial moment. Covey would stand still, breathing lightly, and then he would moan convulsively and punch Frederick in the stomach, sides and face, a volley of blows followed by kicks when Frederick fell to the ground, as he had to if he were to survive.

"Goddamn you. Goddamn you for the evil you've brought to my farm."

He would then flog Frederick, sweat coating his body until he was exhausted.

"Don't you ever tell. Don't you tell, or I'll kill you, and I mean it. I'll kill you and pay Mr. Auld."

He then hurried away, leaving Frederick with his own thoughts of murder, and the suicide that had to follow. There could be no other path. The authorities would hang him after cutting his body into pieces. He heard stories of butchered slaves, forced to eat their own private parts before dying under a tree, or witness the slow flaying of their own skin.

What he feared most was the dark corner to which he mentally retreated, the corner Caroline had warned him about. He now didn't want to read, plan, even think. He even stopped talking with Caroline and Bill. And he could no longer pray. There would be no deliverance, no divine interventions.

Only death could bring relief. He went to the cliff overlooking the bay, its wet wind swirling around him and making his clothes a second skin. He looked down to the rolling, white-capped waves that became gray shells opening to receive him and saw his body inside the shell, protected from the storm, his arms across his chest, at rest, at peace. Frederick stepped toward the edge of the cliff. The wind roared in his ears. He had to find rest. He needed it.

"Frederick!" shouted Caroline behind him. "Get your yellow ass away from that cliff. What in the hell do you think you're doing?"

Frederick turned around. He saw Caroline, wrapped in a blanket, approaching him. He turned to the water, and then turned to her again, uncertain now.

"Get back from that edge, you stupid-ass fool. You can't let Mr. Covey get in your head so bad you want to die. He's not worth it. No, he ain't. Now listen to me, honey. It will be over someday. Don't you believe me?"

Frederick turned and stepped away from the edge toward her. He was grateful that she had saved him from his darkest thoughts. But he was also ashamed that she knew him all too well. He denied her now, saying, "I don't know what you're talking about. I was just looking at my . . ."

"Shut up and get over here now."

He obeyed, and she pulled him toward the house. "I can't keep doing this, following you to the cliff and all. I can't stop you if you're determined. But I'll kick your ass in hell when we get there for not listening to me."

Sundays were especially difficult.

On the Sabbath, he could go to the Bayshore, watch the passing ships with their white sails going north, as he had done not too long ago, dreaming of Baltimore and beyond, where the Edward Coveys and Thomas Aulds could not live, where the air was so pure that only freedom-lovers could survive.

Every Sunday after supper, Covey would convene the entire household in the parlor for evening service, prayer, readings from the Bible, and song. He told them all that he enjoyed Frederick's rich, deep voice, and expected him to lead the singing. Frederick always obliged, trying to please, hoping to placate, still bargaining with a deaf God in heaven. But by Monday morning, the grueling work, the inspections, and the floggings returned, as if Sunday had been a dream.

34.

FREDERICK COULD NOT KNOW by three o'clock this August day that his life would never be the same.

By then, as usual, his head ached, and his legs trembled in the hot, moist air that smothered trees and smeared the sky with a thick, gray haze. Frederick dropped to his knees by the side of the wheat fan and, releasing the tub in his hand, fell on his back, groaning. He closed his eyes, waiting for Bill and the other hands, recently hired, to help him.

The fan had stopped because four men were needed to work it in the treading yard, but the other three didn't move after Frederick's collapse when they saw Covey at the door of his house one hundred yards away. He came forward to investigate, a deep frown on his face. A successful harvest demanded constant work from dawn until the last light of day, when it was too dark to see anything. Failure meant more work, less sleep, less money, or the whip.

Frederick crawled to the nearby fence and lay under the rails. He tried to breathe evenly, but nausea and the wheat dust from the fan made him vomit.

"What's the matter?" Covey asked, standing over him.

"I'm sick. When I stooped down, blood went to my head, and . . ."

Covey kicked Frederick's side with his boot. "Get up, you lazy nigger. Now!"

The blow jarred Frederick's entire body. He was sure some vital organ had ruptured. Nonetheless, Frederick struggled to rise with one knee. He had to get up. He couldn't endure another kick.

But he fell back.

Covey kicked him again with greater force. "Get up!"

Frederick again struggled to rise. He could see his dead body soaked with blood and shrouded by caked wheat dust, straw, and dried sweat.

He had to get up.

Somehow, he managed to find his footing and stumbled over to the fan, where he had dropped the tub. But when he stooped over to retrieve it, he fell again, the head pain now so severe that in one blinding moment it seemed to melt his bones.

Without a word, Covey picked up the hard hickory slab used to level off the wheat at the half-bushel measure and struck Frederick in the head. "If you have a headache, I'll cure you! Get up, damn you, you no-good, worthless nigger. Get up!"

Frederick lay still. He decided that rising now could not change the course of his worthless and miserable life. *Kill me, just kill me*, he silently begged Covey. *End it all.*

But Covey did nothing more and returned to the house, leaving Frederick on the ground. Bill Smith and the other men rushed over when it was clear that Covey would not return.

"Boy, you alright? Freddy, do you hear me?" asked Bill.

Glad to hear any voice other than Covey's, Frederick mumbled repeatedly, "Yes . . . yes . . . yes."

"I ain't ever seen that man so damn mad," Bill said. "What is it with him that makes him do this to you? You now do everthin' he tells you, and still, it ain't 'nough. Damn, he's crazy."

Shaking his head, Bill went on, "The snake's forgotten you ain't his. You is Captain Auld's nigger, not his. He can't just do like he was yo' massa. You the property of Captain Thomas, *his* property."

Frederick started. Bill's rambling words now reminded him of a fact that he had forgotten. He was the property of Thomas Auld, and as property he could expect protection. He had value. Thomas Auld was too cheap and too anxious about material success to allow one of his assets to be permanently damaged by a maniac who could, indeed, break the spirit of a rebellious slave.

"I'm leaving," said Frederick, gently pulling away from Bill.

"Where you going?" asked Bill. No one could leave the Covey farm without Covey's permission.

"I'm going to Captain Thomas. He'll keep me from getting hit again. He won't let this happen again."

"You're crazed by losin' all this blood, that's all. Now just let's help you and stop all this foolish talk about leavin'."

"Don't stop me."

Bill lifted his hand. His voice was resigned. "Boy, I ain't goin' to stop you. If you has to do this, you gotta do it, but I don't think that . . ."

"No, don't say it, please. Just let me be."

Frederick looked to the house to see if Covey watched behind the curtain or stood at the door. "Thanks for helpin' me," he said and started out toward the woods, crossing the open field.

Every few seconds, he looked back to the house, anticipating Covey's discovery, and so Frederick accelerated his pace and increased the distance between himself and the farm. He started to run and stopped looking back, even though blood from the gash started to flow freely over his eyes and nose.

He heard Covey's screaming voice: "Come back! Come back!" I'll beat your nigger ass again! You'll wish you were dead when I finish . . ."

Covey ordered his horse to be brought out and saddled. When Frederick could see Covey riding toward him, he rushed into the thick of the trees, avoiding the main road. He hid in the covered brush and waited until the path to St. Michaels, seven miles away, was clear. His bare feet were cut by rocks and brambles, and the blood from his head wound had soaked his clothes.

He lay on the ground for three quarters of an hour, soothed by the cool breeze, the shade of the trees and dreams of deliverance by Thomas Auld, who had never bothered to write and inquire about Covey's progress. Frederick had nothing else but the hope in Thomas Auld's commitment to the value of his property.

After five hours, Frederick found himself at the front of Thomas Auld's Cherry Street store. Frederick knocked at the front door, and Thomas opened it, grumbling about the lateness of the hour as he held up a lighted candle. Thomas groaned when he saw his slave splattered with blood from head to foot. Frederick's hair was matted, his shirt stiff, and his feet scarred and torn. He looked as if vultures or wolves had shredded his clothes and skin trying to tear him apart.

"Oh, my God. What did this to you? In heaven's name . . ."

Frederick rushed to explain. He started with a general account of how he had spent the year trying to please Mr. Covey, working as hard as he could, never defying him. Then he moved on to that day's incident as another example of his good will and Covey's evil designs. Thomas grimly paced the floor with his hands at his back and shook his head at the mention of ghastly details. "I can't believe it," he concluded, deeply agitated. "Such behavior is beyond a true Christian's way, and he almost killed you. I just can't believe . . ."

"He did this, sir. He did. . ."

Thomas admitted, "I never intended for him to hurt you like this, not like this."

Thomas continued to ramble, and as he spoke, Frederick could see and hear a change in Thomas's face and voice. They seemed to have hardened.

"Mr. Covey is only interested in a day's work, and he just didn't think that you were sick. He is accustomed to niggers faking a day's work. It's better to make sure about such faking with a kick to the side than let some nigger think that dizziness is a good excuse for not working. You probably deserved the beating, knowing you, even if you were sick. It's just like you to anger a man. Today was just the opportunity he was waiting for . . ."

He went on, proclaiming the rights of breakers and the natural insubordination of slaves. Frederick shuddered. The shock of recognition was cold as any swirling wind from the Chesapeake. The brotherhood of the white man, Frederick could see, was a solid circle, fixed and absolute. Even profit had no power to break it.

"Well, what do you want me to do?" Thomas demanded at last.

Frederick hesitated. He could not afford another charge of impudence, not now.

"Well, what do want from me, boy?"

"Please, master, don't send me back to Mr. Covey's. Send me someplace else. I'll work hard. Just don't send me back there. He'll kill me."

"Nonsense. Covey's a hardworking, religious man. He won't break the commandments and threaten his soul. Besides, you can't leave Covey now. I'll lose half the year's rent he paid me if you leave. You still belong to Covey for one year. That's the agreement, and you must go back and stay until Christmas season, come what will."

"But . . ."

"Don't trouble me with more stories about Covey. Now go at once, or I'll have to whip you myself."

Frederick stepped back. "Please, sir, not tonight. Just not tonight. I'll do what you tell me, but I'm sick, and . . ."

Tears filled his eyes.

Thomas relented with a huff. "Oh, all right. But first thing in the morning, you're getting yourself back to Covey, you understand?"

"Yes, sir."

Frederick hoped that the morning light could soften Thomas, make him more conciliatory, more open to persuasion. And a good night's rest could also make Frederick more persuasive, his words, his scars and bruises irrefutable arguments in the light of a sunny day.

As an afterthought, Thomas added, "Oh yes, you'll need to dress that gash." He went behind his counter, reached for a box, and handed it to Frederick. "Use this Epsom salt. The cut will feel better afterward."

"Yes, sir."

"Sleep here in the back on the floor. Don't go in the house or get out of here before sunrise. No one is goin' to see you. And don't think you're going to change my mind. You understand, Freddy?"

"Yes, sir."

Thomas left the store, and Frederick found his corner. Now calm, he realized again that he was hungry. He tensed his stomach, knowing that Thomas had no intention of offering him a piece of bread. He would leave before dawn, hungry still.

Where's Eliza? he thought before he fell asleep.

★

Frederick arrived at Haddon by nine o'clock. As soon as he stepped over the fence, Covey rushed out from a hiding place, brandishing a long cowskin whip and rope. But Frederick, reacting like a rabbit cornered by a fox, immediately jumped over the fence and ran into the cornfield to hide behind the tall stalks.

Covey thrashed the thick leaves as he ranted. "You goddamn black nigger bastard. I'm goin' to get you, and when I do, you're going to wish you had never been born. I'm going to strip the skin off your body. You won't be worth a damn thing after I finish with you. If you know what's good for you, you better come, now, you goddamn, black nigger, you lazy, no-count, good-for-nothin' bastard . . ."

Frederick ran further into the field and successfully eluded Covey, whose bark eventually softened. Frederick could hear only the rustling of the corn leaves now. Covey abandoned his search.

Frederick was not ready yet for the lash. Still exhausted by hunger and the anticipation of Covey or bounty hunters, he retreated into the wood and finally went to sleep.

During the night, he heard footsteps and scurried to hide himself.

"Who's that?" asked a gentle voice. "I know you ain't no animal."

Frederick recognized the voice and came out to the road from the bushes. "Sandy? Is that you?"

"Fred? Fred? What you doin' here?"

It was Sandy Jenkins, a slave belonging to William Groomes of Easton and now hired out to Mrs. Covey's father. He was on his way to spend Saturday night and Sunday with his wife, a free woman who lived in Pot Pie Neck, south of Haddon, in her own house on her own lot.

Frederick described the last two days, and Sandy sympathized with him, shaking his head, and repeating, "Um, um, um, if that don't beat all. . ." When Frederick finished his story, Sandy invited him to spend the night at his wife's house.

Frederick protested: "If Covey finds out, or tells your massa that you were hiding me, they'll give you the thirty-nine tails . . ."

"Dey won't find out," he said. "Mr. Covey will just think you spent the night in de woods, that's all."

Frederick left Sandy's house that Sunday morning. When he entered the yard gate, Covey and his wife, dressed in their Sunday best, stepped off the porch to mount the cart for the long ride to church. Frederick stopped at once and looked for the clearest way to escape. But before he could decide, Covey was before him with a serene smile. Nodding his head once as he looked down he said, "Good morning, Fred. It's a beautiful Sabbath day. I know this is a day of rest, but I need you to drive the pigs out of the lot. They got into the lot early this morning. I'm sure the Lord won't mind and will make an exception. The rest of the day is yours to do as you please."

Before dawn that next morning, Covey shouted his first command of the day at the kitchen door, ordering Frederick to feed, rub, and curry the horses. Frederick rose at once, determined to do swiftly whatever he was told, and hurried to the stables.

He started to climb the ladder to the loft, where the blades were stored, when Covey's hand grabbed Frederick's right leg and pulled him down to the stable floor, trying to slip a knot around his legs before he could draw them up. Quickly recovering from the shock, Frederick grabbed Covey by the throat. Startled, Covey hit Frederick on the side, then on the head. But Frederick would not let go. The raw brutal force of his grip seemed unnatural, demonic, deadly. His fingernails drew blood.

They rolled on the ground, Covey overturning Frederick, then Frederick overturning him. Moaning, Covey punched Frederick again and again, but Frederick would not punch back, determined to only defend himself.

Frederick managed to pull Covey up, hoping that this move would give Covey the opportunity to let go and withdraw. But Covey only kicked at his legs, trying to make Frederick fall. Frederick had to throw him down again, and they rolled in the dust again, gasping for air, sweating, grappling for body parts.

"You mean to resist," Covey said stupidly, as if the obvious had finally penetrated.

"Yes, sir."

"You nigger scoundrel."

To Frederick's surprise, Covey called out for help. "Jimmy! Jimmy, help me! Help!"

Covey's young cousin, ugly, skinny, and stupid, ran into the stable as if on cue. Frederick jumped up, holding Covey by one arm as he prepared to fight Jimmy. At that moment Frederick realized how small a man Covey was. He danced at the end of Frederick's arm like a flopping fish out of water.

Jimmy tried to catch and tie Frederick's arm, but Frederick evaded him by constantly turning around. Prematurely, Jimmy exclaimed, "I've got him! I've got him!"

Frederick kicked the distracted Jimmy in the groin. Jimmy collapsed at the waist, bending over with a deep moan before staggering out of the stable.

"You fuckin' Black nigger. Good for nothing . . . low down . . ." Covey was losing control. His cool strength had ebbed, and he was now just standing there puffing and blowing.

Frederick said calmly, "I won't stand it no longer. I'll never let you beat me again."

"What?" cried Covey. With suddenly renewed strength, he lunged toward the stable door, pulling Frederick behind him. Outside, Covey leaned over to get a large stick, but he was unable to reach it when Frederick snatched him by the collar and threw him into the dung of the cow yard. Now smeared with it, Covey rushed toward Frederick and grabbed him. They fell into the muck and rolled over and over, smearing clothes and skin, each unwilling to release the other, all the while Covey striking at Frederick, Frederick holding back arms and legs as best he could.

Bill Smith entered the yard after spending Sunday night with a woman. Covey called for help. "Get 'im. Take 'im. Do something!"

Bill grinned and asked unctuously, "What you want me to do, Mr. Covey?"

"Take hold of 'im, you fool nigger, take hold of 'im."

"I wanna work, Mr. Covey, that's all."

"This is your work, nigger. Take hold!"

"My master hired me to work, not help you whip Fred."

"Get your ass . . ."

Frederick interrupted, shouting to Bill, "Don't put your hands on me!"

Bill walked away, shaking his head, and saying, "My God, Fred. I ain't goin' to touch you."

Covey screamed at him to come back, but Bill never looked back, deaf and dumb.

Caroline entered the yard for the morning milking, and Covey was revived again. He tightened his grip and ordered her to intervene. "Caroline, get hold of 'im! And do it now!"

"Dat ain't my job." She walked on with a slight swing of her hips, flagrantly ignoring the fact that as Covey's slave she was taking the greatest risk.

"You, Black bitch."

After two hours, Covey gave up. He released Frederick, stood, and announced, as if he had succeeded. "There will be more of this if you don't do what you're told. Now git back to work."

Frederick took a deep breath, trying to get fresh air through the stench of his clothes, and grinned in the gray morning light as he watched Covey go into his house. He was no longer afraid.

If you try to whip me again, Mr. Covey, you will have to kill me. You will have to kill me because I will never let you hurt me.

Covey's fight with Frederick was the talk of St. Michaels and the entire county. Everyone speculated about Covey's refusal to complain to the sheriff or his neighbors. In fact, he behaved as if the fight never happened, barking orders, and making threats as usual. Caroline and Frederick agreed that Covey didn't want whites to know that a breaker, perhaps the most notorious in Talbot County, had lost a fight with a boy. But this explanation seemed inadequate. Such a fight could not be kept a secret. There was little else to talk about on the Bayside. Word had reached St. Michaels, and Thomas Auld sent word to Covey to stop whipping his slave.

And he stopped. Covey never touched Frederick again.

Frederick received another reward. Impressed by Frederick's strength, Caroline offered herself, taking him by the hand to the loft of the barn. "Merry Christmas," she said.

By the year's end, Covey's contract expired, and Frederick was sent to William Freeland's farm nearby for another contracted year. Freeland was not a slave breaker, only a farmer who needed more help. He told Frederick, "I don't beat my slaves. I only want a good day's work until sundown, and what you do after dark and on Sunday doesn't matter to me."

35.

ALTHOUGH SANDY JENKINS WAS older than Frederick by about four years, he looked up to Frederick for his courage, his strength, and, more importantly, his ability to read and write and tell all kinds of stories, especially Bible stories, and his willingness to teach others their letters and how to write their names. They became friends.

Sandy introduced Frederick to a small group of friends, including brothers Henry and John Harris, Charles Roberts, Henry Bailey, no relation to Frederick, all young slaves who wanted to be free.

Frederick organized another school. He and his students met behind Freeland's barn or in the woods on a Sunday afternoon where Frederick taught his eager pupils the alphabet, using discarded Webster spellers, and read from the Bible and his copy of *The Columbian Orator*.

By mid-summer Frederick had twenty pupils. And by winter, the enrollment swelled to almost forty men, women, and children. Frederick was now teaching three nights a week and on Sundays in the house of a free Black man who offered it as a more secure haven. The school remained unmolested. As the months went by, Sandy could tell that Frederick was happy.

As it turned out, he was too happy.

After telling his friends that the new year, 1836, had to be his "freedom year," Frederick explained why.

Slowly, without notice, William Freeland's farm had become a cocoon, sapping his desire to break out. He had become the contented slave. Almost. He wanted to be free. Well treated, though he was, he was still a slave, and a slave for life.

"If I don't leave, I'll be here forever."

Then he shared the possible plans.

He could go by land, travel down the peninsula through Talbot County to Caroline County, or go by sea, sailing north. The first route seemed more reasonable, and thus more predictable. Frederick decided to take the second. As far as he knew, no one had dared to escape that way.

Always ready to interpret dangers in the wind and skies, Sandy listened carefully and objected vigorously. "We could starve or drown or be eaten by dogs, tearing us to pieces with fangs and no mercy. There is scorpions in them woods, and we might get hungry or even starve. We might not have clothes, and them kidnappers might get us, shoot at us, even kill us. We might . . ."

Henry Harris stopped him with a gentle, dismissing hand on his shoulder and a broad smile. "Now, Sandy, you know how your brain runs away with you. Frederick's right. If we just listen to him, we'll be fine. He knows more than we do, and he's been to Baltimore and seen things we knows nothing about. So, try to calm down."

Sandy was jealous, thinking that he should be Frederick's favorite, not Henry, who Frederick openly favored. One day, Frederick had foolishly confessed that he could die with and for Henry and his brother, they were so close. When he realized his error, he added a hasty correction, "And for all of you."

But the damage was done. Sandy said nothing more that night, but throughout February and March, when they met to discuss and polish their plans on Sunday nights, the objections continued from Sandy, who had the most to lose. He had a free wife. His life was easy, settled, and stable. No slave master had ever mistreated him. Frederick answered every objection with the even tone of an experienced teacher or leader, stoic and clear-headed.

As Easter approached, the men overcame their misgivings and became buoyant. They repeated passwords, sang songs, shouted joyous exclamations in unlikely places. The men shouted one song repeatedly and took pleasure in the knowledge that its double meaning protected them from suspicion:

I thought I heard them say,
There were lions in the way,
I don't expect to stay
Much longer here.
Run to Jesus—shun the danger
I don't expect to stay
Much longer here.

Sandy had a dream that he shared with Frederick two Sundays before Easter. He had taken Frederick to the Freeland barn, leading him by the arm, his fingers trembling.

"I dreamed I was awakened by a swarm of angry birds. They made a roarin' sound as they passed overhead, and I saw you, Fred, in de claws of a big bird. That bird was surrounded by other birds with many colors, and they were pickin' at you, takin' pieces of your body with their mouths. You tried to protect yourself, but they kept on pickin'. Then all of them birds flew to the southwest until they was outa sight." Sandy sighed heavily. "That was some dream," he concluded.

Frederick pulled his arm away. "What are you going to do about it?"

"That dream's telling me that we shouldn't go. The escape will lead to nothing but trouble, for us all, and especially for you."

"We'll miss you," said Frederick, turning his head. There was no more to be said.

"Dreams tell it like it is."

"I'm leavin', dream or no dream."

"I can't. I has to stay. I will pray for you all. I want you to follow the North Star and get to freedom land. But I just won't be able to see it."

"Like Moses on the mountain."

"I'm no Moses, that's for sure."

"Our brother always," Frederick said, embracing him quickly.

"Always."

36.

THE OTHERS WERE DEEPLY shaken by Sandy's defection. They gamely tried to accept his reasons, but the unity of the group had been a primary source of its perseverance. Frederick had to spend hours undoing the damage, assuring his friends and fellow conspirators that a smaller group was better to manage in the long run. Their plan was simple but vague: steal a canoe from Hambleton's farm, paddle north up the Chesapeake to Pennsylvania, and trek overland to Philadelphia, even though Frederick had only a vague sense of geography.

At a secret meeting on the Wednesday before Easter Sunday, the remaining five clasped hands and swore to escape together, and to fight and die rather than accept bondage. To seal their pledge, Frederick wrote passes for them all to carry.

The pass read: "This is to certify, that I, the undersigned, have given the bearer, my servant full liberty to go to Baltimore, to spend the Easter holidays. William Hambleton, near St. Michaels, Talbot County, Maryland."

He explained how they were to use the document if they needed to produce it. "Be respectful, answer their questions," Frederick warned them. "But don't show them papers unless the answers you give them hunters, or any white people, just don't satisfy. Don't volunteer. Show it last, when there's nothing left to do."

The men stared at their documents as if Frederick had dusted their hands with gold.

"This is it," said Henry, struck by the enormity of their decision. "We're leavin'. We are really goin' to freedom land." Tears began to well up in his eyes.

"We have to practice what we're goin' to say if they stop us," said Frederick. "We'll do this several times before we leave on Sunday. Now listen . . ." He tried to exude confidence because they all needed it, including himself.

But Frederick was made anxious by waiting. He cursed the sun for rising and setting at its usual pace, ate little, and slept only a few hours a night. By Friday night, he could not sleep at all. He had stirred up his friends with his dreams, conceived a plan that guaranteed nothing, and encouraged them to give up everything they knew and loved—home, family, the sweet air of honeysuckle and roses in summer. Because of him, they could all die, be hunted down by bounty runners, chained, and then strangled by twisted ropes. Or at the least they could be sold at the New Orleans Market, prime bucks going for at least $1,500 each.

The last day of bondage came on Saturday after another sleepless night. Everything was done. Food and clothes were packed, directions rehearsed, the plan finalized, and pledges made. The six men, including Sandy, who had remained steadfast in his decision to not escape, went out to the fields as usual to spread manure. They separated into teams, Sandy and Frederick in one, the Harris brothers in another, and Charles Roberts and Henry Bailey in the third.

Frederick worked his field at a steady pace. There was nothing unusual in the air. Then he felt it, a deep fear that quickened his heart and dried his mouth. He felt as if he had been struck by lightning.

Frederick turned to Sandy Jenkins nearby and said calmly, "Sandy, we're betrayed. Something has just told me."

"Man, that's strange. But I feel just like you."

They both heard the horn that summoned them to breakfast and reluctantly left the field, going to what awaited at the farm.

Near the house, Frederick looked to the lane gate at the main road and noticed six men approaching, four whites on horseback and two Blacks, their hands tied, walking behind. One horse broke away and galloped up the lane toward the house, stirring the dust, obscuring the two men who were now tied to the gate.

Oh, Lord. Frederick realized that the rider was William Hambleton. Hambleton was old and fat and always rode his horse slowly to protect his dignity. Today he didn't care, his jowls, belly, and posterior bouncing on the saddle.

It's all over. Frederick was sure that the men tied at the gate were Henry Bailey and Charles Roberts.

"Where's Mr. Freeland?" Hambleton asked, breathing deeply like he had just emerged from a near drowning.

Without alarm, Frederick replied, "In the barn, sir."

"Sandy. Come with me."

Without another word, Hambleton rode to the barn, and Sandy followed, his face too calm as far as Frederick was concerned. Frederick saw that two of the other white men were the constables Tom Graham and Ned Hambleton.

Frederick turned toward the kitchen. There was nothing else to do but wait inside. He tried to stay calm, unwilling to reveal his complicity in the crime. He desperately struggled to hide his terror. Cold sweat covered his entire body, and he shuddered like a man in the snow of winter. The morning April air was still cool and brisk.

Mr. Hambleton, Mr. Freeland, and Henry were at the kitchen door, followed by the three white men who had charged into the front yard, dismounted quickly, and tied their horses.

Freeland's voice trembled, but he spoke as he always did, like a gentleman.

"Fred, please come forward. There are some men who want to see you."

Frederick obliged, asking, "What do they want, sir?"

Tom Graham pushed Freeland aside and grabbed Frederick by the arms.

"Nigger, you betta not resist," Tom said, gritting his teeth. "You might be in a lot of trouble."

Frederick didn't move. Effort seemed pointless.

Freeland remained rational. Only a true gentleman could ease the difficulties of this day. While Tom and Ned tied Frederick to a chair, Freeland explained what was going to happen next. "They will take you to St. Michaels for an examination before your master, and if the evidence isn't true, then you'll be acquitted."

He smiled indulgently, like a father unable to believe that his son is a criminal. He turned to John Harris and said, "You're next, boy." John was tied without a struggle.

Hambleton, still puffing, said mildly, "Perhaps we had now better make a search for those protections, which we understand he has written for himself and the rest."

How did he know about them, Frederick thought wildly, *Who told? Did Sandy tell? Where's Sandy?*

The impatient Constable Tom turned to Henry and ordered him to cross his hands so that he could be tied.

Henry shook his head and said in a firm voice, "No, I won't."

"Now, won't you cross your hands?" Tom asked.

"No, I won't."

"Sheeeeit," cried the third constable, who pulled out a pistol. "You better cross them hands, nigger, or by God I'll shoot your Black ass down."

Henry looked down at the pistol and said softly, "No."

The cocking of three pistols snapped the air, energizing everyone in a split second. The white men aimed their weapons at Henry's chest. Frederick strained in his chair to free his hands from their bounds.

"If you don't cross them hands right now," said Tom. "I'll blow your damn heart right outa you!"

Henry heaved his chest and shouted into the man's face, "Shoot! Shoot me. You can only do it one time. Shoot, shoot and be damned. I won't be tied!" He raised his arms and knocked the pistols out of their hands. Everyone now rushed forward to pummel Henry with their fists. Henry fell, swinging and kicking. The room rumbled with blows and curses and overturned furniture.

"I'm goin' to kill you," ranted Tom. "Kill you!"

Frederick calculated his advantage. He could get rid of his pass while Tom and the others struggled to subdue Henry. He had only a few seconds. The fight would soon be over, and Henry would be dead or beaten into a pulpy mass of blood, torn skin and muscle. There was nothing he could do about that.

He noticed the crackling fire was a short distance from his chair. He lifted the chair with his legs, since his captors had not bothered to bind them, and dropped it down three times before he was directly in front of the flames. With straining fingers, he probed for the pass in the right pocket of his trousers. Frederick pushed further, stretching to snag the folds of paper between two fingers. Finally, he had it, and pulled the paper out of the pocket.

Frederick looked back at the flame, measuring the distance, and tossed it. The flames consumed it within seconds.

Soon, Henry was subdued. His face quickly swelling with bloody cuts, he was unable to speak.

Mr. Freeland's mother came into the kitchen from the house holding a plate of biscuits. Old but still vibrant in voice and blue eyes, she lovingly whispered to the brothers raised on her farm since childhood and offered them fresh baked bread. "You'll need food on your way to the county jail. Be good. I know you'll be just fine. You didn't do anything wrong. You'll come back to me, now won't you, boys?"

Before they could answer, she turned to Frederick and screamed, "You devil! You yellow devil! It was you that put it into their heads to run away. Thank God, Sandy told us your plan. But for you, you long-legged yellow devil, they would have never thought of running away."

Frederick returned her attack with all the venom his eyes could project, and she cried out, horrified, "You'll burn!"

Freeland now shook his head and asked with deep pain and disappointment, "Why? Why? I know I treated you boys well, better than anyone else in Talbot County. I never thought you could be so ungrateful, so ungrateful."

★

The arrested slaves marched, pulled by ropes behind two horses along the road to St. Michaels, three miles away. Men, women, and children had gathered along the way and jeered. A few threw stones.

The constables laughed, too, and turned around to pull at the ropes of their captives. Tom Graham shouted, "You niggers are goin' to die. We ain't havin' another Nat Turner uprisin' in these parts. Damn, I can't wait to see you hang!"

This time there would be no slaughter of the innocent women and children caught in their beds, paralyzed by the vision of their trusted slaves wielding hatchets in the shadows. No anxious days as rumors spread and militias formed to fight the rampaging Black hordes. Acting swiftly, Tom and Ned and the masters of Talbot County had stopped the insurrection before it started, capturing its leader, and marching him to the scaffold. Maryland would stay safe for white people.

Henry Harris whispered, "What should I do with my pass?"

Startled, Frederick asked, "What?"

Softer, Henry repeated the question.

"Eat it."

"What?"

"Eat it with your biscuit."

Henry grimaced, swallowing an imaginary sheet of paper.

"Pass the word," ordered Frederick. "Own nothing!"

Graham turned in his saddle. "You niggers shut yo' goddamn mouths." He quickened his horse's pace, and the men stumbled behind as the clouds of dust clogged throats and nostrils, making them cough. They stepped carefully, for fear of being dragged like timber.

His hands tied loosely, Henry pulled the pass out of his pocket to his mouth, and started chewing.

"Tell the others," whispered Frederick as Henry struggled to soften the paper.

Henry swallowed, gagging a little, and whispered to Charles to eat his pass also. Soon, all the passes were eliminated.

With the disposal of the most incriminating evidence, Frederick became more sanguine. After all, they had done nothing. They plotted no insurrection, or murders. They talked of freedom, even dreamed of escape, but what slave had not?

"Own nothing!" he said again, reinforcing his resolve.

Soon he stood before Thomas Auld, who paced the porch of his store in St. Michaels, angry and troubled.

"I know that you all are guilty," he said solemnly, as if a claim of knowledge could compel confessions, "and you should admit it right now. It would be better for you all if you did."

"We did nothing," declared Frederick.

Frederick's friends immediately responded in unison: "Nothing!"

"The evidence is clear," Thomas said. "You were plotting an escape. It's so clear that if this was a case of murder, you would all hang!"

Emboldened, Frederick asserted, "But this is not a case of murder, and the cases are not equal. If murder was committed, then someone must have committed it. The thing is done! In our case, nothing has been done! We have not run away. We were quietly at work. Where is the evidence against us?"

Tom Graham's gaped as if a dog had suddenly stood up on its hind legs and made a speech. He rose in his saddle, recovering from the shock. "When are you goin' to shut this nigger up? I can't believe you would allow this nigger to talk to you like he's some white man."

"Take them to the county jail, damn it," sputtered Thomas.

He turned and walked back into his store, leaving the five Negroes in the hands of Graham, who now felt free to abuse Frederick and the others with impunity.

"I ain't goin' to kill you niggers," said Graham. "You ain't my property, but I'm goin to make them fifteen miles to Easton the longest miles you ever took to walkin'. Now get your nigger asses on the road!"

He viciously pulled at the reigns, and the five Negroes were dragged back to the main road, their hands twisted in the ropes.

More had gathered on the road to revile them, their fists raised in the air to punctuate their bitter curses.

Graham and Hambleton joined the citizens in their laughter at their stumbling prisoners as they passed through the neighborhoods.

Negroes were also on the road shaking their heads, standing back without pity, avoiding any threat to themselves, angry that some young fools, by upsetting the white folks, could ruin the peace for the rest of them.

At last, they arrived in Easton, where a crowd waited before the county jail on the public square. The citizens of Easton did not shout or scream, brandish sticks or hurl stones. But their faces were equally ugly distorted by hatred and fear. They whispered, creating a low rumble like the witnesses at an execution.

The county sheriff stepped down the stairs to receive his prisoners and proclaimed, "Let justice be done!"

Only then did the crowd roar its approval.

"Hang the niggers," began the chant, which swelled to a mighty sound within seconds. "Hang the niggers!"

Graham raised his hand to silence it. "People of Easton. There must first be a determination of crime. Then a trial, then a sentence."

"Remember Nat Turner!" shouted one disgruntled man.

The crowd grew ugly, explosive. At any moment things could get out of control. Softly, Graham said to Frederick and the others, "Get inside, boys, before it's too late."

They were hurried inside. Graham put them in two cells, the Harris brothers and Frederick in one, and Charles Roberts and Henry Bailey in the other. The cells were large and comfortable, having three cots and large grated windows that gave them a view of nearby Lowe's Tavern on Federal Street, where they could see Black waiters in white jackets rushing to serve white customers at the tables.

Through the bars of the locked door, Graham informed them of the circumstances. "I'm going to make it as comfortable as possible for you boys while we wait for your masters. There ain't going to be no hangings, even though the folks of Easton would like to see it. The worse that can happen, and I think that's what you're going to see, is that your masters are going to sell you, and you'll be goin' down South, to Alabama or Georgia."

"Oh, God," muttered Frederick, devastated. "They can't do this," he added foolishly.

"Yes, they can," Graham replied. To his point he opened the outer door and allowed in a swarm of slave traders, deputy traders, and agents who rushed forward to laugh and leer through the cell bars. He turned to the eager agents and warned them, "Don't be rough, and keep your hands off delicate areas."

The men laughed before entering the cell while each took turns with probing fingers and measuring sticks to determine health and value. They pried open Frederick's mouth to look at his teeth, poked him in the stomach, squeezed his shoulders, arms, and legs, noting his strength. The Harris brothers stood to the side, waiting their turn. "He's one big fucker, gentlemen," concluded the shortest trader. "He'll get the best price in the market, even if he has a little brain."

Frederick's skin burned, his humiliation as deep as he had ever experienced. He could not hide his offense, and inhaled while flaring his nostrils.

The short trader jumped off the cot, pushed Frederick back against the wall, and yelled out, "Nigger, if I had you, I would cut the devil out of you pretty quick!"

"All right, boys," said Sheriff Graham. "You've seen enough to decide his value. Now you need to move on so he can rest and be ready for Mr. Woolfolk's auction."

Woolfolk? Was he everywhere?

Frederick's despair at what he had lost and was about to lose was so deep that he could not suppress its rise from his soul to his eyes. Nothing but tears could relieve the intense pressure. He fell back against the wall.

"Frederick, Frederick, what's wrong?" pleaded Henry, now that they were all alone again.

"It's all my fault. I'm to blame."

"Man, it ain't your fault," said Henry, approaching him. He put his hand on Frederick's shoulder.

"No, Fred, it ain't," said John, who rarely spoke.

"It was my idea, and now we're losing everything."

"You ain't the only one with the freedom dreams," protested Henry gently. "We grown men. We knew what we was doin'."

"I'm sorry."

"You don't need to tell me sorry. I'm not sorry. We tried. Miss Freeland's wrong. You ain't de cause. She's de fool for thinkin' you de cause."

John, who communicated through song rather than speech, started to sing, his tenor the most beautiful Frederick had ever heard. It comforted and illustrated their yearning to be free. All five prisoners joined together, one by one, to sing their favorite song that promised success in those exciting, heady days when freedom seemed to dance on the wind:

I thought I heard them say,
There were lions in the way.
I don't expect to stay
Much longer here.
Run to Jesus—shun the danger.
I don't expect to stay
Much longer here.

No one interrupted them or called out for silence, and when they were done, they went to the cell door and reached out their hands to their friends in the other cell a few feet away.

"The lions are gone," said Henry. "Gone for today."

On the Tuesday after Easter, Hambleton and Freeland came to Easton for the release of the Harris brothers, Charles Roberts, and Henry Bailey.

"You're going home," said Freeland to Henry, "and there's not going to be any sale or punishment."

"No Woolfolk," said Henry, relieved.

He turned to Frederick, who stood back knowing that the news did not apply to him. Thomas Auld had not come. "What about Fred?"

"He stays."

Sheriff Graham turned the key in the cell door, and Henry stepped back toward Frederick to make one final gesture of loyalty before the final separation.

"You gotta go. It's only right."

"It's not fair. I don't blame you," Henry assured him.

"Take care of your brother," said Frederick, extending his hand to John, who gripped it with fierce determination. It said all that needed to be said.

Freeland said softly, "Boys, it's time."

"Goodbye, my friends."

"Friends, always," said Henry, looking back to Frederick as he crossed the threshold.

"Always."

They were gone, leaving Frederick to contemplate the future. The horror of the cotton field and the sugar plantation loomed before him, a future that was confirmed when the traders returned that afternoon to ask more questions, insulting him with tantalizing remarks. Obviously, they were getting ready for the sale of the season. "One thousand, maybe two thousand," said an impressed trader, who had not been there the first day.

"The bidding will be fierce," confirmed another, nodding his head.

For a week, Frederick waited for the sale, and during that time, he tossed in his sleep, imagining a slow, agonizing torture and finally death from exhaustion and starvation.

Then Master Thomas arrived and, as Sheriff Graham was unlocking the cell, said, "You've been in here long enough. We're going home."

Surprised and relieved, Frederick almost hugged his master, but he resisted the impulse. Thomas hated intimacy of all kinds. He then made his intentions clear, squelching Frederick's enthusiasm. "I've arranged to sell you to a friend in Alabama, who will grant your manumission, on good behavior, after eight years."

Frederick didn't know what to make of this. He never heard of this friend in Alabama and couldn't fathom why a stranger would free a healthy and profit-making slave in eight years. This supposed friend would not be bound to any agreement made with Thomas Auld, who would have to be satisfied with just the bill of sale.

Choosing caution, Frederick did not question Thomas about these arrangements. He would wait and see, and meanwhile enjoy the pleasure of returning to St. Michaels and the comforts of the Auld kitchen. The road back to St. Michaels did not seem to be the same road he had traveled just a week before. The carriage wheels seemed to roll on air, lifted by the high spirits of at least one of the passengers.

Eliza filled him with all the news and dismissed the story of the Alabama friend. But she still had a cautionary story to tell. "I heard Mr. Hambleton in the parlor one night. He was mad as hell and told Captain Thomas to get your ass out of this county or he would shoot you dead himself!"

"And them traders were here day and night, making offers, good offers for you" piped in his stuttering cousin, Tom, the newest member of the household. "But the captain, he said that money couldn't tempt him to sell you south."

"Then he's not goin' to sell me?" asked Frederick.

"No," said Eliza. "We both know he marched the floor the night before he went to Easton to get you out of jail. He was real unhappy, and the next morning, he says to me, 'What am I goin' to do with that boy? I can't let them kill 'im.'"

"He was trying just to scare me," concluded Frederick, amazed.

"He did, didn't he?" asked Eliza.

"What else did he say? What is he going to do, then?"

"I don't know."

Four days later, they found out.

"I'm sending you back to Baltimore," said Thomas in the kitchen before Eliza, Tom, and Frederick, all speechless. "Hugh and I are getting along again, and you can learn a trade in Baltimore. You can't stay here. It's too dangerous. You'll be leaving tomorrow on the next boat."

When Thomas departed, Frederick jumped for joy. "Baltimore! Baltimore! My city!"

Eliza and Tom celebrated with him, forming a dance circle. They understood that he was returning to where he truly belonged. But he had to face another truth. He was leaving his family again, and this time he would never come back. He would die first.

"We have de same blood," Eliza said, taking Frederick by the hand. "But you was not meant to be here, and I was not meant to be there always keeping you clean and making sure that yo ass ain't kicked by some fool. You're a man now. Instead of a big sister over ya, you need a wife."

37.

IT WAS A SUNDAY and Frederick came to the back door. Hugh could hear Sophia's squeal of delight and warm greeting, "Oh, Frederick!" She had overcome her fears of three years ago.

"Now, now, now," said Hugh, "just look what we have here, a buck nigger. They worked you for sure on the Eastern Shore, and you're what we need now in the yards."

"Thank you, sir," replied Frederick, unsmiling. "It's good to be back. I missed Baltimore. How are the children, and where's Tommy?"

They had been friends once, inseparable companions. But that was long ago before Tommy realized he was white and Frederick was Black. "He's at sea. He was hard to handle, like you were when you left three years ago. We don't miss him. You're not going to be difficult this time, right?"

"No, sir."

"Good. I have plans for you. You'll be learning a trade, a trade needed now more than ever. But things are different."

"How?"

"The Irish. The city is crawling with them, there's as many as the colored now. And they take many of the jobs colored use to take, and they hate you colored, *really* hate you. By comparison, we're saints. Anyway, you had better watch that mouth in the yards. The Irish are dumb, hot heads, and they don't hold back, having to prove that somebody is beneath *them*. But that isn't true. *They* are the lowest of the low; and they are as hypocritical as Thomas, filling their churches with pagan statues, smoke, and Latin prayers on Sundays, and then filling whore houses and taverns all week long! At least, I don't *pretend*. I just go."

He continued his tirade, "I'm not afraid of Hell. Could it be any worse than living in this house, living in the city with everything falling apart, with banks closing, with jobs disappearing, with panic spreading like a plague; and the rats are everywhere, Irish rats, nigger rats, abolitionist rats, all rats."

Sophia deflected Hugh's rant. "Fred, you will help us. The money you earn will help, and when you are not in the yards, you can help with the cleaning and the children."

"And they are a handful," continued Hugh, "always squalling, always eating and wanting more and more . You'll start work at the yards as soon as I can make arrangements. You'll have the room under the roof, like in the other house. But, you might not be able to fit, and your big feet will not rest on the bed. But you'll have to make do."

"Yes, sir."

"Take him up, Sophia."

They turned to leave, and Hugh asked, "Are you still saved like Miss Sophia and brother Thomas?"

Frederick didn't answer.

Hugh said, "I expect you'll be going to Church with Sophia and the children on Sundays, and then to one of the colored churches later and during the week. I don't care. Just don't show me how *saved* you are. I won't stand for it, and by the way, that nigger Charles Lawson, the one you spent all that time with, even though I told you not to, he's *dead*. They found him in his hut in the alley. He just died, I heard; stopped breathing. Just might be in hell for teaching you what slaves shouldn't know."

Frederick stiffened, but said nothing.

Sophia dared to console him, touching his arm. "He was a good Christian. Everybody thought so."

Hugh said, "Well, all you saved folks stand together until you all start arguing about what you believe; and then the killing over baptism, the resurrection, the Bible, the Holy Ghost and all the rest starts. Well, I'll I have *none* of it. Why, even the colored churches can't agree about slavery, what you coloreds should do about it: pray for heaven or pray for deliverance. You know the good Lord will not be stepping in real soon to stop it, especially since he's allowed it since the time of Moses and the Pharaoh, if not before that. And if you think *anybody* is going to end it here and now, you already know what will happen, and you can be bloody sure the Irish will be leading the pack."

Frederick didn't reply.

"Good, you *do* know when to keep your mouth shut, after all."

Sophia asked, "May we leave now?"

"Yes, you're still the good wife."

As promised, Hugh found work for him as an apprentice caulker. Two large warships for the Mexican government, the brigs *Independence* and the *Fourth of July*, needed construction workers for a contract that required completion by July.

Trouble with the Irish had started before Frederick's arrival at Gardner's Yard, where whites and Blacks worked together for years doing the same skilled work for almost equal pay. Then the Irish came in large numbers, and they were having none of this. The white carpenters boycotted the yard, insisting that all the free Blacks had to be fired before the whites returned to work.

The free Blacks were all fired; only one Black remained, an apprentice slave: Frederick. The white carpenters did not demand that he go too, but they ordered him about as if they were all his masters and encouraged the white apprentices to torment him as much as possible. Mr. Gardiner told Frederick the eighty white carpenters were now all his masters, and "their word was law."

Frederick needed a dozen hands, and never could work fast enough as the whites called out their orders:

"Fred, come help me cart this here timber."

"Fred, bring that roller here."

"Darkie, heat that damn pitch!"

Frederick endured the racial slurs, the pranks, the loss of tools, the kicks and pushes for months, reporting it all to Hugh daily. Almost every sentence spoken to him had a curse attached. He refrained from being specific about the most profane words, showing the customary deference. Hugh even laughed uproariously with Frederick when he told his story about Ned North, who took a swing at him. He missed, and Frederick, after plowing into him with the butt of his head, and making him lose his balance, picked him up and threw him into the dock. Frederick told other stories about defending himself when attacked, and Hugh never objected.

But then four turned on him at once, and Frederick showed up at the house with his face and shirt splattered with blood. Sophia screamed when she saw him; he had been kicked in the eye. She then covered her mouth with the back of her hand, unable to move.

"Help me," Frederick pleaded once, and fell to the floor, fainting.

"Oh, my God, what have they done? Freddy, you're home, and I'm here. I'll take care of you. Say something, please."

Sophia cradled him in her arms, and when Frederick regained consciousness, he whispered, "Miss Sopha, Miss Sopha, my eye, my eye."

Hugh dropped to his knees beside his wife. "No, no, no, they didn't do this to you. They wouldn't *dare* . . ."

Sophia applied wet cloths to his eye and bruised skin, wiping the blood away to determine the extent of his injuries, giving him a cup of water to drink. She told Frederick, "You won't be blind. You will see again. You'll see. Everything's going to be all right. Don't worry."

"Yes, Miss Sopha," he whispered again.

"What happened?" demanded Hugh. "I need to know. Fred, tell me."

Frederick started to speak, but he winced with pain. Sophia spoke up for him. "Hugh, he can't talk. It's hurting him."

Hugh helped to take Frederick up to his room and reminded them what he expected. "I need a full account, an absolutely full account after you get back up. Do you understand?"

Frederick slept uninterrupted for hours.

Sophia redressed his bandage, and Frederick, although still weak, told the story with graphic details. It all started when Ned Hays, still humiliated after the water tossing, blamed Frederick for bending a bolt, and Frederick snapped back, without deference, "You did it, not me!"

Hays grabbed a large hard ax and rushed at Frederick. "Why you . . ."

Frederick parried his swing with a maul, and they glared at each other, poised for the next move. But neither of them took that step; they knew that it would mean the death of one or both. They separated, still holding their weapons at the sides. But then Hays returned with reinforcements that Monday afternoon near the end of the workday, North in the front with a brick which he tossed from one hand to the other, Steward and Humphries on the sides, and Hays at the back armed with a pike. A crowd of fifty shouted for blood: "Kill the damn nigger! Kill him!"

Frederick struggled to focus on the weapons and simultaneously devise a strategy for winning. But he was disoriented by murderous numbers surrounding him. Suddenly four closed in, and Frederick started swinging wildly at the two in front.

Someone cried out, "Knock his brains out. He struck a white man!"

Hays hit him in the head from behind with a handspike, and Frederick fell to his knees, stunned as the air turned black and red around him. The white apprentices pounded him with fists and bricks. The sound of caving skin, cracking bones, grunts and groans, and the roar of the approving crowed sealed off the world.

Frederick tried to rise, ignoring the searing pain at the back of his head. He had to get up and fight on. Frederick concentrated every vestige of pride and his hatred of white trash flowed freely through his body. He pushed up with his hands and knees. North kicked him in the eye, his boot splitting tissue with such heavy force that bright red blood splattered Frederick's face and shirt.

The crowd groaned and stepped back, horrified and yet satisfied too. The fight was over; nothing more needed to be done. It seemed that Frederick's eyeball had burst and within seconds it was completely shut.

Exhausted, Frederick lay moaning on the ground, his pain matched by the fear that he was blind in one eye, disfigured for life, unable to work as a caulker, and certain he would be murdered for defending himself. Legally, the punishment was thirty-nine lashes, but he also knew about "Judge Lynch's law" which decreed death to any Negro who hit a white man. The mob was judge and jury in Baltimore and preferred a lynching at the nearest tree rather than a hanging at the gallows after a hasty trial.

He slowly regained some strength and jumped up and ran away. No one tried to stop or follow him. As he fled home, pedestrians stepped aside making way for a one-eyed wild man drenched in blood.

Frederick told Master Hugh the complete story then fell back into his chair drained.

Hugh raged against the injustice of this brutal attack. He yelled as if before the court of public opinion, "How dare they do this? Those damn yard men don't respect anybody's property. I'll make them pay for this. I'll get *satisfaction.* They'll regret the day they hurt you. They'll regret to have played with Hugh Auld! I will demand satisfaction for this outrage."

Four days later, when Frederick had almost recovered, Hugh took him to the office of Esquire Watson, the magistrate on Bond Street, where he meant to procure the arrests of North, Hays, Humphreys, and Stewart.

"I want those thugs arrested this minute," Hugh demanded hotly after giving a detailed account of the incident. Frederick could say nothing. He was a slave. "They cannot walk the streets after almost killing a man!"

Watson listened patiently and peering over his square spectacles. "Mr. Auld, who saw this assault you speak of?"

"It was done, sir, in the presence of a shipyard full of hands."

"Have any of them stepped forward to corroborate this boy's story? I am sorry, sir, but I cannot move in this manner except upon the oath of *white* witnesses.»

"But here's the boy," Auld argued, pulling at Frederick's sleeve. "Look at his head and face. They *show* what has been done."

"Mr. Auld," said Watson, still patient, "Maryland law, going back to when Maryland was a colony, decrees that no Black can bring evidence against a white person."

"But he's the victim," Hugh shouted.

"The boy's word is not acceptable, even so. A white man who was there *must* come forward to file a complaint!"

"Not even his *master*?" said Hugh, standing up.

"Mr. Auld, I must insist that the law is the law. No warrants can be served against a white man unless white witnesses make a complaint."

Mr. Watson stood, as if the interview was at an end. He looked down at Frederick who wore his mask of slave indifference. "Even if he had been *killed* by a white man in front of a thousand Blacks, their testimony won't count for anything in a courtroom."

"I'm disgusted that the law won't protect a life, and it's a disgrace when the state won't protect a man's property from a mob. What have we become?"

Hugh did nothing more except withdraw Frederick from Mr. Gardner's shipyard and give him permission to stay at home until mended. "When you're well, and I'll be the judge, I'll ask my employer, Mr. Asa Price, if you can finish training in his yard." Hugh was the foreman there.

"Thank you, sir."

"We need the money."

"Of course, sir. The times are hard."

"The work will be constant. We are building so many ships." He wondered if Frederick would ever find out that the schooner *Dolorez* and the hermaphrodite brig *Teayer* were intended for the African slave trade.

The irony amused Hugh, but it didn't matter.

1836 was difficult. Then 1837 brought the Great Panic and a national depression. Everyone needed work, white and Black. Boycotts were for fools, abolitionist fools.

38.

DURING THE WINTER WHEN he was writing his autobiography, Frederick had spent every waking hour and many nights thinking, talking, and dreaming about his slave masters Aaron Anthony, and the Aulds, Thomas, Hugh, and Sophia. He referenced them, nameless and yet vivid, in almost every speech, and they dominated its pages. When he finished his book on April 28, 1845, Frederick gave it the title, *Narrative of the Life of Frederick Douglass, An American Slave.* He had about one hundred pages of manuscript, tight lines scribbled with some words crossed out in the rush to get everything down. Reading it, Frederick was pleased with his effort and not surprised that so much of his tale had to do with his years on the Eastern Shore; slavery there represented the slavery he had to denounce, hold up as the outrage to justice and Christian values.

Frederick remembered his favorite line and knew when he wrote it that it would stand out as the theme of his book. "You have seen how a man was made a slave; you shall see how a slave was made a man."

It surprised him those distant memories could still manage to chill the skin and sear the heart. But he could not turn away from the anguish of those days, and his determination to be emotionally honest inspired what he considered his most powerful evocation of his inner turmoil: "I was sometimes prompted to take my life, but was prevented by a combination of hope and fear. My suffering on this plantation seems now like a dream rather than a stern reality. Our house stood within a few rods of the Chesapeake Bay, whose broad bosom was ever white with sails from every quarter of the habitable globe. Those beautiful vessels, robed in purest white, so delightful to the eye of freemen, were to me so many shrouded ghosts, to terrify and torment me with thoughts of my wretchedness. I have often, in the deep stillness of a summer's Sabbath, stood all alone upon the lofty banks of that noble bay, and traced, with saddened heart and tearful eye, the countless number of sails moving off to the mighty ocean."

He was proud to have written this; it was a kind of poetry he didn't realize he had within him; and knew he would read it again and again, for his inner world and the Chesapeake Bay itself were even more real through the words he found to describe them.

Words: they evoke, they make meaning; the recreate beauty; they define our humanity. In the beginning was the word.

Now that he was done, Frederick needed readers he respected to give an assessment. He wanted praise, of course, but he also needed to know if he had achieved his purpose—effectively reveal and denounce slavery.

Of all those he considered, he selected Wendell Phillips, whom he greatly admired, for a first reading. After two weeks, Wendell sent a note to come to Boston and hear his assessment. Frederick took the train at once.

He was not prepared to have Garrison and Maria Chapman sit in judgment also, but they were there in Wendell's parlor sitting as a solemn jury about to render a verdict amidst vases filled with roses, tulips, and hyacinths on a beautiful spring day.

"I'm glad that the time has come when the lions write history," said Wendell at last.

"Thank you, sir. Thank you so very much."

"Everyone who reads it will be persuaded by its truth, as are those who hear you speak," Wendell continued, beaming.

"Yes, it is highly creditable to his head and heart," said Garrison, looking to Maria Chapman. "Anyone who reads it without a tearful eye, a heaving breast, or an afflicted spirit no doubt has a flinty heart and must be qualified as a slave trafficker."

Maria Chapman responded to Garrison, "You should write an introduction, testify to its essential truth, that Mr. Douglass wrote it without assistance, or exaggeration. I've not read the entire manuscript, but Wendell read some key passages, and it will sell very well, of course." As usual, she proclaimed its commercial possibilities with the absolute confidence of her other judgments.

"That is a *splendid* idea, of course," Garrison said.

Wendell frowned and said evenly, "I had hoped to write an introduction."

"Then you *both* shall write them," announced Maria Chapman brightly, her decision final. "Your involvements will give it legitimacy, prestige."

Frederick didn't like the implication of Maria Chapman's remarks. He was honored to see Garrison and Phillips vie to write introductions for his *Narrative*, but he didn't *need* their involvement to legitimize his work.

"Mr. Garrison's remarks should go first, of course," said Wendell with a gracious smile.

"Of course," said Mrs. Chapman.

"Indeed," said Garrison, turning to Frederick. "It was I who saw your potential for great things that blessed day in New Bedford four years ago. How fortunate we all were to hear you then, how fortunate the multitudes, the cause. I never hated slavery more than at that moment when you spoke."

"I'm sure it was a *glorious* moment," said Maria Chapman.

"I don't remember what I said," Frederick commented.

"But it was I who had the great idea of inviting you as a speaker for the cause. I saw your potential."

Although this was not how he remembered it, Frederick did not dispute Garrison's version. "Thank you, sir."

"Are there any *problems* with the book?" asked Maria Chapman, turning to Wendell.

"I see none," Wendell replied.

"His discourses on religion and the pro slavery churches are most effective," added Garrison, sitting up in his chair.

"But I hope his comments aren't construed to attack religion in general," said Maria Chapman. "We must maintain the support of our friends and win new friends among people of conscience."

"You can be assured, Mrs. Chapman," said Frederick, "that I make the necessary distinction, and protect the sensibilities of those needing protection." After rereading his manuscript, Frederick found it openly anticlerical and wrote an appendix assuring his readers that he was not against Christianity, just its proslavery ministers who used religion to justify brutality. He considered changing the general text but discarded the idea.

"Then the work will sell briskly," said Mrs. Chapman. "At twenty-five cents a copy, the work should sell by the hundreds!"

Hoping for greater profits, Frederick asked, "Would not fifty cents be more. . . ?"

Before Frederick could complete his question, Garrison announced, "*More*, by the thousands. We will announce its forthcoming publication in the *Liberator.*"

"I will make sure that my friends in magazines and newspapers around town will write reviews of the book to create and sustain interest," said Wendell.

"Thank you, sir. Thank you all for your great kindnesses," Frederick said.

More concerned about the possible consequences for the cause, Mrs. Chapman said, "Perhaps with such success, Mr. Douglass's words should not be limited to the houses in Cambridge, or the huts of Pendleton, Indiana. I suggest this only for your consideration, Mr. Douglass, that it is time for you to go abroad, where our British friends can see you at last. We have written about you, and many have asked that you go. Your trip will continue and hopefully strengthen the ties that connect us."

Turning to Frederick, Wendell said, "You will aid the cause by going to England, and you will see much to learn. England will treat you kindly. You *deserve* this."

"But how will I go?" asked Frederick, eager to see England but believing a trip to be impossible. He didn't have the funds.

"We'll raise the money," said Mrs. Chapman, the expert at fundraising. "That will not be a problem."

"But what about my family?"

"I'll arrange it so that the book royalties go to Mrs. Douglass as a supplement to your *other* income," Mrs. Chapman explained. As much as he appreciated the suggestion, Frederick could not ignore the slight in her remark, a cutting reference to the fact that the cleaning, cooking, and shoe repairs by Anna and Harriet was needed to sustain his struggling family.

"There is another reason you must go," said Wendell, "and we all *know* it." They all turned to him, as he spoke the truth no one was ready to utter. "Massachusetts may not be able to protect you, especially after the attention surely to come after publication of your book."

There was silence as everyone considered the possibility of Frederick's capture and return to Maryland, despite Massachusetts' personal liberty law strengthened after the Latimer affair.

Frederick broke the tension, asking, "How long do you think I will have to stay?"

"We don't know," said Mrs. Chapman. "But it may take a year, or two."

Frederick blurted out, "My God, I can't leave my family for *two* years. We just had a baby; the children are so young, and I leave Anna all the time. Two years . . ."

Garrison and Wendell nodded. They understood Frederick's lament, having left their wives countless times. However, Mrs. Chapman stiffened her resolve. "Sir, you *chose* this life."

"But *two* years!"

"You can stay then, risk capture, and lose everything, including your family," said Mrs. Chapman with passionless logic.

"You can send for them if you have to," said Garrison.

Frederick shook his head. He could not imagine Anna choosing to leave Lynn to follow him to a land where there were only a few Negroes. "No, she won't come."

"Then she'll have to wait," said Mrs. Chapman. "Wives *wait*."

"I can only stay a year," Frederick countered weakly.

"There was this possibility when you started writing the book. Did you not know?" asked Wendell gently.

"Yes, and Anna could see it as well."

"Then she is *prepared* for you to leave as the supportive wife, like my Ann. She sends her regrets today." Frequently ill, Ann Phillips rarely left the house, and for several months Wendell stayed with her and did not travel depriving the movement of his fiery eloquence. Silently, Frederick thanked heaven for Anna's strength. He needed that strength especially now.

PART III: 1845-1855

Julia Griffiths and John Brown

39.

ANNA RECEIVED THE NEWS of his trip with better grace than expected, commenting wryly, "There'll be some changes when you come back, bigger boys, maybe a fatter me. You know how I eat when I worry."

"There's no need to worry," he said foolishly. There was so much to worry about: money; a possible manhunt and recapture on his return, whenever that would be; and bills to be paid, always bills.

And that was that. No tears, no wringing of hands, no promises except her usual one: "We'll do just fine, and you'll be safe there, safe for the very first time, and I have the comforts of the Lord, our boys, and our sister to carry me through."

The children accepted the news of his trip with well-rehearsed good grace. Frederick, Junior announced proudly, "I won't cry, Papa!"

He finalized arrangements for the care of his family. Harriet's presence greatly assured him. She would serve as a bridge between the family and his colleagues, read his letters to Anna, and write her replies.

In August he boarded the *Cambria*, a 219-foot British steamer for the eleven-day voyage from Boston to Liverpool across the North Atlantic. The names of Ireland, Scotland, England, Dublin, Belfast, Edinburgh, Manchester, Newcastle, and London resonated in his ears. They became magical conjurers of kingdoms whose walls he did not need to scale. The bridges were down, the gates flung wide open, and the people inside were cheering his name.

But once aboard the *Cambria* his reveries were made foolish all too quickly. He was denied a cabin and forced to stay in steerage, the least expensive accommodations. His white companions, James Buffum of Lynn and the Hutchinson Family Singers, all agreed to stay in steerage to show their solidarity with him, but the insult festered.

Thankfully, he did not have to endure days of passengers staring at him as if he were a part of Mr. Barnum's show on Broadway. Most of the passengers enjoyed the antislavery singing, and some purchased circulated copies of the *Narrative*. There were discussions about slavery throughout the ship at different times during the voyage. Bt there was no trouble until Wednesday, August 27, the day before the ship landed in Liverpool. Frederick was invited to speak about slavery by the captain, who was responding to a request from several guests, and then threatened by other guests after the captain rang his bell to summon passengers.

"Niggers have no right to speak," shouted one man.

"Someone should shut his nigger mouth," said another.

Others defended Frederick's right to speak, one man shouting, "Since when do Americans decide what can be said on a British ship?"

The heated arguments were only silenced when the Hutchinsons started singing. When they were done, the captain introduced Frederick and expressed his hope that everyone would listen attentively. But after Frederick uttered about five words, he was interrupted by another enraged American.

"That's a lie!" cried a Mr. Hazzard from Connecticut, waving his fist.

Calm, Frederick replied, "I can explain the reason for this man's behavior. The colored man, in our country, is treated as a being without rights."

"That's a lie," repeated Hazzard.

Sarcastic now, Frederick said, "Since everything I have said are pronounced lies, I will substantiate them by reading extracts from published slave laws."

Three white men, behind Hazzard, rushed to the front, brandishing their fists, but the captain stepped in front of Frederick, stopping them. "There are people who want to hear this man speak, and those who do not may go to another part of the ship."

He turned around to Frederick. "Sir, you may proceed."

Frederick began, but he was interrupted again.

Frederick also had his defenders, and soon the heated exchanges became so unruly that the captain threatened to use his irons to quell the mob. He was ignored until he sent for the irons.

By then, Frederick had given up. "I've had enough," he told the captain and walked away, even as he noted the calming effect of the brandished irons.

As they exited, Buffum said to Frederick, "They can't silence you in England, and they know it. You can hear their fear. All will be well."

Frustrated and bitterly disappointed, Frederick now found Buffum's affability and relentless optimism annoying, if not patronizing. "I need to stay angry, thank you very much."

Buffum immediately deferred. "I'm sorry. I did not mean to offend."

Frederick didn't want to talk and turned his back to Buffum when Buffum tried to engage him. He read for a long time, ate a biscuit, and went to sleep, hoping that the undulations of the waves could somehow make him forget slavery's reach across the thousands of miles of open sea under black clouds and the hidden north star. But that night there was no escape from the masters of his native land, whose appointed emissaries in his dreams intoned: "We don't allow niggers in here!"

He imagined he could defy his masters with a repeated, "No!" He covered his ears for them to stop, and they jeered, amused by his folly, the delusions of defiance and the denial of history. He heard Colonel Edward Lloyd, Aaron Anthony, Thomas, Hugh, Sophia Auld, and a chorus of others chant, "You are us, and we are you, now and forever, everywhere. And if the past is prologue, you will always be enslaved."

He did not awaken, but when the *Cambria* finally arrived on August 28, 1845, he was exhausted.

40.

AFTER FREDERICK AND JAMES Buffum landed in Liverpool and toured the city for a few days, they took a ferry to Dublin, where the people were surprised, even delighted, to see an unusual man on their streets. Curious, yes; repulsed, never. Crowds cheered him at the Royal Exchange, the Music Hall, and the Friends Meeting House. Frederick received applause when he entered drawing rooms, the golden glow of the flickering candles adding to the warmth of Irish approbation. He often heard cries of "Bravo" and "Hear, hear" after his comments.

In his early reports, he could have complained about Buffum, a former Quaker who used his wealth, obtained from a highly successful carpentry business, to fund worthy causes. He had donated the money to pay for Frederick's ticket to Britain, and Frederick appreciated Buffum's generosity. But Frederick did not appreciate Buffum's constant talking, his intrusions into every conversation, his comments about every event, a companionship that ignored Frederick's silences, deep sighs, and turns of his body, all cues meant to discourage Buffum's relentless affability. A kind man, Buffum was oblivious to Frederick's need for privacy. Frederick's frustration mounted.

He sometimes worried about saying the wrong thing, revealing his unschooled ways, betraying his lack of formal education or familiarity with social graces in British drawing rooms. He also sensed an immense burden. The first Negro most of the Irish abolitionists had ever met, he automatically became the representative colored man who had all the answers, and the eager Irish behaved as if he were an oracle.

"You are my *first*," said one man, delight in his grin and bright eyes, "and I'm amazed by your eloquence, your bearing, your clarity of thought and speech!"

Sitting at a table across from the eager gentleman, Frederick smiled as he struggled to keep his small teacup steady. He was sure its rattling could be heard across the room. Trying to suppress the noise, he replied perhaps too loudly, "As I am amazed by yours, sir."

The man's smile fell. Frederick immediately apologized. "I didn't mean to offend, sir. The Irish tongue has a beauty all its own."

The man's smile returned, and Frederick vowed to be more careful at hiding a conspicuous fault. Whenever he was uncomfortable, he became stiff and haughty, hiding his inadequacies behind disdain. He never admitted it openly, but he knew he could be, at times, pompous. There was some basis to the charge that he was "uppity."

He smiled again, masking the recriminations that swirled in his head.

Accept their good will.

Stop being such an ass.

Be kind.

Be less judgmental.

Fortunately, three other men joined them, congratulating Frederick as they pulled chairs together. He looked across the room at Richard Webb, his Irish publisher and host, who frowned and lowered his goblet.

Webb's disapproval was apparent from the beginning of Frederick's stay at his splendid townhouse on Great Brunswick Street, with its shining black painted door and brass doorknocker; the well-appointed rooms with mahogany tables and chairs from the reign of Queen Anne; tall, latticed windows with simple lines uncluttered by curtains and other distractions; the carpet imported from the Far East, all proof of his standing in the community.

But Webb seemed to rise from bed every morning with dissatisfaction flaring his nose and curling his lip. At breakfast, after the obligatory opening prayer, he always offered a litany of complaints, from the weak tea and hard scones to a spot on the tablecloth and carriage noises in the early morning. Excellence was always under attack, assailed and undermined by incompetence and mediocrity all around him. Violations of appropriate manners and etiquette could not be tolerated.

After dinner one evening, they were all sitting in the parlor, and Buffum said enthusiastically, "I have so many Negro friends. We should do all that we can to show our love."

"We don't need your love," said Douglass sharply.

Webb's wife, Harriet, gasped, and Buffum turned his head, obviously trying to hide his wobbly lower lip.

"Please excuse us," declared Webb, standing. "I need to talk with Mr. Douglass."

Webb's tone made it clear that he would not tolerate questions or explanations. His oldest, unmarried daughter and Buffum rose immediately and left the room.

There was a long silence.

But Frederick would not look away, waiting as he took a deep breath and rested his hands on his kneecaps. Webb returned to his seat directly across from Frederick.

"Sir, that was unnecessary."

"I'm tired of white people needing to show their approval."

"He is not 'white people.' He is your friend doing important work for the cause."

"You mean hovering over me, checking on me, directing me?"

"He's only kind."

"I don't need his kind of solicitude."

"He raised the money to make it possible for you to come here."

"How do you know this?"

"Mrs. Chapman, of course. But the source is irrelevant. What is relevant is your ingratitude."

"At the very least, you stab me in the front."

"The truth is a blunt instrument."

"What is the truth?"

"Mr. Buffum is only trying to help, and you should appreciate the effort."

"He treats me like a wayward child."

"That's not his intention."

"How do you know his intention? Has he spoken to you about me?"

"Of course, he has spoken to me about you. He needed someone to talk to after helping you cross the ocean and then receiving curt responses and moves across the room to avoid him. Everyone can see you roll your eyes when he speaks. I am not an easy man myself, but this is unworthy of a gentleman."

Douglass stood at his chair and said with a firm but soft voice, "You have made yourself abundantly clear, sir, and I am not an easy man, either. Good night."

"Sir, you dare to end our conversation in my own house?"

"Good night, sir." Frederick had to leave the drawing room quickly. He was afraid that he would say something truly regrettable.

He went to bed but was unable to sleep, reviewing the conversation, creating alternative lines, expressing to Webb the unspeakable.

In the morning, Webb behaved as if nothing had happened. He talked instead about the upcoming Temperance Convention. Frederick was relieved.

★

Webb was an exacting publisher, insisting that he knew best what British readers would accept from an American Negro writer. In a preliminary printing, the *Narrative*'s cover page had an illustration of Frederick as a smiling, almost-white man.

Frederick stared at the illustration. "Wipe that smile off my face. I need to look angry."

"Sir?"

"This drawing makes my skin too white, my nose narrow, and my lips thin. This might bring comfort to some white people, who may need me to be a safe Negro, but I am here to warn, not bring comfort."

"I know what sells, Douglass."

"This is *my* book, sir. And there will be no illustrations about slavery either. My words will describe what happened."

Webb's gray eyes rebuked, but he relented. "Very well, but you will need a new suit. I have an extraordinary tailor on Beale Street. And given where you will be going, only the best will do."

"I can't afford new clothes, sir, and my current clothes will do just fine. No one has complained."

"Of course not, Douglass. No one would dare complain."

"But you . . ."

Webb shook his head. "Color matters not at all here, but class distinctions are measured in multiple ways, large and small."

"Even so, I must watch my expenses."

"This will be a part of my expenses for publishing and promoting your wonderful book."

"Sir, I don't think . . ."

"We all need to be propped up. A good house, a good wife, fine clothes, fine food, standing in the community. These things matter in Britain. Few will care about your color, Douglass, but a misplaced seam in a jacket could mean social ruin, and fewer book sales."

Webb grinned, he understood vanity's pressing requirements.

"Very well, sir," replied Frederick, who rarely allowed a mirror to escape his notice, checking to make sure he looked his absolute best.

That day it was not raining yet—one of the few days when it didn't—and they rode in a horse and carriage over the cobblestoned streets to the shop, passing intrigued pedestrians and the occasional beggar who braved the finer neighborhoods for more generous charity.

"Give nothing," warned Webb. "Once you give, they will hound you, and especially don't succumb to children. They are the worst."

"But . . ."

"I know what I'm talking about, Mr. Douglass."

Once inside a well-appointed tavern, its brass lamps gleaming even in the filtered light, Webb ordered tea without consulting Frederick. After the waiter left them, Webb continued, "Now we'll see the other side of Dublin, beyond the Custom House, the Parliament, and the university. The streets won't be as straight. They will be narrow, filled with dung piles, and crowded with almost-naked children, more beggars than you could possibly help, even if you wanted to. Dirty women will expose themselves, offering their filthy delights. I'm not proud of this Dublin, but these people choose to live this way, drinking their lives away, having more children than they can afford to feed, living in squalor unworthy of pigs."

"Then why are you taking me there?" Webb's mercurial temperament continued to intrigue and frustrate him.

"I'm afraid for my country. I love Ireland and hate her, too."

"Sir?"

"She's beautiful, and she's a mess, decaying, rotten, undisciplined, wild, and disorderly, a wretched island with beautiful churches filled with proud, stubborn supplicants praying for a deliverance that has yet to come after centuries of hounding heaven. I hate what religion does to people. I know you agree. That speech at the Music Hall was splendid."

"Thank you, sir. Yes, I hate a religion that in the name of the Savior covers the backs of men and women with bloody scars."

"I'm a good hater. I hate slavery, mediocrity, poor craftsmanship, bad manners, the Church. But I can also admire, even love, that which I resent. My own house could stand proudly on a London Street in Kensington or near Hyde Park. But if there ever is an uprising for Irish sovereignty, an uprising long overdue, England's armies will destroy us with that cool and orderly efficiency I most admire. And I admire America, and hate her, too, an exhilarating and dangerous place, a vast, abundant continent that builds cities and cultivates farms with boundless energy while enslaving Negroes and killing Indians."

Astonished by Webb's candor, Frederick waited to respond. He took a sip of tea and said, "I have no government to defend. And as to a nation, I belong to none. When I think of America, I sometimes find myself admiring her blue skies, the woods and fields and beautiful rivers and mountains. But my joy turns to mourning when I think of slavery, and I am filled with unutterable loathing."

"Then you'll see my land with clear eyes and hear without prejudice, when we go to Greystones, Wicklow, Enniscorthy, and Wexford." The words rolled off his tongue, and Frederick immediately reached for his little book tucked away in his breast pocket.

"How do you spell them?" Frederick asked.

Webb smiled as Frederick wrote the words and waited until Frederick had finished. "You like these names."

"Yes. Lovely sounds."

"Yes, but they can't hide the ugliness, the famine."

"I hear it's terrible."

"Terrible indeed. You'll see. Thousands are reported dead already because without the potato they starve."

"And thousands are landing in Boston and New York."

"Are you ready for the deluge?" Webb asked. "You better be. If the famine worsens, your country will be overrun by immigrants. And for their votes, your politicians will make an offer they won't refuse: vote for us and we'll keep Negroes down. The Irish will at least be superior to them, and to you."

Frederick tried to see Webb's intention. His assessment was all too accurate. Riots in New York, Boston, Cleveland, and elsewhere were often led by Irishmen energized by anti-Negro editorials and political rants. Frederick could never forget how the Irish treated him and others in Baltimore.

Frederick, although curious, soon dreaded trips outside the Webb house, since the muddy streets were alive with beggars. Some of them had no legs, hands, or arms; and others, down upon their knees with outstretched arms, cast sad looks to the right and left in the hope of catching the eye of a passing stranger in the merciless crowd.

"I've never seen anything like this in America," he reported to Garrison.

But when he took walks, Frederick found it easier to not give money. Rejecting all beggars was easier than selecting the deserving. But the sight of little children, alone and covered in filthy rags, sitting on cold stones, and leaning against brick walls as they tried to sleep, gripped his heart, and he gave a coin now and then. He silently railed against the churches for failing to help them.

He also blamed the Irish for their plight. They were not victims. "They drink too much whiskey," he later wrote Garrison. "The immediate cause, and it may be the main cause of the extreme poverty and beggary in Ireland, is intemperance."

The solution was also simple. A sober man could rise from the depths of poverty, even though an economic system could drive a man to drink.

An individual man could rise above his circumstances. Wasn't Frederick Douglass a living example of this truth?

The Irish could rise, too.

One Irish man did rise, and Frederick was determined to see and hear him—the great Daniel O'Connell, "The Liberator," so named for his successful campaign to get Catholics seated in the House of Parliament. Born in 1775, he had devoted almost his entire life for the Repeal of the Act of Union joining Ireland with Great Britain in 1801. He characterized the English as the enslavers and the Irish as the enslaved.

Enfeebled by prison, O'Connell looked old and tired, his body bent, his skin pale and blotched, his head covered by an obvious wig. His physical appearance at a large gathering of thousands in a packed hall shocked Frederick. But as he paced the stage with outstretched arms giving a speech about American slavery that was, Frederick thought, skillfully delivered, powerful in its logic, majestic in its rhetoric, biting in its sarcasm, melting in its pathos, and burning in its rebukes, the experience seemed to energize the old man, making him taller, more vibrant, more alive.

O'Connell's words were unforgettable.

Frederick repeated one entire paragraph for Garrison to read: "My sympathy with distress is not confined within the narrow bounds of my own green island. No—it extends itself to every corner of the earth. My heart walks abroad, and where the miserable are to be succored, or the slave to be set free, there my spirit is at home, and I delight to dwell."

Frederick noted some of O'Connell's word choices and made sure that they would be included in his book of vocabulary words. Calumniate. Salutary.

O'Connell used a speaking horn, his words repeated by callers shouting at the sides to the back of the house, but Frederick knew that the size of the crowd did not matter. Only the speaker mattered, the speaker who possessed thoughts that breathed, who used words that seared, who told his story and connected with listeners united across the world by their hunger for freedom.

After the speech and a thunderous ovation, Frederick pressed forward to get a closer view of the great man. Buffum, who knew O'Connell, was already at the platform, and he turned to Frederick, saying, "Friend Douglass, I had to put you through. Friend O'Connell wants to meet you. Come forward."

"He wants to meet me?"

Buffum didn't respond, quickly turning away to do his good deed. Buffum and Frederick reached O'Connell, who smiled broadly, extended his hand, and said brightly, "So this is the Black O'Connell, yes?"

Flabbergasted, Frederick replied, "Sir, I am honored to meet you. There is no comparison."

"You are young. You could surpass us all."

"You are a founding father, sir."

"And you wrote a book that people will read long after my speeches are forgotten."

"Legacy matters, sir."

"Time will tell."

"I will never forget you, sir."

"Will you write about me?" asked O'Connell, smiling now.

"Yes, sir."

"Good. Great writing serves humanity, God, and country."

"I will try."

"That's all that anyone can hope for, the trying, the striving."

"Thank you, sir."

The conversation, as if shrouded in a protective cloud surrounding the two men, was over, and the noise and confusion of the platform returned.

"Friend Douglass, Friend Douglass," he heard Buffum say. "We must go and give Friend O'Connell a chance to rest."

Frederick extended his hand and said, "Thank you, sir, for granting me a small portion of your precious time."

"You are most welcome," he replied.

Frederick turned away, determined to keep the inspiration of O'Connell's words and their impact on his listeners alive.

Later, he wrote to Garrison about O'Connell: "Until I heard this man I had thought that the story of his oratory and power were greatly exaggerated. I did not see how a man could speak to twenty or thirty thousand people at one and time and be heard by any considerable portion of them, but the mystery was solved when I saw his ample person and heard his musical voice. His eloquence came down upon the vast assembly like a summer thundershower upon a dusty road. He could at will stir the multitude to a tempest of wrath or reduce it to the silence with which a mother leaves the cradle-side of her sleeping babe. Such tenderness, such pathos, such world-embracing and thunderous denunciation, such wit and humor. He held Ireland within his grasp of his strong hand, and he could lead it wherever he could, for Ireland believed in him and loved him."

I will be the Black O'Connell, one day, thought Frederick. *And one day America will love me as Ireland loves Daniel O'Connell. If I can ever return to a land that hates me.*

After witnessing unbelievable poverty and desperation, Frederick, Webb, and Buffum arrived in Cork, where they were hosted by the Jennings family. Both Webb and Buffum departed after a few days. Buffum said he had unspecified personal business to oversee back in Dublin, and Webb needed to reexamine the distribution of Frederick's *Narrative* and other projects.

Frederick's three-week stay with the Jennings family of Cork after Webb departed lightened his spirits. At last, he could relax in the vast library with a cup of tea and read undisturbed, even in a house with five unmarried daughters, take naps, walk in the gardens, and enjoy conversation about a variety of reforms and causes without Webb silently scoring points, taking notes, and listing grievances.

After three days with the Jennings family, who never made demands or presumed, always asking permission, he spontaneously joined the singing of antislavery hymns one night in the parlor with Isabel, the youngest daughter, at the pianoforte. Smiling, she didn't stop playing, as if they had rehearsed a duet earlier in the day. At the end, everyone applauded, and Isabel said eagerly, "Oh, Mr. Douglass, you have a beautiful voice, a beautiful, deep voice."

"Thank you."

"Do you also play an instrument?"

"Yes, I do. The violin. Not well, but I enjoy making music."

"I hope you will play for us."

Isabel's father intervened gently, "Isabel."

"I didn't bring my violin," Frederick answered. "I didn't want it to get it damaged during the voyage or on the road."

"Of course. But we have violins here, and a viola, even a cello. My sisters try Haydn and Mozart string quartets."

"Isabel?" Mr. Jennings insisted, looking at Frederick apologetically.

"Sir, I don't mind," replied Frederick, charmed by Isabel's eagerness to include him. "I love to play, but I hope there's time to practice."

"We'll find time," said Isabel, clapping her hands, "and in the meantime, I'll accompany you on any songs or hymns you already know. I can play without music, by ear."

"I wish I could do that," said Frederick. Envious, he marveled at this ability.

"You make music with words," said Isabel. "I wish I could do that."

He wanted to stay longer, but he had to cross the sea to Scotland.

41.

AFTER CROSSING THE SEA to Scotland, when Frederick spoke at meetings, many clergymen shifted in the chairs, frowned grimly, shook their heads, and stared ahead, trying to seem unmoved but obviously dismayed by Frederick's remarks, described later as "uncompromising in tone."

Frederick was on a mission to expose the complicity of British churches that remained affiliated with American churches that continued to support slavery, insisting that donations from southern American churches, whatever worthy cause they espoused, were tainted.

No union with plunderers!

No union with slaveholders!

Isolate them!

Send back the stolen money!

Send back the money.

He raised his fist with the last phrase and repeated it. The audience roared, and Frederick realized that he had found the right slogan to repeat throughout his tour of Britain.

Send back the money!

The men and women in the audience lifted their fists and chanted back, again and again: "Send back the money!"

Clerics denounced him from their pulpits. Letters to the editors of local newspapers criticized him. Leaflets were being distributed on the streets. "Send back the nigger!" they proclaimed.

Frederick only smiled, pleased that he was now a threat on British soil, another upstart in a land of kings.

He received word from Garrison that the Massachusetts Society wanted him to stay until at least the summer, when Garrison himself would arrive.

He needed Garrison. Surely his moral clarity would make all things clear: the possibility of his family immigrating to the U.K., thanks to the abolition of slavery in 1833; the festering hostility and mistrust of Americans; the depth of Webb's ongoing hostility. Garrison and Webb were old friends. Perhaps Garrison could intervene on Frederick's behalf.

Frederick continued to hound Webb about the slow production of the *Narrative*. From Perth he wrote, "When the next edition is published, I wish you to have it bound up at once so that I may not have to wait, as I have had to do in the past." He also demanded "better paper."

The *Narrative* was indeed a bestseller in Britain. Thousands of copies were sold, and Frederick naturally assumed that Webb would publish more books to increase his own profits. In Scotland, Frederick had to disappoint many who wanted to buy his book when they came to hear him speak and found he had none to sell. It was embarrassing.

Frederick also assumed that Webb would appreciate having a bestselling author and declare his gratitude, but when Webb came to Edinburgh he had only more grievances.

"Sir, you dared to complain to Maria Chapman about me. After my hospitality, your assertions were inappropriate, and inexcusable," Webb said.

"I only described what I felt, sir."

"Unlike you, I chose to remain silent about what I felt about you. I certainly saw no need to write to Mrs. Chapman. And then she wrote to me telling me that *I* was rude, and I needed to treat *you* better."

"Sir, I cannot be responsible for how she communicated with you."

Webb took a deep breath and smiled, smug satisfaction brightening his face. "No, you cannot, but are you ready for her truth?"

Frederick paused. Webb was about to unsheathe a dangerous weapon.

Trying to sound casual, Frederick replied, "It's unfortunate that she would not tell me directly."

"Then you are fortunate that I am willing to tell you now so you can know what you are dealing with."

"When did she write you?"

"Before you departed for Ireland," Webb said.

"Then you knew all this time?"

"I can be discreet. But more importantly, I waited to see if what she said had any validity."

"You were testing me," Frederick said.

"I didn't know you. None of us knew you, so we were all testing you. Surely, you would know this. You are not a fool," Webb replied.

"What did she have to say?"

Webb took her letter out of his breast pocket, opened it slowly, stretching out his right arm before retracting it for emphasis, and read a passage from her long letter: "Mr. Webb, it is essential that you keep a watch over Mr. Douglass and Mr. Buffum, who might be unduly influenced by the machinations of our British enemies. But because Mr. Buffum is rich, it is unlikely that he will succumb. But poverty has it perils, and Mr. Douglass, always in need, might not be able to withstand the allurements of the London Committee. Sir, be vigilant."

Webb looked up. "Sir, this is a bitter pill dispensed by a difficult woman with whom I have my differences." But his eyes betrayed him; he was enjoying Frederick's deflation.

"This is grievously disappointing," Frederick said, finally. "I supposed I had her confidence, and the confidence of the others of the Boston committee. She trusted me, or seemed to do so at home, so why distrust me abroad? I have never given her just cause to distrust me, and if I am to be watched over for evil rather than good by my professed friends, then I can say, save me from my friends, and I will take care of my enemies."

"Enemy is perhaps too strong a word," Webb said.

"Then she has a strange way of showing her regard."

"She is indiscriminate in her appeals and recriminations. As I said earlier, I am not immune."

"If she is trying to drive me from the Anti-Slavery Society, all she has to do is put me under overseership and the work is done," Frederick said.

"Overseership is too strong a word. That is not her intention. You are too valuable."

"Perhaps you cannot speak to her intention. But you can speak for your own. Why did you read this to me? I can think of no other reason than to drive a wedge between me and my associates, and I think you take pleasure in this. You can leave my room now," Frederick said.

Webb stood. His smile disappeared. "I would have said nothing if you had not accused me. I tolerated your rudeness to my family and Mr. Buffum for a long time, and said nothing to no one, except to my dear wife and sister-in-law. Then Mrs. Chapman writes to me, telling me to be less rude to you! Of all the nerve! She may not be your enemy, but she is now mine, and I will not tolerate her accusing me about you."

"Then all this is about me, not her," Frederick said.

"That is how you, indeed, see it. Everything is about you. Everything must be about you. I'm sick of it. As an egoist, I can't compare to you, a man who acts as if he were born in Buckingham Palace rather than in a shack on Tuckahoe Creek. You are a great speaker and an excellent writer, but you are a *miserable* companion, and certainly not a friend. Good day, sir." Webb could do serious damage as an influential publisher and abolitionist in Britain, so Frederick decided to keep deeper misgivings about him to himself. He did not want more controversy swirling around him. He had enough to deal with.

In the meantime, Frederick heard in March from Maria Chapman, receiving a letter from her for the first time since he departed for Britain. Unsolicited, she he had sent him a copy of *The Liberty Bell,* her annual compilation of anti-slavery writings sold by the Boston Female Anti-Slavery Society to raise funds. He proceeded to write a letter thanking her for the book.

But within a few lines, his gratitude changed to self-defense. "As a humble part of the antislavery machinery, I have even managed to get on, and keep in the fields with very little means—lived in a small house paid a small rent, indulged in no luxuries—glad to get the common necessaries of life. I can thus far challenge the strictest scrutiny into all my movements. I have neither compromised myself nor the character of my friends."

He also assured her that he relied on the sales of the *Narrative*, now 2,000 sold by late March, for his traveling expenses. But on reflection, he despised his need to make a case for loyalty and financial prudence to her at all.

Maria reminded him of Rowena Hambleton Auld. Unlike Rowena, Maria was beautiful and more refined, a product of Boston that no lady on the Eastern Shore could ever match. But at their core, they were the same; their hearts were encased in ice.

As with Rowena, he wanted Maria out of his life. He needed be his own man, answering to no one, especially a white man or woman. If he ever returned to America, he would work for himself as a lecturer attached to no organization or as a writer attached to no single publication or as an editor of his own newspaper. Details remained unclear. He was reluctant to challenge himself to be more specific, fearing consequences. But he sensed an independent future, the fulfillment of an emerging dream.

His health that spring reinforced lingering uncertainties. He never felt very good in the spring, and he wrote Harriet that his health was "only tolerable." In the past, he wondered about the causes, surmising that maybe it was something in the air, dust or seeds. But now he knew. Despite all the triumphs in Britain, his spirit was low. Exhausted by travel, assailed by the criticism and questions of supposed friends, and feeling isolated from his family, friends, and home, he could name the feeling.

Melancholy, what he called "the fog."

He first experienced it in Baltimore, when he was consumed by sin, dark obsessive thoughts, the inability to sleep. Then he was forced back to the Eastern Shore, and the dark thoughts returned with greater force during that terrible stay with Covey. But they returned. They always returned when he felt trapped, deeply alone, or powerless. That powerlessness was now exacerbated by Harriet's news that she was engaged to a man Frederick didn't know. She didn't ask for his permission, only money for a wedding dress. He heatedly replied, reminding her that he was her brother, who had the right to forbid her from marrying some stranger, probably a lowlife with no prospects. She didn't reply.

Distraction came with a walk down an Edinburgh Street and the discovery of an old fiddle in the window of a large store. He stopped as soon as he saw it, reminded of home, where he played his own fiddle whenever he felt the need.

Without another thought, he walked into the store, paid a trifle, and returned to his hotel to play it. He stared at the bridge and strings for just a moment, gently lowered the bow, and struck up "Camel's a Coming," its jaunty rhythms soon lifting his spirits.

Nevertheless, not since his days at Edward Covey's had he ever felt so alone. But he hoped that Garrison's arrival would lift his inner fog.

42.

GARRISON'S SHIP ARRIVED IN Liverpool on July 31, fifteen days after leaving Boston. The weather was clear and the wind fair, a perfect harbinger for the celebrations marking the visit of the royal consort, Prince Albert. All the vessels in the port, an immense number, had colors flying at their mastheads. Crowds filled the streets.

Richard Webb met Garrison at the dock, embracing him as he revealed their anxious wait for his safe arrival. Webb told him how happy he was to see him and immediately took him to the Temperance Hotel in Clayton Square. Garrison could not resist judging the festive spirit all around him. *The attachment to royalty in this country borders closely to idolatry.*

Garrison had asked about Frederick, but Webb's enthusiasm was muted. "His book is doing well." Webb then exploded. "That young man *dared* to complain about me to Maria Chapman. He dared to write a letter to say I was rude. I was rude? After a short time in my house, I found him to be absurdly haughty, self-possessed, and prone to take offense. His treatment of Buffum battered my esteem for him. How Buffum put up with the conduct from one for whom he has done so much is past my comprehension, for I am not a model of forbearance and meekness myself. In all my experience of men, I have never known one so willing to magnify the smallest cause of discomfort or wounded self-esteem into insupportable talk of offense and dissatisfaction. I think his selfishness intense, his affection weak, and unreasonableness quite extravagant. A genius of rhetoric, but he is the least lovable of abolitionists I know. I said nothing for months, and then her letter came, and I didn't hold back, not at all."

Taken aback, Garrison stood before his friend with his head down, averting his eyes as Webb ranted, his words having the power to seal them in a cocoon, the noises of the harbor muted.

Treading carefully, Garrison asked, "Did you reply to her letter, explain?"

"Of course I did, and at length, citing innumerable examples of his poor conduct. And I confronted him too. I read him her letter to me telling what Buffum needed to do, what she feared about Douglass's poverty, his susceptibilities to the enticements of our enemies."

"You read her letter to him? Why did you do that?"

Webb smiled. It was a malicious, triumphant smile that showed Garrison a depth in Webb's character he never knew. "Not all of it, but what I did read brought him down a few notches. He needs to be humbled. He didn't rise alone, without help. He didn't emerge like Athena from the head of Zeus. He's a minor deity, at best. The cause has its leaders, and he is not one of them."

Offended by the references to Greek idolatry, Garrison sputtered, "Sir, scripture reminds that there are no other gods before . . ."

Still smiling, Webb raised his hand. "Fear not, dear friend. I respect the pieties, in my fashion."

"Very well, but what will you say to Frederick when we see him for the Temperance Conference in London?"

"I had my say. What's done is done. I will be at my best. I am a gentleman."

Garrison was reunited with Frederick at the house where Webb was also a guest. The tension between the two was obvious from the first moment Frederick entered the parlor.

"Frederick, you are looking and doing so well," Garrison said. "It pleases me greatly that you have found the approbation here you so richly deserve."

"Mr. Garrison, none of this would have been possible without your work proceeding me," Frederick replied.

"You are famous now. The *Narrative* has made it so."

Stone faced, Richard Webb stood silent. Then he said to Frederick, "Sir, you have me to thank as well."

"Sir, I have thanked you, repeatedly."

"Sir, in your letters."

"Sir, let me thank you now before our friend, Mr. Garrison," Frederick said.

Garrison intervened. "We all have so much to be grateful for, and I am especially grateful that the sea did not swallow me up and make me miss seeing you and all my British friends once more. Of course, if I had succumbed to the power of the deep, I would now be in the arms of our Lord and Savior and know fully the blessing of love and acceptance. But I would miss you still and would have to wait for you to join me in heaven."

"Mr. Garrison, I appreciate the sentiment, but I can't be sure that I will earn the divine embrace you hope for," said Webb.

"Your deeds have earned your place in heaven. Your work for the downtrodden, the enslaved speaks to your salvation," Garrison replied.

When they were invited to the country estate of another British abolitionist, a wealthy man with an extensive garden, Garrison finally found the opportunity to talk with Frederick beyond prying ears.

Garrison needed Frederick to ensure the success of the newly formed Anti-Slavery League. The existing British and Foreign Anti-Slavery Society had tried to strengthen ties between American and British abolitionist societies. But that group was not radical enough and too tolerant of American churches with slave-owner members. The mission of the new league would be adamantly clear: no association with slave owners, whatever their religious affiliations. Given Frederick's success with the "Send back the money" campaign in Scotland, he was perfect for promoting the need for the League.

The implication for Frederick was clear. "Sir, do you want me to remain in Britain?"

Garrison did not expect so bold and direct an inquiry, but he looked directly into Frederick's eyes, counting on his own unwavering, penetrating gaze, "Yes, we need you to stay."

"How long?"

"As long as it will take."

"But my family."

"Is your wife willing to come with the children to England?"

"It is better here for her, for the children, for me, for all of us. I will always be free here," Frederick said.

"Wives should support their husbands. I'm sure she will agree."

"I'm not so sure. I've asked her to sacrifice so much already. I will have to return to convince her and prepare for the move. She shouldn't do it all on her own. I told her I will be back in November."

"Too soon, too soon. There's still so much to do, and we can't be sure about your safety, now that the Aulds know who you are, and where you live. Even if Massachusetts doesn't help returning you, you can still be taken," Garrison said.

Frederick's eyes softened, and his shoulders deflated. "It will give them nothing but the greatest pleasure to see me dragged through the streets of Baltimore or St. Michaels," he admitted with a slight tremor in his voice.

"We will not allow it."

"How?"

Without feeling affronted, Garrison answered, "My friend, my brother, God will provide."

Frederick sighed and lowered his head slightly.

Garrison pressed on, taking care that every word lifted the young man up, not tearing him further down. "We will put our faith in the Lord, and meanwhile you will continue to do your mighty work here. At the public meetings for the League, you'll be asked to speak, and surely you will make a great impression."

Later, Garrison confessed to his wife, "Of course, wherever he goes, he is the lion of the occasion."

43.

JULIA GRIFFITHS HAD FOLLOWED Frederick's career since he had emerged from obscurity, avidly reading her subscription of the *Liberator.* She purchased the *Narrative* and read it in a single sitting, so vivid was his story. But none of this had sufficiently prepared her for seeing and hearing him at the Music Hall in Leeds for the first time, just days before, and spending time with him socially at Ellen Richardson's house in Newcastle, where they were staying as her guests. Now she was disappointed.

Frederick would not hold the manumission papers officially freeing him from slavery in his hands until after the new year. It would take at least two or three weeks for them to cross the Atlantic for him to receive them while still in northern England.

Nevertheless, Julia and Ellen Richardson had received word from Mr. Loring in Boston that the negotiations had been completed and the manumission papers had been filed in Baltimore. They could tell Frederick on Christmas Eve, when they would all be together for dinner and the exchange of gifts. Julia could barely contain her excitement and was afraid that she might spoil the surprise.

At the beginning, when Ellen had asked for her help, Julia didn't realize how complicated the legal maneuvering would be. Julia was an accomplished fundraiser for a variety of causes, but fundraising was the easy part. She found dealing with the American courts and Thomas Auld far more complicated and difficult.

Frederick's cooperation was essential. After Ellen told him of her plan, he suggested that she contact his friend William White in Boston. He could find someone there who could get things done.

White approached Ellis Gray Loring, who then turned to a lawyer in New York. That lawyer arranged for a Baltimore lawyer to approach Hugh Auld for a price. Hugh contacted Thomas, Frederick's legal owner, and Thomas, holding the major bargaining chip and still furious with Frederick for maligning him in the *Narrative*, finally agreed, after a back-and-forth debate about the true value of a now famous slave, to accept 150 pounds sterling, a large amount of money. Hugh gave him the money raised in England in American dollars, and then Thomas filed a bill of sale to Hugh. Finally, Hugh registered a deed of manumission in the Baltimore Courthouse on December 12, 1846.

Now they all had to wait for its arrival. In the meantime, they could celebrate it on Christmas Eve with a confirmed note from Loring.

Frederick was supposed to speak a week earlier but had postponed his talk due to illness. The notice for the rescheduled meeting came with less than twenty-four-hours' notice, so the audience was small. The cold, damp weather didn't help attendance either. Although some speculated that anti-Garrison sentiment in some British abolitionist circles contributed to the poor turnout, Julia didn't care. Seeing and hearing him unencumbered by a crowd, this was better, far better.

He was a huge man, and far more handsome than Julia had imagined, even after seeing his portrait printed in the British edition of the *Narrative*. But it was his voice, that rich voice that made her shift uncomfortably in her chair and dab with delicate and subtle application of her handkerchief at the moisture in the palm of her hand.

For more than a year Douglass had called on the churches of Ireland, Scotland, and England to denounce and dissociate themselves legally, morally, and economically from their denominational counterparts in the American South, and tonight he reiterated his theme, challenging his listeners to reject fellow Christians who embraced the horrors he had come to describe.

At that moment, Julia wanted to stand up and shout out the news of his emancipation, but she did not move, restrained by the powerful momentum he was making. The audience interrupted with cheers and applause, but Frederick didn't smile or bow his head in acknowledgment. He waited for only a few moments, glaring at the audience, as if his hated enemies, slaveholders, and their preaching supporters stood in the aisle right before him. Then he read from the slave codes of the South as final proof of their perfidy: "If more than seven slaves together are found in any road without a written pass, twenty lashes apiece; for visiting a plantation without a written pass, ten lashes; for letting loose a boat from where it is made fast, thirty-nine lashes for the first offence, and for the second, shall have cut off from his head one ear; for keeping or carrying a club, thirty-nine lashes; for having any article for sale, without a ticket from his master, ten lashes."

Julia and the others winced and bowed their heads or covered their eyes with the hands. But Douglass would not have polite aversion only. He would challenge them with a direct affront, make them feel the agony of oppression. "I am afraid you do not understand the awful character of these lashes," he declared with cutting levity. "You must bring it before your mind. A human being in perfect nudity, tied hand and foot to a stake, and a strong man standing behind with a heavy whip, knotted at the end, each blow cutting into the flesh, and leaving the warm blood dripping to the feet, and for these trifles."

"Oh, God," Julia whispered, joining the consternation of the audience.

Perfect nudity.

Shocked and embarrassed now, she silently blamed Douglass for shameless effrontery. But Julia could condemn him for only a moment as he reached his conclusion and basked in the now constant applause and cheers that came to him at the very end: "Only think of a religion under which the handcuffs, the fetter, the whip, the gag, the thumbscrew, blood hounds, cat-o-nine tails, branding irons, all these implements, can be undisturbed. Only think of a body of men thanking God every Sabbath day that they live in a country where there is civil and religious freedom, where there are three millions of people herded together in a state of concubinage, denied the right to learn to read the name of the God that made them, where there are laws that doom the black man to death for offences which, if committed by white men, would pass unpunished. Think of a man standing up among such a people, and never raising a whisper in condemnation of such a state of things, denouncing the slaveholders, or speaking a word of pity. Think, think, think, think, think."

At the end, Julia rose and cheered with the rest.

★

"My dear, Julia," observed her sister Eliza the next afternoon, "you are acting most peculiar. You cannot even decide what jewelry to wear. Why should a dinner with Mr. Douglass rattle you? I know you're an admirer. We all are, but even so . . ."

Eliza was usually the last to dress. But today it was Julia still in her petticoats, having just endured the tightening of her corset at the hands of her sister, who sat imperiously on the chest at the foot of the bed. Although Eliza, at twenty-six, was ten years younger than Julia, Eliza was the voice of feminine rectitude, the upholder of standards, the older one in spirit. Their father said often that Eliza was most like their mother, who died when they were girls. But to Julia, Eliza was a dear but dreary substitute at keeping a distant memory alive.

"Indecision is not confusion," replied Julia. "And besides, when was the last time either one of us had the chance to dine with a famous man?"

"Vanity, beware," said Eliza smugly. "His celebrity will not benefit you or me."

"You are too harsh."

"And so, I remain unmarried," she said, without a hint of pride or regret.

"And when you marry?"

Julia took her sister's hands into hers, and said tenderly, "We will always be together, even after you get married first. And you will get married first, I'm sure of it."

"You are not a good liar."

Julia dropped her sister's hands. "You are never satisfied, even with a compliment. You are younger, more beautiful."

"I am always offending, and men don't appreciate honesty in women, especially women with supposed allurements. I didn't mean to minimize your feelings. You are all I have in this world."

Eliza embraced Julia quickly, her arms pressing against Julia's side, but her hands hovered over Julia's back as if the touch of fingertips were too intimate.

"Let's not quarrel. It's the holidays, and we're about to do something wonderful for a very special man," Julia said.

"I had nothing to do with it and should not be given any credit."

Julia sighed, tired of Eliza's relentless accuracy. "Nevertheless, you can enjoy our pleasure in doing a good thing, can you not?"

Stepping back, Eliza replied defensively, "Of course, I can."

"Good. Now help me with my dress over there," Julia ordered, pointing to another extravagance, a three-flounce gown imported from Paris, a rich burgundy satin, trimmed with black lace and stitched with small black roses.

Julia smiled, enjoying the restoration of her superior position as she watched Eliza gather up the dress. Eliza could be pointedly critical, but she inevitably capitulated to her older sister's maturity, wider experience, and intelligence after brief episodes of autonomy and resistance. Eliza would always stay by her side. "Thank you," said Julia, making sure there was no triumphant sarcasm in her voice.

As she expected, Julia was the most resplendent woman at the Richardsons' that night, since Eliza and Ellen and Anna Richardson all wore black gowns trimmed in white lace with white shawls, a trio of solemnity in a room of golden light and holiday red and green trimmings.

Frederick dominated the parlor, towering over everyone when he stood to greet the Griffiths sisters as they entered the room, windows festooned with garlands, the tables cluttered with candles, candies, and nuts. Extending her gloved hand, Julia immediately cast aside any concern about the first impression she was making. He was the most handsome man she had ever seen, and those large dark orbs, sparkling in the candlelight, brightened his smiling face. Julia noted that this intensely serious public figure disarmed her so casually.

"Miss Julia and Miss Eliza, it is a great pleasure making your acquaintance at last," Frederick said.

"Mr. Douglass, my sister and I are honored to meet you," Julia replied.

"Honor I do not deserve."

"It is the least that we can give. We have something for you," Julia said.

"You should not have," Frederick said.

"I hope you like it," she said eagerly, dropping the pretense of Eliza's involvement all too quickly. "When I saw it, I was sure you could use it."

Julia took the package from Eliza, who had wrapped it with exquisite care, and handed it to Frederick, who sat down to open it. Everyone else then sat down, leaving Frederick alone on the sofa directly facing the fireplace. His large fingers moved deftly, avoiding any rips or tears to the paper, his combination of strength and delicacy impressed Julia even more. Under the paper and ribbon, he found a book, James Prichard's *Natural History of Man*, an illustrated work of anthropology.

"Ah. I've heard of this. Thank you so much. It will be very useful in preparing some of my lectures. I'm no longer just telling my story, as you well know. I'm building a case for the rightful place of the Negro. I'm more than just a slave, *more*," Frederick said.

His voice trailed off as he turned the pages of the book, examining the illustrations placed throughout the text, taking only a second with each picture. Suddenly he stopped at page 157, staring at the engraving there. It was a picture of the head of a statue supposed to be that of the Pharaoh Rameses.

"What is it?" asked Julia.

"This picture . . . it . . . it reminds me . . . it reminds me of my *mother*," Frederick said.

Julia immediately recalled the chilling passage in his book when Frederick mentioned the death of his mother. She almost said, *But you only saw her a few times, long ago, and only at night!* But she checked herself, startled by the confused look in his eyes.

"Is anything wrong?" Julia asked, knowing full well that the memory pained him.

He closed the book and said brightly, "Oh, no, not at all. Not at all. It was so long ago. I just didn't expect to see anything that resembled her. That was a picture of a man, after all, but it still reminded me. Thank you so much for this book. I will study it carefully."

"This leads me to ask some questions about several things you've said," said Julia.

"Julia, please," interjected Ellen, who sat to the right of Frederick with her brother, the serene and notoriously silent Henry Richardson.

Ignoring the objection, Julia asked, "What has been the highlight of your trip here?"

"Julia," pleaded Ellen softly.

"I have no objections."

"Splendid," said Julia.

"The highlight? Not a single event, more a process. I've found another voice. In every town, city, and village in Britain I've been free to speak my mind, and, having spoken, I've learned a new language, my language. I have my own opinions and . . ."

"Are you declaring your independence from Mr. Garrison?" Julia could detect no surprise in his reaction to her question. Clearly, he had thought about this for some time.

"I remain his follower. But I think it is now time to assert that I and other American Negroes need an independent voice," Frederick replied.

"How?"

"A new paper founded, edited, and published by an American Negro."

"By Frederick Douglass," Julia said.

"By Frederick Douglass," he repeated.

"I'll help you," Julia declared at once, making Eliza start, her gloved hands in her lap tightening into another grip of mortification.

"Thank you, Miss Griffiths. I appreciate the offer, but . . ." Frederick said.

"I can raise the money. I can write to friends and associates who admire you and your cause."

"Miss Griffiths, I can't thank you enough, but I have more pressing needs before I begin to even think about starting a paper. Going home."

Julia, the Richardsons, and Eliza looked at each other, assessing if now was the time to announce the good news.

"What is it?" asked Frederick, noticing their unspoken concern.

No one responded to the question, and Frederick became earnest. "What is it? You've heard something. My family, my children?"

Ellen rose from her chair, shaking her head. "Oh, Mr. Douglass, please do not worry about your family. We have no news that should concern you about the welfare of your family."

"Then what is it?"

"I had hoped that after supper . . ." began Anna Richardson.

"Now is the time," Julia declared.

"We have something else for you, Mr. Douglass," said Ellen, going to a table at the end of the room. She returned and handed him an envelope that held the cable from Mr. Loring in her lap. "Great news," she said.

He looked to all of them and started to open and unfold the sheet. Frederick scanned the paper, and his right hand began to shake.

Silent, they waited.

"Free," he whispered. The weight of a lifetime of fear gone. Joy, surprise, and incredulity coalesced in a single word. "Free. Free. Free. Free at last. Thank you for giving back my country."

"Merry Christmas," Julia said, her eyes filled with tears. "And it will be a happy new year when your manumission papers finally arrive."

"I will always be indebted to you. To all of you."

"No. You are free from us, as you are free from them." Eliza reached over to press Julia's hand, as if to restrain her. She hated that Eliza could sometimes read her mind. She wanted to embrace Frederick, feel his heart against hers.

"Now everything is possible, everything. I came a slave. I go back a free man. I won't be able to sit still and remain quiet. In choosing to return to America, I will face even more conflict and greater criticism. But I return gladly. Gladly. I can hold my boys."

"Now we can celebrate with supper," announced Henry.

"And over dinner," Julia said, "I can ask Mr. Douglass more questions, especially about his views about alcohol and its relationship to poverty."

"Julia," admonished Eliza, "he has better things to do than . . ."

"Oh, Miss Griffiths, I have some questions of my own," replied Frederick, unfazed. "Just how did you all determine my exact worth? I was sure that my value matched the crown jewels at the very least."

They all laughed, and it was this laughter that gave Julia permission to take Frederick by the arm as they proceeded to the dining room behind Henry and his wife.

"I understand that you sing, Mr. Douglass," said Julia.

"Yes, I love music."

"I'll be at the piano," Julia replied, before turning around to face Eliza and

Ellen, their faces drained of the holiday spirit. Julia had gone too far, using music to deepen her bond with him. But she didn't care what they thought and turned to glance at Frederick's striking profile.

44.

I SHOULD BE HAPPY. I'm free.

But Frederick was not content, for now an entirely new life was before him, and he wasn't sure how it would turn out. He gave his farewell address to the British people on March 30, 1847, at the London Tavern on Bishopsgate Street. "Wherever I have gone, I have been treated with the utmost kindness, with the greatest deference; the most assiduous attention; and I have every reason to love England."

He paused, allowing the name to hover in the air, a talisman meant to enchant these English patriots, and stoke their sense of superiority. "Sir, liberty in England is better than slavery in America. Liberty under a monarchy is better than despotism under a democracy. Sir, I have known what it was for the first time in my life to enjoy freedom. I say that I have here, within the last nineteen months, for the first time in my life, known what it was to enjoy liberty. With these remarks, I beg to all my dear friends, present and a distant—those who are here and those who have departed—farewell."

Men surrounded him, shaking his hand, and tapping him at the shoulders. The ladies stood at the outer circle, deferential as required, but waved their handkerchiefs, gloves, and bonnets with fluttering ribbons.

Julia Griffiths, Eliza, and the Richardsons reached him, and Julia said, smiling all the while, "Oh, Mr. Douglass, that was so good, and so powerful, but you were not as good as I know you can be."

"Are you my new editor?"

"Are you asking me to come and help you in America?"

"That, Miss Griffiths, is premature."

"When and if you're ready, just summon me," Julia said.

"I will not hear another word," said Eliza, turning away. Then she caught herself, and said to Frederick, "Thank you for a splendid speech, and goodbye."

"Don't mind her. She doesn't like me, that's all. She says I talk too much, speak my mind far too often," Julia said.

"Will she come if you come?"

"Why, of course. She will be my chaperone, and I will be hers. We are inseparable."

"Then she will be joining us for dinner?"

"She wouldn't miss it."

"Good. We can all work to make sure that my last days aren't associated with a rift between sisters. Sisters are too important."

★

In the meantime, he learned that some things don't change.

Preparing for his trip home, he went on March 4 to the London office of the Cunard Line to purchase a ticket. The agent told him only one berth, number 72, remained unsold on the *Cambria* from Liverpool. Frederick paid the first-class price, but asked pointedly, "Will my color prove any barrier to my enjoying the rights and privileges enjoyed by the other passengers?"

The middle-aged man sitting at his desk, replied crisply, "No, sir, of course not."

"Thank you," Frederick said, and left the office, giving his status aboard the *Cambria* no further thought.

When Frederick boarded the steamer with his luggage and inquired about his berth, the clerk checked his roster and said, "Sir, that berth is taken."

"What? How can this be? I paid for it in London!"

"Sir, ticket sales are not my responsibility."

"Then give me someone who is responsible."

"I will send for the captain."

Frederick didn't blame the clerk for reporting a fact, but he needed to stand his ground, intuitively sure there was no mistake. He didn't move, despite the line behind him.

"Sir, please step aside until the captain arrives. Other passengers are waiting."

Frederick looked behind him noticed the frowning faces and stepped out of the line. But he made sure to take only two steps.

Within minutes, the captain approached, introducing himself without extending his hand. "I'm Captain Judkins, Captain Charles H. E. Judkins. And I'm here to inform you that the agent in London did not have the authority to sell you that ticket."

"Whether he had the authority or not, I paid," Frederick exclaimed, enraged but keeping his voice under control. He didn't want a loud, unseemly confrontation, shouts and pumped-up chests making a scene.

"Sir, the resolution of this matter is not up to me," Captain Judkins explained, his face and bearing unchanged, his military reserve on full display for even a minor conflict.

"Sir, I am surprised and deeply disappointed, but I need resolution, so what do you suggest?"

"Sir, you should inquire at the Cunard Liverpool office about what can be done, and I will gladly accompany you to Mr. McIver's office. But even he cannot change company policy."

"What policy?"

"Colored people can't have first-class berths and mingle with the other passengers. This is the American way."

Angrier with himself for forgetting the obvious, Frederick tried to maintain his composure. "Sir, thank you for the offer, but I can go alone after you give me the address."

"We will secure your luggage until you return."

He gave Frederick the address, and Frederick immediately turned away, leaving his luggage behind, too frustrated to think about possible theft.

Mr. McIver, an older Brit with spectacles on a pointed nose, came immediately to his point after Frederick described the situation: "Mr. Ford in London should not have sold you that ticket, especially because it was well known how much trouble you caused aboard the *Cambria* when you crossed the Atlantic two years ago. American travelers communicated their dissatisfaction and made clear that the company would suffer financially if you spoke out again. I can't allow the possibility of trouble, and so if you wish to return to the *Cambria* you must agree to accommodations separate from the white passengers. You can't enter the main dining hall for meals with them, and you can't attend the two Sunday services aboard ship. You must eat alone, sleep alone, be alone. Do you understand?"

Frederick stood silent. He knew he had no other choice. He would return to the *Cambria*, his dignity intact because he was awake once again, a fool no more.

The *Cambria* left Liverpool at noon on Sunday, April 4. The voyage turned out to be more pleasant than he had anticipated, despite the headwinds, the high waves, and the constant fog. The berth he received was much better than many of the other berths he saw aboard ship. All the officers, including the captain, were extremely polite, and the servants were attentive. A few passengers, hearing about Frederick's treatment, made a point to greet him and ask bland, safe questions, the common civilities about food and the monotonous weather.

Frederick landed in Boston on Tuesday night, April 20. After a restless night's sleep, he took the train to Lynn, where he was met at the station by Harriet and his boys, Lewis and Frederick, ages seven and five. When he saw their sparkling eyes and excited, jumping bodies constrained by Harriet's grip, he dropped his bag and rushed to them, catching up Frederick into his arms, and taking Lewis by the hand. And then he ran with his boys to their small house beside the railroad tracks.

45.

"JUST LOOK AT YOU. They didn't feed you right, that's for sure. We need to fatten you up a bit with some home cookin'." Anna saw him at the door, his frame filling it as she had remembered. She rushed to his arms after he lowered Frederick to the floor and released Lewis's hand. "Oh, Fred," she sighed. "You're still such a sight. My, my, my, you're still such a sight." Anna surrounded him with her arms and pressed her chest against his; it was hard and wide, as she remembered it. She held him close for a long time, even though she was distracted by the squeals of her happy sons. She stepped away, holding Frederick at arm's length, and commented about foreign food.

Frederick grinned, displaying those perfectly white teeth. Silently, Anna thanked the Lord that he didn't start smoking over there and ruin that beautiful smile.

"I dreamed about your biscuits every night," Frederick said.

"Papa, Papa!" the boys cried. "Play with us. Read us a story. Please, please, please."

"Now, boys, he just got here," Anna said, turning her head. "There will be time for all that."

"Please, please, please."

Anna approached them, taking two steps in the small room, and said with soft but severe authority, "I *told* you." That was all she needed to do, and they fell silent, looking down to avoid her withering eyes. Her word was law, and Frederick coming home was not going to change that.

"Now, Anna, they're just excited. That's all." Frederick's soothing words made the boys look up and smile, but their response made her bristle. "You know my rules, and that's not going to change 'cause your papa's home."

"Boys, I have some presents for you, all the way from across the ocean. You want to see them?"

"Yes, Papa, yes."

"You'll have to wait until I get all unpacked. Be good and listen to your mama until then, okay?"

Anna frowned. Until then? The rules were the rules, and her authority unconditional. There was no bargaining with her. She would have to have a long talk with Frederick and catch him up with how she and Harriet had managed in his absence.

She saw Frederick's reaction. His smile had disappeared. Anna quickly warmed her tone and said, "We'll have plenty of time for all that later, so just sit down, rest, and tell us all about your trip and those faraway places while I get things ready for some good eatin'. Harriet read your letters, but I just know you have so much more to tell."

Harriet spoke for the first time since they got home, "Yes, Fred, give us more details about England and Ireland and Scotland. Mr. Garrison printed your letter to him about England in the *Liberator*. I read it, and we learned so much, more than we got in your letters." Lest her accuracy sound like criticism, she made amends. "I didn't mean to say . . ."

Frederick raised his hand. "Don't worry about it. I just hoped that I would get the chance to tell you everything."

Tears came to Harriet's eyes. "Oh, Frederick, you got the chance. You're free, really free, and you're home."

"Free," he said, his voice breaking. He embraced her.

When will he say something about the wedding, Anna wondered, and ruin the good feelings all around?

There was silence. The word "free" a one-word benediction that could ease the fraught emotions of reunion. Anna repeated the word, moved by the moment, too.

The children stood still, knowing that this was a time, like in church, when children said nothing and waited for a signal to return to the usual noise.

"Well," said Frederick, and that word gave everyone permission to relax.

Anna said, "Now I'll finish with getting things ready, and Harriet, you check in on Charlie. It's time for him to get up and see his papa. Fred, he's grown so, and since he's the baby, you might just not recognize him."

She laughed, and Frederick replied, "Oh, I'm sure I'll be able to do that. They all look like you."

Black like me, she thought, *black skin with big eyes and big lips, and starting to look fat even when young*. The taunts when she was young back home were constant, and even her brothers and sisters, some of them as dark, would make her cry. "You're a black bitch," one of her sisters had said, to which Anna replied, "I'm a *mean* black bitch, and you had *better* be afraid."

Anna now said to Frederick with the lightest tone she could muster, "We can have some more, and see if at least one looks like you."

The banter embarrassed Harriet, and Frederick immediately turned his attention to her. "Well, Miss Harriet, let's talk about a new marriage. Who is this man taking you from us? What's his name?"

Anna interjected, "He's not taking her away. He's joining our family."

Still joking, Frederick waved his hand, indicating the small space around him, and replied, "Well, he can't live here. We barely have room for all of us."

"No, we can't live here, and I want our own place, just like you. I only hope I can make it as nice as Anna manages."

"*We* managed," corrected Anna. "We'll show that box with our papers and all, the receipts, everything we kept. We made it through."

Frederick frowned, and Anna assumed that Frederick interpreted her remark as criticism of his ability to take care of his family. Yes, money was hard to come by, but every penny helped, money from Frederick, gifts from Mr. Buffum, food and children's clothes from church and the Lynn Anti-Slavery Society, earnings from washing clothes and repairing shoes, vegetables raised in her garden. At first, after Frederick left for England, Anna's pride made her refuse offers of help, but Harriet persuaded her to relent. "These children don't care about your pride, Anna. They want food, clothes, and a roof over their heads."

"My mind was more at ease knowing how many people wanted to help and did help. When I must go away for lectures again, this will ease my mind," Frederick said.

"Now don't start talking about going away when you just got here," admonished Anna, maintaining levity in her lilt that evoked the Eastern Shore.

But Lewis heard only words about his father leaving, and he wailed, "No, Papa, you can't leave! Please don't leave!"

Frederick dropped to one knee and assured his son, "Now, don't you worry. I won't ever be away that long again."

Anna intervened. "Harriet, take Lewis to his room. I will not have him acting this way."

Frederick stood. "Anna, it's nothing. He's happy to see me, and wants more of me, that's all."

"I won't have it."

"Have what?"

"They will respect their father."

"There was nothing to what he said. I heard no disrespect, only disappointment."

"I know our boys."

"And I don't?"

"Two years is a long time. Lots of changes happen in two years."

"I couldn't come back any sooner."

"I know," replied Anna, softening. "Harriet, take the children, please."

She bent down to Lewis and placed her hands on his cheek. "Honey, everything will be fine. He's not leaving, not for a long time."

Harriet pulled the children away to the small room down the hall across from the room she had shared with Anna until today. Her personal belongings were now in the front room to make room for Frederick.

Anna regretted her reaction and prepared herself for a just chastisement. She didn't want to hear it, but at least she didn't have to hear it in front of Harriet and the boys.

"You should not have said that," Frederick gently admonished.

"I know."

"I have to work. I have to go away and give talks until I have enough money to start my own paper, a colored paper for colored people."

"Mr. Garrison and those white folks are not going to let you do that."

"I don't need their permission."

"When you take their money, you do."

"It's my money. I work for them, but it's my money. But I don't want to work for them anymore. I learned over there in Britain that I don't need them. They need me," Frederick said.

"I knew this day was coming. I prayed for you to see that you're better than all of them."

"Certainly, a better speaker, and maybe a better writer, but not a better man."

"No one said you had to be like Jesus," Anna replied, gently correcting.

"Just respectable, a man of standing."

"That won't matter. You could be the president, and white people will still think and say you're just a nigger."

"Don't say that word."

"Why not?"

"I just don't want to hear it in my house."

"*Our* house."

"We'll have to talk about this house."

"No," she said, staring.

"What?"

"No, we're not moving. I've moved enough times for you, three times in ten years. No more."

"Anna."

"I have roots here. I have my church, some friends, my garden. No."

"I didn't say we have to move. But we might, especially if the Committee sees me as competition. Lynn is too close to Boston," Frederick said.

"No."

"We can't stay here if I start a paper."

"I should have known better. I should have known. Every time you cross some water, you do something to make us move. Well, I'm putting my foot down."

"You can't do that."

"You've already decided, haven't you?"

"It might not happen. If I can't raise more money. I have money for a printer, but I need more for rent and paper."

"But if you do, then we're goin."

Frederick paused before answering. "Yes, but it doesn't have to be far, just far enough away."

Anna sat down, absorbing the weight of the inevitable. "You just don't know how hard it is to start over, make new friends, find a church. You are away, so you don't see how hard it is, so hard."

He had been home less than an hour and had managed to ruin their reunion, as if he had pulled a chair from under her.

"Just let me know when we need to start packin'," she conceded at last. "We don't have that much, but we have a house now, or we did."

"We'll have another, a bigger one when the time comes, and that won't be for a while," Frederick said.

That night she took him into her arms, pleased that a kind of peace had been restored, a fragile peace, perhaps, given her volatility and his mood swings, but she didn't want their first day to end with bitterness. Instead, she wanted the day to end in their bed, her around arms his back, his heavy body above her, her complete surrender to passion, love, respect, and adoration.

Anna knew she could be hard, easy to offend, and ready to fight for what she needed. But there was no denying the obvious truth: he was her man, now and forever, to have and to hold until the end.

On the following morning, Anna confided to Harriet, "He still loves me. I worried about that changing, but those people didn't do that over there. But we're leaving Lynn, maybe in the next few months. It might take a while, but it's happening."

Harriet's tears came at once. "Oh, Anna."

"We're leavin' but I'm not leavin' you," Anna insisted, taking Harriet's hands into hers. "You're leaving to marry Perry Adams, anyway, but we're still sisters, you hear? No matter what. Your man and my man can't change that, and I promise to be your sister, no matter how far away. I might just have to learn to read so I can read your letters when they come. Promise you won't forget me."

Anna's tears flowed, too.

Harriet embraced her. "I promise."

"I need you to watch the boys for me," Anna said after she withdrew from Harriet's arms. "We're going to see Rosetta in Albany before Fred goes on to a big meeting in New York. I'll come back after he goes south to the city. Will you do that for me?"

"You don't even have to ask."

"I'm nervous," Anna confessed. "It's been so long."

"You're still her mama," Harriet said, leaving unsaid Anna's great regret—never going to see Rosetta since she went off to school. Anna could have, but she didn't, too embarrassed to be in that house with those educated white women who probably, through no fault of their own, made her daughter ashamed of her. She feared seeing herself in Rosetta's eyes: the ugly, fat woman who couldn't read or write, the mother who would not get on a train and come see her. It took a visit from Frederick, after two years abroad, to get her to go. He had to see his oldest child and asked Anna to go with him.

Of course, she would go.

★

Once Frederick and Anna were seated, Lydia Mott announced, "I'll tell Abigail that you're ready. You'll be so proud of Rosetta. She has learned how to read and write, speaks well, and for one so young is quite poised. You will be so proud, indeed."

"We knew you would be best for her," Frederick said.

"Please excuse me," Lydia said before turning away.

Within moments, Abigail entered the room holding Rosetta's hand. Lydia stood behind them. As soon as Rosetta saw Frederick, she cried out, "Papa!" and broke away from Abigail and ran to her father, her arms extended until they encircled his legs. "Oh, Papa. I'm so happy to see you. I can't believe it. You're here. You're here."

He looked to both sisters as he patted Rosetta's head. "Give your mama a hug," Frederick whispered as Anna stood there stiffly with her hands tightly clasped.

Rosetta looked and quickly embraced her, too. "Hello, Mama. It's good to see you, too."

"I missed you," said Anna, her voice quivering. It hurt her to see that Rosetta preferred Frederick. *I should not have come. Rosetta didn't miss me one bit.*

"I thought it would be a wonderful surprise. I apologize for not preparing her for today. She knew you were coming but didn't know when," Lydia explained.

"No, no, you don't need to apologize for such happiness," Frederick replied as he bent down to embrace Rosetta again. "You are an excellent student, yes?"

She had tears in her eyes. "Yes, Papa. I know."

Frederick laughed lightly, but "Good," was all he could manage to say.

"Are we going home now?" Rosetta asked. "Mama, how are the boys? I have a new brother."

Before Anna could answer, Frederick answered, "No, my dear, not yet. I'm still working and have lectures to do. You know I give speeches, don't you?"

"Of course, Papa. Miss Lydia tells me everything about you, your travels, everything. I want to hear about England. Will you tell me stories about England, the castles, the queen?"

"Yes, dear, I will tell you about England. But I didn't see the queen."

Rosetta became suddenly serious, with a touch of sadness. "But not soon."

"No, not soon."

"When will I see Charles and Lewis and Junior?"

"We can't interrupt your studies."

"May I come home for Christmas?"

Stricken, Frederick looked to Lydia for assistance. Anna felt guilt as she considered that Rosetta had not been home for even the holidays. She didn't send for her or send gifts, as if Rosetta had been banished. Anna looked away, and Lydia stepped forward to take Rosetta's hand, pulling her away gently. "Now, Rosetta, your father is a very busy man, and he has missed being home for the holidays, too, remember. But soon you will all be together."

"We'll be all together?" asked Rosetta, looking to both her parents.

"Soon," was all that Frederick could say.

"I can wait. I know how to wait."

"Be good," Frederick said, embracing her again.

"I'll try, Papa. I always want you to be proud of me. You too, Mama."

Her afterthought stung Anna, reminding her that Rosetta had a long memory of their mother and daughter conflicts, their similarities reinforcing their rigid pride, Rosetta sulking after yet another chastisement from her, Anna sending her to her room, where Rosetta nursed her resentments. Rosetta was glad to leave for school, and she had made her absent father her hero, a shining prince, who could not be tarnished by daily confrontations and disappointments. He was rarely home even before going to Britain.

"Always," said Frederick. He looked to Lydia and added, "We need to leave now. Thank you for all that you have done."

"Our pleasure," said Abigail.

"I'll take that refreshment now," said Anna, taking a seat. "Do you have coffee?"

"Anna, the train."

"We have time, Fred. Rosetta, will you read your mama a story? I hear you read like a grownup. I like stories. Maybe Miss Abigail will help you pick one. Do you have a favorite?"

Anna looked to Frederick, silently daring him to object. Yes, she couldn't read, but she wasn't afraid of books or those who could read them.

Rosetta beamed, rising to the opportunity to show off. "I could read the Bible, but everybody does that. Miss Abigail, what do you think?"

Abigail frowned, aware of the tension and clearly wanting to escape. "Let's go the library and find something."

"And I'll get the coffee," said Lydia, following.

Frederick and Anna were left in the room, silently agreeing to say nothing as they waited, their hands in their laps, their heads down. And they said nothing to each other until perfunctory farewells at the station, where Anna boarded the train for her return to Lynn. Frederick would take the steamer to New York for his series of lectures, more clapping hands, and more money coming in. Abigail Mott was traveling with him and was already on the train.

"I must go," he said at the blow of the whistle.

He kissed her lightly on the cheek, the merest touch of his lips against her skin before he turned away.

"Goodbye," Anna replied, her hands at her sides, heavy as stones.

Only when the train had departed and Frederick was out of sight did Anna allow herself a tear.

46.

WHEN MARIA CHAPMAN HEARD that Frederick wanted to meet Garrison and Phillips at the Boston office of the American Anti-Slavery Society to discuss "serious matters," she invited herself to the meeting.

As usual, she had exchanged information with the zeal of a spy, and the flattered recipients of her inquiries, men and women eager to prove that knowledge was power, continued to share the details of conversations and confidences, even secrets. Virtually every step of Frederick's stay in Britain was offered up to her. It pleased her to know that Frederick's friends and associates could not keep secrets. She had no intention of allowing Frederick Douglass to start his own newspaper, despite his success abroad.

His musings to friends were of course not final decisions, but after he had admitted to another confidant that he didn't have the skills or the money for publishing, Maria meant to pound her sharpest nails into the coffin of his ambition.

Richard Webb wrote to Maria that most British women found their antislavery commitment only through a strong "romantic interest" in Frederick. "From what I hear of her, I wonder how he will be able to bear the sight of his wife after all the petting he gets from beautiful, elegant, and accomplished women in a country where prejudice against color is laughed at." Webb reported that he had questioned his judgments and considered not sending his letter but had reconsidered after reading it to his wife, sister-in-law, and cousin. They all agreed with him. Frederick's "insolence" could not be denied, but they made allowances. Webb's wife said that Frederick was "a child—a savage," and her sister said he was "a wild animal."

And so, Webb sent Maria a detailed denunciation of Frederick's behavior, a virtual chronicle of those first weeks in Ireland, but she could smell between the lines. Maria was an astute observer of male envy, and Webb's jealousy was far too obvious.

The earlier episodes, Frederick's clashes with John Collins, the threats of resignation, his fight in Indiana, his treatment of Buffum, and Webb's open disapproval, were all minor compared to the newest threat, Frederick's desire to start his own newspaper. Maria had to admit that Frederick could write. His letter to Garrison about Ireland, published in the *Liberator*, was particularly eloquent. The words were like the man, powerful without elegance, able to build a case by numbing the senses with vulgar details. Frederick's self-image as the appointed friend of the poor stepping over dirty children begging for food was stunning and almost obscene.

Of course, Frederick Douglass wanted to start his own newspaper! He would probably call it *Frederick Douglass' Paper* and litter the land with his opinions on everything, as if America cared to know what he thought about beyond denouncing slavery.

But the times were not right for such an enterprise. The unity of the Massachusetts abolitionists had to be maintained, and unruly men had to be leashed in. Maria was absolutely confidant in her power of containment. Frederick just needed pruning, like any good rose stem with sharp thorns. The ultimate flower would be worth the trouble.

Maria took one final look in the bedroom mirror, adjusted one stray curl in her hair, and started downstairs for the carriage waiting to take her to the Society office and the meeting with Wendell, Garrison, and Frederick.

She entered the Society office one hour before the arrival of the three men and strategically sat in a center chair to monitor their reaction to her surprise visit. She carefully weighed her options: tell them about Frederick's plans and develop a unified counteroffensive or withhold the knowledge and strike alone, reinforcing her singular power.

As usual, Wendell was calm and detached when he saw her. "Maria?"

And as usual, Garrison sputtered, gesticulating wildly. "Mrs. Chapman. What brings you here? It is our honor to see . . ."

Maria informed them of Frederick's talk of starting a paper.

Shaking his head, Wendell said, "I'm not surprised."

An appalled Garrison started pacing. "I knew it! I just knew it! When we met in England, I could tell those women were feeding his pride, swelling his head. What does he know about starting a paper?"

"I'm sure, Lloyd, that was said about you in 1831," said Maria, unimpressed with the argument. Newspapers proliferated in the land, most of them of disgraceful editorial quality. William Lloyd Garrison was a powerful advocate for abolition, but he was not a good editor. Others did a better job, herself included, and when he was away, the improvements were obvious.

"We need him on the circuit, now more than ever," Garrison insisted.

"Precisely," answered Maria, "and my plan is to organize a tour that will be so time consuming that such foolishness as starting a paper will pass from his mind."

"Good," said Garrison, relaxing. She could see the softening of his gray eyes through those cheap spectacles.

"And, of course, you and Frederick will tour together. Wendell can't leave Boston right now." Ann was ill again.

Entering the office, Frederick's smile immediately disappeared as he saw Maria. He had wanted a meeting of men, and she had ruined his plan. He immediately took the offensive, striding across the room without the customary civilities and came to his point at once: "Mr. Garrison, Wendell, and Mrs. Chapman, I've come here to tell you that I plan to start a colored newspaper with money raised by my English friends."

He outmaneuvered her. Maria's information was not up to date. "How much?" she asked.

"Three thousand," he answered.

Garrison patronized: "A paper, Frederick, will ruin you! Three thousand dollars can be quickly lost. Your family needs the money."

Frederick straightened his back and said with intense calm, "I am supported by my family in this endeavor."

Garrison pressed further. "Then are you saying that the *Liberator* is not enough?"

"Sir, the *Liberator* is a fine paper, but it is not a paper edited and written by colored men. I see a successful colored paper as the best kind of proof that colored people are equal to whites. We colored people need our own voice."

Garrison frowned deeply and began to intone the obituaries of failed colored newspapers. "*Freedom's Journal*, the *Weekly Advocate*, the *Colored American*, the *Mirror of Liberty*, the *Elevator*, the *Clarion*, the *People's Press*, and just recently, the *National Watchman*. The land is full of such wrecked experiments."

Wendell spoke to Frederick for the first time, "We need you now, remember?"

"Wendell, I'm still a friend, a coworker," said Frederick warmly. Maria could see that Wendell still held a special place in his affections.

But Garrison would not relent. "Frederick, you are just nine years out of slavery, without formal education, and trained only as a caulker. Don't you think people will charge you with blatant ambition and presumption?"

"I have been accused of this ever since the moment I realized I was equal to any of you, and that was long ago," Frederick replied.

Maria gripped the arms of her chair and lifted her eyebrows to signal her displeasure. “Editing is a dull, backbreaking job. It’s a form of drudgery that would not leave you much time for public speaking, which is your God-given gift. Your voice is one of the most eloquent in the land, and I never hated slavery more than when I first heard you speak. It should not be stilled now.”

Softening now, Garrison added, “It is impractical to combine the editor with the lecturer, without either causing the paper to be neglected, or the sphere of lecturing to be severely circumscribed.”

Maria smiled, knowing that flattery was Frederick’s Achilles heel and stood to punctuate her victory. “You will need to go west this summer, Frederick. Many of the letters I receive demand that you and Mr. Garrison travel. Thousands are promised to attend your lectures. Garrison and Douglass, returned from his triumphs in Britain. A perfect combination, at a perfect time. Philadelphia, Harrisburg, Youngstown, Salem, Cleveland, Buffalo, and . . .”

“Yes!” exulted Garrison. “We will carry the torch of conscience into the dark places of the West this summer.”

“That doesn’t give me much time with my family after so long a time gone,” Frederick said.

“Your wife and children have become accustomed,” said Maria, unmoved. “Besides, you must leave them for the May annual meeting in New York in any case.” She was bored with this discussion. Frederick had capitulated with only a passing genuflection to the call of family. Despite his protestations, it was clear that family would always be second to Frederick Douglass. His ambition was boundless, given only the limits that race imposed on him. If he had been born white, she decided, he would in no time be a congressman or a senator. When all was said and done, he was a politician, attuned to the needs of his constituents. At this point, his constituents were not the slaves, the free colored, or his family, but three white people in Boston. Despite the welcome home receptions and invitations to speak at Black churches, his most important drive was pleasing *them*.

“Since you are determined to write, why not write for the *Liberator* and the *Standard*?” Maria asked casually, knowing full well that Douglass would bite at the bait. She rose and gathered the folds of her black dress.

“I expect a raise for my added work. It’s only reasonable,” Frederick claimed.

Standing erect, Maria said casually, “Of course, and give my regards to your dear wife, who will, no doubt, benefit from your financial rise in the world. Good day.” She departed, not looking back.

★

On May 11, 1847, Frederick was scheduled to give his first major address since his return from Britain at the annual meeting of the American Anti-Slavery Society in New York. Now officially a free man, he was in a combative mood, and the Society needed his fire. The Mexican War was still raging and there was too much talk of compromise and accommodation with the South. Excluding Wendell, of course, Frederick was the best speaker before the public that day.

In Boston, Maria anticipated controversy as she impatiently waited for news items, letters from delegates, and the exhaustive annual reports. By the end of the month, she learned that at ten o'clock, when the annual meeting opened for business, there were only a few hundred people, mostly delegates, in the Apollo Hall, a part of the vast Broadway Tabernacle that seated almost 4,000 people. Although the empty seats suggested a disaster, the public came later, avoiding the drudgery of prayer and the reading of committee reports.

Garrison introduced Frederick, praising his success abroad, and read long accounts of the farewell meeting at the London Tavern. Exasperated, the audience began chanting, "Douglass, Douglass, Douglass." Garrison's face reddened, but he maintained a stiff smile and cut his remarks. Applauding, the audience came to its feet, and Garrison joined the ovation, turning to Frederick, and said, "Son of my heart, they are yours."

When the tumult subsided, Frederick issued a warning: "I do not doubt but that a large portion of this audience will be disappointed, both by the manner and the matter of what I shall this day set forth. Say what you will of England, of the degradation, of the poverty, and there is much of it there, there is liberty there, not only of the white man, but for the Black man also. The instant that I stepped upon the shore and looked to the faces of the crowd around me, I saw in every man a recognition of my manhood, and an absence, a perfect absence of everything like that disgusting hate with which we are pursued in this country."

Frederick's voice then deepened when he announced, standing absolutely still, "I have no love for America. I have no patriotism. I have no country. What country have I?"

To abolitionists accustomed to Garrison's broadsides against his country, Frederick's attack still came as a shock. Jaws dropped, hands delicately touched arms, and everyone listened. During a war, public patriotism was expected; no, demanded.

Frederick turned to Garrison for a moment, then shouted out: "How can I love a country that dooms three million of my brethren, some of my own kindred, my own brothers, and my own sisters, who are now clanking the chains of slavery upon the plains of the South, whose warm blood is now making fat the soil of Maryland and Alabama?"

No one answered. He avowed: "I have not, I cannot have, any love for this country, as such, or for its Constitution. I desire to see its overthrow as speedily as possible, and its Constitution shivered into a thousand fragments, rather than this foul curse should continue to remain as now." The audience was stunned, and for the first time at a meeting of the American Society Frederick was booed.

Before this day, only whites could denounce the Constitution and call for its overthrow, and now Frederick Douglass did it before a mixed audience, shocking even abolitionists. He expected catcalls from racist rabble, but the open derision of abolitionists disappointed him.

Those most upset kept their distance. The leaders on the stage maintained their customary polite demeanor, but Frederick could feel the chill in their grim congratulations.

He didn't care. He needed to say what he did. It was time and there was no turning back.

Later, Garrison told Frederick, "We'll have even larger crowds in the heartland. They hate nothing more than an ungrateful Negro. It's one thing to be Black, and it's another to be Black *and* unpatriotic." He was not offering caution, just a reminder that Black notoriety attracted dangerous crowds.

"That is not my problem to solve. When we say what white people don't want to hear, they call us unpatriotic," said Frederick.

Reading the various accounts, Maria was thrilled by the potential drama in the heartland and greater publicity for the cause. Of course, she didn't want Frederick to be harmed. Nevertheless, there had to be more noise in the land, rhetorical attack and counterattack, verbal war at its finest.

Within days, Frederick was the object of vilification that shocked even Maria. The *Switch*, a newspaper published in Albany and reprinted throughout New England, printed an unsigned article that began, "Niggers and Nastiness. The offense is rank—it smells to heaven: a depraved portion of the people, and of the press, have for some time past been gratifying their morbid tastes in lionizing a disgusting, impertinent Negro, who styles himself Frederick Douglass. The feelings of the decent portion of the community have, times without number, been outraged by this soot head thrust into their midst. It is needless task for us to recapitulate the instances of this wool head's sauciness." But recapitulate it did, mentioning two events calculated to arouse the hostility of white men especially.

In Albany, before traveling south to New York for the annual convention of the American Society, Frederick had visited the public gallery of the state legislature in the company of a white woman, who, according to the *Switch*, "forgot what was due to the community and to the delicacy of her sex and introduced this offensive creature into the Ladies Gallery, where she left him." The sergeant at arms informed Douglass that he had to sit in the colored section, but "Sambo refused to go." Frederick was ejected forcibly. When his friend and companion returned, she was sent to find him, and soon, as the *Switch* concluded, "they left the Capitol cheek by jowl."

But this story was only a prelude to the more damaging accusation: that Frederick and his unnamed female white companion had arranged to have adjoining staterooms aboard the *Hendrik Hudson* enroute to New York and again on the return trip to Albany. The *Switch* breathlessly reported: "The woman sent the chambermaid to the captain's office for two state rooms, the keys of which the chambermaid delivered to her. The female, on inspection, told the chambermaid that the rooms were not what she wanted—that they must have a door leading into each other. The person in charge of the office, without hesitation, changed their location."

To ensure no misunderstanding, the writer ended with this disclaimer: "We wish it distinctly understood that we cast no imputations on the character of the white woman, who thus gads about the country with a Negro, but she certainly manifests a depravity of taste, that should induce her friends to look sharply after her—and as for this thunder-cloud, he should be kicked into his PROPER PLACE, AND KEPT THERE."

Of course, this account was utter nonsense. Maria wrote immediately to Abigail Mott, the unnamed white woman, who had been invited by Maria to go with Frederick on his lecture tour and sent detailed accounts of what transpired.

Maria expected Frederick to defend himself in print. Frederick was a fighter. The *Liberator* printed his public rebuttal in June. As usual, he was not succinct. But the facts were simple. Suffering from a severe cold and hoarse throat on the *Hendrik Hudson*, he had asked Abigail to book a room because he couldn't get one as he was not white. Without a room, he would have to sleep on deck and worsen his condition.

But the *Switch* was only interested in conjuring up the nightmare of every nervous white man in America. The *Switch* did not need to delineate this image in detail, for it was addressing a vast audience taught about the Negro since childhood.

In the meantime, Frederick assured his *Liberator* readers a thought of impropriety never crossed his mind while sleeping in the adjoining state room. "We needed neither bolts, bars, nor locks, to keep us in the path of virtue and rectitude." By taking the high road, Frederick infuriated the *Switch* editor and other white writers even more. Maria liked this about Frederick, despite her misgivings about him. He always managed to expose the rot in their enemies making the war against them easier.

47.

FREDERICK WAS CELEBRATED, ESPECIALLY in Black communities, as a conquering hero who so dazzled the British that they purchased his freedom. Once his touring resumed, the tightly packed stagecoaches, their constant rolling, the dirt, the endless roads, the humidity and sweat, and the continuous meetings with little or no sleep, all forced a more immediate reaction: he now hated the itinerant life. Tours like this had to end.

A newspaper would reduce his time on the road. He could spend more time with Anna and the children, who were beginning to show resentment for his long absences. Frederick also recognized that he knew little about the business of publishing.

On reaching Ohio, Frederick made speeches every day in towns thirty to forty miles apart, standing under tents, in drafty halls, and in the open air during torrential rains. What started as a scratchy irritation was now a hoarseness that made speeches very difficult to complete. Eventually, he became so hoarse he had to stop talking.

But it was Garrison who had to stop touring in September. He was no longer exultant about the tour. There was too much work to be done, too much traveling, not enough rest. After speaking in a drizzling cold rain, he returned to his room, went immediately to bed, woke from a restless sleep with a fever, the pain aching in his entire body, and took an emetic, hoping that it would relieve his stomach and move his bowels. He sent for a doctor, who recommended absolute rest and no visitors.

Garrison urged Frederick to continue with the tour."We cannot disappoint all those waiting to hear at least one of us," Garrison said, looking so much older now. "Express my regrets and watch that voice, that most eloquent voice."

"Sir, are you sure that I should leave you?"

"I am sure."

"I can stay until you have completely recovered."

"No, you must go."

Still worried, Frederick went on to Buffalo, Troy, Rochester, and other towns in New York. He would attend the National Colored Convention in Troy and finalize his decision about Rochester after meetings with prominent white and colored citizens there. He would have to act quickly. After talking with so many people about a newspaper, he couldn't keep his change of plan from Garrison that much longer. Yes, he had agreed to not publish another newspaper, but a man could change his mind.

★

Pleased that Frederick would be writing more for the *Liberator*, Garrison had announced in the paper as early as July that Frederick abandoned his plans for starting his own newspaper. In fact, Frederick had defended Garrison against charges that he had forced Frederick to stop.

After spending months battling illness and debts, Garrison was feeling more vigorous and more combative. His enthusiasm for the trip with the potential of making new converts and renewing old friendships renewed his body. He had had high hopes for the expansion of the antislavery cause, but on this trip his expectations were deeply personal. Although he traveled with Frederick in England, and celebrated his triumphs as did so many others, Garrison could sense a growing distance between them, and he wanted the restoration of that intense connection he discovered in 1841–1842. He also worried about Frederick, who seemed entirely exhausted; his voice was virtually gone.

By mid-October Garrison was still in Cleveland, and after a confinement of six weeks, he asked his wife Helen, "Is it not strange that Douglass has not written a single line to me inquiring after my health, since he left me on a bed of illness?"

He saw an item in a Cleveland newspaper about Frederick Douglass starting the *North Star*. Garrison closed his eyes, believing for an instant that his eyes were failing like so many other parts of his frail body. Then he looked again. Yes, there it was, in print: proof of Frederick's deception.

Frederick could have had the decency to tell him directly, to explain. Given their history didn't he *deserve* honesty?

Returning to Boston without seeing Frederick, Garrison criticized him privately to Maria Chapman and Wendell Phillips and others in his circle. But they were resigned.

"It was inevitable," said Wendell.

"It will fail," announced Maria.

"He lied to me," Garrison said.

"He will be our spokesman in the west," said Wendell.

"He lied to me," insisted Garrison, disillusionment weakening his voice.

"He's lied before," Maria said, her lips pursed.

On October 1, Garrison opted to be gracious. Helen had urged him to be charitable, and the *Liberator* announced the start of the *North Star* and wished it well, only expressing regret that the American Society was losing Frederick as a lecturer.

Garrison withheld public comment about the newspaper for three months after the publication of the first issue on December 3.

He understood the impact of silence. It could do more damage than thousands of words.

48.

IN 1847 ROCHESTER WAS a prosperous city of fifty thousand people on the Genesee River near Lake Ontario. Frederick had been there in 1843 and 1845 on speaking tours, but only briefly.

His hosts, then and now, were Amy and Isaac Post, the city's most prominent white abolitionists and active participants in the Underground Railroad. Frederick took an immediate liking to Amy and her husband because the couple did not go out of their way to demonstrate their freedom from racial prejudice. They made no announcements about their moral superiority and never declared that Negroes were their "special" brothers and sisters. Members of the colored community in Rochester confirmed this impression. Frederick also could not forget their hospitality in 1843, opening their home to a total stranger.

But it was the report of leaders in the small community of free Negroes that convinced Frederick that Rochester was the place to select as home for his newspaper. They told him that slavery was hated so intensely there that citizens openly harbored fugitives. Of course, there was segregation, but public bigotry was uncommon. Most establishments allowed Negroes to do business with them. A list of the ones to avoid was readily available in a pamphlet passed around the community.

In search of new subscribers, Frederick went on to Troy, where he attended another National Colored Men's Convention, convened for the first time since 1843 but attracting few delegates. At the convention he encountered Henry Highland Garnet, who called for a national Negro press and made it the major issue of the convention, saying, "I'm tired of the short, embarrassing lives of countless colored newspapers. Only a single newspaper, financially supported by the national community, and drawing on the best colored minds in the nation, can forcibly speak for colored Americans to white Americans."

Given the poor financial record of most Negro papers, this recommendation made sense, but Frederick opposed it. He raised his objection during a break in the proceedings. "The community needs diversity," he argued, "not uniformity."

Garnet asked sarcastically, "Do you fear that if you had a paper to offer, we would not select yours?"

Frederick said, "I will abstain during the vote."

"Indeed," said Garnet, "Don't you think you should stand and be counted for all the opinions you so pointedly defend?"

"To not vote is also a decision."

"Very well," said Garnet and called for the vote.

This time Garnet did not fail. Even Massachusetts, home to numerous magazines, papers, and sheets, voted nine to five in favor of support for one Negro journal.

But the resolution had no authority, and so Frederick quietly dismissed it with the belief that if the colored community could only support one newspaper it would be his.

After his victory, Garnet approached Frederick with great charm, smiling still, and said, "You know, Douglass, you and I are not that much different."

Conciliation seemed out of character, and Frederick replied testily, "Our disagreements are fundamental."

"Hold it before we begin another war. Have you ever heard of a white man named John Brown?"

"No, and why should I know him?"

"He's a man who could show you that we do have a great deal in common. He can convince," said Garnet.

"Why are you telling me about this man? If he believes, as you do, about violence and rebellion, then we have nothing in . . ."

"Perhaps, one day."

"Why do you still insist about this? We can never get together," said Frederick.

"Brown is only trying to talk with many prominent colored men," replied Garnet.

"He wants to meet me?"

"When he decides to see you."

Now totally exasperated by these mysterious references to a white man who presumed to summon Negroes, Frederick snapped, "He's wasting his time if thinks he can replace Garrison."

"I said no such thing. But are you afraid?"

"No!"

Garnet whispered once more, "I can't say anymore, but wait to hear from him."

"What?" cried Frederick, but Garnet turned away, leaving Frederick to wonder about a white man who could inspire Henry Highland Garnet to seek Frederick Douglass out as an associate.

"Have you heard of a white man named John Brown?" he later asked Isaac Post.

"A common name, but you must be asking about John Brown of Springfield, Massachusetts. He is serious about helping colored people. He's strange, though."

"How?"

"He's one of those religious fanatics who seem to flourish in the hills. He'll talk to anyone who'll listen about God, Armageddon, and the destruction of slavery," said Post.

"Then you've met the man?"

"My dear Douglass, some people are better left to gossip and rumor. You surely are not considering sitting down at his table? He lives in a shack surrounded by Lord knows how many children."

"Garnet recommended a meeting," said Frederick.

"I don't trust Garnet. And you shouldn't trust him or whomever he recommends."

Frederick was still intrigued. But he had more pressing concerns and soon forgot about John Brown. He needed to return to Lynn, write a prospectus for his newspaper, and tell Anna about the move to Rochester.

After much thought, Frederick decided to call his newspaper the *North Star.* He wanted it to be a beacon of hope to people, especially Black people, as the celestial body helped slaves find their way north to freedom. He wanted white readers, too, but he hoped to attract an unprecedented number of Black ones. He penned a mission statement for potential subscribers and later sent it to other editors, Black and white: "The object of *The North Star* will be to attack slavery in all its forms and aspects; advocate Universal Emancipation; exact the standard of public morality; promote the moral and intellectual improvement of the colored people; and to hasten the day of freedom to our three million enslaved fellow-countrymen."

Frederick wanted to keep to these lofty ideals, but he had to be practical. His future subscribers, most of them working men and women, would want to know the cost, and he added, "The paper will be printed on a double medium sheet, at $2.00 per annum, paid in advance, and $2.50 if payment is delayed over six months."

He was now prepared. The groundwork had been laid. There was nothing more to negotiate; he had to announce the move to Anna and have her start packing up. But before returning home, he had one more person to see.

49.

FREDERICK HAD RECEIVED FROM John Brown an invitation to talk about "urgent matters." Curious and suspicious, Frederick wondered, *How did Brown know where to find me? Garnet must have sent a message.*

In any case, Frederick, as directed, met Brown at his dry good store, Perkins and Brown, near the center of Springfield on a bitterly cold but snowless November afternoon.

Brown had a lean body with a head that seemed too small for his five-foot, ten-inch frame. His coarse black hair, with touches of gray at the temples, was trimmed unfashionably close to the skin and somehow called attention to a mouth with an invisible upper lip as wide as his glaring, blue–gray eyes. At once, Frederick knew John Brown was utterly humorless.

His cold hand gripped Frederick's as he declared, "I have followed your career. God wills that we meet."

Brown turned, leading Frederick to his house on Franklin Street, a drab dwelling with chipped white paint that squatted in a neighborhood without even the hope of pretension. Inside, no cushions, ornaments, or rugs lay about to soften the hard lines of the austere parlor furniture, and no pictures graced the cracking walls. Brown had his wife, Mary, and five of his seven children, all thin like their father, lined up to bow or curtsey as they were introduced to Frederick. When each was done, Brown said, "You may go."

"Yes, Father," they all replied solemnly, including Mrs. Brown. Frederick had never heard a wife refer to her husband as "Father."

Impressed and baffled by the strained atmosphere of these introductions, Frederick observed, "You have a striking family."

"We are not all here," Brown replied, withholding a smile or nod of the head. "Jason and Ruth are in Ohio, and God in his infinite wisdom, has deemed fit to take seven of my children from me."

"I'm sorry."

"Don't be. The Lord giveth and the Lord taketh away. Death comes to us all. Come, let us eat." Brown led Frederick to a plain table, and the two men, served by Mary Brown, ate a simple meal of beef soup, potatoes, and cabbage. They discussed nothing as Brown's wife responded, without hesitation, to his slight waves of hand and subtle shifts of his eye. When done with the meal, Brown said to Frederick, "We both hate slavery, and I have a plan to destroy it."

Mrs. Brown began removing the plates. They waited until she was done.

"Do you follow Mr. Garrison?" Frederick asked, reasserting his principled territory.

"Garrison is a courageous man. But, no, he believes that people can be made perfect. Only God is perfect. Man is naturally depraved, a sinner," Brown replied.

"But a sinner can be converted."

Brown replied forcefully, "Some can never be saved. Some people stand proud before God and cannot be persuaded. The slaveholder will not be persuaded."

"Your plan, then?"

"God will destroy them, using us as His instruments." Brown challenged Frederick, who didn't respond, although he was curious to see to what lengths Brown would go.

"A system of blood and terror must perish by blood and terror," Brown said. The fireplace log had dimmed, and no one attempted to revive it. "As we are told in scripture, Hebrews 9:22, 'Without the shedding of blood, there is no remission of sins.' I have a plan."

Standing by, Mary Brown went to the sideboard, opened a drawer, and produced a map.

"The map will explain everything," said Brown. But before he unrolled it, he said that slaveholders had forfeited the right to life, and this time he quoted the Old Testament, intoning with the burning finality of Isaiah, "By the breath of God they perish, and by the blast of His anger they come to an end."

Brown unrolled the map, pointed to the Allegheny Mountains, and proclaimed softly, "God has given the strength of these hills to freedom. They were placed here for the freeing of your race."

Frederick stared at the mountains, there long before Black slaves arrived in America. He had no idea what Brown meant but said nothing to correct him.

"These mountains are the basis of my plan. I know these mountains well. There are many natural forts and good hiding places." Brown's plan was simple, daring, and outrageous. Brown would strike at slavery by selecting twenty-five men who, in armed squads of five, would periodically leave secret hideouts in the mountains and go to the farms below and enlist the most daring of slaves. His goal was to attract one hundred courageous strong men properly drilled to leave the mountains and gather up even larger numbers of slaves. The brave would stay with him, the weak sent north with the help of the Underground Railroad. The operation would eventually expand to other areas.

He admitted the possibility of treachery, but he considered a precaution: "I will only send people I can trust absolutely. Too many plans have gone wrong because of disloyalty. I will not fail."

Refusing to look away from Brown, used to forcing submissions, Frederick wanted more details. "How will you support all these men?"

Brown responded harshly, "The enemy will support them. This is war, and as in war, I will take whatever is necessary to support my men and free all slaves."

"But, sir, when you free a few slaves, the word will get around, and masters, realizing that their property is not secure, will arm or sell their slaves further south!"

"That's just what I want them to do. I will follow the slaves and get more. Slavery is weakened if we drive it out of one county. Don't you *see* that?"

"They will send bloodhounds into the mountains to hunt you down, to drive you all out," said Frederick.

"We will be in the mountains, hiding. We will be in remote places assisted by the slaves, behind rocks. We'll just pick them off as they come. Once we've killed one group, they will be less inclined to send others."

"You can be surrounded, cut off from supplies."

"They won't be able to do it," Brown objected, then paused, taking deep breaths. "Even if we are surrounded, I can only be killed, and I can think of no better use of my life than to give it for freeing the slave."

There was only the calm acceptance of death in John Brown's eyes. Frederick was appalled, even as he felt a deep sadness. Brown was willing to sacrifice himself and perhaps everyone else around him, including his own family, to his relentless purpose. "There have to be other ways," Frederick said without conviction. He believed in peace, but recognized that death, coming in the night with armed, angry men, might be the only way.

"No. When they killed Elijah Lovejoy in '37, I went to a church meeting and swore to God that I would destroy slavery. Destroy it. Slaveholders will volunteer nothing. They have no shame, no guilt. Their hearts are hardened against the pleas of ministers and Garrisons everywhere. No, only when they are hit against the head will they free the slave. There must be blood, and I am willing to pay. 'For those who are self-seeking and do not obey the truth but obey unrighteousness, there will be wrath and fury,' Romans 2:8."

Brown scanned the room and added, "We live like this because I am saving money for my plan. My wife and children all understand. They all know what I intend to do, and they are willing to help. They all feel as I do, that I have waited too long, too long. How long must the slave wait for freedom to come? How many must die in bonds while you wait for consciences to change?"

Unintimidated by this direct challenge, Frederick noted Brown's remorseless eyes and replied: "Thank you, sir, for trusting me enough to share your plan. But I cannot endorse it, even as we share the same hope."

"How long can the slaves wait?"

Frederick rose and excused himself. "I'm going now. Thank you for your hospitality."

"The Lord will return you to me. I am the instrument of His indignation. Isaiah 13:5."

"Good day."

50.

FREDERICK PREPARED HIMSELF FOR domestic war. Earlier, he had demanded that Harriet leave his house after she had dared to pursue marriage without his permission. He had apologized, writing, "I now wish you to stay in my family."

She stayed until the wedding, never mentioned his threat again, and beamed as he stood beside her during the ceremony, prepared to give her away to Perry

Frank Adams, a free laborer also from Talbot County. Adams was short and dark with calloused, rough hands, but he adored Harriet, wanted a good life for her and their future children, and was openly deferential to Frederick. "Sir, thank you for your blessing as the head of the family."

Anna was happy for Harriet, but after the wedding her silence about Harriet's absence suggested her loss was too painful to acknowledge. One day, Anna surprised herself when she called out Harriet's name, needing her help.

"Harriet, come."

She caught the lapse, standing frozen as Frederick sat in the front room reading the *Liberator*. Surprised, he looked up, and Anna annoyed by her mistake, said peevishly, "I managed before she came here."

Frederick decided to take the offensive, bring the issue of Harriet up, get it over with, and move on. "I was angry because she didn't ask me, but I realized my mistake, and I was there finally." He refused to look away, frowning to convey his intention: *Don't argue with me*.

Anna sighed, "Maybe you can go and see them in Springfield when you're on the road again."

"Oh, Springfield," he said, thinking of John Brown living in the same town. "I can do that, but a visit will have to wait until after everything has been arranged for Rochester."

"Everything? Rochester? What are you talking about?"

The moment had come.

"I've decided to begin a newspaper, and we'll need to move to Rochester, New York, out west, near Canada."

There it was. He was the head of the house, the main source of the family income. His dream was what mattered, and that was that.

Anna sat still, her face dark and foreboding. She shook her head, and muttered, "Um . . . um . . . um. After *all* these years, you still don't know me like I know you. While you was away, I've been putting things away, some linen, dishes. You would never notice. I knew this day was comin' after you started talking about the paper and wouldn't stop. You've been crossing deep rivers all yo' life, and when you come back from a crossin', you want a change, a *big* change, and you always expect me and all the rest of us to drop whatever we're doing 'cause your idea just has to be, just *has* to be, no matter what. So, I can't say I don't know the man I married, and I can't say I'm surprised. I now can laugh at myself for stayin' mad about it so long. I liked being mad at you for a while. But no more, no more."

"Well. You surprise me sometimes," said Frederick.

"I'm always the good wife."

"And it will be a good life for us out there in Rochester."

"Where? You said near Canada? Ain't that north, *real* north?"

"Yes."

"Do you like the cold or somethin'? We keep going more and more north, so far now we're almost out of our own land. I never liked snow and wind. Remember those rooms off Buzzard Bay? You swore you would never get that cold again. And now we're goin' to freeze so that you could write some paper. I hope your fingers stay warm," Anna said. "Do we have enough money? I have some savings from my shoe binding. That can help, but that won't be enough."

"My English friends gave me some money for a printer and paper."

Anna insisted, "But what about us? Will there be enough for your family after the paper? Can you make this all work?"

"I think so. I hope so, but I can't be certain. But I must try. For a time, I might have to do the paper and still give lectures. We'll see."

"When do we leave, and where're we going to stay?"

"I'm looking for a house, but I will be renting some rooms until I find something to my satisfaction, and then I will come back to take you all to Rochester after I get the paper started, after the new year more than likely."

"And we'll get Rosetta from that school in Albany," Anna decided. It was not a recommendation. Her eyes dared him to disagree.

"Yes, we will bring Rosetta with us."

"How long will it all take?"

"I don't know. I hope to have the first issue of my paper in December, and find a house to board us, and then come back for you all before the spring."

"We're moving in winter."

"Yes, and we will be already for spring when it comes, the perfect beginning for our new life. Meanwhile, I will be bringing in money with new lectures. I'm more popular than ever."

"The perfect beginning," replied Anna, unsmiling.

But after she had seemingly agreed to the idea of moving, Anna became increasingly antagonistic toward the idea. She was also not feeling well, and as the time for the move approached, planned for February, she became more and more agitated, repeating sour comments about packing, handling three boys, and, of course, the weather in Rochester.

Frederick had to get there as soon as possible, hoping to have a first edition by early December at the absolute latest. First, he had to find a temporary place to live before Anna and the children followed; and second, he had to find an office space for his printer.

As usual, Anna packed his travel bag with clean linen, biscuits, and cold chicken, but they did not embrace when it was time for him to go. Anna stood at the open door like a guard.

"Goodbye," Anna quietly intoned, and Frederick was out, carrying his bags in both hands.

Aboard the train, he wondered about the upcoming tenth anniversary of their marriage and his escape. The ninth anniversary had passed without comment, but he was sure that ten years merited recognition, if not a celebration. Anna had made his escape possible, and their marriage was a solid foundation for raising a family with free children. Anna was still too hard on them, but she was a good mother, raising them to be respectful, church-going children, who needed to be special in a harsh, judgmental country. Her illiteracy remained a serious problem, but it was still not too late to teach her, and in the meantime the children would receive excellent educations in schools with white children.

He missed the passionate intensity of those first years when they had only each other to survive those first winters in New Bedford. As a cultured gentleman, he was not supposed to admit it, but he liked having sex with Anna, when she was in the mood.

But now he knew. He did not love her as the romantic poets described love. He respected Anna, but he did not yearn to be with her. After ten years, he knew no wife could be perfect. He had to accept Anna's limits as well as his own—and he knew he was not easy. Ending his marriage was out of the question, for the sake of the children and his reputation.

But there was a gnawing ache he could not relieve. He was married but alone. He wanted more than a wife. He wanted a partner.

He and Anna were not equals. They could never be equals.

51.

FREDERICK HAD TO ACT quickly after arriving in Rochester. He found an office to rent at 25 Buffalo Street. He also had to find a place to live. With the help of Isaac Post, he found a shabby but temporary tenement in downtown Rochester before continuing his search for a house to rent for the family so that the issue of permanent housing would no longer weigh on his mind as he finalized the first issue of the *North Star*. But finding the house for a family of six was not as easy as he had hoped, since he wanted to integrate a white neighborhood with only a small number of listings available. He quickly discovered that despite claims for racial liberalism by city boosters, property owners were reluctant, and sometimes hostile, about allowing Frederick and his family into "respectable neighborhoods."

In the meantime, Frederick hired a Black writer out of Pittsburgh, Martin Delaney, to enlist subscribers. But the numbers, though steady, did not come fast enough to meet the sixty-dollars-a-week publication expenses.

Frederick had to decide about the content of the first issue of the *North Star*. After considering several possible approaches, he chose to attack Senator Henry Clay of Kentucky, a slave owner, for supporting colonization. Clay had a long and distinguished career as speaker of the house, secretary of state, and United States senator. His failure to become president after three attempts did not diminish his prestige and dominance in American politics. But a rebuke from Frederick Douglass could get needed attention and attract subscribers.

Frederick was proud of his countless hours writing lines and then scratching them out. When he was done, the letter was almost the entire first issue, save for a few announcements about upcoming events. He judged his essay a worthy introduction to his new profession. It was a loud-enough calling card.

But on the night before publication, he woke up suddenly, his heart beating rapidly, and his mind racing. Maybe he had made a mistake by choosing Henry Clay as his first target for his first issue. Clay had money for good and expensive lawyers. Frederick did not. All of it had to go into the newspaper and support for his family.

Frederick could not sleep.

His night of doubt was forgotten the following morning when the first sheet of his paper rolled off the press. It was beautiful. He received enthusiastic congratulations in person for the first edition, but sales were tepid, one sale after one lecture, two sales after another. Little more.

Frederick was ready to move his family to Rochester in February. The rented house was inadequate, cramped, dark, and without even a small space for a garden, and he continued searching for a permanent residence. But he had a more serious problem: telling Anna that Rosetta would not be coming to Rochester until the end of the school term in June. Enrollment in a new school midyear would be disruptive and damaging for her placement the following year, so she had to stay in Albany.

As he explained his position, Anna took deep intakes of air but said nothing until he was done, and then she hissed, "You *promised*."

"I made no such promise."

"You lied."

"I don't lie. I didn't know when we would move."

"You lie and forget, too," Anna said.

"You forget your place," Frederick said.

"Heard that before, and you did too."

Frederick raised his voice, calibrating it carefully, even though he was outraged by the comparison. "Marriage is not slavery."

"Only you men say that," Anna said.

He turned away, sure that he had prevailed, for now.

In the meantime, Delaney was even less successful with subscribers, not having the benefit of Frederick's fame and charisma. On the road from November to May, he wrote a stream of letters, but Delaney seemed more interested in describing his travels, writing reports about Negro communities throughout the West, and making pronouncements. Subscriptions to the *North Star* seemed incidental, even though he praised the initial issues as "all I could desire—a paper of vast interest and usefulness."

But a divergence of philosophies emerged almost immediately. Delaney wrote letters for the *North Star* that challenged moral persuasion as an effective strategy, implicitly criticizing Garrison and Frederick. Meanwhile, his travel letters became essential parts of the early issues of the *North Star.* Desperate for weekly content, Frederick allowed these letters; and readers told him how much they enjoyed them, how much they learned because they provided graphic descriptions of bigotry and racial violence in the West.

Subscriptions still floundered. Weeks went by without a single commitment, and Frederick wasn't sure if the *North Star* could survive.

There was one good bit of news.

Having not said a word to Frederick since Cleveland or made a public comment about the *North Star* since its first issue, Garrison finally broke his public silence in the Annual Report of the Massachusetts Anti-Slavery Society, published in the spring of 1848. As he read Garrison's comments, Frederick experienced mixed feelings of gratitude, guilt, and relief. In the end, the opinion of Garrison still mattered, especially his praise, belated though it was: "We shall heartily regret, in common with all his other personal and antislavery friends, in New England, his removal to so great a distance. But we shall check whatever is selfish in this feeling, by the recollection that the field of such a reaper is the world, and that, be he where he may, he must find or make a harvest."

Frederick needed as many friends and dollars as he could get. Under the circumstances, he even accepted a subscription and donation from Gerrit Smith, the wealthy philanthropist denounced by Garrison for forming an abolitionist political party.

Smith was already well known for donating thousands of acres so that Negroes, farming the land after promising to abstain from alcohol, would meet the state property requirements for voting. Three thousand had taken his offer of forty acres each, but Frederick was not interested. After his stay with Covey, he hated farming.

Frederick appreciated Smith's generosity and kindness. He also welcomed Frederick to upstate New York and extended an invitation to his home in Petersboro. Frederick looked forward to meeting Smith and was confident that his acceptance of Smith's money was neither dishonorable nor disloyal.

After all, he had to be practical. Some compromises were necessary in an imperfect world. How could a marriage, a family, a business, or a nation survive without it?

52.

ANNA DIDN'T HATE WHITE people. She was certain about that, having lived with and watched the Wells of Baltimore closely. They were kind, honest people trying to do good in a world they didn't create. But white people could not be trusted until they had earned that trust, for they would turn on you when convenient and cry "nigger" without even thinking. Hate was whispered into their ears as they sucked their mother's tit.

Colored people were not all that better, always trying to prove they weren't inferior by outdoing themselves as mean, jealous, and haughty climbers with noses so high they couldn't smell their own shit. She hated that.

Most people disappointed her, so Anna kept to herself and allowed only a select few into her life. Harriet was one. Would there be others? She didn't know, but she was pleased when so many white and colored people in town came to the Lynn farewell party bearing gifts, food, and offers of assistance in the move to Rochester. Frederick was delighted, but surprised, Anna being so private and all. He was Lynn's most famous citizen, but his surprise indicated that he didn't really understand what Anna had done while he was away. She walked among her neighbors and acquaintances with an occasional smile, a few words, and nods of the head proving that she had earned this sendoff as a member of the Lynn community, a well-known cook and gardener, a respected seamstress and shoe binder.

It seemed that Frederick didn't want to see any change in her, as if her clock stood still. His never stood still, but his clock was the only one that mattered. Her husband didn't know her as well as he thought, but Anna held out hope that a permanent life in Rochester would help them get to know each other better.

The trip to Rochester was arduous, a combination of trains, coaches, and cramped boarding rooms. The boys cried, leaving the only home they knew, but they quickly assumed a silent reserve expected of them. As Anna stood before this temporary home, she glanced at her boys, their eyes duplicates of her own: big, sometimes guarded, but most often watching for clues as to their place in their family and new town. Anna was the center of their world, and she had to be respected and obeyed, or they would answer to her.

Her blood was strong, Anna admitted, not at all like Frederick's, whose pale skin, instead blending with hers to make a soft, golden chocolate, was overshadowed in all their children by her blackness. Anna wanted that mix so it would deny that voice in her head she couldn't silence, her father's voice that always reminded her that she was ugly and black. Maybe, just maybe the next babe would be chocolate.

Anna remembered when she first hated her looks. She was about three years old, and she had frozen when her father, angry at Mama, had snapped: "You bug-eyed bitch!" Since she had her mama's eyes, Anna was sure he hated her eyes and that she was a bitch, too.

Her father's eyes were small, golden orbs luminous against his black skin. Anna saw cruelty in them, but no one else seemed to care, especially women. He openly boasted about his good looks and how his eyes made all the difference. "I'm one fine nigger," he said more than once. Even as a child, Anna wondered why he needed to do this. Bambarra Murray was the most handsome man she knew, tall, wide in the shoulders, and thick with muscle in his chest, legs, and high buttocks, all the right places, she heard girls say. Some were even brazen enough to praise his features openly, calling him out like boys before a big-busted harlot. He didn't need reminders about his good looks, but he surely wanted and expected them. "You all should be glad my blood is in you, or you would be even uglier," he had said one night.

Yes, blood was powerful, so powerful that he could not resist coming into her bed and raping her. Anna was sleeping, and then she felt his big, rough hand over her mouth, and heard him say, as if in a dream, "You're so ugly, no man is going to want you. So, I'm going to give it to you so you can know what it feels like. You'll thank me."

Hot tears came to her eyes, but she dared not move. Even before that night, Anna was afraid of him. He was big and loud, and he moved through the cabin like a reckless bull. He roared and cursed, and his wife and children wailed as they begged him to stop. But only drunken exhaustion could stop him, and he would then collapse in a heap, crying and apologizing for what he had done, until the next time when the rampage would come again.

No one talked about the pain and horror of unexpectedly discovering your father on top of you, his hand almost smothering you, his thing pushing deep inside you, tearing your flesh, making you bleed. Her younger sister, Charlotte, was beside her, asleep, thankfully snoring as she usually did. Anna could not understand her father's cruel words or his indifference to Lottie's presence.

Finally, when he was done, he said, "Say nothing or I'll kill your ass."

He rose and left the room. Anna pushed her fist into her mouth to keep from screaming and awakening Lottie. But Anna could hear the screams in her head, and she was sure that she would never return to sleep.

In the morning, she avoided her father, saying little beyond the expected, "Good morn," a requirement if she wanted to avoid another raging scene about respect and good manners. He behaved as if the previous night had never happened.

Anna took her father at his word and didn't tell her mother. She was now afraid to sleep, worrying about his return.

And when he did return a week later, she knew that like during his rages she would learn to distance herself in a dark, deep hole of the spirit. He covered her mouth unnecessarily. She saw no need to protest. It would make no difference, for he meant to have his way. But at least he didn't utter the vicious words of that first night.

One day, she announced to Lottie, "I'm leaving, and I'm never coming back."

"Can I come too?" Lottie asked. She revealed not a hint of surprise.

Is he doing it to you? Anna wondered. But she was afraid to ask, convinced that the truth would break her, and keep her moored to the Eastern Shore forever.

She left at seventeen. She hated leaving her sister and brothers who had not runaway or been sold. She had failed to protect them or her mother from Bambarra's almost-daily outbursts. Her presence could not prevent anything. She could only console them as they cowered in corners, comforting them before they fell into uneasy sleep. She was not the oldest, but they all deemed her the smartest, the most serious, a second mama.

Guilt racked her when it was time to go, but she had to leave if she had any chance for a better life, for staying sane.

After what happened with her father, she did not fear or hate men. Bambarra Murray was so singular in her estimate, so uniquely mean and ugly as only drunks with loud mouths and big fists could be, that no other man came close. She also realized that he married her mother, a plain dark woman, because he wanted to stand out. Despite his size and noise, he was afraid of everybody.

Even so, Anna could not truly escape him and was convinced for a long time that she was too ugly for a man to love. Then Frederick Augustus Bailey came along and swept away all her self-imposed restraints. Falling in love made fools of people, she concluded, and she was determined to marry him before it was too late. She would have beautiful children with such a beautiful man, and she would take them on walks about town taking in the approving nods and occasional compliments.

That wouldn't happen, Anna quickly came to realize, as each one of her children came out looking just like her, all eyes, black skin, and attitude. They cried all the time, demanding her attention, never satisfied with her breast milk, rejecting it like spoiled curd. She ached, and with every birth she had to have her breasts pumped.

If her babies could not be beautiful, they would at the very least be obedient and respectful, no matter how hard it was to mold them. They would be her creation, model boys and girls good enough to make her proud. Now she only needed Rosetta and, hopefully, another girl.

When Rosetta was finally home for good, Anna would reward Frederick. *I'll let him make another baby.*

53.

AFTER MONTHS OF FRUSTRATION Frederick found a permanent home for his family at 4 Alexander Street, near the corner of East Avenue and Main Street, in a tree-lined neighborhood block. Not too far from the office on Buffalo Street, Alexander Street made for convenient walks to work, but only whites lived there, and they made it clear they didn't want Negroes moving in, telling the Posts, who were helping Frederick in his search, that he belonged in "Nigger Town" by the river.

But Frederick would not compromise, even though some of the dwellings by the river were solid, wood-framed structures housing preachers, barbers, mechanics, and other respectable members of the colored community. Finally, the white owner of 4 Alexander sold Frederick his house, saying, "Now there will be three abolitionists on the street, two white and one Black, like a sandwich with dark meat in the center and white bread on the outsides."

Frederick loved the house, two stories, brick, with nine rooms on a one-hundred-foot-wide lot. Nine rooms. It was the biggest house he had lived in since staying with Daniel Lloyd at Wye Plantation.

As soon as he entered, he knew that Anna and children would share his excitement. There was a canopied porch with the front door on the side, then a front hall that led to a formal parlor for guests. Beyond was the dining room and a family sitting room. At the back was the kitchen with an open hearth, and beside it a smaller room, a vestibule for wet clothes and boots. The backyard had a privy, a water pump, and a work bench. Upstairs were the bedrooms, enough for the children and an upstairs office, where Frederick could work away from the more public rooms downstairs. There was also space for guests, all kinds of visitors on the lecture circuit, even runaways on the way to Canada, if necessary.

He was right. Anna loved the house, saying repeatedly as she wandered through it, "Oh, my Lord! Oh, my Lord!"

The children couldn't contain their excitement and ran through the empty rooms unchecked by their mother's usual severities about "proper behavior."

"This is so big and nice, with everything I've ever wanted, and a garden, too, for growing vegetables," Anna declared. "It will take years for me to get everything right, and it will be the best kind of busy work. But how can we afford such a house?"

"Don't you worry about that. It's all taken care of."

They were in the front parlor again, and Anna was feeling the wood of the windowsill, when she turned around and asked again, "How?"

Frederick hesitated before answering. "A loan from my English friend, Miss Julia, Julia Griffiths."

"The same lady that got the money for your freedom papers?"

"Yes. A true friend," Frederick said. He hoped that Anna would not inquire further, because he worried about how he was going to pay Julia back. Money was tight and there still were not enough subscriptions to cover the newspaper expenses.

"Some people say it's not good to take money from family or friends, but true friends understand when things come up," Anna said.

"She'll understand."

"When you write to her, please thank her for what's she done for you, and for all of us."

"I have already."

"For me, too. I mean it."

"I will."

★

Since Anna first arrived in February, she had complained about almost everything, the weather, the food, the small, rented rooms, the churches, the children, and one ailment after another lining up to attack her. But in April, her body and spirit were transformed by her new home. She smiled more. She even giggled a few times. Once consumed by the weight of her complaints, she now stood ready to do the hard work of creating the finest house in town, domestic heaven at 4 Alexander Street.

She was especially happy about preparing a room for Rosetta. The boys could share a room, but Rosetta would have a room all to herself. She needed a quiet place for her studies, Anna told Frederick. He agreed, relieved that Rosetta's delayed return was no longer a source of conflict.

Sad news came from Delaney in May. Earlier, he had explained that his delay in leaving Pittsburgh for the subscription tour was due to his daughter's illness. She died, succumbing to an unnamed affliction.

After reading the brief note, Frederick sighed as he placed it in his lap. The depth of the sigh made Anna look up from her knitting and ask, "What is it? Is it Rosetta? What happened?"

"No, it's not Rosetta. It's Martin's child, his daughter. She's dead. Something took her. He doesn't say. This must be so hard for him, being on the road, and hearing about it, not getting back home in time. I don't know what I would do if . . ." Frederick said.

"Don't say nothing! Nothing is going to happen. I won't let it!"

They stared at each other, fully understanding the foolishness of such a declaration. Children died all the time. It was rare when all children in a family survived into adulthood. Most couples had five or more, just in case. "We can only hope," Frederick whispered.

"We'll do more than hope. We'll pray and pray hard, and the Lord will listen. He has to."

"How's the room coming for Rosetta?" Frederick asked. The mention of her name no longer opened a wound. Rosetta was coming home soon, within a month.

Anna looked up but continued knitting. Her voice was warm now. "It's coming along just fine. She'll like the little desk I found for almost nothing, and that shine will make her want to study even more."

"Good. I'll be enrolling her in Miss Tracy's Seminary, and she will take the entrance exam, pass it of course, and start in September," Frederick said.

"What about Lewis and Junior?"

"I've heard the colored schools are bad, and I don't want them going to bad schools."

"Then what?"

"I don't know yet."

"We need to do something 'cause they can't be playin' in the streets and make people think we're raising some wild animals."

"People will think what they want to think," said Frederick.

"Our boys won't give them reason. There will be no foolishness."

"Of course not," Frederick replied, agreeing with her point but disliking her consistently rigid ways about raising children. He ran free like a wild animal at his grandmother's, and he didn't turn out too badly.

Rising, Frederick gathered the newspaper on the table beside him, and announced, "I'm going to the office. I have work to do."

He loved going to his nearby office on the second floor of the Talman Building at 25 Buffalo Street. He could have gone upstairs at the house, but he loved the serenity and isolation of the office at night, when he could sit at his desk in the corner with cases of type at both sides and hear nothing. He felt about his office as Anna felt about their new house, proud, eager to make everything right, settled at last in his own workspace.

But nothing was ever settled.

Julia Griffiths heard how Maria Chapman, now visiting England, continued to undermine Frederick. Julia was raising money for the *North Star* with a friend, and that friend received a letter from Maria, who urged her to not assist Frederick. Maria had described Frederick as "a selfish person fighting only for his own hand." Julia's friend showed her the letter and she immediately informed Frederick.

He demanded an explanation from Maria, unable to understand why she still opposed him when he was receiving praise from her as "one of the most efficient advocates of the slave population."

Maria said she was misunderstood, and Frederick told Julia and others that Maria's assurances "made him more at ease in his mind."

But he was lying. Her constant backbiting rankled, and he hoped that she would just stay in Britain, where his English friends could effectively counter her schemes. "Americans are innocent abroad," Julia wrote, assuring him. "We have hundreds of years of plotting and scheming to counter even her."

In the meantime, Frederick spent many hours late into the night writing and revising, fretting over a single word or phrase for space on only four sheets of paper. Frederick was excited by the intellectual freedom now his to enjoy and employ. He did not have to depend on editors and publishers or justify his words. And because the *North Star* did not serve as the official publication of any organization, he did not have to adhere to official policies or support resolutions passed by majority vote.

He loved the process: writing, reading, proofreading his own writing for greater clarity and more depth; receiving letters, answering them, testing his ideas, challenging others. He wrote Julia, "It is the best school possible for me. It obliges me to think and read, it teaches me to express my thoughts clearly. I have an audience to speak to every week and must say something worth their hearing or cease to speak altogether."

Letters from readers had to be included as well. Hastily scribbled personal, private notes of acknowledgment and thanks were never enough. If subscribers thought they were being ignored, they would stop subscribing. They wanted to see their own letters in print, and Frederick crammed in as many as he could.

But now he felt the weight of responsibility he publicly assumed as the best voice of the colored community. He had to deliver what he claimed for himself and his newspaper. He had no choice.

He had to be the best voice.

No, he had to be the only voice.

To demonstrate his legitimacy, he continued to comment on the national and international scene, writing editorials about the Mexican War, the upcoming presidential election, party politics, the revolution in France, and other issues. He chastised; he denounced; he scorned, wielding ridicule with undeniable relish.

Frederick also bombarded the colored community with his opinions, calling it to rise to the challenges of education, jobs, elevation; and represent the best so white people could see living proof of Negro equality.

But only a few were willing to buy his newspaper, and by the summer he confessed to Julia Griffiths, "My dear Julia, I seldom can bring myself to say that I have undertaken more than I have the ability to perform. I fear I have miscalculated the amount of support which would be extended to my enterprise. Things have not turned out at all as I expected."

After blaming himself, he blamed Martin Delaney, the ignorance of colored people, and his refusal to align himself with a political party, become its mouthpiece, and receive its financial support. One reader had another reason for Frederick's diminishing prospects: Frederick's scorn for other colored people who disagreed with him.

Frederick countered with his philosophy of Negro uplift: "We must take our stand side by side with our white fellow countrymen, in all trades, arts, professions and callings of the day." This was only possible if Negroes demanded more of themselves and were inspired by honest, even harsh criticism.

Frederick received a reply he did not print: "Sir, if you think by chastising and, yes, demeaning us, you will attract more subscribers, you are in for a very rude awakening. Your version of uplift is a spit in the eye. I receive enough insults from white people. I don't need *more* from the likes of you!"

He was not ready to give up. "I feel sure if I can keep the paper in existence one year I can sustain it permanently," he wrote to Julia. "The *North Star* must be sustained."

By the time he posted this letter, Rosetta was home at last.

Frederick went to Albany to retrieve her. Anna dimly smiled when Rosetta arrived, but she expressed her joy through the food she had prepared, and the room she had scrubbed. Rosetta played with the boys, who were delighted to have a "big sister." His daughter said all that needed to be said when she told Frederick, "I'm back where I belong."

Was I that serious when I was nine? Frederick wondered. Yes, he decided, and he realized that Rosetta, though a girl, would become living proof of his claims about racial uplift.

When he reminded her of the upcoming entrance examination that summer, Rosetta dutifully replied, "I'll make you proud, Papa."

Following Frederick's publication of "What are the colored people doing for themselves" on July 14, Amy Post showed him a call for a Women's Rights

Convention to be held in Seneca Falls and asked him to go. His attendance made sense. Didn't the masthead of the *North Star* declare, "Right is of no sex, truth is of no color"?

When he told Anna and read the convention call, she scowled and said, "Those women have better things to do, and so do you. They have children to raise, husbands to feed, and not make fools of themselves by asking for the vote. Jesus will come back before that's ever goin' to happen."

"There is no mention of the vote. The announcement only says it will be about the social, civil, and religious condition of women," Frederick replied.

"It will come up. Mark my words. Those women want to control things, too."

"The convention is only a start, like the planting of a seed," said Frederick.

"Some seeds don't make it," Anna said.

"You never know."

"No, and from some seeds come rotten fruit."

"Anna, you just don't understand. Equality can never be rotten fruit."

"I'm not dumb."

"I didn't say that."

"In your way, you did. Just because I don't agree with you about rights and all don't make me dumb," Anna said.

"You're one of the smartest people I know."

A hint of a smile touched her face. "That golden tongue of yours is not goin' to change my mind."

"Maybe the ladies at Seneca Falls will change your mind," Frederick said.

"Them white ladies?"

"Why do you think it's just white ladies?"

"Because they never think of us when they start organizing things. We always come later, even when they think they're helping."

"That's not fair."

"You know I'm right. Anyway, our men will have to get their rights before women, white or colored, get theirs," Anna said.

"We can handle more than one right at a time."

"Those white men will give colored men rights before they ever give it to their wives, and you know why? 'Cause they're more afraid of *us*," Anna said.

Frederick paused, startled by a difficult but painful truth. He was about to reply when Anna added, "We know too much. Behind the house door, we see everything, every scratch, every bump, hear every fart, smell your bad breath, clean your dirty underwear."

"Anna, please . . ."

"See what I mean? Even now, with all your talk about equality, you can't stand the truth."

"I'm not talking about truth, only domestic manners."

"We do all the domestic work, and you men *talk* about domestic manners."

Frederick could feel the heat rising under his cravat. An unpleasant disagreement was about to become an argument, so he changed the subject. "I hope to get new subscribers at the meeting in Seneca Falls."

54.

EXCEPT FOR THE CALL for women to be allowed to vote, the July 19–20 meeting at Seneca Falls was a conventional affair of resolutions, speeches, committee reports, and conversation. There was a scattering of men, and Frederick was the only nonwhite person there.

Elizabeth Stanton's call for the franchise was another matter. As expected, the debate about the vote was protracted and heated. The night before the vote, Stanton, a short, plump, young mother of five with piercing gray eyes, told Frederick, "I may need your help tomorrow. I want the votes to not be close, but I can already see that many women oppose me. But you are a most persuasive speaker, and I am not."

"I will do what I can," Frederick promised.

Amy Post, Frederick, and Elizabeth spoke in favor of the franchise resolution. But Lucretia Mott, the beloved Quaker activist, opposed it. She spoke eloquently against the vote, saying it was so radical a proposition that if accepted other goals would be dismissed.

Amy whispered to Frederick, "You must speak. This might go the other way if you don't."

Frederick rose after being acknowledged and said, "There can be no reason in the world for denying to woman the exercise of the elective franchise, or a hand in making and administering the laws of the land. Right is of no sex. I could not accept the right to vote as a black man if women could not also claim that right. The world would be a better place if women were involved in the political sphere. Thank you."

He received tepid applause, but when he sat down, Amy whispered, "Thank you."

The outcome was close. The resolution passed by a two-vote majority. However, most of the attendees, about three hundred, would not sign the declaration. Only one hundred were willing, sixty-seven women and thirty-three men. An anonymous vote was one thing, but a public signature was too damaging to reputations.

Three weeks later, the Rochester Women's Convention organized by Amy Post attracted even more participants, but it went unnoticed in the press, even though it had elected for the first time anywhere a woman as the presiding officer of a meeting with both men and women.

The Rochester meeting reaffirmed the right to vote for women, but participants spent most of their time discussing the uproar over Seneca Falls. Elizabeth Stanton said to Frederick and Amy, "I confess that it was with fear and trembling that I consented to attend the meeting in Rochester. All the journals and newspapers from Maine to Texas seem to strive with each other to make our movement appear the most *ridiculous.* Most of the ladies who attended the convention and signed the declaration withdrew their names and joined our persecutors. Our *friends* give us the cold shoulder. Cowards, nothing but cowards."

Frederick agreed, but he had a more personal disappointment. He was unable to get subscribers for the *North Star* at the two conventions. He went on to the next National Negro Convention in Cleveland with hope for more success.

★

What a difference a year made.

The year before, the delegates had rejected his arguments against a National Negro press. But this year he was elected president of the convention. The honor was a clear recognition of his current standing in the colored community, and Frederick beamed from the glow of approbation. Gerrit Smith extolled him, repeating this observation on numerous occasions, "He has the talents and dignity that would adorn the presidency of the nation."

The delegates reversed themselves and declared the *North Star* the national newspaper needed by colored Americans and urged all to support it.

Frederick actively participated in all the debates. He moved to amend resolution number thirty-three, asking that the word "persons" clearly state that it meant "to include women."

The motion carried, and the delegates gave "three cheers for women's rights."

But again, no one became a subscriber. He received a few vague promises, but no commitments.

Frederick was too annoyed to press his case. His mind was now preoccupied with preparations for writing a letter to Thomas Auld on the anniversary of his escape ten years before. The names and words of specific women and girls from his past pounded in his ears.

While talking to Remond, he closed his eyes for what seemed just a second. He heard Remond raise his voice. "Frederick, Frederick, what's happening? Are you alright?"

Frederick heard anguish and immediately answered, "Please forgive me. I'm fine. Don't worry. Sometimes I hear voices from the past."

"Voices?" Remond asked, his face now even more stricken.

"Memories of things said. I was trying to remember them for inclusion in a letter I'll be writing to Thomas Auld on this tenth anniversary of my escape."

"But why? You have no more obligations to him."

"We're shaped for good and for ill by masters. Thomas Auld helped to shape me, as your father shaped you."

"Are you saying Thomas Auld was your father?"

"No, I'm not saying that! I don't think he was, but he influenced me in many ways even though I hated him."

"Then why do you care what he thinks?"

Frederick paused again, carefully weighing his reply. "It's not about his feelings. He more than likely will never see the letter, considering the ban on abolitionist newspapers in the South. I am using him, like he once used me."

"I look forward to reading it, and I'm sure its publication will enhance subscriptions to the *North Star*. That's the ultimate point, is it not?"

"Mr. Garrison will publish it, too. I proposed and he agreed, saying it would do a great service to our cause." He smiled broadly, again pleased by Garrison's approval.

Remond then took a deep breath and recited lines from *The Merchant of Venice*:

To you your father should be as a god;
One that composed your beauties yea, and one
To whom you are but as a form of wax,
By him imprinted, and within his power
To leave the figure or disfigure it.

"Just what do you mean by this?" asked Frederick, shaken by its relevance and Remond's insight. Frederick leaned forward, his hands gripping the chair, his eyes unwavering as a warning. His friend had gone too far. He had no right to ascribe to Frederick feelings he knew nothing about.

But he did know. "They are like fathers to you, Garrison and Auld, I mean," Remond said.

"No, they are not! And you don't know me well enough to presume to tell me about my feelings."

"I think you protest too much."

Frederick stood. "I have no more to say."

"Be careful. That letter to Auld may reveal more than you realize."

"I know what I'm doing."

"As you always claim," said Remond.

"I thought you were my friend."

"Friends tell the truth, or what they think is the truth."

"Your truth, not mine," said Frederick.

"Still your friend."

"Maybe, or maybe not."

"Oh, Frederick, you named your son after me."

"That might have been a mistake."

"You can be cruel, you know," said Remond.

"A survivor's tool, ready when needed."

"I'm not your enemy."

"I will decide that."

Remond sighed. "Can you afford to lose more friends?"

"They were not my friends. Friends support friends," said Frederick.

"I support the *North Star*."

"Then you are my friend."

"Is everything a transaction with you?"

"You learn that early when you're born a slave. Thomas Auld will be reminded. I will make sure he never forgets."

"You are unforgettable," replied Remond.

"Flattery works with me, you know."

"I know."

★

Sitting alone in his home office and seeing it as a symbol of his rise in the world, from St. Michaels on the Eastern Shore to Rochester, Frederick began his letter to Thomas with civil excuses. The words flowed on this exact day ten years after his escape: "Sir: I intend to use you as a weapon with which to assail the system of slavery—as a means of concentrating public attention on the system and deepening their horror in the souls and bodies of men. I shall make use of you."

He paused, staring at the scribble before him as his pen was poised in his hand above the sheets of paper. He dipped his pen into the ink pot and continued: "I am myself; you are yourself. We are two distinct persons, equal persons. What you are, I am. You are a man, and so am I. God created both, and made us separate beings. I am not by nature bound to you, or you to me. . . .

"Oh! sir, a slaveholder never appears to me so completely an agent of hell, as when I think of and look upon my dear children. It is then my feelings rise above my control. The grim horrors of slavery rise in all their ghastly terror before me. I remember the chain, the gag, the bloody whip. I wear stripes on my back inflicted by your direction. My hands were tied, and I was dragged to jail in Easton to be sold like an animal.

"As of this moment, you are probably the guilty holder in bondage of at least three of my own sisters, and my only brother. Have you sold them? Or are they still in your possession? What has become of them? Are they living or dead? Is my grandmother still alive, the one you turned out like an old horse to die in the woods? If my grandmother be still alive, send her to me at Rochester. Send me my grandmother!"

He stopped, but the essential question of his letter had to be posed and he scribbled on, "How, let me ask, would you look upon me, were I some dark night in company with a band of hard villains, to enter the precincts of your elegant dwelling and seize the person of your lovely daughter, Amanda, and carry her off from you, family, friends, and all the loves ones of your youth—make her a slave-compelled to work, and I take her wages, place her name on my ledger as property, and still more horrible, leave her unprotected—a degraded victim to the brutal lust of fiendish overseers, who would pollute, blight, and last blast her fair soul—rob her of all dignity—destroy her virtue, and annihilate all in her person the graces that adorn the character of virtuous womanhood? I ask, how would you regard me, if such were my conduct?"

Pollute, blight, blast, destroy, annihilate.

Frederick meant to conjure up the fear of rape, a white woman defiled, the fate that Black women like his mother, grandmother and sisters faced daily.

Thomas Auld had to feel the horror.

Frederick reigned in his outrage, resorting to the pleasantries slaves had mastered for generations. "There is no roof under which you would be more safe than mine, and there is nothing in my house which you might need for comfort, which I would not readily grant. Indeed, I should esteem it a privilege, to set you an example as to how mankind ought to treat each other. I am your fellow man, but not your slave." He took a deep breath, leaned back in his chair, and lay down his pen. He was exhausted, but he found the energy to copy it that night. The *Liberator* would have the letter for publication within the month.

The *North Star* would print it, too, but Frederick knew he would have a bigger audience in Garrison's newspaper, as his struggle for subscribers and the paper's survival continued.

★

After writing the Auld letter and attending the Cleveland conference, Frederick's self-satisfaction died when he returned home and asked Rosetta about her first days of school.

Rosetta stood before him in the parlor at a respectful distance, her head down as her eyes surreptitiously checked for the moment when she could answer his inquiry. She was ten years old now, dark, skinny, intense, and humorless. Frederick worried that she would not attract many suitors, boys willing to overlook her plain face and large, sullen eyes. It was especially important that she got a good education.

"Are things going well at Miss Tracy's?" asked Frederick, having been out of town for the few days since her admission to the school. He was still pleased that Rosetta, prepared well by the Mott sisters, had passed her entrance exams with perfect scores.

"Papa, I'm get along pretty well, but, Papa, Miss Tracy . . ." She kept her head down as she examined her father for clues to his disposition and possible reaction.

"But?"

"Maybe I shouldn't say, because I know it is good for me to be there."

"Please tell me. Don't worry about telling me the truth."

Rosetta sighed, then her words came in a rush, as if they had to be spoken as quickly as possible to be faced. "Miss Tracy doesn't allow me to go into the room with the other girls because I'm colored."

"What did you say?"

Rosetta stepped back. "I'm sorry, Papa, but I thought . . ."

"No, no, no," he said, rushing to her, pressing her close to him for the first time in a long time, and hiding his own face, puffed with rage. "It's not your fault. Just tell me what you mean. Please."

He waited, releasing his hold on her, and allowing her to step back and look up at him.

Rosetta started to cry. "I tried to not let it bother me. But she makes me go into a room all by myself, and I get my lessons there alone, all day."

"Why didn't you tell me?"

Rosetta wilted, as if she were the person at fault, and stepped back, her eyes to the floor once more.

Frederick realized his mistake at once, and gently pulled her into his embrace again. "No, no, no. It's not your fault. This should not have happened to you or to anyone else. I'm glad you told me, and I will do something to stop this from continuing. Miss Tracy can't treat you this way. She never said that this would be her practice, and we would not have sent you there if we knew she would do this. I'll see Miss Tracy tomorrow morning." Frederick lifted her face to his, and added, "Don't worry. I will see to it that you be treated like the rest."

When he told Anna about Rosetta's treatment, she asked wearily, "What are you going to do about it?"

"Should I withdraw her? We can't allow her to be degraded this way."

"Then you have your answer."

"But I will insist on a change even when I withdraw her. This can't continue."

"Do Miss Tracy own that school or just runs it?"

"Why do you ask?"

"It just might be her boss's rule, and if she wants that job she will have to do what they tell her."

"Well, I have to start somewhere, and I will start with her."

"Just take Rosetta out."

"No, not yet."

Frederick spent a restless night imagining his confrontation with Lucilia Tracy, who had accepted his money and welcomed Rosetta to her school. Miss Tracy had even said that it was her honor to have the daughter of Frederick Douglass as a pupil, never mentioning separate instructions for Rosetta, the only Black student. He imagined a dramatic but short confrontation, Miss Tracy capitulating at once to his civil wrath.

He marched to Miss Tracy's the next morning, leaving Rosetta at home. As he approached the school, he could feel his anger rise, threatening a loss of control. He took deep breaths. He would not raise his voice, but Miss Tracy would regret her presumption, dearly.

A servant announced him, and he found Miss Tracy, a thin, graying woman, primly dressed in black at her desk. As if prepared for this confrontation, she spoke calmly, "Please sit down, Mr. Douglass, and I will explain the situation."

"Please do, since I pay the same tuition as everyone else."

Objectively, she explained, "When I decided to accept Rosetta, the board of trustees didn't know about it. But when I informed the board, it opposed me, telling me that I had acted improperly. The board said that I would have to keep her separate if she were to stay. As the headmistress of the trustees' school, and as their employee, I could not ignore their ruling. I could not. You know how I feel about antislavery, Mr. Douglass. I have always been a strong supporter of the cause of colored people, and because I am, I thought it best to keep Rosetta away from the other girls. In time, I thought, in a term or two or three, their prejudices might be overcome."

"*Their* prejudices!" snapped Frederick, leaning forward ever so slightly. "You have only talked of the trustees so far. And besides, madam, how can the students' prejudices, if they have any, be overcome if they never see her?"

"Sir, they do reflect the views of their parents."

Frederick stood. "Madam, I want to know directly from the other students if they object to my daughter being in their classroom."

Miss Tracy smiled dimly. Victory was hers, for surely one dimpled bigot could be found in the group. "Very well," she said. "There can be no harm. I will ask each girl. You may sit in the adjoining room. I will leave the door open so that you may hear my inquiry and each response, for they will be free to answer truthfully without concern for your feelings."

She rang a small bell, summoning her servant. "Line up the girls outside the office. Tell them I need to question each one of them."

Like every innocent student summoned to the headmaster's office, the first girl assumed her guilt for some offense known only to her heart and the all-knowing Miss Tracy.

"I have a question to ask you," commanded Miss Tracy.

"Yes, Miss Tracy," she answered, not looking up.

"Would you mind having Rosetta Douglass, the colored girl, sitting in the same classroom with you?"

The girl quickly raised her head, delighted by this revelation. She was not in trouble. "No, madam. No."

All twenty-four girls agreed to have Rosetta in class.

Miss Tracy became more and more irritated with this mounting referendum. When Amy Warner entered her office, Miss Tracy smiled. Her best white hope, the daughter of one of the trustees, had entered at last.

Miss Tracy asked the crucial question, and Miss Warner replied, "No, Miss Tracy, I would not mind."

Startled, Miss Tracy asked, "Did you really mean to vote yes? Are you used to having colored persons near you? Are you accustomed to Black persons?"

"No, madam, I am not, but I'll get used to it."

Then Miss Tracy had another idea, rose from her chair, crossed the room, and opened the door to the waiting line of children outside. "Who wants to sit next to Rosetta Douglass."

"Me, me, me!" they shouted eagerly.

Frowning, she said, "Fine, ladies, but since this is a social experiment, you will have to ask your parents about sitting next to Rosetta Douglass. Have them all write notes telling me of their decision."

She opened the door to Frederick, who stood waiting, his eyes cold. He knew that at least one parent would object, unlike children who were usually free of prejudice.

"If one parent objects, then I have no other choice," Miss Tracy said.

"We all have choices. I will be sending Rosetta to school tomorrow on the hope that human decency will prevail."

He sent Rosetta to school the next day, telling her, "If there is a vote against you, you will not sit in that room alone. Come home with your books and materials. That will be your last day at the seminary."

That afternoon, she came home with her books and a brief note from Miss Tracy. "One parent disagreed. Regrets, Miss Lucilia Tracy."

"Who wrote the note, the one that objected?" Frederick demanded. Rosetta shrank from him, looking to her mother for reassurance. Anna said nothing.

"Amy Warner's father, Henry Warner."

Henry G. Warner, editor of the *Rochester Courier*. Frederick could hear the words he would hurl in a public confrontation sure to embarrass the man: "I should like to know how much better are you than me, and how much better are your children than mine?"

Rosetta's feelings were all but forgotten.

55.

ANNA WAS NOT FEELING well and was sitting up in bed with her back on a pile of pillows. Sick from her pregnancy she complained about constant nausea and frequent vomiting. Never had Frederick seen her so weak.

Even so, Frederick read Anna his letter to Henry Warner. He was going on a trip for six weeks or more and wanted to leave home with Anna knowing that he did what needed to be done to vindicate the honor of his family. Protecting the family's privacy was less important.

"Is it long?" Anna asked. "My eyes are hurtin', but I'm listenin'."

He started slowly and read with increasing fervor. The end of the letter pleased him the most, and he gave to his recitation the tone of denunciation he used on the stage, calibrating the sound for the space of their small bedroom. "I am glad to inform you that you have not succeeded as you hoped to do in depriving my child of the means of a decent education, or the privilege of going to an excellent school. She had not been excluded from Seward Seminary five hours before she was gladly welcomed into another quite as respectable to the one from which she was excluded. Now should I like to know how much better are you than me, and how much better your children than mine? We differ in color, it is true, but who is to decide which color is most pleasing to God, or most honorable among men?"

Anna opened her eyes and gave the expected pronouncement. "It's good, real good."

"Thank you. But I'm not sure about her new school. It takes everybody, you know, and some of the children do not always come from good families."

"Then what?"

"Hiring a private tutor."

"We can't afford that."

"Not now, perhaps, but we have to find the money for a tutor, piano lessons, and the other things needed for a young lady."

"One thing at a time, Fred. Please. She's been through enough changes."

"We wait and see," he declared. "In the meantime, it's good that the boys are also attending the same school. Soon everybody will be able to read to you my letters and the newspapers."

"You just won't let me forget it," Anna said after a long pause, her eyes dark and critical.

"Forget what?"

"You know what."

"It's just a fact of our lives."

"If it's just that, as you say, a *fact* of our lives, then why do you always have to remind me? I know I can't read and write. We all know it. We all live with it and do what we can."

"You can still learn. We can hire a teacher. Even Rosetta can help."

"Do I bring shame on you that much?"

"This is not about me!"

"Everything is about you."

"That's not fair, and you know it. Don't you want to read the Bible? Reading frees the mind, takes it out of the cave of ignorance and . . ."

"So now I'm living in a cave?"

"You know what I mean."

"Yes, I do, and this ignorant woman has heard enough for one day." She turned away from him pulling at her covers, and said sadly, "I'm tired, and I need to get some sleep."

He was about to reach out and pull at her shoulder to face him, but he refrained, for if he tried to win this argument, he could unintentionally reveal the truth: he was ashamed of her.

Before leaving on his trip, he encouraged Rosetta to take care of her mother, keep the house clean as much as possible, and watch the boys. It was a difficult assignment, but Rosetta, only ten, was willing to accept the challenge. "Don't worry, Papa, I'll do everything I can to help."

"I'm not worried. You always do what is best."

"I hope Mama's not sick all the time while we wait for the baby. Miss Post told me that baby sickness lasts just a few months. Things should be good by Christmas. You will be home for Christmas, Papa?"

"Yes. I will be home for Christmas."

★

Frederick spent most of the fall and winter away trying to raise money, build his subscription base, and strengthen support for his opinions, especially now that Zachary Taylor had been elected president of the United States, proof again that the government, in the grip of slaveholders, was rotten to the core.

But after concluding that in the current climate moral appeals alone could not advance the interests of slaves, he recently endorsed the new Free Soil Party, formed to prevent the expansion of slavery in the territories gained by the United States after the defeat of Mexico.

Frederick now maintained that the hearts of slave owners were as hard as coal and could not be moved, and his frustration with the slow pace of change made him open to other strategies.

John Brown invited him back to Springfield that November and Frederick returned, while avoiding calling on Harriet and her husband.

Brown was direct, his steely gray eyes a permanent glare. They faced each other at the table, and he intoned, "You have changed since we last spoke."

"Yes. But I must reiterate that I will not endorse violence, still," Frederick replied.

Brown's immediate response was a quotation, from the ninth chapter of Paul's Letter to the Hebrews: "Almost all things are by the law purged with blood, and without shedding of blood there is no remission."

Here was no lawyer citing precedent. Here was a killer rationalizing murder. Frederick looked into Brown's pitiless eyes. "I will not," he repeated.

"But I've noticed in your paper a growing dissatisfaction with our free colored brothers. I'm not pleased with them, either. Did you see my article?"

Before he could respond, Brown presented him with "Sambo's Mistakes," published in the *Ram's Horn*, a competing colored newspaper. Frederick had somehow missed it.

"Read it," Brown ordered. "I wrote it because I need to help your people see what their problems truly are and how they can learn from them."

Offended by the article's title and Brown's peremptory tone, Frederick arched his eyebrows. But he began reading the four sheets about Sambos who seek the favor of whites by "tamely submitting to every species of indignity, contempt, and wrong instead of nobly resisting their brutal aggressions from principle." Brown charged that Sambos "think themselves highly honored if they may be allowed to lick up the spit of a Southerner."

"Sir, this is outrageous! You have no right to say this in print," Frederick said.

"Am I not right?" Brown asked.

"You have no right!"

"Because I'm white? You have issued similar complaints in the *North Star.*"

"There are some agreements, but this, this . . ."

"In the fight against injustice, color should not count."

"But it does count, and you will not make more friends with us if you sound like one more white man telling us what we should do. We can and will define ourselves."

"You reject my friendship, then, my willingness to help?"

Frederick paused, then answered, "No, of course not. But . . ."

Brown interrupted him. "Someone must speak the harsh truths about compromise and making deals, tolerating the worse in the human heart and the laws that follow it. Besides, very few readers know that the writer is white. Nothing indicates that in the article. Let people believe I'm colored. It doesn't matter. I'm a brother in spirit, anyway. My actions matter, and when they hear of success in the mountains, when they hear slaves have run off to join us, then even a colored barber who refuses to cut Black hair because he will lose business will redeem his manhood."

"How, just how, will all this happen?"

"What other choice do they have? Leaving their hope in the ballot box? The people elected General Taylor and John Tyler of Virginia. And do you really think Henry Clay, John C. Calhoun, and the other slavery hounds will let you vote them out, will let you vote away their slaves?" Brown smiled. "They will fight, and blood will flow. There will be blood."

"You want it. You want blood."

"It is the Lord's will." Brown again quoted scripture, saying with cold serenity, "And he smelled the battle afar off, the thunder of captains, and the shouting. Job 39:25."

"The Bible is their tool, too," said Frederick, suddenly exhausted.

"Then I will quote your own words from a speech in Rochester in August, 'There may, and doubtless will be, many failures, mistakes and blunders attending the transition from slavery to liberty. But what then? Shall the transition never be made? In demolishing the old framework of civil tyranny, and erecting on its ruins the beautiful temple of freedom, some lives may indeed be lost, but who is so craven as to say, it ought never to have been built?'"

Frederick was astonished. The man had memorized his words to use against him, a sneak attack that was as offensive as it was effective. "Good day, sir."

"Brother Douglass."

"Good day," repeated Frederick, his back to Brown. He had to get out of that house. A fanatic, a potential killer, and certainly no gentleman, John Brown was temptation, the dangerous and alluring voice of the reckless abandonment of restraints Frederick carefully imposed after his escape.

But Brown could see through Frederick's façade; the façade cracked aboard the Lynn trains, cracked in Pendleton when he fought back, and cracked when he defied his Boston associates. John Brown could see the rage, and he had dared Frederick to embrace the truth without conditions. And Brown knew that secretly Frederick wanted retribution; he wanted blood to flow.

Frederick hurried home to spend the winter in and around Rochester waiting for the birth of the next, and probably, last baby.

On March 3, a baby girl was born, and Frederick named her Annie, after her mother. According to the midwife, it was a difficult delivery, but Anna rallied, summoned her strength, and said repeatedly, "I've got to stay. I've got to stay."

When Frederick saw his newest daughter, a small brown child with the large black eyes of all his children, he whispered, "Well, you must be like your mother. You never gave up. You're here."

Nothing could compare to the excitement of the birth of his first child, but Frederick felt a special warmth for Annie because he knew instinctively that she would be his last. There could be no more children; any others would kill Anna.

"Annie," he whispered, swaying her in his arms as Anna slept. "You worked so hard to get into this world, I think I should work hard to get to know you."

He thought of the frequent trips away from home. His boys and Rosetta were virtual strangers still. "You're my last chance," he said, drawing the small bundle of soft flesh closer to his chest. "You're my last chance to get this right."

He had another reason to be happy.

Julia Griffiths was coming to Rochester.

56.

JULIA DECIDED. SHE WOULD go to Rochester and help Frederick publish his newspaper. She could be his editor and intellectual partner, challenging him to clarify his thinking and reinforce his characteristic passion and eloquence with trenchant, probing questions.

She would also manage his financial affairs and stay until Frederick no longer needed her. So far, nothing had stemmed the tide of financial dissolution, not even her assumption of the mortgage to Frederick's house.

She had to go.

When it was time to tell Eliza, Julia framed her proposal as an expedition. "We will follow Mrs. Trollope and Mr. Dickens and discover America, the true America."

"But Julia, you haven't asked me yet, not really," Eliza said.

"Surely, you don't intend for me to go into the wilderness alone?"

"Of course not. You will need a chaperone!"

Julia paused, enjoying Eliza's fretful fluttering of hands and darting eyes. "Will you come with me?"

"Why of course. We might see some bears, and maybe Indians," Eliza replied.

"Maybe. But we will see New York first, since we will be arriving just when the American Anti-Slavery Society is meeting for its annual convention. We will have the chance to see and hear Frederick, Garrison, Wendell Phillips, and others."

Eliza's enthusiasm slackened; her eyes now reflected dismay. "These men are right, but they so bore me. I mean everyone except Frederick, of course. But even he says too much, goes on for more than needed."

"That's why he needs an editor, remember?"

"We will see what effect you have on him after we get to Rochester. I hope you are not going thousands of miles only to find him ignoring what you suggest," Eliza said.

"I can only suggest."

"I don't believe that for a minute. You would not go that far just to suggest. You must have your way, as usual."

Julia and Eliza landed in New York on May 3, 1849, following their uneventful first crossing of the Atlantic. After landing on one of the crowded wharves that surpassed in size and noise the Liverpool wharves, they took rooms at the Franklin House on Broadway. Unable to meet them at the docks, Frederick called on them two days later.

He left his name at the desk with a clerk who assumed the worse and pointedly declared, with a deep sniff of his bulbous nose, the letter of company policy.

"Franklin House does not allow . . ."

Frederick raised his hand to stop the man from sputtering on. "Have no fear, young man, but please inform my friends that I have arrived."

Within a few minutes, Julia crossed the room after talking to the clerk, who pointed at him with a curved, dismissing finger. Frederick walked toward her, his hands out to take hers.

Julia's heart quickened at the sight of him. He was so tall and handsome, and his dignity matched his bearing, solid and confident.

"Julia," Frederick said affectionately, taking her hands.

"Frederick."

"Let's take a walk."

"Of course," Julia said, taking his arm without hesitation. "Come, Eliza," now acknowledging her sister, who stood behind looking around the room.

They exited the hotel. They were still talking when they heard a man shout from the front door of Franklin House, "I thought they were gonna kiss that nigger!"

Frederick immediately admonished his companions, "Continue walking."

More shouted insults followed the trio.

"White bitches."

"Whores, no doubt."

"No *lady* would walk with a nigger!"

Eliza pressed closer to Frederick and whispered, "What vulgarity, what rudeness."

"I warned you, Eliza. We're not a common sight," said Julia.

"But *this*!"

Exasperated more than fearful, Eliza blurted out, "What is wrong with these people?"

"Colorphobia," said Frederick.

"We're not animals in a circus or zoo," exclaimed Eliza.

"Ignore them," urged Frederick. "Ignore everything. Don't let anyone see that you're upset."

Eliza straightened her back, held her head high, and smiled, having no trouble demonstrating her superiority to riffraff.

But after a few blocks, Frederick announced that it was time to return to the hotel for tea. There was no objection and they returned.

At the door of the hotel restaurant the head waiter challenged their entry. Lifting his chest and raising his jaw, he declared, "I am sorry, ladies, but our dining room does not allow Negroes into it."

Frederick looked over the waiter's shoulder and declared, "But, sir, there are Negroes in the dining room!"

Incredulous, the waiter turned quickly to investigate. There were colored waiters and porters serving the seated white ladies and gentlemen.

The waiter said hotly, "The rules are definite. No colored people can *eat* at our tables."

Julia asserted, "I am not offended. He can eat at *my* table."

Now three white waiters had gathered as reinforcements blocking the entrance from defilement.

"Julia, the point has been made," Frederick said softly, now resigned to the inevitable. "My readers will hear of this."

The fight was still within Julia. "But this is my moment."

"Eventually they will see that this is not good for business. But in the meantime, I don't want you to get hurt."

Meanwhile, Eliza stood behind, looking for escape. She had enough mortifications for one day. "We must have something to eat."

"Then I will not eat here. I will not stay here," Julia declared, turning to her sister for support.

Startled, Eliza protested, "But Julia."

"I want the manager to know that . . ." Julia said.

Frederick intervened, softly taking Julia's arm and stepping to the side to say, "It's not worth the inconvenience. Don't upset Eliza further. All hotels in New York are like the Franklin. You'll have no place to stay if every hotel must pass this test. That's why we all stay with friends and associates. And soon you'll have friends here and will stay with them. But for this week, just accept this. We'll have our times together."

57.

FREDERICK COULD NOT WAIT to get out of New York, but his scheduled debate for May 10 with Henry Highland Garnet, whom he had not seen in months, could not be missed. Frederick assumed that his increased rise in the world had provoked Garnet, who demanded that Frederick now explain his opposition to ministers, churches in general, and the distribution of Bibles to slaves. Garnet was obviously looking for another fight, and his supporters packed Zion Baptist Church. But Frederick was not intimidated, and the presence of Julia and Eliza, who sat in the front row, made him more determined to win.

Garnet did not make the slightest effort to be civil. When Frederick rose to speak, Garnet suddenly announced that it was time to collect money to defray the cost of the meeting.

Frederick smiled. He now pitied Garnet for showing his hand so crudely and waited patiently for the collection to end.

When Frederick tried again, the chair of the meeting and a friend of Garnet's, Samuel Ward, declared that Frederick now had no right to speak, and then gave a long speech before making requests for donations to his own newspaper.

The collection ended at 10:30 p.m. and Frederick was finally allowed to speak. Standing at the table where Garnet also sat, Frederick spoke briefly, considering the lateness of the hour, reviewing again how southern ministers used religion to support oppression. He looked straight ahead, ignoring Garnet as if he were not in the room. But before he could end, Garnet shouted, "You've said enough!"

The entire audience gasped.

Garnet went on, "I have the floor! I have the floor!"

After the uproar of objections subsided, Ward gave the floor to Garnet, and he harangued the audience with a six-point dissertation on Frederick's enmity to religion, building his case with reference after reference from printed speeches, editorials, and the *Narrative*, the references all preceded by the relevant, proclaimed sin:

Frederick Douglass denies the veracity of scripture.

Frederick Douglass has spoken lightly and contemptuously of the religious conviction of colored people.

Frederick Douglass was once a preacher in the Methodist Church and deserted it.

Frederick Douglass denies the inspiration of the Bible.

Frederick Douglass is unstable.

Frederick Douglass asks colored people to bow down to the unreasonable and unnatural dogmas of nonresistance.

Julia and Eliza faces were stricken with horror and wonder as they watched Frederick sit at the table, his face a mask of contempt and scorn.

What would he say?

What would he do?

Every man and woman in the room seemed to lean forward, waiting.

Frederick took a deep breath, and pounded his fist on the nearby table, rattling it before shouting, "Sir, you are a goddamned liar, and you will hear from me in my paper!"

Before anyone could stop him, he bounded down the center aisle toward the exit door. He would set the record straight in the *North Star* and leave a permanent indictment of Garnet's debased character long after the spoken details of the night were forgotten.

"I don't want to talk about it," he told Julia, when she finally caught up with him.

"But . . ."

"No! I will not apologize or explain my reaction. I will only address his claims."

The torrent of abuse leveled against him were the worst he had experienced, and he worried that matters would get worse once Julia moved in. But Rochester, the last stop of the Underground Railroad, was not New York or Boston, and as a pillar of the community he and his visitors would not be insulted on the streets.

He could not wait to get home.

Nevertheless, they could not avoid trouble on the way to Rochester.

Going to Albany aboard the riverboat *Alida,* they ignored the muttered obscenities made under the breath by outraged passengers in the dining room.

When he sat down, the steward asked him to leave. White passengers moved away from their tables, giving room for the forcible ejection sure to come.

The captain and clerk joined the steward, receiving the applause of the appreciative passengers, and the steward asked him again.

Julia then chastised the staff and passengers, saying loudly enough for everyone to hear, "How dare you force us and Mr. Douglass to experience your base prejudices and unmanly and insulting behavior. The British press will hear of this."

Unintimidated, the steward spoke with the confidence that obedience to long established rules can instill, "This man will be served only as your servant."

"Then bring our food to our room. We paid for it. Come, Eliza. Come, Frederick."

They departed and ate in their room for the rest of the voyage.

When their carriage finally arrived at 4 Alexander Street, the entire Douglass family came out to greet Frederick, Julia, and Eliza.

"Your children look so much like your wife," said Julia to Frederick, who was now waving at his family.

The three boys, Frederick, Lewis, and Charles, stood solemnly at attention, each looking to Anna for the signal to acknowledge their father and his guests. When she nodded her head, the boys grinned and waved vigorously. Anna stood by, scowling. Rosetta's eyes revealed caution, wariness.

"A handsome family," observed Eliza, taking Frederick's hand as she stepped out of the carriage first.

"Help me with the presents," Julia gently commanded her sister.

Introductions were made, and Julia, without waiting to take off her bonnet or asking permission, entered the parlor to offer gifts, explaining why a certain one was the best for this or that child, toys for the boys, a dress for Rosetta.

Unsmiling, Anna objected, "Miss Griffiths, you didn't need to do this."

"Please call me Julia," Julia said, looking up from opening Rosetta's present. Rosetta smiled broadly, obviously pleased with the simple but elegant muslin dress with a thin lace collar.

"Miss Griffiths, you don't need to dress my children."

"Look, Mama," cried Charles, presenting his toy horse. "I can make stories."

"Enough, Charley."

His smile fell, the arm holding the toy dropped to his side, and he looked down, deflated.

Frederick intervened. "There's no harm. You will decide when they play with the toys or wear the dress."

Anna was not appeased and continued to look down with hostile, narrowed eyes on the frivolous display before her.

"Anna, I would like to have a word with you," Frederick said.

She followed him into the hall, closing the door behind her.

"Anna, these are our guests. How could you treat them that way?"

"*Our* guests? They are yours."

Anna reopened the door of the parlor and announced, "It's time to put them things away. Make sure you give thanks to your papa's friends."

"Thank you, Miss Julia! Thank you, Miss Eliza!" shouted the boys.

Rosetta said with utmost seriousness. "Miss Julia, this is the best gift I ever had. Thank you for thinking of me."

Frederick said to all, "This is a great day for the Douglass family. A great day!"

He crossed the room to his favorite chair, sat down, and asked his children to come forward to show their gifts. They surrounded their father's chair, jabbering, giggling, and brandishing their gifts perilously close to Frederick's face. But he didn't object, looking at Julia and not Anna, whose face was unsmiling black stone.

"I'm happy. The work can begin tomorrow, but today I will enjoy this day without it."

Julia insisted gently, "But only until tomorrow."

Anna glared, her offense hanging in the air, the unspoken question: *Who are you to tell my husband what to do?*

Julia only said, "Tomorrow."

58.

JULIA AND FREDERICK WORKED opposite each other at a table and desk in the office, Julia examining every word and line of the drafts submitted to her. She corrected spelling, deleted words and lines, asked probing, sometimes difficult questions to strengthen his arguments and validate his points. She was relentless.

He still bristled at her challenges.

They were also examining a speech he was preparing. He was going to denounce again Senator Henry Clay, who as president of the Colonization Society had recently suggested that all slaves born after 1855 or 1860 be freed on their twenty-fifth birthday after working three years for their fare to Liberia.

"We're supposed to be pleased by such an offer," scoffed Frederick, looking up from his copy of Clay's public letter on the issue.

"Considering your understandable feeling on the matter," said Julia, "your points must be as direct and succinct as possible."

She insisted Frederick stop leaving his major arguments to the emotions of the moment. His spontaneity was a great asset, as she had witnessed throughout his tour of Britain, but it was becoming a disadvantage as he moved beyond slavery to other major issues of the day.

He had to convince men, not just move them. She recommended that he read Walter Bagehot, John Stuart Mill, John Locke, and William Wilberforce.

He resisted her efforts at every step, still believing that his lessons from experience and model speeches learned long ago demanded a long introduction, marked by courtesy and civility, followed by personal references rich in humor, and the relentless stockpiling of examples and references, all in a language as eloquent and elevated as he could make it.

"Too many words. Simplify."

"This is not a simple matter."

"Distill it to what you want them to most remember."

"Audiences are not pleased with short speeches."

"It is long enough," she replied, reaching for her pencil. "You can cut here."

"No more. I will be giving this one, not . . ."

"It's always the lot of editors to be considered uncreative, unsympathetic louts."

"I didn't mean to offend you."

"I have thick skin."

"You talk about arguments carefully laid out. But we are not dealing with reason, even when such arguments come from an intelligent man who believes that every problem can be solved by our leaving. This is our country as much as his, and my people have given blood to this land. We won't let Clay or anyone else take back what we have given. Never," Frederick said.

He paused for a moment. "Why should I now appeal to reasoned conscience when Clay gives every slaver and bigot in this country the opportunity to not change?"

"What are you saying, then?"

"With Clay, Calhoun, and Taylor making the South more powerful than ever since the end of the Mexican War, it is clear that moral persuasion is not enough. Politics requires waiting, and slaves are sick of waiting. I'm sick of waiting," Frederick said.

"Then, what?"

Finally, he whispered, as if speaking an epitaph, "Tyrants know only the fear of death."

"Slaves must fight, then," said Julia.

"Kill," he said, his forehead seeming to bear down on his nose, producing a massive bulge at the bridge that darkened the shadows near his eyes.

"You're no longer a son of Garrison."

"The prodigal son, perhaps. I have not been the same since Pendleton, Indiana. They almost killed me there, and when we rise they will try to kill us all."

"There will be a war," she said sadly.

"And we will win, as in other wars of freedom," Frederick said.

"Freedom will come more easily than equality. I think Americans hate equality more than slavery."

"It will be a long time before people stop staring at you and me on the streets and allow us in restaurants without a scene," Frederick said.

"It's a habit, and habits can change," Julia said.

"You know that it's more than that."

"Yes. You are all a threat, and your self-confidence is, indeed, an affront."

"My own people will hate you for wanting to be my friend, for walking with me on the streets. There will be talk. Most Negroes are prejudiced, too, and will say despicable things," Frederick said.

"In the end, it will turn on something sordid. Why must this business always end with that?" Julia asked.

"There's a malignant tumor in the American soul, but we will stay true to our friendship. Agreed?"

"Always friends, and as a friend I insist that you consider deleting this line," Julia said.

He laughed, and they went back to business, retreating hastily from the emotions their discussion had aroused.

By the week's end, Frederick was off to Boston, and Julia and Eliza were left in the house with Anna, who ruled as the uncrowned queen. Her word was law, and at least the children obeyed without question.

Anna made no effort to talk with her guests at the table, but she was pleased by Eliza's frequent compliments about her cooking, granting a slight nod of the head and an almost demure smile.

But Julia could do nothing to win Anna's acceptance, and participating in the family's domestic routines seemed only to make matters worse.

On the first night after Frederick's departure, the household convened in the parlor for the daily reading of the Bible. As usual, Anna assigned readings to Rosetta and Lewis.

Each read fervidly, proud before their guests, ignoring their mother's stony disapproval of Julia. When done, Rosetta asked brightly, "Oh, Mama, can Miss Griffiths read to us? Please."

Julia immediately objected, "Oh, no, Rosetta, this is your family's special occasion."

"You are part of the family . . . almost."

Anna flinched at this remark, and Julia shook her head more vigorously.

The other boys joined in, "Please, Mama, please."

Anna raised her hand to silence them. They obeyed at once, and Anna asked Julia, "Will you read one of the Psalms?"

Julia selected Psalm 95 and read it slowly.

Rosetta observed, "That's one of Papa's favorites."

"I didn't know that," lied Julia.

Anna then turned to Eliza, who seemed ready to flee the room at any moment.

"Miss Eliza, you'll read a Psalm, too?"

"Of course, Mrs. Douglass. Do you have one in mind?"

"No."

Eliza read a short Psalm, and Julia smiled at her sister's effort to end the prayer session that much earlier.

Anna stood signaling an end to the evening. But Julia was not ready to retire and announced, "Perhaps I can tell the children some stories."

The children turned to their mother looking for approval. They looked in vain.

"All the nights in this house ends with the Lord's word. It's now time for bed."

Julia's face burned, but she maintained her composure.

Anna added, speaking to her children but looking toward Julia, "But if Miss Julia would like to tell you some stories before we come to prayin' next time, then I'm sure it will be a good thing for us all."

Frozen in place, Eliza said nervously, "Yes, yes. Of course. She will. Julia is a good storyteller."

"Good night," said Anna, leading the children out of the room.

The door closed, and Eliza rushed to her sister. "Julia, you can't take over in the way that you do, not in everything. This is not our house."

"I am not trying. I just want to be useful."

"We must be careful, Julia. We cannot upset her, even if you are a problem."

Julia's eyes flashed. "What do you mean?" she asked in a tone that usually intimidated Eliza. But tonight she did not so easily capitulate.

"You know exactly what I mean. You work at the office, spending long hours there with her husband. This is too much for Anna, as it would be for any wife."

"If we are to remain civil, Eliza, I suggest that you never make that allusion again."

Eliza softened. "Julia, you should try being *more* helpful."

"How? I don't like to cook or clean or wash or sew or darn or knit or garden."

"As I promised, I will make no allusions. But Anna *is* his wife."

"And I am his friend," Julia said.

Eliza sighed. "You don't have to convince me."

★

Later that month, on May 31, Frederick created a sensation in Boston's Faneuil Hall at the end of his long speech about the colonization revival. Five thousand people, having come for the 1849 convention of the New England Anti-Slavery Society, sat patiently through most of it, shifting in their seats as Frederick droned on. Then he denounced the Mexican War as "murderous."

He now had everyone's attention, including those hissing patriots who objected to the claim that the war's primary aim was the extension of slavery into the territories.

"A word more," Frederick said to the unsettled crowd, and what followed was his first public disavowal of nonviolence: "When I consider their condition—the history of the American people—how they bared their bosoms to the storm of the British artillery, in order to resist simply a three-penny tea tax, and to assert their independence of the mother country—I say, in view of these things, I should welcome the intelligence tomorrow, should it come, that the slaves had risen in the South, and that the sable arms which had engaged in beautifying and adorning the South were engaged in spreading death and destruction there."

Silence. Absolute silence.

Frederick could hear and see shock. Mouths had dropped as men and women turned to each other and silently asked, what did he just say? Did we hear correctly?

There was scattered applause, and then came uproar, booing, curses, and the pounding of canes.

Sitting down, Frederick turned to Garrison and Wendell, who were looking straight into the audience as if they couldn't face the truth. Frederick had publicly crossed a line clearly marked by Garrison since 1831, but they didn't want to react and show division.

Garrison said kindly, "Dear friend, you got carried away, sir. Ours is a peaceful movement." He said nothing more.

Wendell said, "Patrick Henry is remembered for only one line. I just hope your last line, a longer one to be sure, is not so remembered."

Frederick thought Wendell was more understanding and tolerant than Garrison, and now he had been proven wrong.

When Frederick came home, he had a pile of newspapers to show Julia. "Just look at what they are saying," he said angrily, even though he wasn't surprised by the denunciations in the Garrisonian press.

One paper announced, "There is now only one difference between Frederick Douglass and Nat Turner. Turner *had* the knife!"

"You didn't call for a rebellion," Julia asserted.

"No, I only said I would welcome one."

"Did Garrison have anything to say?"

"He was obviously upset with me, very upset."

"Your next editorial should answer all this. Not a single line of comment should pass unexamined. We shall show them," Julia said.

Frederick smiled. "This will be the proof of a great partnership."

"We'll win, you and me," Julia claimed, standing up with the papers to her chest, as if they were a shield that could hide the intense pleasure the word "partner" had given her.

"What's wrong? What did I say to upset you?"

"No, no, you didn't," she said, turning away and releasing the papers, which fell to the floor.

"Oh, let me get them," Frederick said.

Julia stepped away, fearing that being too close would expose her feelings and ruin everything. "Thank you. It's time that we went to bed. We have important work to do tomorrow." She headed to the door, not looking back.

"Thank you for listening," Frederick said.

She struggled not to turn around and rush into his arms, making an absolute fool of herself. Tears filled her eyes. They were no surprise, even though she was not one to cry often. Months of anguish and self-doubt had come to an end, the internal arguments, the lies, the excuses, the defenses, the anger directed at her sister to hide the truth. No more denials of her feelings about Frederick. And so, she cried from a great sense of relief. Tomorrow could be easier now.

The next morning, after breakfast eaten in silence, she returned to business at the office.

Frederick sat down to write another editorial, and Julia examined the bills, the register of donations, a list of expenses, and other paperwork. She shifted papers, enjoying making order out of chaos. Her desk was behind his, and all she had to do was raise her voice to speak to him a few feet away.

"This will prepare us for what's to come," Julia said.

"What are you saying?" Frederick asked.

"Your creditors and investors are losing patience. Their letters, several from the same gentlemen, demonstrate an obvious transition from forbearance to irritation."

"They just don't understand the complexities of publishing."

"They only understand that you are not paying them and bringing returns on their money."

"Then do what you came to do. Raise the money and keep them off my back."

"I have a list of people to whom I will write immediately. I will flood them with letters, and they will send money just to stop the flow of my appeals."

Julia wrote letters for hours, and money started coming in small quantities day after day. Each letter with money notes was greeted with an exclamation from Julia, a simple, knowing, "Yes," and Frederick always turned to acknowledge his confidence in the future.

But while he was away on tour, a letter from Amy Post arrived, who had been delegated by investors to ask Frederick for an audit of his books. Now after reading it, he remarked, "They don't think I know what I'm doing, and obviously believe I'm hiding something!"

Julia said, "Let them look." Frederick had no interest in the business of running a paper, was behind in his payments to creditors, and matters would be much worse if Julia had not intervened. "You are making a good faith effort. They need to see this if we are to stay solvent," she said.

"But my reputation!" Frederick exclaimed.

"Please."

But Frederick immediately took the offensive when Isaac Post and two other investors arrived. Frederick asked, "So, you don't think I have sufficient experience to know what I am doing?"

"You are inexperienced as a businessman, and an audit can only clarify matters," Isaac replied without defensive bluster. "You have admitted this to Amy on occasion."

"She would be the last person to support a plan that would be degrading to me as a man," said Frederick.

"You know she has the power to compel you to comply, since without the support of the Rochester Anti-Slavery Society you could not continue," Post said.

"Did she say that?"

"It's true, is it not?"

"While I will gladly have a committee kindly see that my books are honestly and properly kept, I can never, will never, consent to give up the entire control to persons who are not responsible for the debts. That would make me a mere cipher," said Frederick.

"We have no desire to take over," asserted Isaac. "Supervision is required during your long absences. Your printer, Mr. Dick, perhaps, can serve, and all correspondence should be directed to him." Frederick had met Dick during his trip to England and invited him to America, his expertise being indispensable for the start of a newspaper, since Frederick knew nothing about printing.

"No, Miss Griffiths will do the job, thank you" Frederick replied.

"We think that Mr. Dick is better suited . . ."

Uncharacteristically silent throughout this exchange, Julia now interjected, "I appreciate the vote of confidence from Mr. Douglass, but if the selection of

Mr. Dick will assuage the concerns of the committee, then I will support the recommendation as a good compromise satisfactory to all parties."

"Very well," Frederick conceded. He was not enthusiastic, but he shook Isaac's hand, demonstrating his support before the auditors departed.

Frederick confronted Julia. He was not angry, only peeved. "Why did you give in so easily? You are far better equipped to do the work than Dick."

Julia smiled. "Committees never run anything well, and it will soon tire of examining the books or running the affairs of the newspaper. Just mark my words."

Frederick returned to his speaking tour, and John Dick never expressed any interest in examining the books. "I'm a printer, Miss Griffiths, nothing more."

By the coming of the holidays, the committee never materialized, the committee audit never happened, and Julia continued to examine the books on her own and raise money with American and English supporters. She started planning an antislavery fair for the western states that would match, if not outdo, the Boston fair organized by Maria Chapman. Its success would certainly proclaim the emerging prominence of western abolition.

On Christmas day, the entire household, including Julia and Eliza and John Dick, rose early to gather in the parlor for the giving of gifts, proceeded by Frederick's dramatic reading of the Biblical account of the birth of Jesus in the Gospel of Luke. Beaming at the sight of his children, who waited in eager anticipation of this family tradition, Frederick read with added emphasis verses twelve and thirteen of Chapter Two: "And suddenly there with the angel a multitude of the heavenly host praising God and saying, Glory be to God in the highest, and on earth peace, good will toward men."

The children, except for the baby who was cradled in Anna's arms, sat in a row, waiting patiently for Frederick to present their gifts, one for each child, simple tokens to reflect the spirit of that day long ago when Jesus was laid in a manger because there was no room in the inn. This tradition, suggested by Anna, held no surprises, but Rosetta and her brothers were always pleased to receive one piece of their favorite candy because candy was so rare in the Douglass house.

"Thank you, Mama, thank you, Papa," said Rosetta, speaking in a stiff, practiced tone for herself and her brothers.

"Breakfast will soon be ready," said Anna.

"Hooray!" shouted the boys. This was their favorite part of Christmas. Anna prepared two feasts, breakfast for the children and supper for adults. The morning meal was for them, planned according to whatever they wanted.

Rosetta started to rise from the floor when Julia stood and announced dramatically, "And now I have a surprise for all of you. Just sit there, and I will bring them out."

Frederick, Anna, and Eliza looked to each other for an explanation. Eliza shrugged her shoulders and whispered, "I have no idea."

Within moments, Julia reappeared with an armful of extravagant gifts, a large, exquisitely crafted doll with large roses on its dress for Rosetta, a toy trumpet for Lewis, an illustrated book of stories for Frederick, Junior, and a hand-painted train for Charles Remond. To Julia, the gifts perfectly matched their personalities and interests, and she thoroughly enjoyed their giddiness receiving them. She sat on the floor and, surrounded by laughter and incessant questions, described the gifts, explaining their significance. Julia was too busy to notice the frown on Anna's face or hear Eliza's groan.

Surprised at first, Frederick recovered quickly. "Oh, Julia, you should not have done this. You didn't need to." There was no reproach in his voice.

"I love your family, Frederick," Julia replied.

"But the cost," he said.

"Say nothing more, please. I wanted to do this. Please understand."

"Oh, Mama," cried Rosetta, "Isn't Miss Julia wonderful?"

Anna stood up, maintaining her composure for her daughter's sake. "Breakfast will be ready soon. You'll need to get ready. Them things will have to wait."

Everyone heard the edge in her voice, the implied criticism, and the noise in the room stopped.

Nervously, Rosetta asked, "Mama, is there something . . ."

Julia responded at once. "Now, children, you'll need to put these things aside. Your mother is waiting for you. You'll have the entire day. And we'll talk some more later. Now go on."

"Thank you, Miss Julia," they all chanted.

"I'll put them on the chair near the fireplace. They'll be waiting right there."

Anna left, followed by Rosetta, the boys, and John Dick, who had said nothing the entire time, as usual. Then came a heavy silence as Frederick, Julia, and Eliza stood in the room avoiding each other's eyes. The wood log in the fireplace collapsed on the grate, releasing a burst of cackling noise.

Frederick crossed the room to Julia, took her hands into his and said, "You care too much. Please understand that you didn't have to. I had no idea that you . . ."

"Please, it was nothing. I don't want to hear another word about it," Julia said.

He released her hands and said, "We are fortunate, all of us."

As he left, the tension between the sisters was palpable.

Eliza whispered, "Oh, Julia, how could you?"

"I did nothing wrong, nothing," Julia replied.

"To use the children so. I just can't believe it."

"Nothing's wrong," she repeated.

"Then why did you keep a secret, even from me and Frederick and Anna? You could not even wait until some later time, or another day. Why now? Don't you remember when we first arrived?" Eliza asked.

Julia's voice hardened. "I will not be reproached by you ever again on this matter. You are not my mother or father. I will do what I like, and if you cannot bear it, you can leave this house."

"I am welcome here," Eliza said.

"And I'm not?"

"You will never be Anna's friend after today. But she will say nothing against you, because you did do something for her children. She loves her children."

"I love them."

"No, you don't. I know it, you know it. Anna knows it. Only Frederick can't see it."

"This will be our last discussion about this matter. My feelings about this family are no longer your business," Julia stated.

"Very well. But your treatment of me will have to change," Eliza said.

"I am who I am."

"But I am not who I was."

"What happened?"

"America happened."

"But you don't like it here. You don't like the weather, the food, the poor manners. I've not heard one compliment about this country from you," Julia said.

"When you're alone here, you'll have to find your own way," Eliza said.

"You are not alone. You have me!"

"Do I, Julia? Do I?"

"We're sisters, and I still love you," Julia said.

"And I love you, but now I can say I know your declarations of love can cut like a knife."

"Eliza!"

"Good day," Eliza said, turning away.

59.

BY THE NEW YEAR, Julia was in full control. As far as Frederick could judge, Julia edited the *North Star* with considerable skill, proofreading, improving style, and broadening the paper's content to include poems, short stories, and essays from Black and white writers. Within one year, she had expanded the circulation of *North Star* from 2,000 to 4,000 copies. Martin Delaney, still on the road and writing travel letters rather than getting subscribers, now seemed incompetent.

Whites and Blacks, free and enslaved, read Delaney's letters, which revealed in graphic details the spectacle of Congress going through fifty-nine ballots before electing a speaker of the House of Representatives. Absolutely disgusted by American politics, Frederick pointed to the right column on the front page of the *Rochester Courier* and said, "Read the latest garbage."

"On, no," murmured Julia, scanning the page. On January 4, Senator James Mason of Virginia introduced a new fugitive slave bill. It required states and local governments to help in the recapture of runaways and punished obstructers with a fine of a thousand dollars.

"Damn them," said Frederick, reflecting the sentiments of millions angry with the South's attempts to impose the protection of slavery on the North. There seemed to be no end to southern arrogance, especially now that some of the Mexican territories, spoils of war, were ready for statehood. Most settlers did not want slavery, but southern politicians like Mason were determined to impose conditions on the nation if the extension of slavery was limited in any way. Some southerners went further and threatened: if slavery can't go west, then we will secede.

"Has a war finally come?" asked Julia.

"There is talk that Senator Clay will save us. He's working on a compromise plan. Compromise, the favorite word of charlatans. If he succeeds, we all know who will be sacrificed."

Julia and Frederick heard the answer when Clay, seventy-four, and at the end of his long career, introduced his compromise on January 21. It provided for the admission of California to the Union as a free state; the organization of the remaining Mexican territory without any conditions or restrictions to slavery; the prohibition of the slave trade in the District of Columbia; and a stronger fugitive slave law.

Reading this, Frederick pounded his fist on the desk. "Damn him! Damn him, and may he rot in hell, the *bastard*!"

Julia started. This was the second time he had uttered a profanity in her presence. "Please accept my apology, Julia. If that law passes, life here will never be the same. Bounty hunters will come all the time and half the colored here will cross the lake to Canada. Some of us can't prove we are free."

"We haven't heard from Senator Webster. He can reject this compromise if he is true to Massachusetts," Julia said.

"Yes, yes. And we must write something for every issue, and write letters to Congress, to Senator Webster, to everybody. We can't let this happen. We can't," Frederick said.

"Webster will set things right," said Julia.

Frederick arched his eyes and said, "Webster's been quiet, too quiet."

"He speaks on the seventh. This may be the greatest speech of his long life. The times require no less."

But Senator Webster spoke for the Union *and* compromise on March 7, 1850, and blamed abolitionists for the crisis. "If the infernal fanatics and abolitionists ever get the power into their hand, they will override the Constitution, defy the Supreme Court, change and make laws to suit themselves. They will lay violent hands on those who differ with them politically in opinion or dare question their infallibility, bankrupt the country, and finally deluge it with blood."

Disgusted, Frederick sat down to pen a brief, nasty editorial for the next issue of the *North Star*. "Well done, Daniel. You've done the work, and it's proper to ask for the pay. You have betrayed innocent blood: why should you be denied your thirty pieces of silver?"

This was gentle compared to what the New England press unleashed. Garrison reprinted every attack on Webster he could find and called him, "the great slave hunter and brazen advocate of slave hunting." But he went too far, charging Webster with keeping a harem of colored women, "big, black wenches, and ugly and vulgar as Webster himself."

"This is bigotry," Frederick lamented, shaking his head. "Pure and simple. I've heard it too many times before. *Big, black, ugly, vulgar*, just the right words to upset white readers of any newspaper. Papers in South Carolina are this crude, but the *Liberator*?"

He paced, the office closed for the evening. "How dare he use colored people to make a point against Daniel Webster, or anyone else for that matter! He's supposed to be our *friend*!"

"He's angry, like all of us. He's beside himself. He doesn't realize what he is saying. Everyone is reckless these days," Julia said.

The nation, indeed, seemed to be going mad.

But most Americans wanted peace and sided with Webster.

Vice President John C. Calhoun was dead, but his compromise, now a formal package of five bills promoted and shepherded by Henry Clay, was the prevailing hope.

It was not a good time for the annual meeting of the American Anti-Slavery Society. Angry and bitter at the rising tide of compromise with slaveholders, Frederick returned with Julia and Eliza to New York more determined than ever to stand up against the rising tide. He could not avoid a rhetorical fight. The times, indeed, were out of joint, but true men had to stand up and declare, *No more compromise. No more.*

Garrison gave the opening address. Never had he wielded his verbal knife with such pleasure. The politicians in Washington had confirmed the conspiracy he had proclaimed since 1831. At last, the truth was clear. The nation was now naked in its slavery to slavery and morally compromised politicians. He then denounced the Catholic Church and all the Protestant denominations for failing to protest the sins of the nation. Garrison pressed on with a slight raise of his hand, as if it could stop the protest sure to follow, "Be not startled when I say that a belief in Jesus is no evidence of goodness."

"Yes, it is," the leader of the Bowery Boys, Isaiah Rynders, shouted above the supportive applause.

"No," Garrison shouted back. "Such belief is a worthless test. His praises are sung in Louisiana, Alabama, and the other southern states just as well as in Massachusetts."

Rynders asked, "What about the nigger prayers to Jesus?"

Garrison replied: "Not a slaveholding or slave *breeding* Jesus!"

Frederick groaned. Garrison was going to end the meeting before it really got started. Clay's compromise bills had not been mentioned yet. Wendell Phillips shook his head before saying, "Mr. Garrison, you *must* desist." Wendell was well known for turning crowds into mobs, so Frederick, sweating under his cravat, took Wendell's warning seriously.

Frederick and the other speakers now stood in front of Garrison to protect him.

The gangsters shouted, "Turn him out! Turn him out!"

Rynders tried to lunge through the human barrier, but Garrison's guards closed ranks. Rynders's fist shook above the abolitionists' heads, trying to rally his forces, but fortunately the police arrived and closed the meeting with no arrests.

"One thing is certain," concluded Wendell in a sitting room of a New York abolitionist who opened his home to delegates, "*we* are the enemy of the people; not slavery." He then pulled out a small pistol from under his coat.

Frederick gasped. "Wendell!"

"I shall kill anyone who touches me," he said calmly, declaring his break with Garrison's pacifist views. "Anyone!"

★

For Frederick, Julia, and Eliza, the dangers became very real the following day as they waited in Battery Park at the tip of Manhattan Island to board the *John Porter* for Philadelphia. They arrived too early.

It was a warm day, and a gentle breeze from the south lightened the humidity. As usual, people stared, pointed fingers, and whispered insults as the three passed arm in arm. But the trio ignored them. They turned toward the steamer, but suddenly six men surrounded them.

"Where do you think you're going, nigger?" growled one tall man with an ugly scar across his forehead.

"Sir, that is no business of yours."

The intruders laughed contemptuously. "Listen to the nigger," said one. "Don't we have *airs*!"

Leering, another said, "Feeling good after having a piece, huh, some good white meat?"

"A whore is a whore is a whore, whore, whore," sang a short skinny man who stood behind the leader.

Julia and Eliza drew closer to Frederick, hiding their faces against his shoulders.

"He's your pimp, ain't he?"

"You like fuckin' Black, don't you?" shouted another man, who grabbed his crotch. "Well, I have more than enough for you bitches, and none of the whores I know complain."

Eliza whimpered.

"Don't," ordered Frederick. "Don't let them see."

The group encircled them, jeering with increasing fervor, baiting them to make a wrong move. Frederick kept the lead, almost pulling his friends toward the steamer.

Julia came to a stop and slowly lifted her head. With all the loathing that she could summon she declared, "Only a blind woman used to living in sewers and cesspools could possibly be interested in the likes of you!"

The jeering stopped, and the thugs pounced, pushing, and shoving. Julia and Eliza screamed, but the men did not spare them. Two men pounded their heads with the flat of their hands.

Frederick kicked wildly, aiming for groins to weaken his attackers. He swung his fists, split lips, and crushed noses. The ferocity of his counterattack surprised the men, and three ran off.

A crowd of spectators gathered, but no one intervened. A few men even cheered.

"Kill the nigger! Kill the whores!"

Eliza and Julia were crying uncontrollably, and Frederick was now the sole object of the group's wrath. One grabbed him from behind, locking his arms, while the two others savagely punched him in the stomach and chest and kneed him repeatedly in the groin. Frederick's pain and nausea made his legs go slack. He could taste blood but didn't care about his face. He was going to throw up.

"Stop them! Stop them!" screamed Julia helplessly to the crowd. "Do something!"

Suddenly a police officer appeared, and the remaining three men ran off, dropping Frederick to the ground. Julia ran to him and cradled his head in her lap. "Oh Frederick, are you alright? Speak, say something, dearest, please. Let me help you." She reached under her dress and tore at her petticoat to make a bandage to wrap around his hand.

Frederick saw the officer and with studied dignity said, "Officer, those men assaulted . . ."

The officer snapped, "Look here, nigger, just get these women off the streets. You were just asking for trouble. Get the hell out of here."

Two of the men who had run off returned to stand behind some spectators. Seeing them, Frederick lifted his body and pointed. "Those two, they were part of it. Arrest them."

"Don't tell me what to do, *nigger*. Just get out of the Battery. If you don't, some other people will get you. And take your women with you."

Frederick yelled at the officer, "Aren't women safe on the streets of New York?"

The officer raised his stick and then checked himself. "Get out of here, you goddamn Black bastard."

The crowd dispersed leaving the three friends stranded in the park like lost, beaten animals. Eliza muttered, "Oh God, oh God, what kind of place is this? Oh Julia, I can't believe this could happen."

Julia turned to Frederick. "It's my fault. I should not have antagonized them. We knew they didn't like what they saw. I should not have added to it."

"No, no. We, you, have every right to walk anywhere in this city. These are *public* streets, and you started nothing."

A man ran up to them from behind and punched Frederick in the face, shouting, "And that's for Rynders!"

He ran off as Frederick fell to the side from the force of the blow. Eliza screamed, but Julia started to run after the man. "Coward! Coward! You're nothing but a low, dirty coward!"

Eliza watched her sister in utter horror, as if Julia were possessed.

Frederick struggled to get up and go after her, but Eliza now calm reached out her hand to stop him. "He's gone. She won't reach him."

Frederick turned to Eliza, stunned by the chill in her voice.

"Julia loves you," Eliza said.

Frederick winced. *Did the attack make her mad? Was she in shock*? Gently touching her arm, he said, "Everything will be all right. I'm sorry. I should not have permitted you to walk with me. It was my fault. I'm deeply sorry."

"She's lost. She loves you in this terrible land. What is she to do, loving you, a married man, a married Black man? She called you dearest. She tore her petticoat."

"She was concerned."

Eliza shook her head again and again and repeated with a soft but deep sadness the word that said everything: "Dearest."

60.

ANNA HAD A HOUSE full. At one point, ten people in all: Frederick, the four children, and herself, John Dick, Rosetta's new tutor, Phebe Thayer, and Julia and Eliza Griffiths.

Later in the year, Anna's sister Lottie would join them.

Only Julia was unwelcome.

The crowded house pleased Anna. This was her world, and she managed it well. She enjoyed arranging sleeping quarters, planning meals, cooking, and scheduling the uses of parlors when there was so much going on, including abolitionist meetings and receptions for visitors, who regularly called on Frederick. She would not allow any servants in her house, even if she could afford them. The work filled her days with purpose and achievement, the smell of good food and clean sheets, the gleam of waxed floors, and the silence of well-behaved children, who were usually not allowed to play outside and give a false impression of rowdiness.

But she had to admit that the house was now too small. They needed more room, especially with all the people coming to see Frederick. She could manage a small house, but there was only so much she could do within the walls of 4 Alexander Street.

Frederick began talk about moving to another house, this time outside the city. He was excited about the land, describing all the trees on ten acres, the space for flower and vegetable gardens, space for the children to play without the prying eyes of neighbors. "The house will be twice as big, for all of us, and guests too," he noted.

"Where is it now" she asked, pleased about the added space, but skeptical about the cost.

He described the spot, and she protested, "Out there, *way* out there? We won't have neighbors."

"You don't like people checking on us anyway."

"But out *there*?"

"We will be able to get everything we need and grow our own food. You'll like that, growing our food, raising our own animals."

"How we going to pay for this?"

"Don't you worry. It's all taken care of."

"You always talk about paying for the paper, and then this? This don't make sense. Buying a house *now*!"

"This is separate. One doesn't have to do with the other."

Anna could tell that he was not going to offer any more information about the purchase of the new house. She waited to see if he was going to invite her out to see the property or seek her advice for its design, since she would be the one living there most of the time while he was on the road.

She waited.

He didn't offer, and again she felt a deep ache. Her body now ached all the time, and parts of her face had started to burn and twitch, causing her worry and sleepless nights. But she refused to see a doctor.

Thank goodness she had some help.

Eliza volunteered for many tasks. None of them seemed beneath her. She admitted, "I should earn my keep. We will always appreciate your generosity." When Anna was too tired to do any more work, Eliza came to her with tea and cakes.

They were not friends, but when Anna didn't have anyone else to talk with, she was willing to listen to Eliza talk about home and Mr. Dick's discreet but growing interest in her.

"What should I do, Anna? I think Mr. Dick likes me," asked Eliza.

"What do you want?"

"I don't know."

"Then when you know, we'll talk."

"How will I know?"

"You'll know," Anna said.

★

Julia was not pretty for a white girl. Her nose was large with a bump on the bridge, her mouth slightly off center, her chin too close to the neck. Those green eyes that seemed to sparkle when she talked were her one good feature, admitted Anna, knowing she had no claims to beauty herself.

But what Anna disliked the most was Julia's mouth. She just would not keep it shut, spitting out opinions about everything. She just had to tell people—and she didn't seem to care who they were-—about the weather, the news, the taste of food, the feel of her clothes, the best ways to raise money and manage newspapers, the abolitionist cause, politics, on and on and on.

Sometimes Anna wanted to slap her and say, "Just shut up and be quiet for once in your life!"

But she didn't, because that wouldn't be right. And when she heard what happened to Frederick and Julia in New York she was horrified. She always worried about Frederick's way of riling up folks, but white women were supposed to be safe on the streets.

Frederick reviewed every detail of the attack and seemed to relive every blow, the taste of blood and vomit, seeing the same scene day and night, falling asleep from exhaustion, and waking in the middle of night with a violent shudder and a garbled scream.

"It will be all right," said Anna, stroking his arm and back one night. "That's over. New York is far away, far away."

As usual, he found some relief and a kind of peace through writing. About his rights at Battery Park and anywhere else, he was unmovable. Letters of support poured in from throughout the country. The letter that most pleased him came from Gerrit Smith, who invited him to his home in Peterboro, New York. "My outraged and inflicted brother, I sympathized with you and loved you before, but much more now."

Smith had invited Frederick and the family last year, but Anna's pregnancy, the prolonged illness of their youngest son, Charles, and a long lecture tour made a trip impossible. Now they could go. He shared the news with Julia, then Anna.

In the pantry, he brandished the letter behind Anna, who was putting away dishes. "Exciting news. Gerrit Smith has invited us all for two entire weeks to Peterboro. We will all need to start packing. Julia . . ."

At the mention of Julia's name, Anna turned to face Frederick, her teeth hurt she was so angry. "Must you always travel with that woman?"

"Anna! This is . . ."

"How much do I have to hear about her? You get attacked in the streets, and then she is with you again, with us, the family when . . ."

"I will not hear of this. Julia is not to be referred as *that* woman, not here."

"I'm not Rosetta, Frederick. I'm your wife."

"I know that."

"Do you?"

"What do you mean by *that*?"

"The way things are 'round here, some can think that you're married to *her*. I'm sure you told her the good news about the family trip before me."

"We're together out of necessity. She respects this family and you and our marriage. But I don't feel that I should defend her."

"She don't have to go to Peterboro with us. Not now, not this time."

"She was invited, too."

"Then I'm not going."

"Then you'll have to stay."

"I see. And you will lie to Mr. and Mr. Smith about the reason for my not coming."

"Of course. A small white lie . . ." Frederick stopped, catching the irony.

"Yes, a *white* lie," said Anna, turning her back.

Suddenly, he roughly turned her around by the arm for the first time in their married life.

Anna looked down at his hand on her arm before speaking, "Has it come to this, that you lie for her and grab me?"

Frederick pulled away and left the room, leaving the question unanswered.

★

Anna's sister Lottie came unannounced to the house one day when Frederick and Julia were at the office. Anna recognized her at once, a thinner version of herself, the large, flashing eyes, the dark skin, the coarse hair parted in the middle and pulled back after a severe brushing into a small bun at her neck.

Stunned, Anna could only mutter, "Oh, my Lord!" Being reunited with her sister hit her like a punch in the stomach, and Anna yelled out in joy. She wrapped her younger sister, younger by one year, into her big arms, forcing her to drop her bags. "Lottie, oh Lottie, it's you. It's really you!"

"I found you, Anna. I *had* to find you. All that talk about them new laws and grabbin' people off the streets."

Before 1850, masters were on their own regarding runaway slaves and often hired bounty hunters, who grabbed people off the streets. But the new law now *required* all government agencies to help slavers. The sheriff, the police, judges, city councils, state legislatures—everybody.

"Then you're still a slave?" Anna asked.

"Yes. But I couldn't take it no more. I heard about the Railroad and a lady from the Shore. She ran away just last year to Philadelphia, and she came back! Yes, she came back for her family, and for other people, too. I found her with the help of some church people. She is something else. I was almost as afraid of her as them bounty hunters. No crying, no talking, all at night. A scared man started cryin', and she pulled out a pistol. Yes, a pistol, and told him to shut up or she would shoot him on the spot."

"Wouldn't that shot bring people around?"

"I didn't think of that at the time. I just thought, she's a general, and we had better do what she tells us. Moses, they call her."

"I thought for sure I wasn't going to see you, not ever!"

"Me too, but I had to go north. I heard your place was on the Railroad."

Anna was struck by a premonition. "Mama and Papa, they're dead, ain't they?"

"Yes."

"How? No, don't tell me yet. Come in and sit down, and then you tell me. I want to sit down, even though the worst part is over, knowing they're gone. It's been a long time, so I was prepared. It just has to settle in while sittin'."

"Your house is so big."

"Yes, but it needs to be bigger, with all them people, the white people around. We're getting a bigger house out of town," Anna said.

"White people?" Lottie asked.

"I'm sure you heard about Fred. You would have to know about Fred. He's in all the papers."

"I can't read the papers. Do you?"

"No,' replied Anna, relieved that she and her sister had another thing in common. "Well, your niece, my Rosetta, all eleven years old, can read the letters and newspapers to us both. She's some reader. Now tell me what happened to Mama and Papa."

"You won't be surprised about Papa. He got drunk again, and got into a big fight, and some nigger—excuse me, that is a word I shouldn't use in your house, respect-able and all, but Papa got taken down by a man bigger than he was, and he cracked his head open with a rock. He died right there in the bloody dirt," Lottie said.

"Did you see him?"

"We all came runnin' when we heard, Mamma and me. The boys had run off or were sold to where I don't know. So, it was just me left. Mamma was carryin' on, crying until the snot came out, rollin' on the ground, like she was at a funeral showin' off. It was such a sight, knowing what he did to her. And all I could think was 'good riddance.'"

Anna swallowed. They had never spoken openly about their father's night visits, but the look on her face when she said "good riddance" suggested that Lottie was also a victim.

But now was not the time to ask. When they were alone, when the house was quiet, then they could talk about the secret. Anna looked to the door of the parlor as if at any moment Eliza or one of the children would interrupt them.

Without prompting or any trace of self-pity, Lottie said, "Yes, he did it to me, and so he can burn in hell, for all I care."

Anna stood. "No more about *that.* Tell me about Mama."

"She was dead before she died, but she couldn't stop crying over him, going on and on. Can you believe that, after all he did to her, after what he did to all of us, and she lettin' it happen? If that's love, then I don't want nothing to do with it," Lottie said.

"He wanted us to think it was love, but it aint," Anna replied.

Looking around the room, Lottie observed, "Well, your man showed you there is some other kinds of love, and for it you got all this. Did you ever think you'd get all this when you met him. It was in Baltimore, right?"

"Yes, and he was a slave then. But I knew he would be somebody, even if I could not see one day he would write books, give speeches across the ocean, and meet all kinds of people, rich people, people wanting to help us be free," Anna said.

"You're proud of him."

"Yes," she admitted. Now was not the time to offer a list of complaints and disappointments. That could come later, if her sister proved to be now what she remembered, a kind, loving, patient listener.

"I'm going to have to make some rearrangements so you can stay here, and you can stay here as long as you like. You can stay here until the day you die, or the day you get married, and who knows when that will be?"

Lottie was her real sister, and they would be together, especially now when Frederick and Julia, and Eliza were going away more and more. While they were in Peterboro, Anna could stay home and enjoy her time with Lottie and not think about what Frederick and Julia could be doing in that big house on that big piece of land that people said looked like a plantation.

61.

PETERBORO WAS SMITH'S PERSONAL village of thirty buildings, stables, shops, green houses, and barns, with scores of employees surrounding his three-story mansion in a forest nine miles from Conastota, the nearest town. The white house had a stately portico supported by six white columns at the front, with a sweeping lawn before it. As their carriage approached the house it seemed somewhat shabby, the white paint now a speckled, peeling gray. Smith was one of the country's wealthiest men, but his estate lacked grandeur.

Smith was a tall, big-boned man standing about six-foot-four with a thick body over two hundred pounds that pressed against his waistcoat and jacket. His hands were huge, larger than Frederick's, with long thick fingers and manicured nails.

But he did not offer to shake Frederick's hand. Once they were seated in the parlor, Smith explained, "Please excuse my not extending my hand, sir. I have constant pain there, and handshakes leave me in agony for days. And I don't need to add more to my ailments, which are many, hemorrhoids, fevers, severe stomach aches, to name a few. My desk drawer is full of bottles of elixirs and ointments, and I'm certain to come to an early demise."

Julia winced. Ignoring her reaction to his candid details, Smith elaborated, "Death and insanity stalk this house. My first wife and two of my four children are gone, as is my father. And my youngest brother, Adolphus, is in an asylum. I might go insane myself, I'm afraid, but I am sure that abstinence from tea and coffee, fish, flesh, gravies, and alcohol will delay the inevitable." He continued, "I hope *North Star* will be successful. Did you get any new subscribers at the meetings?"

Frederick paused, looking to Julia, uncertain whether to answer truthfully. "No, and so I appreciate your donation to my paper even more. But you must know that I remain a devoted follower of Mr. Garrison."

"In the house of abolition, there can be many rooms. Did not our Lord say in the Gospel of John that 'In my father's house are many mansions'?" Smith asked.

"Yes, sir, but . . . ."

"Oh, my friend, let's leave talk about this to another time. I want to hear about what's happened since Seneca Falls. I've invited my cousin Elizabeth to join us. I usually have gatherings with differing people, for I enjoy sociable conflict, but today it will only be you, the Griffithses, the Posts, and dear Elizabeth."

"How do you do it?" asked Julia, intrigued by his warmth and vulgar specificity. She couldn't help her reaction. She liked this man. His honesty was exhilarating.

"I make them all feel important," Smith replied.

"But don't some still object to being together?"

"If they have difficulties, I provide a side table."

Elizabeth Stanton entered the room. Smith, Frederick, and Isaac Post rose from their chairs. Smith smiled and said, "Ah, Lizzie, so pleased that you will be joining us before our simple repast."

Julia was surprised by Elizabeth's stature. She was short, her cheeks were small stuffed bags, and puffy arms filled the sleeves of her dark dress. Her notoriety had made her tall in Julia's imagination. The penetrating eyes revealed her will as a woman not to be opposed.

Elizabeth didn't smile. "I haven't seen Mr. Douglass since Seneca Falls and the Rochester conventions." She behaved as if no one else but Frederick and Smith were in the room.

"Let me introduce my other guests," said Smith, nodding toward the Posts, Julia, and Eliza. Elizabeth nodded her head with each introduction and sat directly to the right of her cousin.

Elizabeth said sourly, "I am pleased that at least for now there are no ministers included in this round of visitations."

Smith frowned for the first time. "Elizabeth, please, not another diatribe."

"You mean a diatribe against all those Bible-quoting hypocrites who use God to justify their tyrannies? He is their ally."

"Oh, Lizzie," sighed Smith. "I am glad that my dearest Ann is away and can't hear such blasphemy. *Her* lord is the Lord of love and justice."

"Where? In the killing of innocent children and entire populations with armies or plagues, the justification for my subordination and Frederick's enslavement, and pronouncements that if I didn't obey Him I would suffer eternal pain in hell?" asked Elizabeth.

Chagrined, Smith turned to Frederick. "Mr. Douglass, you are a veteran of the religious wars. Please explain to my dear cousin the perils of attacking belief in God. Americans are religious, and they will turn away from our causes if we take the path Elizabeth has taken. You had to offer assurances yourself in your book and in Britain that your attacks against the clergy were not meant to diminish and dethrone the Lord."

Elizabeth was derisive. "Another male power. His throne is in the clouds, but he still insists on my obedience, and the obedience of all women to his rules of subordination. I will not stand for it."

"Mr. Douglass, say something," Smith implored, rubbing his hands.

Frederick smiled indulgently and offered a gentle, self-deprecating laugh. "Surely, I'm not one to intervene in a family disagreement. I have enough of my own to deal with."

An awkward silence followed. Julia and Eliza looked at each other and then looked to Frederick for a gracious way to move out of the trap in which they found themselves.

Smith provided an opening. "Be sure to take a walk before every meal," he said and stood up. "It's good for digestion. There is so much to see here, many places where you can sit and relax, be left alone. There is an aviary to the south of here, about a mile away, that I used to go to. If you ever need to get away, that's a spot to think, and the birds are all gone. I've found another place. There is a spot for everyone, so choose well. If not that spot, some spot. Good afternoon. I need to read some new books I received about insanity and the possible remedies through medicine. I will see you this evening at dinner. If you need refreshment earlier, there are radishes and carrots, raw of course, on the sideboard in the dining room."

"Eliza, let's go find that aviary. It sounds charming," Julia said.

"No," Eliza replied, shaking her head. "It's too hot to walk that far. Perhaps, Mrs. Stanton can . . ."

Elizabeth corrected her at once, "Mrs. Cady Stanton."

"My apologies," said Eliza with false civility.

"I'm sure you will remember in the future, and, like you, I choose to not walk in this heat," Elizabeth said.

Julia agreed with everything Elizabeth stood for, but she took an immediate dislike to her after she corrected Eliza. Eliza could be tactless, but she was never deliberately unkind to strangers.

"I can't go alone," Julia said.

"Then Frederick, you go with her," said Elizabeth.

Julia knew that Eliza expected her to decline going on a walk with a married man to a secluded aviary, and she hesitated before giving her answer. But she decided this was another day of independence. They could take walks on the estate of a private citizen and not worry about impressions. Equality in 1850 meant at least this much: a walk together on a friend's private property.

"Let us go then," Julia said.

Frederick and Julia found the abandoned aviary, its roof and supporting pillars hidden by a wall of vines and bushes. They stopped before stepping inside, as if they knew that entering this space could have profound consequences. Frederick pushed back the thicket of leaves and stepped inside, holding out his hand for Julia's and leading her into the aviary, a large structure screened on all six sides and tall enough for them to stand on the wood floor. The air was cool, the humidity softened by the filtered light. The world seemed far away, timeless, at peace.

"Frederick, I have something to tell you."

"What is it?" Frederick asked. She pressed the folds of her dress and looked away, scanning the room for a way out. "Julia, please."

Julia took a deep breath and said, "I love you, Frederick Douglass. I love you."

"I love you, too. True friends love each other."

"No, I'm *in love* with you."

At last, the words were now spoken that had defined countless shared moments, long nights in the parlor reading poetry, arguing over fine points of constitutional interpretation, walks in the street, and their work together. She waited.

"Yes," was all that Frederick said as he took her hands into his.

Julia spoke. "I understand you're married, and I know that I have no right to expect anything. I'm sorry if what I say today compromises you. But I wanted you to know. You have a right to know. I cannot help loving you, and if that knowledge adds in any measure to your life, I am happy, and if . . ."

"And if I love you as you love me . . ."

"I make no demands, have no expectation of return," she said.

"You need not because my feelings for you are . . ." He faltered and said, "I love you, Julia. I love you."

He took her into his arms, and Julia collapsed into them, as if a tremendous weight had been lifted. "Yes . . . Yes."

Frederick stepped away. He lifted her face by the chin with both hands and looked to her eyes. He found tears and kissed them away gently. "We can be happy," he said.

His lips moved down her cheeks to her lips and pressed his own against them. From within him came a groan so soft and deep it almost frightened her. Every nerve and muscle in her body alive, she knew if she did not stop now there could be no turning back. Within seconds he would kiss her mouth with his tongue, touch her breasts, press his groin against her hips. And she would allow it.

Frederick stepped back. "I'm sorry. This should not have happened. I'm married . . ."

Julia felt a rising panic. She looked down as if suddenly found naked.

"Yes, I am married, but I love you. Even in England, there was a feeling . . ."

Emboldened, Julia said, "And now this is our moment, our secret place, our green island."

"And when we leave it, we go back to the way it was."

Taking this as a cue for departure, she composed her body and went toward the exit. "Then let us go," she said.

"No. Not yet. Please stay with me." He kissed her passionately. "Oh, Julia." He caressed her, his fingers searching the confining cloth of her dress, his mouth scanning the soft skin of her neck.

She wanted to feel his body against hers.

"We shouldn't do this," he whispered in contrast to his actions. The sun was going down, and the golden light permitted the casting aside of the day's commandments.

Unbuttoning her bodice, Julia giggled, "My dress will get dirty."

"It could be our blanket."

Images of losing her virginity flashed before her. The endearments, the exchanged sentiments, the encouragements and whispered directions.

Instead, Frederick stepped back, hearing something so powerful in his body he buckled at the waist.

"No. We can't do this!"

He shook his head, and repeated "No," an incantation meant to calm his nerves. "This is not right!"

Julia stared at him feeling a deep well of pity, but not for herself. "I understand," she whispered, her calmness like a gentle breeze, "and I'm sorry if I did anything to put you in this position. Perhaps I should not have agreed to come here, but I'm not sorry for loving you."

"I made a promise ten years ago."

"But you said you loved me."

"I should not have said that."

"Then you lied just to please me."

"Your love made me forget my vows, my reputation."

"So that is what matters, your reputation?" As soon as she asked, she felt like a fool. For a man of Frederick's color and stature, of course it mattered. It mattered every minute of his life, and no one allowed him to forget it. Her long-suppressed emotions were now derailing her poise and judgment.

"Of course, it matters. I know what people want to see happen, but I can't give them proof. They want *this* to happen."

"Do you?"

He paused. "Yes."

"Then I can live with knowing just that, that you want me, even if you can't have me."

"Please, let's not talk about this anymore. It's getting late and . . ."

"Everyone will talk anyway."

"Yes, and if confronted, we won't have to lie. Nothing happened."

"But something happened."

"Words and a kiss, nothing more."

"You sound like a lawyer quibbling over minor details. But a declaration is not a minor detail."

"I don't want to argue with you. We will always be friends, but you are never to mention this episode again," Frederick said.

"I won't, if that is what you want," Julia replied.

"That is what I want, and if you love me, you will do this for me."

"And what will you do for me?"

"I will never ask you to leave me," he vowed.

She looked at his face, that handsome face. Julia took his promise as the best she could hope for. "I love you, still."

"Don't say those words anymore, please. But I can assure you I will not forget them, ever."

"Very well. I promise. I have no regrets expressing them, but I promise."

"But we must return as we once were before we came here. There will be inquiries, suspicions," Frederick said.

"No one will dare to ask. Your friends won't dare. But we still must be careful. Perhaps I should move out of your house?" Julia offered.

"No, that would raise more questions, and I don't want you to leave. You are my friend, my partner."

Julia was unable to resist the next question, but she had to ask it. "If you could have married me, would you have?"

He paused. "Yes," he finally replied.

"That's all I need to know."

"But the past cannot be changed, and if things were different I would not have my children. I don't regret that, and I will not regret that, ever."

"I understand, and I promise I will always be good to them. I wish I could have my own and see in their eyes what I see. They adore you."

"You can get married. Someone will sweep you away."

"Someone already has."

"Don't say that, please. Don't refer, in anyway, to things like that. Once was enough, and unforgettable. But don't . . ." Frederick said.

"Very well, but we must face Anna when we return to Rochester," Julia said.

"We can do that because nothing happened."

"That's not true."

"You know what I mean."

"*Omnia vincit amor*," Julia whispered, loud enough for Frederick to hear.

He frowned, puzzled by the reference.

"Love conquers all," she translated, smiling.

★

When they returned to the house, no one said a word about their absence. Julia tried to find a hint of suspicion in the eyes of Smith or Eliza but found none.

Eliza said nothing about Julia and Frederick's absence in Peterboro until their first night back in Rochester. "What did happen in Peterboro?" she asked without provocation, before Julia took up the candle to blow it out before they went to bed.

"I am not accountable to you," said Julia coldly, startled by the directness of Eliza's accusation.

Eliza was not perturbed. In one year she had changed. She was more critical, more independent. De Tocqueville was right: the American continent had the power to transform character.

"But Frederick *is* accountable to Anna," Eliza said.

"Then she can speak for herself."

"You two think you are so clever. After all, you're just duping an ignorant, illiterate woman."

"Duping? That's absurd."

"Julia, your avoidances are so studied, so artificial. You two were much warmer, more open before going to Peterboro. Now you are business associates who happen to live in the same house. You are working too hard. So dramatic a change can only mean one thing."

Quick to deflect, Julia lied, "We had a serious disagreement."

"About what?"

"About the Constitution and politics. Mr. Smith and I are trying to convince Frederick, but he feels betrayed by the two of us banding up against him, and . . ."

Eliza shook her head and said with pity, "Julia, that is such a lie."

"Then our lives are no concern of yours," Julia snapped. She crossed the small room to confront Eliza with withering scorn.

Eliza did not back away as she always had before. "Julia, you have more secrets now, here in Rochester, than you ever had in England. We used to share our lives in England, and now you shut me out."

"I am not on trial, Eliza, and you are in no position to judge me."

"I will not travel with the two of you again."

"You sniveling, little hypocrite. You live in this house, eat his food, and then sit here and tell me that you wouldn't be seen with him on the streets. Your phony self-righteousness stinks to heaven itself!"

"Then we are both hypocrites. But there are degrees. I will leave you to do as you like—travel together, visit friends. You'll both be free to dig a bigger hole and jump in."

"Why do you hate . . . yes, it is hate. Why do you hate me so?"

Eliza's answer seemed rehearsed, as if she had been waiting her entire life for this moment. "You manipulate me, you manipulate Anna, and you manipulate Frederick, too. You use everybody, and despite all this you are having a wonderful time. It isn't fair. Well, I won't be used anymore, not even to be your chaperone for the world to think, *She's doing nothing. Why, Julia Griffiths's sister is with her all the time.* No more! You will be what you are without my help."

"I never needed you. I could have come without you and would have. You know that very well. You needed me," Julia said.

"Yes, then I could go back to England, or maybe Canada," Eliza replied.

"Then go. You have been nothing but a pain in my side since father died. Now I will be rid of you once and for all. I won't have to be your mother anymore."

Eliza sighed. She said with deep sadness, "I will never be able to match you in sheer, ugly viciousness, Julia. In that you are supreme. I congratulate you."

"Please, don't leave. You're all I have."

"Why, Julia, you are *not* self-sufficient?"

Julia drew back as if she had been slapped in the face. "What?"

"You cannot realize what a pleasure it gives me to see you grovel, at last."

"Eliza!"

"And if you touch me, I will make up for the all the times you bested me."

"You are despicable!"

"I've learned well."

"We will not share a room after today," Julia announced.

Eliza laughed. "Spoken like the mistress of the house you imagine yourself to be. But remember this, Julia: Anna is his wife, and although you underestimate her, she doesn't underestimate you!"

"You've been talking about me to her, behind my back!"

"We talk about many things, and . . ."

"You two cannot have become friends! You are as different as night and . . ."

"Julia, *that* is an unfortunate reference. She is kind, truly kind, something you rarely are."

"Kind? Where in the world have you been? Do you see how she treats her own children? She's like a captain ordering them about, never demonstrating an ounce of affection. Yes, you two must be friends. Two cold, rigid women who don't realize how fortunate they are to know a man like . . ."

"Don't. Don't talk about him to me. You have no right now to extol him to me, and you have said enough about me besides."

"Eliza, you can't go on like this. Everyone will wonder why we are estranged. Explanations will have to be made."

"What other people thought never bothered you before."

"This is different. Anna has to be protected from scandal," Julia said.

"You could care less about Anna."

"Then what about the children? You can't hide feelings from them, not these feelings. After a day, they will be asking about you and me, and surely you don't want them to be bothered with an adult problem between sisters," Julia said.

"You all will have more to talk about after today. I cannot stay, living here with you and Mr. Douglass," Eliza said.

"You are going back home?"

"No, I'm going to Canada."

"But why?"

"I'm getting married."

"What! You can't be serious. When did this happen?" Julia sat back down as Eliza described her relationship with John Dick, her tone soft but urgent, as if she had to speak as quickly as possible before Julia recovered to offer a counterargument.

For months she had developed a friendship with John, shy and awkward but always kind and respectful, glancing her way with a sly smile, becoming more assertive when she smiled his way, but saying very little at the dinner table, in the parlor, at church, or at the antislavery meetings they attended with Frederick. He sometimes talked about starting his own paper and moving to Toronto. Once, he mentioned that he wanted to go there with a wife. Julia never noticed.

At one meeting where women's rights were being discussed, he casually mentioned that he thought Eliza would make a fitting wife, and suddenly asked her if she would ever consider marrying him.

At first, Eliza was stunned by the proposal and the setting in which it was offered. She was not thinking of marriage, and she thought that when a proposal would finally come, it would be during a walk in a garden, some place suggestive of Wordsworth. John Dick was not handsome, and Eliza could not ignore his big hands, large, protruding teeth, and a bulging midsection. But he was her chance to get out of the Douglass house, away from Rochester and from Julia's domination.

"You didn't think it was possible, did you?" asked Eliza as Julia sat before her. "You were sure that I would be the younger sister, the spinster sister of the successful Julia Griffiths. But I surprised you. I will have my own life."

"But he's just a printer. His hands are always dirty. Do you love him?"

"Of course, I do."

"He must be taking advantage of you. I will see to it that Frederick intervenes. This *cannot* happen."

"What is it, Julia? Are you afraid of being alone?"

"I will not be alone."

"Yes, you will, Julia. You will be. This is Anna's house."

"You are marrying to spite me."

"That would give you too much credit, Julia. You have been a powerful enough influence in my life without my binding myself to a man for the next fifty years so I can get back at you. You are already the most powerful influence in my life up to now. You won't be for the rest of it. I will not give you such a victory."

"You can't leave."

"But I will. In June."

"In June? It can't be that soon."

"June."

"Then where will the wedding be, and who will be asked to come?"

"You, of course, and Anna and Frederick, the Posts, a few others. We want no fuss, no bother. We will marry in this house."

"Does Anna know?"

"Yes, of course. I needed to ask if it would be acceptable to marry here," Eliza said.

"And you told Anna before you told me?" Julia asked.

"You will *not* touch this, even with all your plans and organizing. And if you dare do anything for this, I will leave without a ceremony. We will elope."

"You wouldn't!" exclaimed Julia, rising.

"What's another scandal in this family? My activities will always pale in comparison," Eliza said.

As Eliza rose to leave the room, Julia could not resist one final attack, subtle but to the mark. "The wedding will be the highlight of your life when there is so much more you could do with it, if you had the talent or the temperament."

"That is why you will be alone. You will drive everyone away, even Mr. Douglass."

"He is loyal."

"Even the loyal will turn away if they have a shred of self-respect. You almost destroyed mine."

When the door closed behind Eliza, Julia put her fist to her mouth to suppress her cry. She felt deep pain and devastation that the one person she had always counted on had abandoned her.

"Oh, Eliza, how will I live now?"

★

Overruling Anna, Frederick insisted that Eliza and John Dick get married in the parlor of Isaac and Amy Post, a much larger room. Honored by the request, the Posts readily agreed, and Amy made sure that her parlor was resplendent with roses, hydrangeas, daisies, and marigolds.

Before the ceremony, Eliza asked for a moment of Julia's time. Julia hesitated, not wanting to mar the day with another confrontation. Eliza was resplendent in a white gown with white flounces and lace made by Anna with exquisite craft.

They stepped into Isaac Post's downstairs library after knocking on the door and finding the room empty.

"I want to say goodbye now, Julia, just the two of us. I don't know when we will see each other again."

"Today we're supposed to celebrate, not cry or worry about us. Today is your day and Mr. Dick's."

"I have to explain, Julia. I was always upset with myself for caring so much about what you do."

"I didn't help by making everything a competition." She might never see Eliza again, and she didn't want recriminations to be her last memories.

"Perhaps. But I have always cared too much, as if you were my life," Eliza said.

"But we were close."

"But you didn't care in the same way."

Julia braced herself, and Eliza stepped forward to soften her point. "No, don't misunderstand me, please. I didn't come to blame you. No more. I'm to blame. You live your life as you see fit, but I have lived mine always in your shadow, always caring about what you did, what your opinions were. My life was shaped by you, and not by me, until now."

"You have an independent mind, after all. You fought back," Julia said.

"In Philadelphia, I will be free to learn and live my own life," Eliza said.

"Was I so detrimental?"

"You are strong, too overpowering for me. I was weak before you. It was my fault, not yours."

Julia dropped Eliza's hand as her sister continued, "This must be, for my sake."

"I will miss you, too."

"Julia?"

"Yes?"

Suddenly, Eliza's arms were around her sister, and she started sobbing. "Oh, Julia, I do love you. I was angry then, but one thing hasn't changed. I love you."

This was the first time that Eliza had confessed this, and the revelation overwhelmed Julia. She wept too. "Eliza, I love you, too," Julia mumbled, feeling a tinge of jealousy, wishing that she had made the breakthrough first, competitive still.

Eliza stepped away. "Now, now, this is a day for celebrating and no tears. I'm getting married today, the start of a new adventure. And going there will be nothing compared to crossing the Atlantic. Remember that?"

"I hope to never do that again," Julia said.

"Then you will stay in America?" Eliza asked.

"Why, of course. My life is here."

"Yes, indeed it is. Goodbye, Julia."

"Write to me and come visit when you can."

"Yes, I'll write."

They embraced again and left the library together for the last time.

Two days later, Julia and Frederick sat in the Douglass parlor and discussed the implications of Eliza's absence. Julia was not ready to admit that she missed her sister, but she did not have to. Usually talkative, she said little after the wedding ceremony and performed her editorial duties at the office with minimal comments, leaving most of what she had to say to red lines or questions in the margins.

Now Julia declared the obvious as she and Frederick sat across from each other after Anna and the children had retired for the night. "I didn't think her absence would affect me so, but she has been always a part of my life, my sister, my companion, my chaperone."

"Her eyes are no longer watching us."

"What are we to do?"

"There's nothing to do. We will be watched even more carefully now that she is gone. If people assume that something is wrong, they will be especially vigilant. We can't make any mistakes now," Frederick said.

"We will not have to fear the ultimate mistake," Julia said.

"What do you mean?"

"I can't have children," she explained with circumspect references to an illness that her doctors said made her barren. Julia could not look directly at Frederick, for that would reveal a sad inadequacy that embarrassed her. Despite the difficulties, childbearing defined a woman, and she could never do or know what Anna knew, could never love as only a mother could. Julia could feel the pain rising from her chest to her throat, almost making her cry out. She was determined to bend her weakness to her will and took a deep breath. "We never have to worry about that."

"So, you are now granting me permission to commit adultery because you don't have to worry about bearing a child? I told you what I will not do. Don't you take my vows seriously at all?"

Deeply hurt, Julia got up to leave. There was no more to be said. He was not going to express regrets about her physical condition. He was not going to embrace and comfort her. She had tried and failed by testing a man who had so much to lose with an invitation that compromised her own standing in his eyes. She was now appalled at what she had become. She was no better than a conniving seducer.

"No. Don't leave, please stay," Frederick said.

Still unable to face him, Julia said, "I was happier at Peterboro than I thought I could ever be. I have been happier here with you than I have been my entire life. If you could only understand what you bring to life in me."

"I cannot take responsibility for your feelings, only my own," Frederick said.

"What *are* your feelings?"

He paused. "I love you for yourself, for being all that I ever wanted. But a declaration will have to suffice. It must suffice, even when I want to take you into my arms."

"Your words are enough," she said, lying again.

"Don't demand that I repeat this, for I will begin to resent you. Just remember what I said, and don't expect me to offer reminders, another order that I have to obey. I'm done with that, and you know why, and we will never return together to Peterboro. Never."

"I understand."

"But you will be with me by my side when we work, when we take walks, when we go to meetings."

"By your side."

He turned to reach for the teacup sitting half-filled below him, took a sip, and then left the room.

62.

BY LATE SUMMER OF 1850, it was clear that the new fugitive slave bill would become law, and concerned, outraged citizens wrestled with the same question: how should we resist?

From the pulpit, and in countless editorials, angry northerners proposed ways to circumvent the law or make it difficult to enforce. Even William Lloyd Garrison, the unrepentant pacifist, now acknowledged the legitimacy of self-defense and offered his readers a regular forum for obstruction of the law or overt civil disobedience. He and others proposed to harass slave catchers through civil suits; publish the names of all northern officials appointed to enforce the law, embarrassing them; boycott anyone who obeyed the law; deny food and shelter, carriages and other services to slave hunters and collaborators; publicly ridicule slave hunters by following them in the street with placards; circulate handbills that identified slave masters who hoped for anonymity; and demand unceasingly the repeal of the law.

The details of the Fugitive Slave Act demonstrated the degree to which politicians in Washington had capitulated to slave owners: commissioners appointed by the U.S. circuit courts could grant certificates for returning slaves; the law fined U.S. marshalls if they did not enforce the law and made them personally liable for the value of the slave if the slave escaped custody. Slave owners only needed a description of a fugitive to obtain an arrest warrant, and fugitives could not speak in their own defense. Anyone trying to prevent apprehension could be arrested, fined, or imprisoned, while commissioners ruling on fugitive cases would receive $10 if they ruled in favor of a master and only $5 if they ruled in favor of the fugitive.

Alone in his office, Frederick reacted with stunned silence and then rage, the feelings of betrayal so deep and disappointment so vast that pacing of the floor gave no relief. The unrelenting hatred of the United States was now law.

Frederick was as angry with himself as he was with Congress for the passage of the Fugitive Slave Act in September and the celebrations for the salvation of the Union that followed. He was a damn fool for believing that it could have been any different.

When rumors reached Rochester that hunters were on their way to take Frederick back to Maryland, he rushed to the loft to find the bill of sale proving his purchase from Thomas and Hugh Auld. After four years, he had forgotten where he had put it. He never imagined he would ever have to use it. He had often referred to it in his speeches, brandishing the unseen paper above his head as a symbol of the system that required its necessity. Now he needed to carry it always to save his freedom.

He remembered that the bill of sale was in the large strongbox under a pile of old clothes in the northeast corner of the room. He quickly brushed the clothes aside and opened the large box to find within it a smaller, wooden box. He found the thick parchment declaring that he was bought from Hugh Auld at $750 in British gold. He read the paper again and again, trying to detect some flaw in the language, some loophole that would give federal agents a reason to arrest him.

Finding none, he sighed with relief, and his hands started to shake. There he was, a desperate man in a dusty, crowded loft, holding the only insurance he had, a mere piece of paper that could burn, fade, or disappear, a document that could be contested in courts now eager to keep slave owners happy. He was helpless, a mere pawn in a political game for white men only.

In that moment, Frederick completely abandoned the last vestiges of non-resistance. He would fight back. Garrisonian principle was futile, an empty gesture that could only mean enslavement.

Like Wendell, he bought a pistol. However, words would remain his primary weapon, and so he dared anyone to arrest him when he went to Boston and joined five thousand other people in Faneuil Hall on October 14 to rally against the new law. Hundreds were denied admittance because the building was not large enough to accommodate the white and Black crowd.

In a November 9 letter to a slave owner, widely reprinted in the press, President Millard Fillmore declared that if any state opposed or obstructed the law, "it would be his duty to call forth the militia and use the Army and Navy for overcoming such forcible combinations against the laws."

There at last was the terrible, unvarnished truth: force was all that mattered. On a Sunday evening, December 8, in the major public-lecture venue in Rochester, Corinthian Hall, Frederick declared at last what he knew to be true. Looking at the audience below, he could tell that many were shocked at the violence of his words, a violence that was spoken with a soft and mellow tone that cut to the quick. But he did not flinch. "In the spirit of genuine patriotism, I warn the American people, by all that is just and honorable, to beware! I would warn the American people, and the American government, that the time may come when those they now despise and hate, may be needed; when those whom they now compel by oppression to be enemies, may be wanted as friends. What has been done, may be again. There is a point beyond which human endurance cannot go. I warn them, then, with all solemnity, and in the name of retributive justice, to look to their ways; for in an evil hour, those sable arms that have, for the last two centuries, been engaged in cultivating and adorning the fair fields of our country, may yet become the instruments of terror, desolation, and death throughout our borders."

The applause was thunderous, and the sound was like a roaring flame that chastened as it burned.

★

At first, the escaped slaves came in small groups, two or three, to Rochester on their way to Canada, and some of them stayed at the Douglass house, receiving food, clothing, and solace as best as he and Anna could provide. Although Anna said little about politics, the movement, or the Fugitive Slave Law itself, she responded to the arrival of her temporary guests with eager open arms, organizing the sleeping arrangements, cooking the food, and cleaning clothes as if her reputation as a housekeeper were at stake. "We won't turn away nobody," she said proudly. "One day one of our people might show up. Thank the Lord, Lottie got here before all this craziness."

As winter approached, the stream of arrivals thinned out, but the entire community, organizing itself through a network of houses, churches, and meeting halls as unofficial parts of the Underground Railroad, prepared for large numbers to come in the spring.

Frederick also thought constantly about his own intellectual transformation. He knew he could no longer adhere to his past conceptions of the Constitution, American politics, and the entire antislavery movement.

Smith continued to send donations for the *North Star* as well as argue for the U.S. Constitution as an "antislavery instrument," contending that the intentions of the framers were irrelevant because they had created a document that allowed the people, through its representatives, to change it. The preamble was all that mattered. Everything else was the relative consequence of time and political circumstance.

Julia agreed, citing letters Smith had written her as well. She refused to analyze the U.S. Constitution as a sacred, inviolate text, and studied its words, phrases, sentences, and entire paragraphs with the eyes of a lawyer building a case before one skeptical but patient judge, Frederick. She came to Smith's conclusion. The Constitution could be used to abolish slavery, even though the framers were slave owners and built slavery into the document without mentioning it.

Frederick listened.

He informed Smith on January 21, 1851, that he agreed with him. Smith reacted by donating more money to the newspaper.

Frederick was ready to announce changes in his thinking and plans. He was about to reap a whirlwind because the man who famously called the U.S. Constitution "A covenant with death, and an agreement with hell" would share the same stage. He went to Syracuse, where the American Anti-Slavery Society would meet for the first time. They could not meet in New York City. No halls were available.

From the beginning, Garrison was in a combative mood. When his long-time friend Reverend Samuel J. May recommended Gerrit Smith's newspaper, the *Liberty Party Paper*, be added to a list of endorsements that included, the *North Star*, Garrison jumped up, shouting as in a courtroom, "I object! I object on grounds that this journal, this *Liberty Party Paper*, doesn't stand for the dissolution of the Union. And worse, it continues to maintain the antislavery character of the U.S. Constitution. I urge the Society to *only* endorse papers which assume the proslavery character of the Constitution."

Frederick raised his hand to be recognized.

The moment had come. "After two years of study, ladies and gentlemen, I have concluded that the Constitution, construed in the light of well-established rules of legal interpretation, can be made consistent with the noble purposes of the preamble. In short, the U.S. Constitution is *inherently* antislavery and should be used on behalf of emancipation."

His face red, Garrison cried out, "There is roguery somewhere!" There was silence. Even his strongest supporters looked down or to the side. He had gone too far. But Garrison offered no explanation, refusing to clarify or justify his point. "I move that the *North Star* be stricken from the list of endorsements," he demanded.

"Point of order!" said Frederick. "There are other resolutions on the floor."

A Garrison loyalist, Francis Jackson, the chairman of the meeting, announced that there had been no seconds for the other motions.

"I second the last motion," said Wendell, standing up beside Garrison. The vote was called. Without discussion, the *North Star* was stricken.

Frederick was unprepared for Garrison's unyielding rejection. His mentor had revealed no sign of struggle. It was simple: openly disagree and be cast out. Relationships did not matter. Perhaps they never did. He sat down. He had given his heart and mind to William Lloyd Garrison for twelve years, and now Garrison could stomp on them without even a twitch of regret.

Frederick said nothing more and avoided any serious discussion with his old associates. Garrison avoided Frederick entirely.

Frederick suddenly felt the room becoming a small, cramped stage on which players mumbled the lines in a farce. He could hear the cruel laughter behind their white, derisive masks. Today, he hated them all.

63.

DURING A CARRIAGE RIDE with Julia, Frederick found the perfect spot two miles south of the center of town on a hill on South Avenue approached by St. Paul's Road with no other houses within sight. The maple trees would have to be cleared, but Frederick looked forward to the physical work of building a new home. Gerrit had loaned him the money, and Frederick could pay him back at any rate over an indeterminate length of time.

"We can see for miles," Frederick said, helping her down from the carriage. "There will be enough room to hide fugitives, too. I'll have a barn, an orchard for fruit trees, vegetables, and flowers, too, like the garden at Wye Plantation, full of roses."

Frederick turned and started to walk around the site, showing Julia where the rooms would be.

"And upstairs facing the north will be your room."

"My room?"

"Of course, you'll always be living with us. You're part of my family, you know."

"I'll live here as long as you will have me."

"Forever. There will be no neighbors, just you and me."

"And Anna and the children. And when you are away or in town, I will be out here all alone. There is another side to this isolation."

"No, don't, Julia. Let me enjoy my dream."

"I'm sorry. But in the meantime, I have an excellent idea for raising money. I'm going to collect pieces written by good writers, like yourself, include your autographs, and sell the book as a souvenir. *Autographs for Freedom*, that's what I'll call it."

"You never cease to amaze me. Who else is on the list?"

"There will be some obvious but necessary omissions."

"Yes. The Massachusetts hosts."

Julia stepped closer to him and said with equal emphasis, "We don't need them, like they needed you. Some of them might even beg to be included, and we'll be generous and allow them in. Of course, you will write something."

"I will write something new. Not a speech, maybe a story."

"Yes, something new."

"I've been thinking about slave revolts, about Nat Turner, the Amistad mutiny of 1839 and Madison Washington's mutiny on the Creole ten years ago. I want to write a story about a great man, and I think I will call it 'The Heroic Slave.'"

"There is even more reason now."

"And we can hide fugitives out here, on their way to Canada. This will be the perfect place for them. During the night we'll take them to town and the lower falls. A boat will be waiting to take them away to freedom."

He took her by the hand and stepped toward the end of the bluff looking out to the hill that rolled toward the Canadian border. "Freedom," he whispered.

Julia pressed his hand, saying nothing as they looked to the horizon.

"Freedom," he repeated.

In September they all needed that bigger house. The most famous fugitives since the passage of the Fugitive Slave Act came knocking at the Alexander Street door.

Their story filled all the papers, and the news wires carried bulletins about the Christiana Revolt on the hour. White people murdered in cold blood, the reports said. Shot in the back like dogs.

Sick with bronchitis, Frederick came down from his bed to receive their leader, William Parker. He told Frederick that he knew him as Frederick Bailey in Maryland, heard him speak in Baltimore, and was inspired to form a mutual protection society. "I have never listened to words from the lips of a mortal man which were more acceptable to me."

Parker's story, as told to Frederick, Anna, Lottie, and Julia in the parlor, began with a Maryland plantation owner named Edward Gorsuch, who had freed some slaves and hired them out for wages, a common practice. But four of them escaped and established themselves in a small Black colony near Christiana, Pennsylvania.

Forming a party of six that included a son, a nephew, and a cousin, Gorsuch rode to Christiana and found his slaves barricaded and armed with pistols, muskets, and knives. Surrounding the house with the help of a U.S. marshall, Gorsuch called for surrender. The slaves answered with the blowing of a horn, a signal for help from the neighbors, and the Gorsuch posse started firing.

After an exchange of bullets, the Black neighbors overwhelmed Gorsuch and his party, killing him and one other, severely wounding his son, and driving off the rest. The slaves and their supporters celebrated, for the time had come to defend freedom, oppose the law, even die if necessary.

Parker concluded his narrative with a chilling observation: "A story went about that Gorsuch shot his own slave, and then his slave shot him. But that ain't true. His slave struck the first and second blows, then others sprang upon him. The women put an end to him. But we ain't murderers, no sir. We're not."

"No, you're not," replied Frederick, his throat hurting. He wrapped his blankets more tightly to him. "You did what you had to do."

Parker smiled, his eyes still cold, dark pools.

Abrupt and stone faced, Anna rose and went into the kitchen to prepare food. Frederick followed her. "What did that mean exactly? That look of disapproval. I've seen it enough times before."

"I don't believe half the stuff he says. Oh, he is important. Listening to him, you would think those white folks just sat around and listened to him talk, and then when all those white folks got tired, they just started runnin' when he started shootin'."

"Why should he lie?"

"Because he's a cold-blooded killer. That eye don't fool me none. He has to be a cold killer to talk about those women just finishing those white people off, as if that was the most natural thing in the world."

"In a fight, a *freedom* fight."

"Nobody should be shot in the back!"

"Not everything you hear is true."

"People died, one in the back."

Frederick exploded, ignoring what felt like a rip in his throat. "I can't believe you! I just can't believe you. No, I should believe you. You never knew what it is to be a slave, what it makes a man do, and now you sit here in judgment."

"What makes us better if we be cold-blooded killers?"

"Christiana will be a warning to others. They had better stop trying to capture slaves."

"I want them out of my house. I don't want my children to know them."

"They will stay until we can make arrangements. I'll send Julia out to see if a boat can be ready for Canada. They will be gone tomorrow night."

Anna flinched at the mention of Julia's name, "Go back to bed. You can't help nobody if you're sick."

He returned to bed, still stewing about Anna's unrelenting hostility toward Julia.

By the next night, all the arrangements were in place, organized by Julia and a neighbor, James Porter. The men would go down to the landing on the Genesee River at night and board the steamer for Toronto. The captain and crew took pride in doing their part to oppose the Fugitive Slave Law. It had made abolitionists of more white northerners than any lecture from Frederick or Garrison.

Frederick wanted to do his part and dressed himself to ride the three men in his small carriage.

"You can't go. You're sick, too sick! You'll get your death," Anna protested, sure he had consumption.

"I must do this," he said, thrilled by breaking the law.

"I thought Mr. Porter would do it."

"I have to."

"Then let me go with you. If you get any sicker, somebody will have to be with you."

"I'll be fine. Stay here with Julia and Lottie. It's not the time for women to be out trying to help men escape. It's too dangerous."

Julia said, "No one here has been deputized yet to arrest them. But it could happen at any moment."

Anna turned to leave the room.

"Anna," Frederick said weakly.

"It's time, Frederick," Julia said.

Outside, Julia said, "Oh, Frederick, we're all worried. Be careful."

"She didn't have to make a scene," he replied.

The three men said nothing during the ride to the landing. They seemed to trust their companions. But arriving fifteen minutes before the departure of the steamer gave all of them time to suspect every bush as a hiding place for marshals, every passenger as a hastily deputized assistant.

Frederick silently cursed the moon for being out that night. He tried to comfort the men as best he could, but they remained nervous until the captain ordered Frederick to disembark before the hauling of the gangplank.

Frederick shook all the hands. Parker pulled a gun out of his coat pocket and gave it to Frederick, saying solemnly, "It fell from Gorsuch's hand when he died. Remember Christiana, as we will always remember you."

"I will treasure this," Frederick said.

When they returned to the house, Anna had gone to bed, sleeping with Rosetta. For two days she didn't say anything about the ride to the Genesee River, then she confronted Frederick as he lay in his bed, still sick with a hacking cough.

"I want that woman out of this house!"

"What?" He sat up at once.

"You heard me, Fred. I've had enough of her."

"Don't talk about Julia in that way. She's not some child."

"I have a right! As far as you're concerned, I'm your housekeeper, the mother of your children, your nurse and gardener and everything else but. You treat Julia with more respect, more care, and I am sick of it."

"Anna, you don't know what you are talking about."

"I know, and I've always known. You'd rather be with her than with me, even when I asked, Frederick, about going down to the Genesee. I asked, Frederick. Didn't that count for *somethin'*?"

"You couldn't leave the children. It was not safe for you or for any woman. And you didn't trust Parker, anyway. Besides, there was no room."

"You've left the children often enough. I could leave them once. Lottie has her way with them. But that don't matter, now does it?"

"I had to go."

"Don't tell me again about what you *had* to do. I've gave up everything for you, gave up my own life and family, *everything* for you. And I'm not going let Julia Griffiths sit back and enjoy all that I've worked for."

"Anna, you've said enough. I'm tired."

Anna stepped forward, her fists balled at her sides. "You don't care about *me*! You cared long ago, but no more. You only care about her, what she thinks, how she feels. I'm the shadow. That's all."

"I have a right to friends."

"You are more than friends."

"We are good friends, close friends."

"Maybe more."

Frederick leaned forward, rearranged the covers, coughed twice, and said coolly, "Anna, please leave. I have no more to say."

She shouted now, "What do you think I am? Some dog that jumps 'cause you say 'jump'?"

"Anna, you're beside yourself. Calm down. Get some tea. We can talk about this some other time, tomorrow."

"What do I have to do? I've given all that I could give. I even hoped that keepin' quiet would prove somethin'. That I believed, trusted, but, no, you just saw more reason to spend your every wakin' hour with her, at the office, in the parlor at night."

"I'm too tired, Anna, to continue. I need rest. I see no point in going on."

She took a step and was now above him, looking down at his stricken face. "I accepted your life. But that didn't mean I had no say in it."

"You knew what it would mean from the beginning."

"It did not include Julia Griffiths at the beginning."

"You will have to accept my friends."

Calm now, she said, "You will send her away from this house."

Frederick fell back, coughing. "I will *not* send her away. And my decision is final." He rolled away from Anna.

She did not immediately reply, but then she pulled the blanket at his shoulders.

"This is not right, you treatin' me like I don't matter."

"Anna, please. You matter a great deal, but on some matters I have the final say."

"I don't have to see you two in my own house."

Frederick pounded the covers and shouted, "This is my house, too!"

Anna smiled. "It's her house, remember? She has the paper, not us, and when we move into the new house, she probably paid for that too."

"Then that fact makes it more obvious she has a right to stay."

"Right?"

"I have nothing more to say."

Anna huffed and left the room.

Frederick wanted to send for Julia. They now talked about almost everything. But he did not have energy to talk with her, respond to her emotions, and control his own reactions. Julia didn't need to know anyway. The news would only upset her. He could count on Anna to say nothing, even though she despised Julia. Her pride would not allow it. Better that Anna show her silent contempt and force Julia to flee.

But he would convince Julia to stay.

64.

JULIA WAS DEEPLY WORRIED. No, she was frightened.

Over several months, Frederick's body and mind were deteriorating. He often complained about the pain in his right hand; and he complained even more about his throat, a precious instrument that could not sustain his demands on it, the two- and three-hour speeches in halls that filled hundreds and sometimes thousands.

He also experienced rheumatic inflammations that swelled his joints and limbs and made him unable to control his movements. He fell in the house, turning over a table as he tried to keep his balance. Forced to rest in bed, he objected vigorously to "all the fuss." But when he fell two more times during the summer he no longer protested and accepted a man who came to wash him twice a day when he could not walk at all.

Frederick agonized about the possibility of never walking again, never speaking before audiences, unable to financially support his newspaper or feed his family.

He now talked about money whenever he saw Julia, who called herself the banker of his newspaper. She freely reviewed the ledgers of donations and bills to be paid and reported her relentless appeals for money from supporters in America and Britain.

He now admitted that Julia's constant appeals for money embarrassed him, even though he recognized their necessity. But Julia was not offended. "No one could possibly think you are less of a man because you must raise money. You were not born wealthy, and your rise is an inspiration to many. Don't worry. You will prevail."

There was a steady stream of small donations, especially from Gerrit Smith, in increments of $10, $25, and $100. When Smith occasionally sent $200, Julia and Frederick rejoiced, praising Smith's generosity and reminding him that more was "always welcome."

But joy couldn't last.

Numbers, ledgers, lists, and letters only gave temporary comfort before another barrage of questions and doubts, followed by sullen silences, sighs, and heavy intakes of breath from Frederick.

Concerned, Julia began reporting Frederick's condition to Gerrit Smith. She told Smith that Frederick was "extremely depressed" and suffered "immense anxiety (pecuniary and familial)."

But then Frederick started to wander around the house, murmuring about going crazy.

Now Julia ached from rising terror: If Frederick Douglass could go mad, anyone could go mad.

She sat at his bedside for hours. She read his favorite Robert Burns poems. They read together scenes from Shakespeare.

Her interventions provided only temporary relief, for she discovered that a crisis of faith deepened his despair. With deteriorating health, a fear of madness, and the possible loss of his livelihood, he now felt a deep sickness of the soul. "I have been for the past year under a cloud," he muttered.

At first, he was reluctant to talk about it, but then he speculated that his attacks against the clergy had "destroyed in myself that very reverence for God and for religion."

He was once confident about the will of the Lord, whose interventions saved him again and again from slavery's worst cruelties.

But something went terribly wrong.

In the process of demeaning religious defenders of slavery, he had diminished the God they all claimed to revere, and His religion had become a tool to keep people down.

Frederick feared the loss of his Negro followers if they ever learned of his doubts, but he feared more the loss of God's love, for now he was convinced he *deserved* abandonment.

Gently, Julia asked, "Why? You've done nothing that can't be forgiven. We are all sinners."

"I have a cold heart. I love nothing, no one. No, I only care for myself. God sees, and I am being punished for the lie I've lived, and I hate him for knowing me, for truly knowing me like no one else can. I've spent my entire life making myself, but he's not fooled. He's not fooled. At night, I see those all-seeing eyes. I'm coming apart, and I know I can't gather it all together again. I can't. I hate myself for telling you this, and I hate you for hearing my disgusting self-pity. This is what I've become, a wreck trembling before a God who won't save one child from cruelty, not one."

"Frederick, you don't mean . . ."

"Don't tell me what I don't mean! I know what I mean all too well."

Julia placed her right hand on the top of his hand resting on the coverlet. His intense eyes softened when he looked down to her hand and he whispered, "And you still love me."

"Yes, still."

"You shouldn't."

"You can't stop me."

"I don't want you to."

"You're getting better. You can see reality and feel it, too."

"Through a dark glass." he said, alluding to scripture.

"But then face to face," Julia replied, continuing to reference 1 Corinthians 13:12.

"Your face."

"And yours, too. Now get some rest."

In December, when Frederick could write again using a portable desk in bed, he surprised her with an editorial.

He admitted to his readers that he was "extremely unwell," his illness making work at the newspaper office impossible. He gave full credit to "my friend Julia Griffiths" for its continued publication and, by implication, his improving spirits.

"You are most kind," she said, truly touched.

"It's only the truth. And I will tell everyone and anyone, even when I go back on the road."

"Are you sure about this? Maybe you should wait a few more weeks."

His illness and recovery had strengthened their bond, but Julia remained afraid to reveal her own doubts about God and religion, worried that her skepticism would create a permanent fissure in their relationship.

After reading David Hume, Thomas Paine, Voltaire in translation, and many other Enlightenment thinkers, Julia had concluded that the God of the Old Testament was too demanding and vengeful, and certainly His need for adulation and praise was not worth her respect.

She was saddened by the obvious truth: she and Frederick were not as close as she wanted. True partners should be able to share *everything*.

65.

THE SILENCE FROM BOSTON was unusual. Except for one reference in the *Liberator* to "party spirit having made some havoc of the character of Frederick

Douglass" from an unknown correspondent, there was no public criticism of Frederick's new political views. But when Frederick marked his declaration of intellectual independence in his newspaper with its new name, *Frederick Douglass' Paper*, direct, personal attacks began.

Stephen Foster confronted Frederick in Corinthian Hall when he was sent in March to investigate the start of an independent New York Anti-Slavery Society.

Foster declared with the melodramatic flamboyance for which he was notorious, "Sir, I have come here to test you, and demand that you show cause for not uniting with us. Your disloyalty, sir, is already well known. You and your *political* kind are a carbuncle on the body of our cause, and you must be hacked off, if necessary."

Frederick smiled. The last thing he wanted was a debate with a man known to disrobe in public, roll in the mud, bark like a dog, and call himself Jesus. Nothing that Frederick could say now would be remembered once Stephen S. Foster decided to dramatize his own point.

"My respects to Mrs. Foster," said Frederick with a slight nod of his head, hoping that Foster detected his disapproval of Abby Kelley's 1845 marriage to him. He once thought she had better judgment.

"But, but, but," Foster sputtered.

Foster had unwittingly confirmed a conspiracy to attack, snub, or humiliate him. As if on cue, Garrison, Wendell, and Abby all turned their backs when Frederick entered the room.

He took a deep breath and selected as his own target of the day Charles Remond, his travel companion in the early days. He offered his hand as he approached, saying, "Friend Remond, how are you? It's been a long time." He had not seen Remond in months.

Remond stepped back as if Frederick had offered a cup of reeking urine. "I am fine, sir. I have business to take care of, if you will excuse me."

"No," said Frederick, blocking his path by stepping in front of him.

"I beg your pardon?"

"Shouldn't you be begging mine?"

Frederick was loud now, drawing the eyes and ears of other delegates nearby. He was enjoying Charles's lost composure. "You didn't take my hand. Even though I must be careful since that break in Indiana, I still accept courtesies."

Charles quickly grabbed Frederick's hand.

"Have a good day," Frederick whispered, releasing the fragile hand with its spindly fingers.

Frederick took his seat prepared to challenge any man or woman who dared to provoke him. He would not be a model of Christian forbearance like Uncle

Tom in Mrs. Stowe's new novel, its message of Christian forbearance annoying and impractical in times that demanded defiance.

After the fall of the opening gavel, Garrison soon gave Frederick reason to remain surly and argumentative. Garrison's opening speech praised the "generous spirit" of the American Society toward the world and its members.

This hypocrisy could not remain unchallenged, and Frederick raised his hand to be recognized when Garrison was done.

The chairmen, Francis Jackson, acknowledged him, and Frederick went to the front table, bowed his head toward his former mentor, who sat in the center, and asked everyone assembled, "If what Mr. Garrison says is true, then why am I treated as an alien here?"

Frederick sat in one of three chairs at the table. Garrison crumpled a piece of paper in his hand, and Charles Remond, Stephen Foster, Robert Purvis, and three others in the front rows, as well as Wendell at the table, rose at once and declared: "I have reason. I have reasons."

Each man was assigned a turn by Mr. Jackson, and Remond began, his voice high and sharp: "Mr. Douglass has demonstrated that both his spirit and acts are reprehensible, and I suggest that only the darkest motives can explain his recent character."

Foster interjected: "Yes: avarice, faithlessness, treachery, ingratitude."

"You are out of order, Mr. Foster. Please wait your turn, sir," said Jackson, forcefully. He took pride in running effective meetings. It was no surprise that he was elected year after year as the Society's chairman.

Remond continued, enjoying the pause before the final assault: "Since he left us to start a paper in this city against the well wishes of his associates, Frederick Douglass has made himself an alien, and proved himself an enemy of our enterprise."

After giving a general description of Frederick's career, its outline familiar to almost everyone, Remond concluded, "Since the start of the *North Star,* Mr. Douglass has been in fellowship with the deadliest enemies of the American Society."

The wealthy Robert Purvis, a pale Negro so elegant in dress he seemed out of place in the drab, middle-class trappings of Corinthian Hall, stood again and said, "Mr. Douglass allowed himself to be patted on the shoulder at the recent Buffalo Liberty Party Convention and has accepted a *bribe* from a colonizationalist!"

The audience stirred with gasps and frantic whispers, but Frederick sat still, visibly unperturbed, his stomach only turning at the thought of an attack by Wendell. Purvis had only money, but Wendell had genius. Frederick had always pitied Wendell's targets, so withering were his sarcasm and exaggerated analogies. Now he was about to become one.

But Wendell waited, allowing others to offer a litany of complaints:

"He changed his opinion about the Constitution."

"He let Gerrit Smith know about these changes privately before he answered the charges in his paper, all of which can mean only one thing."

"He joined in the formation of a separate society in this state, not an auxiliary to the American Society."

"His paper is not an antislavery paper but a Liberty Party paper."

"The former *North Star* is now a *political* paper," said Abby, the word "political" a blasphemy. "And now Mr. Douglass has the effrontery to call it *Frederick Douglass' Paper*. He uses his own name, his very own name!"

Finally, Wendell stepped forward and began his remarks softly, his scalpel sharp: "Frederick Douglass's major faults are his pride and ingratitude. We recognized him, nurtured him, assisted him, and in return we have received his removal from our midst, the establishment of a paper against our wishes, the publication of a paper inimical to our views, and the association with men who work against our highest hopes. We have tried to steer him against the tests of public recognition and self-congratulation. But we were heeded not, for vanity seduced him, taking him from us, and he has embraced it willingly. In the end, he ignores his former friends, ignores their work, refuses to acknowledge their part in his career, and glorifies himself over the work of his fellows. A north star has indeed fallen, and Frederick Douglass has risen in the firmament. But, oh, how inglorious is such an ascent."

The room fell silent, and Wendell turned directly to Frederick, his eyes soft now, his face drawn and darker than usual, a final farewell.

Frederick's heart pounded wildly, but he summoned his deep inner strength to reply with the utmost self-control to every charge. It would have been so easy to explode as he did in New York against Henry Highland Garnet, but today he would give no one the satisfaction of seeing him ruffled, disoriented, or vindictive. He cast aside the pain of lost friendships and the fear that he perhaps had never had them. He focused instead with the facts of his philosophical transformation. He was dispassionate, even dull, making point after point without gestures, maintaining an even tone, refusing to attack anyone personally.

But his conclusion was delivered with the force of anger hiding deep pain: "I contend that I have a right to cooperate with anybody, with everybody, for the overthrow of slavery in this country, whether auxiliary or not auxiliary to the American Anti-Slavery Society. If I happen to be found in company with anybody who entertains a spirit more narrow than my own, I will *not* withdraw from him, but do what I can to enlarge his spirit, remove his prejudices, and impart to him more universal ideas than he had previously entertained. And this, do not mistake me, I hold to be sound whatever the agents of the American Anti-Slavery Society may say to the contrary."

There was a spattering of applause coming from the back of the hall.

A single, "Hear! Hear!"

More applause—scattered but strong—then a crescendo. Frederick smiled, nodded his head once, and sat down.

Neither Garrison nor Wendell turned their heads to face him.

Later, during the first break, Remond crossed the room to speak to him, his face as cold and disdainful as it was on that first day they met in Boston. Frederick was alone. Others had greeted him but did not linger.

"I can see you gloating from a distance, and I have to correct a false impression before you leave for the day," said Remond.

"Sir, by all means."

"I am sure that you will interpret the applause as another one of your many personal triumphs, an easy capitulation to your eloquence and intelligence. You need to reconsider. Allowances are being made for you. You are being *patronized*."

"And what are they doing to *you,* since you remain with them?"

"There are some things more important than the brotherhood of the race, Mr. Douglass. Some things you will never understand, like honor and principles. I find it fascinating but predictable that in your discovery of negritude you have cast these virtues aside."

"You are jealous, Charles, *still*."

"I pity you, Douglass. You can't see what we all see. You, more than anyone, want his approval. You want it desperately, and you can't be honest even now when you will never get it ever again. If not, why do you come back? You dare to tell me it's pride, that you are determined to be your own man? You are a son of Garrison, his boy, still."

"Then what are you? His . . . ." Frederick took a step forward, the word *bastard* about to explode from his mouth.

Remond smiled even more broadly. "Go ahead, Frederick, do it. Prove it once and for all. Pendleton was just a taste, surely, of what's to come. Let everyone know what we all know---you're an effective speaker, but you're *common*, and the dirt of Tuckahoe will always be on your hands."

Frederick took a deep breath. "A while ago, Charles, you said that I was the better speaker and you the better man. Now we both know that you were wrong. Whatever my faults, I never tried to hurt your spirit. I named a son after you. You justly belong in this room of mean-spirited men and women. Goodbye, sir."

"I will never speak to you again."

"So be it," said Frederick before sitting down for the remaining business of the day.

Later, Frederick was nominated to the board of managers of the American Society, taking some pleasure in the public acknowledgment of his prestige, even after a display of rancor unparalleled in the history of the Society.

Frederick wrote that night to Gerrit Smith: "I will not tell you how I met the onset. Suffice it to say, that I stood it all, with spirit unruffled, and have the pleasing satisfaction to know that I was elected a manager in the Society with but one dissenting vote, and that was the vote of my old, jealous friend, Remond."

66.

FINALLY, THE HOUSE ON South Avenue was ready. The wooden farmhouse was solid and well-proportioned in the latest country style, bracketed Italian with a broad gabled roof protecting the walls and an ornamental veranda on ten acres surrounded by trees.

For weeks Anna had organized the move, packing, arranging, deciding where every piece of furniture would be. She had not been to the house during construction, insisting that she only wanted to see the finished house, and instead examined the pile of drawings for deciding where things would go. If changes were to be made, she would make them *after* the move.

The tension in the old house was as thick as smoke, and Anna was now openly hostile with grunts, rolling of eyes, puffed cheeks, and long silences when Julia entered a room. Anna never spoke directly to her and didn't allow the children to interact with Julia without her there. At first Frederick objected, but now he was no longer willing to fight with Anna about her treatment of Julia. He felt exhausted, worn down by Anna's seething bitterness.

Julia was tired, too. Without her sister or friends, she spent countless hours at the office working. More and more doors were closed to her, despite all the hard work for the Rochester Anti-Slavery Society. Even Amy and Isaac Post had stopped inviting her to their home.

Only Ann Smith, Gerrit Smith's wife, desired her company and one afternoon came out to see her and the new house after sending a note announcing the date and time. Ann did not write to Anna, knowing that she could not read, and expected Julia to receive her. Julia didn't want to tell Anna, fearing another uncomfortable silent accusation and condemnation. But she thought better of it and told her. Not telling her would be worse. Even so, when the moment came, Julia cringed.

Anna's back was turned, and Julia said, "Anna, Frederick's friend, Ann Smith, Mr. Smith's wife, is coming to see the house. She hopes this will not be inconvenient. She can only come tomorrow afternoon."

Anna did not turn around, and Julia waited, the silence awkward and insulting.

At long last Anna turned. Her eyes were the usual cold stones. Julia was nothing to her. She might as well have been dead.

"Tea?"

"Make it yourself."

The next day, while upstairs, Julia saw Ann arrive in her small carriage. She was so happy to see her that she went down the stairs as quickly as she had ever done, holding up the folds of her skirt almost to her waist, an indecent height, so that she could skip a step or two.

Outside, she looked up to the cloudless sky and said to Ann, who was stepping out of the carriage, supported by the hand of her taciturn, young, and handsome driver, "It's a beautiful day, a perfect June day."

Looking at the house, Ann said, "It's beautiful and worth every penny."

Julia didn't respond. Surprised, Ann declared, "You don't know how much it cost to build this house."

Julia was not poor and had managed money successfully for years, but she never became accustomed to the brutal arrogance of the very rich. It didn't matter that Ann Smith was religious and charitable. When it came to money, she was like all the rest, insensitive and clueless, a blunt instrument of privilege.

"Three thousand, including the materials and labor for the house, and the land," Ann asserted confidently.

"Welcome to Frederick's house," was all Julia could manage to say.

"And Mrs. Douglass?"

"Indisposed."

"That's unfortunate. Please give her my regards."

"I will."

"I hear she is the gardener, growing flowers in the front and vegetables in the back."

"Yes."

"I must talk with her about seeds and how she manages to be so successful. I love gardening too, you know."

"I know."

"May I see the children?"

Julia paused, not knowing how to respond to the unexpected question. "The two youngest are asleep, and Anna gave orders for the oldest to not disturb us."

"Very well."

They sat down in the front parlor, the humid air filling the room as Ann looked around, taking note of the room, and obviously waiting for the offer of more abundant refreshments. There was tea in a plain white teapot with two cups and nothing more.

Anna came into the room holding the youngest, Annie, in her arms, with the other four children behind them, accompanied by Anna's sister Lottie. The family resemblance was remarkable. There was no denying that all of them, except for the little girl, were related to Anna. Annie was different; she had golden brown skin, small, inquisitive eyes, and a radiant smile that immediately charmed and disarmed. The others stood there as silent props in Anna's show, grim and uncomfortable, shifting in the shoes, impatiently waiting for their performance to begin and end quickly.

Julia stared, unable to speak. Not only had she been exposed as a liar, she was dumbfounded by Anna's entrance.

The children stepped forward one at a time, prim and respectful. Their skins shined from a thorough cleaning, their clothes starched and immaculate. With a slight curtsey or bow, each child announced their name followed by the same refrain: "Good day, Mrs. Smith and Miss Griffiths."

When done, Anna told Lottie to take them upstairs. Once they departed, Ann said to Anna, "You must be proud of them."

"Yes. We're proud of them, me and my Frederick. I know if he was here he would want you to see them. I'm doing this for him." Then she left as well.

Julia looked down and said nervously, "Of course, with a houseful there can't be a tour. There are several rooms that have wonderful views of the valley, especially to the northeast. On the clearest of days, you can see Canada."

She opened and closed her hands repeatedly, drying the sweat in her palms.

"Julia, what is wrong with you?"

"Nothing. You must come back to Rochester on July fifth. Frederick is preparing a major address of the Ladies Society. We asked him to speak on the fourth, but he refused, and you will understand his reason once you hear it. It's an excellent speech, a bit too long, but he continues to work on it. He sometimes takes my advice. I'm more successful with the newspaper than with the speeches. I don't think he's going to leave anything to the moment this time, however. This speech, he says, is the best speech he's ever done."

"He never fails to impress."

Ann rarely traveled, so the comment took Julia by surprise. "When did you last see him speak?"

"Gerrit can't stop praising him. As you know, the cup of his enthusiasms always runs over," said Ann.

"Then you and Mr. Smith must surely come to Corinthian Hall," Julia replied.

"Coming to Rochester can be so tiring. And this house is even farther, I'm afraid."

Julia felt the intense pain of her isolation, the house now the embodiment of separation from everything that mattered: her sister, Frederick's children—in the same house but not allowed to be alone with her—Frederick himself when he was so often on the road, her friends back home in England. She willed her face not to react to Ann Smith's comment, hiding her bitter truth. She was alone.

"But I will return with some seeds from our greenhouse," said Ann. "Mrs. Douglass and I can become friends, as Gerrit and Frederick have become friends. I think she and Frederick should come to Peterboro. Don't you think?"

"Yes, without me."

"They are a couple, after all."

"Yes."

67.

BEFORE A CAPACITY AUDIENCE of six hundred, who had paid 12.5¢ each to hear his denunciation of the Fourth of July holiday, Frederick sat waiting on the stage of Corinthian Hall, the most impressive building in downtown Rochester, its pillars and tall windows accenting grandeur that made it attractive to speakers throughout the country. Reverend Robert R. Raymond of Syracuse preceded him with an opening prayer and a reading of the Declaration of Independence. Then Frederick rose and waited for absolute silence.

He looked down from the stage to the first row, where Julia sat beside Ann Smith. Julia sat perfectly still, her face having the soft radiance of pride that lightened Frederick's way through a long, tangled dialogue of argument, historical reference, and passionate anger. She had played an essential part in the development of this speech, his best, a summary of a career forever changed by meeting her and now at a turning point whose aftermath she would probably not share.

Their life together was coming to an end. He could see it in her renewed interest in English politics and literature; her desire to serialize *David Copperfield* in the newspaper; her periodic references to the consistent generosity of the English subscribers and the need for more money, which she said only England could provide.

Julia might never come back. Frederick understood. The rumors and accusations about her, and about them, were becoming more and more virulent. He could see the strain in her eyes and hear it in her voice every time she handed over the mail to him.

Frederick would deny the most outrageous charge about their relationship until the end of their days. Anxious whites wanted to find a sexual predator stalking white flesh, defiling it for retribution's sake. Blacks wanted a whore determined to bring him down, the emasculating bitch trying to roll in the gutter with a pillar of the community.

The truth was simpler: he loved her and aspired to pass beyond the racial and moral categories even as he made a mistake by betraying Anna's trust, and foolishly believing, like a selfish child, that Anna could not be hurt. Yet Anna had eyes and ears. She could see the gestures, the silences.

But in Julia Griffiths he found a friend like no other. She listened, encouraged, challenged, and understood him. Frederick got from Julia unconditional love despite his flaws and frailties, that same unconditional love he got from his grandmother, a love that needed no explanation or defense.

Silently saluting her with a nod of the head, Frederick now addressed his audience. "Fellow citizens, pardon me, allow me to ask, why am I called to speak here today? What have I, or those I represent, to do with your national independence?"

He had, of course, the answer, and he shouted it over the front rows to the back of the hall and beyond to the readers of newspapers across the land, refusing to appeal to their vanity: "Your high independence only reveals the immeasurable distance between us. The blessings in which you, this day, rejoice, are not enjoyed in common. The rich inheritance of justice, liberty, prosperity, and independence, bequeathed by your fathers, is shared by you, not by me. This Fourth of July is yours, not mine. Do you mean, citizens, to mock me, by asking me to speak today?"

Then, softly, he said, "There is no man beneath the canopy of heaven that does not know that slavery is wrong for him."

There was a heavy silence in the room. Frederick waited for his point to sink in, and then unleashed his stern rebuke: "What, to the American slave, is your Fourth of July? I answer: a day that reveals to him, more than all other days in the year, the gross injustice and cruelty to which he is the constant victim. To him your celebration is a sham: your boasted liberty, an unholy license; your national greatness, swelling vanity; your sounds of rejoicing are empty and heartless, your denunciation of tyrants, brass fronted impudence; your shouts of liberty and equality, hollow mockery; your prayers and hymns, your sermons and thanksgivings, with all your religious parade, and solemnity, are to him, mere bombast, fraud, deception, impiety and hypocrisy—a thin veil to cover up crimes which would disgrace a nation of savages. Go where you may, search where you will, roam throughout all the monarchies and despotisms of the old world, travel through South America, search out every abuse, and when you've found the last, lay your facts at the side of the everyday practices of this nation, and you will say with me that for revolting barbarity and shameless hypocrisy, America reigns without a rival."

Frederick reiterated his attack on the slaveholder's use of religion to defend slavery, and after denouncing their ministers as false prophets, scribes, Pharisees, and hypocrites, hurled this challenge to the beams of the rooftop: "For my part, welcome infidelity! Welcome atheism! Welcome anything in preference to the gospel, as preached by those Divines!"

But Frederick could not leave them with his anger, and so he said, soft again, "I do not despair of this country. There are forces in operation, which must inevitably work the downfall of slavery. I leave off where I began, with hope."

He spoke for over two hours, reading a manuscript that when printed was thirty-two pages long, a speech that reviewed America's revolutionary past, the troubles of the day, and his fears for the future. On most occasions, he spoke without notes. While preparing this speech he decided that the occasion required deliberate argument, solemn eloquence carefully built on a scaffold of carefully chosen words that revealed a deep study of the Bible and Shakespeare and the giants of antislavery. He had rehearsed this speech, memorized key passages, and made sure he concluded with quoting Garrison's "The Triumph of Freedom," unable to deny his debt to him. Frederick's career was, indeed, made possible because of Garrison's faith in him and his faith in Garrison, dreamers of the same dream.

"God speed the year of Jubilee the worldwide over," Frederick concluded, quoting Garrison's first stanza as his own peroration: "When from their galling chains set free, the oppressed shall verily bend the knee, and wear the yoke of tyranny like brutes no more."

He stopped, his body suddenly drained by the hours. Then hope lifted his spirit again, and he pressed on through three more stanzas.

At the very end, he proclaimed the words of historical and personal triumph, affirming his purpose and the will of God:

"Until that year, day, hour arrive,
With head, and heart, and hand I'll strive.
To break the rod, and rend the gyve,
The spoiler of his prey deprive—
So witness Heaven!
And never from my chosen post,
Whate'er the peril or the cost,
Be driven."

Julia was first to her feet, and the rest followed, creating a thunderous wave of sound, the sound of it rolling over him like the waves of the Chesapeake, mighty, unbound, free.

He knew he had given the greatest speech of his career.

★

Julia's stay at the house came to an end in November. Anna's ultimatum was offered quietly with a clarity of purpose that surprised and impressed even as it angered him. As he sat at his desk in the upstairs office, Anna tapped at the door. He acknowledged her, and she entered, closing the door behind her before speaking. The room was cool, the fire in the fireplace was low, and he was in no mood to revive it.

"She's gotta go, and I'm not taking no for some answer. When everybody in town is talkin' about our private business, when she is talkin' about our private business to Ann Smith and heaven knows who else, well, I'm done." There was no equivocation in Anna's voice.

Frederick didn't want an argument, but he offered a weak protest. "Anna."

"I'm not asking you, do you hear me? I'm not asking. She goes."

"Or?"

"There's no or. If she don't leave after she finds a place, and is all packed, I will do what I has to do."

"You can't threaten me."

"I ain't threatening. I'm promising. If she don't get out of this house, I will go to every house in Rochester and tell them what everyone is saying is true, that you two are more than friends, that you two spend all the times together day and night, and I found you in the parlor acting like animals, kissing on the floor and rolling around . . ."

He started to rise, his voice now loud and belligerent. "That's a lie, an abominable lie!"

Anna did not flinch. She stepped forward, prepared for him to do something hurtful, to push her away, slap her face. "I dare you. Just do it, and I will have even more to tell."

Deflated, Frederick fell back in his chair.

"I don't care what you do at the office, how much time you spend together there or at those meetings, or on the road when you make them speeches. But she will not live under our roof. She will pack tomorrow, and she will go where she can go after you find some place for her. One of your many friends will take her in, and if they ask questions you will tell some story to keep them from asking more, even though they will surely talk. And *are* they talking."

"How do you know that?"

"Mrs. Porter told me after Mr. Porter told her."

"Why didn't he tell me to my face?"

"You ask him, but with all your talk and excuses, why should he bother? You don't listen to nobody."

"Anna, you've said enough."

"More than enough. You don't listen to me, but you better listen and listen good. I mean what I say, and if you don't do as I tell you, you will be the loser, not me. I don't care what people say, but you do. Lord, you care, and I know it. So, don't make me do it. But I will if I has to. Now get some rest and tell *that* woman tomorrow to get out of this house in the best way you can. And you won't have to lie to her. She already knows I can't stand her, and I've wanted her out for months."

"You *told* her?"

"I don't have to. She's not stupid. But she stayed because you wanted her to stay. I'm sure of it. So now you can tell her. I'm not goin' to waste my time with her. And I won't make some scene. Don't you worry about that. I won't have to, 'cause if I don't see them bags, you will know what I'm going to do, even if I has to walk and knock on every door in town. I mean it, Frederick, and you know I mean it," Anna said.

Frederick went downstairs to the parlor. He knew he would find Julia there reading or writing late into the night. He opened the door without knocking. Julia looked up, and Frederick decided he would not repeat the details of his argument with Anna. He said evenly without emotion as it all had been drained from him, "Anna wants you to leave the house."

Standing up, Julia replied, without any indication of dismay, "You know, I've expected this. After Parker, I knew that she had enough of me."

"I don't want you to leave. You know that."

"I know. You've been most generous, and so has she. She opened her home to me, treated me as a guest should."

"You are more than a guest."

"But I betrayed everything that being a guest means. I took food, shelter, and . . ."

"You didn't take me," Frederick said, reaching out to take her hand.

Julia stepped back, withdrawing her hand. "No, please don't."

"You will still work for me, with me in the office," he said.

"If you will have me."

"If? If?"

"I've done enough in this house, and I've lost more by coming into it. Maybe it's time for me to go back to England. Start over."

"No, don't talk about England. You have a life with me. Please, don't leave. Anna is just upset, and if you leave Rochester now you'll live under a shadow."

The tears came to Julia's eyes. She turned away. "I didn't mean to cry. It doesn't help, I know. I'm sorry."

"Please don't be sorry."

Julia stepped away. "Don't think I don't want you to comfort me, because I do. I'll always be selfish about that. But I can't be selfish about it anymore. I can't be. I lived here and loved you on borrowed time. I knew that all along, and I always knew, deep inside, that it would end. I want my part to end gracefully, without a fight or struggle. She's fighting for you, Frederick, and I understand. I would fight for you, too, if I were in her place."

"If only . . ."

"No more ifs. It was not meant to be, Frederick. We live in the wrong time, the wrong place. You're from the Eastern Shore of Maryland, and I'm from Newcastle, England. For a while I pretended that all this wasn't so. It was a dream, a foolish fantasy."

"After Peterboro, it was real for me. It filled my day, my dreams, even though I couldn't tell you, since I was the one who declared prohibitions."

"But we hurt the innocent. We did. She could see it, that look in my eye. You would enter a room, and I would turn to you as if everything bright and warm and strong had come in. I thought I could hide that, but Anna could see it, and I could see it, because I saw that same sun in her eyes. She loves you, Frederick."

"You're my friend. You will always be my friend, no matter what other changes take place. That I promise."

"You're a fortunate man, Frederick Augustus Washington Bailey Douglass. Two women love you."

"I love you, Julia."

"And Anna, too, in your own fashion. I'll find a place. Perhaps the Porters can provide a room until I make permanent arrangements, maybe with another Quaker family."

Before he could reply, Julia was out of the room. Frederick stared at the closed door, feeling a great stab of pain in his chest thinking of Peterboro.

68.

THE POLEMICAL WAR BETWEEN Frederick and the Garrisonians intensified.

Frederick fondly remembered the days when he eagerly anticipated the arrival of every issue of the *Liberator*. Now he dreaded it, fearing personal attacks and the invasion of his privacy. He was also ready for a fight.

After Frederick had branded Charles Remond "a practical enemy of the colored people," Garrison printed his first public attack. Frederick was an aggressor, a specimen of low cunning and malignant defamation, a man of inflamed passion and the lowest moral debasement. Garrison even suggested that Frederick used his black skin to "hide the blackness of his treachery."

Garrison offered his explanation for Frederick's fall from grace. He observed, "The history of the antislavery struggle has been marked by instances of defection, alienation, apostasy, on the part of some of his most efficient supports for a given time; but by none more signal, venomous, or extraordinary, than the present. Mr. Douglass now stands unmasked, his features flushed with passion, his air scornful and defiant, his language bitter as wormwood, his pen dipped in poison; as thoroughly changed in his spirit as every 'arch angel ruined,' and as artful and unscrupulous a schismatic as has yet appeared in abolitions ranks."

But history was not a sufficient explanation, and so Garrison plunged into suggesting an unnamed temptress: "For several years past, he has had one of the worst advisors in his printing office, whose influence over him has not only caused much unhappiness in his own household, but perniciously biased his judgment; who active, futile, mischievous, has never had any sympathy with the American Anti-Slavery Society, but would doubtless rejoice to see it become extinct; and whose sectarianism is manifestly paramount to any regard for the integrity of the antislavery society."

Julia Griffiths. She was the cause.

Back in September, the *Antislavery Standard* had called her "a Jezebel whose capacity for making mischief between friends would be difficult to match." Now the accusations cut even deeper. Garrison said that Julia was the cause of "domestic trouble" in Frederick's household.

Frederick could not let this charge remain unanswered. His reputation and honor and the privacy of his family had to be protected. His solution: forge a letter from Anna denying that Julia was any cause of trouble.

When he first suggested the letter, Julia cautioned him. "It's unnecessary and will make matters worse."

"But I must defend my family, my private life," he objected.

"You can defend it without using Anna. She will find out and there will be more trouble."

"How can she find it? She doesn't read."

"Oh, Frederick, she doesn't have to. Ann Smith reads. Amy Post reads. Rosetta reads. Someone who knows Anna will tell her because they all know she can't write."

"I'll write the note and sign her name. She can sign her name. I've had to do this before, write for her and get her signature."

"Don't do this, Frederick."

"I'm doing it."

That evening, he scribbled, signing Anna's name, "It is not true that the presence of a certain person in the office of Frederick Douglass caused unhappiness in his family."

He didn't expect Garrison to print it in the *Liberator*.

Anna found out and confronted Frederick with a copy of the *Liberator* provided by Amy Post. He was in his upstairs office, and she didn't bother to knock.

"This was the dumbest thing you've ever done," she declared. "I can't think of nothing that comes close."

"What are you talking about?"

"Don't start this with me, not now. You and Julia wrote a letter saying she was not the cause of unhappiness in the family."

"We did no such . . ."

"Stop lying for her. Please, stop lying."

"She didn't write the letter," Frederick said.

"Mr. Garrison is right even so. She did make trouble between us."

"He said she made me change my mind about my beliefs."

"Then he's a fool, too. Nobody, not nobody can *make* you change your mind. You do that all on your own."

"He and his friends don't think so."

"Well, you didn't have to use me for telling them the truth about that," Anna said.

He paused, took a deep breath, and then confessed. "I wrote the letter. Julia was against it."

Anna paused. She said, "You should have listened. But you never listen, especially when *we're* right. No, us women are not equal, not to you, or other men, colored or white. You're all the same when it comes to us. Even so, you will have to clean up your own mess, and you won't be able to get my help in this. I'm not lying for you. If somebody asks me, I'm not going to say, 'Go ask Frederick.' I'm going to say, 'No, I didn't write that letter.' And if they ask, 'Did Julia cause trouble?' I will say, 'Yes.' You better hope nobody asks. Probably nobody will. I'm just your no-reading, no-writing wife, living in this big house alone on this hill, cooking and cleaning and raising children while you go about lying about whatever you need to lie about."

"That's not true. I tell the truth about what matters most."

"What matters most? Slavery?"

"My family."

"Liar," Anna whispered. "That may have been true long ago in New Bedford, those early years back in Lynn. But not now."

"It will always be true."

"Liar," she repeated and left the room dropping the *Liberator* to the floor.

That letter was also the last straw for Amy Post. She told Frederick that she could no longer receive Julia as a guest in her house, and she could not countenance Frederick's forgery and using Anna as the excuse for it. "You are no longer welcome here, either," she said.

Frederick did not try to explain or defend himself. There was no excuse for what he had done.

Nevertheless, one charge wounded him deeply. Garrison said he was selfish and cared for nothing but his own ambition. Frederick wrote his most emotionally raw, public response:

"Was it selfish, when in England, surround by kind friends, and strongly invited by them, to make my home among them, with every provision made for my comfort and security in a land where my color was no crime—I say, was it selfish in me to quit the shores of that country, and return to this, to endure insult, abuse and proscription, with the rest of my oppressed people?"

When he read the passage to Julia in the office, she paused for a moment, and then said, "Excellent. No, superb, but. . ."

"But, always but," said Frederick, disappointment by another editorial intrusion.

"But it won't make a difference or change their minds about you," Julia said, her tone direct but kind. Since her departure from the house, she worked even more zealously to raise money and edit the newspaper with scrupulous care, convinced that any mistakes would provide ammunition to Frederick's enemies. "They are determined to make you the villain, a combination of Cain, Brutus, and Judas. We can fill the next issue with entire columns answering their charges, but a better answer to the questions about your identity would be another book, another autobiography, an expansion of the *Narrative*, a more comprehensive story of your bondage and freedom, your life as a slave and a free man."

"Another book? I don't have time for another book. I had enough difficulty finishing "The Heroic Slave."

"But you stayed the course and wrote a wonderful story about a slave rebel. You can do the same now."

"I don't have time."

"You'll *make* time, and I will do what I can so that you don't worry about the newspaper and pour as much as you can into your story, this time with more details, more character description, less argument but more reflection. I can't wait to read it, and I know it will be better than *Uncle Tom's Cabin* because it will be true."

"People don't want the truth," asserted Frederick. He sounded more bitter than he intended. The extreme popularity of Stowe's novel irked him. She had written to him asking for more information about slave life, then transformed her material into a religious melodrama that made it too easy to excuse and forgive slave owners. The true monsters were not Simon Legree and other overseers with a whip, men easy to identify and condemn. Far more monstrous were characters from his life like Rowena Hambleton Auld, the mastermind behind sending a cripple away to die; jealous wives selling the slave sons and daughters of their husbands; pious men yelling hymns in church while crawling in the grass to frighten boys.

Hypocrites all.

He hated Hugh Auld, but at least that cruel drunk was honest. Better to be called "nigger" to your face than be stabbed in the back with a smile, like William Lloyd Garrison.

"The source matters," Julia said. "You were there. Mrs. Stowe wasn't."

"I have to give her credit. She has opened eyes."

"She wants to see you. She asks that you come to her home," Julia said, turning to reach for a letter on her desk and giving it to Frederick. She opened all letters addressed to him at the office, and he had accepted this practice long ago. He had nothing to hide from her, and she sorted the letters so he could answer them more efficiently.

"Why?" he asked before reading the letter for himself.

"She wants to talk about the training school for Negro boys. And Garrison."

"She's Garrison's friend."

"Just see what she has to say. There can be no harm."

"She'll report back to him."

"Then you make sure that what you say is what he should hear."

"I've said all that I need to say in the paper, and I don't care about what he thinks, not anymore."

"Are you certain?"

Julia's candor inspired him to say, "No, I'm not certain. I want to be, but I'm not, and the proof is the amount of time I think about him and all the ink I have used to explain myself to him. I still believe I can change his mind. I'm ready for a fight. I can defend myself."

"Of that I have no doubt."

It was late. Julia stood, turned to her desk to pick up some papers and said, "It's time for me to go. Good night."

He ached at the sight of her fleeing the office. It reminded him that she was alone, truly alone. He called out, "Please go see your sister. I'm sure she misses you."

She turned, and he thought he saw that soft beginning of tears.

"Thank you and Merry Christmas," was all she managed before going through the door.

★

Two years before, when *Uncle Tom's Cabin*; or *Life among the Lowly* first appeared as a series of articles in the *National Era*, Harriet Beecher Stowe, already a subscriber to the *North Star*, wrote to Frederick asking for his perspective on slavery. She wanted details from a former slave. However, most of her letter addressed his "regrettable sentiments" about the church and her hope that she could change his mind after admitting that she had a "considerable share of feeling of reason" for his position.

Stowe conceded that the church as a body might be considered "proslavery," having the power to put an end to evil and not doing it. But most members in many denominations, she argued, were good people of "intelligence, probity, and piety."

Her praise of ministers came naturally. "I certainly ought to know something of the feelings of ministers," she wrote, the daughter of a minister, whose six brothers were also ministers.

Her belief in the power of religion to transform lives was unmistakable. Stowe concluded her letter with the religious eloquence she brought to her novel, "After all, my brother, the strength and hope of your oppressed races do lie in the church. In hearts united to Him of whom it is said He shall spare the souls of the needy—and precious shall their blood be in his sight. Everything is against you—but Jesus Christ is for you—and He has not forgotten his church misguided and erring tho it may be. I have looked all the field over with despairing eyes. I see no hope except in Him. This movement must and will become a purely religious one."

Uncle Tom's Cabin took the nation by storm, inspiring many converts to the antislavery cause despite the vituperative attacks from slavers and their political enablers. The novel was gripping, with powerful scenes and memorable characters, and Frederick could not put the book down, reading several chapters in a single sitting late into the night.

Nevertheless, he found Uncle Tom's piety cloying and his martyrdom ineffective. Stowe presumed that religious Blacks, models for others, would inspire whites to relinquish slavery, and then as missionaries immigrate to Africa to convert Black heathens. Uncle Tom dies in the book, forgiving his master and the overseer that beat him, but people like him could change the world, insisted Stowe, who wrote a great story and an apologia for colonization and missionary zeal.

Frederick knew better.

Whites would never relinquish slavery without a struggle.

And Black people would never leave the United States to go to Africa or anywhere else.

But Mrs. Stowe, now a world-famous, bestselling author, had her own kind of power, and Frederick went to her house in Andover, Massachusetts, eager to see and hear how she would wield it as an enthusiastic supporter of Negro uplift. "I want to do something practical in the wake of *Uncle Tom's Cabin*," she had declared.

The granite house facing colleges on a beautiful public square with many trees, was large, plain, and gray, with a bulk that suggested an imperishable fortress. The interior was equally plain, the furniture finely carved but simple, almost severe in design. There were few frills, no pillows, and no flowers. The only sign of ostentation was the large wood cross hanging from Mrs. Stowe's narrow neck.

Frederick sat across from her and said solemnly, "Mrs. Stowe, with all due respect, I must make one matter very clear before we proceed on the matter of the education of my people. I must speak to you about colonization."

At the end of her novel, she had expressed the hope that colonization would be the solution to the problem of slavery and race in America, as Henry Clay, now dead, also believed. Frederick did not question her deep hatred of slavery, but her hopes for colonization suggested a moral laziness he found deeply disturbing.

Mrs. Stowe paused, and he waited for a nod, a smile, some gesture. He didn't want to be rude. Finally, she asked "Yes?"

He answered, keeping his voice soft and even, "There is little reason to hope that any considerable number of the free colored people will ever be induced to leave this country, even if such a thing were desirable. The truth is, dear madam, we are here, and here we are likely to remain. Individuals emigrate—nations never."

He then succumbed to ardent advocacy, "If then, the question for the wise and the good, is precisely the one that you have submitted to me—namely: what can be done to improve the condition of the free people of color of the United States—then I am ready to discuss and offer solutions."

Frederick noted Stowe's dim smile and intense blue eyes when he used the phrase "the wise and the good." Flattery worked once again.

"Yes?" she asked, leaning toward him. "Please continue."

"The plan which I humbly submit in the hope that it may find favor with you, and with many friends of humanity who honor, love, and cooperate with you—is the establishment in Rochester, or in some other part of the United States equally favorable to such an enterprise, an industrial college in which shall be taught several branches of the mechanical arts. This college is to be opened to colored youth. I will pass over, for the present, the details of such an institution as I propose. It is the peculiarity of your favored race that they can always do what they think is necessary to be done. I can safely trust all details to yourself, and the wise and good people whom you represent in the interest you take in my oppressed fellow countrymen."

Mrs. Stowe smiled again. “Even the wise and good can lack imagination when it comes to details.”

“Your support is more important. Your understanding of the pressing need, and making sure your friends understand it, too, will do far more good. They all must realize that free Negroes must learn trades or die. One thing is certain. We must find new methods of obtaining a livelihood, for the old ones are failing us very fast.”

“Very well. Are you now ready to discuss Mr. Garrison?” Mrs. Stowe asked.

“Madam?” he asked weakly, expecting to continue the elaboration of his case.

“Mr. Douglass, your comments today and your editorials have all given me sufficient arguments for persuading others about your proposal for a school in Rochester or elsewhere.”

“Please accept my apology for saying too much, perhaps . . .”

“No, you don’t need to apologize for *this*, but I do need to understand your break with Mr. Garrison. He came to see me earlier this month, and he’s devastated by what has happened.”

“He has a strange way of showing it. You’ve read the *Liberator*.”

“Yes. I admire its frankness, fearlessness, truthfulness, and independence, but at the same time I regard with apprehension and sorrow much that is in it. There are sentiments there that I find distasteful, for I fear that the *Liberator* takes from poor Uncle Tom his Bible and gives him nothing in its place. It is a grief and sorrow of my heart that anyone who is distinguished in the antislavery cause should be rejectors of our Bible. He said he didn’t understand my objection. If the Bible is all that I claim it to be, then being anxious about its just appreciation is unwarranted. The more the Bible is sifted, he said, the more it will be prized, if it be all holy and true.”

Frederick nodded his head. Despite all that he found objectionable in the man, he could not deny his powers of persuasion.

Mrs. Stowe admitted as much. “He has a remarkable tact at conversation, as do you.”

“Thank you, madam, but we have profound disagreements, and he is fierce, even ruthless, when opposed.”

“I’ve read the newspaper, but you tell me why.”

“I can only speak for myself, and I will explain my thinking that has changed, if you don’t mind hearing about the Constitution and politics again.”

He slowly reviewed his case, needing to make sure she understood the breadth and scope of the disagreement and the struggle to arrive at this moment after careful examination of a variety of issues.

She listened with hands folded and unwavering but uncritical eyes.

When Frederick was done, she said, "I feel bound in justice to say that my impression of you is far more satisfactory than I anticipated, and I am satisfied that your change of opinion is not a mere political one, but a genuine growth of your convictions. You have a vigorous, reflective mind, and you hold no opinion which you cannot defend. Your plans for the elevation of your race are manly, sensible, comprehensive. You have carefully observed and thought deeply. My unfavorable view of you, sir, was wrong, and I must admit my error, and extend to you an apology. There is abundant room in the antislavery field for you to perform work without crossing or impeding the movement of old friends. Perhaps in some future time meeting each other from opposite quarters of a victorious field, you may yet shake hands together."

"That, madam, will be up to him, not to me."

She lifted her right hand and gently stroked her cross. "Can you forgive him?"

"No."

69.

FREDERICK REREAD THE *NARRATIVE* for the first time in years and found it thin, simplistic, and shallow, its characters all puppets in his severe moral drama, their lives without ambiguity, resonance, or shades of gray, only victims in the quarters and oppressors all around them.

By the spring of 1854, at thirty-six years old, he changed his mind and decided to write another book. His story now had to be a rebuke to any claims to Black inferiority. "Not only is slavery on trial, but unfortunately the enslaved people are also on trial. It is alleged, that they are, naturally, inferior; that they are so low in the scale of humanity, and so utterly stupid, that they are unconscious of their wrong, and do not apprehend their rights."

He had no new records to go by, but this time he spent hours taking notes, making lists, preparing an outline. He would not write his new book impulsively, producing pages only through sudden bursts of emotion. This book would be carefully planned, and every tale would have rich detail: the sights, sounds, and smells of Maryland, nothing distilled down to just a moral lesson, more Dickens, and less Hawthorne.

Even the book cover had to reinforce his case. He could not leave it to the publisher to find an artist to draw a likeness. He would find a photographer to produce a daguerreotype for engraving on the title page, an unsmiling portrait of a sitting, prosperous gentleman with glaring eyes facing the reader, his eyebrows arched; the furrow at the top of his nose and the lines under his prominent cheeks dark and deep; his mane of black hair brushed back and parted at the side; his thick neck obscured by a closely cropped beard, a high starched collar, and a silk cravat tied with a prominent pin; his shoulders and chest covered by a white, crisp, and tight shirt, mostly hidden by the cravat and waistcoat; and a double-breasted, wide lapelled jacket buttoned at the waist. Every piece had to look expensive. And he would make sure that his hands were fists in his lap.

His recollections excited him. What had been ignored before now assumed pride of place. He refashioned his grandmother and mother in his new book, especially honoring Harriet Bailey. He admitted, "I cannot say that I was very deeply attached to my mother; certainly, not so deeply as I should have been had our relations in childhood been different." He also admitted that he didn't know her well and remembered little. But he described her anyway as "tall, and finely proportioned; of deep black, glossy complexion; had regular features, and, among the slaves, was remarkably sedate in her manners."

He needed to write this tribute, a testament to her essential place in his identity, for he was more Black than white. He was the man he became because she was his mother, not because the unnamed white man was his father.

His grandmother was not given a similar honor, even though he had lived with Betsey Bailey for six years and knew her as only a favorite grandchild could. But when he now recalled the moment she left him—leaving him in a strange place without warning—that deception still rankled. He understood her actions. She had to obey her master. But he could not forgive. Not yet. He wondered if he ever would.

About the Lloyds of the Wye Plantation and his time spent there, Frederick remembered details unobscured by sentimentality. He had to recreate the sights and sounds of Wye Plantation and the Eastern Shore with powerful, unforgettable images, and expose the emotional costs for everyone there, the enslaved and the slavers. For horror and disgust, for shame and provocation, for enlistment and donations, Frederick had to devote pages to the casual cruelties of Colonel Lloyd, the hatred of Aunt Katy, the sinister viciousness of Edward Covey, the gross religious hypocrisy of Thomas Auld, and the near lynching in St. Michaels. This was his chance to match and even surpass the graphic, dramatic power of *Uncle Tom's Cabin.*

But the present intruded on these reflections and forced him to stop writing and take to the road again. Current politics could not keep Frederick on the sidelines. He crossed the northeast blasting Senator Stephen Douglas's proposed legislation, the Kansas–Nebraska Act. The wall to the western expansion of slavery created by the Compromise of 1820 would crumble the moment Congress passed the Douglas's Act and grant power to slave owners and their political supporters to vote on slavery.

Frederick was not alone. Most northern whites had come to accept the Compromise of 1820 as an inviolate, solemn protection against slavery's intrusion in the territories and a guarantee of free soil for free white people. This new law obliterated this protection. Thousands denounced it in letters and at public rallies. A new political party against expansion, the Free Soil Party emerged and then transformed into the Republican Party.

Editorial protests, speeches, and rallies proved futile, and Congress passed the Kansas–Nebraska Act in May. Frederick unleashed invective that broke the bounds of rhetorical control he had carefully crafted over more than a decade. "A bolt that bound the North and South together has been surged asunder, and a mighty barricade, which has intervened between the forces of slavery and freedom, has been demolished by the slave power itself; and for one, we now say, in the name of God, let the battle come . . . Let the old parties go to destruction. Let their names be blotted out, and their memory rot; and let there be only a free party, and a slave party, and the bloody flag of slavery and chains shall then swing out from our respective battlements, and rally under them our respective armies, and let the inquiry go forth now, as of old, who is on the Lord's side?"

At last, he was a prophet of freedom. This was his calling.

And now, personal and political events pushed doors open.

The break with Garrison and his followers; the realignment of American politics with the collapse of the Whig Party; the emergence of the Free Soil/ Republican Party; the roiling debate over the Kansas–Nebraska Act; and the writing of a new autobiography reinvigorated Frederick.

The new president, Franklin Pierce, was determined to show his commitment to federal law when a runaway slave named Anthony Burns was arrested and tried in Boston that June. Supporters attacked the Court House, and a man deputized as a U.S. marshal was killed. Pierce sent thousands of troops, who marched Burns in handcuffs through the streets to the ship waiting for his return to Virginia. Nearly fifty thousand people lined the streets held back by marines and police officers. People spit on the soldiers from upper windows, and crowds shrieked "Shame! Shame!" at them as they walked by storefronts draped in black.

This spectacle of federal power moved Frederick to dismiss the death of the marshal, proclaiming to a stunned audience, "We hold that he *forfeited* his right to live, and that his death was necessary, as a warning to others liable to pursue a like course. Every slave hunter who meets a bloody death in his infernal business, is an argument in favor of the manhood of our race. Resistance is, therefore, wise as well as just."

Later that summer Frederick pushed deeper into more dangerous territory, writing his editorial "True Remedy for the Fugitive Slave Bill." He defined the "true remedy" as "A good revolver, a steady hand, and a determination to shoot down any man sent to kidnap. Let every colored man make up his mind to this, and live by it, and if needs be, die by it. This will put an end to kidnapping and slaveholding, too. Is it right and wise to kill a kidnapper? If any one truth is more firmly established in the American mind, it is this: resistance to tyrants is obedience to God."

In cities and towns throughout the northeast, citizens shaken by the brute force administered by the Pierce administration over the return of just one man now applauded Frederick's calls to arms throughout the northeast and sent hundreds of letters of support. He returned to his second autobiography with renewed vigor. When he finished writing, he had a book four times longer than the *Narrative,* almost five hundred pages, to be sold for $1.25. He dedicated his work to Gerrit Smith.

Frederick had an introduction to *My Bondage and My Freedom* written by Dr. James McCune Smith, who was also born a slave and the son of a white father. Smith had a remarkable career, receiving advanced degrees from the University of Glasgow and practicing medicine for whites and Blacks in New York City, where he lived in a mansion near Broadway. Frederick anticipated a positive review after Smith agreed to write the introduction, but he was flabbergasted by the length of the essay, the depth of its insights, and the extent of its praise.

Smith opened his long introduction by asserting that Frederick's life was indeed representative. "Dear reader, it is my privilege to introduce you to the life of Frederick Douglass, recorded in the pages which follow. It is not merely an example of self-elevation under the most adverse circumstances; it is, moreover, a noble vindication of the highest aims of the American anti-slavery movement."

Frederick was truly American: the self-made, self-reliant man celebrated by Emerson.

He gave the complete manuscript, the introduction by Dr. Smith, and his plan for the appendix to Julia, who announced her verdict sitting across from him in the office. "It's good, very good. Some will prefer the other book because it's shorter and written so soon after you escaped. There was an immediacy."

He frowned, disappointed that her praise was so short lived.

"But this is better, more reflective, and far more insightful. Slavery's heart is here, and so is your heart. You love Maryland, Baltimore, the Eastern Shore, the Chesapeake. It's all here."

"It's in my blood. It made me who I am."

"Your book will make anyone believe what you believe. Well, most . . ."

"I'm a better writer now."

"All good editors make sure of that. Now that it's done, and after I wield my editorial pen, as you expect me to do, I can go back home to England."

"What?" Frederick asked. Julia had more than once said that she missed England and needed to go there to raise money, but he couldn't accept her statement. "You can't be serious?"

"It's time."

"No."

"Yes."

Avoiding her eyes, too ashamed to reveal his need so nakedly, he whispered, "Please, don't leave."

"I'm sure you will not miss my ruthlessness as your editor and critic."

"No."

"I must. You know that. Your friends there just need to be asked personally to give you money for your work," Julia replied.

She had tried almost everything to save Frederick financially. Becoming the secretary of the Rochester Ladies' Anti-Slavery Society, she had organized bazaars. She also collected articles, essays, letters, and poems from William Seward, Horace Mann, Gerrit Smith, Reverend Theodore Parker, Ralph Waldo Emerson, Reverend Henry Ward Beecher, his sister, Harriet Beecher Stowe, and others for her gift book, *Autographs for Freedom*. Frederick contributed his story about the slave Madison Washington.

But the famous names made little difference. It sold poorly in 1853. The second volume, published a year later, did no better.

"You will come back?" Frederick asked.

"There are no guarantees," Julia said.

"Do you want to come back?"

"Of course. To work with you, to help you."

"I'll miss you."

He reached for a piece of paper on his desk and quickly scribbled three words and gave the paper to her: *I love you*.

Julia's eyes filled with tears, and she turned her back away from the open door of the outer office, where Frederick's oldest sons were now working.

"I should not have. We agreed," he said.

Since her visit to his new house outside of town, no endearments or intimacies had passed between them. They were friends and colleagues only. In the office, their discussions about politics and national policy were as impassioned as ever, but they maintained a careful distance, never touching, never probing below the surface of office civility, never taking a stroll on the streets, never being alone together for any reason.

Gently, she tore up the incriminating piece of paper. "Don't apologize, but I know one day, very soon, I will regret that I didn't keep this paper, something to hold on to, something to take out and treasure."

"Then you will . . ."

"Don't. Saying goodbye is hard enough."

"You talk as if you'll never come back."

"I didn't leave England with the idea of never returning. I came to do a job and I did it, and now the job requires me to go back. My work is done here. I can be of better use over there."

"You'll do well."

"The work is *most* important."

He wanted to shout his denial of their pretense, at least now, when he was about to lose her. Love should matter more than duty.

"The work is . . ." Frederick mumbled.

"There are arrangements to be made, introductory letters to write," she said.

He heard the desolation in her voice, the longing for what could have been. He looked down searching for a needed distraction.

They went back to work, saying nothing more about the separation to come.

Four weeks later, with all arrangements finalized, her departure was stiff, formal, and without public tears. Before she boarded the train for Albany, Frederick declared, "Julia, I'm going to take your hand."

She didn't resist him as he took her gloved right hand and raised it to his lips. As usual, there was the sudden turning of heads, as if all eyes had been waiting for the anticipated moment, another public scandal, more gist for parlor gossip and whispered asides about Black and white sex. But Frederick didn't care. All that mattered was the tenderness in Julia's eyes and that delicate, knowing smile.

"You are my friend," he said.

"Always," she said.

"Always," he repeated. She was gone, stepping into the train car, not looking back or coming to the window. There was a loud blowing of the whistle, and a sudden rush of white, billowing steam as the train slowly lurched east toward Albany.

PART IV: 1855–1861

Ottilie Assing

70.

MY BONDAGE AND MY Freedom sold well, five thousand copies in the first two days alone, and fifteen thousand in the first three months. Frederick serialized parts of the book in his newspaper, and on lecture tours sold it for $1.00, a good price for brisk sales. The reviews were complimentary. He was most pleased with the assessment of Harriet Beecher Stowe, who wrote in an essay for the *New York Independent* that he had "a natural genius for writing."

His public fight with Garrison was still roiling in the abolitionist press. Garrison's review of the book in the *Liberator* declared, "It is a volume remarkable, it is true, for its thrilling sketches of a slave's life and experience, and for the ability displayed in its pages. But in its second portion, it is reeking with the virus of personal malignity towards Wendell Phillips, myself, and others, and full of ingratitude and baseness towards as true and disinterested friends as any man ever yet had upon the earth."

Frederick laughed bitterly. Of the twenty-five chapters, only the last three mentioned the abolitionists at all, with Wendell and Garrison referred to as "true friends" for urging him to flee the country. Obviously, Garrison was peeved that he had not been mentioned enough.

There were other disappointments that summer, including the news from Julia.

She reported from England that her old friends had too many causes and journals to subsidize. She could only send small amounts of money and apologized for not sending more.

More serious was the growing change in the tone of her letters. Progressively, they became a formal collection of business and travel reports with details about the changes in England since 1849. She withheld intimacies, and endearments came only with her salutation and closing remarks. "My dear Frederick" and "Your friend always" were all he had to satisfy a longing intensified by her absence.

He now hated going to the office and seeing her empty desk. For a few days, he found himself looking up from his work and without thought saying, "Oh, Julia, how about . . ." At home, he was sullen and irritable.

Of course, Anna knew the cause, but never mentioned Julia's name. She did not have to say it, but as far as she was concerned, Julia was dead.

And Frederick hated Anna for winning her war.

Frederick also struggled to make his children fit into his picture of a successful, happy family. Rosetta was dark and plump like her mother and sullen and sharp tongued when provoked. Her brothers always irritated her and drew signs of her disdain—the roll of her eyes, the sharp intakes of her breath, and a wave of her right hand.

"Boys!" was all she needed to say before asking to leave the parlor. She would always leave to return to her studies.

The boys were not as ambitious or intelligent as their older sister, and they never seemed able to do anything right without direct supervision or dire warnings. Frederick could not let a day pass without a cross word to them.

Frederick had them work in the newspaper office, but they were mediocre workers, unable to sweep the floors without supervision. The boys seemed incapable of holding themselves to high standards of performance. Just getting by was good enough. At the office, he often asked them, "Can't you do it right? Can't you do just *one* thing right?"

Frederick, Jr., and Lewis never complained. They only said "Yes, Papa" and listened carefully to Frederick's corrections. Charles, the most sensitive, seemed ready to fight his brothers, or anyone else, at any moment.

Sometimes, Frederick would relax and play with the children. He sang songs like "My Old Kentucky Home" or "Nelly Was a Lady," or played his violin. The children vigorously applauded their father's voice and fiddling.

Because Sunday was the day for church and Sunday dinner, it was not his day of rest. Saturday was supposed to be the day when he could read and think without the pressure of getting the paper edited and printed. But the children wanted time with him.

"Papa, Papa, play with us, please. How about hide and seek, how about . . ."

At first, the answer was always, "No, not now," or "No, I'm too busy."

"Please, please."

And he would relent. "Just one game, and then you need to know how to have fun on your own time."

They learned to turn to their mother for almost everything, avoiding Frederick's curt replies or long, boring lectures. Even when Anna, as the dutiful wife, said "go ask your father," the children interpreted his consent as a formality. After all, he was busy and didn't want to be bothered with the details of raising a family. Mama was in charge.

Annie was the only real pleasure for him. She only had to smile, and he would do anything for her and forgive everything. For her he made exceptions, never dismissing her with the familiar, "I'm busy." He found her fumbling mistakes charming and played games whenever she wanted them. She also loved books, and he read stories to her almost every day.

No one pointed out the injustice of his favoritism, but Frederick supposed that favoritism was in the order of things when a couple had five children. Annie possessed an unearned and obvious distinction. She was temperamentally always happy, so unlike the rest, as if she did not harbor some dark family secret and resent life for being unfair. She was a miracle, a sun who cast no shadows, and Frederick eagerly anticipated each afternoon when he arrived home and heard her excited, joyous cry, "Papa!" That one word had the power to make him forget, for at least a moment, the trials of the day.

Once, thinking about his friend Doctor Smith, who lost three children in one brutal summer, Frederick impulsively took Annie into his arms when she came into the parlor. He pressed her so tightly against him that she asked gently, "Papa, why are you squeezing me? It hurts."

Frederick started, as if her words awakened him from a nightmare, and apologized. "I didn't mean to, sweetheart. I just love you so."

71.

OTTILIE ASSING FINALLY MET Frederick at a meeting of Black abolitionists at James Pennington's Shiloh Presbyterian Church in New York on May 6, 1856. When she first came to America in 1852, she didn't think it would take four years, but thankfully, her moment had come at last.

When she read the notice for the meeting she hurried to the familiar church. Her arrival caused a stir. There were no other women present, white or Black. But Ottilie didn't care. A radical feminist and free thinker, she liked causing trouble.

She was on a mission. She had to find Douglass, introduce herself, and ask if she could come to Rochester for an extended interview. Ottilie didn't know if or when she would have the chance to hear his voice and its impact on audiences, because the meeting had no scheduled speeches.

Speed was essential, and she assessed the room for opportunity. He was standing in a group at the side of the meeting hall and turned his head toward the front door, where delegates grumbled about the entrance of a white woman.

Ottilie went directly to him and declared, "I'm Ottilie Assing, a journalist from Germany now living here in New York. I've read your wonderful *Narrative*, but *Bondage and Freedom* is the greater book, and I want to translate it and write an introduction for my German readers. May I come to Rochester for an interview?"

As she expected, he was stunning. However, the descriptions of his unusual height, the broad shoulders, and large head covered with a mane of peppered, brushed back hair did not do him justice, for they failed to capture his physical presence. He smiled, pleased by her bold attentions despite her effrontery. He paused, then replied, "Of course, any time, as long as I am not on a lecture tour."

"Then I'll find you."

"You flatter me," Frederick said, then looked over her head, signaling that their conversation had come to an end.

"My praise is deeper than flattery," Ottilie declared. She refused to look down or away, a habit most men found disquieting.

Frederick's face revealed no displeasure, but Ottilie felt judged somehow, characterized as a needy supplicant.

"I expect to see you in Rochester soon," he said, nodding his head before stepping away. "Let me know when you are in town. Goodbye."

Ottilie took a deep breath. She was embarrassed but not ashamed. Her mother, a free-thinking woman who taught her to name hundreds of plants and animals also raised her to understand her body, recognize its signs. Ottilie knew her reaction was more than infatuation. This was adoration and desire.

As a young woman she had fallen in love with the great actor Jean Baptiste Baison during his engagements in Hamburg as Hamlet. He was extraordinarily handsome, thin, almost frail, with flowing blond hair and scalding blue eyes, a man granted lavish endowments, one of Nature's favorites. The embodiment of the passionate but sensitive hero, he spoke lines as if they were the spontaneous expressions of his very soul.

Ottilie had to have him, so she moved into his house as the governess of his children and slowly seduced him. After all the careful planning and waiting, nothing else mattered. He was her soulmate. Her favorite novels described such a love, and the great philosopher Immanuel Kant defined it as "the sublime."

She envisioned a similar domestic arrangement for herself and Frederick Douglass, with modifications appropriate to her life in America. As an independent journalist who needed to work and travel, she would continue living in New York, her favorite city, and every year she would go to Rochester and stay at his house for weeks, talking about politics, history, literature, slavery, and abolition, spending hours on the translation of his books and speeches, and waiting for him to realize that she was his true, natural wife.

That was the plan. Its fulfillment was only a matter of time. And what about Anna, his legal wife?

Ottilie heard the gossip. Anna Douglass was black, ugly, illiterate, uninterested in Frederick's public life. How could she possibly be his intellectual partner, his soulmate? Yes, Anna was the mother of his children and keeper of the house. But these were not great achievements, they only made her as common as most women. And Ottilie Assing thought of herself as anything but common.

She was the oldest daughter of the vivacious and beautiful Rosa Maria Varnhagen Assing, who taught her girls that living with a lover was legitimate if he had an exotic background and possessed the true spirit of the Romantic age. But even her mother's lessons did not prepare her for the sudden death of Baison, who, after complaining of severe stomach pain and headaches, collapsed and died in 1849. After the funeral, she was ordered to leave the house by his wife, who had tolerated the affair.

Ottilie now had to find work. She wandered throughout Germany, taking whatever journalistic assignments came her way. At the age of thirty-four in 1852, she decided to go to America, hoping with so many other immigrants to start over and create a new life. She was disgusted with Germany. It was now even more stifling, conventional, and repressive. The promise of America, especially after reading the rich utopian literature about the new world, beguiled her.

She made a list of what to see, whom to meet. Wendell Phillips was at the top. He was America's greatest orator. Frederick Douglass was next.

Ottilie understood America's faults, the contradictions that its great Declaration of Independence could not obscure, contradictions Phillips and Douglass exposed with knives of eloquence matched in her own country only by Friedrich Schiller. She meant to go there as an instrument of radical change. She would introduce the glories of European culture to a culturally impoverished land. Her readers in Germany expected full reports of her triumphs.

On arrival to America, she took a four-month trip from New York to Ohio. On her return to New York City, she rented two expensive rooms in Manhattan. They were too expensive, but she had no regrets about coming to America, because it gave her so much material from which to work. She dutifully sent her articles to her editor. In the meantime, she found a large, creative, and intellectually stimulating community of German expatriates living across the river in Hoboken, New Jersey, on the heights overlooking the Hudson River, with panoramic views of the city and its countless ships.

She went there almost every weekend and spent hours talking to her new friends about her new country, slavery, the reform movements, including abolition, and, of course, Frederick Douglass, whose *Narrative* caught her attention. It was the best of the slave narratives, eloquent, riveting, a powerful indictment.

After finally meeting Frederick Douglass in New York City, Ottilie arranged to stay with a distant cousin and left for Rochester. She arrived at Frederick's office with only his general invitation to come see him. She sent no note. He gave no explicit directions for time and place. He was not in when she arrived and was told he was at home. Without a second thought, she walked the two miles to the house on South Park Road, noting the sites of the bustling town on the Genesee River, and daydreaming her future as his companion, confidant, and lover.

Yes, she would seduce him as she had seduced Baison. She would bide her time, carefully waiting for the moment when she would declare her love and signal it was time for their love's consummation, the true union of kindred spirits, the triumph over dead categories and boundaries about women and race only a daughter of Doctor David Assing, a Jewish convert to Christianity, and Rosa Maria Verhangen Assing could expect to achieve. Reviled as Jews by birth and choice, they nonetheless taught their daughters that individuals could choose their identities and places in the world. Autonomy, integrity, and self-liberation mattered.

When a young woman with dark skin and large brown eyes answered the knock at the door, Ottilie declared boldly, "I'm here to see Mr. Frederick Douglass. He expects me."

Puzzled, Rosetta asked, "Is he? He said nothing about a visitor today. And who are you?"

"Ottilie Assing. We met in New York, and he invited me."

Still skeptical, Rosetta didn't invite her inside. She said, "Please wait here. I will tell my father."

Within seconds, Frederick stood before her, his presence commanding. "Why, Miss Assing, this is a delightful surprise. Please come in and you will of course forgive my daughter. I have far too many peddlers and solicitors coming here. She's the guardian of the gates."

"Of paradise," Ottilie said.

"Excuse me?"

"I'm where I am supposed to be," she said, looking around to the walls and roof of the entry hall.

"Miss Assing, you worry me. You are far too grand. Even when I met you, I found your declarations, brief though they were, somewhat ominous."

"I love to laugh, too."

"Good. These are serious times, and we all need a good laugh now and then. Even I sometimes forget."

"We will laugh together, then."

"Good. Then there's no danger of an outbreak of solemnity, at least today."

"No danger."

"Would you like to have some tea?"

"Yes."

"I will return shortly."

He left the room, and Ottilie quickly took note of the piano and the violin resting on the top, portraits on the walls, and the many books with markers.

Frederick returned, followed by a large Black woman with thick lips, large eyes, and a bandana covering her hair and the top of her forehead. She held a tray with a tea pot and two cups.

"Thank you, Anna," Frederick said when the unsmiling woman placed the tray on the table and chairs in the front of the piano.

"Miss Assing, let me introduce to you my wife, Mrs. Douglass."

Ottilie thought the woman was the maid, since she stood at attention as if waiting for direction. Confused, Ottilie began to object. "Oh, for a moment . . ." Realizing this was Anna confirmed her sense of mission. She would *save* Frederick from this ugly, Black woman. No wonder he never described her in his books, leaving her to two lines between them. "I'm pleased to make your acquaintance," lied Ottilie, quickly putting out her hand.

Anna took it, whispering politely, "How do you do."

"Miss Assing is from Germany, and she hopes to translate my book."

"Good," said Anna before leaving without saying another word.

When the door closed, Ottilie returned to her seat, paused for a moment as she made sure there wasn't a trace of self-pity in her observation, and said, "She doesn't like me."

"Miss Assing, you can't possibly know that."

"I could see it in her eyes. Her vague smile was one thing, but the eyes said something else entirely."

Frederick sighed. "Miss Assing, if we are to continue a working relationship, you will say nothing more about my wife."

She recognized at once the terms of their future together. There could be no disclosure of private matters, however deep the love they developed. She would share details of her past, seeing so many parallels between her life story and his. But secrets would remain. "Very well. I understand. Let's have our tea before it gets cold," Ottilie said.

72.

OTTILIE WAS NOT BEAUTIFUL, but her vigorous opinions and small dancing brown eyes created a distinct, arresting face composed of thin lips, a narrow, pointed nose, and scant eyebrows. She also loved to talk, and Frederick could not resist.

"Translating a long book into German will take time. We will need to discuss every phrase and sentence, every word, to capture the eloquence that flows naturally from the facts of your life," Ottilie said.

"I don't know German, but I'm willing to do whatever you need," Frederick said.

"German is a rich language, with long phrases that capture the complexities of life itself. Translations are, therefore, difficult. It will take weeks for us to come to agreements. I must return in the summers and stay close at hand to review my work with you."

"You will stay with us here, of course," Frederick said, still taken aback by her boldness, and delighted too. "You can stay as long as you need. We have rooms for guests."

"For the Underground Railroad?"

"Yes, and fugitives come every week, not as often as they came in 1850–51, but they still flee from a land that will not love them. This country is difficult to love."

"I love America."

"Is that a rebuke or a provocation?"

"A provocation, of course."

"You and I see a different America."

"I'm here to take your eyes and put them in my head for my pages."

Frederick grimaced at the image.

"Be assured. I'm not Dr. Frankenstein," said Ottilie.

"That's a relief. When did you read Mrs. Shelley?"

"When I was a youth. But more importantly, I've read almost all your worthy writers, Cooper, Hawthorne, Emerson, Thoreau, Melville, and Whitman. Hawthorne and Melville are especially subversive," Ottilie said.

"*Subversive*? What do you mean exactly?" Frederick asked.

"Hawthorne and Melville are like philosophers raising essential questions about the nature of society and our relationship to God and Nature. You have no great philosophers like Hegel, Fichte, Schelling, and Kant in my country, but . . ."

Frederick interrupted. "We have Emerson."

Ottilie waved a dismissive right hand. "His essays are not extended arguments."

Frederick frowned, and Ottilie changed course, brightening her tone. "At least your great writers *dramatize* the great ideas and are thus more accessible. We can read them together. And I must confess even most Germans don't read Kant or Hegel, either."

"And Mrs. Stowe? Surely, they have read her?"

"She writes drivel, pure drivel."

"You can't be referring to *Uncle Tom's Cabin*?"

"Of course, I am. The characters are stereotypes, the language is clichéd, and the plot *so* predictable."

"But her book opened eyes, and it sold by the thousands, a bestseller in fact. Probably the most-sold book in our history, and no doubt read by thousands in your country, too." Frederick didn't want to sound defensive. He was enjoying their banter despite her self-righteous pronouncements.

Ottilie was not deterred. "*The Scarlet Letter* and *Moby-Dick* did not do as well, but they will last because Hester Prynne and Captain Ahab embody protests against society and a God that Uncle Tom can never know or understand."

"God?"

"Oh, let's leave the nature or existence of the Almighty to another time."

"Existence? Surely, you don't *doubt* . . ."

"We, indeed, have so much to discuss, especially when I return next summer to work on your book. For now, let's talk about Kansas."

He smiled. "So, I see, you know the diversion tactics of war as well."

"When it serves me. Of course."

They discussed the Kansas crisis, as did most people that summer of 1856. John Brown was at the center of it all. Commissioned as a captain in the First Brigade of Kansas Volunteers by an agent of the New England Emigrant Aid Society, Brown was unofficially a marked man. The news coming back to Rochester in clippings, letters, and editorials denounced Brown and told stories of brutal war, conspiracy, and murder.

President Franklin Pierce was at war against free Kansas. In a special address to Congress, he asserted that Kansas's troubles were the fault of the eastern emigrant-aid societies and called the free-state government revolutionary. He said that he would consider armed resistance to the proslavery government at Lecompton "treasonable insurrection."

What was the truth?

Frederick carefully read everything he could get his hands on and tried to piece together for his readers, and himself, an outline of the most controversial aspect of the war, the Pottawatamie murders. A border army from Missouri had marched into Lawrence, the center of free Kansas, and, meeting no resistance, looted stores and burned buildings. Retaliating, one group of Free Staters went to the houses of five unarmed proslavery men on Pottawatomie Creek, pulled them out of bed, and killed them in cold blood.

Three members of one family were hacked to pieces, their heads split open, their arms cut off. The father was shot in the forehead as he lay on the ground, mortally wounded or dead. Later that night, the group took another man from his wife and children, slashed his head and side open, cut his throat, and dragged him into the brush about one hundred fifty yards from his house. On Sunday, this same group arrived at the house of James Harris, spared him but selected a guest staying with him, mutilated his body, and threw it into Pottawatamie Creek.

The government and citizens of Lawrence denied any complicity in these murders, and the free-soil press unanimously condemned them. The proslavery press called for blood. A full-scale war began. Missouri raiders and their southern allies pillaged, burned, and killed in the search for the Pottawatamie killers, and free-state settlers evacuated southeastern Kansas, or formed their own armies to pillage, burn, and kill. John Brown was a captain of one of these armies, the "Kansas Regulars," and now he was a wanted man on the run.

Ottilie was cautious. "I've seen revolutions fail completely. I saw what happened in Germany. The soldiers mowed people down in the streets. The King of Prussia invaded Berlin. The Parliament passed laws to remove rights. It's a familiar story, the failure of dreams when politics and keeping power is more important than what is right, what is true."

"John Brown is different, even if America is not so different," Frederick said.

"Maybe. We can hope."

"We need more than hope. We need a commander with a plan."

"Like George Washington?"

He didn't like the tone in her voice. She seemed to mock his faith in Brown, a heroic but troubling man. "No, like Nat Turner."

"But he was executed."

"But because of him white people wake up at night in fear, waiting for the next Nat Turner. And he will come, as surely as the night comes."

"But Brown is white."

"That makes it even better."

73.

OTTILIE'S HOBOKEN HOME WAS on Washington Street. She rented two rooms for herself and had a third room set aside for visitors. Ottilie told Mrs. Marks, her landlord, about Frederick, making sure that Mrs. Marks understood that he would be a frequent visitor. He always needed a place to stay when he was in the New York area. An admirer of Frederick and an ardent supporter of the antislavery movement, Mrs. Marks raised no objections. "He is always welcome here at our table," she said, her subtle smile acknowledging that Ottilie and Frederick would be together now and then.

Of course, there was nothing from Frederick that indicated he knew what Ottilie envisioned in that room, but Ottilie was willing to bide her time despite her impatience. Destiny was sometimes slow, but nothing could stop her goal in life: becoming the *true* wife of Frederick Douglass, the breaker of all the false barriers and taboos of conventional America.

When Frederick came to New York for meetings in May 1857 and was scheduled to speak, she made sure she was there. Finally, she had the opportunity to hear him before an audience. She enthused to her readers, "The lion of this season was Frederick Douglass, this excellent mulatto whom I have mentioned repeatedly in my reports. Having hitherto known this talented, brilliant man only from his writing and personal intercourse, I heard him for the first time as a public speaker who gave me an appreciation of his great and general importance. Among the many great orators in this country, he is one of the greatest."

After watching Frederick, Ottilie wrote, "Although he is one of the best, although he belongs to the true intellectual aristocracy, although he enjoys fame and reputation throughout the nation, and although he is gifted with a great mind and prodigious talent, with a commitment to action, personal charm, and a spotless character—so called society shuns him because he is a 'nigger.'"

Frederick also spoke against the Supreme Court's March decision Dred Scott v. Sandford. After Dred Scott, a slave, was taken by his master into Illinois and Wisconsin, where slavery was prohibited, he sued for his freedom in Missouri, claiming that his four-year stay in free territory granted it. A lower court agreed, but the Missouri Supreme Court overturned it. The decision was appealed to the United States Supreme Court under Chief Justice Roger Taney, a Maryland slaveholder. His final ruling, supported by a seven–two majority, stunned the nation.

Taney declared that, as a Black man, Scott was a not a citizen and could not, therefore, sue in federal court. But the court went further, asserting that Negroes had no rights. Taney reasoned, "They had for more than a century been regarded as beings of an inferior order, and altogether unfit to associate with the white race, in either social or political relations, and so far unfit that they had no rights which the white man was bound to respect."

"This is a decision too monstrous to stand," a furious Frederick declared in New York. "The Supreme Court is high, but the Supreme Court of God is higher. It cannot undo what God Almighty has done. He has made all men free and has made their freedom self-evident."

Once back in Rochester that summer, Frederick also spent hours discussing with Ottilie her translation of *My Bondage and My Freedom*, but not a day would pass without Frederick interrupting their work with outbursts about the Dred Scott decision, which also asserted that Congress had no power to close slavery to the territories.

Ottilie was careful, avoiding the issue of God's intervention. At times, Frederick seemed like a child who could not fathom that his father would not save him. He would acknowledge uncertainty, admitting he did not know and could not know the time of deliverance. His anger was always there, burning below the surface and occasionally exploding in righteous tirades. But she concluded that he was fundamentally a man of hope. He could not remain pessimistic and afraid, even when talking about death and destruction. He could only rise. Rise through his rhetorical art. That art compelled her to comment, "I've talked to singers, artists, actors, and they tell me that when they feel that spirit, they no longer fear critics; they no longer worry about doing their best; they become the music, the words, and everything *flows*."

"Have you ever felt that flow?" Frederick asked.

"Sometimes, but only rarely when I'm writing. Most of the time, writing is laborious work, the craft of putting words and sentences together, like building a good table."

"Have you built a table, *too*? Your talents are broad indeed."

"No, but you know what I mean. My work is like building a table or making a dress. But when *you* speak, the words just come. I've seen it. You have notes, I know, but I know the words just come, and I'm sure that if not, when you reach those moments, you know it. You surely remember them, with amazement, curiosity, and the hope that they return. That's what great artists want, and we in the audience return to watch and hear it happen."

"I'm not like that, a great artist."

"Oh, yes, you are, and humility is not required."

"But if you're a vessel, then humility *is* appropriate."

"Perhaps now and then. We don't want the anger of the gods who punish the presumptuous."

"But there is only one God."

"There are many gods in Greek mythology."

"The Greeks were wrong, as pagans are wrong."

Ottilie stood, realizing that she had inadvertently entered territory that could ruin everything. She had led them to an argument about the divine in a matter of minutes. How could she be so reckless, so stupid?

"Let's read to each other, perhaps something light, amusing, or let's play violin sonatas with piano," Ottilie suggested.

"Oh no, not duets now. There will be no flow, for sure. I will have to work at not making a fool of myself. I need to practice first."

"We can work together, and then we can give a concert for the family. We will practice, and then, if we do the hard work, then maybe, just maybe, we'll have our moment. Let's at least try."

"Not this summer. We don't have that much time. The translation must take priority."

"Very well," Ottilie agreed, happy that she had successfully deflected further inquiry into her religious views. How long would she, an atheist, be able to delay a heated conversation about God? At the very least, she would delay it until after he fell in love with her.

★

Frederick had few other white visitors that summer, but he reminded her about the fugitives that would suddenly come knocking at his door. His house was the last important station on the Underground Railroad, and this summer would have more fugitives after Dred Scott. "We have folks coming almost every other night now. Those poor people are so frightened and hungry. But I can see their excitement of being near freedom. Lord, my life was comfortable compared to so many others. And Anna is never happier than when she is cooking, washing, and cleaning for these people. It's her way, perhaps her only way, of showing how she hates slavery, and wants it dead. She's an abolitionist, too, in her own way."

Ottilie was struck by the gentle pride in Anna that softened Frederick's voice. There was also regret, an acknowledgment that her definition of abolition could never be his, that Anna's small world could never match his larger one. Then he changed the subject, a signal to her that he had perhaps revealed more than he intended.

On that very night, four fugitives arrived at the house, shaken and hungry. Their stories were heartrending to Ottilie, and she listened with great care, seeing the brutality of slavery that even her closeness to Frederick and hearing his story didn't convey. She witnessed firsthand the effects of a system that separated and destroyed families for profit; fugitives forced to abandon their homes and drag their children hundreds of miles through swamps and over mountains; mothers who killed their own children rather than have them live another enslaved day.

Ottilie wept when she heard their stories and she continued to weep night after night throughout that unforgettable summer. When her stay finally came to an end, it seemed too soon. But Frederick offered an invitation that alleviated her disappointment. She could come to Rochester for eight weeks next summer. And he would come stay at her rooming house when he was in New York for a round of meetings, including the State Convention of Colored Men.

"Oh, Frederick, this makes me so happy. I won't have to wait a year to see you again, and you will be with me in Hoboken," Ottilie said. He was famous and popular and had multiple offers of accommodations in town. Even so, he was staying with her!

But he did not come that fall. He wrote a note explaining that Dr. Smith had insisted that he stay in Manhattan so they could finalize strategies for resolutions denouncing the Dred Scott decision and make plans for another Colored Men's convention in 1858.

Ottilie was deeply disappointed.

But she recovered. She understood that she had not sufficiently charmed him. One interview in the summer of 1856 and four weeks in the summer of 1857 was not enough time to fulfill her dreams of Frederick falling in love and taking her into his powerful arms. They were colleagues and friends, nothing more. She continued to yearn for him, but Frederick seemed afraid of her, as if he knew that lowering his guard would unleash a torrent of emotions sure to violate commandments. She was an admittedly impatient woman, but she could also bide her time when the prize was a man as vain as Frederick Douglass, who loved being loved.

74.

IN JANUARY 1858, JOHN Brown arrived without warning at Frederick's door. Gaunt and frizzled, he had aged. His hair was streaked with gray and combed harshly back, and his upper lip was twisted as if he had survived a stroke. "I need your help, Douglass," Brown said dispassionately.

He had spent almost the entire year crisscrossing the northeastern and midwestern United States begging for money and supplies, receiving more promises than cash from enthusiastic supporters. "Ralph Waldo Emerson said I'm a hero, a true hero," Brown reported, the pleasure of such praise brightening his eyes like polished glass.

"What's a true hero?" asked Frederick, frowning.

"A man who believes that it's better that a whole generation of men, women, and children should pass away by violent death than a word of either the Bible or the Declaration of Independence be violated in this country."

"Did Emerson say this?"

"No, he didn't. I did, but he agreed."

"How did it go, speaking to the Massachusetts legislature?" asked Frederick, deflecting.

Brown frowned. "You should know. They applauded, passed no resolutions, appropriated no money. And after that, I had to go into hiding. There were rumors the U.S. marshall was coming to arrest me for what happened in Kansas."

"What happened?" Frederick had heard rumors about the Pottawatomie Massacre.

"I have a constitution to write for a provisional government that will lead the slave rebellion. I will need at least three weeks and absolute privacy. I will not stay unless you allow me to pay board."

"Of course, you can stay, and you do not have to pay."

"I insist. Three dollars a week."

"Then it's three dollars a week."

"Good. Now we'll carry war into Africa if we must." Brown paused for a moment and then added, "I have only a short time to live—only one death to die."

"What?"

Brown said, "Cowards, all of them, nothing but cowards. The antislavery people in Lawrence just sat around watching those gangs come in and burn the town. I had to do something to prove that some of us weren't afraid, that slavers would pay."

"Pottawatomie, did you?" Frederick asked.

"That was decreed by God, ordained by eternity."

"Did you?"

"We were justified under the circumstances."

"Then you ordered those killings."

"My way was a restraining fear."

"Did you kill?"

"No," Brown said, never looking away. "I only shot old man Doyle in the head, after he was dead."

"I see," Frederick replied, disillusioned.

"But he deserved to die, like all the rest. And those deaths are nothing compared to the deaths of the slaves suffered every day. What of those? Who remembers those? Are five white slavers so important?" The five murdered men did not own a single slave, but Brown was fighting a just war. The innocent die in war. "Except for Owen and Salmon, my own boys acted like sniveling women. Frederick cried and just watched. Jason, with his damn abnormal conscience, wouldn't go, and John, Junior, refused to go to the Creek, argued with me, and told me to do nothing rash. And when we came back, John went to pieces, running out of the cabin and hiding in the brush like some dumb dog."

Frederick replied, "There are others who want to help, Captain Brown," who smiled at the reference to his military title as Frederick continued, "but they have misgivings about the raids, the cattle stealing, the. . ."

"The spoils of war, Douglass. As the Lord says in Deuteronomy, 'But the women, and little ones, and the cattle, and all that is in the city, even all the spoil thereof shall thou take unto thyself; and thou shall eat the spoil of thine enemies, which the Lord thy God has given thee.'" Frederick didn't respond, and Brown asked, "Do you have misgivings?"

"No."

"Too many whites are bigoted, weak. But your people, when given the call, will rise. I want you to help me arrange some meetings with colored leaders—when I give the word. Here are some names."

Brown pulled out of his pocket a small notebook and read the names of those he deemed the "military" abolitionists: Frederick Douglass, Henry Highland Garnet, Jermaine Loguen, Martin Delaney, Harriet Tubman, George T. Downing, and Reverend James Cloucester. "These are men," he concluded.

"There is one woman," Frederick observed.

"Yes," Brown admitted. "They call her Moses. Have you met her?"

"No, not yet. I hope she comes on the railroad. But in the meantime, I will do what I can, but you will have to talk to them directly. No reading of letters. You must stand in front of them."

"Good, good, good," Brown intoned. "I want the meeting to be at Chatham. I hear most Negroes who go to Canada live there."

"I'll see what can be done."

"Good. The Lord will provide. And after Chatham the arms of the wicked shall be broken." Brown quoted Psalms 37:17 often.

Anna was not consulted about Brown's extended stay, but she received the news with more irritation than anger. "He's strange, that one," she said.

Defensive, Frederick snapped, "He'll do what others . . ."

"Another white man to put your hopes in. He'll let you down like the rest of them. They'll not be what you want."

"What?"

"They're all the same, these white men, always older, with something you want they can't or won't give. Thomas Auld, Hugh, Captain Anthony, Mr. Garrison, now Brown."

"You don't know what you're talking about, and I won't have you talking about them. How dare you even put them all in the same group?"

"None of them will be what you want. None of them will be your father. Even Mr. Smith, a good man, can't be. Now it's Mr. Brown's turn. They ain't never goin' to be what you never had, and what you will *never* have. That's just the way it's goin' to be."

"This conversation is over. Prepare his room. He will have his meals in his room. He has letters to write and . . ."

"They all make you mean, these white folks, and some of them I don't want no more under my roof, but you will have your way. He's crazy, but at least Mr. Brown in willing to die for us. You and Mr. Brown and Mr. Garrison are all the same. You all kill in your own ways."

Frederick was so angry he didn't speak to Anna for a week and would not sleep in the same bed with her. After that, they exchanged few words but nothing more. It still rankled. They could tolerate each other's presence in the same room for appearance's sake, but they could not hide their lingering resentment from the children, who exchanged nervous glances at the dinner table.

Brown stayed in his room the first week writing letters and his "Provisional Constitution." Anna cooked meals and delivered food to him. By the second week, he joined the family for suppers. Anna set the table, served the food, and then left for the night, not returning even for prayers. Frederick and Rosetta led Bible readings in the parlor. Brown never asked about Anna's absence. Finally, his constitution was ready, and he read the entire document to Frederick, every line, every word.

The provisional government was patterned after the current U.S. government, with a few modifications, a one-house congress, a president and vice president, and a supreme court. The president, however, was not commander in chief, a separate position that would be appointed by the president, the vice president, the supreme court, and a majority in congress. The commander was the most important position in the government. Brown intended to be the commander. There were forty-eight articles. He made several provisions for the fair treatment of captives and their property, and he condemned profanity, fornication, rape of female prisoners, and desertion. He expected the strict observance of the Sabbath.

Brown's reading took hours, but Frederick never interrupted or asked a question until Article 46, which proclaimed that the flag of the provisional government "shall be the same that our fathers fought under in the Revolution."

"Why the same flag, Captain Brown?"

"We are all Americans. I don't want to overthrow any states or dissolve the Union. I want to abolish slavery and establish a nation of justice and racial equality under God," Brown replied.

"I see," was Frederick's response, irritating Brown. He wanted more than respectful silence and a single question. He wanted a glowing affirmation of his mighty work.

At the end of the evening, Brown was wide awake, energized by the prospect of absolute victory after slave uprisings that would include raids of plantations and enlisting bands of runaways throughout the Alleghany Mountains as he had envisioned in 1848. He said, "But this I say, my brother, the time is short."

"When?" asked Frederick.

"You'll find out soon enough. Remember Kansas."

"Pottawatomie?"

"Remember Kansas," Brown intoned, meaning to silence objections, inspire unfettered loyalty, and stoke blind faith.

Frederick stayed silent. He needed John Brown.

Brown left Rochester hoping to get money and weapons throughout the northeast, offering his reputation as "The Terror of Kansas" as credentials.

75.

THE SUMMER OF 1858 finally arrived, and Ottilie took her translation of *My Bondage and My Freedom* to Rochester. It proved her professional acumen, but more importantly, it would provide her the opportunity to read aloud to him his own words in German so he would know the beauty of the language of Schiller and Goethe. In a New York bookstore, Ottilie found a volume of well-translated Goethe, and she anticipated long evening conversations with Frederick about Faust, Egmont, Tasso, Iphigenie, and other heroic characters.

Ottilie worried about packing too many books, but she had to bring her two-volume set of the *Grimms' Fairy Tales*. She was sure the Douglass children would enjoy her reading them, translating them by sight in the parlor at night before they went to bed.

When Ottilie arrived on a sunny Saturday afternoon, the orchards were full of ripe pear trees. She had a family recipe to make preserves and to give to the Douglass family and guests. She also had small gifts all carefully wrapped for each member of the family, a cigar for Frederick, German candies for the children, and a newly invented kitchen utensil for Anna, an eggbeater with rotating parts.

When she stepped out of the hired carriage, the driver unloaded her two big cases that she could not carry on her own. Frederick's oldest sons came running out of the house and down the hill. What a difference a year makes, she thought, as they came toward her.

"Hello, Miss Assing, welcome back. We're here to help," said Lewis, smiling.

Before she could reply, they bounded up the hill with her bags. Ottilie paid the driver and walked up the hill. Frederick stood waiting on the porch. He was smiling as broadly as if her arrival had truly brightened his day.

He reached out with both hands, taking hers into his. "Welcome back, Ottilie. It's so good to see you. The family is waiting in the parlor to greet you, everyone except Anna. She's not feeling well."

"I'm sorry to hear this," she replied, relieved that she would not have to face Anna's scowling presence, hoping Frederick would draw her into his embrace.

He didn't.

"Come," he said.

"Wait," Ottilie replied.

"What's wrong?"

"Nothing. I have gifts for you and your family. I just want to make sure that's it all right with you."

"Of course, it's all right. What do you have for me?" Frederick grinned.

"It's a surprise, but I think you will like it. I'm sure you will like it. But Anna has strict rules for the children."

"Don't worry about that, not today."

"I don't want to be the cause . . ."

"Don't worry."

Frederick's five children assembled in two rows of chairs, the girls at the front, and the boys behind them. They sat perfectly still, with hands folded in laps, backs straight. As Frederick and Ottile stood before them, they greeted her individually, from the oldest to the youngest, "Good afternoon, Miss Assing."

"It's so good to see you all again, and I want to tell you all the things I want to do with you this summer. Last summer was all work, and this summer I will have so much more time when you are free from family chores and work at the office downtown, especially on the weekends." Ottilie hesitated, looking for approval from Frederick, even though she hadn't reviewed these details with him.

Frederick assured her. "Don't worry. I'm sure whatever you plan will be just fine."

Ottilie relaxed, straightened her back, and shared her plans: "I hope I can be a helpful guest, and we can have fun and learn many things, too. I can learn from you because I still don't know as much as I need to about your country. And I would love to tell you about mine, how I grew up, what it was like to be a child in Hamburg. I love stories, and I will tell as many as you're willing to hear. And I love to read, and I can read to you all kinds of books and stories—Dickens, James Fenimore Cooper, and I will tell you about Cinderella, Hansel and Gretel, Rumpelstiltskin, Sleeping Beauty, Snow White, Rapunzel, and so much more. I will read one each night. And you will tell me stories, too. We can play games. I love games, especially croquet, and we can also run around the garden, playing chase and hide and go seek. I can teach you more serious things because I'm also a tutor."

Frederick interrupted her warmly, "Now, Miss Assing, you will tire yourself out just talking about all you're going to do. You have over two months, besides."

"And for my German lessons I will give each of you, if you are interested, my undivided attention, separate sessions for each of you."

Annie applauded. "I'm so happy to learn more!"

"There's always something more, sweetheart," said Frederick. He clearly adored his youngest child.

His sons, now eighteen, sixteen, and fourteen, still unmoving in their chairs, now looked uncomfortable in their adolescent lumbering. She could see that they were curious, but they looked to their father for a signal to speak. Frederick was oblivious, more interested in his daughters. Ottilie engaged them, nonetheless. "If it's all right with your father, I want to hear from you boys what you want from me." She turned to Frederick, and he nodded his assent, indicating no displeasure for being put on the spot.

"Lewis, Frederick, and Charles, tell Miss Assing, one at a time, from the oldest to the youngest, one thing, and just one thing Miss Assing can do with you or for you."

"I don't know yet," said Lewis. "I'm sorry."

"I don't know yet," repeated Frederick, Junior.

Frederick frowned.

"I want to speak French," said Charles. "I want to speak French when I go into Canada. Do you speak French?"

"Yes, I do, and I can teach you words and phrases to tell you when you go. And Frederick and Lewis, you don't have to an answer right away or at all. You're almost grown men and you probably have better things to do than endure my going on and on." They seemed relieved and smiled. Both boys avoided their father's stern demeanor.

Frederick interrupted, "Now that's enough for one afternoon. You all can go and do what your mama wants. I'm sure she's told you, even from her sickbed. Go on, now."

Well trained, they left.

Ottilie observed, "They're so well behaved."

"That's their mother. I can't take the credit. They know what to do, and they also know if I tell her that I am not happy there will be consequences from her."

"I will be sure to tell her myself how well behaved they are."

"Be careful. She's not happy you're here, not after Julia Griffiths."

"Oh."

"You appreciate candor. It's best you know."

"I will cook with her, if she lets me. I will pick the fruit. I will clean and wash. I've had to live on my own. I know what it takes to do what needs to be done. This is a big house, and there is a lot to do."

"Even if she agrees, and I don't know if she will, she won't thank you. Her pride won't let her."

"She won't have to. It will be my way of saying thank you for letting me stay."

Frederick changed the subject. "Now sit down with me and let's talk about capital punishment. Murder is not the cure for murder, and lying and stealing will not cure lying and stealing. So, what do you think?"

Ottilie agreed with him, but even so, their discussion lasted for hours, the first of many to do so. As the summer went by, due to deep conversations with Frederick, readings and games with the children, songs and piano playing, picking fruit and cooking preserves with Anna, Ottilie had never been happier. For her, the Douglass house on the outskirts of Rochester became a special place.

76.

"YOU KNOW I'M WILLING to fight the good fight, but I need rest, too. I should enjoy time with my family, and I need your company too," Frederick told Ottilie one evening. "I'll return to the fray this fall, but now, I want to go to lectures, attend concerts, all with you."

Ottilie paused, and for the first time Frederick noticed her flush. She said, "I enjoy your company more than you can imagine. But this house is not a refuge for everyone. Rosetta wants to leave."

"She spoke to you?"

"Yes, she confides in me, too."

"I want her to be happy, but I don't want her to leave yet. You understand."

"I do. Even though I don't have children, I do understand."

"You are so good to mine. They love being around you; the games, the readings, the lessons, all of it. Without having children of your own, how did you know how to do what you do?"

"I took care of a family in Germany, the family of a great actor and his wife, also an actress. They had three children."

"I see. Then your future children will be fortunate."

Ottilie paused. She straightened her back, lifted her head, and declared evenly, "And that will never happen because the children I would want to have would be with a man who's already taken."

She departed. Frederick fell silent for a moment and wondered, *Who could be the man she loved?*

That night, he awakened with a jolt to his heart and sat up in bed. *Oh, my God. How can I be so blind, so stupid? She was talking about me!* But he knew he was not in love with her. He admired her. He loved her friendship and the time they spent together. He did not yearn for her, as he had yearned for Julia and that consummation that could never be. He had dreamed of it, and he had ached with pent-up desire.

Even though their relationship was not sexual, he and Julia shared an emotional and intellectual intimacy that he never had with anyone else. He always wanted to be with her, talk to her, hear her comments and questions. The very air they breathed in the office and in the parlor when no one else interrupted them seemed to fill them with an energy that, if not contained, could lift them from their chairs. As in the old spiritual, they could indeed fly. Love could make them fly.

Ottilie did not inspire these reactions. He was flattered, he was touched, and he was grateful for her companionship and the challenging intellectual stimulation that came with it. When he and Ottilie were out together at meetings and concerts or on walks, she gave him her undivided attention, as if every word spoken mattered. She didn't care that people stared or pointed at them as they passed by. In fact, she enjoyed it. "Isn't it wonderful that *we* excite their otherwise boring lives?"

Yet he struggled. He was a gentleman, a pillar of the community who could not risk his reputation, his standing in the community, or allow his recklessness to damage that community. He was the representative Negro, and if he fell, the ensuing white scorn would never end. But that was the reasoning that kept him from Julia. He loved her deeply and wanted to sleep with her but couldn't allow it. Now he regretted that decision. Having lost Julia, he would not repeat the mistake.

Ottilie was certainly not Anna, now growing fat, still refusing to learn how to read and write, no longer interested in sex. After Annie was born, Anna slowly withdrew from sex. Frederick was on the road for weeks at a time, but when he was home, they used to have sex at least once a week. Then it was once a month. Then months passed. And now, nothing.

At forty, Frederick was not ready for abstinence, seeing himself as a vigorous, passionate middle-aged man. He needed love, needed attention, needed fingers stroking his sweaty back. He wanted to hear the gasps and grunts of excitement, feel the moist inner space that had to be caressed and filled.

Why refrain? Why?

Frederick could summon all kinds of reasons, but he decided that he would not refrain with Ottilie. He would have Ottilie, a fascinating, provocative, attractive woman. Was he in love? Not yet, he decided, but for now attraction and infatuation were enough. He would go to her in Hoboken, leave his separate room near hers, tap on the door at night, take her into his arms, and lead her to her bed where she would submit to him, grateful that he had come to her at last.

Ottilie would keep their secret. Mrs. Marks would say nothing, even if she understood that a third room was a ploy for discreet, easy access to interracial delights. She had confessed to a room full of friends, including Ottilie and Frederick, "I don't care what people do behind closed doors, as long as they pay their rent on time."

★

Frederick returned to New York in late January and stayed at Mrs. Marks's boarding house. On that first night, a group of Ottilie's liberal friends, German and American, had gathered to show their support for Douglass. They talked about the Haitian Revolution, Nat Turner, and the European revolutions of 1848, but neither Frederick nor Ottilie mentioned John Brown or his plans.

On the second night, after giving a speech at the Shiloh Presbyterian Church, Frederick returned to Hoboken for a late dinner and conversation with Ottilie and Mrs. Marks, who excused herself early. Frederick and Ottilie continued talking in the downstairs parlor until they both agreed it was time to retire.

Frederick's heart was beating rapidly.

He knew intuitively that this was the night for tapping on Ottilie's door and taking her into his arms.

"Good night," he said softly, and took an oil lamp with him up to his room. He wondered if he should have waited and allowed her to go first, a simple courtesy expected of male guests. But he had to get out of the room. He was sure that she could detect his excitement.

Frederick waited for an hour, sitting in his night robe and long shirt. He blew out his lamp, went to the door, and looked out into the hallway. It was completely dark, and the chill of the January night gave him pause. But for only a moment. He stepped in the hallway and hurried to the door directly across from him and tapped gently.

As if she had been waiting, Ottilie immediately opened it, stepped aside to allow him entry, and placed her oil lamp on the table beside the bed. He looked for a place to put his lamp until she took his hand and led him to another small table near the window, maintaining a distance from it so their shadows could not be seen from below as he blew the lamp flame out.

Frederick looked to the other lamp, but Ottilie whispered, "No, I *must* see you."

Frederick pulled her into his arms. She lowered her hand to touch him and said only, "Oh." Surprise and delight in that single word.

Frederick held her head in both hands, searched her small eyes, shimmering from the light of the oil lamp. She was ready. Frederick told himself, *I must give her the pleasure she deserves after months of waiting. This night is hers more than mine.* He kissed her forehead, then both cheeks, brushed his lips against hers, luxuriating in the sweet taste.

"I love you," he lied. He wanted to thank her for being an important part of his life, and sex was his way of doing so. Frederick anticipated the pleasure of other nights, perhaps tomorrow, and certainly during future visits. He made a few decisions. No more denial of his needs, no more denial of sexual pleasure, no more worries about what people thought or whispered. His enemies were going to think ill of him anyway. His reputation was solid, and a secret could be maintained with two willing participants. He had to seize his remaining days. At forty, he was not getting any younger. Already there were streaks of gray in his mane of hair. He didn't feel old, but he was beginning to look old.

There was one more thing, truly important.

He and Ottilie could never be intimate in Rochester at his house on South Avenue.

Never, no matter how many summers she would be spending there.

Never.

77.

FREDERICK AND OTTILIE WERE visiting Gerrit Smith in Peterboro, and John Brown was on all their minds. Having fled to Kansas, he was back in the news.

"He's a brave man," said Ottilie at Smith's house, meeting Gerrit for the first time, that summer of 1859.

"Don't talk about him," said a skittish Smith, now wearing a long, gray beard. "It's too dangerous. We can't be too involved."

"But we *are* involved," protested Frederick. "We've given money, written letters . . ."

"I should have never agreed to anything, and writing letters was one of my most awful mistakes. We could die for this, and . . ."

"Nothing has happened, not here," interrupted Frederick with kindness and worry. His friend was known to get depressed and sick over trivial matters.

Smith's left leg shook. "He showed me those maps of the South, designations for operations in specific places like Augusta, Charleston, Washington, D.C., St. Augustine, and a place in Virginia called Harpers Ferry. They have federal arsenals or forts there. He said an attack at one of these would be *interesting*."

"*Interesting*?" quizzed Frederick. "That's what he told you? When I was in Detroit, he asked to see me and mentioned Harpers Ferry. I told him that I could not support any plan that included arsenals. Besides, he's too experienced in military matters to attack an arsenal!"

"He didn't say he would, but those eyes worried me. I could see destruction, even death. And he was smiling when he talked about the possibility. For a moment, I thought he was mad. And as you know, I'm familiar with madness, *too* familiar," Smith said.

Frederick and Ottilie turned to each other, more concerned about Gerrit's mental condition than Brown's. Thankfully, Gerrit's daughter, Elizabeth, now married, broke the tension when she entered the drawing room wearing a Bloomer outfit.

Elizabeth came forward, her hand extended to Ottilie's. "Miss Assing, I heard you were coming. I am thrilled to hear all about your travels, your adventures, everything you would be so gracious to tell me." She behaved as if her garment was unworthy of mention, although as she sat down she said, "I've just come in from a walk, and this makes for easier stepping, especially over rocks and other nuisances on a beautiful summer afternoon."

"I'm not quite ready to dress like a man," said Ottilie, smiling, trying to sound self-deprecating.

Elizabeth Miller touched her bosom with her hand, and without the slightest trace of offense, said, "Of my femininity, there is no doubt."

"But Baroque, eccentric appearances can only confuse those who doubt our equality."

Frederick frowned, and Ottilie could see the consternation in the faces of both men. Still smiling, Elizabeth asked, "Isn't that a problem for men to overcome, to see beyond appearance? Mrs. Stanton and Miss Anthony tell me . . ."

"I take issue with them because . . ." Ottilie said.

Gerrit stood, looking about. "Let's have some tea. It's hot, but tea cleanses the body and the spirit on even a hot summer afternoon."

When Frederick and Ottilie were at last alone, sitting on the veranda in the late afternoon as dinner was being prepared, Frederick rocked in his chair and said, "You don't have to push every conversation into being about you. I can't have you upsetting my friend. I know Gerrit likes you. He told me so. But there are limits when he's so fragile these days. Please keep your opinions to yourself for at least one day."

Ottilie was quiet as she looked out to the luxurious green lawn before them. She was unable to face him, trying to hide the hurt she felt. He had never rebuked her for speaking her mind. He had encouraged it. "I believe in the equality of men and women as you do, Frederick. But I can't abide the claims of Stanton and Anthony that women are morally superior and must channel our superiority to win our rights."

"That is not what Elizabeth said. She just happened to mention their names," Frederick said.

Ottilie took a breath before she replied. "You're right. I've read Stanton and Anthony, but I should not have reacted as I did. Elizabeth is a lovely person, and I need to watch my tongue in the house of one of your closest friends. I am sorry."

"That is not too much to ask."

"I will apologize."

"The matter will be closed when you apologize to her *after* you apologize to me."

Ottilie hesitated. Frederick sounded like other cruel men she had known who demanded subservience. She had heard the tone of her Uncle Karl, a martinet who financially supported her after her parents' deaths. "I'm sorry," she whispered.

Frederick stood, satisfied. He said with a broad smile, "Now, let's go back inside for some refreshment before dinner. I wonder what kind of berries Ann Smith is growing this season. She told me she had some seeds for Anna. Isn't that kind of her?"

Ottilie didn't answer as she turned to enter the house before Frederick.

★

Frederick's Detroit meeting with Brown had been more disturbing than he could admit to Ottilie or Gerrit Smith. Their relationship had almost been destroyed there.

President Buchanan had offered a $250 reward for Brown's capture, and the proslavery press, quiet for almost a year, was now hysterical again, denouncing him as a dangerous troublemaker and a thief of human property. Even some abolitionist newspapers condemned Brown's raid into Missouri.

But Brown was not deterred. He offered interviews to *New York Tribune* reporters and wrote a public letter about his exploits. His march to Canada with eleven fugitives had been accomplished in the open, and he was cheered in packed houses for the rescue.

Emboldened by such stories, Brown came to Detroit triumphant, expecting a warm reception from Negro leaders there. Knowing Frederick's schedule, Brown had asked him to come with some of "his colored friends."

When Frederick saw him for the first time in almost a year, he was startled by the deep lines in Brown's tanned face, the white hair no longer closely cropped but full and wild. He had a thick white moustache and a long white beard. Thin and slightly stooped to the left in his shoulders, Brown had aged, but his will had carried him across the country.

"Gentlemen, I have summoned you here for a mighty task, ordained by providence. The destruction of slavery is at hand. Will you help me?" Brown asked.

"*How* will you destroy slavery?" asked George de Baptiste, a large man who was a successful barber, baker, steamship steward, and Underground Railroad operator.

"By war, sir, with Black and white men tired of words," Brown said, unfazed. He described his plan for raids on plantations that would begin a chain reaction of slave escapes to the mountains. This was the Allegheny plan of ten years before. Brown ended his review with scripture, quoting Psalm 108:13, "Through God we shall do valiantly, for he it is that shall tread down our enemies."

The men listened intently, never interrupting, but as soon as Brown stopped, Baptiste objected, "Your proposal doesn't go far enough."

Startled momentarily, Brown asked with an undeniable chill in his voice, "Sir, do you have a better plan?" Brown was certain that Baptiste had nothing more to offer.

Baptiste continued, his words slow but distinct, like a teacher explaining a lesson, "I suggest that first we blow up fifteen large churches on a specified Sunday, signaling Blacks to leave the plantations and causing complete confusion with the white folks in the area."

Frederick and the others objected immediately.

Brown waited for the murmurs to die down, then he replied with solemn conviction, "Sir, I cannot participate in such a thing, for reasons of humanity. I don't wish to shed blood unless it is necessary, *absolutely* necessary."

Unappeased, Baptiste became sarcastic. "We are talking about war, are we not? And in war, blood must be shed. Consider Nat Turner. It was the blood he spilled that almost brought the Virginia General Assembly to its knees and abolished slavery."

"Sir, this is a holy war, a crusade, and there must be rules of engagement."

Baptiste replied, quoting Isaiah at his most chilling. "But thus saith the Lord. Even the captives of the mighty shall be taken away, and the prey of the terrible shall be delivered: for I will contend with him that contendeth with thee, and I will save thy children. And I will feed them that oppress thee with their own flesh; as they shall be drunken with their own blood, as with sweet wine."

No one stirred. The sound of divine, ruthless revenge had muted them all.

Brown turned to Frederick, "What do you think, Douglass?"

"I am against Baptiste's plan for the same reason you are, Captain Brown."

Brown nodded with a slight smile, but it immediately disappeared when Frederick continued, "But I am also unsatisfied with your original plan. There are too many problems that have not yet been resolved. There are too many opportunities for things to go wrong. There isn't enough preparation. How will the slaves get the guns? How will they get the news about the other escapes? Who will read the telegrams for those who can't read? What about provisions after they leave the plantations?"

No one moved. His friendship with Brown was well known, and it now seemed to rupture before everyone.

Brown's voice quavered with the sadness of deep hurt. He asked Frederick, "Sir, have you no courage?"

Frederick mustered absolute control of his voice and said with deliberate emphasis on each word, "Courage has nothing to do with this. Feasibility is the issue." The attack was personal, but Frederick was determined to keep their disagreement a matter of difference about tactics.

"*Feasibility*," Brown repeated with contempt.

"Yes, that has to be considered if you want success. I never see much use in fighting unless there is a reasonable probability of whipping somebody," Frederick replied.

"If you don't have courage, no plan will succeed, however *feasible*."

"My courage does not need demonstration, sir."

"I will be the judge of that!"

"Who do you think you are talking to?"

Baptiste intervened, stepping between the two men. "Gentlemen, gentlemen, there is no need to attack each other's character. There can be honest differences without this kind of . . ."

"Captain Brown doesn't recognize honest differences of opinion," declared Frederick. "There is only one opinion, *his*."

Another man pleaded, "Douglass, please."

Brown became indulgent. "My friend, you are indeed angry, but you don't realize what you're saying."

His patronizing tone made Frederick angrier. "I know exactly what I'm saying, Captain, and I also know I'm wasting my time talking to you, and that you're wasting your time talking to us. You are going to do what you want anyway, so why do you bother even coming here? We don't have to listen to you, work with you, or help you. We may choose to do all these things, but we don't have to, and you cannot compel us. We are not, and we will never be, soldiers under your command. That is why almost nobody of significance came to that meeting in Chatham you called for last year. Remember?"

Brown looked to the others, verifying whether Frederick had spoken for them all. They raised no objection to Frederick's passionate rejection. "We have nothing more to discuss," Brown said before stalking out of the house.

The men were quiet for a few minutes after his departure. Frederick experienced the regret of recognition. Once again, he had to fight another man who tried to control him, another man who wanted to help him and his people but demanded that he be compliant, subservient. He was not going to submit. He had submitted many times, for many legitimate reasons. But no more. Those days were done and done forever.

Baptiste finally spoke, "Douglass, what are you doing? We *need* him."

"But you opposed his plan."

"Yes, I opposed his plan, but not him, not *him*. Do you know any other white man who's willing to die to make us all free, a man who is not a man of just words, but deeds? I'm not sure he has all the answers as to how the changes should come, but he knows he must face death itself, and not flinch. I don't know anyone else like him these days. It will take a man like him to bring the slave system down, to strike fear in the hearts and minds of every white man in the land. He will make them afraid, and they should be afraid, very afraid. He is *our* Nat Turner. There is no one else," Baptiste said.

"What if he unleashes the whirlwind and we are all caught up in it?" Frederick asked.

"It will come. It's only a matter of time. It will come, and we need to be ready. Captain Brown is ready, and more of us need to be."

"Now is not the time."

Baptiste said, "It won't be up to us to decide that. When white people start killing each other, *that* will be the time."

★

Frederick regretted his argument with Brown and continued to raise money on his behalf, collecting small sums at various Black churches and lecture halls. He didn't offer details, but people were willing to give money for a grand if vague campaign to free slaves. The Missouri rescue on a much larger scale was a cause worth at least a few dollars.

Brown was now writing constantly, badgering supporters for more funds and weapons. There was a heightened sense of urgency in his requests, as if a major event in the war against slavery was imminent.

Ottilie's arrival that summer came as needed relief. Yes, they had a disagreement in Peterboro, but they had managed to move beyond it and continued to talk for long hours, take walks along the river, attend concerts and lectures, and work together in the office. She was an excellent editor, even though English was her second language, and reviewed his articles with the same scrupulous eye she gave to translation. Like him, she loved words, and her celebration of their power was inexhaustible. They read poems and plays for hours, searching for meaning, and asking questions. "They're more important than the answers," she once declared.

For one who acted as if she had all the answers, this was an odd, if not hypocritical, assertion, and Frederick challenged her. "Really? Coming from you, of all people? Really?" Enchanted by her sense of humor, honesty, and intellectual curiosity, he wanted to believe he was falling in love.

The dialogue would continue long into the night, at home and at the office. As the days passed, he could also feel the tension rising in him. He wanted to feel her skin, to kiss her breasts, to luxuriate in the contours of her mouth.

He would keep his promise. They would not have sex at the house. But there was the office, and it was customary for Frederick to remain in the office long after his sons and the other workers had gone for the day. He had stayed in the office after hours with Julia so often that now no one seemed to notice or care that Ottilie stayed after hours as well. Even Anna didn't bother to comment about the arrangement.

They were in the office late one night when Frederick looked up from his pencil-marked copy and said to Ottilie, who sat across from him on the other side of the desk, as Julia had, "I *need* you now."

There was a sofa on the other side of the room. He had slept there many nights when he decided it was more convenient to remain in the office until the morning to continue working.

Saying nothing, he led Ottilie by the hand to the sofa. She followed without a word, then sat down and looked at him, waiting for a signal. Frederick leaned over and lightly kissed her lips. Their bodies jolted by an undeniable impulse, they frantically groped at buttons and stays, lifting cloth, pushing and pulling away impediments. He opened his trousers. She pulled at her crinoline, stepped out of it, then lowered her laced pantaloons to her knees and fell back against the sofa, her eyes pleading with him to hurry.

Afterward, Frederick lifted his body off the couch and began dressing, his back turned. Ottilie stood, and Frederick heard the light rustle of crinoline, wondering about the inconvenience of wide, flounced skirts. *That Bloomer outfit would make things easier*, he thought, amused. He crossed the room to his desk and waited for Ottilie to finish dressing and return to her desk. Then they resumed their editing at the exact spot they had left it.

Until the end of her stay in early October, he would, at least once a week, wait until the office was closed and the staff had gone home, and take Ottilie by the hand, crossing the room to the sofa.

Frederick was enjoying himself. Even so, these were not the best of times, and he continued to worry about John Brown and the gross incompetence of President Buchanan and his administration. But he would not deny the joys of that summer of 1859. He was a freer man, a guiltless adulterer.

But a glorious summer must end, and this one was ended by the distant hand of John Brown, who sent his oldest son, John, Jr., to Frederick's house. At thirty-eight, John, Jr., didn't look like his father, having instead a wide face and heavy jaw. His neck was thick like a tree stump, and his hair was curly, not straight. He also didn't have the self-possession of his father. Sitting across from Frederick, John, Jr. said, "My father wants to give you something."

He reached into his satchel and pulled out a hand-written copy of the Provisional Constitution. Frederick already had his own copy, after Brown had allowed him to make one. But this document was written in Brown's own hand. Frederick stared at the small handwriting, unable to read some lines. The parchment was thick and heavy, expensive, and carefully crafted, a precious gift.

John, Jr., inquired nervously, "Is anything wrong?"

"Oh no, nothing's wrong," Frederick replied, conflicted. *Was this a gift, a peace offering, or a bribe?*

The son confirmed Frederick's suspicion. The gift had conditions. "He wants you to come and see him."

"Oh, when and where?"

"August nineteenth in Pennsylvania, near a town called Chambersburg."

"Why there?"

"I'm not free to tell you. He'll explain."

Brown's penchant for secrecy always annoyed Frederick, and he revealed that annoyance now, "What is the urgency, after all?"

"The time is short."

"Short for what?"

"Sir?"

"Does your father plan to strike now, or in September, or October?"

"I don't know."

"Will the captain answer all my questions if I come?"

"If? You have to come!"

Frederick relented, not wanting more trouble for this anxious messenger. "You can tell your father I'll be there."

The son smiled. His father had never smiled so broadly. In fact, Frederick could not remember the last time he saw Brown's teeth. His jaw was clenched most of the time.

"How will I find him?"

"You're to go the barbershop of a Mr. Watson in town. He'll direct you."

"On August nineteenth, correct?"

"Thank you. There is one more thing I forget to tell you."

"Yes?"

"Father wants you to bring that colored man you know."

"Who?"

"Shields Green."

Puzzled, Frederick said, "But the captain only saw Green once here, way back in January of last year. I doubt that three words passed between them." Green was a fugitive from South Carolina whom Frederick had hired to help with the house and yard now that the boys were in school or at the office. He shrugged his shoulders, wondering why Brown wanted Green.

"Isn't Green your friend, the man Father wants to come with you?"

"Yes, but . . ."

"He insisted, and you know how he is. Once he makes up his mind about something, there's no turning back."

78.

BROWN HAD EXCLAIMED BEFORE the New England Anti-Slavery Society in Boston, "Talk! Talk! Talk! That will never free the slaves. What's needed is action." He repeated the last word, a pointed emphasis: "Action!"

Now it was time to tell his eighteen recruits, gathered at a farmhouse in northern Maryland, about his planned assault on the arsenal at Harpers Ferry, five miles to the south.

Most of them knew Brown. Three were his sons; two were neighbors from North Elba, where his wife and other children now lived; and the rest had joined him in Kansas or Iowa. They were all white men under thirty, who revealed a wide range of qualities and temperaments. But they all shared an abiding hatred for slavery and believed in the mission of waging war to destroy it.

Brown had a new Secretary of War, John Henry Kagi, a twenty-four-year-old teacher, who was the only one who knew exactly what Brown planned to do. The rest assumed the Virginia mission would start small as the guerillas took groups of freed slaves into the mountains, followed by a stampede of local outbreaks as the news spread.

"Gentlemen, there has been a change in plans for the start of our holy war," Brown announced as he stood in the crowded main room of the farmhouse. His tone was casual, as if he announced a change in the weather. "The federal arsenal at Harpers Ferry will be our first and primary target. We will seize the town and its weapons before we begin freeing slaves and taking them into the mountains."

There was stunned silence for a moment, then his three sons raised the loudest objections. Having lived in the area for several months, scouting and spying, they were familiar with the entire layout of the town between two rivers and the strategic placement of the arsenal on the heights.

"You can't be serious!" exclaimed Watson, the twenty-four-year-old who left his wife and son at the family farm in North Elba. Like Brown's other sons, he had been raised to be obedient and respectful, but in the past few years he had rarely seen his father and had remained in New York during the Kansas wars.

"Father, no," said Oliver, the youngest of the sons. He had fought with his father in Kansas and had come with his seventeen-year-old wife to reduce suspicion by giving the impression they were new tenants at the farmhouse with frequent visitors.

The second oldest, Owen, had also fought with his father in Kansas, and was now the bluntest. "This will be like Napoleon's march to Moscow. We know how that ended."

More men nodded their heads and muttered agreement. The chorus of rebellion grew louder. Another Kansas veteran shouted, "I'll be damned. I'll be Goddamned."

Brown stood before the agitated and confused group as the men tried to absorb his announcement.

Kagi broke his silence, "I stand with the captain. I have talked with many of the locals. They're antislavery, and I'm sure they will rise with us when the time comes."

Brown declared, without a trace of anger or disappointment, "Then I will resign, since so many of you oppose me, and you should appoint another commander." He waited and didn't move. The air in the crowded room was dense with heat and tension. Brown stared one by one at his men. This was a test of loyalty, and he thought he knew his sons and the other men. They would not abandon him now at this crucial moment, when they were about to fulfil their very destinies under *his* leadership to the end.

Kagi called for a show of hands. "Who will go with the captain?" he asked, raising his own. Then began the show of hands one by one at first, then small groups of two and three until Brown had unanimous support.

Owen wanted assurances.

His father had to agree that the railroad bridges to the town had to be burned to prevent anyone coming to its defense. And he would have to accept a letter from the men about the condition of his continued leadership. Owen volunteered to write it.

"Very well," Brown replied, indulging his red-haired third son, the one who always stood his ground, a confident boy who often spoke back and never cried out under the lash despite Brown's Old Testament discipline.

Brown found himself more forgiving, more willing to compromise with imperfect men, especially his sons, relatives, and neighbors who came to Virginia to sacrifice their lives for the only cause that mattered. Potential death had paradoxically softened him, for he was comforted by their shared connection, a brotherhood of men about to face the ultimate Judge, even as they hardened their bodies and hearts, preparing to storm a federal arsenal.

The demanded letter read:

Dear Sir,

We have all agreed to sustain your decisions, until you have *proved incompetent,* and many of us will adhere to your decisions as long as you will."

Your friend, Owen Smith

Owen had been using Smith as an alias since arriving there weeks before.

Brown read the letter twice, folded it, and put it in the chest pocket of his jacket without comment. The letter merited none. Their loyal obedience was all that mattered.

Brown needed at least two or three Black recruits to show his war was founded on the principal of racial equality. Unlike most abolitionists, he had visited the homes of Negroes and invited them into his home as well. He had never subscribed to the assumption that Blacks could not and would not fight. In fact, he believed the sin of slavery could not be eradicated without Blacks fighting for their own liberation. "Give a slave a pike and you make him a man. Deprive him of the means of resistance, and you keep him down."

Brown had high hopes that John Anthony Copeland, a free man who attended Oberlin College in Ohio, would soon join the raid. He also wanted Shields Green, that taciturn but agreeable young man who worked hard for Frederick Douglass.

But most importantly, Brown needed Douglass to be an active participant in his holy war, fighting with him at his side. The symbolism alone would persuade the cautious and inspire fighters white and Black.

John, Jr., had assured his father of Douglass's arrival, a day connected to pre-scheduled lectures nearby. Nevertheless, Brown now paced the floor of the Kennedy Farmhouse, waiting for his meeting.

Frederick came to Brown at the abandoned granite quarry west of Chambersburg on August 19. The sky was a dirty sheet of gray, and the dark clouds seemed ready to release a drenching rain. The wind rattled Frederick's tailored coat, and he pulled the sides close to his body. At the entrance stood three armed guards who pointed to Brown below, saying not a word.

Frederick sat down on a rock and said lightly, "Well, Captain, the citizens of Chambersburg were surprised to see me, wondering why I would come unannounced to their town. But I gave a speech to justify my being here."

They shook hands.

Brown frowned and said, "I'm here to pick up two hundred Sharps combines, two hundred revolvers, and a thousand pikes."

"I'm reminded, Captain, of the time when you came before the Convention of '55 and asked for money to buy arms for the fight in Kansas. You had that same look. I remember how impressed we all were by your reading of your son's letter and that last line, 'We need arms more than we do bread.'"

Brown smiled for the first time and reached out to pat Frederick on the shoulder. "Now it's you, Frederick, who we need more than bread," he said affectionately.

Frederick shifted uncomfortably on the rocks, "How?"

Brown wasn't ready to answer directly and instead passed Frederick a deeply creased piece of paper, a letter from Charles Robinson, the head of the Kansas Free State Party. It read:

"Captain John Brown:

"My dear Sir, I take this opportunity to express my sincere gratification that the late report that you were among the killed at the Battle of Osawatomie is incorrect. Your course, so far as I have been informed, has been such as to merit the highest praise from every patriot, and I cheerfully accord to you my heartfelt thanks for your prompt, efficient and timely action against the invaders of our rights and the murderers of our citizens. History will give you a proud place on your pages, and posterity will pay homage to your heroism in the cause of God and humanity."

"I don't understand this. How will you free the slaves, now that you are out of Kansas?" Frederick asked.

Brown felt slighted. "I'm not prepared to die alone."

"Who are your new friends?"

"Kansas still needs me," said Brown, deliberately ignoring the question. "A fugitive there tried a rebellion with only scythes and hoes. They need guns, and I'm here to get as many as I can. The mountain plan will no longer work. Something big must get the slaves' attention all at once. The best way is to attack the arsenal at Harpers Ferry and occupy it for a few hours. That will be the signal for the final battle to begin."

"Harpers Ferry? The federal arsenal?"

"Yes. After capturing it, we'll cross the Potomac, and after attracting all the slaves who will join us, we'll return to my hiding place on a farm in the Maryland mountains."

"This is impossible! You're going to attack government property with a handful of men. All of you will be wiped out. Freeing the slaves is one thing, but this—this makes no sense. You cannot do this."

"We can do it, and we will, and there's no turning back."

"How can you succeed? You'll be going into a perfect steel trap there between those two rivers. You'll be surrounded at once. Escape will be impossible."

"No. A small group can fend off a much larger force. Besides, the arsenal is guarded by civilian watchmen in a town with no interest in politics."

"But you are in slave country, in the very middle of it. Slave owners could form an army against you in an hour!"

"Even some of the whites there will join us. The poor whites there want to form a separate state in that mountain area. Even the Governor of Virginia said that he has a greater fear of a poor white rebellion," Brown replied.

"Sir, it is not just the state of Virginia you have to worry about. The whole country will attack you if you attack a federal arsenal. You'll be waging war against the United States," Frederick argued.

"What's happened, Douglass? You never objected before all this time. You knew that."

"I agreed to your earlier plan, to free slaves and then hide them in the mountains before smuggling them north to freedom."

"They will need guns."

"But not from an arsenal. That arsenal is there for a reason. It's hard to get to, and all they will have to do is close those bridges and cut you off."

"If we must, then we'll take prisoners, hostages, and with them we'll bargain our way out."

"Virginia won't care about you or your hostages. They'll kill you all rather than let you hold Harpers Ferry. Don't you see that?"

"I see that the slaves have to know that we mean business, that we have come."

"How will they know? Have you warned them about the attack and made arrangements?"

"They will know, they will hear."

"Captain Brown, this is rash, unwise . . . *wild*."

For the first time, Shields Green stirred and frowned at the man who gave him shelter in Rochester. Frederick pressed on: "There were problems with the other plan, but it had a chance for success, at least a chance. Return to that plan. I'm willing to be a part of something that might succeed, but *this*?"

"This will rouse the nation. The sparks will fly," Brown insisted.

"They'll destroy you."

"I said before: I'm ready to die."

"What good will there be in death?"

Brown rose. "Come with me to Harpers Ferry, Douglass."

Frederick shook his head. "No. I'm going to England instead, on a lecture tour. Didn't you know this?"

"Douglass, this is the great mission of my life. I know it is. God has prepared me for this moment. Kansas was nothing, this is everything."

Frederick shrank a bit, taken aback. He asked, "Do your supporters in Boston know about this?"

"They don't want to know specific details. They're just willing to support the idea of an assault on slavery," Brown answered.

"Then you didn't trust any of us."

"No, I wanted to make sure I had the support I needed so that when I told you, you could see the chances for success."

"But if they don't know now . . ."

"They will come."

"And what if they don't? I saw friends in New York and Philadelphia before coming here. Some of the same people were at Chatham, and they said that they weren't going to participate in whatever you planned, no matter what it is."

Brown flinched but put his arm around Frederick. "Then you come with me, Frederick. I need you. I'll defend you with my life. Imagine what we can do together. When I strike, the bees will swarm, and you'll hive them. Come with me, please." He repeated the word "please," his soft, urgent voice violating his Calvinistic standards of behavior.

"No, I can't. I just can't. Your plan won't work. It can't work."

Brown's arm fell heavily to the side. For a moment he felt a deep sadness, but he recovered his composure, and asked, "Then what about Green?"

Frederick turned around and asked his companion, "What do you want?"

Green looked to each man, and quietly replied, "I believe I'll go with de old man."

Frederick turned to face Brown and said, "Farewell."

He walked away, cautiously finding his way over the rocks. Brown watched him climb to the top of the old quarry, and quoted a favorite hymn, a dart from his heart to Frederick's:

"Happy is the man who hears. Why should we start and fear to die? With songs and honors sounding loud." He watched Frederick disappear, the sun had sunk close to the horizon, and Brown accepted that his friend was a coward after all.

"Goodbye, my friend," Brown whispered. "Goodbye."

79.

ON OCTOBER 17, THE *Philadelphia Evening Bulletin* carried a telegram from Baltimore about rumors of a slave insurrection in Virginia the day before. Frederick's heart sank, fearing Brown's death and the disaster that could fall on the Negro community once it was known that abolitionists had supported

Brown with money and arms. Innocent people could be arrested or hanged, as they were after Nat Turner's revolt almost thirty years before.

He didn't fear for himself so much. He never kept his relationship to Brown a secret, publishing his letters from Kansas in his newspaper, renamed the *Douglass Weekly*, and writing editorials in response to them. There was no direct link between him and Harpers Ferry. He was invited but rejected the offer without equivocation.

Furthermore, he was the most well-known and respected Negro in the country, a self-made, respectable, middle-class Negro with close ties to the white and Negro communities. He was safe, he believed---as safe as a free Negro could be in 1859.

Frederick decided to go about his business and gave his scheduled lecture on "The Self-Made Man" on the evening of October 18 at National Hall on Market Street in Philadelphia. He spoke for two hours before a crowded room of whites and Blacks. He had given this talk many times before, trying to give young Black men hope, encouraging them to not accept the shackles of their condition, insisting that they strive and become the best that they could be.

As he spoke, Frederick could still feel the force of Brown's unspoken questions, which pounded the back of his head behind his right eye and gave him a headache he tried to ignore. *Am I coward? Who is the greater man, one who gives his life in a futile battle, or one who wisely ignores the battle to continue the struggle in print and on the stage? Who am I, and what have I become?*

He faced these questions the next morning as he opened an elegantly written note from Amanda Auld Sears, the daughter of his former master, Thomas Auld, now married to a coal merchant in Philadelphia. "Dear Mr. Douglass, I heard you last night at National Hall, and would like to see you again after all these years, if it is at all possible. Please come to my husband's office and arrange a visit. Thank you."

He was incredulous. Amanda Auld had reached out to a former slave who had struggled beside her trying to make life bearable in the unbearable home of her stepmother Rowena. He remembered Amanda's gentle soul and inability to protect herself when Rowena waged war around her.

The sights and sounds of Baltimore and the Eastern Shore, along with the familiar faces from that time, filled him with innumerable questions and renewed a deep longing to get final answers. *Where was his oldest sister, Eliza? What happened to the rest of his family, his brother Perry, his other sisters? And Gram Betty? Was Aaron Anthony his father and Lucretia Auld his sister? Could he be an uncle to Amanda Sears? Had his white family finally come to terms with his existence? Were they ready, at last, to accept him?*

Frederick needed to validate his past beyond his own memory. As the years passed, he could recall less and less. Details blurred and mistakes became more obvious. A comparison of the *Narrative* and *My Bondage and My Freedom* revealed discrepancies. Which book was truer, the one closer to the events, or the more specific second account?

But there was a more disturbing fear: Once he was dead, the only evidence of his life would exist in two books and some printed speeches. This was not enough. He needed hard evidence and he saw Amanda Sears as opening the door to some final answers.

He dressed quickly the morning of October 19 and hurried to the Sears's office, standing tall and proud, to show that he had become more than Rowena Hambleton Auld could ever imagine. But John Sears was not happy to see Frederick and did not want to talk with him at all.

"But, sir, your wife . . ." Frederick said.

"She did this without my consent or knowledge," Sears replied.

"But she came to my lecture."

"I was not there."

Frederick felt pleased. He left St. Michaels before he knew the outcome of Rowena's campaign to crush Amanda, but apparently it had failed because Amanda was not a weak woman. Maybe she had learned a few lessons from him and Eliza?

Frederick insisted, "Please, Mr. Sears, allow me to see your wife. She asked me to come to you first. We have a history that . . ."

Sears reddened. "Speak not to me of *your* history. In them you dared to viciously attack my father-in-law, who treated you well, much better than most. He sent you to Baltimore and gave you a chance when he could have sent you to Mississippi instead. And all he received from you was ingratitude and mockery throughout the world in books and lectures. And he still mentions you in his letters. Why should I make it easy for you to see his family and get more stories for your lectures?"

"But he was Amanda's father and . . ."

"How dare you use my wife's Christian name!"

"I meant no offense, sir. But Mrs. Sears, nevertheless, wants to see me."

"That is her folly, but she is a good woman and doesn't ask for much. I will agree on one condition."

"Anything you ask, sir."

"You will not write or give a speech about the meeting with Mrs. Sears."

"Agreed. Then you will allow me to call on her?"

Sears stared at him for a few moments and turned to scribble on a sheet of paper that he thrusted toward Frederick.

The note gave the address. John Sears said, "Come at noon tomorrow. She won't have all day."

"Thank you, Mr. Sears," said Frederick, offering a handshake.

"She will not be alone," Sears replied, refusing to take it.

"Of course."

Married women could receive gentleman callers without chaperones, but Frederick understood that his color would require a chaperone's presence. On the following day, he was startled to enter a parlor filled with people, all white and openly curious.

A Black servant opened the door and retreated to the back of the house, leaving Frederick to look around the large room, scanning the faces for Amanda. Which one was she? What did she look like after all these years?

Then he saw her standing with a small group before the fireplace. He recognized her at once. She looked the same as she did in St. Michaels, like her mother, pale and thin with an understated beauty, her smile brightening her blue eyes and auburn hair. Amanda stepped forward, both hands extended to greet him. "Oh, Mr. Douglass, how good of you to come."

Frederick smiled, abashed by the warmth of her courtesy. "No, Mrs. Sears, it was your gift to invite me."

"I hope you don't mind that I have invited some friends. They all wanted to meet you. They all agree with me that slavery is a terrible wrong. Come, let me introduce you." She took him around the room, introducing him with words of praise for his accomplishments since the old days. Frederick was amiable, and answered all inquiries, however redundant, with great patience.

They were most interested in hearing about the controversy with Garrison and Frederick's move toward political abolition. What did he think of the Republican party now that it would have a candidate for the presidential election? Would the South give up slavery peacefully if an antislavery president was elected? What did he think of Abraham Lincoln?

Frederick was not interested in Amanda's guests. He wanted to talk to her about the old days, alone. He saw his opening when she said, "Oh, Mr. Douglass, I most appreciated what you said about my mother in your books. She had a tender heart and tried to do her best, even though her father had slaves. I told Father I would be seeing you."

"If we could have a few moments to talk," Frederick replied.

Amanda smiled and led him to a divan near the front window. When she sat down, her broad hooped skirt, now the fashion rage, covered almost the entire seat. She nodded toward the small space remaining where Frederick was to sit. "We should not avoid our friends for too long, but I understand that you might not consider me a friend, and . . ." she said.

Excited, Frederick cut her off. "Can you tell me anything about my family? Where are they? My sister Eliza, my brother Perry? Are there any records?"

Amanda maintained her poise, revealing no sign of offense. "I'm afraid, Mr. Douglass, that I can't tell you very much. Your family belonged—please forgive me for using this word to describe the situation—to my father, and whatever records there are about your family are with him in St. Michaels. Like you, I had to leave there. I could not live around slavery."

"I'll be satisfied with what little details you may recall, anything," Frederick persisted.

"It's been some time, but I know there are many Baileys still in St. Michaels. Your sister married and had several . . ."

"She's alright then. Is she still a . . ." He could not say the word "slave." It seemed profane now, even though he never shirked from using it when needed.

Amanda replied, "After your second book was published, Father made a point of writing to tell me what he did for you and your sister."

"I remember your father selling Eliza to her husband, Peter Mitchell, a free man," Frederick said.

"She's free, Mr. Douglass. Father said she worked off the money some time ago. He was pleased by selling her to her husband because that virtually made her free, too."

Frederick frowned. This was the kind of reasoning that infuriated him about Thomas Auld. Nothing he did was open and honest. He was still a hypocrite, seeing charity in the selling of another human being, using technicalities to keep his grip on the Bailey family. He ignored the fact that if Thomas had freed Eliza outright, she would have had to leave the state according to state law.

Amanda added, "I make no excuses for him."

"I'm not here to criticize, madam. Please believe me."

"Sir, I know that, and you've demonstrated your generosity by coming today, and not blaming me for what he did."

"But I could never blame you. You too had a difficult time, in a different way," Frederick said.

"Father has followed your career most closely. We all have."

What was she saying? That he was more important than just another slave who happened to escape? That Frederick was part of Auld's family? "I appreciate that, but is there more to tell, surely," he countered gently.

"I'm sorry, Mr. Douglass, there's not much more that I can tell you. One day you'll have to go to the Eastern Shore yourself and get the full story. Maybe one day you and Father . . ."

"I will never go back until . . ."

"That day will come soon. It has to come, Mr. Douglass. What did Mr. Lincoln say, 'a house divided against itself cannot stand'?"

"There will be war, then, like in Kansas."

Amanda stood, "Oh, Mr. Douglass, let's not ruin the day with more talk of war and rebellion, or John Brown or any of that. Today was meant as a kind of celebration. Let's return to our guests, who all came to see you because you're Frederick Douglass."

"I meant no offense."

She smiled sweetly. "If anyone has a right to be offended, it's you, Mr. Douglass. When I think of what my family did to you and your family, I am amazed that you were willing to come here at all. You honor us by coming, and I don't want to continue the Auld tradition of taking offense at you for speaking out when you had to."

"You are, indeed, like your mother, "Frederick said.

"The memories are fading, but your books help. Come, let me share you with the others again. This is a rare opportunity. Do you realize how famous you are?"

Before he could answer, they were back in the center of the room, where Frederick stood proudly as the object of curiosity and admiration in the house of one of the Aulds.

He was blissfully unaware that he was under arrest.

80.

THAT SAME AFTERNOON, WHILE Frederick was talking with Amanda Sears, James Hurn, a telegraph operator on the other side of town in Philadelphia, took down a message coming from Washington, D.C. When he was done, he quietly exclaimed, "Oh, my God" and immediately knew what he had to do.

The telegram had directed the sheriff of Philadelphia County to arrest Frederick Douglass for his complicity in the attack on Harpers Ferry. It said letters were found with John Brown that proved Frederick's involvement.

Hurn had a bright future, according to his supervisor. But he was also an abolitionist who admired Douglass. And now Douglass was in trouble. Hurn could warn him about the telegram and withhold delivery for as long as possible, maybe two or three hours. Give Douglass time to get out of town and escape arrest, return home, and reach safety somewhere. *Where was Douglass staying? Who was that Negro who organized the meeting at National Hall? What was his name? Thomas Dorsey. That's it: Thomas J. Dorsey, who owns that catering business.*

Hurn hoped that he could find Dorsey and Douglass quickly. The Negro community in Philadelphia was close and tightly organized. Everyone seemed to know everyone. Certainly, everyone knew Frederick Douglass. No one wanted to see him arrested by the governor of Virginia with the help of President Buchanan. *May they both rot in hell.* He put the piece of paper in his coat pocket and looked around to the other two desks in the office.

The other operators were sitting and waiting for more transmissions. And his supervisor, Mr. Trotter, was in his own office either reading the paper or eating, his two favorite pastimes.

"Mr. Trotter, I must deliver a message," Hurn said.

Trotter obliged, without lifting his head.

Within an hour, he found Dorsey's house and pounded on the door. "Please let me in. I have an urgent message. It's a matter of life and death. Please."

"What's going on here, young man?" Dorsey asked.

Hurn reached for the paper. "I have a telegram. Please, you've got to show this to Mr. Douglass. I know he's staying here. He's in great danger. I work in the telegraph office."

Dorsey let him in, taking the telegram from his hand at once and reading it as he stepped away from the door.

"Frederick! Frederick! You have to leave. We must get you out of here," Dorsey called out.

Frederick quickly appeared, hurrying down the stairs and entering the parlor, where Dorsey showed him the telegram. Hurn was struck by the size of the man he admired and by the fact that he was standing not more than three feet away from him.

"This young man got that telegram from Washington."

"It just came in. I can keep it for about three hours before I have to deliver it to the sheriff. It came on my line. I don't know what would have happened if it had come to one of the others."

Frederick stepped forward with his hand extended. "Thank you, young man. You turned luck to my advantage. I will always be grateful."

"Thank you, sir." But then Hurn added, "I need to get back, not raise suspicions. No one will know when it came. I can't destroy the telegram. I would lose my job. But no one would know when it came."

"You're taking a great risk, young man," said Frederick.

"No greater risk than you have, sir." Hurn departed.

Dorsey said, "We must get you to the Walnut Street Wharf and the ferry to Camden."

"I'll pack quickly."

The immensity of the news hit Frederick. He was under arrest for treason. They would put him in jail and find a reason to kill him before a trial. He would never have a chance for justice in Virginia. He had no rights in federal court anyway. He thought bitterly of the Dred Scott decision and fixated on the possible incriminating evidence.

What did they find? Did Brown bring letters to Harpers Ferry? Were they found with him when the troops stormed the arsenal? If so, why did he not destroy them before he was captured? Is Brown trying to take revenge on me for not coming with him?

His mind spiraled off into wild speculations. Fear gripped his stomach, but he tried to stay calm. He had to think clearly. *How will I tell Anna and the children? How can I protect them? What about the papers in my desk, especially my letters from Brown over the years, and a draft of Brown's constitution for a new government?*

"Hurry. We don't have much time," said Dorsey unnecessarily. "I'll get my neighbor Mr. Turner to help."

Soon the three men were on their way to the Walnut Street Wharf, with Turner quickly driving the carriage through crowded streets. The men said little as they scanned the crowded streets for policemen or bounty hunters. Frederick could hear his heart and taste bitterness in his throat. He was sweating profusely. *I'll hang if they catch me. They'll hang us all.*

It was all too clear. Nothing infuriated white men more than the thought that he could escape their justice. Nothing else mattered: not fame, reputation, connections, achievements. He was the scapegoat who had to pay.

When they arrived at the ferry landing, Dorsey said, "Goodbye, Frederick, and good luck. I can't wait around. You understand."

Turner, the tall Black neighbor, said, "I'll stay."

"Thank you," said Frederick, too stunned by Dorsey's quick departure to say more.

"Stay calm," said Turner. "Get quickly out of Camden. Take the train to New York."

"They could arrest me on a train to New York. I'll take the steamer. It will be slow, slow enough for the news to reach New York. A train has too many stops, too many times for the police to come on board and take me. I'll be trapped."

"Then how will you get home from New York?"

"I don't know. A train to Rochester will also be a trap."

"You must have friends in New York. They'll figure out a way."

Frederick purchased a ticket and boarded the ferry for Camden, where he would board the steamer for New York. He had to wait for another half hour before departure. Frederick paced the deck, keeping his eye on the streets, anticipating the sudden appearance of a mob calling out his name.

"All aboard! Last call! All aboard!"

He was off to Camden, close, and yet far away.

Upon arriving in Camden, Frederick quickly boarded the steamer for New York. As he expected, the steamer was painfully slow, and he worried every second of the trip.

He had to get out of New York. Frederick rushed to the Barclay Street Ferry and crossed the Hudson River to Hoboken. He hurried on foot to Ottilie's boarding house late that night. When he knocked on the door, Ottilie took him into her arms. "Oh, Frederick, you're safe. Come in. Mrs. Marks and I have been waiting ever since we heard the news. But Mrs. Marks finally went to bed."

Ottilie had bad news: the New York papers, especially the *Herald*, had printed a letter from Douglass to Brown that seemed to prove his complicity in the raid. Editorials denounced him as a traitor and called for Frederick's arrest.

"They found a satchel in the house where he was staying before the raid. He had letters from everybody, Mr. Smith, you, Theodore Parker, and others. And the *Herald* printed most of them. Here's your printed letter," she said.

Frederick read the letter dated December 7: "My dear Captain Brown, I am very busy at home. Will you please come up with my son Frederick and take a mouthful with me?"

Frederick slapped the *Herald* with the back of his right hand, "I wrote this *two* years ago. Leave it to the *Herald* to omit the date. This proves nothing, certainly not a conspiracy to go to Harpers Ferry."

"But Mr. Smith is not so lucky," Ottilie replied. "The *Herald* printed a letter dated June fourth. He calls Brown a dear friend and promises him two hundred dollars. And it gets worse."

There were details of Brown's activities with Smith, Samuel Howe, Theodore Parker, Higginson, and two others—meetings, donations, references to rebellion and slave governments, all provided by Hugh Forbes, his disgruntled former secretary of war, who abandoned Brown when his financial supporters would not give him money to bring his wife to America. The *Herald* righteously proclaimed: "Enough it seems has been ascertained to justify a requisition from Governor Wise of Virginia, upon Governor Morgan of New York, for the delivery over to hands of justice of Gerrit Smith and Frederick Douglass, as parties implicated in the crime of murder and as accessories before the fact."

Frederick grabbed Ottilie's arm. "You have to send a telegram to Rochester for me. Brown's papers are in my desk, a constitution and other pieces sure to incriminate me. There's a telegraph operator at home, a Mr. Blackall. I trust him. He can get a message to Lewis to secure all the papers in my high desk in the study. But I can't go back to the city."

"No, you shouldn't even take the train in Jersey City. We'll borrow a carriage and drive to Paterson. From there you can go north, west of the Hudson. Fewer people, less news."

"Everyone knows."

"And many will help. I didn't come all the way from Germany to let the president of the United States take you away from me. What I think doesn't matter. You must get home, and then decide what to do. Your wife and children need you, and you must get some rest."

"Ottilie . . ."

"Your room is ready. I will get to the telegraph station first thing in the morning. Here are some of the other newspapers you can read. The country is going mad."

She left, leaving Frederick to sit and read the accounts on the raid and its aftermath. He doubted he could sleep. From a quick scanning, he learned that Brown was still alive, but his sons Watson and Oliver were dead, as was John Kagi.

There was so much to absorb, the details providing some distraction. Nevertheless, he could not subdue the low but steady pounding of his heart and only deep intakes of breath deflected the rising panic that could make him cry out, terrified.

Frederick finally retired for the night. He tossed and turned, dozing off now and then, but never relaxing into sleep. On the following morning, Ottilie went to the telegraph office with Frederick's message and returned with a carriage to get Frederick to Paterson.

Before he boarded the train on the Erie Railroad line, one not usually taken to Rochester, Ottilie said, "Remember this. They're more afraid than you are. Wise, Buchanan, Chief Justice Taney, and all the rest, they know there will be other John Browns, more Harpers Ferries. Slavery is *finished*."

"I wish I could be so sure," Frederick whispered, holding her hands.

"Not today, but soon. You must be around to see it, my friend, so do what you have to do, even if it means leaving the country, going to Canada."

"I can't leave! This is my home. My family."

"Take them with you."

"No, no, no, once I get back home and take care of my affairs, my papers, and maintain the necessary contacts, everything will be fine. I'm sure of it. There will be no need to leave, to go to Canada. Goodbye, Ottilie. And thank you for everything."

"I'll do anything for you."

★

Back in Rochester, Frederick went immediately to his house. Anna and the children gathered in the parlor. The children had been trained by Anna to show no fear, but they could not hide it. Anna's fear could be heard in her hollow, exhausted voice, "What are you going to do?"

"My desk. Lewis, you got the message and did . . ."

Lewis interrupted him for the first time in his life, "Yes, Papa. I had to force it open. It left . . . a mark, I'm sorry."

"Don't worry, son. You did what had to be done. Where are the papers?"

"In a box that I buried in the yard. They can't find them there."

"Get them for me. They're important, but I couldn't have them taken while I was trying to get here."

"Why did he leave them papers? Why did he do it, leave them papers so that peoples could find them?" Anna implored, having learned the news through Rosetta and Lewis.

After hours of speculation, Frederick was sure he understood Brown's motive. Brown wasn't careless or vindictive, leaving letters to ensure that if he failed others would hang with him. Instead, he anticipated a hurried entrance into the arsenal, a triumphant exit, a swift outbreak of slave rebellions, the collapse of federal authority in the area, and the sudden emergence of his provisional government. The proof of his esteemed participants and their supporters would be in the hundreds of letters.

Frederick replied, "There's nothing we can do about that now. We'll have to wait and see. Just wait."

"Wait," Anna repeated. She turned to Annie, who now wailed, "Papa, Papa, I'm afraid. Are they coming to take you?"

Rosetta held Annie, wrapping her arms around her waist and gripping her hand. Tears were in Annie's eyes as she tried to be brave for her father, but she could not hold her emotions in check. She pressed her small body forward, still restrained by Rosetta, "Are you going to die?"

Frederick rushed to her, embracing her with his head beside hers. "No, sweetheart. They are not going to do that. I'm safe. We're all safe."

"Then why are Rosetta and Mama crying?"

"She's just worried. That's all. Now that I'm home, we'll make everything better. We just need to wait and see."

"Yes," Anna said, "We'll has to see. Amy Post said there's lots of talk, but so far there's nothing to it. Now you all need to let your father rest. It's been so long, and he needs his rest. Rosetta, please help get Annie ready for bed, and you boys need to do whatever your father needs, like Lewis did. I'm proud of you, Lewis."

Lewis beamed. It was probably the first compliment he had ever received from his mother.

"Yes, Lewis, I'm proud, too," Frederick said. "Now let's get some rest." He went to his separate bedroom. He had no expectation that he and Anna would share a bed, even on a night such as this. He and Ottilie had departed together just three weeks before, and Anna had ignored them for days at a time. When they left, Anna didn't bother to say goodbye to either of them.

The next morning, Anna placed mush on the table for breakfast. "What are we going to do?" Fear wobbled her voice.

"I don't know. I really don't know," Frederick answered.

On October 22, Amy and Isaac Post came to the house with a letter from William Still of Philadelphia, a Negro active in the Underground Railroad. He had addressed the letter to Amy Post for fear of writing Frederick's name on anything. This letter could not be intercepted.

Frederick respected William Still and pondered his words carefully: "Dear Frederick: You must leave the country for Canada secretly and at once." Still explained: the federal government was convinced that Brown was part of a national conspiracy that included prominent white men in the northeast. Three of them had already fled to Canada, and others now faced arrest. If whites were not immune, then a Negro could be arrested and killed long before a trial. "You are not safe in your own land, Frederick, and you must leave for your own good," Still declared.

Frederick looked up from the letter and said to Anna and the Posts, "It's time to go. I'll pack a bag, and I'll take the ferry."

"We'll take you to the landing below the falls," said Isaac.

Frederick turned to Anna. "I'll tell the children. I must do this. Bring them here."

The boys were stoic and stood awkwardly before their father, not knowing what to do with their bony hands.

Frederick suddenly regretted the missed opportunities to get close to them.

"Boys, you take care of your sisters."

"Yes, Papa."

Annie would especially need them. Distraught, she pleaded, "Take me with you. I'll be good. I promise. Don't go, Papa." Anna and Rosetta had to take her from the room, her arms flailing like a puppet with tangled strings. Anna returned and told Amy and Isaac that she needed to be alone with Frederick.

They replied, "Of course," and went to their carriage.

When they were alone, Anna said, "I won't go down to the wharf. Annie needs me here. The boys need me, too, though they won't admit it. I'll stay. It's easier. This way I can make it into just another one of your trips. There have been many. This is just one more, with more to come." As usual, she was determined to take care of what she could control, manage the household, provide security during a crisis. Anna's path was clear, even if Frederick's future was uncertain.

Frederick told her the truth. "Canada may not be safe enough. I could be kidnapped. England might be safer."

Anna reached for his hand, and said tenderly, "And each time you crossed, it got better for you. You didn't know it then, but it did."

He pressed her hand in his, and embraced her, holding her close for the first time in months. "Oh, Anna, you always had hope, believed."

"I can't help myself. It's you, Frederick, *you*."

"Nothing will keep me away for long."

"I know," Anna replied, kissing him on the cheek.

"I'll come back. This is our house, our home. This is my country, too, and yours. We belong here."

"I know."

"I'm crossing another deep river," he said, referring to one of his favorite songs, whose words about crossing the river Jordan to safety and peace in the promised land had consoled him as a child. But now he insisted, "Home is *not* over Jordan. It's *here*." His voice cracked on that last word because Frederick felt the inescapable pull to Rochester, to his America, to home.

Anna repeated: "I know."

81.

FREDERICK LEFT CANADA FOR speaking engagements in England planned before Harpers Ferry. But he had a more pressing reason for leaving. The Posts and other friends had verified that the United States government meant to send agents into Canada to arrest and return him, ignoring Canada's sovereign right to protect a fugitive now deemed a traitor. Only the Atlantic Ocean and British law could protect him now.

On November 10, he boarded the *Nova Scotian* in Quebec for Liverpool. During the fourteen-day trip, the endless ocean rose and fell, making mountains that collapsed into foam and engulfing waves. At night, the starless gray sky joined the sea and the steamer seemed like a piece of wood drifting for a moment before disappearing in the vast, indifferent expanse.

Finally, he landed in Liverpool, taking comfort in being on solid earth while simultaneously dreading the return voyage that he would have to endure one day. Hopefully soon, after John Brown was dead, after Governor Wise and President Buchanan had other crises to manage, after his name was no longer in the paper every day.

Now he was in Newcastle with Julia and her husband and would be a guest in their house until the end of January, when he would start his tour; enough time to discuss all the current issues, review the latest news in the English and American press, and talk about the past, carefully.

Reverend Crofts was a slight man with narrow, stooped shoulders, and a shallow chest. He was a pale creature, squinting through round spectacles sitting on the long nose of his pasty white face. But he had a strong, resonant voice, as deep as any Frederick had heard on the river or stage, as if nature had compensated him for his short stature. Crofts listened with undivided attention, never interrupting, always waiting until it was clear that others had finished.

Frederick wanted to dislike him but couldn't. Julia was fortunate to have Henry Crofts as her husband. After dinner and two hours of conversation that first day, Crofts gently pressed Julia's hand before rising and said, "You two have much to talk about without me. You were friends and partners in America, and a marriage can never change that. Good night, Mr. Douglass, and come up when you're ready, Julia. Don't stay up too late, although I know that late night talks were the usual in Rochester. There is so much to do tomorrow."

He left, leaving them sitting quietly in the warm glow of the late evening fire. Frederick and Julia avoided each other's eyes.

"He admires you very much," Julia spoke first.

"He's a good man," Frederick replied. He turned to the window, unable to think of what to say next. The howling wind and snow distracted him for a few, needed moments. He decided to be honest, and added, "But I'm still jealous."

Julia pressed her hands together, and said firmly, "I do love him."

"I believe you."

Her eyes flashed. "I don't need your absolution."

"Then why did you need to make a declaration?"

"You know why. The past is past. We cannot return . . ."

"To Peterboro."

She shook her head and raised her hand to stop him. "Don't mention that place ever again if we're to remain friends. Don't."

"I'm sorry."

"You can stay only if you do not try to make me say something I will regret."

"How can I make you? Four years is a long time, and there can be no obligation. You're married, and so am I."

"Yes. But I cannot love you as I loved you, and I will not be disloyal now."

"I understand."

She gave a wan smile and lifted her bosom as if relieved of a burden. "Now it's done. We can move on."

"Can it be that simple?"

"It will have to be. I will break no more hearts. Henry is upstairs, waiting for me, trusting me. How can I not honor him?"

Frederick bowed his head. "I am a fool."

"You're selfish, and so am I. I will have both of you in my own way."

"Then I am a fortunate man."

"I will always be your friend, and true friends are rarer than husbands and wives."

"And to be cherished even more." Frederick rose slowly, his body heavy from mutton, potatoes, bread, and false hope. He said lightly, "This will be a wonderful Christmas, indeed."

"Not as good as a Christmas with your children."

He froze as if she had slapped him in the face. "You still see it as your duty to remind me of reality." He tried to not sound harsh, but resentment was in his voice.

Julia approached him, her eyes suggesting deep tenderness. "Yes," she replied, gently touching his cheek with the palm of her hand. "Those who love you should. Who else is there to do the difficult work?"

Frederick closed his eyes, luxuriating in the softness of her hand, trying to permanently imprint her touch. He sensed that it would be the last of its kind.

"I will never touch you this way again," Julia said.

"I love you," he said softly.

Her hand fell away. "Do not ever say that again. And if you do, I will ask you to leave, and I will refuse to see you as long as I live."

He took a deep breath. He wanted her to remain in his life, and he would ensure that future by conceding to her wishes. "I promise."

"As your friend, I will always love you. Good night."

He stood motionless, and said, looking at her as she crossed the room, "Good night."

Julia Griffiths Crofts was still a remarkable woman, and he was truly fortunate to have such a friend.

English abolitionists, riveted by the news from America, gathered in parlors throughout the land to read newspapers, journals, and letters from their American friends, and speculate about the future. John Brown was going to die on December 2, and between his trial and execution a restless anticipation of martyrdom seemed to make some Americans impatient, as if they feared that Brown would receive a reprieve and deprive his admirers of a "glorious death."

Henry David Thoreau complained, "I almost fear to hear of his deliverance, doubting if a prolonged life, if any life, can do as much good as his death."

"It's easier to celebrate death when it's not yours," said Julia in the drawing room with Henry and Frederick.

"I'm sure the judge regrets giving Brown so much time between the verdict and the execution," observed Frederick, holding the *London Times* in his hands. "Captain Brown has certainly made the most of the opportunity. He has a *new* reputation after the trial and his last speech, and after all those published letters and interviews. He couldn't organize a rebellion, but he knows how to prepare for the gallows."

82.

WHILE HE WAS IN Glasgow, the letter from Rosetta trembled in his hand. Her words, tender and yet harsh in their young adult brevity, became a blur of gray lines as tears filled his eyes. Annie had died.

He couldn't believe the news. Just that December, Annie had written a short note proudly telling him that she was a good student, its words reflecting the charm and vibrancy of her character. In a recent letter, Charles had remarked how much he enjoyed the company of his younger sister, who was not "tense and serious, like Rosetta."

Frederick dropped Rosetta's letter, the anguish and despair weakened his fingers and legs, forcing him to sink to his knees and double over, his arms across his midsection to keep from crying out like a wounded bull. But his grip failed, and a deep cry rose from his gut and weakened his clenched teeth and jaw. It started as a low moan and ended in a raw protest about the injustice of God and his own impotence: "No!"

If he had been there, he could have patted Annie's head, told her stories to pass the time, and held her in his arms. He could have stopped the course of the illness, obtained proper medical treatment, carried her off to a safe, secure place beyond the reach of whatever had attacked her frail body.

If he had been there.

Now he was angry at everything that had separated him from Annie: the federal government, slavery, John Brown, his own fear, and the flight to Canada. He had failed her as a father, and he cursed himself. She was dead and there was nothing he could do about it.

Frederick struggled to remember happier times with Annie—their strolls in the woods, the games in the parlor, the snow fights, the songs during other Christmases, the bedtime tales, her simple smile that beguiled him.

He lifted his head and inhaled deeply. He had to go home, get back to his family. He rose to his feet, vowing to be a better father and husband, to never cross the ocean and leave his family again. He didn't care that he was still under threat of arrest, that the Mason Congressional Investigating Committee was still deliberating, that arrest warrants were issued to four men, including John Brown, Jr., who refused to testify.

After returning to Newcastle to say goodbye to the Crofts, Frederick returned to America, arriving in Rochester on April 11 numbed by grief and guilt, and yet relieved to learn he was no longer facing arrest. The Mason committee had dropped Frederick's charges as a pressing matter. The government was no longer interested in creating more martyrs.

The boys rejoiced at his return, but they lost interest when he asked questions about Annie. After the required mourning period, they no longer dressed in black and had adjusted to her absence by resuming the rituals of their daily lives. They wanted Frederick to tell them stories about England or play games, not talk about Annie and a funeral. She was five years younger than Charles, and after the novelty of a new baby had worn off, the boys had ignored her.

Rosetta confessed that her loneliness was difficult to describe, but she explained to her father that she missed her sister and could not console her mother.

Anna was thinner and her eyes failed to deliver the usual cold, harsh assessments that made the children quake and immediately shut their mouths. Her frailty shocked Frederick, who believed that Anna would be the pillar of strength through it all. But grief had eaten her up.

She told the story of Annie's death with no emotion, no sighs or ringing of hands: Annie became sick in January. The doctor could find no reason for it. In March, she was gone. After her brief account, Anna picked up the Bible, which she still could not read, from the stand beside her, stroked it once, and said, "The Lord giveth, and the Lord taketh away, blessed be the name of . . ."

Frederick snapped, "Don't say that!"

She continued, unintimidated, "Blessed be the name of the Lord."

"I will not bless Him for taking her."

"This is my way."

"His way is what I won't accept."

"You were not here."

"Does that make you better, being here to see it?"

"If I could trade places, I would. You don't have them days to remember."

"Did she blame me for leaving her, for not coming when she wanted me?"

"Yes, she blamed you. She was a child, and her daddy was far away, unable to comfort her."

Frederick started, "She couldn't understand, near the end with that fever and all."

Anna stood. She said scornfully, "Why must I make it easier for you now, make it less ugly than it was? Death ain't pretty, you know that, and killing my child is the ugliest thing that anybody can do, and even the Lord has some answerin' to do when I meet Him. Do you want me to lie to you about everything?"

"It wasn't my fault that I wasn't there."

"I didn't say it was your fault. My baby is dead. Annie's gone . . . Dead, and the Lord is punishing me. He is punishing me by taking my baby."

"But Anna, what are you talking about? You said that the Lord took her and . . ."

Anna continued, her voice shaking, "She loved you more than me, her own mother, and I was always with her, beside her every day, and she loved you more, and sometimes I didn't want her with me, near me for just one evil minute, always crying, always pleading for you, and de Lord heard my wish, and took her. He gave me what I wanted, what I wanted when I had my evil thought. He's punishin' me. Why didn't he take me instead? Why? Why?"

"Anna, you don't know what you're saying," he said. He went to her and touched her arm, resisting the impulse to embrace her, finding no signal from her that she wanted him to do that. "You're just upset. You don't believe what you're saying."

Her strong faith in God's benevolence returned, and she fell back in her chair. She asserted with ferocity: "No, the Lord is good, and there is a good reason for this, a good reason, and it will come to us to know in His good time, if he so wills that we know, and if we never know, there is somethin' in that, too. No, there is some good in what happened to my Annie, and I will wait for my Lord. I will wait for . . . my . . . Lord."

He stepped away, leaving her to commune with a personal God he now rejected. That God was still the Lord of creation. History rolled out, revealing his grand designs, and Frederick was still sure that the end of slavery was an element of His plan. But as surely as the sun rose each day, the Lord God was indifferent to the pleas of his creation. If He heard Anna and Annie at all, He did not intervene to relieve their anguish, to stop the pain, to suspend the pace of inevitable decline and eventual death. All powerful, He could have suspended time itself, *but why should He*? And if He were to intervene for Annie Douglass, why did He not intervene for Augustus Bailey, his uncle who died as a child, or for the many other children killed and abandoned? Why did Annie Douglass deserve a special dispensation, a mercy the Lord withheld from others?

Because she was the daughter of Frederick Douglass?

Frederick knew this to be an absurdity.

He had achieved much, but even his reputation could not move the Almighty to make an exception, and Frederick did not believe that God existed to serve him, to be at his beck and call like a divine servant or heavenly bellhop.

Frederick settled for a different answer.

We are as insignificant in His eyes, as ants are to ours. We are born, we eat, we reproduce, we struggle, we die, and the world rolls on. Occasionally, he spoke through his prophets and son.

Occasionally.

It all made sense now.

God was the creator and nothing more.

He was not a friend, a succorer, a confidant.

He was only power, just as Job had said long ago.

Frederick could accept and respect raw power. But he would not love it, seek its advice, or whisper pleas or endearments. As earthquakes and storms did not care about his feelings, it was time to stop hoping that the Lord would. In fact, He never did.

Frederick admitted all this to Ottilie in a letter, and she sent him a copy of Ludwig Feuerbach's *The Essence of Christianity,* a translation by George Eliot found in a New York bookstore. "When I come to Rochester this summer," she scribbled in a brief note accompanying it, "we have so much to discuss."

83.

OTTILIE STILL FRETTED ABOUT revealing her atheism to Frederick. Over the years, she had alluded to it, and now she had sent the Feuerbach book as an indication of her position, but she had never declared her rejection of God's existence. Frederick's most recent letter after Annie's death had eased her mind somewhat. He had not rejected the existence of God, only the existence of a personal one. That was a good start. *Maybe I should just leave it there. After all, does it really matter?*

But Ottilie could not resist her missionary zeal. His belief was the last barrier between them. Their love was intimate and deep, but the removal of this last barrier, this one obstacle, would perfect their relationship. At the very least, she had to be honest and confess what she had believed since she was an adolescent. True love required this.

When they were at last alone that July, they embraced in the parlor of Frederick's house.

"A thank you note is never as a good as a direct expression of the heart," Frederick said. He stepped away and looked at her directly. "I will always appreciate what you did. It was selfless, truly loving."

"I would die for you."

"Oh, Ottilie, you're a woman of such passionate extremes. Your death will not be necessary."

It was clearly a gentle joke; nonetheless, Ottilie stepped away, offended. "I was being honest."

"I know that."

"I must always be honest."

"About everything?"

The moment had come. She would tell the truth about what she believed about God. "I'm an atheist. I always have been." She waited and looked at his face for a reaction. She expected the beginning of a heated debate, argument and counterargument, then resolution, *her* resolution.

His face remained kind, without that withering glare he casted upon intellectual foes. "I'm not surprised. I always suspected as much, and the arrival of the book sealed the assumption. But surely you know it doesn't matter to me."

"But it does matter to me."

"Why? We don't have to agree."

"True love requires consensus on fundamental values, shared beliefs."

"Who says?"

Ottilie paused. She knew there was one thing she could never share with Frederick: her attempted suicide as an adolescent. Finally, she replied, "I do."

Frederick maintained his distance, and Ottilie could see his anger, subdued though it was. "I will respect your opinion, and I will seek to understand it, but you *dare* to ask me, *require* me, to abandon the faith of my family and my mother and grandmother, a faith that kept me going when I had nothing else to sustain me? Yes, I have changed, and, yes, I no longer believe as I once believed. My path is not unique. There are many others who have concluded that God is a minimalist, a creator who leaves it to us to create our own lives and make our own world. I have read Jefferson and Franklin, Theodore Parker, Voltaire, Thomas Paine, and Feuerbach, too. I agree that the God praised in most churches is a projection of our own needs and desires, a creature of our own vain imaginings, and we have enlisted him to justify all kinds of horrors and cruelties; and the churches that have been built in His name have oppressed, and continue to oppress through the centuries as its members sing, cruel in its irony, about a loving, just God. I have released myself from the shackles of any gospel that requires my intellectual and emotional enslavement, and I said years ago that I would welcome infidelity, atheism, welcome anything in preference to any gospels preached by any man who demands my subservience. But for *you* to insist that I *cannot* acknowledge that there is a force greater than ourselves, that it moves the universe in mysterious, unfathomable ways, that I must put *all* my hopes in small, petty men and women who cannot see beyond their ambitions, greed, and selfish desires, I will not, not even for *you*."

Ottilie had not experienced such a rebuke since adolescence, when her uncle slapped her. She said, "I am *not* a child. I do not deserve to be treated in this way by you, or anyone."

"You *declared* the conditions of our disagreement. I am not asking you to agree with me, only understand. Why can't you do the same? And, please, do not deflect the course of an honest disagreement of opinion by shifting the issue to how I am *treating* you. You've insisted on the primacy of the message over the messenger often enough."

"I will leave tomorrow."

"No, you won't. You can never resist a good fight, a true battle of mind and heart. You still think you can convince me to change my mind, if not today, tomorrow, or the next day, or next month. Be honest."

"I can be persuasive," Ottilie confessed.

"Then we should enjoy the journey, not the end. If we claim to reach it, then we stop growing. Isn't that death?"

"What about heaven?"

"Let's stay with the living, please. We can know nothing about heaven, since no one has come back to confirm its existence."

"Then I have something else to tell you."

"What is it?"

"I'm applying for American citizenship. I want to be an American, like you. Will you sign the certificate?"

Frederick took her into his arms again. "Oh, Ottilie, this is great news. I will proudly sign the certificate."

She would not tell him that she saw her application as another kind of marriage vow, a permanent token of her affiliation with him and the land of his birth. After her announcement, Ottilie ached for its consummation on the office sofa. Months had passed since they had been intimate. Harpers Ferry, Frederick's exile, and Annie's death had made that impossible.

But now surely enough time had elapsed.

Ottilie pressed both hands against his cheeks and looked to him for a signal. He gently pulled her hands away, stepped back, and whispered, "No, it's still too soon. I will not kiss you in this house, and when we go to the office I will not go to the sofa. Please understand."

"I have waited this long. I can wait more if you will have me."

"There's no doubt. We have the memory of Hoboken."

Ottilie took his hands. "Yes, there's always Hoboken."

By the last week in August, they waited no longer and that sofa was theirs to enjoy again.

★

With Frederick driving his carriage, they went to city hall to sign the application for Ottilie's American citizenship.

It was a beautiful summer day. A gentle breeze stirred the trees.

"Are you sure you want to do this? You're entering a burning house, you know?"

They had followed the collapse of the Democratic Party that July. A faction known as the Southern Democrats nominated Stephen Douglas of Illinois for president after breaking off from the Democrats of the north, who nominated John C. Breckenridge of Kentucky. As author of the Kansas–Nebraska Act, Douglas still supported the right of citizens to decide on the expansion of slavery. Like most Southerners, Breckenridge insisted that the federal government had no right to limit slavery's expansion and warned that with the May nomination of Abraham Lincoln, a Republican committed to restricting slavery, the very survival of the South was at stake. Already, there were threats of secession and war if Lincoln was elected.

"It's our house and it will survive. Mr. Lincoln will save the Union."

"I was for Senator Seward," Ottilie responded. "He's a true abolitionist. Lincoln is not. I don't trust him, and I suspect that he will sell your people out to save the Union. He's already promised to allow slavery in the South. That's his platform, that's the Republican platform."

"Mr. Lincoln said that a house divided against itself cannot stand, that it cannot endure permanently half slave and half free."

"Yes, but he said that when he was running for the U.S. Senate. It was easy enough for him to say that to an audience in Illinois. No, I don't trust him," said Ottilie.

"I think that speech helped him get nominated. Even if Mr. Lincoln can't be trusted, I know that Southerners are taking him at his word. They know he wants to destroy slavery in due time. And that's the problem, in *due* time," Frederick exclaimed. "How long will we have to wait? How many of us will have to remain slaves before white people say we can't be the land of the free with slavery, too? How long?"

"Not too long. Southerners are *ready* to fight."

"He will appease them," said Frederick, his voice deep with agitated anger. His hands gripped the reigns. "He knows that white people will never fight a war to free us. As long as the war is about the Union and not about us, they will fight, but if it ever becomes about us, then he will hear their message loud and clear: 'I'm not giving my life or sending my sons to die for niggers.'"

Ottilie was struck by his use of that word. She was sure he had never said "nigger" in conversation with her. She kept her eyes on the road. "If

Southerners secede, they will all become traitors, and that will be enough for most of us."

"That will not be enough for me, but it pleases me to hear you say 'us.' You *have* become an American."

"Despite the German accent."

"Just one of many others. Isn't it amazing that we can be one nation with so many different peoples, that you and I can both be Americans?"

"Yes, and that's an idea worth fighting for," said Ottilie. At first, her application for citizenship was only a personal transaction, another way to bond with the man she loved. But now she sensed a deeper connection as a member of a broad community of people sharing similar ideas in a political and cultural family. The European revolutions of 1848 had failed to achieve what the revolution of 1776 had achieved: the creation of a new nation that welcomed everyone. Indeed, America had redefined the meaning of family. It was the broadest, most expansive family in the history of the world. No wonder millions were coming to its shores. This was a nation that had to survive.

She would do her part, enlist as a citizen and explain her new country to the old for as long as possible. It needed allies.

When they arrived at City Hall, people still turned to take notice of them, even though they were a common sight in town during the summers when they shopped together and attended various events. Inside, the quick turns, the side glances, and the whispering continued. But Ottilie also noted the tips of the hats, the respectful nods, the occasional, "Mr. Douglass," "Good day, Mr. Douglass," and "Good morning, sir." No one acknowledged Ottilie or spoke to her. She was invisible, as if recognizing her existence would verify their worst fears.

"Ottilie, are you ready?" Frederick asked.

"Yes, yes," she reached in her small purse for the papers she had brought with her from New York. She only needed the signature of another citizen in the presence of a local official to finalize the application process. She hesitated, her hand with the pen poised above the document.

"Is there anything wrong?" Frederick asked.

"No, no. This is a momentous step, a happy occasion."

"Then even more reason to sign quickly."

The clerk asked, "Do you wish for me to mail it, Miss Assing?"

"No. I will take it with me back to New York. It will be in safe keeping. Thank you for offering."

"It's my pleasure, Miss Assing. And good day to you, Mr. Douglass."

They walked out of the building into bright sunlight, and Ottilie turned to Frederick and asked, "And when will I be able to vote as a citizen? When will that time come?"

Frederick stopped, and as if he had been prepared for this inquiry, answered, "After white men decide that Black men won't have to pay two hundred and fifty dollars to vote. That's when."

A referendum to reverse this requirement was before New York state voters in November.

"Women should be able to vote," Ottilie replied.

"You know I agree, but first steps first."

"But . . ."

Frederick raised his hand. "Please, let's not argue about this, not today. I'm already in trouble with Elizabeth Stanton and Susan B. Anthony, who insist that women and Blacks should get the vote together. But today we should only be happy."

"Yes. We should savor this day, for I'm afraid there won't be many others."

84.

OTTILIE RETURNED TO NEW York in late September, and Frederick returned to the lecture circuit as the presidential election hurled toward its climatic last days. The more Frederick followed the campaign, the more he didn't trust Abraham Lincoln. Like most politicians, Lincoln said what he needed to gain votes, often catering to the prejudices of white voters, proving he was not an abolitionist, always confirming that whites were superior to Blacks. He was on the record as far back as the Lincoln–Douglas debates a few years before.

Even so, Lincoln was the best hope for a political solution to destroy the reach of slavers now controlling the White House and Congress. Frederick wrote for his *Monthly,* "The slaveholders know that the day of their power is over when a Republican president is elected."

Lincoln's election would enrage Southerners and drive them to extreme measures like secession and war. Politically, this would destroy slavery. Frederick was convinced of this. But he hesitated to give Lincoln his vote, revealing the prevarications and inconsistencies that frustrated his friends and delighted his enemies, opening himself again to charges of hypocrisy, deception, or gross stupidity.

For more than ten years since meeting Gerrit Smith, Frederick recognized that only politicians through their political parties could end slavery. But no party was sufficient to the task, not even the Liberty Party, whose platform under the guidance of Gerrit Smith was a pure abolition platform, could do the job. It never received enough votes to make any difference.

Frederick tried to find his way through this political morass. But for a man of principals, for any man who hoped to wield political power for good, this was a sorry, frustrating spectacle that required voters to hold their noses, vote, and hope for the best.

He continued to believe that a vote should be a moral decision that best reflected consistency with principal. He could justify voting for the Republican William Seward, who opposed Lincoln for the nomination, but after Lincoln won the nomination, Frederick still couldn't cast his ballot for him. Finally, he gave his vote to Gerrit Smith, a man who could never be president, a man who was not even on the official ballot.

Lincoln's victory was decisive, even though he did not win the majority of the popular vote. Between the four candidates, Lincoln won 180 electoral votes to a paltry seventy-two for Breckenridge, an embarrassing thirty-nine for John Bell of the Constitutional Union Party, and a mere twelve for Stephen Douglas.

A season of disorder began.

The electoral count would not be official until January, and Lincoln's inauguration would not come until March, but threats of secession and war intensified. While southern legislatures debated secession, frightened northerners offered compromises to save the Union, found scapegoats in abolitionists and Negroes, worried about a dithering president currently in the White House, and waited for Lincoln to say something decisive about the unfolding crisis. There were threats to Lincoln's life, too.

The spectacle disgusted Frederick.

Yankees provided ample proof for the hunger of compromise in Boston on December 3, when Frederick came to Tremont Temple for a commemorative speech on the anniversary of John's Brown's death. The year before, on the day of Brown's execution, church bells tolled, guns fired salutes, ministers preached sermons, and thousands bowed their heads in silence. But now the city was tense, roiled by rumors of secession and war.

It was bitterly cold; ice and snow on the roads had been pushed against walls to make room on the sidewalks. Attendance was thin when Frederick arrived just before the official 10 a.m. opening of the first session of John Brown's memorial. Negro men clustered in small groups throughout the hall, looked nervously over their shoulders for signs of danger. Frederick approached one of the groups and noticed Wendell Phillips talking with an interracial group at the back of the stage.

He stopped, his heartbeat accelerating. Frederick had not spoken to Wendell in six years, since that terrible moment when he declared Frederick a fallen star, a traitor to the antislavery cause. The hurt was deep and the insult unforgivable. Frederick had sworn to never allow himself to feel that kind of anguish again. Wendell Phillips was as good as dead.

Wendell had changed. His hairline had receded farther back on his forehead, streaks of gray lightened his hair, and he was heavier. But he was still the elegantly dressed, formal gentleman. He was ready to honor and defend John Brown, as he had done the entire year, according to news reports. Reading these accounts, Frederick found Wendell's words still eloquent and searing. Despite his rage against his former friend, he could not undo his professional respect.

Frederick was still not ready to speak to him. He decided to sit in the audience instead, five rows from the platform, avoiding what now seemed inevitable. Eventually, he would have to mount the stage with the other speakers and say something, offer a perfunctory greeting, make an inquiry about his wife Ann. But for now, Frederick would stall.

Soon the auditorium was full and hot, women crowding the upper galleries, speakers and other dignitaries packing the stage. Cheers for the Union filled the hall. The tumult of whoops, shouts, roaring chants, and shrieks of patriotic joy made it almost impossible to hear speakers. Order seemed impossible, but the organizers persisted and elected a meeting chair. As if on cue, a large posse of policemen entered the temple.

The chair made it clear that the Union had to be saved, compromise was essential, and the issue of slavery had to be avoided. In the audience, Frederick rose to speak, and the chair acknowledged him with a nod and warning, "Be brief."

As Frederick approached the platform, several white men dressed in coats, cravats, and top hats, blocked his way as they closed ranks with arms across puffed chests. Without lifting his hands, Frederick lowered his head and shoulders and battered through the wall of men too caught off guard to resist him.

On the stage, he tried to speak, but hecklers stood on their chairs and interrupted almost every sentence. Undeterred and outraged by this attack on free speech, Frederick yelled above the roar, "It seems to me as though some of the white men of the North have gone to the devil. They murder liberty—kill freedom."

White men seized chairs and rushed the stage, hurling them into a heap as if intending a bonfire at the back of the platform. Wendell was quickly surrounded by supporters and hurried from the hall. More men rushed the stage and grabbed a Black man and tossed him on the pile. Frederick was knocked down. When he got up he grabbed a chair. A policeman and five others tried to wrest the chair from him, but Frederick held on, while another man grabbed him by the hair.

The chief of police stepped forward. "I am requested by the chair to clear the stage. If you retire, you will stop the police from performing a very unpleasant duty."

Released, Frederick raged against the obvious bigotry of the police. Only Negroes were being grabbed and forced off the stage. He shouted above the din of screams, curses, and laughter. No one was listening, but Frederick didn't care. Only open defiance mattered.

More police reinforcements arrived, and the hall was finally cleared, except for reporters, officers of the building, and eighty police officers. There were no arrests, just warnings of future apprehensions if the abolitionists continued to make trouble before the hall was locked up. Unfazed, Frederick and other veterans of the brawl agreed to meet that night at the Joy Street Church.

Later, thousands of Bostonians gathered outside the church as city policemen patrolled the streets and shouted warnings about an infantry battalion on alert.

Wendell Phillips arrived. He apologized to the group for not staying to speak. Fearing for his safety, friends had surrounded him and forced him out. A week before, he had been followed by a mob and had to hire a police escort. He approached Frederick with a kind, knowing smile, all traces of animosity erased as he reached out his hand to shake Frederick's. "Douglass, we need your courage, such as are the times."

"Thank you," Frederick replied, taken aback, realizing that he wanted reconciliation with old friends when everything was falling apart, despite his avowals to never forget or forgive.

"Let's not have any discussion about what happened years ago. Let's not examine. Just let it be," Wendell said.

"You don't have to do this for me."

"I'm doing this for me, my friend," said Wendell. "We are different men, in different times. I've learned that you can't demand of your friends what you demand of your congressmen. Those you care about aren't required to be consistent. Didn't Mr. Emerson once say, 'a foolish consistency is the hobgoblin of little minds'?"

"It's done," Frederick agreed, enjoying the sudden warmth of their renewed connection.

The riot received national coverage, most of it hostile. Frederick grinned when he saw the December 15 issue of *Harper's Weekly* and its depiction of the riot under the heading "The expulsion of Negroes and abolitionists from Tremont Temple." The black and white wood print depicted an unnamed, generic Negro, well dressed in coat, vest, and cravat, raising his hand to the cheering women in the galleries.

Frederick was clearly that illustrated colored man of the hour as the nation teetered on the brink of catastrophe and waited for Lincoln to speak. There were no others as famous or as effective. Henry Highland Garnet had moved to Jamaica, and Martin Delaney to Canada. Charles Remond had retired from the lecture circuit. James McCune Smith was busy working as the doctor of the Colored Orphan Asylum in New York.

I am back where I belong, after flight and exile, infuriating opponents, saying what white people don't want to hear. Frederick wanted to boast this from rooftops. He was the preeminent Black leader in America. But even he could not predict the speed of the nation's collapse.

South Carolina voted to secede from the Union on December 20, with church bells, marching bands, fireworks, and bonfires celebrating the political and cultural divorce. President Buchanan declared secession illegal, but said he had no right to stop it, as if giving other southern states permission to leave the Union.

"What's going to happen?" asked Rosetta. "Will other states leave? Will Mr. Buchanan finally do something, or will we have to wait for Mr. Lincoln?"

"I don't know," replied a worried Frederick. Despite his bellicose language that fall and winter, he didn't like being under the collapsing roof of a house on fire.

"Well, Mr. Buchanan and South Carolina surely know how to ruin Christmas, or at the very least, dampen the holiday spirit," Rosetta said.

"They can't do that," replied Frederick, as the family sat in the parlor for the traditional Bible readings. "We won't let them."

Anna knitted and said nothing during the reading, but now she looked up. "There will be no Christmas in this house this time."

Puzzled, Rosetta, asked, "Mamma, what do you mean?"

"Christmas is for children, and we don't have none, no more now that Annie . . ."

"But Mamma . . ."

"We're still in the mournin' season, and decorations, and parties, and dinner, gifts, and all that would be wrong, a disrespect for my baby."

Frederick intervened gently. "The living need Christmas, Anna. And Annie wouldn't want us to be unhappy." The children all looked to each other. Frederick had already given them money to buy presents now secretly stored away.

Anna stood, the ball of yarn falling from her lap. "Fine. Do what you want, but I'm not cookin', not fixin' decorations, making things."

"I didn't have Christmas last with you. I need it, especially now. We all do," Frederick said.

"You had Christmas last year, didn't you, with Miss Griffiths?"

"Yes, with her and Reverend Crofts."

"You bein' away couldn't be helped, but you could have stayed away from them, knowin' about how I feel," Anna said.

Rosetta stood, too, looking to her brothers. "Mama, we are leaving now. We don't need to hear about this. This is between you and . . ."

Trying to remain cool, Frederick said, "Yes, I don't think this is talk they should . . ."

"There you go again: I, I, I, and I'm sick of it."

"Anna, they should not . . ."

"Yes, let's pretend. Let's just keep shutting out the light. Let's just hide another story. How many other secrets do we need to put away?"

Turning to his sons, Frederick insisted, "You will leave now. This minute. I insist."

Anna said, "Stay."

"Leave."

Rosetta and her brothers hesitated, turning to each of their parents for signals of compromise, a resolution that could make it possible to leave without angering one or the other. They hurried from the room, Rosetta leading the group.

Anna sat down and picked up her needles. "They surely know how to disrespect me when you're 'round. But when you're gone, they don't. They know better. And you'll be gone again, and it will be like it was before."

"You will drive them away."

"I know already Rosetta is leavin'."

"How do you know?"

"I know. She can't help it, packing, organizing, being all nice and all. I know."

"She's an adult. She can do as she pleases."

"Will you give her your blessing, or have you already?"

Frederick hesitated, and Anna said, "Another secret between you two. How many more agreements have you made with my children?"

"There are no agreements, but you don't give them reason to come to you and make agreements. You're too hard, and they feel comfortable . . ."

Anna stood again. "Here's the truth. It's easy for you to be their friend. When you're away, they make you special. Annie, poor Annie, she did that. They all do that. Living with a real person is so much harder."

Feeling pity for her, Frederick pleaded, "Anna."

Anna lifted her hand. "Don't! I'm done with the lyin', especially the lyin' you tell yo'self. Done!'

She bent down to retrieve her needle and ball of yarn and turned to leave.

"Anna."

"Done," she said and left the room, leaving the door open.

Frederick didn't want to spend time thinking about what Anna had said, parsing the meaning of every word. He meant to summon the children and tell them that they would continue celebrating Christmas as they always did. They would decorate the tree on Christmas Eve and exchange gifts, go to church on Christmas morning, and return to the house for Christmas dinner.

Anna stayed in her room. She didn't cook, make gifts, or even go to church with them on Christmas day.

Rosetta and her brothers dutifully decorated the tree, adding ornaments and stringed popcorn. They were afraid to comment or make jokes as they were used to doing. "Let's give our gifts now," said Rosetta, her voice straining to brighten the atmosphere. They sat in chairs before the tree to take turns retrieving a gift and presenting it in the traditional order. As she was the oldest, she was the first to give a gift, but when she handed a small package to Charles, the youngest, as family tradition required, she started weeping. Her hand wavered.

"What's wrong, Rosetta?" asked Charles.

"Annie. This should be her turn."

"It's not my fault," replied Charles, understandably defensive but still gentle. They treated Rosetta as a second mother, giving her love and respect when not driving her to distraction and enjoying her frustration.

"I know. I didn't mean to upset you," Rosetta said.

"Annie would want us to be happy," Frederick said, "to enjoy each other, unwrapping with all the fun and excitement that she had, that you all had before what happened."

"Yes. We will do our best for Annie."

"For Annie," repeated Lewis, and then the others, including Frederick.

By the end of the exchange, levity had returned, and Rosetta offered another assurance. "I will be doing my best for Annie, too, in the kitchen, but I can't promise you that I will succeed, since I have not inherited Mama's skills, and it didn't help that I refused to be a good student."

"Now, Rosetta, let's not get serious again," pleaded Frederick, Jr.

"I'm just saying. You'll need resolve and a strong stomach."

"This isn't promising," said Charles.

"You've all been warned."

As predicted, Christmas day dinner was a disaster, the meat and biscuits dry, the vegetables either boiled to a pulp, or overcooked and hard as rocks. The desserts were too sweet, and the coffee too bitter. When Lewis took a bite, frowned, and looked to his sister, she said, "I told you."

Frederick smiled, admiring her honesty. She enjoyed being right, as he did.

South Carolina had coincidentally reinforced Frederick's righteousness the day before. After giving no reason for secession on December 20, the convention offered on Christmas Eve its reason, declaring, "An increasing hostility on the part of the non-slaveholding States to the institution of slavery has led to a disregard of their obligations, and the laws of the General Government have ceased to affect the objects of the Constitution."

Slavery.

Not state's rights, not protecting the homeland, not independence.

Slavery.

It was that simple, Frederick noted smugly. *Only a fool could think otherwise.*

Yes, he enjoyed being right, and never did vindication feel so good.

He would also do his duty with stoic persistence in the Douglass family tradition, and so he and his children ate their Christmas day dinner silently, frowning, casting side glances, and refusing to make comments on the horrible food and ruin the rest of their holiday. They still had to read the Bible and sing songs later that night.

Anna never came down.

85.

BY FEBRUARY 1, MISSISSIPPI, Florida, Alabama, Georgia, Louisiana, and Texas followed South Carolina. The marches, parties, picnics, and fireworks continued as Southerners appointed themselves the true heirs of the first American Revolution.

That winter, Frederick gathered as many news clippings, letters, and telegrams as he could, fascinated and appalled by the effort to make slavery essential to freedom. One Richmond newspaper boldly asserted, "Freedom is not possible without slavery."

Such nonsense deserved ridicule, and Frederick delivered it, telling Southerners that secession, though celebrated with pyrotechnics, music, and dancing, "was not a thing as easily done as leaving a society of Odd Fellows, or bidding good night to a spiritual circle."

Having harshly criticized his country, Frederick was now an ardent American nationalist who denied any constitutional "right of secession," and smelled treason like an eagle smells its prey from miles away. "Revolution in this country is rebellion, and rebellion is treason," he wrote in an editorial, "and treason is levying war against the United States, and with something more than paper resolutions. There must be swords, guns, powder, balls, and men behind them to use them. If there is not wisdom and virtue enough in this land to rid the country of slavery, then the next best thing is to let the South go and be made to drink the wine cup of wrath and fire, which her long career of barbarism and blood shall call upon her guilty head."

Not all Northerners appreciated public acceptance of war. Mobs formed in many cities, and in Rochester the police had to close Corinthian Hall after an anti-abolitionist crowd disrupted a meeting there.

Politicians tried concession and appeasement, filling "the air with the whines of compromise," said Frederick, who scorned every proposal. Congress wrangled for months, paralyzed, and confused, stoking Frederick's fear that schemers would do anything to save the Union.

Lincoln was elected on the platform that restricted slavery and said it was not within Congress's power to forbid future changes to the Constitution. Such a grant of power was unconstitutional on its face.

What would Lincoln say in his March inaugural address about secession of southern states from the Union?

Lincoln's train to Washington for the inauguration arrived in Rochester on February 21. When the president-elect appeared on the rear balcony of the train before a crowd of fifteen thousand, Frederick cheered the tall, lanky man he had never seen before. He wanted to show his support for Lincoln and the country.

Appreciating the irony, Frederick later learned that Lincoln had to enter Washington secretly like a fugitive on the Underground Railroad, changing schedules, routes, and conveyances as he approached an armed city full of slaves and defiant, raucous rebels. "We have no censure for the President at this point," noted Frederick. "He only did what braver men have done."

Frederick's empathy soured into scorn and contempt as he read Lincoln's inaugural address. He decided to write a scathing denunciation and print Lincoln's entire speech, proof of Lincoln's perfidy, for the *Monthly*. Frederick expected Lincoln to expose and rebuke the enemies of his country, especially the men who were bent on destroying it.

But Lincoln did not. Frederick wanted another Oliver Cromwell, commanding, righteous, and ruthless. But instead, he got another James Buchanan, another Franklin Pierce, a dissembler, a prevaricator, a compromising stooge.

Lincoln had opened his address by announcing his complete loyalty to slavery in the slave states and declared that he had no lawful power to interfere with slavery there. But he went further and denied ever having "the least inclination" to interfere.

"Mr. Lincoln was in a position that enabled him to wither at a single blast their high blown pride," Frederick asserted in an editorial. "The occasion was for honest rebuke, not for palliatives and apologies. The Republican president bends the knee to slavery as readily as any of his infamous predecessors. What an excellent slave hound he is."

Frederick also acknowledged Lincoln's deep commitment to his oath of office. He would preserve and protect the Constitution of one nation; defend all properties and places belonging to the federal government; and meet with force any use of arms against the United States.

Seven states had seceded, but Lincoln did not recognize their right to do so and believed those states were still a part of one country. He closed his address with an eloquence that Frederick could not deny, even as he hated this song of appeasement: "We are not enemies, but friends. We must not be enemies. Though passion may have strained it must not break our bonds of affection. The mystic chords of memory, stretching from every battlefield and patriot grave to every living heart and hearthstone all over this broad land will yet swell the chorus of the Union, when again touched, as surely they will be, by the better angels of our nature."

Frederick predicted the consequence of this appeal, "To parlay with traitors is but to increase their insolence and audacity."

The entire nation now waited for a resolution of a crisis in Charleston Harbor as a delegation from South Carolina demanded the surrender of Fort Sumter, now manned by only eighty soldiers, as hundreds of militia men on shore vowed to drive the Yankees out if they did not surrender and leave.

Major Robert Anderson from Kentucky, a former slave owner but still loyal to the Union, commanded the garrison at nearby Fort Moultrie and decided to move his command, under the cover of darkness, to reinforce Sumter and forestall an attack.

The rebellious South Carolinians were enraged. Northerners celebrated, insisting the surrender of Sumter would bring shame and dishonor to the country. It seemed as if everyone had a raging fever.

The day after his inauguration, Lincoln learned that the Fort Sumter garrison was running short of supplies. He had to do something: resupply the garrison and provoke a war or order a withdrawal, destroy Republican support in Congress, and divide Northerners even more.

Lincoln had a divided cabinet, and one cabinet member leaked to the press that Lincoln planned to surrender Sumter. This was not true, but the northern press and Republican constituents exploded. "Have we a government?" thundered one newspaper. The *New York Times* proclaimed, "The Administration must have a policy of action." Telegrams and letters flooded Congress and the White House.

Lincoln ordered the resupply of Sumter. Anderson rejected surrender and before the arrival of the resupply fleet, the Confederates opened fire on Sumter at 4:30 a.m. on April 12, 1861. After thirty-three hours of bombardment, Anderson surrendered, watching the American flag go down and the Confederate flag rise over Fort Sumter on April 14.

On April 15, President Lincoln called for 75,000 militia men to put down the rebellion.

Relieved after weeks of waiting, Frederick exclaimed, "Thank God!"

"You insult de Lord," Anna observed, frowning deeply after Frederick had summoned the family to the parlor for the important news.

Rosetta had moved to Philadelphia that March, having accepted a teaching position there.

Before he could reply to his parents, Lewis declared to the assembled family, "I have important news, too. I'm going to enlist." He stood erect, lifting his chest as if in military formation.

This was the face of war: his son, eager to leave, ready to die. Suddenly, all of Frederick's bellicose words became foolish, stupidly abstract.

"No!" cried Anna, standing.

"But it's going to be over soon," Lewis protested. "They can't last!"

"No," repeated Anna, staring with the eyes that once could shut him down. "I'm not going to sit about waitin' to hear that your body is lyin' in some ditch with your head shot off."

"Anna," murmured Frederick, shocked by her graphic cruelty.

"But, Mama."

"What makes you think you'll live when thousands will have to die?"

"Nothing's going to happen."

"You don't know that, and I don't know that, but you don't have to wonder about that." She turned to Frederick. "You're not going to let him go, are you?"

A rejection was the only permissible answer, and Frederick said, carefully, "Son, we don't know yet if colored boys can join."

She demanded again of Frederick, "Are you?"

"I can't stop him. He's twenty, a man."

"Then I hope Mr. Lincoln will stop him, and not let colored boys join. Them white boys won't stand for niggers fighting beside them."

Lewis objected, "Mama, you don't know *what* you're talking about."

Anna inhaled deeply and suddenly slapped his face, twisting his head to the left. The room became very still. No one moved or breathed. She said, "Yes, I know. I know that I don't wants you to get killed, and if Mr. Lincoln don't want no colored boys in his army, that's fine with me. He don't care about colored people, never did. So why should you care about him?"

Lewis blinked at his mother, rubbed his face, and tried to hide the humiliating tears. "It's *my* country."

She stepped back, as if momentarily stopped by his fierce patriotism. "It don't love you."

"It's my country, and you can't take that away from me."

She turned away, and when the door closed behind her, he still said, louder than before, "It's *my* country."

Frederick started to move toward his son, but Lewis raised his hand, saying, "No, Papa, you can't change my mind. I'm a grown man now, and I will leave to do what we all should do, even without your blessing."

Frederick turned to his two other sons, who were still immobilized. "Boys, you need to leave. I want to talk with Lewis alone."

They hurried out, relieved to be gone.

"Lewis, I understand, but your mother is right about one thing. We don't know if Mr. Lincoln will let you fight."

"Then you'll have to change his mind."

"I doubt he will listen to me, after what I've said about him recently."

"Well, Fort Sumter has changed everything. He will need us. There are only so many white boys for fightin', and if the slaves join in, then Captain Brown's dream will come true for sure."

"Maybe so, Lewis. We'll have to wait and see. For now, this war is a white man's war, and it will only change when enough of them die."

Lewis frowned. "There are some things worth dying for, isn't that so, Papa?"

Frederick hesitated. He didn't want Lewis to think he was willing to sacrifice his sons for a cause. "Yes. There were times in my life when I realized that it had come to that. But war is different. It's brutal slaughter. The guns, the bayonets, the shells coming down."

"It will be over soon, Papa. There are far more of us than there are of them. They call us cowards, but those rebels are in for a big surprise. The battle cry of freedom will keep us going far longer than the battle cry of slavery."

"Those Southerners say they're fighting for freedom, too."

"If that lie keeps them going, then let them keep saying it, I suppose. But we know better, don't we, Papa?"

Pride so warmed his heart, Frederick wanted to embrace Lewis, but, never knowing the embrace of his own father, he refrained. He feared that he would not react well if Lewis, surprised by his action, rejected his embrace.

"Son, I'm proud of you. But I'm not sure if our country deserves your sacrifice. I don't think I could accept that sacrifice."

"Where would we be without the sacrifices of others, Papa? All those men and women on those slave ships coming over, all those who worked the fields, built the land, raised the crops, raised families, and tried to run away. You had to sacrifice things, too, didn't you? Leave your home and your family to come here; try to make a living for all of us; go all over the country and speak until your voice was raw and almost gone; run away to escape capture, to the North, to Britain, and back again. You know sacrifice, Papa, and we've learned it from you."

Seeing his son as a mature, reflective young man for the first time, he didn't know what to say. "I didn't know that you knew . . ."

Lewis smiled. "Papa, I've read your books. And when you work at the paper, I read all those editorials and speeches. I don't know everything about you, and I'm sure there's more to know, but I know your sacrifices. You gave up so much so we could have a better life. We have a better life, a life far better than most colored people, I think."

"I appreciate what you've said. I really do. Thank you."

"No, thank you, Papa."

"May I shake your hand, Lewis?"

"Of course, Papa."

Frederick approached him, put out his hand, grasped Lewis's, and then, suddenly, he pulled Lewis into his arms and hugged him, feeling his son's surrender as he rested his head on his father's chest. At five feet nine inches, he was not as tall as his father. "I love you, Lewis," Frederick said, his voice wobbling.

"I love you, too, Papa."

Frederick gently stepped away. "And you know your Mama loves you, too. Will you forgive her?"

"I know that, too, Papa. She's just scared."

"I'm scared, too."

"We all are. I'm only hoping that the rebels are even more scared because they have more to lose and will give up quicker."

"That's my hope. We have more people, more land, more money. We should win this."

"We will win this. God is on our side, the just side."

"They pray to the same God," said Frederick, being careful. He didn't want this moment to descend into a theological dispute. He had Ottilie for that.

"But He doesn't listen to everyone, only the righteous. In Peter, scripture says, "For the eyes of the Lord are on the righteous and his ears are attentive to their prayer, but the face of the Lord is against those who do evil."

"You continue to surprise me, son."

"Well, Papa, what other outcome could you expect, after all those nights of Bible reading? Something had to stick. Besides, we believe in America. We really believe the Declaration of Independence."

"Keep on reading."

Two weeks later, the secretary of war announced that his "Department has no intention at present to call into service of the government any colored soldiers."

Frederick became even more determined to make the war to save the Union a war to end slavery and the inequalities it demanded. It had to become a crusade for freedom, and Frederick intended to use every means at his disposal—his pen, his body, and his voice on the lecture circuit—to educate the public, make it realize that emancipation and colored enlistments were indispensable for a union victory, and force Lincoln to change his war policy.

"The cry now is for war, vigorous war, war to the bitter end," Frederick announced in May. "Let the grim visage of a northern army confront slaveholders from one direction and a furious slave insurrection meet them at another, and starvation from still another."

Frederick had his own civil war to wage.

Holy war.

PART V: 1862–1877

Abraham Lincoln, Andrew Johnson, Ulysses S. Grant, and Rutherford B. Hayes

86.

THE WAR CONTINUED, BUTCHERING soldiers in open fields, lengthening the casualty lists, dashing hopes, squandering resources, exposing fools. The slaughter was unbelievable. Even with scattered reports of Confederate casualties, the numbers surpassed the combined totals for the American Revolution, the War of 1812, and the Mexican War.

Frederick tried to not think about this too much. Now at forty-four years old, he had editorials to write and speeches to give as he grappled with Lincoln.

The president had a grossly incompetent and insubordinate commander in General George McClellan, who would not fight and take Richmond, the Confederate Capitol, from the east as he was told to do. Lincoln refused to fire McClellan, and in May 1862 assured a congressional delegation from the four slaves states still in the Union that the federal government would financially compensate them if a successful war, with their assistance, ended slavery. Ottilie concluded that Lincoln, his cabinet, and McClellan were all traitors.

Frederick refrained, unsure of Lincoln's motives as he tried to hold the rest of the Union together while facing defeats at the hands of superior Confederate generals like Robert E. Lee, Stonewall Jackson, and others.

Lincoln signed the Confiscation Act in July. The law freed all slaves who had escaped to Union lines and all slaves who had disloyal owners in Confederate territories held by Union soldiers. To Frederick's astonishment, the law also authorized the president to employ Blacks when "necessary and proper for the suppression of the rebellion." If this was not the moral highroad, at least military necessity was building a bridge to it.

But August news from Washington dashed Frederick's hope that Lincoln supported the hopes and dreams of Black people. "Damn it!" shouted Frederick, slapping his hand on his desk, "Damn him, damn him, damn him!" He had just read an account of Lincoln's August meeting with a delegation of Negro ministers in the White House, a historic first.

"What is it, Papa?" asked Lewis from his typesetting desk on the other side of the room. "Is it Mr. Lincoln again?"

"Yes, it's Mr. Lincoln *again*."

The president had invited the press to record this unprecedented meeting, where he read an hour-long lecture asking Black people to *leave* the country. He allowed no discussion or questions and issued his comments as a formal White House statement. The five obscure preachers, local Baptists from the Washington area, said nothing.

What would have happened if Lincoln had summoned me, Charles Remond, James McCune Smith, Martin Delany, and Henry Highland Garnet? Frederick imagined a heated exchange that challenged every point. The delegation would remain civil, but it would not cower before the most powerful white man in the country.

Frederick realized that Lincoln knew what he was doing. His essential audience was not the Black ministers summoned to the White House, or Black readers across the country. He was speaking to and for white people, assuring and mollifying whites in the North as defeat loomed and southern whites smelled victory in the approaching summer. Yes, he was indeed the white man's president, the champion of their bigotry.

According to the White House and newspapers, the president shook the ministers' hands and declared, "You and we are different races. We have between us a broader difference than exists between any other two races. Whether it is right or wrong, I need not discuss, but this physical difference is a great disadvantage to us both, as I think your race suffers very greatly by living amongst us, while others suffer from your presence. In a word, we suffer on each side. If this is admitted, it affords reason at least why we should be separated.

"Your race is suffering, in my judgment, the greatest wrong inflicted on any people. But even when you cease to be slaves, you are yet far removed from being placed on an equality with the white race. I do not propose to discuss this, but to present it as a fact with which we have to deal. I cannot alter it if I would. I need not recount to you the effects upon white men, growing out of the institution of Slavery. I believe in its general evil effects on the white race. See our present condition—the country engaged in war!—our white men cutting one another's throats, none knowing how far it will extend; and then consider what we know to be the truth. But for your race among us there could not be war. Without the institution of Slavery and the colored race as a basis, the war could not have an existence. It is better for us both, therefore, to be separated."

But for your race among us there could not be war. Frederick could feel one of his severe headaches coming. But he had to stay focused and prepare for a sharp, ruthless response. He intended to reprint Lincoln's entire statement in his newspaper. The claims that the mere presence of Blacks had caused the war, that prejudice is a natural condition, that Black people are physically disposed to function better in warmer climates, all had to be refuted as illogical, hypocritical, and contemptuous.

Frederick was not alone. Black people throughout the North attended protest meetings and wrote letters to newspapers and magazines, to their congressmen, and to the president himself.

When a combined force of over 130,000 men under the commands of McClellan and Lee converged on Antietam more than 20,000 men were left dead or wounded. It was the bloodiest single day of the war. Piles of twisted and dismembered bodies photographed by Matthew Brady confirmed the horror of war and heightened one of Frederick's greatest fears that more gruesome battles would increase public demands for a peace settlement allowing the Confederacy and slavery to survive.

Five days later, in September, Frederick read from a telegram Lincoln's Emancipation Proclamation: "That on the first of January, in the year of our Lord One Thousand, Eight Hundred and Sixty-Three, all persons held as slaves within any State or designated part of a State, the people whereof shall then be in rebellion against the United States, shall be then, thenceforward, and forever free." He jumped from his office chair. "Lewis, Lewis," he yelled, brandishing the telegram and an edition of the *New York Tribune* for good measure, "He did it! He did it!"

"What Papa? Who are you talking about?"

"Mr. Lincoln is going to free the slaves. He's freeing them."

"What? I thought . . ."

Frederick hugged his son, who stood stiff-armed. He stepped away and, still gripping Lewis's shoulders, said, "We must get home. We must tell everyone and shout for joy."

During the two-mile drive to their house, Frederick read aloud every word of the *Tribune* article that described the new policy and the two years of defeat and disappointment that brought Lincoln to his decision.

At home, they bounded up the hill to the house, calling out names. Frederick was out of breath when he reached the open door and saw his second son. "What is it, Papa? Is something wrong?" Junior asked.

"Where's your mother?"

"Where she always is, in the garden with that new man."

"Go get her and bring Nathan, too. Hurry!"

"Yes, sir."

Frederick and Lewis went into the parlor and waited. Frederick paced the room, unable to sit down, looking at the telegram, scanning key words. Lewis stood at the door, looking down the hall for his mother and brother's return. Anna appeared signaling disapproval. She had unfinished work to do in the gardens and hated disruptions of her domestic routines. "What is it now, Frederick? Is Rosetta alright? Did Mr. Lincoln do something bad again?"

Nathan Sprague, a twenty-year-old gardener who also worked in the nursery next door, remained in the hall, respectfully holding his sun hat.

"No. Rosetta is fine, as far as I know. I have a telegram. I have joyous news. He finally did it. The president finally did it. He freed the slaves. He *freed* them!"

"*All* of them?" asked Junior, turning to Nathan Sprague, who was born a slave.

"No, but most of them. Free forever on January 1. That will be the day of deliverance for millions!"

Junior clapped his hands. "Oh, Papa, finally it's here, but what will this mean for us, since we're free."

"I don't know. We'll learn more later. But now's the time to celebrate. Is it not, Anna?"

Anna sat down, staring ahead. She rocked in her chair as tears streamed down her cheeks. Frederick, Lewis, Junior, and Charles stared at her. Anna said slowly, "What a day, what a day. The day of jubilee. And our people will come out of Egypt, and your family and my family, all those still alive we can see again. We'll be together again before kingdom come. *Before*! Oh, I can see them now."

She shifted in her chair. "Maybe, maybe your brothers and sisters will come too," she said to Frederick. "So many people will come together. Isn't this what that paper means? People can do what they want to do. They will know what we know, and they'll love freedom even more because it didn't come in a bed born free, it came as a blessing from the Lord, the Lord's hand through Mr. Lincoln. Lord, Hallelujah! Lord, Hallelujah!"

"But our people are from Maryland," protested Charles. "It's not in rebellion, and so they aren't free."

"Yes, you're right," Frederick said, "but this document is a first step, a very important first step, for surely once slaves are freed in the deep South, it will indeed be impossible for slaves to be kept slaves anywhere else."

"Very well, Papa," replied Charles, who retreated sullen and withdrawn. He wore his intelligence like armor and used facts, figures, and quotes as weapons, making sure that everyone knew how smart he was. Of all his children, Charles was the hardest to love. Frederick sensed their growing alienation because Charles was so like him, an unnerving mirror to his own blatant faults.

Lewis asked, "Will he take it back? Will Mr. Lincoln change his mind?"

"No. Mr. Lincoln may be slow, but he is not a man to reconsider, retract, and contradict words above his signature. We must confide in his word."

Frederick turned to Anna and reached for her hand. "Come, Anna, let's celebrate with some good coffee and biscuits and jam. I'm so glad you're back to cooking. It makes us all happy that you're feeling better. And this is the best time to celebrate. Yes, January 1 will be the day of Jubilee." Anna's health had improved, her face and figure had their familiar shape, and her dark skin was no longer marred by rashes and blisters.

"Now, you know I don't like you all watchin' me cook, so stay here and talk about Mr. Lincoln and his paper, and read it to me, *every word*, when I call you in. I don't want no disappointment. I want to make sure hope is on solid ground in good dirt. You know good fruit don't grow in weak dirt."

"Don't worry," Frederick said as she went to the kitchen, Sprague following her.

But he did worry as the weeks passed. Frederick had sleepless nights about the grace period that allowed the Confederacy to surrender and reenter the Union, even as runaway slaves, hearing about the Proclamation, abandoned plantations and swarmed Union camps.

What will happen to them? What if rebels returned to Congress and, with pro-South Democrats still eager for compromise, overrule the president, reverse the Proclamation, and legislate removal?

Democrats gained seats in state legislatures in the November elections. Runaway slaves were being hunted down, recaptured, and sometimes executed as traitors; and colonization schemes still emanated from Washington. President Lincoln also reminded citizens in his annual message that December that he could not "make it better known than it already is that I strongly favor colonization."

Damn it. Why can't the president comprehend the obvious? We're not leaving.

Hope floundered while waiting for January 1, but Frederick was determined to keep it alive relying on Divine Providence and the course of history to sweep imperfection aside and fulfill destiny. He assured Ottilie that the Proclamation was a moral bombshell, the beginning of the end and not just a declaration of military necessity after a year of Union defeats. "Let the conflict go on! There is no doubt of the result, and though the war is a dreadful scourge, it will make justice, liberty, and humanity permanently possible in this country."

But triumphant words could not assuage the anxious waiting. President Lincoln's public actions did not help to relieve the tension. He did not reaffirm in any public comments that January 1 would indeed be the day of emancipation. He also claimed that the rebellion was "already substantially suppressed." He continued meeting with border-state men and proudly avowed a readiness to change his opinion.

Fearing betrayal again, Frederick threatened Lincoln writing in the *Monthly*, "if Mr. Lincoln shall thus trifle with the wounds of his bleeding country, he will be covered with execrations as bitter and as deep as any that ever settled upon the heads of any perjured tyrant ancient or modern." Frederick donned his emotional armor to guard against potential disappointment and deep betrayal and went to Rochester's Zion Church on December 28. He then planned to attend a mass celebration of the Emancipation Proclamation in Boston on New Year's Eve.

Frederick stood before the Black church packed with Black and white citizens, determined to express hope and possibility. He didn't care that his voice slightly trembled. "This is scarcely a day for prose. It is a day for poetry and song, a new song. These cloudless skies, this balmy air, this brilliant sunshine, making December as pleasant as May, are in harmony with the glorious morning of liberty about to dawn upon us."

He mentioned his childhood, a rare reference now. "Among the first questions that tried the strength of my childhood mind was first why are colored people slaves, and the next will their slavery last forever. From that day onward, the cry that has reached the most silent chambers of my soul, by day and by night has been, How long! How long oh! Eternal power of the universe, how long shall these things be? This will be answered on the first of January 1863."

Four days later, he didn't go to Boston's Music Hall, where Henry Wadsworth Longfellow, Oliver Wendell Holmes, John Greenleaf Whittier, Francis Parkman, Emerson, Garrison, and Harriet Beecher Stowe sat in the balcony to the cheers of the throng below before a concert of Mendelssohn and Beethoven. Frederick avoided Garrison and chose an alternate venue for celebration, a Black-organized meeting at Tremont Temple, where 3,000 people assembled.

Poetry, choir singing, and speeches filled the morning and afternoon sessions. Frederick was the last speaker of the afternoon. After the break, even more people arrived formally dressed in coats and gowns, as if attending a grand ball. They embraced, reminisced, and sang songs. But the mood began to sour as people waited and wondered, will Lincoln sign the Proclamation? Will he change it? Will there be damaging compromises with the Confederacy?

Hours passed.

No news.

People became more and more restless, exchanging rumors. Doubt sounded like distant thunder.

Frederick spoke again about the significance of the hour, but he knew it was not logic people wanted to hear. They wanted to hear the trumpet of jubilee, see a bolt from the sky, watch by the dim light of the stars for the dawn of a new day, shout for freedom, and sing anthems of the redeemed.

Eight, nine, ten o'clock came and passed, and Frederick imagined a shadow falling over the crowd.

Eleven o'clock, still no news. As speakers took turns, everyone kept turning their eyes to the doors, expecting to see a runner bringing news from the telegraph office downtown.

"We won't go home until morning," announced Frederick.

Below him, Frederick saw and heard one man grip his neighbor and implore, "It's gonna happen, isn't it, isn't? It's true, right?"

"When is it coming?" shouted another man. "*When*?"

The audience began a chant, "When? When?"

Unwilling to wait for a messenger, Judge Thomas Russell went to a nearby newspaper office but quickly returned, running into the hall, and shouting, "It's coming. It's on the wires! It's here!"

The entire audience was on its feet, cheering, applauding, embracing, dancing, laughing, crying, tossing their hats and bonnets into the air, drowning out the long-awaited words Judge Russell tried to read.

Frederick hugged everyone around him, including Charles Remond. He went into the audience and gave and received more. He shed tears, too. He returned to the center of the stage and declared, "This is a day for poetry and song." He began the refrain of a familiar song, his deep voice projected to the rear of the hall, its tone conditioned by years in church choirs and the forests of the Eastern Shore, its beauty commanding attention as the song swelled from the front rows to the back until the entire audience tempered its raucous joy through rhythm and harmony and soaring melody, praising their Lord:

Blow ye the trumpet, blow
Sweet is the work, my God, my King.
I'll praise my Maker with my breath.
O, happy is the man who hears.
Why should we start, and fear to die,
With songs and honors sounding loud.

Reverend Charles Rue sang a psalm with a light tenor that suggested the innocence of youth. His voice comforted Frederick as it bolstered courage needed to face all the fear and promises of a new day.

"Sound the Loud Timbrel over Egypt's dark sea," Frederick sang, joining the preacher. "Jehovah has triumphed, his people are free."

When the song ended, Frederick turned to Rue and whispered the word, "Free."

Frederick repeated, "free," and the word that began as a whisper reverberated throughout the audience and the temple as the reality of the word sank in.

Free.

Free.

Free.

Free.

They sang "Glory Hallelujah," "Old John Brown, his soul is Marching On," and other songs. Frederick knew his voice sounded good. He wanted to sing late into the early morning hours. Many people didn't want to leave, even though Tremont Temple was only rented until midnight. When it was relatively quiet, Reverend Leonard A. Grimes, the minister of the Twelfth Baptist Church for almost three decades, suggested adjourning to his church to continue the revel.

Someone shouted, "Let's go to Twelfth Baptist!"

The crowd poured out into the light snowfall, singing, humming, laughing, and hugging for the twenty-minute walk to the Twelfth Baptist Church on Phillips Street in the Black section of Boston. Grimes supervised the all-night party in his packed church, providing food and organizing the music. Frederick spoke and sang until almost dawn. He was exhausted, his bleary eyes ached, and he could barely walk to the train station.

And yet his body felt light, almost weightless.

Frederick knew he would not sleep on this New Year's Day, as the memories of one of the happiest days in his life filled his mind.

He thought about Mr. Lincoln, the man who made this day possible, and wondered if he should offer a public apology for the harsh, insulting words of that season of waiting. Lincoln had proved him wrong, and an honest man should swallow his pride and admit his error.

No, Frederick decided. He would wait.

Lincoln had more to prove. *Will he actually call men of color to arms? Will he allow the sons of Frederick Douglass to serve*? But he would not allow his questions to cloud the bright and fair morning of this day. *At last, millions of my people are free. At last.*

87.

FREDERICK BELIEVED THE NEW Proclamation was "the greatest event of the century," and throughout January and early February he traveled over 1,000 miles calling for Black soldiers: "Let the black iron hand of the colored man fall heavily on the head of slaveholding traitors and rebels, and lay them low. Give them a chance! Give them a chance! I don't say they are great fighters. I don't say they will fighter better than other men. All I say is, give them a *chance*." Secretary of War Edwin Stanton gave Black men that chance by granting John Andrew, the governor of Massachusetts, permission to mobilize the first Black unit, the 54th Massachusetts Infantry Regiment.

Eighteen-year-old Charles Douglass signed up for the 54th on February 9 as soon as he heard the news. He proudly told his father, "I was the first. I have the honor of being *first*!"

"I'm proud of you, son, so proud!" Frederick shook Charles's hand vigorously. He never anticipated that his youngest son would enlist first or enlist at all. Charles had a mind of his own, never agreed with his father, even during Frederick's passionate harangues about the war and the need for Black men to fight, and he never expressed interest in fighting, guns, or play battles. Although the youngest, Charles was the peacemaker, arguing even as a boy that conflict was a waste of time and energy. "Only stupid people fight."

"What did your mother say?"

"She's changed since Fort Sumter. Even then, she knew there was nothing she could do about us going, but the Proclamation helped. Her mind is hard to change, but she's willing when she must. That's her way, 'No, no, no,' at first, and then . . ."

"You're wise, son."

"Maybe, but I watch. The youngest ones always watch and learn because we get ignored in big families."

"But Annie . . ."

"She was a girl, and we all knew she was your favorite. She was all our favorite."

Charles had never spoken about his sister this way. Frederick was touched. "I miss her."

"We all do, Papa."

Frederick faced the prospect of losing another child, this time to a war he wanted. He said weakly, "You don't have to go."

"Of course, we do. How could we not, after all that's been said?"

Frederick bristled at the implication of personal responsibility. Indeed, he had been calling for men to arm, and as the most prominent Negro in America the pressure on his sons to enlist was undeniable. He wanted to enlist, too, but was too old. He tried not sounding defensive. "I can't make you do anything."

"We know that papa. But we still want your blessing."

"You have it, son. I can't be prouder."

Charles put out his hand for a handshake and said, "Thank you, Papa." Frederick gave him two brief shakes, and Charles left the room. Frederick was relieved that his lecture schedule would prevent excessive worry about his son.

He still had so much to say about the Proclamation.

Within three weeks, he had another job.

★

After the Massachusetts legislature provided funds for recruiters, the governor of Massachusetts asked George Luther Stearns, one of the Secret Six supporters of John Brown, to supervise recruitment. Stearns came to Rochester in late February to enlist Frederick as a recruiter. He offered $10 a week for expenses. Frederick thought he deserved more and frowned. Stearns hastily told him that he would be joining the distinguished company of Charles Remond, Henry Highland Garnet, Martin Delaney, William Wells Brown, and other prominent Black men.

Despite his displeasure, Frederick decided that he and Stearns had a crusade to mount. Their campaign included recruitment speeches that Frederick delivered in the northeast at mass meetings publicized by posters and banners that proclaimed Frederick's words, "MEN OF COLOR! TO ARMS! TO ARMS! NOW OR NEVER for Three Years' Service" with his name featured prominently at the bottom. Stearns tallied the number of attendees and offered a $3-dollar second-class ticket for each soldier's transport to the training site of the 54th Massachusetts in Readville, near Boston. Frederick travelled to mass meetings throughout western New York and the Hudson Valley, and went as far as Boston, New York City, and Philadelphia.

He could see skepticism in the eyes of some of the men. They had heard stories. They would not receive equal pay, despite Secretary Stanton's promises. They would not be able to be officers. Only white men could lead them, and some northern officers were already making it clear they would never lead coloreds because they were all cowards anyway. Confederates were going to capture Negro soldiers and hang them as traitors as an example to slaves thinking about running away.

Frederick pressed on, sure that an anthem to freedom, patriotism, history, and martyrdom would sway them. Applause always followed, but not his usual thunderous ovations. Sometimes, as the applause diminished, he simply asked the men to come forward to sign up. Frederick celebrated even one enlistment, and often he only obtained one or two. Some apologized for not signing, since there were so many jobs available because of the booming economy. But the numbers added up.

It took almost three months for a complete regiment to be assembled, and in the meantime, families boarded trains, carriages, and wagons to visit the training camp and watch their sons. Tourists were also attracted, eager to see Black men march, point rifles, and salute.

From Boston, Frederick went to the camp daily for two weeks in May, proudly introducing his sons to anyone and everyone. Anna and Rosetta also visited for a week, and all three stayed together with an old church friend living in Boston.

Anna's arrival in Boston astonished Frederick, who was convinced that Anna would never leave Rochester. Rosetta said, "Oh, Papa, Mama wanted it to be a surprise. Isn't it wonderful? She's so much better, and she said she couldn't miss seeing her boys in uniform."

When Frederick came into the parlor where Anna was staying, she was sitting and knitting as usual, but she stood when she saw Frederick. "I had to come," she said with a dim smile, but her bright eyes gave her delight away. "I wanted to see that look when you can't plan everything."

"Oh, Anna," Frederick hurried across the room and embraced her. "It's a surprise, all right. A good surprise."

"I know I've been hard on them in the past, but that's over. I want them to know I want only the best. I care," she said.

"They know."

"But still, I want to say it in my way, by coming."

"They will be happy to see you, I'm sure."

Anna turned to Rosetta, "You didn't tell your brothers I was comin', did you?"

Rosetta shook her head. She enjoyed this rare moment of banter between her parents. "Oh, no, Mama, you said you wanted to surprise them."

"Good." Anna turned to Frederick. "Now, can you arrange to see some people so I can have them for myself just a little while, just a moment, that's all?"

"I'll see what I can do," he replied.

"Good. Now Rosetta come on in and tell your father what we've been doing at home while he's been gone."

"Yes, Mama."

Later, when they were alone, Anna said to Frederick, "I need to talk to you about Rosetta."

"What is it?"

"Rosetta wants to move back home."

"That's good news. She's been unhappy and lonely away from home."

"She told me about what she's been feelin' away from home. Rochester is her real home, but . . ."

"You don't want her to come?"

"I do, I do. But I think she has her eye on de boy that helps me with the gardening work."

"Nathan, the gardener?"

"Yes, he makes her smile all the time. Yes, he's some looker, not as good looking as you, but fine enough for all the ladies always lookin'."

"How do you know *that*?"

"I'm not blind. I just see it when the ladies come to the house and get fruit from the trees and want to buy fruit and some of my jams. You know I sell most of the fruit, don't you? We can't eat all that fruit, and he helps me sell it, and when we're sellin' Rosetta's always there, sneakin' side glances. She's lookin' for a man, I think. She's that age."

"But not a gardener! She can do better than a gardener!"

"She'll do what she wants. She's that way."

"She won't marry without our permission."

"You mean your permission." Anna's voice was calm as she stated the obvious between them. Neither of them forgot what happened with Harriet's wedding.

"Don't you want to have some say?" Frederick asked.

"It's not up to us."

"She'll want our blessing."

"And we'll give it to her because she wants it, even though I think, like you, she can do better than Nathan Sprague. He's a good man, as far as it goes, but everybody, especially girls, should be marryin' up. I did."

Frederick smiled. "I was a slave."

"Not for long, and I just knew, knew it deep down in my soul, you would be somebody. Just look at you now. Just look at you! And now I want my boys to know I love them."

"Tell them," Frederick said.

"It's hard," Anna replied.

"I know."

"You've told them?"

"Yes, we need to tell them."

Anna said, "I don't know if I can bear another . . ."

"You can do anything if you can survive *that,* and you would want them to have that memory of you telling them what they so want to hear before they leave."

"We should pray for them."

"We can if you like."

Curiosity crossed Anna's face. "If I like? Don't *you* want to pray for them?"

"We need all the help we can get," he said.

"Well, I have said enough for one night, for two and three, too," she concluded and rose. Anna smiled at Frederick again before asking, "Are you goin' to give a talk sometime while I'm here? That's somethin' I haven't seen or heard in a long time. Are you still *good*?"

Frederick was delighted by Anna's playfulness. "Well, of course I'm still good. The times require it."

"Good. You can't be embarrasin' your whole family now like some of them preachers who don't know when to stop after they lose the fire."

"The fire still burns," Frederick said.

"Good. Now, don't stay up too late," Anna said.

As house guests, they shared a bedroom and bed, but Anna's message was understood. She would go up first, and after an appropriate time, Frederick would follow and find her asleep.

88.

FREDERICK WENT TO THE regiment headquarters to ask if his sons, in different companies, could be summoned at a certain time for a family surprise. When he asked to see the commander, Robert Gould Shaw, and presented his identification card, the young captain at the reception desk recognized Frederick and stood a bit straighter, his chest wide and adorned with gold buttons. He paused for only a second. "Yes, sir. Just a minute. I'll see if the colonel can receive you." He was gone for only a moment, then returned, saying, "The colonel will see you now."

Colonel Shaw was a strikingly handsome young man, twenty-five years old with flowing blond hair and the most luminous blue eyes Frederick had seen since Thomas Auld's. He was short, thin, and dignified, wearing a smart, pressed uniform worthy of his celebrated survival of the battles at Winchester, Cedar Mountain, and Antietam. Colonel Shaw extended his hand, "Sir, what an honor it is to meet you. You deserve our nation's gratitude. Thank you for your recruitment work."

Frederick was invited to sit down. He immediately made his request, asking for a small meeting room for a discreet reunion with his sons' mother. He emphasized discretion because it was a surprise, and also because he didn't want his sons embarrassed and later mocked for receiving a special favor from the commander of the regiment.

Colonel Shaw was taken by the opportunity to help Frederick. "It is the very least I can do for you, sir, and you can be sure that discretion will be the order of the day. I will give an order to my captain outside to say nothing, and when I send for your sons, Privates Douglass, I assume, they will not know the reason. This will concern them at first, I'm sure, but that will be forgotten quickly enough, when they see their mother. Some of the men will never see their mothers again. Their comrades will understand."

"But if their comrades find out I had a say . . ."

"Mr. Douglass, all these men understand orders, follow orders. It will be *my* order that they come here, and that will be that."

"Thank you, sir."

"When do you want your surprise?"

"Within the week. Mrs. Douglass returns to Rochester at the end of it."

"We have serious trainings tomorrow, but the day after can work. The afternoon will work best because your boys will need rest after what I will be putting them through. We have to be combat ready."

"Thank you, sir," said Frederick, who presented his hand. For years, this gesture had been a subtle way of testing the possible aversion to Negro touch. The blinking eyes, the immediate look at the hand, a quick intake of breath, were giveaways. But Shaw didn't hesitate, maintained his smile, and shook Frederick's hand with two vigorous pumps.

Two days later, Lewis and Charles were summoned to headquarters and ushered into a small room, where their parents and sister waited. They had seen their father briefly the day before because he had been coming to the camp almost every day, but they could not restrain themselves when they saw Anna and Rosetta, hugging them, not caring about the family decorum that required reserve.

Anna had something to say. "Just look at the two of you, all grown up now, dressed like grown men in the uniforms that make you look even more handsome than you're already. I'm so proud of you two, still findin' your own way." She turned to Frederick, "We did some good work."

"Thank you, Mama," said Lewis.

"And I needed to say it."

"Thank you, Mama," said Charles. "I didn't *need* to hear it, but I appreciate it anyway."

"I brought a basket for us to share 'cause I know this Army food is terrible, just terrible. With all those mouths to feed, I'm sure you get food even pigs don't like. Now, I have here some fried chicken and some biscuits and pie. Nothing large, just somethin' to carry you through."

Lewis clapped his hands. "Yes, this is what I was hoping for."

"Yes, there's nothing like a family picnic, and we haven't done one in years!" Anna said.

"Let me see if the captain can provide some area," said Rosetta, taking charge. She went to the door and called out to the captain, "Sir, perhaps you can help my family. We need your services." She returned, and the family turned to each other with knowing looks. Rosetta was in her element, leading, making demands, giving orders. Frederick realized that he didn't have to worry about her, and if Rosetta were interested in Nathan Sprague and did marry him, she would lift him up to match and even surpass her. But would she respect him if he didn't learn to read and write, or enlist like her brothers?

★

The 54th Massachusetts had all the men it needed by May 18, and trains from Boston and Providence brought dignitaries, including Garrison and Wendell Phillips, to the ceremony for the presentation of the colors at Camp Meigs. So many thousands came, the morning locomotive had to pull nine extra cars.

Frederick greeted Garrison but said nothing more. Garrison, equally cool on a bright, warm day with a slight breeze, the perfect day for a celebration, nodded and said, "Mr. Douglass," before turning away to talk with Reverend Samuel May, who stood beside him. Chagrined, Wendell pulled Frederick aside and whispered, "He'll come around."

"I'm not holding my breath," Frederick said.

The governor and the other dignitaries reviewed the men standing ramrod with their new Enfield rifles, some of the non-commissioned officers with swords. When the review was completed, the men were dismissed. Frederick went to find Lewis and Charles. He found Lewis first, who said, "I don't know if I will come back, but the governor will never have reason to regret the steps he has taken in raising the regiment."

"Please, son, no talk about not coming back."

Away from his brother, Charles had little to say. "I'm glad that's over with."

"But you *are* proud?" asked Frederick.

"Yes, I was first, remember? But I didn't sign up for parades."

"That's part of it."

"And that will be over none too soon," Charles said.

"But I will be there for that incredible sight, a thousand armed Negro soldiers marching the Boston streets before cheering thousands, to glory." *Or death*. "Be careful," said Frederick, suddenly shaken.

"I'll try, Papa," Charles replied.

"Do more than try."

Charles softened his tone, and said, "I'm not going to ask you to not worry about me, because you should worry, as all parents should. But I do want to come back, Papa. I do."

Frederick grabbed his son and held him against his chest, his hand on Charles's head. Charles didn't resist, but his limp arms made for an awkward moment. "*Please*, come back!"

"Yes, Papa, but I need to go."

A week later, Charles became so ill he was hospitalized, and the doctors said he would have to stay at the camp hospital and miss the Boston parade and the regiment's departure for South Carolina on May 28. Frederick found his son weakened by fevers and severe stomach cramps.

When Charles saw his distressed father, he tried to assure him with humor. "The doctor's assured me it's not the food. But how do they know? Mama was right, as usual." But his bitterness got the best of him, and he said," "They won't let me go, Papa! I can't go with Lewis to Carolina." Charles took a breath as his face and body twisted from pain, and continued through clenched teeth, "I lied, Papa. I want to be in that damn parade. I want to be there. I deserve to be there. I was first, remember?"

"It's only a parade, son. You'll get to Carolina when you get better."

"There won't be any other like it. It's a first, too!"

★

May 28 was another bright and clear day, so bright that shadows seemed etched into the cobblestones in early morning. Since dawn, thousands of people had lined the streets on the parade route and entered the viewing stands. Frederick had stayed in Boston and arrived early, too, hoping for the best seat. Everyone was excited, men and women, adults and children, all swept up by the historical importance of the day, ready to cheer and wave handkerchiefs, banners, and flags. Frederick heard delighted expressions at this incredible fulfillment, the dreams of thousands. "Can you believe it? Can you believe what's happening? At last!"

The trains carrying the men of the 54th arrived at Providence Station at nine o'clock. Colonel Shaw mounted his horse and ordered his men to form a line. Once in formation, the men marched behind the renowned Patrick Gilmore Marching Band and a large squadron of the city police and its chief. As soon as the columns entered Boylston Street, decorated with national, state, and regimental colors, the cheering started, as spectators on the sidewalks, windows, and balconies near the Boston Common waved flags and white cloth. People packed the narrow streets.

When the regiment passed the Essex Street house of Wendell Phillips, Colonel Shaw saluted William Lloyd Garrison there on the balcony, his hand resting on a bust of John Brown and tears flowing down his cheeks. Just beyond the Phillips house, a woman rushed into the street and presented a bouquet of flowers, masses of zinnia and dianthus, to Shaw. He grabbed the bouquet and managed an awkward salute.

After the regiment marched around Pemberton Square, it entered Somerset Street, where some members of the conservative club, offended by the sight of Black soldiers, hastily drew the window curtains.

At Beacon Street, in the front of the State House, Shaw paused to acknowledge Governor Andrew waiting for them at the front portico. He escorted the governor and his staff down the hill as the cheering continued.

At the West Street Gate, the 54th entered Boston Common, where thousands filled the review stands. Frederick sat in the middle so he could get a panoramic view of the parade and hopefully see Lewis. The band played continuously, and the cheering never stopped. Whites and Blacks together, proud parents, friends, and supporters, all witnesses to a moment in history that defined their identities as Bostonians and Americans.

The sight of Black soldiers made strangers hug.

Finally, the 54th marched to Battery Wharf, where the men had to wait to board the new steamer, the *De Molay*. The public was not allowed on the wharf, only family and friends. Many of the men had no one to bid them farewell. So many had come from poor families unable to buy tickets to Boston or had parents who needed to work that day. These men huddled together, reviewing the day, wondering about the future.

Frederick managed to find Lewis, but he wasn't willing to leave his comrades. "Most of them have nobody." Frederick gently pulled Lewis aside and said, "You all looked splendid today, and make us proud. Too bad your mother and sister had to go back to Rochester. Stay safe."

Lewis looked back to his waiting friends, and then shook his father's hand. "Don't forget to write, Papa. The best part of our day is when letters come. We write so you will answer."

"I will write. But it's not yet time to say goodbye. A few of us have permission to go on the ship into the bay."

Lewis was pleased by this revelation. "Then I'll see you aboard." He returned to his friends.

Frederick boarded the *De Molay*, and the brass and drums of Gilmore's Marching Band played again. The group of family and friends cheered, applauded, and waved flags and handkerchiefs for the last time. The sun continued its descent in the late afternoon, and the *DeMolay* moved toward the horizon as the sounds of celebration dimmed.

Frederick thanked Colonel Shaw for allowing him and a few other civilians to board the *De Molay*. "You are an honorary member of this regiment for all that you have done," said Shaw. "And truly, I ought to be thankful for all the happiness and success in my life so far. And if the raising of colored troops proves such a benefit to the country and to Blacks, I shall thank God a thousand times that I was led to take my share in it."

"Perhaps we're all children of fortune," Frederick said.

"Time will tell. Goodbye, sir."

Frederick remembered what Lewis had said about his comrades. So many had no one, and in the remaining time he had on the ship, he went around to the men he had recruited and wished them a safe return.

When he came to Lewis, he tried to control his voice, but it quivered. This could be the last time seeing his face, hearing his voice. "Goodbye,

Lewis," Frederick whispered, his voice cracked by emotion. "Stay safe and come back."

Lewis's voice was firm. "I'm not a coward, Papa."

"I know, son, but come back."

"I will try."

"I'm proud of you, Lewis."

"Thank you, Papa, and I'm proud to be your son."

"A father's greatest gift."

It was time for Frederick to board the tug for the city he could not see because the ship was so far out. He boarded reluctantly as he looked up to the faces looking down at him. He continued looking at the *De Molay* until it was out of sight. Despite the words of pride and patriotic duty, Frederick felt deep sadness as the sea rolled on. *I invited this war into our house. War kills, and it breaks the heart. What will I be able to say and do when this guest turns on us and takes my sons*? He silently prayed, *"Please, Lord, protect my boys? Please, let them live."*

89.

TROUBLES FOR THE 54TH Massachusetts began almost immediately after its celebrated departure in Boston. In early June, the War Department issued its policy for soldier pay. White privates would receive $13 per month, Black privates $10, from which a $3 clothing allowance would be deducted. Frederick was outraged. Secretary Stanton and George Luther Stearns had assured him that equal pay would be government policy, and Frederick had assured thousands of reluctant Black men. Disenchanted Black soldiers wrote protest letters to Frederick, Stearns, governors, congressmen, and the president.

Now a noncommissioned sergeant, Lewis was incensed by his discovery that he was paid less than a white private and asked his father to do something about this inequity. Units of Black troops were refusing unequal pay, including the 54th Massachusetts.

Weeks passed as the troops waited and prepared for the order to attack Fort Wagner. While they waited, they heard about Gettysburg, Vicksburg, and the Draft Riots in New York. Like most soldiers, Lewis received scattered news through rumor, letters, and official notifications. Frederick had more information, and it became clear that July 1863 was a terrible, frightening month, despite victories on both sides.

After a victory at Chancellorsville in late June, General Lee invaded Pennsylvania, and with great trepidation the entire North followed the accounts of the three-day battle at Gettysburg, from July 1 to July 3. A Lee victory would mean foreign recognition of the Confederacy and a negotiated peace settlement, if not the fall of Washington and a Union defeat.

But after two days of success, Lee and his troops were finally defeated, and they retreated to Virginia on July 4. Combined with the news of General Grant's victory at Vicksburg after a forty-seven-day siege, July 4 was a great day for celebration.

Even so, few could ignore the appalling losses. More than 51,000 men were either killed, wounded, missing, or captured at Gettysburg, over 23,000 on the Union side, over 28,000 on the Confederate side. At Vicksburg, there were 19,000 estimated casualties.

Never had the nation seen the spilling of so much blood in three days. No wonder few men in a crowd of 5,000 came forward to enlist after Frederick's appeal in Philadelphia on July 6.

As the Confederacy mourned, the Union cheered. But the cheering stopped for Frederick and Black people when news broke a week later about draft riots in New York City.

While working with Black troops at Camp William Penn, Frederick already knew about the seething resentments against the new draft, especially its provisions allowing men to purchase exemptions and find substitutes.

On Saturday, July 11, the first draft names were drawn and listed on Sunday. On Monday morning, as new lots were drawn, a mob of 500 mostly Irish white laborers gathered at the draft headquarters at Third Avenue and Forty-Seventh Street. Led by the volunteer Firemen Company 33, known as the "Black Joke," the crowd threw large paving stones through windows, rammed through the doors, and torched the building. When the official fire department arrived, rioters dismantled their vehicles, killed horses pulling streetcars, and smashed the cars. Telegraph lines were cut. The Bull's Head Hotel and the Tribune Building were attacked as well.

But what started as an anti-draft riot quickly became an anti-Black riot as mobs attacked, maimed, tortured, and killed scores of Black people, including one man who, surrounded by 400 men and women, was beaten with clubs and paving stones, then hanged from a tree and burned. Another man was found hanging from a tree with toes and fingers sliced off and gashes everywhere. All of this happened while men, women, and children watched and cheered, sang songs praising Jefferson Davis, and jeered "the niggers."

Much of the riot details Frederick would learn later, but what he heard and read about in Philadelphia made him worry for his own safety. He had to go through New York for his return to Rochester. He did not know how long the riots would last or how long it would take for the military units called in by the governor to quell the rioters and restore calm to a city well known for its pro-South sympathies.

Lincoln did nothing.

Frederick telegraphed Ottilie for assistance, and she arranged for his travel through Newark, getting him to the Hudson River Railroad before he could be attacked by mobs who were now dragging people off buses and from homes, assaulting any Black person within sight in the upper parts of Manhattan.

"Saved by you, again," said Frederick to Ottilie as he boarded the train at the Chambers Street Station in lower Manhattan, a few miles away from the center of the riots. "And you put yourself in danger again just by being with me."

"I had to see for myself that you got here safely," Ottilie replied.

"It's a sad day when the fire of the enemy opens in the rear of the loyal army."

"I don't know if I can love this city anymore."

"Love is always tested," Frederick said.

"But not everyone survives disappointment," she said.

"Then maybe it's not strong enough."

Ottilie frowned and looked away from him as he stood at the top of the steps to his car.

"I better sit down," he said, glancing at the interior of the car. "I'll write when I arrive."

"Yes, and I will eagerly wait for it."

The whistle blew. "All aboard!"

The train slowly moved north to Rochester, where Frederick would receive more bad news, this time from South Carolina. There was an assault on Fort Wagner near Charleston and Colonel Shaw and three other officers were killed. Many more soldiers were also killed, wounded, taken prisoner, or were missing in action.

As details of the assault became available, Frederick, Anna, and Rosetta were stricken by fear. *Was Lewis dead? Did he survive? Was he wounded? Was he a prisoner about to be executed, as ordered by the Confederate secretary of war, who demanded executions for all captured Black soldiers? If alive, was he tortured and then enslaved, lost to the fields of Alabama and Mississippi?*

Only Anna remained hopeful. She insisted, "The Lord won't take him. No, he won't take no more of my babies."

Frederick tried to get answers, sending telegrams to George Luther Stearns, Governor Andrew, his congressman and senators, Secretary Stanton, and the president himself.

No response.

After two weeks of anxious waiting, Frederick and Anna received word from Lewis in a letter dated two days after the assault. "I cannot write in full.

Shells fly overhead, and we expect a counterattack. We made the most desperate charge of the war on Fort Wagner, many killed and wounded and missing three hundred of our men. The splendid Fifty-Fourth is cut into pieces. Good-bye to all. If I die tonight, I will not die a coward. Goodbye."

As he read the letter to Anna and Rosetta, Frederick's hand shook as relief, joy, and horror coursed through his body. Lewis had been through hell and survived.

"Praise de Lord," whispered Anna, clasping her hands tightly as she rocked in her parlor chair.

Tears came to Rosetta's eyes, and she asked, "*How* did he survive? And he's waiting for another attack! Why do men do such things? *Why*?"

Frederick didn't answer, but rage followed joy and relief when later he learned that the Confederate secretary of war had condemned all captured Black soldiers to death, and the president was doing nothing about it, even after the 54th Massachusetts had received universal praise for courage and valor under fire.

Nothing!

But the assault on Fort Wagner had changed public opinion about Black soldiers.

Shaw was now a martyr, and his men had proven, once and for all, their courage.

The sable arm was more than reliable, it was indispensable, and deserved special protection. Frederick wrote his most blistering attack yet against the president: "The slaughter of Blacks taken as captives seems to affect him as little as the slaughter of bees for the use of the army. What has Mr. Lincoln to say? What has he said? Not one word."

Frederick went further in another editorial and demanded orders of retaliation. "'For every prisoner slain in cold blood, Mr. Jefferson Davis should be made to understand that one rebel shall suffer death, and for every colored soldier sold into slavery, a rebel shall be held as a hostage. For the government to do less than this," he concluded, "is to deserve the indignation and the execration of mankind.'" He then made a decision. He could no longer work for a government that forced his sons to fight with halters about their necks.

He would resign as a recruiter.

90.

IN HIS AUGUST 1 resignation letter to George Luther Stearns, Frederick asked, "If the president is ever to demand justice and humanity for Black soldiers, is not this the time for him to do it? How many 54th's must be cut to pieces, its mutilated prisoners killed, and its living sold into slavery, to be tortured to death by inches before Mr. Lincoln shall say: 'Hold enough!'"

Frederick received a prompt reply. Stearns told Frederick that at the end of July the president had issued General Order 100, ordering that "For every soldier of the United States killed in violation of the laws of war a rebel soldier shall be executed, and for every enslaved by the enemy or sold into slavery a rebel shall be placed at hard labor on the public works."

Frederick issued a correction, but not an apology. "What ought to have been done at the beginning, comes late, but it comes. It really seems that nothing of liberty, or humanity can come to us except through tears and blood."

Stearns also urged Frederick to go to Washington and directly make his case to the president for the fair treatment of colored soldiers. Stearns didn't know Lincoln, but he knew Lincoln constantly received uninvited visitors, supplicants, and applicants filling the halls of the White House. He offered the support of Kansas Senator Samuel C. Pomeroy, a friend and former Massachusetts state legislator. Pomeroy was an ardent opponent of slavery and had introduced the legislation that became the Confiscation Act. Pomeroy would escort him to the offices of Secretary of War Edwin Stanton and then to the White House.

Frederick agreed, and on August 9 without a White House invitation, he boarded the overnight train to Washington through Baltimore. He stayed in the car when it stopped in Baltimore, looking out to the President Street Station and the city he had not seen since his escape in 1838. But he could not leave the train. Slavery was still legal in Maryland, and Black people were being abducted off the streets and taken south.

The train departed, and Frederick arrived in Washington on the morning of August 10. When he stepped out of the train at the B&O station on New Jersey Avenue and C Street near the Capitol, Frederick had spots of soot on his crisp white collar, and he could already feel sweat under his shirt and black overcoat. The humidity was thick. Crowds of people, mostly Black, filled streets littered with garbage and excrement that attracted flies and mosquitoes. Frederick hurried by, clutching his small travel bag, covering his mouth with a piece of cloth.

The city was like an armed camp. White soldiers were everywhere. There seemed to be little discipline, as if the heat made it impossible. It was hard to believe that this city was the nerve center of a vast military enterprise. But the unfinished Capitol dome, its reconstruction suspended at the beginning of the war and renewed last year, gleamed in the morning light as it waited for the installation of the Statue of Freedom scheduled for December. And despite the scattered ladders and remnants of scaffolding, the building on the hill at the end of Pennsylvania Avenue suggested the majesty of government isolated from the teeming masses below.

After checking his bag at a boarding house, Frederick found the small office of Senator Pomeroy in the Capitol Building. Pomeroy had kind blue eyes. He received Frederick warmly, shaking his hand immediately and promising to escort him throughout the visit.

They went first to Secretary Stanton's Office at the War Department in President Park near the White House. Pomeroy warned him, "the man can be brusque. But take no offense; he's like this with everyone."

"I see," Frederick said, resolving that he would not be intimidated. His mission was too important.

"He holds a special affection for Mr. Lincoln. Mr. Lincoln is the only man he truly admires and respects."

"What do you think, sir?"

"Of Mr. Lincoln?"

"Yes."

"He's a good man, slow to action, too slow. I had to plead with him to issue the Emancipation Proclamation. But he does the right thing, in time," said Pomeroy.

"Then there's hope," Frederick replied.

"He *is* hope, if anything."

Lincoln's character was the object of speculation throughout the country. There was no consensus. He was a wise, ambitious politician or a simpleton, a kind and sensitive gentleman or a coarse country lawyer. His choice of advisors was peculiar, if not outrageous, his choice of generals, worse. He treated everyone kindly, including Black people, but he told jokes that made fun of them, too. He was a courageous man almost broken by the death of his son Willie last year, and yet he continued as commander in chief to press his generals for more vigorous attacks against the rebels. He was a harried husband, browbeaten by his southern wife with Confederate sympathies, and an inveterate liar with political skills that brought him to the White House. Yet he was well known as "Honest Abe."

When Frederick and Pomeroy finally entered the antechamber of Stanton's office and presented their ID cards, the military aide left immediately and returned quickly. "You may go in now." They entered the room and found Stanton reading at his desk. He continued reading as they stood near the door. Finally, Stanton turned to them and looked through his horn-rimmed glasses. He said, "Douglass, I know of you. You have thirty minutes of my time. Thirty minutes."

Stanton did not smile, offer his hand, or acknowledge the senator. He had thick sideburns connected to a long beard that fell to his wide chest, but no moustache. His beard was the longest Frederick had ever seen, longer than John Brown's, and only Stanton's penetrating blue eyes and severe demeanor kept him from looking ridiculous, as if the tail of a gray fox was suddenly attached to his thin, lower lip.

"State your business, sir," said Stanton, who didn't offer them seats.

Frederick and Pomeroy glanced around and sat in the chairs nearest them.

Frederick cleared his throat. "Sir, when the government recruits, it needs to understand two extreme images of Black people that keep others from seeing them as competent or courageous. We are not all pious angels, benevolent, saintly, and self-sacrificing. We are not all Black devils ready to do all forms of evil. Black soldiers are like white soldiers. Some are brave, some are not. Some are ambitious, and some are not. The policy of the government should conform to these essential facts, and . . ."

Stanton interrupted, "How does it not, sir? What are the conditions with colored troops that demonstrate our ignorance?"

Frederick remained calm. "Unequal pay, sir. And regulations confine them to the dead level of privates or non-commissioned officers."

"Dead levels, sir? Privates and non-commissioned officers can serve honorably."

"Yes, but not if they are forced to remain there."

"Well, it is difficult to institutionalize equality. Difficulties and prejudices must be surmounted, prejudices among soldiers and politicians must be considered. Nonetheless, I have tried to obtain the same pay, rations, uniforms, and equipment for your boys, our boys. I even personally drafted a bill to achieve this. Unfortunately, it passed in the House but failed in the Senate."

Frederick saw an opening and tried a more conciliatory tone. "I appreciate your effort, sir, but in the end, there are things more important than pay or rank. We want freedom now and recognition as citizens of the United States."

"I truly want equal pay for colored soldiers. In fact, merit should be the basis of promotions for all soldiers, colored and white. As a show of good faith, I will promote any colored man recommended by his superior officer, and I will do more than that. I will hire you as a commissioned officer. You should be an assistant adjutant helping in the recruitment of freedmen in the South," said Stanton.

"Sir?" At first, Frederick was too stunned to say more. He almost jumped out of his chair. He turned to Pomeroy, who sat there frozen in astonishment. This appointment was one of the most significant events in Frederick's life and in the lives of Black men in the country. He would not be the first to get a commission. That honor belonged to Major Alexander Augusta, a surgeon, who received his medical training in Toronto after the University of Pennsylvania refused to admit him. But very few people knew about Major Augusta. The appointment of Frederick Douglass would send a clear message throughout the country. Southerners would be furious.

"You are needed. How soon can you be ready?" Stanton asked.

Frederick could see Stanton's resolve. He paused for only a moment and answered, "In two weeks, sir."

"Good." Stanton wrote a quick note, summoned his aide by a small bell, and handed it to him. The aide left.

"You will report to General Thomas in Vicksburg, Mississippi, and you will cooperate with him in raising said troops," said Stanton crisply.

"Please send the papers to my home in Rochester, sir."

"Of course. You must also see John Usher, the secretary of the interior, who will give you a pass for free travel anywhere behind Union lines. Good day, sir."

Stanton turned his back and resumed reading documents.

Frederick and Pomeroy glanced at each other and rose simultaneously.

"Thank you, sir," said Frederick to Stanton's back.

"Thank you, Secretary Stanton," said Senator Pomeroy.

Stanton didn't respond, and they left the room.

Outside, Pomeroy exclaimed, "You were amazing, Mr. Douglass, amazing! Very few people impress Mr. Stanton, very few. You *earned* that commission even though, by the end, he was trying to get rid of us."

"He's a busy man. I still can't believe what just happened."

"But it happened, even though he lied."

"About what? Did he offer a fraudulent commission just to get rid of me?"

"No, no," said Pomeroy, shaking his head, his face stricken by Frederick's interpretation. "He didn't lie about the commission, or he would not be sending us to the Office of the Interior. No, he lied about sending a bill to Congress. We never voted on such a bill because there never was one."

"Why would he do that, lie?"

"He's not an elected politician, but he's one anyway, and we say what we must to get what we want."

"I see. But why lie to me?"

"Perhaps he was impressed by you, too. But I can't be sure. Mr. Stanton remains inscrutable, as is his ardent support of Mr. Lincoln. They are a most unlikely pair: Mr. Stanton, cold, efficient, all business, and Mr. Lincoln, kind and deliberate, too slow for me, but honest and committed to his duty. You know I wasn't for Mr. Lincoln's nomination. I supported Mr. Seward."

"I think I heard this."

"Once I met him, I changed my opinion. He has a way with people. He filled his cabinet with rivals, and those men have been changed by the man. You'll see why."

They reached the Office of the Secretary of the Interior, and John Usher, who had been notified of their arrival, came out of his office, shook Frederick's hand, and presented a document. He smiled as Frederick read it:

Department of the Interior
Washington, D.C. Augt. 10, 1863

To Whom It May Concern.

The bearer of this, Frederick Douglass, is known to us as a loyal, freeman, and is, hence, entitled to travel, unmolested.

We trust he will be recognized everywhere, as a free man, and a gentleman.

Respectfully,
J. P. Usher, Secy.

"Thank you, sir," said Frederick, looking up.

"By all means," replied Usher.

"May I read it?" asked Pomeroy, reaching for the document without waiting for an answer.

He read it and said, "I will sign it, too. Give me a pen."

Pomeroy went to the desk and signed his name below Usher's. Pomeroy signed in a larger and wider script, taking three lines with" JC Pomeroy," then "USS" below it, then "Kansas."

"Let's get to the White House," said Pomeroy. "There will be a mob there waiting to see the president. Some wait for hours."

"Thank you, Mr. Usher," Frederick said, and he and Pomeroy left the office.

As they were about to leave the building, they ran into Montgomery Blair, the postmaster general who tried to enlist Frederick's help in a federal government colonization plan, assuring him then that there "was no question of superiority or inferiority in the proposed removal." They had never met, but Blair recognized Frederick at once. "Ah, Mr. Douglass," said Blair with a slight nod of his head but offering no handshake. "It's a pleasure seeing you."

"Thank you, sir. I have just received a commission for the recruitment of colored soldiers, and I have this pass from Secretary Usher," Frederick said. He presented the pass to him.

Blair read it, and said, "I will sign it, too." He turned to the officer at the main desk, reached for a pen, and signed with a small, tight script on the bottom two lines of the sheet, "Pass this bearer, Frederick Douglass, who is known to me to be a free man. MBlair, Postg."

"Thank you, sir," said Frederick. Now that he had signatures from three of the most powerful men in the country, he was even more determined to see the president.

Frederick and Pomery reached the White House. Frederick paused before entering, taking a moment to reflect on the span of his personal story, a man born a slave about to enter the residence of the most powerful man in the country, a poor white country lawyer now president of the United States. He was sure that Lincoln, when not overwhelmed by the terrible burden of war, paused to consider his own remarkable path as a self-made man rising from a log cabin in Kentucky to a mansion in the nation's capital, the absolute height of prestige and power. This historical occasion stirred within Frederick a pride that took his breath away,

The reception room was packed with white men, and they all scowled when they saw Frederick, who presented his card to the aide and watched him scurry up the stairway. He expected a long wait, at least hours, maybe half a day. Two minutes passed before a messenger called his name, "Mr. Douglass, the president will see you now."

The white men stirred, heads turned, whispered to one another. One man said loudly, "Yes, damn it, I knew they would let the *nigger* through."

With Pomeroy at his side, Frederick entered the office and found the president sitting in a chair not meant for a man with a six-foot-four frame. His arms dangled at the sides, and his feet seemed to be in a different part of the room. Frederick was struck by his very long legs. President Lincoln's overcoat and trousers were rumpled and dusty, the untailored cuts reflecting either the president's indifference or his tailor's incompetence. The room, cluttered with books, maps, and other documents was the perfect frame for the disheveled man at the center of it all. Three secretaries hovered, whispering, and handing him papers to sign.

Lincoln rose, towering over his guests. His deeply lined face softened with a smile as he reached for Frederick's hand, "Mr. Douglass, I know you. I have read about you. Mr. Seward has told me all about you. Sit down. I am glad to see you. Now, tell me what brings you here. What's the object of your visit? Please sit." He seemed well balanced between cordiality and reserve. Frederick felt immediate ease. He sat with Senator Pomeroy at his side, but the president gave his undivided attention to Frederick, who revealed his reasons for coming. "Sir, I have been assisting in the recruitment of Black soldiers, and I have been very successful in getting men to enlist, but now it is not easy to induce colored men to enlist because the men feel that their government does not treat them fairly."

"Please give me particulars, Mr. Douglass." The president's eyes suggested genuine interest.

"Sir, there are three reasons for their feelings. First, colored soldiers ought to receive the same wages as white soldiers; second, colored soldiers should receive the same protections when taken prisoner and be exchanged as readily and on the same terms as any other prisoners; and third, when colored soldiers perform great and uncommon service on the battlefield they should be rewarded by distinction and promotion precisely as white soldiers are rewarded for like services."

"You do know I've issued the Order of Retaliation."

"Yes, sir, and we thank you for it. But you were somewhat slow."

Pomeroy flinched, but Lincoln maintained his smile. The president continued: "You made a speech in New York, I think, and it got into the papers, and that speech said many things, but one of the things you said was that if you were called upon to state what you regarded as the most disheartening feature of our present political and military situation, it would *not* be our present political and military situation, it would *not* be the military disasters in the field, but it would be the tardy, hesitating and vacillating policy of the president of the United States." He paused, and added kindly, "Mr. Douglass, I have been charged with being tardy, and the like, and I am charged with vacillating, but, Mr. Douglass, I do not think that the charge can be sustained. No man can say that having once taken the position I have contradicted it or *retreated* from it."

Frederick cleared his throat. "Yes, sir, I made those remarks at Cooper's Institute in February last year, and time has confirmed your conclusion."

"Thank you, Mr. Douglass, but I need to address the other matters. The employment of colored troops was indeed a great gain to colored people, but it must be understood that the employment of colored troops could not have been successfully adopted at the beginning of the war. Their enlistment was a serious offence to popular prejudice, and equal pay would have exacerbated that offence. You know, sir, that the colored man is hated and despised throughout this land, and you surely know that if I had come out with equal pay at the very beginning, all the hatred which is poured out on the Negro race would be visited on this administration. Preparatory work was needed, and preparatory work was done. Remember this, Mr. Douglass. Milliken's Bend, Port Hudson, and Fort Wagner are recent events, and these were *necessary* for the equal protection proclamation and the coming of equal pay. Ultimately, colored soldiers will receive the same pay."

"Thank you, sir," replied Frederick. He wanted to listen more and talk less.

"About the relation order and equal protection, I must offer my misgivings. Retaliation is a terrible remedy, one that is very difficult to apply. Once begun, there is no telling where it will end. If I can get hold of specific Confederate soldiers who have been guilty of treating colored soldiers as felons, I can easily retaliate, but to hang a man for a crime perpetrated by others revolts my feelings. Thankfully, I have received word that colored soldiers are receiving better treatment as prisoners of war, and I remain convinced that less evil will be done if retaliation is not resorted to."

Then why did you issue the order? Frederick wondered, but added nothing more about the matter, impressed by the president's confession of his moral struggle with a needed policy. His nickname, "Honest Abe," was earned indeed.

Frederick waited, and then the president said brightly, "About that third matter. I will sign any commission to colored soldiers whom the secretary of war recommends to me."

Frederick reached for the pass in his pocket and presented it to the president, saying excitedly, "Secretary Stanton has offered me a commission, and I intend to go to the South and help recruit the freedmen."

Lincoln read the pass, turned it sideways, and wrote, "I concur. A. Lincoln. Aug 10, 1863."

"Thank you, sir," Frederick said, marveling at his document with the signature of the president, two members of his cabinet, and a United States Senator.

Lincoln stood. The interview was over. "Come back and see me, Mr. Douglass. I am eager to hear your reports about the recruitment work down South. Good day. Good day, Mr. Pomeroy." The president returned to his uncomfortable chair.

Outside the president's office, Pomeroy enthused, "A decent, honorable man, as I told you. Yes, we in Congress have had to put a little fire under his chair now and then, but I would rather have a slow wise man than a hasty fool. I fear for the country if something happens to Mr. Lincoln."

"Thank you, sir. I need to get home as soon as possible," Frederick said. He rushed down the corridor and stairs, ignoring the whispered "niggers," pausing only to adjust to the bright light, the intense heat, the awful smell outside. He had to get home and get ready for the promised commission and the trip south.

Frederick boarded the next train out of Washington. When he arrived home, he received a letter from Stanton telling him to go Vicksburg and report to General Thomas. "It's de Lord speaking to you," said Anna, confirming destiny's hand.

But there was no word about a commission, or mention of rank, pay, or specific duties. He wrote to Stanton for clarification on August 14. Convinced that answers would come, Frederick wrote his farewell letter to his "Respected readers" two days later. He had to answer the most fundament question: Why was he ending his publishing career after all these years and going south?

Before answering that question, he assured readers that his paper was still strongly supported, having received generous help from the very beginning. He told them he was not motivated by a love of change or adventure. The historical moment required more than words; the moment required action and sacrifice. He could no longer remain on the sidelines. If he could not fight, he could help organize units that would bring honor to the men and inspire the nation, as the 54th Massachusetts had done.

But these new units would do even more, for, unlike the 54th, a regiment of free Negroes from the north, these new units of former *slaves*, ready to fight for freedom, were a slave master's worst nightmare.

Given all the sweat and hours he had given to the publishing and editing newspapers since 1847, his valedictory letter seemed inadequate, but he trusted his readers. They would accept his motive because they trusted him to do the right thing now.

Then he waited.

The silence unnerved him.

His anger simmered as he tried to understand why Stanton would offer a commission and then say little more. *Did he realize he had made a mistake? Did he discover opposition in the administration that even he, with all his power, could not deflate?*

Frederick could not blame the president, who said that he would accept any commission that came to him. But the commission had to come from Stanton, and clearly Stanton was the culprit.

He had made a fool of Frederick Douglass.

Later, he learned from Senator Pomeroy that Stanton had changed his mind after several generals lodged protests. Many of them were still not ready for Black officers, especially an officer as famous as Frederick Douglass.

Frederick's anger boiled.

When he paused to consider the events of the past month, he could not avoid self-recrimination. Obsessively reviewing past conversations, he realized what had happened.

He had been so swept away by his mission on behalf of colored soldiers, by a signed document with the signatures of important men, by his entrance into the White House and his meeting President Lincoln, that he had succumbed to flattery by the powerful. He had lowered a guard carefully developed over decades, and now he was empty handed. No commission, no job, no newspaper; nothing but the bitter taste of folly and disillusionment. He made a decision. He would not go south without documented distinction in standing or rank. An officer of the United States Army would have more protection in a war zone than a civilian, he reasoned.

Earlier that year, he had mentioned in a letter to Julia that he might enlist if the state of New York guaranteed equal rights. She responded vehemently, "By everything dear to you dear friend, do not take any commission that leads you personally into the fighting ranks. Never go south—or killed you most assuredly will be. You are a marked man. The pen is greater than the sword—the head is greater than the hand—your work is with your pen and tongue." When she heard the news of his decision to not go, she was ecstatic. She wrote, "Dear friend, my relief knows no bounds. You are safe for the good you will still do, thanks be to God."

Even so, he had little to show for all his efforts by the fall of 1863, and any explanations or excuses seemed especially hollow when he considered the sacrifices of his three sons.

91.

THE YEAR ENDED AS it began, with a celebration. But the marriage of Rosetta to Nathan Sprague on Christmas Eve was a small, quiet affair muted by separations, painful memories, and distant war.

Frederick sat in his office and waited for Rosetta to begin their descent to the parlor and their guests, the Posts, the Smiths, the Porters, and the officiating minister, Reverend Thomas Bentley. Frederick recalled the terrible events of that summer and fall and recognized that Rosetta's blooming romance and eventual engagement were anticlimactic but came as needed relief.

He had continued his recruitment work and given lectures until just weeks before the wedding, so he missed seeing how Rosetta's love for Nathan developed. But her engagement came as no surprise. He had been warned by Anna, and Rosetta was indeed happier when Nathan was nearby. Every time he came into a room, she smiled, her surreptitious glances failing to hide her feelings. "He is *fine*," Anna reminded Frederick. "Just look at that *face*!"

But Nathan had no prospects, at least none assuring Frederick that he could take care of Rosetta and their future children, although he talked vaguely about owning a gardening shop. But Frederick did not hold this against him when Nathan finally came to ask him for Rosetta's hand. Frederick had one condition, even though he never meant to prevent the marriage and upset Rosetta. "You *must* enlist. You must join the 54th Massachusetts. All able-bodied, young men should do it, for country, for family pride." Frederick said this despite what happened to the 54th during the assault of Fort Wagner.

"I will enlist, sir. I just need a little time with Rosetta before I go off," Nathan replied.

"Then you have my blessing, sir," said Frederick, vigorously shaking his hand.

On the day of her wedding, Rosetta dressed in a splendid white gown made by her mother, its beading and embroidery surpassing the work done for Eliza Griffiths. She was a vision of loveliness and joy that stopped Frederick's brooding about the past year.

"Oh, Papa. I'm so happy, and I feel so beautiful."

"You *are* beautiful," he assured her. "Are you ready for a brave new world?"

"Yes, Papa. I'm ready."

As agreed in advance, Frederick rang the small bell on his desk to start the wedding march on the parlor piano. Frederick and Rosetta left the study and slowly stepped down the stairs, her right arm in his left.

"I wish the boys were here," Rosetta whispered. "My day would be perfect."

"I wish they were here, too. But let's just be happy in the moment."

"Yes, Papa."

Despite his advice, Frederick could not stop thinking of his sons. Lewis was more injured than he admitted at first. By September, he was so sick that he was sent to an army hospital in New York. Frederick asked his friend Doctor Smith to examine him. In October, Smith diagnosed Lewis with "gangrene of the left half of his scrotum," and declared him unfit for service.

Frederick rushed to New York, staying with Ottilie, and went with her to see Lewis. Frederick spent the next three weeks at his bedside, assuring him of his love and pride, hiding his guilt and fear, suppressing his outrage. There were hundreds of wounded men who lay in bandages moaning for hours, unattended by an overwhelmed staff, unvisited by family or friends. Frederick could only imagine what conditions were like in hospitals near battlefields, where many died *after* medical treatment.

Lewis never complained about the hospital or the staff. He insisted the doctors and nurses were doing all that they could do under the circumstances. He expressed one regret. "I can't be a father."

Meanwhile, Charles languished in an army camp outside Boston, often sick, hating army life—the poor food, the hard cots, the constant mud, the smells, the endless hours of mindless and meaningless work. He complained that the men of the 54th Massachusetts left behind were "treated worse than dogs." He also lost weight. "I fell away like a skeleton," he reported, alarming his parents.

Only Frederick, Jr., who never served as a combat soldier, remained unscathed.

By the end of their descent down the stairs on that Christmas Eve of 1863, Frederick forced himself to focus on Rosetta's imminent marriage. He could not forget his sons, but he could not allow his concerns to mar the most important day in Rosetta's life.

The room was decorated with dried hydrangeas, primroses, hollyhocks, and daisies from Ann Smith's garden, the one concession Anna made over having complete control of the arrangements for the wedding and dinner. Frederick had asked for pieces by Schubert and Mozart to be played, and Anna reacted with an emphatic "No!" with those wide, intense eyes that crushed her opposition. "Church music only."

The ceremony was short and simple as Anna required. "No sermons, no long speeches. We don't need to hear them ministers talk about what they know or believe. This is about Rosetta and Nathan, not what they have to say. And we won't remember anyways."

If Rosetta had any ideas about her special day, she kept them from Frederick.

★

After the New Year, Frederick decided to return to the lecture circuit, continuing what he had started in early December. After reading the president's brief but eloquent "Gettysburg Address," given on the battlefield on November 19, specifically three short paragraphs dedicating the war to a "new birth of freedom," Frederick needed to reinforce, in his own words, the mission of the war as both men were now defining it.

The war was a moral struggle, a second revolution that had to make sense and give meaning to the appalling statistics facing the nation. At Gettysburg alone, 6,000 had died. There were 27,0000 wounded, and 12,000 missing. The cause had to be worthwhile. Such slaughter could not be in vain.

After considerable thought, Frederick went to Washington to give his "Mission of the War" speech to a packed audience of almost 1,000. Hundreds of former slaves waited outside. He entered to the playing of "The Star-Spangled Banner" and mounted the pulpit as if on a crusade. After reading "The Gettysburg Address" and respectfully telling his audience of his meeting with the president, Frederick told his enraptured audience, "We are not to be saved by the captain this time, but by the crew. We are not to be saved by Abraham Lincoln, but by that power behind the throne, greater than the throne itself. You and I and all of us have this matter in hand. Men talk about saving the Union and restoring that Union as it was. They delude themselves with the miserable idea that that old Union can be brought to life again. That old Union can never come to life again. It is dead, and you cannot put life into it. We are fighting for something incomparably better than the old Union. We are fighting for unity, unity of object, unity of institutions, in which there shall be no North, no South, no East, no West, no black, no white, but the solidarity of the nation."

Frederick redoubled his efforts on the lecture circuit, reiterating his—and the president's—mission of the war and demanding the vote for freed slaves. He knew this last proposition would be the most controversial with northerners who often claimed that Negroes were too ignorant to vote. Frederick scorned this specious claim, especially given the ignorance of white immigrants who were allowed to vote. If a man knows enough to be hanged, he knows enough to vote, asserted Frederick. If he is good enough to fight for his government, he is good enough to vote.

Frederick continued his crusade, spending weeks away from home. He missed the day Lewis returned to the house for rest and recuperation, and he missed the day when Lewis received his formal discharge, dated February 29, 1864.

He missed Nathan's departure for the training camp of the 54th Massachusetts.

He missed Rosetta's announcement of her pregnancy.

He missed the first arrival of letters from Charles.

Charles was still alive, but he was sick almost constantly. He was discharged from the 54th Massachusetts and transferred to the Fifth Massachusetts Cavalry now serving in Virginia. Like his brother, Charles was appointed to the rank of First Sergeant, and with that noncommissioned rank, he became more eager for battle. He escaped the slaughter at the battles of the Wilderness and Cold Harbor and performed guard and picket duties. Boredom made combat more attractive.

Charles fell ill again and was transferred to the hospital complex at Point Lookout. During his stay there he was given leave to cross the Chesapeake Bay to St. Michaels, and he reunited with the Bailey cousins, the first Douglass to do so.

Frederick wanted to ask the president to discharge Charles from the army, but he was reluctant to make his request after attacking Lincoln in June for the first time since their meeting.

He had praised Lincoln publicly for months, telling eager, applauding patriots that their president was an honest, fair, and just man. But now the president's reconstruction plans for Louisiana were too charitable, too willing to ignore painful facts. Abraham Lincoln still appeased traitors by vetoing a congressional bill that restricted the organizing of state governments in the South to states where there was a loyal majority. Lincoln demanded only one tenth of the white voters support the new government. Lincoln still prevented Black voting and equal pay. Lincoln still refused to retaliate against the cold-blooded murder of colored soldiers.

Frederick's faith and patience were now threadbare. He wrote a letter charging the president with betrayal of his promises. "The president has virtually laid down this as a rule of his statesmen: *Do evil by choice, right from necessity.*" He did not intend the letter for publication, but somehow Garrison obtained a copy and published parts of it, demonstrating to him Garrison's unrelenting campaign to impugn, if not destroy, his reputation. *Once an apostate, always an apostate.*

Then Lincoln invited Frederick to the White House.

Frederick stared at the official White House stationery. Lincoln called the meeting of August 25 urgent. Stunned and embarrassed, Frederick knew he had to comply. This was a summons from the president of the United States.

92.

THE TRAIN RIDE TO Washington gave Frederick considerable time to consider the president's possible motives. He didn't know what to think, since Lincoln offered no explanation about the meeting's urgency. He could only hope that Lincoln needed his advice and respected his opinion.

Frederick fretted all the way to the White House.

When he entered the president's office, Frederick was flabbergasted. Lincoln had aged. His hair was grayer, his large frame sagged, deep lines and hollow cheeks marked his face, dark eyebrows and bags under his eyes converged to form wells of sadness so intense Frederick almost turned away. The president had seen too much.

And yet Lincoln smiled, and Frederick quickly approached him to shake his hand. "Sir, it is so good to see you. Thank you for the invitation."

"I think very highly of your mind, sir. You are a reflective, eloquent, and honest critic, and I need your advice. Please take a seat."

"Thank you, sir, for your trust."

They sat down and Lincoln came to the point.

"I want your advice about a letter I wrote. I'm being accused of protracting our war and failing to make peace when offered the opportunity. There's growing impatience. So many are dying, and the battles, especially in Virginia with Lee and Grant, seem to settle nothing. Many are saying that a peace settlement is not possible with the rebels because the war is now a war to end slavery, and our platform requires the adoption of a constitutional amendment ending it everywhere. If the Democrats nominate McClellan at the end of the month, I may very well lose the election."

"Sir, that can't happen. That *won't* happen," exclaimed Frederick.

"It can. My nomination was not assured with Secretary Chase running against me. And the carnage in Virginia has depressed everyone. The Democrats, if they stay united, have a real chance," said Lincoln.

"They are not united, sir, and Mr. Chase's resignation demonstrates your power."

"Give a man power, and his character is tested," Lincoln said.

Frederick was not sure if he was referring to Chase or himself. He said, "It's a refiner's fire, sir, and your character is clear to us all, especially to the colored people of this nation, slave and free. If we could all vote, we would all vote for you." Frederick meant to do more than flatter the president. He wanted to remind him of the potential political power of Black voters. They would surely become Republican voters.

"The vote, that will come too, eventually. In the meantime, I need your advice about this letter. I must address the peace clamor being raised against me," Lincoln said.

The president handed the draft of his letter to Frederick, who read it slowly.

Although supporting negotiations, the president's letter made it clear that potential negotiations would not include revocation of the Emancipation Proclamation or re-enslavement. "As a matter of morals, could such treachery escape the curses of heaven, or any good man?" Lincoln wrote. "As a matter of policy, to announce such a policy would ruin the union cause itself."

Frederick silently agreed, but the next assertions deeply troubled him. The president reassured critics that he did not have the power to abolish slavery everywhere. Only the people through Congress and the amendment process could do that. He also didn't think Congress would allow him to make the abolition of slavery an absolute prior condition for peace. The future of slavery was not up to him.

"Shall I send this?"

Frederick didn't hesitate. "Certainly not, sir. It would be given a broader meaning than you intend to convey; it would be taken as a complete surrender of your antislavery policy and do you serious damage. In answer to your accusers, your friends can make the argument of your insufficient power, but you cannot wisely say a word on this point. Address their concerns, yes, but send this, no."

"Thank you for your advice," Lincoln responded. His face revealed neither approval nor disapproval of Frederick's assessment, and he moved on. "I have another important matter to discuss."

There was a knock at the door, and Lincoln replied, "Come in."

His secretary, John Hay, said, "Sir, Governor Buckingham is waiting to see you."

"Tell Governor Buckingham to wait because I want to have a long talk with my friend Frederick Douglass."

Frederick started to rise. "Sir, I can step out, if you need to see the governor of Connecticut."

"No, he can wait."

When the door closed, Lincoln said, "I have something else to talk with you about. I wish to confer with you about the most desirable means, outside of the army, of some ways to induce slaves to come into federal lines now. The slaves are not coming so rapidly and so numerously to us as I had hoped, and with increasing opposition to the war, and constant calls for a peace settlement, I fear that many slaves don't know about the proclamation and will remain enslaved if there's a forced peace."

If there is a forced peace. Frederick was struck by the president's honest apprehensions, and he deflected his concern about Lincoln's political future. "Slaveholders keep proclamations and news from slaves. Probably very few slaves know about your proclamation, sir."

"Well, I want you to set about devising some means of making them acquainted with it, and for bringing into our lines what John Brown said he wanted to do—*before* Harpers Ferry."

The old John Brown plan. Frederick appreciated the irony, since Lincoln had called Brown a madman and a criminal.

"Will you do it?" Lincoln asked.

"Yes, sir," Frederick replied.

"Good. Send me your ideas when you can, the sooner the better."

"Yes, sir."

"You will organize scouts, colored scouts, to go into the rebel states, beyond the line of our armies, and urge slaves to come within our boundaries. John Brown had no lines, except Canada; our lines are everywhere. We should get thousands. And when they hear about my plan for a constitutional amendment banning slavery everywhere—and it must be abolished everywhere—we will gain even more soldiers. We need more soldiers, and the bare sight of 50,000 armed and drilled Black soldiers on the banks of the Mississippi would end the rebellion at once," Lincoln said.

"My son Frederick is trying to recruit freedmen in Mississippi," Frederick said.

"Please extend to him my appreciation. How are your other sons doing? I understand they enlisted as well as your new son-in-law."

Frederick's admiration deepened. He didn't think the president, with all his responsibilities, would know anything about his family. "Thank you for asking, sir. My oldest son survived the assault at Fort Wagner but has been sick ever since and is now recuperating at home. My youngest son, Charles, has also been sick, so sick he has not been able to fight. He wants to fight very much, to prove himself and his devotion to our country."

"The devotion of our sons, and the sons of all of you is incontestable now. There is a witness in every white man's bosom that he would rather go to the war having the Negro to help him, than to help the enemy against him. We are in your debt. Now tell me what Lewis had to say about the Wagner assault," Lincoln said.

There was a knock at the door. The secretary entered to remind the president that the governor was still waiting.

"Have him wait," Lincoln said.

"Sir, I can leave," Frederick said.

"No, not yet, Mr. Douglass. Mr. Hay, tell the governor he should wait until I'm finished here with my friend."

"Yes, sir."

Frederick and Lincoln spoke for almost two hours. Finally, Lincoln said, "Well, I must do my duty and meet with a duly elected governor." His tone was mischievous.

"Thank you for sending for me, and I will send the plan you asked for as soon as possible."

"Good and extend my regards to Mrs. Douglass back in Rochester."

"Thank you, sir." Frederick left the room elated. The president had deeply impressed him.

Later that day, after working on his commissioned project, Frederick paced the parlor floor trying to explain his impressions to his host, Thomas Dorsey. He couldn't settle down, his excitement agitated him. Frederick said, "I've just come from President Lincoln. He treated me as a man. He did not let me feel for a moment that there was any difference in the colors of our skins. The president is a most remarkable man."

"Indeed, he is," said Dorsey.

"Remarkable. Wise, kind, and free of personal prejudice," Frederick added.

★

Frederick sent his four-part proposal to the president on August 29. Squads of slaves would work as laborers and eventually as soldiers under the general agent, the unnamed Frederick Douglass. Subagents selected by Frederick would conduct squads of slaves to the North. Union generals would have close ties to the subagents. And a roving commission would make sure that proper food and shelter were provided to all freedmen in the campaign. Frederick wrote to the president: "This is but an imperfect outline of the plan, but I think it enough to give your Excellency an idea of how the desirable work shall be executed. Your obedient servant, Frederick Douglass."

Pleased with his August meeting with Lincoln and the warm feelings it engendered, Frederick seized the opportunity to ask the president for a favor.

He asked him to discharge Charles. On September 10, the president sent a terse command to the War Department. "Let this boy be discharged. A. Lincoln." On September 15, Charles informed Frederick and Anna that he was honorably discharged and would be home within two weeks.

Always thin, now Charles looked terrible, a skeleton with huge eyeballs. But he had never seen a battle, his dreams of warfare unfulfilled. Charles was bitter and said, "I never had a chance to prove myself. Lewis will always have that over me!"

Far less competitive, Lewis was no longer the proud survivor of battle. Now home, too, he was weary and deeply sad, asking plaintively while his parents sat at his bedside, "Will I smell death for the rest of my life?"

Frederick never heard from the president about his scout plan, but he rationalized Lincoln's silence because recent events seemed to make the "old John Brown plan" moot.

The day after General McClellan, finally fired by Lincoln, was nominated in Chicago as the Democratic presidential candidate, Atlanta fell to General Sherman. The nation celebrated the victory, which changed the national mood after months of stalemate. Praise for Lincoln, especially among white soldiers, rose. McClellan hoped to get their vote, and sensing slippage in his appeal, turned to race baiting, calling the Republicans "the nigger party."

Republican operatives in New York state didn't want Frederick's active participation in the campaign, fearing that it would lend credence to the charge of "Republican niggerism." Frederick wanted to campaign for Lincoln but didn't want to be a distraction. He bowed to pressure and said little about the election during his fall speaking tour.

Frederick was in Rochester on election day, November 8, and as allowed by NY state law because he met the property requirement for black suffrage cast his ballot for Lincoln. He then walked to the telegraph office to follow the returns. It was a landslide. The president carried the popular vote of 2,206,938 to McClellan's 1,803,787. The Electoral College vote was even more overwhelming. Lincoln won 212 votes to McClellan's 21.

He returned to the lecture circuit that fall ready to review his celebration of Lincoln's election. Starting his tour at the AME Zion Church in Rochester, he mounted the pulpit on the Sunday afternoon of November 13 with the rapid, light step of a man eager to share good news. Frederick intended to highlight the significance of Lincoln's reelection by announcing major news: his imminent return to Baltimore, a symbol of the new era. Now he could leave the train and walk the streets and reunite with family, friends, and his former masters, the Aulds. Maryland had abolished slavery by a narrow margin of 30,174 to 29,799 in a state referendum on November 1. Frederick could return without fear of arrest and deportation.

Frederick's speech conveyed the joyousness of dreams fulfilled, the once impossible now possible, a miracle giving rise to great expectations. "What a wonderful change a few short years have wrought," he said to the packed church. "I left Maryland a slave. I return to her a freeman. I left her a slave state. I return to find her clothed in her new garments of Liberty and Justice, a free State." He hoped for a public meeting with Thomas Auld surrounded by the city fathers, all of them acknowledging the new era.

He was now ready to return to Baltimore.

On November 17, as the choir of the Bethel AME Church on Saratoga Street in Fells Point sang "Home Sweet Home," he walked up the center aisle arm in arm with his sister Eliza, accompanied by thunderous applause. He had not seen her since 1836, when Thomas Auld returned him to Baltimore from the Eastern Shore. Now fifty-two, Eliza was the free wife of Peter Mitchell, who had devoted years of hard work to purchase her from Thomas. She had traveled fifty-six miles from Talbot County to see her famous brother. Frederick didn't notice her in the crowd because he had been receiving city officials, old friends, and well-wishers in the reception hall before his speech.

Frederick had immediately recognized James Mingo, the founder of the Baltimore Improvement Society. He was still a tall, dignified man, impeccably dressed. His hair was closely cropped but completely white, but his skin, like Frederick's, didn't show signs of age. It was lineless and dark brown with a glowing sheen. Mingo said in his deep resonant voice, "Well, my friend, you're not a Senator yet, but you will be. I'm sure of it."

Frederick grabbed Mingo's hand with both of his, shaking them vigorously. He exclaimed, "Oh, my friend, it's been so long. I never thought I would see you again, ever. We talked of New York, California, South America."

"And here you are. My, my, my," Mingo replied.

As Mingo was speaking, Frederick could see a dark and attractive woman, taller than the other women in the line of well-wishers, waiting her turn, and his heart stopped as their eyes connected. She smiled. Frederick knew who she was.

Frederick called her name as he approached her, passing the others in line. "Eliza."

"Yes, your sister. Your *big* sister," she replied.

He laughed at this reminder from the past. She knew her place, and so did he. Frederick took her into his arms and held her close and long as if she would vanish into the very air. "Eliza, Eliza," he whispered, his voice cracking with emotion. He was thrilled and shaken by the realization of a dream long put away as a foolish fantasy of adolescence. All the years of separation had closed within a moment. Tears rolled down his broad cheeks, and he was not ashamed. He stepped away. "How? How did you find me? I can't believe it. I just can't believe it."

“We all heard about your coming. We know all about you. Sixty miles ain’t a long way to come,” Eliza said. Those around them had stepped discreetly away, allowing the two to have a private reunion in a public church.

“Tell me about the family, tell me all that you can, please,” Frederick said.

“I have nine children of my own. I named one of my girls Mary Douglass Mitchell after you,” Eliza said.

“I’m honored, and I have four of my own. I had five.”

“Your Charlie told us when he came last year. I was sorry to hear about Annie. My children are doin’ just fine, thank you very much, and my family is free. We bought our way out from Captain Auld. We worked and worked till it was done, Peter and me.”

“And what are they doing now?”

“Oyster tonging, working on the farms. That’s what John, Edward, and Pete are doin’, and Susan and Mary are out to service. And we all never stopped hearin’ and talkin’ about you, that’s for sure. Captain Thomas, he never could stop talking about you, either, about how you was spreading lies about him and his brother Hugh,” Eliza said.

“Guilt makes a man forget the truth, and even if I stretched the truth, it was needed,” Frederick said.

“Still, Mr. Thomas wants to see you. He’s sick, but he said he wants to. He knows all about what happened since you left.”

“But that didn’t stop him, now did it? Still selling, separating Baileys, I hear. What about the rest, what about Perry and the others?” Frederick asked.

“Sold to Mississippi and Louisiana, somewhere. I don’t know where exactly,” Eliza replied.

“Can I do something for you and for your children? I want to do this.”

“No, nothin’. You don’t need to. We just glad to know that we have you here.”

Eliza patted his hand and pulled at her shawl, as if preparing to leave. “I never forgot you, and I’m so proud you is my brother. You became somebody, as I knew you would, from the start, as if the Lord had his hand on you.”

“You’re somebody, too,” he said. He took her large, rough hands into his, feeling the lines, cuts, and callouses that defined her life’s work.

“Yes, I know. But you showed them that you is as good as them. No, you showed them you’re better.”

“I’ll come to see you again.”

“And don’t stay away so long.”

“I won’t.”

“Remember this, Frederick Augustus Washington Bailey, we is always family,” Eliza said.

"Walk with me down the aisle. It would mean so much to me," Frederick said.

"I'm not one for showin' off."

Frederick laughed. "Well, you know that's not true for me. Never was."

"Ain't that the truth? Some things don't change."

"Still on that high horse."

"And nobody can knock you off now," Eliza said.

"Now, let's go and show our people a reunited family," Frederick said.

On that "day of wonders," as he called it, he admitted his love of Maryland. From the pulpit draped with American flags and a large sign saying "Welcome Home," Frederick declared, "I left Maryland in a hurry, shaking the dust from my feet, as if leaving a doomed city; now I return to greet with an affectionate kiss, the humblest pebble from the shores of your glorious Chesapeake. I did not leave because I loved Maryland less, but freedom more."

Over the next two weeks in Baltimore, Frederick gave six lectures offering practical advice for the demands of the hour. To Blacks he emphasized education, hard work, and perseverance. To whites he offered a refutation of white supremacy: "I deny that the Black man's degradation is essential to the white man's elevation. I deny that the Black man should be tied, lest he outstrip you in the race of improvement. I deny the existence of such a necessity and affirm that those who allege the existence of any such, pay a *sorry* compliment to the white race."

Two days later, Frederick approached the Auld house on Ann Street after receiving a reply from Benjamin Auld to his note asking permission to visit. He now doubted the wisdom of his return to this house, the sagging wood and peeling paint further proof that success continued to elude Hugh Auld. Frederick chided himself for hoping that the Aulds, or at least Sophia, would overlook years of denunciation in the press and on the lecture circuit and embrace him as a member of their family, the prodigal son returning home at last. For a moment he considered leaving Ann Street forever. But his pride would not allow a retreat, and he knocked hard at the door, still eager to show that he had become somebody.

A stocky, unsmiling man opened the door. He had the blond hair of Sophia, and the incredible blue eyes of Hugh and Thomas. Frederick said, "Mr. Auld, I'm here to see Miss Sophia. I'm Frederick Douglass."

Benjamin Auld scowled and stepped back, allowing Frederick into the dark hallway. He remained silent as he led Frederick to the parlor and stood before the fireplace in the drab room.

"Sir, Mr. Auld. I'm here to see Miss Sophia, and Tommy," Frederick said.

"Tommy never came back, died at sea, and you *dare* to come back here," Benjamin replied.

"I didn't know, but I want to thank . . ." Frederick said.

"You will not see her today, or any other day, sir, after you have slandered my family," Benjamin interrupted.

"I even wrote to your father . . ." Frederick had finally written to Hugh in 1859 to say that he felt a strong desire to write him and learn something of the position and prospects of his children.

"He cannot tell you to your face that you are a liar, *you* who called him a 'foul imp of a slaveholder,'" Benjamin said.

"Sir, I was sorry to hear that your father . . ."

"You don't care about him. You never did, even when you wrote that guilt letter. Did you really think that they believed you? You spent years attacking them, even my mother, who you said treated you like a brute. A *brute*? She taught you, made you who you are. Your whole life is built on lies!" He interrupted Frederick yet again. Prepared for this moment, Benjamin Auld pulled a sheet from his trouser pocket and read the offending lines with cutting sarcasm: "Your dear children were dear to me—and are still—indeed I feel nothing but kindness for you all. I love you, but hated Slavery." Benjamin looked at Frederick and exclaimed, "Good God! And now you come back, and for what? So that my mother will forgive you? That will never happen. So, get out of our house."

"Sir . . ." Frederick said

"Get out!"

"Sir, tell her that . . ." Frederick said, never raising his voice.

"Get out!"

"Sir, will you tell her I was here?"

"She will *not* see you. Get out!"

Frederick departed, holding his head high and back straight. He did not turn around when Benjamin shouted with all the sullen, petty belligerence of his father, "May you rot in hell for what you did to my family!"

Ten days later the newest member of Frederick's family, his first grandchild, entered the world. Rosetta named her Annie in memory of her sister.

93.

FREDERICK WAS NOT IN Washington on January 31 when the House of Representatives passed, by one vote, the Thirteenth Amendment, abolishing slavery throughout the United States. He was on tour. Frederick resolved to not miss Lincoln's second inauguration on Saturday, March 4.

Frederick arrived on a packed train two days before the inauguration. A band played "The Battle Cry of Freedom" at the B&O depot despite the heavy rain. He had to walk carefully to the home of his hosts, the Dorseys, as the streets were rivers of stinking mud, and thousands of Black fugitives still huddled in shacks and under fragile tarps. Thousands of Confederate deserters were homeless, too, as the war seemed near its bloody end and Union victory was close at hand. Even so, the jubilant mood in the capital was muted, almost somber. There was talk of southern desperation and plots to kill Lincoln. The crowd was silent, its leaden stillness reminding Frederick of a funeral. Everyone huddled closely together, trying to stay dry during a soft but cold rain.

The tall doors of the Capitol swung open, and a mass of people emerged from the Senate chamber, where new senators and the vice president had been sworn in. Everyone cheered, though Lincoln was not yet in sight. He then came out with Andrew Johnson, his new vice-president, at his side. Lincoln smiled, graciously taking the hands of those extended to him. He now seemed like an old man, tall but fragile in the bend of his head and back. He looked to the crowd, scanning for familiar faces. When he found Frederick's, he nudged Johnson and pointed, smiling with a distinct nod of his head.

Unable to hide his initial reaction, repulsion crossed the face of the former senator from Tennessee. Frederick refused to break eye contact, unembarrassed by the vice president's raw contempt. He waited to see how Johnson would react to his scrutiny. Johnson regained his political composure as quickly as he lost it, with a practiced grin and nod. Frederick's companion, Mrs. Dorsey, commented slyly, "Whatever Andrew Johnson may be, he certainly is no friend of our race."

The sergeant at arms bowed before the crowd, and it fell silent. Mr. Lincoln stepped forward acknowledging the applause from below with another nod of his head, and started to read his address as the sun broke through the clouds and painted the platform with light. His voice high and clear, he began: "Fellow countrymen: at this second appearing to take the oath of the presidential office, there is less occasion for an extended address then at the first." It was a mundane beginning, but soon eloquent, Biblical cadences followed, earning applause and bringing tears to the eyes of Frederick and Mrs. Dorsey and many others there. Lincoln continued: "Truly do we hope, fervently, do we pray, that this mighty scourge of war may speedily pass away, yet if it be God's will that it continue until the wealth piled by the bondsmen by two hundred and fifty years' unrequired toil be sunk, and until every drop of blood drawn with the lash shall be paid by another drawn with the sword, as was paid three thousand years ago, so it must be said that the judgments of the Lord are true and righteous altogether."

The war was God's punishment for the nation's original sin.

At last, everyone heard the complete identification of the war with emancipation. If the nation was to survive, slavery could not survive.

Frederick was now ready for the reconciliation that Lincoln offered like an olive branch in the climax of his address: "With malice toward none, with charity for all, with firmness in the right, as God gives us to see the right, let us strive on to finish the work we are in, to bind up the nation's wounds, to care for him who shall have born the battle, and for his widow and orphans, to do all which may achieve and cherish a just and lasting peace among ourselves and with all nations."

A roar of cheers and applause surrounded the president. Standing there, Frederick decided that he would return to the Eastern Shore and, in the spirit of Lincoln's speech, see Thomas Auld. It was now possible for lambs to venture into the lion's den without the danger of being eaten. When silence was at last restored, the president turned to Chief Justice Chase, held up his right hand, placed his left on the Bible supported by the chief clerk of the Supreme Court, and repeated the oath with a loud, ringing emphasis on the last words, "So help me God!" He bent forward and kissed the book. The crowd cheered, and artillery saluted the president with cannon fire as Lincoln departed.

"Shall we go to the reception?" asked Mrs. Dorsey. "The public is invited."

"Negroes have never gone before," observed Frederick. "But this is a new day, and someone must lead the way."

Later that night, 2,000 people pressed against the White House gate, and when the gates were finally opened at eight o'clock, they stampeded the front portico. Swooning women in pounds of crinoline had to be lifted and carried over the heads of the crowd. The vestibule of the White House was littered with feathers, flowers, lace, and slippers, battered remnants of the crush. The crowd formed a long line into the East Room, where the president waited to greet his guests. When Frederick and Mrs. Dorsey entered the building, a policeman grabbed Frederick by the left arm. "Stand back! We have orders. No coloreds allowed!"

Frederick jerked his left arm free. "There must be some mistake. President Lincoln would never give such an order."

The sergeant gritted his teeth and encircled Frederick's arm like a metal vice. "Listen, nig . . . Listen, mister, orders are orders!"

The sergeant looked about him, embarrassed by the commotion Frederick was causing and angered by the horrified faces of spectators, who wanted something to be done immediately. The sergeant whispered in a polite show of confidence, "All right, mister, then come this way with me."

He led Frederick through the Blue Room to a window where wood planks served as a temporary exit ramp. Frederick stopped. "Sir, you have deceived me," he shouted, making sure that he was heard throughout the room. "I will not leave until I see the president!"

The sergeant pushed him forward on to the ramp. Mrs. Dorsey followed, saying nothing. Frederick looked over his shoulder and called out to a white man who knew him, "Sir, please inform Mr. Lincoln that Frederick Douglass is being detained at the door."

The acquaintance hurried off, hopefully to the East Room, where the president was receiving the public.

The sergeant relaxed his grip, whispering, "Frederick Doug . . ."

"Yes, Frederick Douglass," said Frederick boldly.

The sergeant snapped, "I don't care who you are. I'm just following orders. No Negroes."

An officer ran into the Blue Room, came directly to the sergeant's ear, and whispered, "the president wants to see him." The sergeant released Frederick's arm and returned to his duties without apology.

Frederick pulled at the cloth of his jacket to restore his best appearance before talking to Lincoln. He was escorted by another sergeant to the entrance of the East Room and waited patiently, relieved that he had not been forced to return to the end of the line. Frederick slowly approached the president, who pointed to him and said to a man near him, "Here comes my friend Douglass."

"Mr. President," Frederick said.

"I am so glad to see you," Lincoln said, shaking Frederick's hand. "I saw you in the crowd today, listening to my address. How did you like it?"

Lincoln's hand was cold, his face emaciated, but the warmth in his voice encouraged an attempt at brief conversation. Frederick replied, "Mr. Lincoln, I must not detain you with my poor opinion, when there are thousands waiting to shake hands with you."

"No, no, you must stop a little, Douglass. There's no man in the country whose opinion I value more than yours. I want to know what you think of it."

"Mr. Lincoln, it was a sacred effort."

"I'm pleased that you like it! Let me introduce you to Mrs. Lincoln. Mary, this is my friend Frederick Douglass."

The short, plump woman, splendidly dressed in a cascade of flowers on her head, bowed her head slightly, and said with the dimmest of smiles, "Mr. Douglass." She did not offer her hand.

Frederick started to move away, and the president took his hand again. He said gently, "Please excuse the sergeants for their behavior. They had no orders. Habits are often blind."

★

"Frederick! Frederick! Frederick!"

He jumped up from his chair. Isaac Post's voice was loud with pain and horror. Frederick took a deep breath, bracing himself. Bad news was coming. He immediately thought of Frederick, Jr., still in Mississippi. The war was over. Lee had surrendered to Grant at Appomattox, but it would take weeks before word reached every rebel that far south, and surely some rebels, stirred by the revenge of ignoble defeat, would try to kill every Yankee still alive.

Isaac burst into Frederick's upstairs study shaking telegrams in his hand. "Someone shot the president! He's dead, Frederick! Lincoln is dead, shot in the head. Oh, my God, I can't believe it! He's *dead*!"

Frederick was struck by an incomprehensible horror. He felt sick as Isaac garbled about murder and conspiracy, sputtering out what he knew. "A southern actor shot Lincoln in the head . . . at the theater . . . somebody stabbed Secretary Seward . . . Grant was killed on a train . . . the cabinet wiped out."

"No! This can't be true! We have to find out more. We need to go back to the telegraph office," Frederick cried.

Isaac took a deep breath and soldiered to attention. "Frederick, he's dead. Nothing we do or say will change that. Mr. Lincoln is dead, cheated out of the victory he had worked so hard to achieve. He's dead."

Frederick allowed the word "dead" to sink in as memories of Lincoln flooded him. The tall frame, the wry smile, the long arms and huge hands, the high but determined voice, his keen intellect, his compassion, his dedication to the union and the abolition of slavery, phrases from the second inaugural address, the words, "my friend Frederick Douglass."

"Being out here, the news might not have reached you for hours. I didn't want you to find out casually if you went to town today," Isaac said.

"We need to go get as much information as we can. My carriage is downstairs." Frederick's house was far out of town. A walk would take hours, and he didn't want to be alone. Isaac could leave his horse tied to the post at the end of the road. "Thank you, Isaac, for coming. How are you doing?"

Isaac collapsed, convulsed by sobs. Frederick rushed to hold up his friend, as millions did throughout the devastated nation. Together they returned to town, where they learned more about the assassination. Lincoln had been shot in the head Friday night during a play. The assassin had escaped. Lincoln died early Saturday morning in a building across the street. Although the secretary of state had been stabbed in his home, he survived. And the rest of the cabinet was safe. Grant was unharmed.

By three o'clock that afternoon, a massive throng gathered at City Hall as bells tolled. Many said they didn't know what else to do. Hundreds had to wait outside because the room could not accommodate them. Mayor Daniel Moore had quickly organized the meeting and had asked several clergymen to speak.

Frederick sat in the back, intending to just listen. But people saw him in the audience and a chant began. "Douglass! Douglass! Douglass!"

Startled, Frederick looked around. He understood in their soft chants the belief that he could best articulate their feelings and could find the words to give meaning to incomprehensible tragedy. The chant grew louder, and Frederick rose. As the north star rose every day responding to the laws of nature, he too had to rise, to do the right thing.

The people parted for him as he approached the platform. Some nodded their heads, and some whispered their thanks. Frederick nodded his head from time to time, still not knowing exactly what he would say. He reached the platform and shook the hands of the mayor, a federal judge, the president of the Rochester Theological Seminary, and the rector of St. Luke's Episcopal Church. Frederick turned to the audience and looked down to the first rows and saw hope amidst desolation, a need for higher ground, where memories of a noble life would triumph over aching loss.

He began calmly, his voice even, controlled. "This call to address you on this occasion was quite unexpected to me, and on which I find impossible to respond. If you have . . ." He stopped, his voice gripped by painful grief, surprising him because the time it took to ride into town had seemed to calm his shattered nerves.

Frederick closed his eyes, drawing on his emotional and intellectual strength, and resumed: "If you have deep grief in the death of Abraham Lincoln, I feel it as a personal as well as a national calamity because of the race to which I belong. This is not an occasion for speech making, but for silence. I have scarcely been able to say a word to any of those friends who have taken my hand and looked sadly in my eyes today. A dreadful disaster has befallen the nation. It is a day for silence and meditation; for grief and tears. Yet I feel that though Abraham Lincoln dies, the republic lives; though that great and good man, one of the noblest to walk God's earth, is struck down by the hand of the assassin, yet I know that the nation is saved, and liberty established forever."

The sound of applause cracked the silence, and Frederick continued, giving a speech despite his earlier disclaimer. It was shorter than usual, but he could not resist using the gift God had given him: "When the heads of this Rebellion are swept off, in their tracks will spring up their luckless sons, to whom they will bequeath some infernal passions like that which has caused our great bereavement. By their hand other officers of the government will be stricken down. What is our remedy? It is here: Know no man hereafter by his complexion, but know every man by his loyalty, and where there is a patriot in the North or South, white or black, helping on the good cause, hail him as a citizen, a kinsman, a brother beloved. Let us not remember our enemies and disenfranchise our friends. The black man will not only build for you ramparts of earth and solid stone, but they offer you ramparts of flesh, and fight the battles of the nation amid insult and persecution. Let us not forget that justice to the Negro is safety to the Nation. For the safety of all, let justice be done to each. Let it be done."

Frederick mentioned seeing the president, shaking his hand, and hearing his great inaugural speech, the last paragraph of which he quoted from memory, "With malice toward none and charity for all." Most of all, Frederick needed his audience to remember the lesson of Lincoln's life and death. Punctuated by cheers, Frederick noted, "Today, today as never before, the American people, although they cannot have indemnity for the past—for the countless treasure and the precious blood—yet today they can resolve today to exact ample security for the future. And if it teaches us this lesson, it may be that the blood of our beloved martyred President will be the salvation of our country. Good man we call him; good man he was. If an honest man is the noblest work of God, we need have no fear for the soul of Abraham Lincoln."

Five months later, a gift from Mary Todd Lincoln arrived. The entire family and Ottilie gathered that August morning to witness the opening of the long and narrow box. Before doing so, Frederick read aloud the brief note that came with it, "Dear Mr. Douglass: Mr. Lincoln always wanted to present you with some token of his high regard for you. Please accept his walking stick in memory of him." Frederick held the memento and said, "Oh, sir. Oh, sir."

94.

WHEN FREDERICK HEARD THAT Garrison was going to propose the formal dissolution of the American Anti-Slavery Society at its thirty-second annual meeting in May, Frederick went to New York City's Church of the Puritan ready to wage another war, perhaps his last, against him.

Ottilie was in the audience. He had reviewed his major points with her the day before, and her approval bolstered his confidence. He didn't need her support, but he appreciated it because she understood his complicated history with Garrison. She criticized carefully, offering her latest assessment with that combination of insight and audacity that provoked and excited him all at once.

Garrison, always thin, stood straight as a flagpole. His pale skin now tight over prominent bones revealed a gaunt old man, but his voice was as strong as ever, a veteran of oratorical war. "We are organized expressly for the abolition of slavery. We called ourselves an antislavery society, and now I believe slavery is abolished in this country, abolished constitutionally, abolished by a decree of this nation, never, never to be reversed," Garrison said.

"Sir!" interrupted Wendell Phillips, "The Thirteenth Amendment is not ratified yet!"

"It will be, as you well know," Garrison replied.

Wendell persisted, "Sir, the South is not converted. You cannot kill off all the white men who cherish hatred toward democratic institutions. You can only flank them as Grant flanked Lee; flank them with the Black vote, divided lands. Sir, prejudice is very rife. All over the country, the colored man is a pariah. *Your* abolition must be only the technical end of slavery, but *my* abolition, when I pledged my faith to that Declaration of Sentiments and the constitution of the American Anti-Slavery Society, was absolute equality before the law, absolute civil equality. And *I never* shall leave the Negro until, so far as God gives me the power, I achieve it." Loud applause from the crowd greeted these remarks, and Wendell accepted them as usual with a slight bow before turning to Garrison for a reply.

"I am sure that the government will insist that reconstructed states protect the freedmen, give them the right to vote, eventually," Garrison said. He usually responded to challenges with a heightened, almost propulsive, vigor, but now he seemed listless, unfocused, purged of the fire that drove him for more than thirty years. He seemed unwilling to challenge Wendell's public rebuke.

Frederick had not been there to witness the deterioration of their relationship and was astonished to see it now. He jumped up. "Eventually? Eventually?"

Garrison's demeanor was unforgiving, penetrating, and as cold as ever. "Yes, *eventually*," he replied evenly. "The freedman is not yet ready to vote; he is unschooled, unprepared for civic responsibilities."

"Sir, white Americans are not too particular about foreigners. Foreigners get the vote as soon as they land, even though they can't read or write, or even speak English. How much do we have to know in order to vote?" Frederick countered.

Garrison responded as if an unruly, misinformed student had spoken out of turn. "Sir, you speak as if the elective franchise is a natural right, not a conventional one. States grant the right to vote, and they have the power to take it away."

Stephen Foster, a staunch Garrison supporter until now, blurted out, "Sir, you make compromise with the devil himself!"

Amused by Foster's sudden allegiance with him, Frederick waved his hand to reply to Garrison's remarks. "Gentlemen, a question has been asked which merits an answer. If the Negro knows enough to fight for the flag and the government, he knows enough to vote. If he knows as much when he's sober as an Irishman knows when drunk, he knows enough to vote. Without the vote, his liberty is a mockery."

"Mr. Douglass, the issue is not the vote," Garrison said, "but our part in getting that vote, which I don't deny the freedman needs eventually . . ."

"Eventually!" thundered Foster, repeating the word as conclusive proof of Garrison's fall. "Eventually!"

Garrison rolled his eyes. "This is an abolition society. The vote and other needs should be left to Negro-aid societies. To keep an antislavery society alive after slavery is abolished would seem, in our judgment, to be folly."

Wendell Phillips stood again. "A man is still a slave until he can protect his freedom with the ballot. Therefore, an antislavery society has every reason to continue until that freedom is completely his."

Frederick agreed and warned the audience about the new form of slavery: laws passed by states to ensure the degradation of the Black man under the new constitution; restrictions of testimony against whites; limits to bearing arms; constraints on meetings; state's rights in full flower.

The debate continued for two days, and when the roll was called Garrison's motion went down to defeat, 118 to 48. Trying to make amends and reduce the smart of defeat, Wendell called for Garrison's election as president of the society. Hungry for harmony after two acrimonious days, the Society reelected Garrison as its president. But he refused to accept the job, saying with wounded pride, "I have already announced my intention to withdraw from this society, and this election will not keep me in it." He marched out with a few loyal followers, declaring those who remained unregenerate, deluded, excommunicated apostates.

Wendell was elected president but didn't relish the victory, for it marked the end of his long association with Garrison. "I knew this day would come," he explained to Frederick during a late supper after the society's adjournment. "We started disagreeing during the war about Lincoln, you know. Because of the Emancipation Proclamation, Lloyd was willing to ignore and forgive everything. He was so eager to celebrate, *too* eager."

"Is that why you stayed away from the jubilee celebrations?" Frederick asked.

"I didn't see much to be thankful for . . ." Wendell said.

The absolute arrogance of this statement stung Frederick to the quick. "Wendell, you're in no position to say anything about gratitude."

Wendell raised his hand to stop the beginning of a tirade. "Please, dear friend, don't misunderstand me. I, too, felt the emotions of January '63, but sometimes our joys make us blind to details. That emancipation was not the jubilee I expected, and you, too, saw its limitations. Lincoln was too lenient with the South, too willing to let the traitors back into the Union without making Negro suffrage a precondition for readmission, too willing to forgive, perhaps even to forget."

"But . . ."

"Let us recollect that he was human and that he welcomed light like most men and was more honest than his fellows and with a truth to his own convictions much as few politicians achieve. With all his shortcomings, I point proudly to him as the natural outgrowth of democratic institutions. Coming time will put him in that galaxy of Americans which makes our history the day of the nations, and history will add his name to the bright list, with a more loving claim on our gratitude than either Washington or Jefferson or the rest. For not one of those was called upon to die for his cause."

Frederick was silent for a moment. "You have taken the full measure of Mr. Lincoln."

"We all must try, now that he's gone."

"But the things you said during the war."

"My opposition was political, never personal. And Lincoln had a capacity for change. But Garrison cannot bend, cannot move from his own narrow rock. At one time, that persistence was courageous—yes, inspiring. The war is over, the Thirteenth Amendment will soon be part of the Constitution. And he feels entitled to a rest with a perfect celebration. The biggest day of his life was when the government invited him as a guest of honor to attend the ceremonial raising of the Union flag over Fort Sumter. Three thousand freedmen greeted him in Charleston, and he was carried on shoulders to the speaker's stand in Citadel Square. But Lincoln was shot that very same day. John Wilkes Booth, you, and me, we're all spoiling his greatest moment," Wendell said.

"And slavery is back, going by the name of 'freedmen labor laws,'" Frederick said.

"And he will not forgive us for reminding him that he was wrong. The end of slavery is only the beginning. And yet, and yet, how different history would be if he had not taken on slavery and discrimination, almost alone, in the spring of 1831. Abraham Lincoln, John Brown, and William Lloyd Garrison will be remembered and honored for their courage."

"And you with them, my friend," added Frederick, suddenly realizing that Wendell was the underappreciated great man. "It is only fitting that you belong there."

"No, you're the originals, the creators. I remain the follower, explaining, defining, but never inspiring."

"You underestimate . . ."

"No, I do not. I am a minor star in this galaxy."

"You are too close to judge. What appears small in our eyes now will look larger later when we have better eyes," Frederick said.

"You are kind," Wendell replied.

"And the light which puts out our eyes is darkness to us."

"Ah, Thoreau," sighed Phillips, smiling. "Another difficult original, like you."

Hearing praise and not criticism, Frederick extended his hand and quoted Thoreau once more, "And there's more day to dawn. The sun is but a morning star."

95.

OTTILIE NEVER LIKED LINCOLN. His pictures did not flatter. He was very tall, a fact that only called attention to his ugly face, ungainly posture, disheveled suits, big hands, and big feet. A self-trained lawyer, he always looked like a country bumpkin out of place in a capital city of a great nation. He often told jokes and told long-winded stories and was known to refer to Negroes as "niggers," even after meeting Frederick. As a wartime president, he was indecisive. And as a thinker, he was inconsistent, sometimes confusing. Now that Lincoln was dead, stories about him were being printed almost daily.

His assassination was a shock, of course, but the period of mourning had been protracted. The omnipresence of black bunting on buildings along with so many black-clad bodies was oppressive and boring. Walking the streets of Rochester that summer with Frederick at her side, Ottilie found herself wanting to shout out as she passed one sad countenance after another, "Live, people. We need to *live*!"

It didn't help that Frederick was still grieving Lincoln's death, too. His anguish bewildered her. After all, he had had only two conversations with the president and only met him one other time, when they exchanged a few words in a reception line just weeks before the terrible night in Ford's Theatre. Lincoln's second inaugural address had changed Frederick's perception of the man. He called it the greatest speech he had ever read or heard, for it carried in its lofty sentences the weight of history, the judgment of the Almighty, a profound hope in the redemption of the nation.

When Ottilie finally reunited with Frederick in New York a month after the assassination, Frederick was still in shock. He seemed lost, unsure about his and the nation's future. "What are we going to do now? How are we going to live? A man in my situation has not only to divest himself of the old, which is never easily done, but he must also adjust himself to the new, which is still more difficult," he asked. Frederick even talked about moving back to Maryland. His depression deepened by news from Washington and the South.

Lincoln was barely in his grave when as the new president, Andrew Johnson, changed Lincoln's reconstruction plans with astounding speed and revealed a deplorable willingness to give power back to Confederate traitors during the congressional recess. Johnson issued an amnesty for Confederate leaders, invited the ex-Confederate states back into the Union with the acceptance of the Thirteenth Amendment as the only requirement for readmission, and ignored the increasing elimination of Black rights and freedom in the South.

Emboldened legislatures, dominated by former slaveholders, then passed "Black Codes" that virtually re-enslaved freedmen. When freedmen were not at work, they were arrested. When they couldn't pay fines or bills, they were hired out. When they quit work before the expiration of a work contract, they were jailed for breach of contract. Children of parents deemed to be too poor to care for them were bound out as apprentices until the age of eighteen or twenty-one. Laborers without contracts were deemed "vagrants" and had to return to their former masters. Freedmen couldn't vote or appeal to the courts when lands granted during the war were seized by whites. Hooded gangs raped, plundered, and lynched with impunity.

President Johnson did nothing to intervene.

Back in Rochester, Ottilie and Frederick talked constantly about Johnson, reviewing the details of his career for earlier signs of betrayal and hypocrisy. After one such session when Frederick recalled many details of Johnson's past and they were alone and unable to be overheard, Ottilie called Frederick by his pet name, "You never cease to amaze me, my Big Bird."

"Well, my Pig Tail, my memory always had its uses," Frederick replied, using her pet name in return.

The conversation suddenly turned serious. "You don't like sharing me," said Frederick. "You are happiest when we are alone, in Hoboken."

"But I'm eager to come here. I'll stay as long as you let me, even if Anna doesn't like me. She tolerates me, that's all. But I don't expect more. Why should I expect more? She understands jealousy. I certainly do. I can bear what must be borne."

Ottilie's equanimity had been tested the morning Lincoln's cane arrived as a gift from Mrs. Lincoln. Anna asked her to come to the kitchen after breakfast and all the plates were washed and put away. Now a pot of tea and two cups were on the table and Anna sat at the end. "Come in. I have somethin' to say. Sit," she commanded.

After tea, Anna would be going to her garden, where she would spend most of her day like a common laborer. *Where she belongs*, thought Ottilie.

"Yes, I talk, just not to you. Sit," Anna said again.

Ottilie sat on the side at an angle near the teapot and cups. Anna poured the tea and said, "First, I want to give thanks."

"To the Lord, of course," Ottilie said.

"No, no, not this time. I want to thank you," Anna replied.

"Me?" Ottilie took a sip, the tea was dark and delicious.

"Yes. You've been good, real good, to my children, telling them stories, reading and teachin', and all. They talk about you all the time, especially Rosetta. I was jealous, but no more, at least not on account of them." She paused, watching Ottilie, who tried to mask her surprise. Anna continued, "And I've been good to you, too. When that package came from Mrs. Lincoln, the cane you know, Fred gathered us all up and said this was just for the family and not Miss Assing."

"He couldn't have said . . ." Ottilie replied.

"But he did, sayin' that you didn't like Mr. Lincoln anyway, and he thought it was a time for only people who felt the way he felt, who love . . ."

"This . . ."

"But I stepped in, saying that leavin' you out, even if you didn't like Mr. Lincoln, was not right." Anna was smug in her generosity.

"How do you know what I thought about Mr. Lincoln?"

Anna grunted. "He talks to me about things, about politics, and the war, and Mr. Lincoln. You're surprised. Yes, he talks to me, as a husband should with his wife. He talks about you, too."

"He does? What does he say?"

"Ask him," Anna said.

"I will." Ottilie wanted to look away, but she dared not give her the satisfaction.

"What could you know about a man and wife? You are just—what's that word you white women say about folks like you? *Spinster*?"

Ottilie straightened her back. "You are cruel."

"Yes, I'm mean. You have no idea how mean," Anna said.

"I don't deserve this kind of treatment. I'm Frederick's friend," Ottilie said.

"You're more than a friend."

"I don't know what you're talking about."

Anna grunted again. "I'm not dumb. I know about Hoboken. Rosetta's always excited with news when them letters come from you, the news, the stories. You never stop telling about Fred's visit to your boarding house and his own room there when he comes to New York."

"He does have his own room!"

"Rosetta is smart about some things, and not about other things. But if you turn against her somehow, even if you stop writing to her because I told you, I'll hate you even more. I'll find more ways to hurt you."

Ottilie moved away from the table. "Anna!"

"You have some nerve talking about me. Yes, I'm mean, has to be, ugly and black with five children in this world. But you and Fred gets the prize for mean, going about as if I don't live, as if I don't matter."

"That's not true," Ottilie said.

"Stop, just stop. I'm no dumb fool," Anna said.

"Frederick will hear of this."

"I'm sure he will, but I don't care. No more. I don't care, because he'll get tired of you. You'll get old and cold, like me, and he'll toss you aside like he did Miss Julia."

"Don't mention that name."

"He didn't fight for her. He let her go, and he'll get tired of you, like he got tired of me. You can't stop flappin' your mouth, and you'll keep on writing them letters—"

"I've heard enough."

"I'm not done."

Ottilie returned to her chair.

"Today is the longest time I will ever say somethin' to you besides 'Good morn" and 'Good night.' I have some manners, even if you don't. I'm not your friend, and never will be. I hate it when you come, can't stand it, after weeks, after months of puttin' up with you. But then you go back home, and you're gone. He never mentions you, at least not to me. After you're gone, it's as if you're dead. But he wants you to come, and you'll come year after year. You do some things for him that I don't do. Those talks. The books. Them meetings. He needs them. But I has some satisfaction. He'll never leave me for you, even if you come every summer for twenty years, and every fall he goes to that room in Hoboken. Why? Because family is more important. My family, his family. We matter more than you, and always will," Anna said.

Ottilie stood to her full height. "Thank you for the tea." She left the room, holding her head high, her back straight. Tempted as she was to tell Frederick about Anna and align him against her, she decided to not tell him about the tea. Frederick didn't need more to worry about.

She resolved to continue her campaign: ingratiate herself; tutor the children; read stories; play games; accompany Frederick at the piano; bear gifts, even for Anna.

Ottilie Varnhagen Assing was worth the wait.

Upsetting news came at the end of the month. Without explanation, Mrs. Marks, in a brief note, told Ottilie she could no longer rent her rooms. "You will need to find other accommodations," she wrote in a scribble.

Ottilie informed Frederick, who was not concerned. "There are always rooms to rent in and around New York."

"Of course, I can find rooms to let. There are big houses everywhere. But there are not that many who will provide rooms for the both of us. Mrs. Marks was special in that way."

"Don't worry, Miss Assing, we'll find another Mrs. Marks."

Ottilie softened. "When you say 'Miss Assing,' like now, I almost melt."

Their candid intimacy made her want to embrace him, but she restrained herself, knowing that he would resist her in his house. She would have to wait to hold him in her arms until they were in her new home with two rooms somewhere back East. That fall he would come to New York on tour, and she would take him to her bed, renewing her vow to be his forever.

Unfortunately, after taking the train to New York that October, Ottilie learned she no longer had a job. Her newspaper had ceased publication.

What can I do now?

1865 ended with too many unanswered questions.

96.

FOR THE FIRST TIME since the death of Abraham Lincoln, Frederick returned to the White House.

It was bitterly cold that February morning. Under gray skies, Pennsylvania Avenue was a river of ice, mud, and manure, its stinking syrup an affront to the faded majesty of the federal buildings. Frederick worried that he would encounter a similarly cold reception in President Andrew Johnson's Executive Office. He vividly remembered Johnson's scorn when locking eyes with Frederick at Lincoln's second inauguration.

The accidental president of the United States waited for a delegation appointed by Black men from Alabama, Florida, Pennsylvania, Maryland, New York, the District of Columbia, Wisconsin, and the New England states, who met at the Fifteenth Street Presbyterian Church in Washington and selected Frederick, his son Lewis, and three others to call on President Johnson at the White House. Johnson received them on February 7, 1866, in the conference room adjoining the Oval Office, where a white stenographer would record comments for later distribution to the press.

The president shook the hands of each delegate, his grip firm, his smile kind. Johnson seemed comfortable and confident with the powers invested in him. Once seated at the conference room table opposite the president, George T. Downing, the leader of the delegation, told the president, "It is our desire for you to know that we come feeling that we are friends meeting with a friend. We cherish the hope that we may be *fully enfranchised*, not only here in the District, but throughout the land. We respectfully submit that rendering anything less than this will be rendering to us less than our just due; that granting anything less than *our full rights* will be a disregard of just rights and of due respect of our feelings. With confidence in the triumph of justice, we base our hope." Downing was a skilled president of numerous conventions, an owner of successful restaurants in New York and Newport, and now manager of the dining room in the House of Representatives. He was confident in his authority.

The president listened without moving his body, his eyes fixed on Downing, his hands on both knees as he sat away from the table.

Frederick made a brief statement, "Mr. President, we are not here to enlighten you, sir, as to your duties as the Chief Magistrate of this Republic, but to show our respect, and to present in brief the claims of our race to your favorable consideration. Your noble and human predecessor placed in our hands the sword to assist in saving the nation, and we do hope that you, his able successor, will favorably regard the placing in our hands the ballot with which to save ourselves. The fact what we are the subjects of Government, and subject to taxation, subject to volunteer in the service of the country, subject to being drafted, subject to bear the burdens of the State, make it not improper that we should ask to share in the privileges of this condition." Frederick noticed that the reference to Lincoln irritated the president.

The president stood, cleared his throat, and looked directly at Frederick. "If I know myself, and the feelings of my own heart, they have been for the colored man. While I say that I am a friend of the colored man, I do not want to adopt a policy that I believe will end in a contest between the races, which if persisted in will result in the extermination of one or the other. God forbid that I should be engaged in such a work. Yes, I have said, and I repeat here, that if the colored man in the United States should find no other Moses, or any Moses that would be more able and efficient than myself, I would be his Moses to lead him from bondage to freedom; that I would pass him from a land where he had lived in slavery to a land, if it were out of reach, of freedom. But I am not willing, under either circumstance, to adopt a policy which I believe will only result in the sacrifice of his life and the shedding of his blood. God knows that anything I can do I will do. In the mighty process by which the great end is to be reached, anything I can do to elevate the races, to soften the ameliorate their condition I will do, and to do so is the sincere desire of my heart."

Frederick tried to remain emotionless, but he saw dismay on the faces of the delegates, for they all had heard the president, claiming to be the Moses of Black people, oppose the Black vote because he feared a violent white reaction. He again resorted to flattery, "I have to return to you our thanks, Mr. President, for so kindly granting us this interview. We did not come here expecting to argue this question to your excellency, but simply to state what are our views and wishes. If we were disposed to argue the question, and you would grant us permission, of course we would endeavor to controvert some of the positions you have assumed."

Downing turned to Frederick, "Mr. Douglass, I take that the President, by his kind expressions and very full treatment of the subject, must have contemplated some reply to the views which he has advanced, and in which we certainly do not concur, and I say this with due respect."

Frederick said, "If the president will allow me, I would like to say one or two words in reply. You enfranchise your enemies and disfranchise your friends."

Johnson was once the only southern senator who refused to resign and join the Confederacy. Now he was returning power to men he had consistently branded as traitors throughout the war. And these traitors were refusing to allow Blacks the right to vote.

Downing gasped but maintained his poise. He watched the president go to the end of the table, stand over Frederick, and say, "Now, let's get closer up to this subject, and talk about it. What relations has the colored man and white heretofore occupied in the South?" The president wanted a debate, but Frederick felt the president was unfairly using his body to emphasize the weight of his office.

Looking up at Johnson, Frederick asked, "Mr. President, do you wish . . . ?"

"I am not quite through yet," interrupted the president. "Slavery has been abolished; a great national guarantee has been given, one that cannot be revoked. I was getting at the relation that subsisted between the white man and the colored man. Have you ever lived upon a plantation?"

"I have, your excellency," Frederick replied.

"Then you know slavery creates hate between Blacks and whites, especially those whites who are poor and don't benefit from the monopoly that slavery creates."

"Yes, but it is not so simple, and . . ." Frederick noticed the others silently urging caution.

"Do you deny that first great principle of the right of the people to govern themselves?" the president insisted. "Will you resort to an arbitrary power, and say a majority of the people shall receive a state of things they are opposed to?"

"There is, under some circumstances, the tyranny of the majority, and . . ." Frederick said.

"I might go down here to the ballot-box tomorrow and vote directly for universal suffrage; but if a great majority of the people said no, I should consider it would be tyrannical in me to attempt to force upon them without their will. It is a fundamental tenet in my creed that the will of the people must be obeyed. Is there anything wrong or unfair in that?"

"A great deal that is wrong, Mr. President, with all respect. "

Frederick was surprised when the president suddenly became conciliatory, almost friendly, and said, "I merely wanted to indicate my views in reply to your address, and not to enter any general controversy. Your statement was a very frank one, and I thought it was due to you to meet in the same spirit."

"Thank you, sir," Frederick said.

"I think you will find, so far as the South is concerned, that it would be better for your people to live and advance in civilization elsewhere," Johnson continued.

Frederick could not allow another appeal for mass migration to go unchallenged. He responded, "Those who live in the North do not intend to leave our country, sir, and those who live on the former plantations cannot get away. Those former masters decide for the Negro where he shall go, where he shall work, how much he shall work—in fact, he is divested of all political power. He is absolutely in the hands of those men."

"If the master now controls him or his action, would he not control him in the vote?"

"Let the Negro once understand that he has an organic right to vote, and he will raise up a party in the Southern states among the poor, who will rally with him. There is this conflict that you speak of between the wealthy slaveholder and the poor white man. Together, poor whites and poor Blacks will make a powerful force to be reckoned with," Frederick said.

"We want the same ends, but we propose to do so by following different roads. Thank you, gentlemen, for coming today." Johnson returned to his seat, bringing the meeting to an end.

Frederick and the other delegates stood to leave, and he said, "The President sends us to the people, and we go to the people."

The president said emphatically, "Yes, sir. I have great faith in the people. I will believe they will do what is right."

The five men said not a word to each other until they were out of the building, and then they railed against what they had witnessed. Shock, incredulity, outrage, offense, and more poured out. At Frederick's hotel, they decided to answer the president's comments with a printed response. The presence of a stenographer certainly proved that Johnson intended his remarks to be disseminated; proof of his presidential acumen, proof of how to treat insolent coloreds. Downing urged the men to get others to sign the document as well. Naturally, they turned to Frederick to compose most of the sentences. He began, "Believing as we do that the views and opinions you expressed in that address are entirely unsound and prejudicial to the highest interest of our race as well as our country at large, we cannot do other than expose the same, and, as far as may be in our power, arrest their dangerous influence."

Frederick thought for a moment, and as if the president stood before him, said, "Men are whipped oftenest who are whipped easiest. Peace between the races is not to be secured by degrading one race and exalting another, by giving power to one race and withholding it from another; but by maintaining a state of equal justice between all classes."

Frederick looked at the delegates and considered the weight of his next words. He said, "The president hates me. I'm just another nigger, another unruly nigger."

97.

BECAUSE PRESIDENT JOHNSON DID nothing to punish the rioters after scores of Black people died during race riots that summer in Memphis and New Orleans, Frederick denounced him in the press and on the lecture circuit, where he was in high demand and earned the highest fees of his professional career. "The Negro still has a cause," Frederick claimed, "and he needs my voice and pen to plead for it.'

Frederick's ascendency was not universally appreciated. For some in Republican Party circles, it was inconvenient, controversial, and politically problematic. When Southern Democrats, many of them former Confederate officials, rallied around President Johnson's policies at a convention in Philadelphia that September, Republicans organized a counter convention in the same city. Party members in Rochester unexpectedly selected Frederick as one of hundreds of honorary delegates expected to attend. He was delighted, but Thaddeus Stevens, the leader of the Radical Republicans in Congress, urged the Rochester Republicans to not send Frederick. His visibility was too controversial and would open the Republican Party to charges of excessive integration.

Frederick issued a public statement before leaving Rochester: "If this convention will receive me, the event will certainly be somewhat significant progress. If they reject me, they will identify themselves with another convention." On the train to Philadelphia, a group of western and southern delegates, led by Oliver Morton, the governor of Indiana, approached Frederick. The governor and his associates were deferential as they expressed their "respect and high esteem" for "a great American." Morton voiced concern that if Frederick came to the convention as a Republican delegate the party would be seen as advocates for social equality. This would lead to Republican losses at the polls. He concluded, "You do understand our dilemma."

Frederick took a quick breath and said calmly but emphatically, "Gentlemen, with all respect, you might as well ask me to put a loaded pistol to my head and blow my brains out, as to ask me to keep out of this convention, to which I have been duly elected. Then, gentlemen, what would you have gained by this exclusion? Would not the charge of cowardice prove more damaging than that of amalgamation? Would not you be branded all over as dastardly hypocrites? As a matter of policy or expediency, you will be wise to let me in. Everybody knows I was elected to be a delegate, and if I am not admitted, you will find that inquiry more difficult to answer than any charge brought against you for favoring political and social equality." Saying nothing more, the entire delegation left the car, leaving Frederick, the only Black delegate, wondering what was in store.

He soon found out.

Frederick arrived in Philadelphia and was warned about the procession from Independence Hall through the historic streets that would open the convention the following morning. As planned, the delegates gathered before the march, and it soon became clear that hundreds of delegates were determined to ignore him. An announcement was made: "For the march, gentlemen, two abreast. Two!" Frederick stood alone as two lines formed. He felt like a child rejected for play on city streets, as he was conspicuously avoided.

The editor of the *New York Independent*, the tall, handsome, golden-haired Theodore Tilton, approached Frederick, offering his arm. "Mr. Douglass, I'm so glad to see you again. It will be my distinct honor to accompany you this morning."

Pleasantly surprised, Frederick fell into formation. Some men scowled, others snickered. But the crowd roared when Frederick and Tilton passed by.

At the corner of Ninth and Chesnutt streets, Frederick recognized the face of Amanda Sears, the daughter of Thomas and Lucretia Auld. She was with two children at the front of the crowd waving. He broke ranks and ran to her. "Amanda, Mrs. Sears, I am so happy to see you. What brought you here?"

"I always wanted to see you again after your last visit before the war, and so when I heard you were to be here, I came to see you walk in the march. I'm so glad I did," Amanda said.

Frederick turned around to discover that a smiling Tilton had stepped out of line and waited patiently for him.

"Children, this is the famous Mr. Douglass. Mr. Frederick Douglass. We knew each other when we were children together," Amanda said. The boy and girl, both under ten years old, were intrigued by the sight of the tall colored man with a mane of silver-streaked hair and a moustache talking to their mother.

"Pleased to meet you, sir," said the boy, prompted by his mother with a slight touch on his shoulder.

"Pleased," said the girl with a slight curtsy.

"Thank you for coming, all of you, but I have to rejoin my friend. Thank you," Frederick replied.

At the convention, Northern Republicans now acknowledged Frederick after the crowd's popular approval made it safe to do so. Frederick nodded his head and shook hands, leaving aside a tendency to hold offences for another day. When the convention was called to order, there was, as expected, extensive debate about the franchise for Black men. For three days, the Northern and Southern delegates met separately, and Frederick gave three lengthy speeches. He was introduced by Theodore Tilton as "the runaway slave who was apprehended and brought before the bar and tried for the crime of being a wonderful genius."

By the fourth day, Frederick was hoarse, but his condition didn't prevent him from upsetting a subcommittee meeting of the Southern loyalists, along with Theodore Tilton and Anna Dickinson, a twenty-three-year-old Quaker. The interracial trio attended to rattle the Southern loyalists. Sensing the coming defeat, some Southerners bolted the convention, including the elected president of the convention, who futilely declared the convention adjourned. The remaining delegates elected a new president, and the convention endorsed the Black vote. Delegates thanked Frederick and Dickinson for the final outcome.

When the tumult subsided, Dickinson said to Frederick, "Friend Douglass, now it's our turn. We deserve the vote, too, and there will be another battle for it."

"I support women's suffrage, and have done so for years, as you probably know," Frederick replied.

"Yes, you were one of the few men willing to sign the declaration Mrs. Stanton created. What if we insist on getting the vote when you do?"

"As you should."

"But what if men are willing to give it to you, but not to us?"

"One step at a time, Miss Dickinson. One war at a time."

"That's what I am afraid of. What if my step takes years after your step?"

"The current crisis demands our step."

"And the times do not demand ours? We need thee, Friend Douglass. As in '48, we need thee."

"I will discuss this matter with Elizabeth and Miss Anthony at their meeting in November," Frederick said.

She smiled, her dimples dazzled. "Dear sir, I don't think the ladies, especially Miss Anthony, will allow equivocation."

Frederick was not prepared for the ferocity of the coming battle.

★

When Frederick went to the state meeting of the Equal Rights Association in Albany, he still had no news about the birth of his second grandchild. He was hoping that this time it would be a boy bearing his name. Frederick waited for the good news at any moment and was somewhat anxious but still amiable, smiling broadly as he reunited with women who had done so much for the antislavery cause before and during the war. Elizabeth Stanton was delighted to see him. She was larger than ever after seven children, but her intense curiosity, keen intelligence, and sparkling wit created an undeniable glow. Her smiling face belied the anger that made her once tell an audience that marriage, as currently constituted, was "nothing more than legalized prostitution."

Elizabeth Stanton prepared to petition the state legislature to allow women and Negroes to vote for delegates to the state constitutional convention that would eliminate the $250 property qualification for voting and extend the voting right to women. She asked Frederick, "Where do rich white men get the authority to forbid poor men, ignorant men, and Black men, the exercise of their rights?"

He waited and she answered for him, "All this talk about education and property qualification is the narrow assumption of a rotten aristocracy."

"You're right, as usual," he replied. Frederick enjoyed Elizabeth's eloquent sarcasm as he noticed Susan B. Anthony approaching them. He had known Susan since she moved to Rochester in 1849 and still found her unrelenting severity unpleasant and exhausting. As an ardent abolitionist, Frederick appreciated Anthony's tireless energy and mania for planning. Any good cause needed a Susan B. Anthony, unmarried, undistracted, focused on victory without concern for casualties. Her father died during the war, and she still wore black. Frederick doubted she would ever wear any other color. Grief was a cause, too.

Frederick and Elizabeth had seated themselves at a side table when Susan finally arrived. He stood for her.

"Frederick, you've been with us from the very beginning," Susan said warmly.

"And I will be with you both until the very end, when universal suffrage is won," Frederick replied.

"And if we fail here in Albany, we will go next year to Kansas," said Elizabeth. "I still find it incredible that a state will have a vote to allow women to vote."

Susan stiffened. "If they allow us to . . ."

"When we go, they will be persuaded," Elizabeth said. "No country ever had or ever will have peace until every citizen has a voice in the government."

Frederick chuckled. "My dear Elizabeth, that sounds ominous."

"We need not worry about stoking their fears," interjected Susan. "They're already afraid, very afraid. They can imagine what it would be like if we're the majority and have the vote. And sadly, all of our old abolitionist friends, with scarce an exception, are sure we're wrong. Only time can tell, but I believe we are right and hence bound to succeed."

"I'm one of the exceptions," declared Frederick, his voice conciliatory.

"Yes," replied Susan. "And I only wish there were more Frederick Douglasses."

Frederick laughed. "I don't. One of me is surely enough, at least for President Johnson and his cronies. And I would rather not have too many competitors."

"At last! Peace restored between friends," Elizabeth said.

"Not a war, Elizabeth, just disagreements," said Frederick.

"For now," said Susan. She looked at Frederick as if to warn him that she was ready for battle if war was to come.

"Oh, Susan, please," chided Elizabeth. "Even revolutionaries can relax for a moment." Susan and Elizabeth were like sisters, their relationship fraught with tension and yet solid like iron.

With a faint smile, Susan replied, "Brothers and sisters can disagree and stay united if there's a shared understanding of first principles. And our first principal is universal suffrage, for men and women, together. There's a shared understanding. Men and women together."

"Yes," said Frederick. He agreed on principle and withheld the caveat that if white men insisted that Black men could have the vote but that women, white or Black, could not, Black men should not, could not, refuse it. He hid his presentiment. He knew that Anthony, as true a believer in equality as anyone he had ever met, would never accept second place in the march toward political equality. Their conversation spoke of a future battle, and Frederick shuddered at the prospect of becoming the public enemy of Elizabeth Stanton and Susan B. Anthony.

98.

ANNA HAD A STROKE in April. She was at the sink and suddenly fell across it. "My head," she said, and vomited. Charles's wife, Libby, rushed to her and struggled to raise her as Anna mumbled about her head hurting and saying other things that didn't make sense. Nathan's sister, Louisa, raced a carriage down the hill to Rosetta's house and drove her back to South Avenue. Nathan stayed with Annie and the baby, Harriet, born in November.

Rosetta found Anna in bed, with Libby holding her hand. Rosetta asked repeatedly, "Mamma, can you hear me?"

No response.

Rosetta brought her two children to the house and stayed for weeks caring for Anna. At last, Frederick arrived, taking a break from another tour. "She can't die. She can't."

"She won't, Papa. The doctor said she will survive. She'll be just fine."

"I won't leave again until I'm absolutely sure she's fine, when she can recognize us, talk to us," Frederick said.

The wait wasn't long.

"Where's my Fred?" Anna asked one afternoon. Rosetta was at her side and immediately went to his study to retrieve him.

"Freddy, you're . . ." Anna said.

"Yes, Anna, I'm here," he replied.

"Good. That headache was a good thing, brought you back, brought you all back."

"Not everybody," Frederick said.

"So, Charles is still back east when his wife is with child, and his mamma is close to her grave? What are we going to do with that boy?" Anna asked.

"Now Anna, don't get all upset. You need your strength," Frederick said.

"I'll need my strength for all of them when they get back home and live here with us. That will make me happy when they're all here, under one roof."

"We'll see. Our boys can be stubborn."

"Me too," she said, smiling. "That's why I'm still here, ain't I? I wasn't ready to go, not yet. This house is meant to be filled with children and grandchildren, and more comin'.

"There will be more, a fuller house this summer." He told Anna and Rosetta his plan for his brother Perry, whom he had not seen since the family was divided when Aaron Anthony died and his three children inherited the Baileys. "He's called Perry Downs now and lived in Maryland for years until he was sold to someone in Texas. He managed to get back to Maryland, and he wrote to me. Actually, someone wrote for him, and he asked if he and his family could come here and live with us. He has four children."

Rosetta blurted out, "And you said *yes*?"

"Of course, I said yes. He's a lost brother, and now he's been found," Frederick replied.

"And we're his people," said Anna. "Strangers no more We're only doin' what the Lord want us to do. When do they come?"

"This summer, probably July," he said.

"Good," said Anna. "A full house, and more work for me in a good way, a real good way, all that cleaning, all that cooking, growing vegetables. It will be like a holiday. The girls will have cousins around, and there will be new babies, too, Libby's and Rosetta's, and we can have picnics and play games on the back lawn."

"Now, Anna, you'll need to keep your rest. The Douglass Hotel will be open, but you'll still need your rest." Frederick would not mention Ottilie's return in July.

"I'll get plenty. There's Rosetta and Libby and Louise and Perry's wife to help. Now what's s her name?"

"Maria," Frederick stated.

"Is she a Mexican girl?" asked Rosetta.

"I don't know. Does it matter?" he asked.

"No, it don't matter none," Anna replied.

"Yes, Mama," Rosetta said.

★

After Anna's recovery, Frederick had resumed touring. His bones ached. He had traveled thousands of miles, given over one hundred lectures that spring before Perry and his family arrived in July. In the heat of summer, he could not bear another moment of train engine smoke, pressed bodies in coaches, bad coffee, and cold chicken gobbled down in the mad rush to the next engagement. He washed himself every night, but he wanted to sit in a tub for hours, allowing skin, bones, and muscles to relax as if nothing mattered in the world.

When Frederick finally returned home, Ottilie was there waiting for him. She frowned and said, "You look terrible. Get some rest before you see your brother and his family. First impressions matter, and you need to be prepared for your brother and his family."

"Are you warning me about them?" Frederick asked.

"Forty years is a long time. And so much has happened," Ottilie replied.

"I understand. We're different men, but his reunion had to happen. I made sure of it."

"I hope you're not disappointed."

"Why should I be?"

"His life was hard, so hard after Maryland."

"I'll talk to him myself after I go up. Let Anna and Rosetta know I'm home. Rosetta is still here, yes?"

"Yes."

Frederick entered his bedroom and went to the mirror to untie his cravat and remove his collar. For the first time, the sight of his gray hair high and brushed back covering his ears with a streak of white above his right eye made him feel old. His moustache was still black, and the goatee that he had worn during the war was now shaved for the sake of a more youthful appearance. But the two parallel lines that defined the foundation of his high cheekbones were now signs of time he could not reverse.

Perry was older than Frederick by about five years, but he couldn't be sure. Perry didn't know his birthdate, and Frederick didn't know his. Perry had been identified as his brother and he acted like a big brother, bossing him around and at times protecting him when Frederick was harassed by older boys. He couldn't remember much more about Perry.

But Frederick could never forget that terrible afternoon when he and Eliza watched Richard Anthony, in a drunken rage, stomp Perry's head with his boot as Perry lay on the ground and blood flowed from his ear. Moaning, he had remained still, waiting for the storm to pass. Perry hadn't complained about it, as if he implicitly understood that nothing could be done and he wanted to survive. It was a cruel trick of fate that Perry was sold to Richard Anthony when the Aaron property was divided. Perry's life must have been a bitter hell beyond anything Frederick endured with Hugh or Thomas Auld.

Frederick removed his jacket and turned to his bed, where he needed to take just a brief nap, maybe a half hour or so. He didn't discover that an hour had passed until Anna nudged him, whispering, "Fred, it's time to get up. They're waiting downstairs. They've been waiting since you arrived. Come on, now, you can get your rest later. You have more family to meet. Rough 'round the edges, but good people." He rose to put on his jacket, cravat, and collar.

Frederick entered the parlor. Perry stood and gestured for his wife, daughter, and grandchildren to rise too. Perry was as tall as Frederick but thinner, his brown face deeply wrinkled. Perry's wife was short, about half his size, and her smooth complexion suggested she was half his age. She was pretty, and her thick black hair was tied in a long braid that fell over her chest. Their daughter, about the age of Rosetta, and three grandchildren stood beside them in a line from oldest to youngest, all nerves and curiosity in darting eyes and the quick rubbing of fingers.

"Perry," Frederick whispered.

Frederick crossed the room and stood before Perry. He studied his face and wondered if he should take Perry's hand in a gentlemen's handshake or fully embrace him. Perry wrapped his arms around Frederick, and Frederick quickly enfolded his brother in response. Anna, Rosetta, Ottilie, and Libby applauded. To Frederick, the sound seemed far off, strangely intrusive. His arms dropped to his side. Perry stepped back and smiled at Frederick. "What a sight you is. Dressed up and all. My, my, I still can't believe this is happenin'," he said.

"Me neither," said Frederick. He shook his head and scanned his brother's eyes.

"Thank you for takin' us in, for bringin' us all here. This house is beautiful. Ain't it, Maria? Frederick, this is Maria," Perry said.

Maria put out her hand, and Frederick gently took it. He pulled her close and kissed her on the cheek. "Welcome, Maria, to your new family," he said.

"Thank you, sir," she said and stepped back with a radiant smile.

"No, it's Frederick, or Fred."

"Or Freddy, "said Perry. "That's what I 'member."

"Or *Fred*," replied Frederick, who never allowed anyone to call him Freddy. He could still hear Katy, Thomas, Rowena Auld, Hugh Auld, the workers at the shipyards, and so many others using that name to cut him down to size.

Perry told his grandchildren, who had been trained to be silent and respectful, "This is yo' Uncle Freddy. Now introduce yo'self, one by one like yo' gramma told you."

Frederick had so many questions about Perry's past, what he knew about their mother and grandmother, and so much more, but he had to wait because Anna clapped her hands and announced it was time for dinner. "You two can talk yo' heads off later. We gotta get some of my food in them bellies." Frederick noticed that Anna had reverted to using the words and intonation of the Eastern Shore.

They sat around the large dining room table, including the grandchildren. Anna insisted on serving the meal with the help of Louise. Perry and Maria didn't ask any questions about Ottilie. Perhaps Anna had informed them while Frederick was sleeping. Frederick noticed they all ignored Ottilie. He also noticed that Rosetta and Libby stopped smiling once dinner was served and conversation began.

Rosetta and Libby looked at each other and rolled their eyes as they watched Perry and his family slurp soup, eat meat with their hands, gulp down coffee, and break every rule of standard English grammar. Perry and his family seemed oblivious to their slights.

Later, Frederick summoned Rosetta to his upstairs office as he could not allow such blatant disrespect. Controlling his voice, he told Rosetta, "I will not allow you to show such disrespect to your uncle. That look of yours said everything. I don't care how crude, uneducated, and unsophisticated he is. He cannot help if he had a hard life. Just think, I would have been him if I had stayed. Let him be a reminder of your good fortune, Rosetta, I love you dearly, but you disappoint me sometimes."

Tears formed in Rosetta's eyes. "Father, I am sorry. I just wasn't prepared for how different we are from them. I am sure I will become accustomed to their ways."

"Your mother is very happy having them here. The more the better, and there will be more when your brothers return," Frederick replied.

99.

ONE EVENING IN JULY, when it was still uncomfortably humid, Frederick and Ottilie read aloud alternating paragraphs from John Motley's multivolume *Rise of the Dutch Republic*. Frederick paused and sighed heavily. He told Ottilie, "I think it's time Perry and I do something together, something with our hands this summer. He doesn't talk much, and he's hard to understand at times. But he let me know, very carefully, that he thinks it's time to move out, give the family more room, get outta folks' hair. When I asked him about being made to feel unwelcome, his eyes answered for him, and he just said, 'It's time.'" He acknowledged the hardship and sorrows of Perry's life, but Frederick admitted to Ottilie, "His forty-year separation from me is as complete as if he had lived on the moon."

"It's for the best," Ottilie said.

"The work will keep my mind off other things," Frederick replied.

"What other things? Is it Charles?"

"Yes. I have another letter. He's been hearing about Perry from Libby, maybe Rosetta. He dares to say this about his uncle, my own brother." Frederick reached for the sheet of scribbled paper and read, "'I don't understand how in any way those people you have at home are related to you." Frederick looked up and said, "*Those* people. No wonder Perry feels the need to move out. And then Charles, after insulting me, dares to ask for money, again. His salary isn't enough. One hundred dollars a month is just not enough."

"I hear its expensive in Washington and getting more expensive by the day," Ottilie said.

After working in the army hospital there, Charles always wanted to live in Washington. The district was growing by the thousands. It had granted the vote to Black men, and opportunities for political and economic advancement abounded. Negroes were not in the majority, but it could happen.

Both Charles and Lewis wanted to work for the Freedmen's Bureau, the agency that provided essential services like food, clothing, medical care, and education to four million freed slaves. Charles couldn't get a job there. He begged his father to use his influence. Frederick reached out to the head of the Bureau, General Oliver Otis Howard, who had supported the recruitment of Black soldiers. Frederick did not explicitly ask Howard to hire Charles. He only reported that Charles, an admirer of the Bureau, hoped for a job there.

Charles was hired as a clerk. He proudly told his father, "I am the second colored man in the government that has been given a first-class clerkship."

The joy of Charles's announcement soon evaporated. "I arrived here, and there was a pile of letters from Charles," Frederick complained to Ottilie, the volume of Motley remained open in his lap. "I was happy for him, of course, but he cannot stop telling me about his debt, financial worries, expenses, and hopes for future loans, and for future investments." Charles had suggested Frederick invest $1,800 in a building association to eliminate monthly boarding house costs all together.

"He needs to rise on his own," said Frederick.

"The American way," Ottilie said, her sarcasm light but clear.

"What does that mean?"

"No one rises on their own, not even you. I was alone, but I found a distant cousin to help me, and I made friends in New York and New Jersey. If we rise, we rise with help."

"Yes, there's help, and there's gross dependency, becoming a parasite, an ingrate."

"That's harsh, Frederick. Are you saying this about Charles?"

"I fear it."

"He needs help, that's all. Sometimes you can say yes, and sometimes you can say no."

"He sounds entitled. I'm supposed to always say yes. That's why he hounds me," Frederick said.

"Then tell him to stop writing to you about money," Ottilie said.

"And when he's not writing about that, he's writing about getting me a job in Washington. He thinks I could do a better job than Major Howard. He sounds disloyal, manipulative, like a schemer. Is this what the Washington of Andrew Johnson does to people?"

Charles had written to Frederick, "My hope is, that you won't refuse the position if tendered." Frederick understood the use of flattery and a child's need to curry favor, but he worried that Charles campaigned behind the scenes to remove General Howard from his post to make way for his father.

"Why is Charles involved here?" he asked Ottilie. "He should just keep his head down, do his job, mind his own business, save some money, and stop pestering me about it. Besides, General Howard is a good man."

"Good advice," she said.

"I will tell him so, but it is a good job. It pays $3,000 a year, and I would supervise two thousand employees. But I don't want to get a job by forcing out a decent man through secrecy, confidential letters, and gossip. Charles is obviously not bothered by this stinking mess. Or maybe he is being duped?" asked Frederick.

"By whom?"

"By a vengeful but canny politician, the president."

"I thought you said that the president isn't smart," Ottilie said.

Frederick said, "He can be dumb and cunning. He hates me, wants to control me through an appointment." It was now common knowledge that the president had referred to him as "that nigger" after the February meeting with the delegation of five.

Frederick's misgivings only deepened when he received another letter from Charles that summer. "My position here will depend on the policy of the successor of General Howard, and friends and reporters in the press are saying that if you accept the offer the job would at once be given." Charles then asked for $800.

Frederick told Ottilie, "He writes as if the deed is done. This is a stab in Howard's back. Maybe if the president manages to appoint a Black man to head the Freedmen's Bureau, it would, more than all other acts of his, demonstrate his purpose in being the Moses of the colored race in the United States."

Ottilie tittered. "Will you accept?"

"Of course not! The president hasn't offered the position directly, anyway. I will tell Charles the answer is no." But Charles did not accept his answer. "Reconsider," insisted Charles in a one-word telegram.

Frederick was furious. He wanted to get on the next train to Washington and confront Charles with the obvious. An employee in the federal bureaucracy was in no position to make an enemy of President Johnson, who had not reached the end of his wrath now that Republicans had majorities in both houses of Congress and were eager to override every presidential veto. Retaliating, he could fire anybody. And no laws, rules, or organizations could protect him. "Charles is a damn fool," he told Ottilie.

Proud of his decision not to engage in politics regarding General Howard, Frederick wrote a private note to Theodore Tilton of the *Independent*. Tilton printed Frederick's note anyway and offered an editorial compliment, "the greatest Black man in the nation did not consent to become a tool of the meanest white. For this prudence and firmness, Mr. Douglass is entitled to the thanks of his country." Frederick was not angered by Tilton's indiscretion. He publicly wanted to add his own voice to the growing chorus of alarm about Johnson's abuse of presidential power. General Howard deserved protection.

There was more and more talk about a Tenure of Office Act preventing the president from firing members of his cabinet without Senate approval. Maybe all jobs in the federal government needed rules to protect workers. Such rules could prevent Charles and others from resorting to behind-the-scenes duplicity and machination to avoid dismissal or advance themselves.

Ottilie challenged his role in what he now named *the Bureau affair*. "You marked your note *private* to Tilton, but you knew he would print in anyway, didn't you?" she asked.

"I thought he might," Frederick replied.

"And you didn't castigate him for doing so. Correct?"

"Correct."

"Then we're all schemers. It's the spirit of the age. We use others for our own purposes."

Frederick started to object. "I didn't—"

"You used Tilton for a good purpose, but you manipulated him even so,"

Ottilie interrupted.

"There are degrees."

"The ends justify the means?"

Frederick arched his eyebrows. "You said *all* earlier. To what scheme are you alluding?"

Ottilie hesitated. "Us. Here."

"I do not want to discuss *that*, and I mean it."

"I understand."

100.

FREDERICK MET CHARLES IN the lobby of the Wormley, where he resided. "I expect an apology from you about what you said about your Uncle Perry." He gestured to a table and chairs at the side of the lobby. As they crossed the room, Frederick nodded his head toward a gentleman who had recognized him.

"Father, you are the most famous man in town," Charles said.

"Flattery will get you nothing, Charles, not this time. Now tell me. What is it between you and Rosetta? She wrote me a letter about the conflict between you and your brothers. And Junior is involved, too? How can that be? If this is about money, surely, he has none, having failed out West, as I expected."

Charles looked at the tablecloth. "He had enough money to lend to Nathan."

"What!"

"And I loaned Nathan money, too," Charles said.

"You? You never liked him, and . . ."

"Rosetta, she asked us. She pleaded."

"She asked you? Why didn't she ask me?"

"She was too ashamed."

"You don't have any problem with shame," said Frederick. He immediately regretted his sharp tongue.

Charles stared at his father and took in the insult. "But I will pay you back, every last cent. You have my word."

"Good," Frederick said.

"I am managing."

"Good."

"There is so much happening here now with the president asking for Secretary Stanton's resignation and . . ."

Frederick cut him off. "I have an appointment with my friend Senator Sumner, and he can fill me in with all the details since he is closer to what's happening."

Charles looked down. Frederick moderated his tone. He continued, "I appreciate your detailed letters, Charles, and your interest in government and policy is most refreshing."

Charles retorted, "Does this surprise you?" He shifted between subservience and defiance within seconds, a habit most often revealed with his father.

"No, absolutely not. Your keen intelligence has found a worthy subject, and one day you might include your observations and insights in more than letters to me, in articles and essays for publication."

"Thank you, Father. I would love to write for you someday. Will you ever start another newspaper?"

"I'm thinking about it," Frederick said.

"Another newspaper in Rochester?" Charles was both dubious and scornful.

"I do need to be closer to the center of events."

"Are you moving here?"

"No, no, not yet. Rochester is home. The house, the garden, your mother, the family."

"But you're never there, except in the summers when Miss Assing comes."

"Charles, my schedule is none of your business."

"I'm sorry, Father. I was excited by the prospect of you being close and working together, that's all."

"So, what are you doing when you're not working?"

"I'm still looking for a permanent place for Libby and baby Charles, and will send for them when I do, and . . ." Frederick took a deep breath, preparing for another appeal for money. Charles continued, "I keep myself busy by reading every newspaper I can."

Frederick stood. "Good. I need to see Senator Sumner."

Charles looked up for a moment, then stood, too. "Of course, Father. May we take a ride around the District this week and have a meal together and—"

"Maybe. We'll see."

"Of course," Charles said, deflated.

Frederick extended his hand. "Good seeing you, son. I'll send a note as to when I have time. Sumner, Chief Justice Chase, the representatives from New York, and others require my attention."

★

SUMNER WAS THE MOST ardent, uncompromising advocate of Black suffrage and equality in Congress, and Frederick, like most Black Americans, had worried that his injuries from 1856 would prevent him from fulfilling their dreams. After Preston Brooks caned Sumner on the Senate floor, his injuries made service impossible for three years. When he returned, Sumner complained of extreme headaches and remained in bed for days. Many had hoped he had learned his lesson after giving a speech that enraged the South Carolina congressman, but Sumner never tempered his words. He insulted routinely and antagonized opponents, which deepened their resolve to oppose him. When Sumner submitted Civil Rights legislation again and again, his enemies would not permit his bills to come to the floor for a vote, most often citing his intemperate, insulting speeches during debates as reason for not staging another spectacle of invective and recrimination.

Supporters and constituents feared another attack. But Sumner was unafraid, and few doubted his courage. Nevertheless, he made friends and supporters wary and cautious. Sumner was bombastic, egotistical, self-righteous, rigid, and humorless. From his Olympian heights, Sumner had no equals. Admiration, or even reverence, was possible; true friendship, the bond of brothers, almost impossible.

Frederick measured his time carefully whenever they met. Sumner was exhausting. Yet his political power was undeniable, and Sumner relished it as he marshaled his forces against anyone who stood in his way. He was the best ally of the oppressed because his hatred of oppressors was pure, principled, ruthless, selfless. "I'm the best hater," he had told Frederick two years before during the inaugural celebrations for Lincoln. "I have no ambition save the absolute and total defeat of the enemies of colored people. I am General Sherman in the halls of Congress; and I will only accept total surrender."

Frederick appreciated Sumner's relentless resolve, but today he was uncomfortable. Even praise smacked of condescension. Sumner never called him Frederick, only "Douglass."

"Douglass, I see you are giving your speech, 'Sources of Dangers to the Republic,' throughout the East. It's being printed in many newspapers. I consider this comment your best: 'a government that cannot hate traitors cannot love and respect loyal men.' Indeed, Mr. Johnson is a traitor," said Sumner.

"We've had bad luck with vice presidents," Frederick replied.

"Aaron Burr, John Tyler, John C. Calhoun, Millard Fillmore, Johnson," Sumner intoned. "Eliminate the office."

"We must change the Constitution. It puts the liberties of the American people at the mercy of accidental presidents, bad and wicked men. The Founders said they didn't want a king, but they made one anyway with the president's absolute power to hire and pardon. He can get people to exchange their souls," said Frederick.

"I will not be beholden to any man, to Buchanan, to Lincoln, to Johnson, to you, to no man."

"But to the people."

"Through their *elected* representatives."

"Without the vote, my citizenship is but an empty name."

"There must be another constitutional amendment, and I will do everything in my power to get it first passed in Congress. The Negro vote is absolutely imperative," Sumner said.

"Thank you, sir."

"And we will override the president's veto."

"But if Republicans lose seats in the midterm elections . . ." Frederick said.

"Then we will find other means," Sumner said.

"Impeachment?"

"Mr. Johnson should have been impeached a year ago for allowing traitors to regain control of southern legislators and then depriving freedmen of their rights. I can list at least ten articles of impeachment for his betrayal of the reconstruction we envisioned, a reconstruction of the new South based on equality and justice. We now have enslavement by another name. Yes, impeach the scoundrel, but don't impeach him on some law, some mere technicality. His crimes and misdemeanors are crimes against your people."

"Surely, if it comes to that, sir, you will not oppose Congress's desire to curb the president's power?" Frederick asked.

"Of course not, Douglass. Congress is an equal branch of our government, but more importantly, I abhor the president. But I am a professional hater. I hate with certainty and rigor, and the Tenure of Office Act is a strategy only, a strategy without rigor. We must embody hatred against our enemies. It needs to be our essence, our very being in the war against evil." Sumner's words evoked memories of John Brown.

"We should hate as we love. That's what I said a few weeks ago in Philadelphia," Frederick said.

"That pleased me when I read it the *Evening Telegraph*. Our hatred requires that we will not compromise about the removal of the president, as surely as there is a God in heaven. From the beginning of our history, the country has been afflicted with compromise. It is by compromise that human rights have been abandoned. Congress cannot equivocate about the rights of the freedmen. And Mr. Johnson must be removed to protect your *people* from his willingness to give their rights over to white people for his political gain. I will crush him."

"If New York allows for universal Black suffrage, I will be able to work with you, sir, against our common enemies." Admitting his political ambition to Sumner, Frederick surprised himself, never anticipating that this day and time would be the moment for a private declaration. But the process of building support had to begin somewhere, and Charles Sumner, despite his fractured relationships within the Republican Party, had considerable influence.

Sumner leaned forward. "The Republican Party of New York will never allow you to run, sir, for it's too afraid of being branded as Black, too Black. And Democrats will come out to make sure you do not win, since race always works to their advantage. Didn't you say yourself that hating Negroes can be brought into an election with telling effect. It's already happened in Ohio. Why, sir, they want freedmen to vote in the South, but not Negroes in Ohio, where there are only a few. Your effectiveness is best outside the political house."

Frederick thought Sumner would be his champion. This rebuke stung, and he weakly protested, "But you're inside the house."

"Massachusetts is not New York, sir, and you chose to move to Rochester long ago. But Fourteenth and Fifteenth amendments, over a presidential veto, will change everything, even for you!"

Frederick stood, too rattled to remain. "Thank you for your time, sir. Please give my regards to Mrs. Sumner." Sumner, a bachelor for most of his life, had just married for the first time last year.

"She is rarely home to receive your salutations, as she travels about town with her friend, that German diplomat," Sumner said.

Only a deep bitterness could explain Sumner's indiscretion about such a personal matter, and Frederick said nothing, too taken aback to reply. His feeling deepened when Sumner added, "you should know about such matters."

"Sir?"

"Germans."

"Good day, sir," was all Frederick managed to say as he turned away, furious. He knew Charles Sumner was notoriously rude, but he never thought that Sumner would allude to his personal life, and especially to his public friendship with Ottilie.

"My regards to Mrs. Douglass," Sumner said.

101.

BY THE END OF 1866, Frederick's energies were depleted, and he was too drained to board the train for Albany and Rochester. He found refuge in the new home of Ottilie and her hosts, the Koehlers. They were delighted to receive him, and showed him the room where he would be staying. The room was spacious with large windows. The light made the room seem even larger. The huge stove provided ample heat. It was quiet. The Koehlers pointed out the prints of Lincoln and Douglass himself above the bedframe, ignoring the fact that the bed was too small.

Didn't Ottilie tell them I need a big bed? Frederick regretted the thought.

Everyone was doing their best to make him feel welcome, excited they had a famous lecturer and writer in the house. They had eagerly anticipated his arrival and were going to celebrate his birthday on New Year's Eve with bountiful food and good cheer.

It was Ottilie's idea. "This is your fiftieth year, Frederick, a major milestone in anyone's life. *Fifty* years," she said.

"I think it's fifty years. You know I don't know my birthday. I wish I did. From other events, I think it's February 1817. But I can't be sure."

"Well, your guess is good enough for me and the rest of us. We'll have a birthday cake and celebrate you and the coming of another year when the world is blessed to have Frederick Douglass in it. And we will be *together*."

"I love you," Frederick whispered. She pressed his hand. As soon as he said the words, the spell was broken, for he knew the words didn't match the love he saw in Ottilie's eyes or the love he still had for Julia, the love that made him quiver every time he received a letter from her. They still corresponded regularly, and he eagerly anticipated Julia's letters. Ottilie's letters did not inspire the same response. He enjoyed her visits, her letters not so much.

He went to her room that night. She had placed a blanket on the floor. Looking to the bed, she whispered, "Too much noise, even with just me." Ottilie helped him lift his nightshirt over his shoulders and dropped to her knees looking up to him in the candlelight.

Frederick groaned, luxuriating in the touch. He felt the tension and heat course through his entire body, and his legs shivered slightly as if they could not bear the weight of desire. As soon as he penetrated her, he was done. "I'm sorry," he whispered, his head beside hers.

"Don't be. We're both getting older. We can enjoy each other in other ways, a touch . . ." Ottilie replied.

"No funerals for loving just yet," Frederick said. He was mortified by his inadequate performance. He felt vigorous, potent at fifty, and didn't expect a premature response. This was supposed to happen years from now. "Good night," he said, reproaching himself for reducing love to function. He did not feel shame, for he was convinced that Ottilie wanted only what was best for him.

"Good night, with love," Ottilie whispered.

On the following night at the party, Ottilie raised her cup and toasted, "Tonight is for Frederick. To Frederick Douglass."

They all raised their cups, including Frederick, whose cup remained empty of alcohol after years of abstinence. No one badgered him about it or tried to make him conform.

"To Frederick Douglass," they exclaimed. And he said, "To friends," as they repeated his name. The party continued for some time until Frederick and Ottilie were the last in the parlor, as if the entire household understood that Frederick and Ottilie needed time alone.

"These are good people," Frederick observed.

"Yes, and they want us to be happy," Ottilie said.

"Us? Surely, you didn't talk about us?"

"There's an understanding, as with Mrs. Marks. We Europeans are so much more open and tolerant of such things."

"But . . ."

"Frederick, please, no arguments. Not tonight. Happy birthday, and happy New Year."

"Tonight was good for me. The world is mad, but we can still enjoy good food, the company of friends," he said.

Two days later, Frederick continued his tour, holding the letters Charles and Rosetta had forwarded to Ottilie for safekeeping. Ottilie assured him that she would hold any letters arriving after his departure. Frederick told her, "I will be back here before I leave for Rochester. I don't know exactly when, but I will telegram you when I know."

When he returned to Hoboken, he found a pile of letters filled with news. Charles spent most of his letters relating the political drama in Washington. Most of the news was familiar, but Charles had firsthand knowledge of the response of the colored community in Washington. He was irritated by its indifference to the Tenure of Office Act and the future of Secretary of War Stanton. He summarized their position in a single line from a neighbor: "all of this white man's stuff has nothing to do with our daily lives."

As a government employee, Charles did not have the luxury of apathy or indifference. He was invested in the outcome of the battle between the president and Congress over jobs in the federal government. The president had informed Stanton that his services were no longer required, and Stanton, invoking the Tenure of Office Act, refused to resign, and told him he would wait for Congress to reconvene in December. In the meantime, the president appointed General Grant as the interim Secretary of War. Grant refused.

Charles was adamant. "Don't people realize how important this all is? The president has fired the military commanders in charge of southern Reconstruction districts and replaced them with Confederates, with *traitors*? He can't get away with unlimited appointment powers. This is bigger than Secretary Stanton. By appointments alone, the president can destroy Reconstruction entirely. He can use the courts as well. Look what happened with the Supreme Court under Justice Taney ten years ago? The president must be stopped."

He described the president's December 3 annual message to Congress. He copied the most offensive passages, even though the message was reprinted verbatim in every Negro paper in the country as the most egregious public expression of racism from a president in the history of the Republic. About Black self-government, the president had asserted:

"The peculiar qualities which should characterize any people are fit to decide upon the management of public affairs for a great state have seldom been combined. It is the glory of white men to know that they had these qualities in sufficient measure to build upon this continent a great political fabric and to preserve its stability for more than ninety years, while in every other part of the world all similar experiments have failed. But if anything can be proved by known facts, if all reasoning upon evidence is not abandoned, it must be acknowledged that in the progress of nations Negroes have shown less capacity for government than any other race of people. No independent government of any form has ever been successful in their hands. On the contrary, wherever they have been left to their own devices they have shown a constant tendency to relapse into barbarism."

Frederick was equally aghast that a president would articulate such views so openly, but he was not surprised by the deep racism and hostility to threats to his power. Charles wrote to Frederick in early February, "The city is in the wildest excitement in consequence of Johnson's last drunk. Before you receive this, he will be impeached." On February 24, the president was formally impeached by the House of Representatives, and the trial started in the Senate chamber on March 23. Eight hundred tickets were available to government workers each day, and, according to Charles, workers at the Freedmen's Bureau could easily obtain them. Charles obtained tickets for April 16, asking his father to join him.

Frederick agreed to come and made arrangements to stay at the Davis Hotel. Charles arranged for time off that day, but Frederick did not show up. He had decided his presence would be a distraction and later apologized to Charles. Charles accepted the apology, but the slight lingered, reinforcing Charles's conviction that his father did not respect or like him, despite his efforts. Frederick had left him waiting for hours worrying about his safety.

The trial was unfortunately an excruciating bore, mind-numbing in its procedural, repetitious excessive points of order, and reading of documents for the record. Frederick missed nothing of note, but even so, he could have sent a note or paid a call. Charles had to inquire through a telegram. "Are you safe?" he gently asked. Charles feared never winning Frederick's approval, never measuring up to his high standards. But he was too stubborn to give up. Maybe, just maybe, his father would look at him like he looked at Lewis, just once.

102.

WHILE WAITING FOR A Senate conviction in Johnson's impeachment trial, Frederick attended the 1868 annual convention of the American Equal Rights Association in New York. He was concerned about Elizabeth Stanton. She started a newspaper, the *Revolution*, funded by George Francis Train, a notorious racist and Democrat, and was more radical than ever. In January, she wrote in her first issue, "The male element is a destructive force, stern, selfish, aggrandizing, loving war, violence, conquest, acquisition, breeding in the material and moral world alike discord, disorder, disease, and death. The idea strengthens at every step, that woman was created for no purpose than to gratify the lust of man. Society as organized today is one grand rape of womanhood under the man-power."

Elizabeth Stanton once told Frederick she was "naturally very timid," but her fierce opposition to men had withered timidity, and now, at least in print, she was an inflexible female warrior. Even so, she could be amiable and charming on occasion when she reunited with old friends. She was a natural storyteller; the knowing twinkle in her eyes enraptured listeners.

Talking with Frederick and Ottilie in a hotel sitting room where association delegates were staying, Elizabeth related her three-month stay in Kansas the year before, where she went with Susan B. Anthony to promote a referendum for women's suffrage, the country's first. After relating her travails about food, bugs and mice, miserable accommodations, and hostile men, she noted, "We will be forever grateful that George Francis Train came to our rescue, offering to pay all our expenses. He's a marvelous specimen of manhood, like you, Frederick, so tall and so fine looking."

Frederick bristled. "That was a mistake, Elizabeth, a serious mistake accepting his money and, worse, associating with him."

"All of the other men who once supported us abandoned us there. We lost, but he helped us win votes in Kansas, and we were willing to accept Democratic votes if they supported us. He's a Democrat, but it didn't matter, and it still doesn't matter. He's for our movement, for the vote."

"Train is a bigot, Elizabeth, the grossest kind of bigot."

Elizabeth didn't answer. Frederick continued, "Must I quote the racist doggerel he offered with Miss Anthony at his side?"

"No," she replied, defiant. "Did you come here prepared like a lawyer to make a case against him?"

Frederick answered, quoting Train's warning to white men: "And then he held his nose and said, 'Keep your nose twenty years on a Negro and you will have hard work to smell a white man again.'" He asked, "You tolerate a man who would say such things about a friend in the presence of your dearest friend?"

Elizabeth stood, reached for her purse, and said, "So long as Mr. Train speaks nobly for the woman, why should we repudiate his services, even though he utters words I would not use? And Miss Anthony can speak for herself."

Elizabeth turned and walked to the door of the sitting room. Frederick and Ottilie watched, saying nothing until she was out of sight. Ottilie turned to Frederick and touched his hand on the table, forgetting their agreement to avoid gestures of intimacy in public, and said softly, "I'm so sorry."

Frowning, he looked to her hand, and she immediately withdrew it. "So am I," he replied.

"Your equality is not her equality," Ottilie said.

"I thought we understood each other. I thought we shared the same agreement on principle."

"You can remain friends and still disagree," Ottilie replied. "We remain friends."

"But Train hates me and all Black people. How can they be his friend and mine too?"

"Are you no longer their friend?"

"I want to be, but . . ." Frederick trailed off.

"I never liked them, but I'm still your friend," Ottilie said.

He chuckled, acknowledging his inconsistency. "We all make allowances, don't we?"

"Yes."

Susan B. Anthony avoided Frederick throughout the association gathering, and he didn't try to engage her. Neither one anticipated that their next day together would be defined by a public defense of George Francis Train by Olympia Brown, the first woman ordained as a minister by the Unitarian Church. It was as if Elizabeth had reported her conversation with Frederick to her colleagues and they strategically decided it would be best for a third party, who had no personal connection to Frederick, to confront him.

Frederick had never met Olympia before, but her reputation preceded her as an eloquent, incisive preacher, abolitionist, and supporter of women's suffrage. No other women had attempted ordination and received the wholehearted endorsement of her congregation without schism. She had traveled to Kansas as well.

At the Association meeting, where attendance was small in a somewhat shabby rented space, Olympia raised her hand for recognition, receiving it from the association president. She rose and turned to Frederick, sitting two rows behind her and challenged him, "Mr. Douglass, I wish to understand why you didn't join me and Mr. Train when we were in Kansas working for the cause of women's equality?"

Frederick stood and was convivial but firm. "He hates the Negro, and that is what stimulates him to substitute the cry of emancipation for women. And it should be noted that Mr. Train's Democratic Party opposes the impeachment of President Johnson and wants a white man's government."

"The fate of the president is not at issue here," replied Olympia, resolute, unequivocal, demanding subservience.

Frederick raised his voice just a notch, keeping it convivial and firm. "But indeed it is, madam. Conviction will be a hopeful indication of the triumph of our right to vote and will mean that the South shall no longer be governed by traitors and the Ku Klux Klan but by fair and impartial law. The survival of Reconstruction depends on it. President Johnson and his supporters, like Mr. Train, should not succeed."

Olympia softened. She replied, "Sir, your opinion of Mr. Train is yours to own, but we remain convinced that for our cause, the cause of equality for women, we need to welcome allies from all quarters."

"We all want equality and the vote for all," said Frederick.

"But when for all?" Olympia asked.

"In due time," replied Frederick.

"In due time," scoffed Olympia, "the eternal call for delay and the death of revolutions."

Before he sat down, Frederick added, "Let's see what the next few days will tell us all. The fate of Mr. Johnson will determine the fate of the rest of us in ways big and small." Elizabeth and Anthony avoided him for the rest of the day, even as he was elected vice president of the Association. Ottilie told him after the vote, "They still need you."

"Defuse the enemy with flattery," Frederick said, his sarcasm pointed. Then he turned serious. "But the Black vote cannot wait, and it will come if Johnson is no longer in our way."

★

A WEEK LATER, ON May 20, the Republican Party met in Chicago and nominated General Ulysses S. Grant for president on the first ballot by all the delegates. Everyone left Chicago sure of victory in November, even though the platform was as bland as unsalted porridge. The platform denounced President Johnson, but it avoided support of federal Black suffrage, stating instead that northern states could choose to grant Black men the right to vote. This genuflection to states' rights—again—deeply disappointed Frederick, but he accepted Grant's word about federal Black suffrage.

The Democrats scuttled Johnson for renomination and selected the governor of New York, Horatio Seymore, as their candidate. Johnson's impeachment trial finally ended on May 26. The United States Senate acquitted President

Johnson. Thirty-five senators voted guilty and nineteen for acquittal, one vote short for removal. After weeks of procedural wrangling, the verdict seemed anticlimactic, like the tepid end of a long and boring play.

In his remaining months, Johnson, using the power he still possessed, fired generals in charge of the military districts supervising Reconstruction and replaced them with pro-South, anti-Black officers, since the Tenure of Office Act only applied to the cabinet.

Ottilie fretted. "What if he pardons General Lee or, worse, Jefferson Davis just before he leaves office? And what if he pardons without any conditions? What if they can never be charged with treason?"

Frederick was bitter. He said, "It would be his last laugh."

The summer of 1868 was the best summer Ottilie had had at the South Avenue house. There were no other long-term visitors, and Anna ignored her, spending hours in her garden, cultivating, mulching, pruning, and picking. There were flower bouquets in every room, and meals were served with fresh vegetables every night. The abundant pear trees provided fruit for pies, cookies jams, jellies, sauces, relishes, and salads.

Frederick and Ottilie spent hours together reading again from Motley's *Rise of the Dutch Republic*, deepening his love of history and softening the pain of his lack of formal education. They also read Dickens's *Hard Times*. Frederick was writing more for journals like the *North American Review* and *Atlantic Monthly*, and Ottilie enjoyed reviewing his manuscripts and suggesting edits.

Frederick was asked to contribute to a collection, *Scenes in the Life of Harriet Tubman*, and was inspired to do his best work for a remarkable woman whom he had never met. Before writing his tribute, he told Ottilie, "It's about time. She inspired so many who wanted freedom. We all owe her our deepest gratitude. This woman of Maryland deserves nothing less."

Once he finished the work, solicited by Harriet for the book, he proudly read it aloud to Ottilie: "You ask for what you do not need when you call upon me for a word of commendation. I need such words from you far more than you can need them for me, especially where your superior labors and devotion to the cause of the lately enslaved of our land are known as I know them. The difference between us is very marked. Most of what I have done and suffered in the service of our cause has been in public, and I have received much encouragement at every step of the way. You, on the other hand, have labored in a private way. I have wrought in the day—you in the night. I have the applause of the crowd and the satisfaction that comes of being approved by the multitude, while the most that you have done has been witnessed by a few, trembling, scarred, and footsore bondmen and women, whom you have led out of the house of bondage, and whose heartfelt 'God bless you' has been your only reward. The midnight sky and the silent stars have been the witnesses of your devotion to freedom and of your heroism. It is to me a great pleasure and a great privilege to bear testimony to your character and your works, and to say to those to whom you may come, that I regard you in every way truthful and trustworthy."

Ottilie heard the deep emotion in his voice, and any comment from her seemed inadequate, but she managed to say, "Splendid."

She had much more to say to her sister. That summer, Frederick inspired her to write, "I see little of the world, and I am so completely satisfied with the garden of life I live here that I have not the slightest desire for change, especially since this whole garden holds a whole universe for me. The summer on the green magic island passes with incomprehensible speed, but I am happy."

103.

FREDERICK WAS GETTING MORE agitated about what he was hearing. Susan B. Anthony told Theodore Tilton, who then quoted her back to Frederick, "I would sooner cut off my right hand than ask the ballot for the Black man and not for woman." Elizabeth was reported to have asked, "It becomes a serious question whether we had better stand aside and see Sambo walk into the kingdom first?"

Sambo?

Offended by such rhetoric, Frederick wrote to the Association secretary: "As you well know, woman has a thousand ways to attach herself to the governing power of the land and already exerts an honorable influence on the course of legislation. She is the victim of abuses, to be sure, but it cannot be pretended I think that her cause is as urgent as ours. Miss Anthony's and Mrs. Stanton's position is: that no Negro shall be enfranchised while woman is not. Now, considering that white men have been enfranchised always, and colored men have not, the conduct of these white women, whose husbands, fathers, and brothers are voters, does not seem generous."

He didn't expected an answer and did not receive one, but the comments later made by Elizabeth in the *Revolution* revealed the hardening of her position. It seemed like a direct response to his letter. She wrote, "Black men and immigrants should not get the vote denied to women because to do so would exalt ignorance above education, vice above virtue, brutality and barbarism above refinement and religion."

Embarrassed by these words, and gently opposing such intransigence, Lucy Stone, a friend of Elizabeth's and Susan's, suggested the formation of a New England Woman Suffrage Association and asked Frederick, Stephen Foster,

Foster's wife Abby Kelley Foster, Thomas Wentworth Higginson, and others to join her in Boston that fall.

Frederick accepted Lucy Stone's invitation.

Wary of Foster and Abby since the rancorous break with Garrison in 1851–52, Frederick found, to his great surprise, the radical couple congenial and courteous, as if the disputes of the past no longer mattered. These firebrands, who hated politics and considered almost all politicians morally bankrupt, actively supported the Republican Party as the only acceptable option for the Black vote. Time had mellowed them, making them more pragmatic.

The Bostonians regretted that victories for Black and women's suffrage could not come hand in hand but agreed that opposing the Fifteenth Amendment—the all-or-nothing approach of Anthony and Stanton—was untenable. Other equal rights associations formed to stem the radical tide were taking similar stands.

Frederick campaigned for Grant throughout the summer and fall of 1868, while keeping a wary eye on the growing split between efforts to ensure the enfranchisement of Negroes and the women's suffrage movement. Moderates throughout the land celebrated when General Grant won the presidency in an Electoral College landslide, 214 electoral votes to Seymour's paltry 80 votes on November 3.

In spring, after the inauguration, the party faithful who worked hard for Grant's election expected their rewards: appointments and jobs. Frederick anticipated inquiries of interest and then appointment telegrams within the next few months. Some called this a gross feeding from the political trough, political corruption at its worst, or, kindlier, patronage. Those more realistic with knowledge of historical transitions, when transfers of power were not met with riots and bloodshed, called this the working of democracy.

While he waited, Frederick celebrated the election and the coming of the new year with Ottilie and their German friends. The Lowenthals hosted the party this time, and everyone laughed and sang songs into the early hours of the morning. Eventually, Ottilie and Frederick were left alone in the parlor after everyone else had retired for the night. This was the unspoken arrangement. After a sufficient pause, Ottilie and Frederick could go upstairs unnoticed, and in the morning the Loventhals and their guests could legitimately say they saw nothing scandalous.

But surely they heard through thin walls how this New Year's Eve ended with the prolonged pleasures of sweat and heat, Frederick and Ottilie indifferent to whether they could be heard seeking fulfillment in the dark.

They didn't know yet that on Christmas Day President Johnson had issued unconditional and "without reservations" full pardons and amnesty to all soldiers and leaders of the Confederacy and restored all their "rights, privileges, and immunities under the Constitution."

Happy New Year!

★

The president-elect announced potential appointments before the March inauguration, and there were rumors about Frederick, but nothing more. He fretted and expected satisfaction as a party loyalist, but he had to make alternative plans. He considered moving to Washington and starting another newspaper, the *New Era*.

Frederick told Ottilie during one of his more frequent sojourns to the East, "If I start another newspaper, you can work for me as my copy editor and an editorial contributor."

"Another newspaper?" she asked in New Jersey.

"I miss publishing. I miss writing editorials, commenting on the issues of the day. I even miss the feel of typesetting. And the travel is only misery," Frederick replied.

"Can you get your old office back?"

Frederick shifted in his chair. "No, someone else has it. But I don't think I want to have another newspaper in Rochester."

"Then where?" Ottilie asked, thrilled.

"Washington. If it all works out, it will be Washington, and I will hire Lewis to be my printer. He's good, you know."

"But why Washington and not New York?"

"Everything that matters happens there. Whatever is going to make the country change will be decided there. Would you leave New York?" Frederick asked.

"For you, of course!"

"Well, nothing has been decided yet. And if President Grant appoints me to a post after the inauguration, the newspaper will have to wait. Grant has absolutely endorsed Black male suffrage and will see it through Congress and ratification. I think he'll have more clout than Mr. Lincoln. He could only manage to get the House of Representatives to pass the Thirteenth Amendment by one vote," Frederick said.

"More speeches, more trains, and carriages after it passes in Congress. The States ratification will take months," Ottilie said.

"The Fifteenth Amendment must come out of Congress first. What an exciting time to be alive!" Frederick declared.

"Indeed," Ottilie agreed.

He went off to Boston, and she to Washington for her first visit as a tourist, both expecting a reunion that spring for the next Equal Rights Association meeting in May, if not before.

Congress formally passed the Fifteenth Amendment on February 26, 1869, and the debate about its ratification intensified.

Elizabeth Stanton became even more impassioned, more strident, telling readers in the *Revolution* that if politicians denied the vote, they "degrade wives, and daughters below unwashed and unlettered ditchdiggers, boot-blacks, hostlers, and barbers." She asked readers to imagine "Patrick and Sambo and Hans and Yung Tung who do not know the difference between a monarchy and a republic, who never read the Declaration of Independence making laws for refined Anglo-Saxon women."

Frederick was more than disappointed. He was appalled. Elizabeth Cady Stanton was a racist through and through. Not only did she subscribe to white supremacy, she subscribed to white female supremacy. He didn't want a public battle with her and Susan B. Anthony. But they had to be confronted now. He was prepared but anxious, nonetheless. Friendships were about to die. He was sure of it.

Frederick stayed with Ottilie from Monday to Friday during that week of the Association meeting. The highlight of their evenings together was a performance of *Othello* at the new Booth Theatre, with Edwin Booth performing the title role. After what Ottilie thought was a splendid performance, she and Frederick walked arm in arm on Sixth Avenue, vibrant with noisy vendors, carriages, omnibuses, and loud conversation. They talked about the play's meaning.

"It is also about a great man destroyed by his own insecurities, his own torment," Ottilie observed.

"Why was he so willing to believe his wife was guilty?" Frederick asked, his hand gripping Ottilie's arm when he stopped. "How could Iago so quickly dupe this man? Did Othello believe he was essentially unworthy of her because he was Black? And because he couldn't face that truth, he destroyed her instead?"

Ottilie looked down to his hand, and he immediately released her. "I don't know," she whispered.

They continued walking, and Frederick stopped again. "Those words of farewell, farewell to pride, pomp, and circumstance, they ring in my ears. I worry like him that my occupation is gone, that I'm no longer whole."

"But this can't be true."

What was happening to him? "This feeling will pass. It always does," he said, exhaustion in his voice. "And I will be ready for tomorrow's battle, and others, too."

★

The battle lines had been drawn in New York City before Frederick uttered a word. After a year of public and incendiary comments from Stanton and Anthony, the meeting attracted a large raucous crowd that pushed into Steinway Hall and called for a showdown.

Stephen S. Foster, more conciliatory in Boston, returned to his old ways, standing up from his chair in the audience and challenging Elizabeth, who was presiding as first vice president. "I demand, madam, that you and Miss Susan B. Anthony withdraw immediately from this organization because you have repudiated its fundamental principles." Gasps, cheers, applauses, and boos ensued. Foster grinned and nodded his head, appreciating his role as disrupter, holy fool. Louder now, he continued, "And how did you do this? By espousing that only educated Negroes should be allowed to vote and by branding the Fifteenth Amendment 'infamous.' Furthermore, Miss Anthony needs to clarify her expenditure."

"That is false!" shouted Susan, propelled from her seat. "Everyone who knows me know I am frugal, I am forthcoming, and I have always kept meticulous records about every expenditure, public and private. How dare you, sir?"

"You are out of order, Mr. Foster," declared Elizabeth, slapping her hand on the table, "and you must sit down! Now!"

Foster looked all around him, still grinning, obviously pleased by the uproar he had caused before returning to his seat.

The husband of Lucy Stone, Henry Blackwell, traveled with his wife and lectured with her throughout the country on behalf of women's suffrage. He was well liked and admired for his conciliatory manner. "No one, and I mean no one, can seriously question the commitments of Mrs. Stanton and Miss Anthony to the cause of equal rights. And as a member of the executive committee, I can assure one and all that it is satisfied, fully satisfied, with Miss Anthony's skills as a recordkeeper and money manager," he said.

An approving murmur passed through the hall, as if the crowd was relieved that the blood sport for which they had come had been averted. But Elizabeth was not ready for peace. She said, "I call for this convention to declare Mr. Foster out of order for accusing Miss Anthony of mishandling funds. Such a vote will be a vote of confidence on behalf of Miss Anthony."

Frederick had never seen Elizabeth so enraged. Her fat cheeks seemed about to explode.

She received an immediate second, and she called for a vote from the convention floor. There was no debate, and the convention confirmed her ruling.

Frederick spoke: "I must say that I do not see how anyone can pretend that there is the same urgency in giving the ballot to women as to the Negro. With us, the matter is a question of life and death. It is a matter of existence, at least, in fifteen states of the Union. When women, because they are women, are hunted down through the cities of New York and New Orleans; when they are dragged from their houses and hung upon lampposts; when their children are torn from their arms, and their brains dashed out upon the pavement; when they are the objects of insult and outrage at every turn; when they are in danger of having their homes burnt down over their heads; when their children are not allowed to enter schools; then they will have an urgency to obtain the ballot equal to our own."

Loud applause greeted him as well as a shouted question, "Is that not all true about Black women?"

Frederick replied loudly, "Yes, yes, yes, it is true of the Black woman, but not because she is a woman but because she is Black."

Susan stood, stone faced, single minded, and ruthless as a snake. "I want to say a single word. The old antislavery school and others have said that women must stand back and wait until the other class shall be recognized. But we say that if you will not give the whole loaf of justice and suffrage to an entire people, give it to the most intelligent first . . ." There was applause here. "If intelligence, justice, and moralities are to be placed in the government, then let the question of woman be brought first and that of the Negro last. When Mr. Douglass mentioned the Black man first and women last, if he had noticed he would have seen that it was the men that clapped and not the women. There is not the woman born who desires to eat the bread of dependence, no matter whether it be from the hand of father, husband, or brother; for anyone who dares so eat the bread places herself in the power of the person from whom she takes it."

Applause.

Susan continued, "Mr. Douglass talks about the wrongs of the Negro; how he is hunted down, and the children's brains dashed out by mobs; but with all the wrongs and outrages that he today suffers, he would not exchange his sex and take the place of Elizabeth Cady Stanton." There was again applause and laughter, the sound of truth resounding. Susan continued, "there is a glory . . ."

"Will you allow me a question?" Frederick asked, unflummoxed by this shift from politics to biology.

"Yes, anything. We are in for a fight today," Susan replied, reigniting the battle for which so many had come. Gloves were off, and the crowd wanted a winner and a loser.

"I want to inquire whether granting to women the right of suffrage will change the nature of our sexes?" Frederick asked.

Susan answered, "It will change the nature of one thing very much, and that is the peculiar position of woman. It will place her in a position in which she can earn her own bread, so that she can go out into the world on equal competition in the struggle for life, so that she shall not be compelled to take such positions as men choose to accord her and then take such pay as men choose to give her. Your Fifteenth Amendment would put two million colored men in the position of tyrants over two million colored women, who until now had at least been the equals of the men at their side. If you do not give the whole loaf of justice to the entire people, if you are determined to extend the suffrage piece by piece, then give it first to women, to the most intelligent and capable portion of the women at least, because in the present state of government, it is intelligence, it is morality which is needed."

Lucy Stone's words mirrored the conciliations of her husband. "But we are lost if we turn away from the middle principle and argue for one class. Woman has an ocean of wrongs too deep for any plummet, and the Negro too has an ocean of wrongs that cannot be fathomed. There are two great oceans; in the one is the Black man, and in the other is the woman. But I thank God for the Fifteenth Amendment and hope it will be adopted in every State. I will be thankful in my soul if anybody can get out of the terrible pit."

Susan rose from her seat and approached Frederick. Applause and nervous laughter signaled a desire for an even uglier confrontation. He, too, was surprised. "Frederick, you must stop this now," she said.

"No, no, Susan. Why? Because you are losing?" he asked. Frederick loudly mocked her after she returned to her seat. "You see when women get into trouble how they act? Miss Anthony to the rescue, and these good people have not yet learned to hear people through. When anything goes against them, they are up right away."

His tried-and-true mimicry landed well with the crowd, and they laughed and applauded. Frederick noted Susan looked immobile. The fight was too important to worry about her wounded pride.

Elizabeth, always the reliable supporter, came to her aid. "Let the record show that not another man should be enfranchised until enough women were admitted to the polls to outweigh those already there. I do not believe in allowing ignorant Negroes and ignorant and debased Chinamen to make laws for her to obey."

Frances Watkins Harper, a poet and novelist and a Black suffragist, one of the few there, commented, "I regret the fact that the nation cannot seem to handle more than one question at a time, but since it is a fact, then I would not have the Black woman put a single straw in the way, if only the men of the race can obtain what they want."

"I call for the vote of the two submitted resolutions," said Susan coldly. She understood imminent defeat after years of experience in halls that had moved against her. The convention voted down the call for educated suffrage and approved the ratification of the Fifteenth Amendment with few dissenters.

Susan refused to look at Frederick. Their relationship was over. But Elizabeth was not deterred and made it clear to him that the battle was not finished. "We will form our own organization. It will continue to oppose the Fifteenth Amendment. And will call for a Sixteenth Amendment that will specifically recognize a woman's right to vote, demand equal pay for working women. We will do whatever it takes to obliterate in divorce law the notion that women belong to their husbands. And most importantly for our organization, no man will be permitted to hold office in our organization. We will forever repudiate a man's counsel. A woman must lead the way to her own salvation with courage and determination that knows no fear nor trembling. We must not put our trust in men while we are regarded as his subject, his inferior, his slave."

Frederick rose and said, "Surely, dear Elizabeth, you can hear the ironies."

"I thought you were my friend. Perhaps I should be grateful that you stabbed us not in the back but before the entire world. We are antagonists from now on," Elizabeth stated.

Frederick had anticipated this moment, but he had hoped that it would not be so ugly and that charm and past agreements could still save the day. "Elizabeth . . ." he tried.

"No, Frederick. I will not be appeased or patronized. You're a traitor. That's what you are. A traitor." Elizabeth turned her back and walked away.

104.

THE TALK ABOUT FREDERICK being appointed minister to Haiti came to nothing. Grant gave the job to the thirty-six-year-old Ebenezer Don Carlos Bassett, a teacher from Philadelphia. Bassett was the first Black U.S. diplomat anywhere in the world. Ironically, Frederick had submitted his name to government officials when Grant made it clear he wanted to appoint Negroes to posts in his administration. Bassett had worked to recruit Black soldiers during the war. Frederick never anticipated that Grant would give one of the most prestigious jobs in the State Department to him.

Frederick was furious at being overlooked. He resumed plans for the *New Era*, seeking investors, looking for a permanent office. He had misgivings about the inadequate funding, and working without a salary was another burden he didn't need. But neither exhaustion nor intellectual muddiness could deter Frederick's ambition. He felt he could still be the preeminent voice of Black

America as the corresponding editor. And even better, Lewis could be the paper's printer and at last be able to make his mark.

The New Era was finally launched on January 13, 1870, with Frederick using the newspaper to urge the ratification of the Fifteenth Amendment, which finally took place on March 30, 1870. One hundred guns boomed in the capital as the president wrote a message to Congress. "This measure is indeed a measure of grander importance than any other one act of the kind from the foundation of our government to the present day. The adoption of the Fifteenth constitutes the most important event that has occurred since the nation came into life." A torch light procession of thousands marched down Pennsylvania Avenue and gathered in front of the White House. The president came out and described the amendment as "the realization of the Declaration of Independence."

Frederick celebrated with countless others at conventions, meetings, and rallies throughout the East and Midwest. He observed on one such occasion, "I seem myself to be living in a new world. The sun does not shine as it used to." But joy was tempered by a heightened awareness of responsibility. Now that Black men had the power to determine their future, they had the responsibility to fulfill the great expectations that came with that power. "No more excuses" became Frederick's rallying call.

He accepted the racial realities. The overwhelming majority of whites, raised as haters, still demanded the recognition of their superiority, and many southern governors and legislatures, alarmed by Black power, especially in states with Black majorities, intensified efforts to restrict and intimidate voters. Membership in the Ku Klux Klan soared. The backlash was a whirlwind.

Frederick was convinced that ambitious, determined, and organized Black men could shift public scorn as they succeeded in political and economic life. At the final meeting of the American Anti-Slavery Society in April, delegates dissolved the Society because the Fifteenth Amendment made it obsolete. Frederick said, "We must depend on ourselves, make our own record, make our own future. I have no doubt that we will. We have already made great progress."

He was hoarse that day and thought he would not be able to speak before the audience of mostly women in New York's Apollo Hall. But the presence of old friends and enemies, Wendell Phillips, Lucretia Mott, Abby Kelley Foster, Stephen S. Foster, and Henry Highland Garnet, stirred him. He said, "In fact, I could not very well keep away from here. I know no place in the world where today I could be half as happy as here; to see these faces; to hear these voices; and these faces bring up other faces to memory dear but passed away."

After the prayers, speeches, and songs, the delegates gathered in an adjoining room. Leaning on his cane, Garnet approached Frederick. They had not spoken in years. Garnet's hairline had receded dramatically, but his straight back, high forehead, wide nose, penetrating eyes, and thick white muttonchops that ended below his chin, affirmed his commanding presence. Now a pastor at Shiloh Presbyterian Church in Harlem, he was the first Black minister to preach to the United States House of Representatives, addressing members a month after passage of the Thirteenth Amendment.

Frederick could not forget their New York shouting match of twenty years before, and he remained convinced that only Lincoln's second inaugural address was greater than Garnet's 1843 speech calling for slave rebellion. His was the standard for the galvanizing power of eloquence.

"I was sorry to hear about your loss," said Frederick, offering his hand. Garnet's wife, Julia, had passed away in January.

"Thank you for your condolences. She held on to see the New Year but had to go on January 7. She's in heaven celebrating our new day," Garnet replied.

"And we all join her in celebration."

"And we must thank God for the Fifteenth Amendment, for making its passage possible."

"I will not thank God. God had nothing to do with it. Men passed the Fifteenth Amendment," Frederick said.

"Men inspired by God," Garnet countered.

"How could you know that?"

"Still fighting the Lord, I see."

"Just giving credit where it's due. I want to express my gratitude to God by thanking those faithful men and women who have devoted the great energies of their souls to the welfare of mankind. It's only through such men and such women that I can get any glimpses of God anywhere," Frederick said.

Garnet grinned. "Our people don't like such talk."

"I was not meant to be a preacher."

"You would not have lasted."

"We're successful in different spheres."

"Are you congratulating me, at last?"

"Yes," said Frederick said.

"Why, thank you, sir. But heed my warning: if asked, and you won't thank God, there will be a storm," Garnet replied.

"I'm used to storms. Like you, sir."

"Indeed."

As Garnet predicted, the press of several Black churches and ministries denounced Frederick as a hater of God, Jesus, the Bible, and religion in general. He was again asked to thank God for the Fifteenth Amendment and, again, he refused.

Frederick also remained an unrepentant supporter of the separation of church and state, saying to an audience in Philadelphia that April, "My command to the church, and all denominations of the church, whether Catholic or Protestant is, hands off this government. And my command to the government is hands off the church." He explicitly called for the removal of Bibles from the courts and public schools.

Despite the controversy, colored people filled halls and auditoriums throughout the East. Frederick Douglass was still the most respected and honored Black man in America. Two celebrations for the Fifteenth Amendment that spring in Albany and Baltimore were especially memorable.

A committee of Black men and women made elaborate preparations and decorated Albany's Tweddle Hall with banners, flags, and countless flowers. When Frederick was introduced, the band played "Hail to the Chief." He told the audience, "We cannot be too grateful to the brave and good men through whose exertions our enfranchisement has been accomplished. It would, of course, be impossible to do justice to all who have participated in this noble work." Frederick tried to name and honor as many as possible, acknowledging William Lloyd Garrison, Wendell Phillips, Theodore Tilton, Anna Dickinson, Charles Sumner, Thaddeus Stevens, President Grant, Owen Lovejoy, Abraham Lincoln, John Brown. He didn't name Jesus or God.

Following Frederick, Charles Remond came to the platform. His comments were brief and unmemorable. Afterward, Frederick extended his hand. It was time to heal old wounds. "Brother Remond," he said, making a point of congratulating him.

Remond was always thin, but now he was fragile and spindly. His face was tight with prominent bulges and furrows topped with a tower of black hair on the side. "Friend Douglass," he said.

"We are all together now—not we colored particularly, but all of us. We are fellow citizens. What a country," Frederick said.

"Yes, what a country," Remond said.

"And we'll be united in defending it from all its enemies, whether from within or without."

"Yes, of course. And how's my namesake, your son?"

"He's doing well," lied Frederick. He was still rattled by Charles's lost job with the Freedman's Bureau and his confessions that his wife, Libby, was "insanely jealous" and accused him of dalliances with friends in their social circle. Charles was now the father of two sons. Frederick sent unsolicited money for his growing family. "And your family?" Frederick asked.

Remond noted Frederick's deflection with a raised eyebrow. "I've had my losses, a wife and child. But I endure with a new wife and three other children," he said.

"We endure," was all Frederick said, unwilling to share his own losses and disappointments with a man who, after all these years, still clenched his teeth as if standing before a pile of dung. This reconciliation was not going as he had hoped.

"As we must. Farewell," Remond said.

"Farewell," whispered Frederick, sure that he was seeing him for the last time. He was no doctor, but Remond seemed to be ravaged by cancer. Frederick hoped that when his own time for death came, it would come suddenly, without warning. He didn't want to suffer, linger with pain.

The celebration in Baltimore resonated even more for Frederick than Albany. He had not returned to the home of his enslavement since 1864. It began with a parade of 10,000 Negroes, who marched to Monument Square representing regiments, fraternal clubs, drum corps, secret lodges, and trade unions, their banners proudly displayed in bright colors and huge letters and symbols.

When Frederick spoke, he reminisced about his past, "Forty years ago, I sat on Kennard's Wharf, at the foot of Philpot Street, and saw men and women chained and put on the ship to go to New Orleans. I then resolved that whatever power I had should be devoted to the freeing of my race. I am here today to pledge myself that whatever remains to me of life shall go in the same direction." He was tired, but the cheering never stopped.

Frederick continued his celebration tour for three more months, speaking almost every day, building his bank account for his family. He rushed back to Rochester when Rosetta went into labor to be there for the birth of his fourth granddaughter on August 11, Estelle Irene Sprague.

105.

ANNA TOOK GREAT PRIDE in preparing meals for fugitives, guests, and family members on numerous occasions, and on his return from yet another grueling trip Frederick deserved his favorite meal of pork chops, collards, biscuits, and gravy. Even if that meal included Ottilie. After five summers, Anna understood that as long as Frederick was home meals would include Ottilie, who could never say Anna didn't know how to cook, whatever her other faults.

Anna didn't completely avoid meals when Frederick and Ottilie were together, but she limited herself to sitting with them in absolute silence on Sundays only. She sat at one end of the table with Frederick and Ottilie at the other. They never tried to engage her in conversation, accepting the unspoken ground rule. They had no problem ignoring her as they talked about the issues of the day.

Anna listened, for she was, contrary to what others might think, interested in what was happening in the country, and what Frederick was doing. She just was not going to talk about it, or ask questions, with *them*. Rosetta remained her window to the world.

When Rosetta and Nathan came for dinner, they sat in the middle of the table, and Anna would talk only with them. Swallowing his pride, Nathan had finally agreed, for the sake of Rosetta and his girls, to return to living at the house after living separately at the Alexander Street house Frederick still owned.

After another uncomfortable Sunday dinner, Rosetta demanded. "Mamma, what's happening with you? What's going on?"

Anna sighed, sat down at the kitchen table, and said, "Of all your father's friends, I will not talk with her. She's your father's guest, and she can come here, but I will not speak to her."

"What has she done to deserve this?"

"Rosetta, I don't need to talk about what everybody knows."

"Mama, how can you say something like this? This is . . ."

"They are more than friends."

"What? You can't be serious." Rosetta leaned back, as if preparing for a slap in the face.

"I'm not sayin' more. It will do no good to talk to him about it. It's no good to talk to you about him. He's your father, and there are things between wife and husband the children should not know. It's private."

"Then why did you say this, Mama? You could have given me any number of reasons for what you've been doing and saying. I would have not known the difference. You wanted me to know because you know how I feel about Papa. I never, never thought you could be so mean. And Miss Assing's a part of the family. She helped to raise us! It can't be true."

Anna maintained her composure. "She comes to this house and eats at our table, but I have to do something to show I can't accept their arrangement, and so this is my way."

"Oppose! This doesn't make any sense, Mama. If this is true, what does all this say about you, Mama?"

Anna slapped her hand on the table. "Now that is enough, girl. You've clearly forgot your place. I'm your Mama and this is my house, and my life, and if you don't like it . . ."

"What, Mama? Are you going to force me away if I don't go along?"

"You will go along if you want to live here. I make the rules of this house because your father is here only part of the time. He accepts my place and has said nothing, and I mean nothing, about my not talking at the table. He knows. He don't push because he wants it both ways. He wants me and her."

Rosetta placed her hands over her ears. "Stop this talk, Mama, just stop it."

"You clearly have lost your mind talkin' to me in that way, but I knows what shock can do. But the rule is the rule since you asked. I'm not talking to them at the table, not to them. And you, nor your father, and sure not Ottilie Assing, can make me do different. All you has to do is sit, watch, and eat my good food."

"You shouldn't have told me," said Rosetta, defeated.

"You shouldn't have asked."

"Oh, Mama, we'll never be the same now."

Rosetta left the room, and Anna felt deep regret. *I could have said something else. Why did I put a rock, the heaviest burden, between her and her father? Am I that hateful?*

Rosetta was now even more unpleasant when, on rare occasions, Perry and his wife were included for dinner while Frederick was away. It did not surprise Anna when Perry came to her one afternoon after Frederick and Ottilie went to town and told her about returning to Maryland. He said, "We can't stay here no more, Anna. The family—no, let me say it—Rosetta and Nathan and that white lady, they don't want us here. I tried to make it right, but I'm not going to change for them. This is what I am, and this is what I'm going to be. I thought the family of my own brother would accept me, but no."

"I accept you!" Anna replied.

"I know, and I thank you for yo' kindness, but in Maryland, they don't hate family. We're all family there 'cause we're not that different. We're too different here. Blood don't matter here like it matters there," Perry said.

"What about Fred?"

"He's too far away most of the time. And the truth is—and I know he won't see it, he's with them, with Rosetta and Nathan and the white lady. He wanted me to be here, but he really don't want a brother here, not a brother he has to make excuses for and keep away."

"He didn't help build that house to keep you away!"

"Didn't he? He thought it would be easier for me to have my own house away from the big house. It was, but, really, it was easier for him, easy so he didn't have us around to make excuses for day after day. I want a real family. This is not a real family," Perry said.

"No family's perfect," Anna said.

"But don't family forgive?"

"There's nothing to forgive."

"Oh, yes there is," said Perry raising his voice, sounding like his younger brother. "They can't forgive us for being not like them. They still hate us for being what we is."

"Do you hate them?"

"We better than that," Perry said.

"You forgive them?" Anna asked.

"Yes, but I don't have to stand being 'round them."

"I'm sorry."

"Don't be. Not your fault, and you don't hate yo' roots."

"They make us strong. But Rosetta and the rest don't know Maryland."

"They don't want to know us or Maryland. Has they asked? Has they ever asked? They don't, 'cause they ashamed of our past, of us. I bet they don't ask you 'bout yours, either," Perry said.

Anna reflected on the truth of his words. Life for Rosetta and the boys began in New Bedford and Lynn, and those years in Baltimore and on the Eastern Shore meant nothing to them. But she felt the need to defend her children. "But Charles went to the Eastern Shore and met your sister's family right after the war. He was first. Not even Fred's been back to the Shore."

"Do Charles talk about them? Written them? Gone back?" Perry asked.

"No."

"Have you? What about yo' kin?"

"There's no goin' back for me," Anna said.

"Why?"

"I can't explain. They're dead to me. Too much hurtin', too much grief. Some things need to be cast aside, like a stone on yo' back."

"I'm sorry."

"Don't be. It made me, but dead is dead. Some things can't come back from the dead."

"The Lord Jesus promises we'll all meet again."

"In heaven, if some of us are not in hell." Anna thought of Bambarra Murray, and she hoped he was in hell burning for what he did to his wife and children. No, there was no forgiveness for him, and if her refusal meant her own damnation and eternal separation forever from Frederick, her children, and her grandchildren, so be it.

"Jesus forgave his killers," Perry said warmly.

"He was Jesus."

Ottilie Assing. Bambarra Murray. She hated them deeply with a righteousness so hot and hard, like a flaming cinder caught in her throat, she could not imagine in her life expelling it. "Maybe someday," was all Anna could manage.

"He'll take you into his arms like you did us. He'll remember the good you did. We will." Perry embraced her and hurried from the room.

When Frederick learned of Perry's decision, he approached Anna. "He's leaving in September, and he said there's nothing I can say or do to change his mind. I think he blames me for being away for so much of the time."

"No, he doesn't blame you. He's proud of you, and he knows what your job means. But even if he didn't tell you, you know the reason, and there's nothing you can do that will change the way they feel about him. You can't order them to change their feelings," Anna said.

"This is not what I wanted. Why are our children so difficult?" Frederick asked.

"We raised them."

"This is our fault? Is that what you're saying?"

"It ain't all about us. They may want to say that, but we know better. We raised them good, I think, but they decide who to love, who to like. I want to make them my way, and I sure tried, and so did you, all the rules, the speeches. I can see them now, all eyes and ears, taking it all in, and waiting till they could get away, like we did. We got away. They're independent, too," Anna said.

"Not that independent," said Frederick scornfully. "Taking our money."

"Oh, Fred, that ain't goin' to change. It's our blood. Please don't be too hard on them."

"And you're not? I'm the softer one."

Anna chuckled. "That's the truth. So you be soft, I be hard, and get what we both want. A happier family, together, if it all works out."

"I don't think the boys are coming back here. They all like Washington."

"I have my dreams," said Anna, standing. "I need to see my garden."

"But you went to the garden earlier today. You're there before dawn, almost all day."

"I need it." She reached for her bandana.

Anna's gloves and tools were in a small shed next to the kitchen door. Larger tools were in the garage. She didn't intend to do heavy work. For now, she wanted to walk under her pear trees, walk among the flowers, check the vegetables on the vines, feel the air on her skin as butterflies fluttered on the wind, smell the aroma of the earth alive with worms. She removed her slippers and burrowed her toes into the soft mud after a light rain. Sunlight dappled England aster, Red columbine, Swamp milkweed, blue mistflower, the foamflower stalks jutting up like towers among sweet William, cranesbill, Vernonica, and other wild flowers, a profusion of luxurious color that made her forget her troubles.

Anna loved roses most of all, the majesty of red and white hybrid tea stems, and the abundance of floribunda bushes. But the fullness of their season had passed in the summer heat, and now the humidity thickened the air. For a moment, she thought she could fly, rising on wings, soaring above the green earth, seeing her home below and all she cherished in it. Instead, she dropped to her knees, and her body convulsed with the anguish of rejection and regret.

Frederick did not love her, not as he loved Ottilie. The force of this insight, long held as a tight truth under a shield of self-protection, now engulfed her as a mourner at a funeral faces the dead and accepts their loss.

Perhaps Frederick loved her when they were young and desperate and he found relief in the warmth of her ample flesh. Now he tolerated her more like a son placating his overbearing mother than a husband grappling with the aging process together, raising an extended family of children and grandchildren, facing the setting sun of their lives together.

He was grateful, nothing more.

She and Frederick were not partners now, nor had they been for many years. But today the pear trees planted long ago could not protect her from the storm raging within her heart. It was crushed, and she wept because she had deeply wounded her daughter by giving her the fruit of knowledge like the snake in the garden.

Rolling back and forth, Anna prayed, "Lord, please forgive me what I did. I was evil, needing to bring him down in her eyes. Please, lord, give me the strength to wait for her forgiveness, and the will to accept if it never comes."

106.

FREDERICK WAS IN WASHINGTON to review potential sites for the new journal. Charles had selected three for his consideration. He hoped that his father would select the most expensive because it was closest to the Capitol and breaking news. But Frederick chose the cheapest printing office, in Uniontown across the Anacostia River to the southeast. Done with the inspections and selection of a site, Frederick made a major announcement to Charles and Lewis, "I'm moving here to Washington."

"What!" they exclaimed simultaneously.

"I need to be close to the office, to the two of you, to the news here. Rochester is too far away," he said.

"But what about the . . ." Charles checked himself. It was his childhood home, and he didn't want it sold. It was bad enough that Frederick was allowing Nathan, Rosetta, their children, and two cousins to live there. Charles despised Nathan, sure that he was a lying scoundrel who was scheming to embezzle the family fortune. He turned to Lewis, as if Lewis could read his mind.

"Are you selling the house in Rochester and moving the entire family here?" Lewis asked.

"No. I'll have two residences, two homes, a place for me when traveling out West and a place here. It all makes sense. We can all vote for President Grant using the South Avenue address, since we can't do it here. Besides, your Mama will never leave Rochester. She won't leave Rosetta and the girls. You'll need to help me find a place, Charles. I'll stay here while we look. I want the house to be near the Capitol, even if the office isn't."

"Yes, Father. The city's booming. You'll have some excellent choices to consider," Charles said.

"We'll be spending night and day finding a house and starting the paper," interjected Lewis. Forever the peacemaker, Lewis suggested, "Father, with so much going on, maybe it will be best to not let Mama know about the other house until after the newspaper is up and running. She has enough to worry about, and she will have more to worry about if she knows about two homes. She may not leave Rochester, but she will come here just to make sure everything is just right. That's what she does. That's what she always does."

"Yes, there's no hurry in telling her yet. It will be easier to plan for the house, the furniture, her garden once we have a specific place. No point in making it more difficult now. She'll just worry. You're right," Frederick replied.

"I think so. That first issue will come upon us soon enough. How much copy do you have for me to print, Papa?" Lewis asked.

"I'm still working on some editorials, but I have my welcome letter to readers," answered Frederick.

"Good, let's see your first piece," said Lewis, "and we'll see if we'll still have jobs when we find some errors. Or maybe we'll get fired after we print errors." Lewis smiled and read Frederick's justification for the new journal: "Such a journal, published from week to week in the capital of the nation, inspiring its readers with manly sentiments, ennobling aspirations, reflecting the highest intellectual and moral resources of the colored people, will serve as a pillar of cloud by day and a pillar of fire at night . . ."

Lewis looked at Frederick and said, "Tall order, Papa. But we can live up to the call."

He handed it to Charles to read.

Charles finished reading his father's words and looked at him and then his brother and said, "Yes, we can. We will do this."

★

Following Christmas day in Rochester, Frederick spent the remainder of the holiday season, including New Year's Eve, with Ottilie and their German friends in Hoboken. When he returned to Washington, he received a telegram from the secretary of state, Hamilton Fish. President Grant wanted to see him at the White House.

Frederick arrived at the White House and met first with Fish, who prepared him for the interview with the president. The former governor and United

States senator from New York was a handsome, distinguished man, the features of his long face perfectly proportioned and highlighted by a thin beard touched with gray connected to sideburns. A product of great wealth, Fish wore the finest tailored jacket, trousers, and matching waistcoat money could buy. Ten years older than Frederick, Fish looked ten years younger now that Frederick's hair was almost all white. The secretary's frame was still thin, missing the added midsection pounds of middle age that Frederick carried.

"Please take a seat, Mr. Douglass, and let me explain briefly why you are here." An easygoing gentleman, Fish didn't speak like a self-promoting politician in love with the sound of his own voice. "The president wishes to interview you for the position of secretary to the commissioners for Santo Domingo."

Thanks to Senator Charles Sumner, chair of the Senate Foreign Relations Committee, the Senate defeated President Grant's treaty for the annexation of Santo Domingo, the Spanish republic west of Haiti. Sumner argued that annexation would increase the wealth of the U.S. and more pointedly the wealth of Grant's rich friends. Sumner prevailed, but now the president recommended the formation of a commission to investigate conditions in Santo Domingo and ascertain if its people as well as its leaders desired annexation. On January 9, the resolution for an inquiry commission passed the House, and the Senate approved three days later.

The new resolution authorized the president to appoint three commissioners and a secretary versed in English and Spanish, and it would require only a simple majority for passage rather than the two-thirds majority for treaties.

"I am honored to be considered, sir," Frederick told Secretary Fish.

"No one else is under consideration, sir. That is how confident the president is with his choice. The interview is a mere formality. You will accept if asked?"

"Yes, but my acceptance can't be interpreted as automatic support of annexation, sir. I am disposed to support it, for I do believe that annexation will benefit both the United States and the people of Santo Domingo. But I have not finally decided," Frederick said.

"Understood. This is a commission of inquiry, and it will report its findings to me, the State Department, and to Congress. You will be working with three distinguished men, men of great integrity: Andrew White, the president of Cornell University; Benjamin Wade, the former senator of Ohio; and Dr. Samuel Gridley Howe, whose work for the blind is well known. I'm sure you know Dr. Howe as a longtime abolitionist."

"Yes, I do know him. These are all distinguished, honorable men."

"Dr. Howe and Mr. White actually oppose annexation. Their public stand will thus give no credence to claims that the commission is being stacked by the president in annexation's favor," Fish said.

"Then why me, sir?"

Fish smiled. "Oh, Mr. Douglass. That is an easy question to answer. You are the most famous and distinguished colored man in the country, and because issues of race are unavoidable in this context, there is no better man to explicate them for the public in the commission's report than you, sir."

"You honor me, sir, but this possible appointment places me in an awkward predicament," Frederick said.

"Senator Sumner, yes?" Fish asked.

"Yes, Senator Sumner."

"Well, if the predicament is too awkward, then you have no choice but to *decline* the president's invitation."

"I informed the senator I support the inquiry. And despite his vote against the commission, I still support the inquiry," Frederick said.

Fish stood and reached for his walking cane. "Then let's go and see the president. He's waiting." They had a short walk down the hall to the Oval Office. One of the president's secretaries sat at a small desk and looked up when he heard them approach. He was in army uniform, a part of the staff Grant brought to the White House.

"Please inform the president that Secretary Fish and Mr. Douglass are here to see him now," Fish said.

The soldier stood, towering over both of them. He went into President Grant's office and quickly came out saying, "The president will see you now." He held open the door, allowing Fish in first, then Frederick. The president was behind his desk with a coffee cup in his hand, his large moustache and beard obscuring his mouth. "Mr. Fish. Mr. Douglass. Sit down," he commanded. Grant had sent thousands to their deaths. Equivocation was foreign to his nature. Two chairs had been placed at the front of the desk.

"Mr. Douglass has been informed, sir, about your intention," said Fish.

"Then what say, you, sir? Yes or no?" Grant asked.

"Sir, I am honored to be considered, but there are some . . ." Frederick replied.

"Yes or no, sir. If no, then we have no more to discuss. If yes, then I am open to hearing your concerns. Even so, I don't have all day. Just be aware the commission is scheduled to depart from New York on January 17."

"Yes, sir. I accept," Frederick replied.

"Good. Make the arrangements, Fish," Grant said.

"Yes, sir," said Fish.

Grant focused on Frederick, as if about ready to take aim and fire. "Your concerns, Mr. Douglass?" Frederick hesitated long enough for Grant to jump into the breach, "Mr. Sumner, I take it."

"We are friends," Frederick replied.

"What do you think of his opinion about annexation?" Grant asked.

"Mr. Sumner sincerely believes that in opposing annexation he is defending the cause of colored people of all races, as he has always done." The president seemed unsatisfied. Frederick continued, "What do you, Mr. President, think of Senator Sumner?"

"I think he is mad," Grant stated.

Secretary Fish was rattled by the president's candor. He interjected, "Sir, perhaps . . ."

The president waved his hand. "I am not his friend, and I cannot be a friend of a man who quotes the Bible as if he wrote it. But I do not hold his friendship against you, Mr. Douglass."

"Thank you, sir."

"As the president, however, I issue you this warning. Do not trust the man," Grant said.

Fish interjected again, "Sir, perhaps this is not the time to address . . ."

"Mr. Fish, do not interrupt me."

"Yes, sir."

"Now, Mr. Douglass. I will repeat my warning because he made the issue of my going to his house last year a public affair during his most recent speech. You know the reference?"

"No, sir," Frederick lied.

"I did go to his house to talk with him about the treaty. There were others present. He said in his speech he was honored to have his president come to his house. But since that time do you know he has been telling senators I came that night to his house drunk? Did you know that?" Grant demanded.

"No, sir. I didn't know. How could I know?" Frederick said.

"Such a man can't be trusted, I tell you. Such a man will, behind my back and yours, say that I am using you to curry favor with him. Let me assure you, I have no hope of winning his favor or vote. He remains only one member of the United States Senate. He has made his opposition abundantly clear, but the commission report may sway others when I submit another treaty for annexation later this year after the commission returns."

Frederick was taken aback. The president confirmed what Sumner claimed. The commission's purpose was to defend annexation and ultimately force consent from the Senate the next time a treaty came forward.

Fish leaned forward, being careful, "Sir."

Grant leaned back in his chair, aware that he had gone too far in revealing his ploy. "I say the commission report *may* sway senators. The objectivity of the commissioner's report may sway. The report does me no good if it's perceived that I deliberately tried to slant its findings. I will do no such thing and give

Senator Sumner more fuel for his rantings."

Fish said, "Sir, since you have your answer from Mr. Douglass, may we go now? I need to finalize all the preparations for his departure for Santo Domingo."

"Yes," Grant said.

★

Frederick arrived at Charles's house, where Charles and Lewis waited for him. When he announced his new appointment, Charles was indiscreet, as usual. "What, Father? Just the secretary? You should have been one of the commissioners. How insulting, you a secretary to three white men."

Frederick didn't want an argument. He wanted support. "*Congratulations* would've have been a better first response, Charles," he said.

"Congratulations, Papa," Lewis said. "Of all the people, he could have selected as secretary, he's nominating you. What an honor."

"Thank you, Lewis," said Frederick.

"I'm sorry, Father. I didn't mean to detract from your excellent news," Charles said.

"I know. And I won't allow your indiscretion to change my mind about you accompanying me to Santo Domingo," Frederick replied. He understood that Charles genuinely believed he deserved the highest honors.

Charles stepped back. "What did you just say? How? I mean, I can't believe . . ."

Frederick explained, "Mr. Fish said as secretary to the commission I could have one staff person accompany me, and since the law specifically says the secretary needs to have a command of Spanish, I thought of you. Thank goodness, the senators confirming me did not hold my lack of Spanish proficiency against me. But Miss Assing taught you well, and I know you studied it on your own throughout your army days and afterward. That was so smart of you."

"I will do my best, Father. I promise," Charles said.

"I will try to keep a journal. I've never been to a tropical island. This is going to be truly an educational experience, and I will write about the trip for the paper," said Frederick.

"Yes, Papa," said Lewis.

"Congratulations, Father," said Charles.

A month later, when they returned from Santo Domingo on March 27, the president invited the three commissioners to the White House for dinner, but Frederick was not asked to attend.

107.

"WHAT AN INSULT, FATHER," Charles exclaimed when Frederick informed him about the White House dinner. "Surely, you will protest this slight. Colored people here will not allow this outrage to go unnoticed. For a man who has dined with statesmen and scholars in this country and Europe, what happened at the White House should not be ignored."

"I appreciate your support, Charles. But this a minor incident after what was a successful, enjoyable journey. We learned a great deal, and I returned supporting annexation," Frederick replied.

"For that reason alone, Father, Mr. Grant should have invited you!" Charles insisted.

"The commissioners called on the president, and he spontaneously invited them to dine with him. Had I been with them, an invitation would have been extended to me as freely as to any of the other gentlemen. I am sure of this."

"But, Father . . ."

"Enough, Charles. The Commission Report and my explanations in the *New National Era* will reveal the benefits of annexation for our country and Santo Domingo. It's a beautiful place with its blue bay, mountains, deep green trees and plants, hot weather, and beaches."

At the mention of the beach, where Frederick had bathed on numerous occasions, Charles flinched. "But you almost drowned, Father."

"I knew I shouldn't have told you." Frederick had stepped out too far on the rocks, and a heavy wave had overwhelmed him and swept him from the shore as the rocks bruised his arms, legs, and chest. "But I found my strength to get back to the shore and escape being dinner for the sharks." Frederick chuckled, but Charles was not amused.

After the meeting between the commission and the president, Frederick and Secretary Fish were summoned to the White House. Grant wanted Frederick to tell him personally what he thought about the commission's trip to Santo Domingo.

The president sat in his chair in the Oval Office, taciturn as ever. He had his cup of coffee nearby, and he glared at Frederick and Secretary Fish as if they were co-conspirators. "Well, Mr. Douglass, what do you have to say about the commission's findings? Be brief. I don't have all day," he said.

"I came back supporting annexation, sir," Frederick reported.

"Good, but that is not what concerns me today. What do you think of the Dominicans and the Haitians? Some say that the Dominicans threaten freedom-loving Haitians."

"That is Senator Sumner's opinion, but . . ." Frederick replied.

"Don't mention him. Go on," Grant interrupted.

"The government in Haiti is despotic and has no interest in us. But Santo Domingo desires our relationship, and such a relationship, indeed, will strike a blow against tropical slavery," Frederick said.

"Still the abolitionist, sir," Grant replied.

"Yes, sir."

"I'm pleased the commission's report sustains my views on annexation. But I will only ask Congress to print and disseminate your report. No action will be required, and thus I will end all personal solicitude upon the subject," Grant said.

Frederick did not look at Fish but stared straight ahead because he knew the president was lying. It was common knowledge that Grant used his loyalists in Congress to get his way. The commission's report and publication was his show of indifference. He was going to have his way with Santo Domingo no matter what. He would not allow another defeat by Charles Sumner, a man he hated. Referring to the senator now without using his name, the president said, "A faithful public servant, supported by his own conscience, can bear with patience the censure of disappointed men."

"Yes, sir," Frederick replied, daring to look at Secretary Fish, who kept his eyes on the president.

"You may go. I'm done," declared the president in his peremptory manner. "Thank you for coming and sharing your views."

"Thank you, sir, for inviting me," Frederick replied.

The president grunted, sipped his coffee, and turned his chair to the window.

Secretary Fish stopped outside the Oval Office before walking down the corridor. He said to Frederick, "The official work of the commission is complete. The report has been written and submitted. You will need to resign."

Frederick was thrown off by Fish's brusqueness. He didn't expect this abrupt end to his first official association with the administration. "Yes, sir," Frederick managed to say.

"Send a brief note addressed to me at the State Department," Fish said.

"Yes, sir," Frederick replied.

"I need to return to the president. He's expecting me." Fish turned, knocked on the president's door, and, without waiting for an answer, entered his office.

Frederick formally resigned, informing Secretary Fish he regretted that his "services in the capacity authorized by the terms of my appointment were inconsiderable and unimportant." Nevertheless, he assured Fish that whatever the commissioners asked of him he rendered "promptly and cheerfully." Frederick closed with a pinch of obsequiousness because it could help with a future appointment and certainly could do no harm: "I am, dear sir, very respectfully yours, your obedient servant."

Frederick wrote seven articles in the *New Era* and gave several speeches about his support for the annexation of Santo Domingo, essentially making the case that a democratic government committed to freedom and equality could ensure the strengthening of democracy on the entire island. The economic benefits for the United States and Santo Domingo were secondary.

Frederick offered a vision of American influence: "The natural thing for Haiti, Cuba, and for all the islands of the Caribbean Sea is to come as soon as possible under the broad banner of the United States and conform themselves to the grand order of progress upon which this great Republic has now earnestly entered."

Sumner challenged Frederick, writing that his vision was nothing more than the same bloody and dirty garment of "manifest destiny" celebrated in the 1840s. Sumner also repeated from Garrison's article on Frederick's position: "Of course, Frederick Douglass favors the measure and already has his reward. It is not the first time his ambition and selfishness have led him astray." The Garrison comment stung Frederick. He thought he no longer cared, but he still wanted Garrison to accept him, respect him as he once had, or as he thought he had.

Frederick did not reply, but Sumner continued his epistolary siege, writing as if Frederick was another political enemy he had to destroy, "Your ambitions for appointment are well known, but Mr. Grant has proven himself unreliable. Your fate in the administration is irrelevant as well. Mr. Grant, a colossus of ignorance, will not prevail in the matter of annexation. I am a force with which he must reckon." Sumner had his way and convinced a majority of senators to reject annexation again.

President Grant swiftly punished Sumner by getting his Senate supporters to depose him as chair of the Senate Foreign Relations Committee. Sumner erupted and blamed the president in a three-hour rant on the Senate floor. He again accused Grant of presidential abuse of power, and compared him to a Klan wizard. Frederick was grateful for not being in the Senate gallery during Sumner's tirade. Afterward, Sumner summoned Frederick to his house.

Frederick arrived at Sumner's house not as a friend, but as a curious, skeptical off-the-record reporter. The butler told him to go to the library and wait in the chair next to the writing desk. Apparently, Sumner wanted a barrier between them. Sumner entered and offered no salutation. He sat at his desk.

"Good evening, sir," Frederick said, stunned by Sumner's bloated face. He seemed to be suffering from a hangover, even though he didn't drink.

Sumner didn't reply. He stared at Frederick. "He did this to me," he said, low and soft, as if broken by grief. "He has sunk to unparalleled depths of viciousness and cruelty. I should have expected this from a drunken soldier." Sumner seemed flabbergasted. He had underestimated the president. Frederick thought of Goliath stupefied by David and his slingshot.

Frederick asked carefully, "Sir, should you not direct your rage against your Senate colleagues?"

The question seemed to restore Sumner's vigor. "Yes, they've betrayed me. Nothing has aroused me more since the Fugitive Slave Bill and the outrages in Kansas. And I will no longer speak to or work with Hamilton Fish. He is a gentleman in aspect with the heart of a lackey, the blackest heart," Sumner replied.

"And the president?"

"I will introduce a Senate resolution calling for a constitutional amendment limiting presidents to one term."

Astonished by Sumner's brazen affront to presidential authority, Frederick waited a moment before asking, "Will this not be seen as another personal slap? The Senate will not support this."

"No more challenges from you, I see. Your effort at objective inquiry could not endure more than a minute," Sumner said.

Frederick was rattled. "Sir, I'm used to saying what I need to say directly and . . ."

Sumner interrupted, "Good for you, and so let me tell you this: I tremble for my country when I contemplate the possibility of this man being fastened upon us for another four years."

"But we can't risk the president losing the election. If the Democratic party wins, our new-born liberties will be strangled in the cradle. I had better put a pistol to my head and blow my brains out than to lend myself in any ways to the destruction or defeat of the Republican Party," Frederick said.

"I will grieve for you at your funeral, my friend, but I have every intention to join the Liberal Republican movement." This movement, launched in 1870, called for the end of radical Reconstruction, considered too divisive in a country exhausted by race issues, and demanded instead the concentration on civil-service reform and reduction in the tariff.

"You can't be serious, sir. All of your work, our work, will be destroyed by men calling for a general amnesty for former Confederates, for traitors," Frederick said.

"Your people are not satisfied with the current Republican Party. It won't even support my Supplemental Civil Rights Bill. The party cares more about profit and refuses to execute plans for land distribution in the South. Many Black voters would follow me into the new party. Their loyalty has been taken for granted. Besides the amendments, the party has done virtually nothing," Sumner said.

Frederick became more agitated and leaned forward. "You can't do this. You can't. Yes, I admit there is good ground for complaint against the Republican

Party and the assumption that we should just be satisfied with the right to vote. And I can admit much more against the Republican Party."

"All the more reason for a new party."

"If in the course of time the party should become faithless to its own principles, and another party should spring up that should promise to be a better custodian of the rights and liberty of the people, we shall certainly join it, and urge all others to do so, too. For the present, there is none, not the Liberal Republicans and certainly not the Democratic Party."

Sumner smiled for the first time. "Well, well, well, Douglass, you have the blind party spirit that should carry you far as a true lackey."

Frederick jumped to his feet. "How could you say this? Has your hatred of President Grant and anyone who supports him so blinded you to common decency that you insult a man who had always believed you as steady as the North Star. Damn you, sir. Damn you!"

108.

PRESIDENT GRANT NOMINATED FREDERICK for a two-year term to the Territorial Legislative Council, an advisory board to the House of Delegates responsible for passing municipal laws for the District. It was a minor bureaucratic post without power or salary. Frederick accepted the offer and quietly seethed, having worked tirelessly for the Republican Party and Grant's election. He would work equally hard for Grant's reelection, but Grant's ingratitude rankled. *Was there a deeper issue? Was Ulysses Grant another president who, deep down, was a racist? Was this president also intimidated by the most famous and influential Negro in America?*

Frederick deemed his concerns as ultimately irrelevant. President Grant was an ardent supporter of the Fourteenth and Fifteenth amendments of the U.S. Constitution and vigorously opposed the Ku Klux Klan's efforts to deprive southern Negroes of their rights by sending troops to enforce equality under the law. Unlike Lincoln, Grant did not quibble or prevaricate. The law was the law, and as the commander in chief he used the military when necessary. Most people admired him for being a general and not a politician and seemed willing to overlook the machinations of his wealthy friends until their schemes affected them personally.

Frederick accepted this compromise, too.

★

Washington was now Frederick's second home. He had rented rooms at the Wormley Hotel and then stayed with Charles. Now he finalized the purchase of a three-story rowhouse near the Capitol at 316 A Street Northeast. On the first floor was a parlor with large bay windows and a large office at the rear. The second level had three bedrooms. And the third had two more bedrooms plus a large sitting room in the rear that could serve as a guest room when needed, especially when Ottilie was in town. Lewis, Amelia, and Frederick, Jr., now the owner of a store, would live with him there, too. Anna would not. She made it clear she would never move to Washington.

Adjacent to 316 A was another three-story rowhouse, 318 A. Frederick planned to purchase it and expand the original house by opening the dividing walls on each floor. There would be room for family members and distinguished guests on long visits as well as space for Frederick and Ottilie to work when they were not at the *New National Era* office.

The *New National Era* was not yet a financial success. In fact, it was always close to bankruptcy. Expansion beyond a Black subscription base had not materialized, and subscribers were fickle, inconsistent, undependable, and complained about everything, as they had with the *North Star* in Rochester. Thankfully, Gerrit Smith always contributed something.

The motto of the *New National Era* was to the point in two sentences: "Free men, free soil, free speech, a free press, everywhere in the land. The ballot for all, education for all, fair wages for all." The paper was being published in an era of deep uncertainty. Frederick asked himself, *If war among the whites brought peace and liberty to the Blacks, what will peace among the whites bring?* He had no illusions. In any peace settlement, whites would sacrifice Black people for their own comfort and convenience. This fear drove him to speak out at the third national celebration of Memorial Day at Arlington National Cemetery on May 30, 1871.

Arlington House, the former home of Robert E. Lee, was festooned with eucalyptus, pine, and other evergreens. The soldiers' graves were adorned with wreaths and the badges of the military corps in which they served. A procession of dignitaries walked to the main stand at the rear of Arlington House under a grove of oak trees, where hundreds sat, including President Grant and his cabinet, to hear speeches before they walked to the Tomb of the Unknown Soldier covered by a canopy of flags.

After another round of prayers, Frederick was the last scheduled speaker. On this national stage, before the president and a large audience, he seized the opportunity to remind people of the tremendous weight of history and the danger of forgetting it: "We are not here to applaud manly courage only as it has been displayed in a noble cause. We must never forget that victory to the rebellion meant death to the republic. We must never forget that the loyal soldiers that rest beneath this sod flung themselves between the nation and the nation's destroyers. If the star-spangled banner floats only over free American citizens in every quarter of the land, we are indebted to the unselfish devotion of the noble army who rest in these honored graves all around us." There was polite applause, and the marine band played on.

The president sat absolutely still. Was he absorbed by memories of war and those he sent to their deaths? Or was he determined to not reveal through the slightest physical gesture his absolute boredom at yet another official function? Grant remained an enigma, but it didn't matter. Frederick intended to devote the next months to his pen and voice for Grant's reelection. The survival of Reconstruction depended on it. The future of political and racial equality depended on it. The Republican Party, the party of historical memory, had to defeat the Democratic Party, the party of treason, and its cancerous appendage, the Liberal Republican Party. The stakes were even higher now that Senator Sumner wrote public letters urging Negroes to follow him and become Liberal Republicans.

Frederick could not stay on the District Legislative Council. He was bored with the council's work and he was restless. He knew that his best work was speaking to the public. After only two months on the council, Frederick formally tended his resignation, citing "imperative engagements elsewhere." Frederick canvassed the land, speaking day after day, month after month. When the Democratic Party nominated Horace Greeley and Charles Sumner endorsed him, Frederick became more energized.

Grant was the only viable option. Frederick praised Grant as a leader. "I have been in the presence of Ulysses S. Grant. He is a good man, a true man, a steady man. You know what he is today, what he was yesterday, and what he will be tomorrow, for he does not turn with every wind of doctrine, and for that reason we want him." He campaigned exhaustingly for the reelection of Grant and his attention. Nothing stopped him, except devastating news from Rochester.

On June 3, Frederick received a telegram about a fire. No one was hurt, but the house and barn were gone, burned to the ground the day before. His family was safe, sheltered by friends, but he rushed to Rochester nonetheless, feeling agitated and sickened with dread over the possible loss of books and original copies of his newspapers.

The Posts and the Porters had taken in his family. He found Anna at the Posts. He woke them from their sleep, embraced Anna, and received as much information as they could tell him. Around midnight, the fire started in the barn and spread to the wood-framed house. Anna, Rosetta, pregnant with her fifth child, and Nathan rushed to save the couple's four young daughters, who were in their bedrooms. Rosetta, Nathan, the neighbors, and firemen had managed to save most of Frederick's massive book collection that included complete sets of Robert Burns, Dickens, Shakespeare, and several volumes of Bible commentary. They also pulled out one of the pianos and some furniture.

The fire destroyed everything in the barn, scorched the groves of trees and the vegetable garden that were Anna's pride and joy, and in the house burned much of the furniture, many personal letters, and sixteen volumes of original copies of the *North Star* and *Douglass Weekly*. Flames were seen for miles, brightening the horizon and casting shadows on the trees. The fire company's horse-drawn wagon did not have enough water to stop the inferno, and the house was lost as the Douglass family and neighbors watched. Still in shock, Anna mumbled as Frederick held her hands, "We couldn't save them papers, Frederick, your newspapers, them government bonds. We just couldn't. I'm sorry."

"Don't blame yourself," he assured her, although he wished she could have saved the newspapers that constituted half his life. "It couldn't be helped. You're safe, and Rosetta and the girls are safe, and Nathan. You lost things of your own, too, your clothes; your flowers, your pear trees."

Frederick felt apprehensive and yet curious as he walked from the Post's home through the thick mud to his house the next morning. He found smoldering remains, shattered brick walls and stone foundations that made him imagine a besieged fallen city. Frederick marveled at the power and speed of fire and shuddered to think about what could have happened. The thought of the demise of his entire family, including an unborn baby due in two months, sickened him, and he bent over hands on knees and tried to breathe in the acrid air.

Frederick bolted upright. *How did this happen? Why? Who did this? Was this an accident?* The more he thought about it, the more convinced he was that the fire was arson. Nathan had reported that no light or fire had been used in the barn since last winter. Frederick went to the police with his suspicion that the fire was a racially motivated act, a statement against another successful Black man.

The officer objected carefully, "Sir, Rochester has been open to Negroes for decades. It is one of the most open, most liberal cities in America. The Underground Railroad alone proves . . ."

Frederick was always irritated by the familiar reference to the escape network. He interrupted the officer, "the overground railroad, you mean, sir, and my house was an important part of it, but that was then, and this is now, when Rochester has its full share of the Ku Klux spirit, which makes anything owned by a colored man less respected and secure than when owned by a white citizen."

"Mr. Douglass, I object to your characterization, and you yourself, in the newspaper, thanked the police and fire departments for making every effort to save your property, and you also thanked your neighbors, all white, I may add, for doing everything in their power to give relief to your shelterless family. Didn't you thank them, sir?" The officer maintained his reserve, calm, and respect.

"Yes. The *Union and Register* captured my sentiments exactly," Frederick replied.

Vindicated, the police chief refrained from showing smug admission. "You can be sure, sir, that if we have any lead to the fire as a crime, we will follow it to the full extent of the law."

"I expect nothing less, because my family was attacked by the spirit of hate, the spirit of murder, the spirit that would burn a family out of their beds."

Frederick's insistence soured the officer, and his voice darkened. "If true, sir, this would be forever a stain on our town, a town we both love."

"Love no longer, sir," said Frederick. He left knowing that his connection to Rochester went up in flames that night. He would not rebuild. He would sell the land and move the entire family, including Rosetta's family, to Washington. Even though Frederick had just lost $4,000–$5,000 in real estate, the purchase of 318 A Street Northeast was now essential.

Frederick was able to recover $11,000 of bonds that Anna kept in the light box under her bed. He invested in them as well, and Ottilie had recorded each bond's number for safekeeping. Frederick telegraphed her about the fire and asked her to come to Washington from Boston, where she was visiting her old friends the Koehlers, and stay at his new house once his family moved in.

Ottilie was given her own room over Anna's unspoken objection. Her black eyes never failed to communicate her feelings, which Frederick ignored as usual.

"Oh, Frederick, I've lost my summer home," Ottilie complained, more wistful than petulant when they were alone. "What am I going to do?"

"You'll be here working with me at the *New Era*, writing, editing. You said you wanted to be at the center of things, so here you are."

Ottilie stayed until the day after the election.

Grant won his second term reelection in a landslide.

109.

DESPITE THE TRAUMA OF the Rochester fire, there was excitement that summer and fall at 316 A Street in Washington, D.C. Frederick had more reason to purchase the house next door and expand it to make room for Anna, the rest of his family, and Ottilie. Excited, he showed her interior plans for both houses and designated the large room overlooking the rear garden hers.

"You'll have peace and quiet for writing, and time for yourself away from the children, especially when Rosetta comes with the new baby," Frederick said.

Ottilie wouldn't admit her concerns regarding aging and health and how Frederick's absence depressed her. She dreaded the coming of late fall and winter, when he was away on tour. Not only was she lonely, but she seemed to get sick every winter. Before she returned to Hoboken that November, she got a cold. Her nose ran, and she had a fever, but what most worried her was a constant ringing in her ears.

She wrote to her sister Ludmilla: "As beautiful and rich as this summer turned out for me, so bad has been my winter so far. The incessant ringing has not stopped in weeks; this makes it almost impossible to do any kind of intellectual work and often drives me to despair. I had no idea that one could be exposed to such torture, and that while free from pain, from fever and in perfectly good health."

Dr. Freunstein, her physician and friend, prescribed rest. He assured Ottilie that she would not experience permanent deafness, but the possibility terribly frightened her. She could not imagine a world without being able to hear Mozart, Schubert, Beethoven, or Frederick's voice. Despite the crowded house in Washington, she eagerly anticipated her return from Hoboken to the summer warmth of Washington. She was ready to move there permanently in 1873. She needed to be with Frederick even in the small house.

Hoboken was no longer her home. Ottilie's friends were fighting each other over the outbreak of war between France and Prussia in 1870. They also objected to her support of Grant and her opposition to the Liberal Republican movement led by Charles Sumner. Ottilie didn't tell Frederick, but she thought Grant was a crackpot without political skill, an old warrior whose time had passed.

Ottilie's misery deepened when Ludmilla boasted about her forthcoming marriage in December to an Italian twenty years her junior. Ottilie sent her congratulations even though she was skeptical. Ludmilla was not as young or as attractive as Ottilie, and her history with men suggested their interest lay with her money. But Ludmilla sent money now and then to Ottilie, helping her pay bills. She used some of that money to assist Charles, Lewis, and Rosetta, despite her complaints about their financial dependence on Frederick. Ottilie worried that Frederick would find out about the gifts, called loans even though she didn't expect repayment, but so far the children hadn't exposed her.

Ludmilla's wedding announcement generated a comparison that saddened Ottilie, who was alone that New Year's Eve of 1872. Frederick was on tour out

West, and Ottilie wrote her sister: "Every day I think that this might be your wedding day, and I keep repeating my hope that your Grimelli will prove as true, as faithful, and as thoroughly good and noble as Douglass. Seventeen years, in defiance of all external adversity, with people and prejudices of all kinds against us, this is what be called a true ordeal by fire."

Ludmilla informed Ottilie that she was married on December 1, 1872. Ottilie replied sincerely, "Really married then! My warmest, heartfelt congratulations. How lucky you are that no external conditions are in the way of following your inclinations. That mere will is enough to transform the wish into reality." But her sister's good news again touched a nerve, for Ottilie's will could not change her circumstances with Frederick. She continued, "How differently have I fared. Unmarried for seventeen years and yet united in a deeper love than many who are married, without the slightest perspective that it will ever be different. And what is worse, we are separated from each other by a true monster, who herself can neither give love nor appreciate it. What a terrible fate. If I were superstitious, I would believe that my name is somehow fatal."

Ottilie could not resist her competitive impulse. She wrote, "I do have certain presentiments and usually see sharply when looking into the distance as well as into the future. When you are so intimately connected with one man as I am with Douglass, you will get to know men as well as women from a perspective that would never be revealed to you otherwise, especially if it is a man who has seen so much of the world and who was loved by so many women."

She offered her sister proof that Frederick loved her: "Douglass, who is just adding a large wing to his house, which means he will gain six spacious room, feels that I should move in with him for good. You will imagine how happy it would make me to be together with him always. It would be the purest happiness, yet I must consider seriously whether it would be prudent to live continually in proximity to his charming wife. So far, I have been able to maintain the most friendly terms by means of diplomacy and feeding her with gifts, but with people so ignorant and uneducated you never know what weird notions hit them."

Ottilie returned to Washington for her usual summer visit in 1873, but she didn't stay long, for there were too many Douglass family members in that small house: Frederick and Anna, Nathan Sprague's sister Louisa, who had become quite close to Anna, and an army of grandchildren. It was too much. Ottilie arrived there in late August and left in late October, her shortest visit to date.

A separate bedroom in a future new wing and long days at the Library of Congress could not cloister her from turmoil. Anna was more and more open in her hostility. As Ottilie and Frederick played their instruments for family entertainment, Anna declared, "I will not watch you two enjoy yourselves even for the rest of the family." She remained in her room until the performances were done and it was time for the evening Bible reading. Ottilie went to her bedroom, believing that Frederick's domestic life was untenable and that he would leave Anna for her.

110.

OTTILIE REVIEWED FREDERICK'S NEW itinerary for the upcoming fall season and following year and cried out, "Are you mad?"

"No, not yet. I'm working less for myself than for those around me. I find my continuous working power in some measure failing me. My health is rather uncertain as I grow older," Frederick replied.

"You're not old," Ottilie protested.

Frederick glanced down to his expanding waistcoat and its slightly pulled buttons. "I feel old. Over fifty, that's old. If only I didn't have to sit on my fat backside for hours on carriages and trains. And I still eat like an insatiable horse. After all these years of eating whatever I like and not getting fat, my body is warning me. I want to travel less. Surely, I have done enough."

Frederick continued to wait for President Grant to reward him with a post, a sedentary post. But the fall and winter of 1872–73 passed without a hint of recognition, as Grant and his administration became embroiled in scandal after scandal.

Frederick had no illusions. He lamented to Gerrit Smith, who had abandoned Washington years ago after one term in Congress for similar reasons, "The moral atmosphere here in Washington is more than tainted, it is rotten. Avarice, duplicity, falsehood, corruption, servility, fawning and trickery of all kinds, confront us at every turn. There is little here but distrust and suspicion." Nonetheless, Frederick believed that once inside the Grant administration he could successfully influence policy makers who needed to protect Negro rights and Reconstruction even more vigorously.

Frederick found some comfort in his appointment, by its board of directors, as president of the Freedmen's Saving and Trust Company or Freedmen's Bank, a private company charted by Congress.

But the March 1874 appointment quickly became a disaster.

He should have listened to Anna.

More amused than dismissive, she scoffed at the news of his appointment. "What do you know about money? I've been handling the money for years, and when it became too hard I asked Rosetta to help. This is foolishness."

"The board said I will attract more customers and investors because colored people trust me," Frederick said.

"And you trust dem white folks? Everybody's grabbin' for whatever they can find all over the country, so I hear."

"What do you know about . . ." He stopped himself, but it was too late.

After thirty-six years, Anna knew her man, his blind spots, his prejudices. "There you go, thinkin' I know nothin' about this place, what's going on. I don't care about this town, but I have eyes and ears. Your children talk. You know that. Even Charles talks to me if he has nobody else. He sure don't have Libby to listen to him. She's turned out to be a pain to him, to me, and to all of us with her complain' about money and other women."

"He talks to you about . . ."

"See? There you go again. You just can't believe he would come to me and keep things from you. He wants me comforting him, like boys always want their mamas doin'. He probably tells me more about things 'cause he wants you to think of him as handlin' everything right all the time. That's what boys do with their papas, always wanting to be good as their papas, equal, even better. I just listen 'cause he needs me. But he's like a minister at the front of the church, goin' on and on. I pick things up, and this bank has a smell to it."

"The office is one of the most impressive in town," protested Frederick, referring to the bank's five-story brownstone on the east corner of Lafayette Square at 1507 Pennsylvania Avenue across from the White House.

"Another big house," sniffed Anna. "Just like them mansions in Baltimore, looks goods on the outside but hiding nothin' but mess behind them doors."

Rosetta had returned to Rochester a year earlier and lived in a house purchased by Frederick as an investment. She wrote to him about his new assignment as president of the Freedmen's Bank and was as dubious as Anna but more careful with her words, "Papa, your prestige will add luster to the bank's image, but I doubt, given your indifference to mathematics, you will contribute to its financial solvency." Indeed, he didn't have experience with banking, but he represented the rise of the Black middle class.

Frederick liked his title and enjoyed going to his large office on Pennsylvania Avenue every morning, sitting back in a fine black leather chair under the high white plaster ceilings, and watching well-dressed tellers behind filigreed walnut cages take deposits.

But the bank teetered on a stack of playing cards.

A congressional charter represented the federal government's commitment to the bank, but Congress basked in the fantasy of helping Black depositors, mostly farmers, sharecroppers, and clerks, and did not rein in overzealous promoters and speculators. In fact, Congress amended the bank's charter to allow mortgage loans, especially since Washington was growing rapidly and needed more construction.

No one told Frederick until it was too late that when he became president of the bank it was already in financial trouble, due to poor investments by some members of the board of directors. The full board of fifty trustees never met, and most of the white trustees had resigned.

Congress launched an investigation, and Frederick became the public face of Black financial failure as the entire country reeled under the weight of the Panic of 1873 and the depression that followed. On July 1, 1874, the trustees voted to close the Freedmen's Bank. Frederick felt humiliated and betrayed. He blamed the trustees, calling them conniving plunderers, and claimed that some of his clerks embezzled money. "I was married to a corpse," he concluded.

Frederick's misery deepened with the failure of the *New National Era* under the management of Lewis and Frederick, Jr. While Frederick continued to lecture, the newspaper lost subscribers at an alarming rate. Ottilie tried to help by writing articles and editing copy. Frederick could not expand the subscription base to white readers, and his Black readers often failed to make payments.

Frederick's theory for the weak support from Black readers was that they preferred white newspapers, that they preferred whiteness in most things. He trusted Gerrit Smith enough to confess in a letter, "Our confidence is in the white race. White schools, white churches, white theology, white legislators, white public journals, secure our highest confidence and support."

To make matter worse, Frederick received a disturbing letter from Ottilie's doctor, who expressed concern about Ottilie's emotional and physical health. "I am worried about her health, but I think with warmer weather she should recover her philosophical calmness within the cranial cavities of her auditory system for at least the summer months. She has, as well as everyone of us, an Achilles heel in her body. Her self-slaughterous tendencies remain unabated, notwithstanding her improvement, and it is useless to reason with her on that nonsense, for it is nonsense itself to reason on nonsense."

Self-slaughterous tendencies?

Frederick knew about the ear ringing and recognized her hypersensitivity and emotional flamboyance. But self-slaughterous tendencies? He didn't know what to make of this. Was the doctor alluding to the excesses of self-criticism or, worse, suicide? Frederick could write him a letter, but he decided to wait. While Ottilie worked for the *New National Era* Frederick saw no indication of emotional instability. Work seemed to energize her.

But nothing could stop Frederick's financial bleeding, and he lost at least $10,000 when he closed the *New National Era* in October. Lewis and Junior were unemployed again. At the same time, Nathan was arrested for stealing mail, pleaded guilty, and was sent to prison for a year, leaving Rosetta pregnant with five children and dependent on Frederick to finance a household in Rochester and fend off an army of bill collectors.

Financial loss was nothing compared to the deaths of colleagues, friends, and family members. Charles Remond had passed away from cancer in late 1873. Once friends, then bitter enemies, he and Frederick tried to reconcile near the end but failed. They were the preeminent Black abolitionists of their day, a heady time when youth and eloquence, courage, tenacity, and sheer nerve impressed even the skeptical.

Frederick did not grieve Remond's death for their paths were too complicated, too fraught with competition and envy. But remembrance was an appropriate tribute for this giant of the abolitionist era. Frederick would remember him daily because his son bore his name.

On the other hand, Frederick grieved the death of Charles Sumner, who died of a heart attack at his home in Washington in March of 1874. Arrangements were made for his body to lie in state in an open casket in the United States Capitol rotunda, the second senator to receive such an honor, after Henry Clay in 1852.

These deaths and tribulations made for a terrible year, and Frederick yearned for 1875. Surely, 1875 would be better. Then came news that Gerrit Smith had died suddenly in New York City on December 26. Frederick had long ago forgiven Gerrit for his denial of involvement with John Brown. He had objected to Gerrit's contribution to the bond for the release of Jefferson Davis after he was arrested for treason. He disagreed with Gerrit's insistence on literacy tests as a prerequisite for Black voting, although he supported Negro suffrage. But up to the very end, Gerrit was one of the most generous philanthropists in the country, giving thousands of dollars to a variety of causes. He had always supported the Negro press and Frederick's newspapers from the beginning, and in the last years he donated generously to Cornell University, Howard University, Hampton Institute, and his own alma mater, Hamilton College.

Of all the men Frederick knew, notwithstanding the casual attribution of "Friend" to almost every man in polite conversation and correspondence, there were only two men he considered true friends, whom he trusted with his mind and heart, his doubts and fears, his hopes and dreams, questions and beliefs. The first was Henry Harris on the Eastern Shore, Frederick's student and confidante, who was willing to escape with him and die for him. And the other was Gerrit Smith. There was a private family burial for Gerrit at Peterboro, and Frederick sent a condolence note to his wife Ann.

Frederick wondered if this giant of the abolitionist movement would be remembered.

Would Sumner?

Would any of that generation?

Would he be remembered?

The Senate passed Sumner's Civil Rights Bill a year after his death. It became law, signed by President Grant on March 1, 1875, prohibiting racial discrimination in all public accommodations and public transportation as well as prohibiting racial exclusion from jury duty.

In May, Rosetta finally had the son she always wanted. She named him Herbert Douglass Sprague. Frederick sent a telegram. "Congratulations. Your sixth, and a boy, at last!"

Only two months later, Frederick received news from Rochester of the sudden death from meningitis of his six-year-old granddaughter, Alice. She was Rosetta's third child, who had lived on and off with Frederick and Anna from birth. Like the death of Annie, who also died when he was far from home, Alice's death brought Frederick, weeping, to his knees.

Frederick feared grief's power. It could break the will, darken the mind, and weaken the body, as it did to him when Annie died in 1860. If he returned to Rochester, the city of fire and loss, he would be going to not one funeral but two. To survive, he needed to freeze his soul to escape the pain. He saw himself at Mount Hope Cemetery a shattered man, his body broken into pieces of ice. Death would demand his collapse, the price he needed to pay to prove his love for his girls. He was so determined to keep his emotional and physical distance, he refused to travel with Anna and the rest of the family to Alice's funeral.

Frederick wrote to Rosetta to explain his decision. But he was not honest about his fears and resorted to platitudes about death: "Death is the common lot to all, and the strongest of us will soon be called away. It is well. Death is a friend, not an enemy. The real price is with the living, not with the dead. The best any of us can do is to trust in the eternal powers which brought us into existence, and this I do, for myself and for all."

He told Anna about staying in Washington instead of going to Rochester. She was dumbfounded. She shouted, "How can you do this to your own daughter, your own flesh and blood? She needs you now more than ever."

Frederick stepped back from her because she seemed wild, ready to pounce. "You will be better for her, stronger," he said.

"So you are leaving everything thing to me again, to take care of everything?" Anna asked.

"I can't leave the house unoccupied. There's too much crime near the Capitol. We could have another fire, and if we are burnt out a second time, I have no more strength to start over again. We are not among friends here any more than in Rochester."

Anna opened and closed her hands as she inhaled quick breaths. She, too, took a step back as if to stop herself from clawing his face. "Just listen to yo'self. Just listen to your self-pity and excuses. You want me to believe this, this crazy excuse, when you and I know this house won't be empty with that woman here in it?"

"A woman should not be here alone to protect it," Frederick answered.

"You left me alone enough times! You didn't worry about me then."

"But New Bedford, Lynn, and Rochester are not Washington."

The palm of her right hand shot up. "I've had enough of this! Rosetta adores you more than anybody else in this world, and you can't be bothered to take a few days and comfort her at the worst time of her life. You didn't do it for me at my worst day. You could do it for hers."

"I couldn't come to you. I was across the ocean," Frederick said.

"That's what makes this far worse, far, far worse. You have no ocean, no fear of the white people grabbing you. No, you're a sad, sad, no-good father, and I will never, never forgive you for this. I used to care you chose Miss Assing over me, wanted her to be with you. But to choose Miss Assing over Rosetta? I can't believe it. I just can't believe it," Anna cried.

"This has nothing to do with Rosetta," Frederick said.

"Shut your mouth, do you hear me? Just shut your mouth."

"Anna . . ."

"But I know Rosetta will forgive you, will continue to love and make excuses for you. What is it about you, Frederick, that us women will make absolute fools of ourselves over you? What is it?" Anna didn't wait for an answer, leaving the parlor, the cloth of her simple smock rustling in the humid air.

111.

FREDERICK DID NOT CONCEAL his despondency. He wrote and talked about death, destruction, disappointment, public humiliation. The past four years were terrible, but his failure to get a government position that supported his large family and sanctioned his standing before the nation struck a heavy blow to his self-confidence.

By 1876, he knew President Grant would not deliver an appointment or nomination and resigned himself to exhausting tours as "the self-educated fugitive slave." Frederick also knew his audiences essentially came to hear about slavery and his escape. Some of his new lectures were good, some not. His "Self-Made Men" and "Composite Nation" were well received. His lectures about William the Silent, the history of religious wars in Europe, Emerson, or ethnography received only tepid applause.

Frederick's self-esteem was boosted when he was invited to give the dedication speech for the unveiling of the Freedmen's Memorial Monument to Abraham Lincoln in Lincoln Park on April 14, 1876. The skies were clear and bright with the sun at high noon and the air brisk but not cold. A perfect spring day.

Flags above the Capitol and other government buildings flew at half-mast on the national holiday. A massive crowd, mostly Black, assembled at Seventh and K streets to form a parade headed by twenty-seven mounted police followed by three companies of Black militia, a marching drum corps, and several Black fraternal orders. A large banner with a painting of Lincoln led the horse-drawn carriages carrying Frederick and other dignitaries to Pennsylvania Avenue. They passed thousands of cheering people and ended at a field where a crowd waited before a tall statue covered by bunting and flags.

A podium and a stage for dignitaries were built next to the statue that seated the president, most of his cabinet, several U.S. Senators, many members of the House of Representatives, all the justices of the U.S. Supreme Court, scores of federal and civic government officials, diplomats, clergymen, and former Union generals.

Ottilie arrived very early and stood at the front so she could see everything. The master of ceremonies droned on and on, making the crowd restless. He finally told the audience that he was supposed to unveil the statue, but he wanted the honor to go to the president.

Grant, always inscrutable in public, revealed no surprise and went to the front of the stand to pull the cord. The flag fell away to reveal a ten-foot bronze statue of Lincoln standing in formal attire with a half-naked slave on bended knees before him. The audience cheered, cannons boomed, and the band played "Hail to the Chief."

Ottilie winced.

A white sculptor had depicted Lincoln with his right hand on a podium holding the Proclamation and his left arm extended out as if offering comfort or a benediction over the bare back of the emancipated slave. His broken shackle lay nearby. At the base below them was the word *EMANCIPATION*.

When the master of ceremonies introduced Frederick as "the orator of the day," he gave one of his finest, most candid speeches. He initially intended to praise Lincoln as well as review his history of slow responses to abolition and the war for freedom. During that time, Frederick had criticized Lincoln unsparingly, but after his assassination he refrained from publicizing Lincoln's deficiencies. But today, he would not spare Lincoln or the Republican zealots who demanded absolute, uncritical devotion to the man who saved the Union and emancipated millions by the stroke of his pen.

After eleven years, so much had been forgotten.

Frederick now intended to speak the truth: "It must be admitted, truth compels me to admit, even here in the presence of the monument we have erected to his memory, Abraham Lincoln was not either our man or our model. In his interests, in his associates, in his habits of thought, and in his prejudices, he was a white man, and he was preeminently the white man's president entirely devoted to the welfare of the white man. He was ready and willing at any time during the first years of his administration to deny, postpone, and sacrifice the rights of humanity in the colored people to promote the welfare of the white people of the country."

Ottilie heard gasps and exclamations from scattered whites.

There was also appreciation from colored people, as if in church.

"Speak it, my brother."

"His truth is marching on!"

There was also confusion and suspicion.

Frederick then declared, "My white fellow citizens, you are the children of Abraham Lincoln. We are at best only his stepchildren, children by adoption, children by force of circumstances and necessity. You have the prime responsibility of honoring Lincoln, but let the stepchildren have their place in this commemoration."

As usual, Frederick's speech was too long, with too many details about shifting war policies, but he had the gift of ending his speeches well, and that day his peroration soared, for it seemed that Frederick had freed himself from the burden of ambivalence and unresolved contradiction. He no longer tried to resolve them, accepting them as the reality of his memories of Lincoln, confounding, messy, yet inspiring.

Frederick closed, "Dying as he did die, by the red hand of violence; killed, assassinated, taken off without warning, not because of personal hate, for a man who knew Abraham Lincoln could not hate him, but because of his fidelity to Union and liberty, he is doubly dear to us, and will be precious forever."

The applause was not the most thunderous he had ever received, but few could deny his rhetorical greatness in a country that revered great orators. The audience gave him his due with a loud but not extended ovation.

Ottilie found Frederick, who was unsmiling. "It was a great speech, Frederick," she said.

"I hate that statue. Hate it!" Frederick replied.

"Why?" She knew the answer.

"That white man made us look servile. The Negro here, though rising, is still on his knees and nude. What I want to see before I die is a monument representing the Negro not on his knees like a four-footed animal but erect on his feet like a man. There is room for another monument in Lincoln Park, and I will say so in a letter to the *National Republican*."

Ottilie thought Frederick's manner seemed lighter, having effectively just made his own declaration of independence before the Washington luminaries as well as a final break with Grant and his administration.

Frederick beamed and said, "No Black man has ever spoken before so many, before a crowd that included the president and almost every government leader in the country. May I be the first and last for a hundred years!"

Challenging Frederick was always Ottilie's way of showing her love. She asked, "Wouldn't it be a sign of progress if it happened more frequently, with you and other Black leaders?"

"I prefer the singular distinction," Frederick replied.

"But one hundred years?"

"From the gates of heaven or hell, I won't be surprised by the one hundred years. Not at all."

Seeing Frederick so ebullient, Ottilie decided it was time to tell him about the decisions she had made. She would not live permanently with Frederick and his family. The loss of friends, corruption in Washington, and her own beleaguered body made Ottilie decide to tour Europe and reunite with her sister. He was excited for her. He said, "Yes, definitely go. It will be wonderful!"

"Please come, too. I know you can't until your winter tour, but it would please me so much—no, make me very happy—for you to join me in Paris," Ottilie said.

"That sounds delightful," Frederick said.

"Promise me."

"My schedule, the family."

"Please."

"Very well. I will come in the spring. I might arrive in time to see the tulips in the Netherlands before arriving in Paris."

"Oh, Frederick that will make me so very happy."

"Good, and in the meantime we can get a glimpse of what it will be like to travel together—and hopefully not kill each other in the process—by going to see the Centennial Exposition in Philadelphia. I understand it's quite special. There is a bust of me by that Rochester artist J. M. Bundy that I must see. Obviously proud of his work, he has urged me to see it."

"A splendid idea," Ottilie said.

"You will go first, and then I will join you there for about three days. What do you think?" Frederick asked.

"Of course," she replied.

Their trip to Philadelphia left Ottilie with fond memories of their one night together: the passion that belied the old age Frederick feared, the surrender that confirmed her devotion. She reviewed all that was said and done for she knew that other than an occasional letter there would be nothing else from Frederick until they met again.

She boarded the *Friscia* on July 5,1876, but Frederick never went to Paris.

112.

AFTER YEARS OF WAITING and hoping, Frederick was granted a job from the president of the United States. The offer came from President Rutherford B. Hayes, who had lost the popular vote to Samuel J. Tilden but won the Electoral College in the election of 1876 after a season of accusations, claims, and counterclaims about stolen ballots and alternate electors from three southern states. The disputed election went to the House of Representatives, and Hayes became president by one vote.

Hayes was inaugurated in a small ceremony at the White House on Saturday, March 3, 1877. There were concerns for his safety and the possibility of civil unrest after the House vote and details of the compromise, worked out behind closed doors, came to light.

Congress gave the White House to a Republican and gave the South to the Democrats, who were now free to govern without direct federal supervision or troops. Successful in keeping Negroes away from the polls, the Ku Klan Klan and their political allies accelerated their campaign of terror and disenfranchisement.

Even so, Frederick was delighted when the new president nominated him as the United States marshal for the District of Columbia. Hailed as "a credit to his race and the best representative of his people in this country," Frederick now held the highest honor ever bestowed by the government on a Negro in the nation's history.

The post was administrative and ceremonial. The marshal remanded prisoners between jail and the courts, posted all bankruptcies in the District, and introduced guests at White House receptions. His family and friends were delighted. Congratulatory letters, telegrams, and editorials poured in.

President Hayes's appointment did not please everyone. Some white lawyers complained that Frederick had no legal experience, and other whites said he lacked "business capacity." A few Black leaders said he was "too high toned" to represent the Black masses. One newspaper was amused by the irony of a former fugitive from justice being a constable.

Frederick was amused by the uproar. Objections from the whites was another absurd mask of their racial fear of having a Black man introducing guests of the president of the United States in the White House. The nomination succeeded in the Senate. However, President Hayes buckled under the pressure from critics and redefined the job, appointing a white man to announce guests. Frederick did not protest the decision. Hayes was president because of agreements made between politicians, and this was just another one, a minor one at that. Besides, Frederick didn't want to be a butler.

Anna was skeptical. She dismissed Frederick's explanations with a weary voice and a languid wave of her hand. "If you say so. If them excuses make you feel better."

"Now that I have this job, I'm looking into buying land across the river in Anacostia," Frederick said.

"And doing what?"

"There's a big, porched house, the old Van Hook mansion, and from the front there's a wonderful view of the Capitol and all of Washington below. The house is so big there will be space for everybody, including guests; and there will be so much more yard space for the grandchildren."

"What about all the work done for this house, adding on and all? We just got here." Anna said.

"It's crowded, even so, and it has been five years," Frederick replied.

Anna asked, "Haven't you lost enough money already?" Frederick didn't answer her. She tried again, "How much is this place going to cost?"

"Six thousand dollars." It was better to just say the amount and move on as quickly as possible.

"Where are you going to get that kind of money?"

"I don't know yet," Frederick lied. A bank currently owned the property, and Frederick intended to borrow the money from the wealthy Dr. Purvis, a former Freedmen's Bank board member who would allow Frederick to pay back the money through monthly installments.

"Tell me when we're moving," Anna conceded.

"I didn't say we were moving. I'm just looking," Frederick said.

"Your saying is already telling me. Tell me when we're moving."

Feeling more patient and charitable because historical public recognition was now his, Frederick said nothing more. He had Maryland and its Eastern Shore on his mind.

★

Frederick Bailey would return to the Eastern Shore with his head held high, reunite with the Bailey family, give a speech to the colored and white citizens of St. Michaels, and face Thomas Auld for the first time in forty years. Auld had invited him after Frederick's Senate confirmation as U.S. marshal. He accepted the invitation with the hope of some kind of reconciliation, and to get answers about his past. Frederick made sure that a reporter from the *Baltimore Sun* accompanied him. The world needed to know about this triumph. This trip required vigilance, and Frederick planned to control the reporter's content and manipulate him with charm.

He boarded the steamer *Matilda* at Fells Point on the afternoon of June 16, 1877, prepared to impress the citizens of St. Michaels. Over one hundred Negroes were returning to the Eastern Shore that afternoon, and many passed the time laughing, eating, drinking, and dancing. Strummed banjos and stomping feet accented their good spirits, and scores, having no place to sleep, celebrated all night.

Frederick did not approve. A tea drinker himself, he objected to public drunkenness, preferred Mozart violin sonatas to popular songs, and could not abide men tossing chicken bones over the side or relieving themselves over the rail. The *Matilda* was an old sternwheeler, and accommodations were crude at best. No one had a cabin, but Frederick struggled to hide his disgust and alienation.

He was not one of these people. He was not them.

By sunrise on Sunday morning, the *Matilda* docked at the steamboat wharf on Navy Point in St. Michaels Harbour. St. Michaels was still a little harbor town with a new canning plant and a steam sawmill. But there was a significant change. A mixed crowd of white and Black men, women, and children had come to the dock to greet him and wish him well.

"Mr. Douglass," said one old white man, his eyes sparking with the pleasure of their meeting, "I remember you as a boy, and I just knew you were going someplace and would be somebody to make us proud. We're from the Eastern Shore."

"Thank you, sir," Frederick replied.

"Uncle Frederick, Uncle Frederick," cried a chorus of Mitchells, the children of his sister, Eliza, who had passed away just last year. Frederick smiled and waved and pressed forward to shake hands and touch the heads of the small children. He was told many names and remembered none of them. It seemed that he had scores of cousins in St. Michaels, but he felt like a tourist with a crowd following him.

The old streets were familiar to him—Willow, Cherry, Cedar, and Mulberry. Storefronts proclaimed the ownership of the families in power in 1836—Hambleton, Haddaway, Dawson, and Dodson. Frederick anticipated criticism for being there, the usual charges of appeasement and race betrayal. But nothing could deter him from the most important purpose for coming back to St. Michaels—making peace with Thomas Auld.

113.

AS ARRANGED, FREDERICK WAS met by Thomas's servant, Mr. Green, who led him to the brick house on Cherry Street where Thomas lived with his daughter Louisa and her husband, William Bruff. The crowd followed them to the front door, where Louisa and William waited to greet Frederick. The *Baltimore Star* reporter was behind Frederick furiously jotting notes.

"You are welcome to our home," said Louisa, an infant when he first came to St. Michaels in 1833, and now an older woman crippled with arthritis. She had a tight smile, but her voice was warm and gracious. "I will take you to see Father."

Frederick turned to the reporter. "Wait in the parlor until I'm done, and I will give you details about what happened." He passed through the neat and well-furnished house to Thomas Auld's bedroom at the back. William opened the door and allowed Frederick to enter without closing it. He and Louisa waited at the door listening silently.

Frederick found Thomas Auld in bed, a frail shrunken man with waxen skin and palsied hands. He was almost unrecognizable but for his eyes, small, bright, and cobalt blue. As striking as they ever were.

"Captain Auld," Frederick said.

Frederick's former master called out in a light, quavering voice, "Marshal Douglass!"

"Not marshal. Call me Frederick, as you used to." Frederick extended his hand, and Thomas took it gently and started to weep. His tremulous hand held Frederick's.

Thomas apologized for his emotional outburst. "I didn't mean to upset you."

"No, sir, please, it isn't necessary," Frederick replied.

"So much has happened."

"Let's talk about some of it. We don't have much time."

"Yes." Thomas wiped the tears from his cheek. The effort touched Frederick, reminding him of the kinship all human beings shared as they faced the deterioration of their bodies and remorseless death.

"How did you react to my escape?" Frederick asked.

There was a long pause. "Frederick, I always knew you were too smart to be a slave, and had I been in your place I should have done the same as you did," Thomas said.

"Captain Auld, I am glad to hear you say this. I did not run away from you but from slavery. It was not that I loved Caesar less but Rome more. Please understand."

"I understand."

"Now, I must apologize for something, and this is not easy for me. I am proud, perhaps too proud, but I now know I made a mistake when I claimed you were cruel and ungrateful to my grandmother, leaving her to die. You didn't do that. I know that now, and I'm sorry for it. I said all that because I thought that she went to you after Captain Anthony died," Frederick said.

"I did foolish, stupid things. But I never owned your grandmother. She was awarded to my brother-in-law Andrew Anthony, but I brought her down here and took care of her as long as she lived."

"I corrected the mistake as soon as I found out the truth. I never intended to do you an injustice. We all were victims of slavery."

"Oh, I never liked slavery. I meant to emancipate all of my slaves when they reached the age of twenty-five," Thomas claimed.

He did not, but Frederick chose not to bring that fact up. He also chose to ignore that awful night when Thomas Auld beat his cousin Henny again and again and sent her away.

"I'm sorry for all of my mistakes," Thomas continued, "but I could never force Betsey Bailey out. She was a special woman."

At the mention of his grandmother's name, Frederick's heart skipped a beat. To deflect his pain, he asked for information, "Did she tell you about my birthday? When was it?" After all these years, Frederick still didn't know when he was born, and this still troubled him.

Thomas answered, "It was February 1818. I know that."

"Not February 1817? Miss Lucretia said I was eight going on nine when I was sent to Baltimore, and I know that 1825 was the year of the launching of the great ships, and . . ."

"No, 1818. There are records," Thomas interrupted.

"Where?" Frederick was startled by this news.

"Captain Anthony. He kept lists of all of the Baileys."

Frederick recovered quickly, sensing that he did not have much more time. Thomas's voice was getting weaker. "What do you mean?" Frederick asked, trying to control his voice as he realized that there was proof of his birth.

"He had books, listing your entire family. Why you Baileys go back hundreds of years. It's all there," Thomas said.

"Where?"

"It's been years now, but I think Amanda has some, and Benjamin. I'm not sure. Much was lost when Lucretia died."

"Then you know who my father is?"

"There was talk all around."

"I heard the rumors, but I didn't believe them."

"There's no proof. He never said he was, and Lucretia never told me either.

I'm sorry I can't say for sure. Maybe you can find out if you see my family in Baltimore."

"When I last saw Amanda, she didn't know much, and Miss Sophia's son won't let me see her," Frederick said.

"Then I don't know what to tell you," Thomas said.

"What do you think? Was it Captain Anthony?"

Thomas paused, glancing down for a second. "I think so, and Lucretia said I should take care of you. From the very beginning, she treated you as different. It bothered me. No, it angered me, but now I understand. But she never told me for sure. I think she worried about what I would do if I knew, if I had proof."

Frederick felt weightless, as if a giant boulder had been lifted from his shoulders. "Thank you, sir," he said. He was unwilling, for the moment, to complicate the matter with further inquiries or speculations. He just wanted to revel in the knowledge of his existence, his birth year, even without the specific day. But he was unable to resist the impulse to ask, and so he asked Thomas another question. "Did my grandmother know?"

"Know what?"

"About my father?"

"Whatever there was to know, she knew. And whatever we knew, we weren't supposed to say. We thought you knew. You acted like you knew," Thomas said.

"I didn't know. I was just being myself, full of hot air. My sister Eliza never could stop reminding me."

"I'm sorry about Eliza, and I'm sorry to hear about your house in Rochester. Did they ever find who was responsible?"

"No, sir."

"That happens." Thomas said wearily.

"But fires make it easier to start over, as I've had to do many times," Frederick said.

"The future belongs to those who can start over. I've had four wives. Four." Thomas was proud and tough in spirit, even if his body was now weak and frail.

Frederick asked, "How old are you, sir?"

"Eighty-three, Frederick, eighty-three."

"You've seen many changes."

"Not as many as you have, and I know for sure now, as I did not know then, and could not know then, that my world is altogether different because you were part of it," Thomas said.

"Are you thanking or blaming me, sir?"

Thomas laughed, and his blue eyes brightened. "When you get to my age and look at the face of the man who will keep my name alive for years after I'm gone because he is Frederick Douglass, it makes you wonder." He laughed again, enjoying the irony. He shook his head before adding, "No, I should thank you. Thank you."

"Thank you for sending me to Baltimore," Frederick replied, acknowledging that fateful decision that had forever changed his life.

"It's what Lucretia wanted."

"But she was dead when you sent me there the second time," Frederick corrected gently.

Thomas didn't seem to mind the correction. "She understood you from almost the beginning. You were born here, but you belonged there. You're a voyager. That's who you are. I wanted to be a captain, but I was really a merchant, stuck to the land, never looking beyond the horizon. I was not like you. You were always restless."

"But I'm getting older, too, and settled, living in Washington," Frederick said.

Thomas had closed his eyes, and Frederick stood, startled by the possibility that Thomas had passed away. "Captain," he cried.

The captain opened his eyes and smiled, as if enjoying Frederick's consternation. "Marshal Douglass, I'm not dead yet. But keep your eyes out there, over the river, across the bay and sea."

Louisa knocked on the door. "Mr. Douglass, it's perhaps time for you to leave. My father gets tired easily."

"Goodbye, sir," Frederick said.

"Goodbye, Marshal," Thomas replied.

"And thank you again for everything you did for me," said Frederick. He felt almost giddy now that his greatest fear, to never know the details of his birth and heritage, had been faced and conquered at last.

That Frederick's knowledge was dependent on Thomas Auld even now did not matter. To his own satisfaction, Frederick knew his personal history. He was not just the creation of his own will and imagination. He was more than a character of countless lectures and two books. He was the son of Aaron Anthony and Harriet Bailey, an integral part of two families whose histories went back hundreds of years. Frederick Augustus Washington Bailey Douglass felt, for the first time in his life, that he stood firmly on the shoulders of proud, imperfect but enduring Black and white people strengthened, and forever changed, by the crossing of two, deep family rivers somewhere near Hillsboro on the Eastern Shore of Maryland.

Frederick held his head high that afternoon, and his "Self-Made Man" speech delivered at the local Black church resonated for him with greater power and significance.

Indeed, something good had come out of a union he could never fully understand. But he could accept it, as he could accept nature in its wild, luxurious abundance teeming with messy life, that eternal challenge to the illusion of purity embraced by charlatans and fools.

He was now ready to continue his personal journey and life in Washington. He would complete the purchase of a ten-acre estate across the Anacostia River that he now called Cedar Hill because of its abundant evergreen cedar trees, and next year he would go to Easton, where he was jailed. He would go to Wye House and face the descendants of Colonel Edward Lloyd. And, finally, he would go to the Anthony farm near Hillsboro and find the cabin of Betsey Bailey, where he was born.

Frederick knew what he would do at that spot. He would gather up a handful of soil, a remnant of the land from which he had to escape, the land to which he had to return and leave again, and take it back to his new home in Washington.

Frederick could never live on the Eastern Shore, having seen the great bay, where from its banks he admired the white sails that seemed to float above the deep, shimmering water, and dreamed of his true home on the other side of Jordan.

He knew the land that defined him could never be the same again, for Frederick Douglass now had different eyes, and with them his world, once limited to a farm on Tuckahoe Creek, was made forever new, changed by his journey across the deep rivers flowing to home under limitless skies and the North Star rising.

PART VI: 1877-1887

Helen Pitts and the Douglass Family

114.

ROSETTA WAS EXPECTING ANOTHER child after becoming pregnant when Nathan was released from prison, before he went to Nebraska to seek his fortune. In her letter to Frederick, Rosetta referred to Nathan's departure as a "marital separation," alluding to adulteries. She wanted to remain in Rochester, but life there became untenable when, after refusing to sign for one of Nathan's bills, a constable arrived to confiscate furniture. She came to Washington with her five children, moving into the 316 A Street home. The move could not come soon enough.

Frederick informed Anna about the completion of the transaction for Cedar Hill. Their crowded house created the perfect opportunity for the announcement, but he muted his excitement. She would not be as excited as he was. She was never as excited as he was. "It's all done, Anna, and I want to show you our new house. You'll love it. We should go on a Saturday morning."

"It's not a good idea to leave Rosetta. She might go into labor while we're gone," Anna said.

"We don't need to worry. If there's a problem with the baby, Louisa will take care of it." Louisa Sprague, Rosetta's sister-in-law, had become Anna's friend and a major support for the entire family.

"All right. Should I pack a lunch?"

"Yes."

Frederick hired a carriage for the September ride from Capitol Hill to Anacostia across the river. They said little during the entire trip. Crossing the new Navy Yard Bridge, he tried to engage Anna, observing, "A marvel of engineering just finished three years ago. No more wooden bridges. This iron bridge is the future, and trains might cross on it one day. Just imagine that."

Looking ahead, Anna did not reply. Frederick considered demanding an explanation for her silence, but he thought better of it. He didn't want to ruin his introduction to the new house above Uniontown, a suburb consisting of churches, stores, no sidewalks, and a motley collection of Victorian houses and shanties with wild dogs by the hundreds running around. Blacks and whites lived there, but more and more whites were leaving as Blacks moved in.

Going farther south, they arrived at a high hill. To reach its top, the carriage needed to go around the hill to the south and approach the house from the rear. The Victorian, built in 1855 with brick, was L shaped and had a gabled roof. There were large windows throughout, and the covered front porch was supported by four thick white rounded columns.

From the beginning, Frederick planned to expand the house in the rear, adding two wings. Eventually, if all went as planned, it would have fourteen rooms, space for children, grandchildren, and visitors. He also hoped to expand the acreage of the estate by seven or eight more acres. As they approached the house, he broke the silence. "Isn't this place beautiful? And the space. Just look at this space. You will have a wonderful garden, for flowers, for fruits and vegetables. And I'm going to garden, too, when I have time. And then I will press petals and leaves and create a catalogue of everything!"

"Yes, it's beautiful," Anna replied.

The forty-three-foot porch extended across the front of the first floor. Frederick intended to sit in his rocking chair under the canopy decorated with latticework, enjoy the northern view of the city and the Capitol, and read his beloved Dickens. As they looked to the city below, he said, "I'm going to walk to work and back every day. Yes, I'm going to rise at five, walk my grounds, come back, write letters, eat breakfast, and walk to work. That will bring down the pounds."

"You need to lose some of them pounds, and I do, too. But I'm not walking to Capitol Hill. That would kill me. We can take walks all 'round here when I'm not feeling bad," Anna said.

They had not walked together in years, and her observation touched him. "Yes, we'll do that."

"Let's go inside," Anna said.

There were three main rooms on the first floor, the center stair hall was flanked by east and west parlors with the dining room and library behind them. Upstairs, there were five bedrooms, the largest for himself, another for Anna, and the rest for family and guests. They walked through all the empty rooms. Frederick identified every room according to the house's original design and his own preferences.

When he identified the large bedroom at the rear of the house overlooking the expansive yards to the south as the guest bedroom, Anna stopped to look out the window. "So much light. It'll be beautiful for the people staying here on visits." She didn't say Ottilie's name, but she was the only consistent guest year in and year out. "When will we move in?"

"It will take time. With all that must be done, maybe next year," Frederick said.

"We need the time. 1878 will be a good year."

"So, you're glad I did it?"

Anna smiled for the first time that day. "My dream will come true: everybody will be here, even more than South Avenue. I never thought we would live in such a house. My, my, Frederick, we've come a long way from those two rooms above Buzzard's Bay."

"Yes, a long, long way."

"And this will be our last."

He didn't have to make a promise. He knew that Cedar Hill would be their last home. It was fitting that his last days would end in so splendid a place. "Yes, our last."

They returned to Capitol Hill, again in absolute silence.

Two days later, Rosetta went into labor. Rosabelle Mary Sprague came into the world on September 25, 1877.

★

Cedar Hill was a difficult project, and the coming winter would force delays for weeks, if not months. He feared the move to Cedar Hill would probably take a year. Meanwhile, Amanda Sears, the daughter of Thomas and Lucretia Auld, was gravely ill, and her husband, John, asked Frederick to come. She wanted to see him before she died. Frederick immediately boarded the train for Baltimore.

John Sears met him at the door. This time he was gracious and gentle, so unlike the surly man Frederick met in 1859 after Harpers Ferry. Grief had softened his features and his voice, and Frederick could see his effort to maintain his composure. He took Frederick's hand. "Thank you for coming, Marshal Douglass. I'm sorry for the haste, but she told me she had to see you before the end."

"I'm so sorry, Mr. Sears. I wish I could have come more quickly, sir. But we can't fly, yet," Frederick replied.

"No apologies are needed, sir, and . . ."

Frederick interjected, "It's Frederick, Mr. Sears."

"Then it's John."

"Then it's John," Frederick repeated.

"Come," he said, leading with an extended right arm down the main hall to a bedroom at the rear of the house.

Prepared for her visitor, Amanda lay in bed sitting up against several pillows. Her skin was quite pale, almost translucent. Her hands were spindly and veined, and her voice was thin but clear. In the corner of the room stood her two adolescent children, their heads down. Frederick had felt the anguish of mourning, especially when he was a child. He had not been moved by the death of his mother, as he barely knew her. But the losses of his grandmother, Lucretia Auld, Sophia Auld, and his own grandchildren resonated when he saw this grieving family. He turned to offer some kind of consolation to the Sears children, but Amanda interrupted him. "Thank you for coming to see me, Frederick, no, Marshal . . ."

He gently corrected her, approaching the side of the bed. "No, it's Frederick, always Frederick, as you knew me long ago."

Amanda gripped his hand. "I don't have much time, so please tell me as much as you can remember about my mother. Tell me what she looked like. I have only the vaguest memory, and tell me if my children look like her." She looked to the corner of the room. "Don't cry, my darlings. Mama is going to a better place."

Frederick glanced at the girl, who was about fifteen, and said to Amanda, "She looks just like your mother, her form, her features, all like Miss Lucretia."

"Her name is Lucretia, after my mother."

"A loving, fitting tribute."

Amanda nodded. "Thank you for coming to see me. You didn't have to, but you came, and I appreciate that my life has been a happy one. I'm glad you saw Father. He told me he was pleased to see you. It meant so much to him." She closed her yes.

"Amanda, Mrs. Sears." Frederick thought she passed away, but she opened her eyes and turned to her husband standing at the other side of the bed. "John," she said before reaching for his hand.

Instinctively, Frederick stepped away and then hurried out, leaving the immediate family to face her death.

When Amanda finally died a few weeks later, Sears and his son hoped Frederick would come to the funeral, but he did not go. He could not shake his fear of funerals and dreaded the arrival of telegrams. When Frederick received a telegram from Charles about his wife's death, Frederick felt relief as well as sorrow. Only thirty-one, Libbie was buried in her plot on Long Island. Charles was the only Douglass family member present, and he didn't tell his father about Libbie's last request. "Tell them after I'm gone," she had insisted, dying from tuberculosis. "I want only my family and you."

★

The new house was soon ready for occupancy, and Frederick, Anna, Rosetta, and her children moved to Cedar Hill the last week of September 1878. Ottilie came a week later to see it. There was still so much in the house and grounds that needed work, but everyone was happy with the latest results. Everyone except Anna. And it was because Ottilie was there.

Anna rarely mentioned her name, but after Ottilie's arrival she commented dryly one evening, "The door barely closed behind us before she shows up."

They were sitting in the west parlor on one of those rare occasions when they were alone. Anna was knitting, Frederick was reading, and the remark came without warning, for they had not been talking for several minutes. When they did talk, it was not about Ottilie. It seemed as if Anna had been waiting for her shot in the dark, for an opportunity to say something bold. He ignored Anna, continuing to read.

"Didn't you hear me?" Anna asked.

Frederick looked up, not replying.

"I don't want her here," Anna continued.

"I know that," Frederick said.

"But it don't matter what I want."

"No, not about this." He had never been so bold in his insistence about Ottilie's presence in his life.

"It's settled, from now on, *she* will be here," Anna said.

"Yes, every summer and early fall," Frederick said.

Anna stood. "No, this is my house. And every day as I sit there I will be her reminder that this is my house, and you are *my* husband and the father of *our* children. And when she is gone, I will not mention her name, and you will not either, not to me, never to me. Just spare me and the grandchildren finding you two holding hands or doin' what we used to do a long, long time ago."

"Anna!" he shouted and stood. He looked toward the door for eavesdroppers, outraged by her declaration about something that had never happened in their home.

"I've made my peace with it," Anna said, starting toward the door.

Frederick blocked her way, his anger so intense his eyes ached. He inhaled deeply. "This . . . is . . . not . . . peace. You didn't . . . you didn't have to say . . ."

Anna's face was serene, and she said, "But I did 'cause I want you to know my peace is knowing you and her will never have peace. Now get out of my way, or you'll have to knock me down."

Frederick stepped aside.

She opened the door and stated, "I will never talk about this again. Never. I'm too old, and too tired. No, I will not hide in my room. I will be here for every visitor, every neighbor, every dinner, every meetin' while she's here. Rosetta and Louisa will make sure I look my best, even if every bone in my body is achin'. I will be there as the mistress of Cedar Hill, and nobody else, for one hot minute, will think otherwise, not even you, and certainly not her!"

115.

FREDERICK AND ANNA'S NEIGHBORS to the southeast of Cedar Hill sent a note asking if they could come introduce themselves. Trying to make peace, Frederick consulted Anna, and they agreed to receive Hiram and Frances Pitts for afternoon tea, which also included Ottilie. The Pitts arrived with their niece, Helen, the daughter of Hiram's brother Gideon, who had recently moved to Washington to live with them while looking for employment as a federal government clerk. Hiram was a clerk in the Treasury Department but could not secure her a position there. This information was revealed almost immediately by Frances, who did not work but seemed determined to establish her family's social standing as neighbors of "the great Frederick Douglass."

"Our family has known you for years," Frances began. "My brother tells me that you came to Honeoye now and then during your lecture tours. Helen remembers you coming then. She was young, but she remembers. Isn't that so, my dear?"

"Yes, I remember. But I can't expect Mr. Douglass to remember. I was just a girl, and he was traveling far and wide," Helen replied.

"I'm sorry, Miss Pitts, I don't remember," Frederick confessed.

"That is not your fault, sir," Helen said, looking directly at the man she admired. There was a pause as if the group was immobilized by a spell cast upon the room.

Frances's high, insistent voice broke the spell. She was determined to carry on: "And standing comes from family history, too, as it comes from our heritage as descendants of John and Priscilla Alden, who came on the *Mayflower*. Hiram's grandfather, Peter Pitts, earned the title of captain for his service during the Revolution, and for that service was granted land in western New York near Honeoye Lake. Hiram and Helen were born there." Hiram and Helen sat stone-faced in their chairs, teacups held tightly. Frederick sensed mortification. Frances Pitts sounded like a hapless bore who didn't know when to stop talking.

"Some of us have the privilege of good fortune," Frederick acknowledged with warmth.

Ottilie responded coldly, "I wonder how much land of the Natives was taken, no, plundered, by your family in Plymouth and New York to establish your wealth."

"I would not call it wealth," objected Hiram.

Although the others looked at Ottilie with reproval, she was unruffled. "Sir, you have an *estate* next door," she countered.

"Even so, we all work. We all serve in our own ways," Helen answered, turning to her aunt and uncle, defending them with a nod of the head and a delicate smile. "We *contribute*."

"How?" asked Ottilie. She looked at Helen as if chastising a wayward child who had forgotten her place as an ornament at an adult function.

Frederick, displeased with Ottilie's rudeness, almost intervened. But he was curious how Helen would handle herself. Over forty, Helen was not a young woman. Frederick did not think she was conventionally beautiful like the gorgeous Kate Chase, daughter of the chief justice, the unofficial queen of Washington society. Nonetheless, Helen was attractive and seemed at least ten years younger than she was, the cinched waist of her bustled dress accentuated a youthful, trim waist below a full bosom. She had flawless pale skin, and her ample, golden hair fell in a curl on either side of her face. Her bright gray eyes seemed alert and curious, and her lilting but strong voice captured his attention.

Frederick had no doubt. Ottilie was jealous.

"I was a teacher once, raised by parents who expected me to serve others, especially those in need. I went south during the war to teach freedmen, who so wanted to learn to read and write," Helen said.

"The need remains. Why are you not still there?" asked Ottilie.

"I almost died. Disease. My father had to come get me."

"I'm sorry you were ill," said Ottilie, sounding genuinely concerned.

"Thank you, but I now want to devote myself to the cause of women, improving our lives, our health. I'm now the corresponding secretary of the Moral Education Society. Are you familiar with its mission to strengthen women through education and activism?" Helen asked.

Ottilie became cold again. "The Society that publishes the *Alpha*."

"Yes," said Helen.

"You actually associate yourself with that journal?"

"Yes, and why do you object?"

"I object to its tone, its assumption of the moral superiority of women as the religious guardians of our society."

"You support women's rights, don't you?"

"Of course, I do. We all do. Frederick has been dedicated to it his entire life." Ottilie turned to Frederick and smiled.

"Since we are all in agreement about women's right to equality and access to the ballot," Helen continued, "then I don't understand your hostility to the Society and its journal."

"We are doing God's work," said Frances, intervening hotly.

"And that, Mrs. Pitts, is precisely the problem. You educate women about their bodies, telling them what to do in the privacy of their bed chambers in graphic details unworthy of a respectable enterprise, in the name of Christian values," Ottilie said.

"Miss Assing," said Hiram. "I would never allow my wife to be involved in anything unrespectable, anything that would bring dishonor to us."

"I see," Ottilie retorted, "*You* would never *allow* . . ."

"Are you a prude, Miss Assing?" asked Helen.

Ottilie flinched. "No, I am not. But there should be limits to what is said in print."

"Are you claiming that what is said there is dangerous, obscene, something that the laws should shut down?" Helen asked.

"Yes."

"I have heard enough," said Frances. She stood and placed her teacup on the table. "You are Mr. Douglass's guest, and you are entitled to your opinion. But when we asked to be invited here, I did not expect—and I will not tolerate—an inquisition from a stranger. Good day, Mr. Douglass. Come, Hiram. Come, Helen. Thank you, Mrs. Douglass for the refreshments. If you and Mr. Douglass are disposed to have us return, we will gladly accept an invitation if we can be assured that Miss Assing is not here."

Without waiting for Helen, Frances and Hiram turned to the door. Frederick rose to see them out, but Hiram was brusque. "We can see ourselves out, sir. Good day."

Helen stood and addressed Ottilie. "Miss Assing, we are not pornographers, and the Comstock laws have allowed us to send our journal through the United States mail. It bewilders me that as a friend of Mr. Douglass you hold us to standards worthy of the pilgrims and Puritans you so clearly despise. We will not be acquaintances and certainly not friends. And if Mr. Douglass requires us to accept you as a condition of our friendship, then that will be too high a price to pay, and we will remain just neighbors." Helen added, "Thank you, Mr. and Mrs. Douglass for your hospitality. I will see my way out as well."

Frederick followed her. "I'm so sorry."

Anna and Ottilie remained seated, staring at each other. "Well, well, well. A jealous woman can sure make a fool of herself in somebody else's house," Anna said.

"Jealous? I have no reason to be jealous," Ottilie replied.

"Lie to yourself all you want."

"I'm not a child to be reprimanded."

"No, you're a mean bitch. That's what you are. Takes one to know one. I'll tell Louisa to bring you some hot tea. You'll need it. I can tell he likes Miss Pitts and will want to defend her."

"And you're not jealous?"

"Why should I be? I have you." Anna smiled and left the parlor.

Frederick returned, furious. "Ottilie, that was outrageous, unnecessary, unacceptable."

"I'm sorry," she replied.

"No, you're not. And don't try to explain, because your explanation will only make me angrier, as you expose yourself with excuses and rationalizations."

Wounded, Ottilie muttered, "Please don't. Please."

"I will be glad when you're gone," he said.

"Don't say that."

"It's the truth. I don't need this kind of stress in my life."

"Are you sending me away? I can leave tomorrow."

"And make me the villain in your narrative? No, I won't give you that satisfaction."

Frederick left the room. Ottilie stayed until November, and they never spoke about Helen and the Pitts family again. After she left, they continued their usual correspondence. Frederick told her that Helen had moved to Indiana to be with her sister Jennie and serve as a substitute teacher.

Ottilie's vicious letter in reply stunned him: "There is a distressing lack of genuineness about her. She is scheming to use your good name to bolster a project that is a disgusting hodgepodge of radical feminism and religious hypocrisy. I should rejoice to see you keep aloof from anybody and anything at all connected with that infamous *Alpha*. If you have read it as I have, notwithstanding my disgust, just for the sake of having a right to denounce it, you would agree with me that no good and pure-minded woman can advocate those monstrous doctrines, allow her imagination to run always in that same channel, read all that obscene stuff hidden under religious language without being shocked unless she is so irredeemably stupid as to be considered altogether irresponsible."

Frederick didn't reply. He also didn't tell Ottilie that he was corresponding with Helen and hoped to see her in Indiana when he was there on his upcoming speaking tour.

116.

IN EARLY NOVEMBER, FREDERICK boarded the overnight steamer *Highland Light*, slept in a stateroom assigned by the steamer's white captain, and arrived at Easton Point, Maryland, on a Saturday morning, November 23, 1878. He had expressed a desire to return to Easton, and the mayor and city council invited him to speak at the courthouse. He lectured first at the new Bethel A.M.E Church, telling his Black audience, as usual, to work hard and save money.

Frederick returned to his hotel and received white callers, some of them telling him that they knew him when he was a young man. No one admitted to being part of the mob that stormed his Sunday school or called for his hanging at the Easton Jail.

That evening, he repeated his earlier lecture at the Ashbury A.M.E. Church before retiring for the night and a restless sleep. He was too excited about the next day. Frederick had hired a horse and carriage, and on Monday morning, he and the driver, Louis Freeman, who had been a slave on the farm owned by a grandson of Aaron Anthony, rode twelve miles up Tuckahoe Creek to the crossroads known as Tapper Corner.

"It's a little ways up, near here," Freeman said, pointing.

Freeman exclaimed, "Stop!" when they came to a deep, curving gully that rose toward the road. "There! That's Aunt Betty's lot."

Frederick stepped down from the rig, and as his boot touched the ground the sound of pebbles brought memories of childhood. "Where's the big cedar tree?" he asked.

"Down there, near the edge of the ravine," Freeman replied.

"Let's go."

Frederick hurried into the underbrush. Within minutes, they found the tall tree, and he stopped and took in the wide branches, its height and circumference. He walked toward the creek, where he remembered Betsey's cabin stood. There was no log hut, and the well was gone, too. To the right was a new house. "But this is the spot. This is where she raised me. This is where I was born," he said.

"Yes, sir," said Freeman.

Frederick fell silent and stood with his eyes closed. He heard the rustling of leaves and the light breeze of autumn. He heard his own voice as a child running through the high grass arriving home from a day's adventure. *Gram Betty, I'm home.* He opened his eyes and bent to scoop handfuls of earth that he put in a bag he had in his pocket. Frederick fulfilled his plan to find this exact spot and take dirt back to Cedar Hill, thus uniting Tuckahoe and Washington on the road to freedom. He whispered aloud now, "Gram Betty."

Freeman waited respectfully, and Frederick turned to him. "I'm ready. Let's go. I have to get back to town."

"You're going to talk at the Courthouse tonight, sir. Yes?"

"Yes."

"I'll be there. Lots of folks will be there."

That night his formal address was "Self-Made Men." Black and white listeners provided occasional but polite applause at the description of his arrest, the mistreatment of the slave traders, and the kindness of the sheriff, who was in the audience. Provoked by the racial separation before him in the audience, Frederick became almost vociferous, but controlled his voice with the mastery gained over his career, "If you see the Negro going to church, let him alone! If you see him going to school, let him alone! If you see him going to the ballot box, let him alone! Do not form your Ku Klux Klan, and your rifle clubs, to drive him from the polls! *Do not!*" He received prolonged applause. The Black members of the audience gave him a standing ovation. About half of the white audience stood. A few seemed irritated, if not insulted. But no one objected or expressed contempt.

After his speech, several well-dressed white men, leaders of the town, approached Frederick and offered their hands, congratulating him, thanking him for coming, and bringing prestige to Easton as the U.S. marshal. One man boasted, "We have never had so distinguished a visitor. No, sir. I will tell my grandchildren, sir, of this day."

Sheriff Graham, over eighty and bent, approached him, extending his withered hand. Frederick recognized him at once.

"Sheriff."

"Marshal."

"Thank you for what you did for me," Frederick said.

"You honor us for coming. How could we know what you would become? But I knew you had to leave or die."

"Thank you."

"No, thank Mr. Auld."

"I did thank him."

"Good."

Frederick also reunited with his brother, Perry, that week and was shocked to discover how old and feeble he had become. His back was bent, his shriveled hands trembled, and a frequent cough shook his thin body. His wife, Maria, had died, and his other children, except one daughter, had moved away. Frederick always wanted to bring his brother to Washington. Dying, Perry was grateful and did not mention the family's previous treatment of him.

Ottilie, however, wrote about Perry's return, "It's just like you and natural enough under the circumstances. Among all the leeches that feed on you, he is one of the most harmless and least expensive, and since you are wisely going to put him in the little house, you will not be greatly troubled by his presence."

Frederick didn't reply. He was too angry. He made a decision: Ottilie would never come back to Cedar Hill.

117.

FREDERICK BEGAN TO DREAD the arrival of Ottilie's letters. He now found them distracting and exhausting. Her criticism of the financial dependence of his boys, especially Charles, was unrelenting. In another letter, she called them "parasites." And yet she could be astute in her analysis of American politics and encouraging about his career. "I should much rejoice if you would employ your leisure in writing the sequel of your autobiography. I have no doubt you could make it a highly attractive book. The long winter evenings are favorable for such work."

This prompted him to start writing *The Life and Times of Frederick Douglass*. He perceived the trajectory of the story, the unfolding life of a self-made man, a life of struggle to define his life on his own terms against the great evils of his time, human bondage, and racial inequality.

He had begun his book when he learned that William Lloyd Garrison died in May 1879. Frederick was not surprised that he did not feel grief. Regret, yes, but not grief. Gratitude seemed the most appropriate response for the pivotal role that this great man had played in his life. But Frederick could not forgive Garrison for rejecting him. He did not go to Garrison's funeral in Boston, where flags flew at half-mast, and 1,500 people, Black and white, packed the service and heard the eulogy given by Wendell Phillips.

Frederick needed to make a public statement about Garrison. Before a mixed audience gathered at Washington's Fifteenth Street Presbyterian Church, he said, "this is not the time and place for a critical and accurate measurement of William Lloyd Garrison," and then he gave a pointed assessment anyway: "Speaking for myself, I must frankly say I have sometimes thought him uncharitable to those who differed from him. Honest himself, he could not always see how men could differ from him and still be honest. To say this of him is simply to say that he was human, and it may be added when he erred here, he erred in the interest of truth. He abhorred compromise and demanded that men should be either cold or hot."

Frederick continued his remodeling and gardening projects at Cedar Hill. Away from a full house and the back lawn, where family and friends played croquet, Douglass built a small, windowless, stone room with a fireplace. He placed within it a chaise lounge and a writing desk from the estate of Charles Sumner. He named it the "Growlery" after Mr. Jarndyce in Dickens's *Bleak House*, who described his own refuge as the place where he went to "come and growl."

Cedar Hill attracted family and visitors. Charles was back, looking for a job without success, as his children became more and more attached to Anna and Frederick. Lewis and Amelia had their own room, as did Louisa, and Rosetta's older children came for extended visits while their parents tried to reconcile in Rochester after Rosetta had her seventh child. Now Perry and his daughter were living with him, too, and Ottilie was scheduled to arrive in June for her annual visit. He had to tell her she could not come this summer.

Frederick finally informed her. There was not enough room in Cedar Hill. There were too many family members living there. Also, he could not entertain any guests. He was too busy writing. "Wait for further instructions," he wrote her.

Ottilie sent a telegram. "I do understand."

He was relieved that she didn't press the matter, and their correspondence continued. During one of the most challenging periods in Frederick's postwar career, Ottilie remained brutally honest in her criticism of his opposition to the Black exodus movement of 1877–79.

Hundreds of thousands of Black people in the South, without resources and protection, began an exodus after the withdrawal of federal troops. Frederick received the harshest criticism of his career as he stubbornly insisted that Black people needed to stay, work hard, and wait until white people saw the truth about equality. Coming from a former fugitive, his philosophical words proved hollow, and a new low was reached when he avoided a September meeting of the American Social Science Association, where he was asked to defend his opposition.

Initially, Frederick accepted the invitation, but three days before his appearance, Frederick canceled. Instead, he sent his paper "The Negro Exodus from the Gulf States" to be read at the conference and published in the *New York Times*. He did not want debate and controversy at the meeting, and he also feared being booed. There was a time when a hostile audience energized him. Now he could not face the professional scorn of Black and white intellectuals. He avoided controversy as much as possible, intending to keep his job for the remainder of the Hayes administration.

★

Frederick made a detailed outline for *Life and Times*, revising his first two autobiographies while updating the narrative from 1855. He eagerly anticipated the work ahead. This book was going to be his longest, best, and most comprehensive work. Frederick credited Ottilie for moving him forward, and he extended an invitation for her return to Cedar Hill, where she could read and edit an early draft. He could now forgive if not forget her cruelty.

Reflecting on his life story since 1855, Frederick thought of the deaths of John Brown in 1859, Hugh Auld in 1861, Lincoln in 1865, Charles Dickens in 1870, Charles Remond in 1873, Charles Sumner in 1874, Thomas Auld in 1878, and William Lloyd Garrison and Amanda Sears the following year. The losses in his immediate family, starting with Annie in 1860, were almost too painful to contemplate. His sister Eliza died in 1875, as did Rosetta's third daughter, Alice, at six years of age. Frederick, Jr., lost three children in five years. Charles endured the deaths of his one-year-old daughter, Annie, in July of 1872; his wife, Libbie, in 1878; and his one-year-old son, Eddie Arthur, in 1879. Though Frederick deeply grieved the deaths in his family, he did not write about them or share his sorrows.

Despite Anna's crucial role in his escape from slavery, Frederick did not name her in his first autobiography, the *Narrative,* only mentioning that he had a wife. In *My Bondage*, he wrote simply, "my intended wife, Anna," which he included in *Life and Times*. Although Anna received barely a mention in his third autobiography, Julia, and Ottilie ("Miss Assing") were included three times each.

Frederick focused his third autobiography on the Civil War, Reconstruction, and his present. He anticipated almost 500 pages. His references to his children could fit into a single short paragraph. Rosetta and Nathan Sprague were not mentioned at all.

He had two priorities for 1880: Finish *The Life and Times of Frederick Douglass* and campaign for the Republican Party, the best hope for Black people in a country growing tired of Black people.

118.

FREDERICK REMEMBERED HIS MOTHER giving him a heart-shaped cake in February, and in lieu of documentation he decided that February 14 was his birthday. He now knew that he was born in 1818, not 1817. On February 14, 1880—his sixty-second birthday—Frederick was not in a celebratory mood. He had been summoned to testify before a select committee of U.S. senators about the collapse of the Freedmen's Bank six years before. Testifying before a Senate committee was another first in his life, but he was not thrilled. After six years, he was still mortified by the public criticism he endured as the bank's president for its failure after months of mismanagement and fraud by the trustees.

Long after Frederick's departure and the bank's closure, there were still problems that Congress needed to resolve. All too familiar with corruption, the press demanded answers, and a Senate committee, headed by the Black senator of Mississippi, Blanche K. Bruce, who had stayed at Frederick's house when he first came to Washington, was convened to call in witnesses to answer questions. The opening questions, led by Chairman Bruce, were perfunctory and illustrated a history already known to all. Under oath, Frederick related the facts as he remembered them.

Only when a white Democrat, Senator Garland of Arkansas, who served in the Confederate Congress and was pardoned by President Johnson after the war, began his examination did Frederick, already uncomfortable, feel embarrassed. His hands sweated as Garland, courteous and deferential, probed his knowledge about banking: "Mr. Douglass, had you given the institution any examination as to the conduct of its business before you were called upon to be president?"

Frederick replied, "No, not at all, sir. I had no business there. I had no banking experience. I knew nothing about banking. My life had been a theoretical one rather than a practical one—on the stump—and I hesitated about it until I was persuaded that as the colored people of the country generally had confidence in me, I might strengthen the bank, after the run had been made upon its reserve, by consenting to occupy the position of its president." This exchange trigged mortification because forever in the congressional record would be evidence of his ignorance and inexperience. Only his popularity would account for why he was given the job as president of the bank.

Bruce later assured Frederick, "You did fine, my dear friend. You did just fine. Preparing for legislation is hard, and it requires patience from legislators."

Frederick was not comforted. He was agitated by the hearing and wanted distance from the legislative process. He wanted to stay in government service, but legislative work did not appeal to him. He did not have the temperament for banking or for Congress. Life at home was not as nerve-wracking, even as change continued to surprise, annoy, and excite him.

Rosetta had moved her entire family to Cedar Hill, leaving Rochester permanently and separating from Nathan without getting a divorce. Rosetta and Charles had reconciled. At least it seemed so, because they no longer argued openly and now sat pleasantly together at dinner. Anna was happy, and they all adored Laura, Charles's new wife, who was far more congenial than Libbie.

Perry had passed away on August 18, after telling his brother he was glad to go. He thanked Frederick for making his last days "so comfortable and peaceful."

★

Frederick embarked on the 1880 fall campaign trail, championing a man he had never met, saying to a cheering Black crowd at the Cooper Institute in New York, "James A. Garfield must be our president. He is right on our questions, take my word for it. He is a typical American all over. He has shown us how man in the humblest circumstances can rise, and win." The Republican nominee from Ohio had won the nomination on the thirty-sixth ballot, when it became clear that neither Grant, tarnished by scandal but still popular because of his war record, nor Senator James Blaine could get the majority of delegate votes. A relative unknown who did not seek the nomination, Garfield became the consensus candidate.

Frederick heard about a group from Fisk University, the Black university founded in Nashville, Tennessee, singing spirituals for Garfield at his modest farmhouse. Garfield proclaimed, "And I tell you now, in the closing days of this campaign, that I would rather be with you and defeated than against you and victorious." This response moved Frederick and confirmed Garfield as the better man for the presidency. The election was the closest in American history. Garfield prevailed over Winfield S. Hancock by fewer than 2,000 votes. His Electoral College victory was much stronger, since he carried the northeast and upper Midwest.

The tranquility of the Douglass household was tested when on an unseasonably warm afternoon in late November, lame-duck President Hayes, his son Rutherford Platt Hayes, age thirty, and his secretary of the treasury, John Sherman, made an unannounced call. Frederick was in the library when Rosetta knocked rapidly on the door to tell him the president had come. "Papa, Papa, the president is here. President Hayes is here!" she whispered.

"What did you say?" asked Frederick. He bounded from his chair and quickly opened the door. "President Hayes? He's here! I can't believe this. But why?" He didn't wait for her to answer, and she hurried off to inform the rest of the family.

Rosetta had escorted the president and the others into the formal east parlor, where family and guests gathered on rare occasion for weddings and funerals. Frederick rushed in, taking in deep breaths. "Mr. President, gentlemen, please accept my apologies for not receiving you as soon as you arrived. I didn't know you were . . ."

Hayes, always genial and comforting, gently interrupted, raising his hand but not his voice, "No apologies are needed, Marshal Douglass. We are interrupting your day. We should apologize for coming uninvited. But we were in the area and saw no harm in paying a call, hoping you were home."

"No, no, no apology is needed. This is an honor, sir, quite an honor. The president of the U.S. has come to my house. I've been to yours, but never in my dreams thought a president would come to mine," Frederick said.

"This lame duck, without power, can give some joy in these remaining months."

"We'll provide refreshments shortly," Frederick said, looking around as if servants were within his hearing.

Rosetta appeared, followed by Ottilie, whom Frederick had invited to celebrate Garfield's victory. Frederick said, "Our guests need refreshments as soon as possible," and Rosetta immediately turned to do what needed to be done.

"Mr. President, this is our house guest, Miss Ottilie Assing, a journalist who has translated my work. She hopes to translate my next book, too."

"Pleased to meet you," said the president.

Anna entered the room wearing her finest wig and one of her few expensive dresses and approached the president without waiting for an introduction. "Mr. President, I'm Mrs. Douglass. You do us all the greatest honor by comin' to Cedar Hill."

Frederick's mouth almost dropped open, he was so taken aback by her assertiveness. Whenever they had guests in the past, Anna remained in the kitchen preparing food and assigning others to serve it. She said to the president, "I'm a shy woman, Mr. President, and usually stay back in the kitchen, but there's nothin', and I mean nothin', goin' to keep me back from meetin' and sittin' with the president of these United States in my own house!"

Still smiling, the president shook his head and replied, "It's always nice to know when you're welcome. There are places where I am not."

"Then shame on them," said Anna. She turned to Ottilie. "Miss Assing, after the food comes, I'm sure the president will like to hear you play the piano for him and the rest of our guests across the hall in the west parlor. You will do that, won't you?"

"Yes, of course," replied Ottilie, looking at Frederick with astonishment.

"Good, and thank you, Miss Assing. Mr. President, Miss Assing is quite good at the piano, and Mr. Douglass just might play his violin with her, or sing. He has a fine voice, just so fine a voice. Will you, Frederick, play or sing?"

"Yes, I'll sing."

"You can do both," urged Anna, her voice warm and pleasant. "The president should know all that you can do before he leaves this house." She turned to the president for approval.

"Yes, all your talents should be on display," he said.

Rosetta appeared at the door. "Louisa has prepared some tea, cookies, and sandwiches. We'll eat in the dining room."

"Good," declared Anna. She looked at the president, who knew what to do next. "Come, Mrs. Douglass," he said, offering his arm. Anna took it and looked at Frederick and Ottilie, enjoying her social triumph.

In the dining room, the guests talked about the future Garfield administration and Hayes's plans for his post-presidential life. Anna added almost nothing to the conversation. At one point, President Hayes encouraged her participation and she replied, "I'm doin' just fine, sir. You folks just keep on talkin'. I'm learnin' by listenin'. Listenin' is a good part of learnin'."

"Everybody needs to listen more and talk less," said Hayes, before returning to the conversation.

Later, the president, his son, and the treasury secretary rode off in their carriage, and Anna waited until Ottilie and Rosetta and Louisa had gone inside. She then said to Frederick, "I'm Cedar Hill."

119.

AFTER GARFIELD WON THE election, Frederick informed him that there was "an earnest effort" to prevent his reappointment as U.S. marshal. "In respect to this movement, I want to say whatever may be the ostensible reasons given for it, the real ground of opposition to me is that I am a colored man, and that my sympathies are with my recently enslaved people."

President-elect Garfield didn't reply, but as U.S. marshal, Frederick attended the Garfield inauguration on March 4, 1881.

It was a high point of his life.

Frederick gathered in the U.S. Senate chamber with President Hayes, President-elect Garfield, Chief Justice Morrison Waite, Vice President William Wheeler, and Vice President–elect Chester Arthur, a host of congressmen, and other dignitaries. He met Garfield for the first time, exchanging pleasantries and nothing more. A tall, handsome, amiable man, Garfield was dignified and poised. He looked around and whispered, "I can't believe this!"

It was time to march to the East Portico of the Capitol through the rotunda. As tradition required, President Hayes and President-elect Garfield stood side by side, with the U.S. marshal before them. Silence fell in the room, and the procession proceeded quietly out of the room and down the hall. As he walked, Frederick was struck by the enormity of the moment, for himself and for all people of color. Here he was, the highest-ranking Black man in the federal government walking before the president of the United States and his successor. In a moment, they would appear before a multitude, as a symbol of racial integration.

Frederick heard the fanfare and introductions for the dignitaries and officials. He was moved by the moment. He was an equal, at least for this occasion, with all involved in the peaceful transfer of power. Tears almost came to his eyes. James Garfield was introduced, and the responding roar was loud and prolonged. The marine band played. Cheers and applause resounded through the cool but sunny day before thousands of excited people.

While he waited to hear from President Garfield about his appointment, Frederick carefully prepared the publication of *The Life and Times of Frederick Douglass*. He selected fourteen illustrations and insisted the publisher use the finest print and quality of paper. He concluded his book by observing, "Like most men who give the world their autobiographies I wish my story to be as favorably towards myself as it can be with a due regard to truth."

President Garfield invited Frederick to the Executive Mansion on April 3 to discuss "the matter of appointments." He was ushered into the Oval Office by the president's private secretary and found Garfield standing before his desk. He was smiling. His blue eyes revealed the kindness that Frederick had observed the month before. Away from the excitement and pomp of the inauguration, Frederick took in the full measure of this tall, broad-shouldered, barrel-chested man with a short beard, a former soldier born in extreme poverty, having no shoes in the Ohio snow until he was four, and now celebrated by Horatio Alger.

"Thank you for coming," Garfield said, extending his hand for a handshake. "I have received your letter of application, and others have written on your behalf, including a letter from Mark Twain."

Garfield opened the letter from Twain, asking Frederick to take one of the two seats before the desk. The president sat in the other, and in an even and firm voice read the letter: "A simple citizen may express a desire with all propriety, in the matter of recommendation to office, and so I beg permission to hope that you will retain Mr. Douglass in his present office of Marshal of the District of Columbia, if such a course will not clash with your preferences or with the expediencies and interest of your administration. I offer this petition with peculiar pleasure and strong desire because I so honor this man's high and blemishless character, and so admire his brave, long crusade for the liberties and elevation of his race. He is a personal friend of mine, but that is nothing to the point; his history would move me to say these things without that, and I feel them, too."

Frederick had no idea that Mark Twain held him in such high esteem or considered him a friend. They had met casually at gatherings of the Literary Society and at the office of James Redpath, their mutual publicist and booking agent. When done with his reading, the president looked up and smiled, his eyes vibrant with delight. "What an honor to receive such accolades from such a distinguished American, Mr. Douglass. Congratulations! Have you read *Tom Sawyer*?"

"No, sir. Not yet."

"A splendid book. My childhood is there. One of our great writers, whose opinions matter."

Garfield paused and his smile disappeared. He added softly, "But . . ."

"But?"

"Yes, as Mr. Twain has indicated, federal appointments must reflect my own preferences, despite your distinguished service to the nation and your support during the election."

"I see."

"I wish to appoint a close friend to the office of marshal."

"Sir, I withdraw my application immediately."

"As you should, sir, but I intend for you to serve in my administration in another capacity. You have my assurance, and you will soon receive notice of my nomination, which will require Senate confirmation, for recorder of deeds in the District, a new position we have created just for you. You will be the first."

"Thank you, sir," Frederick replied, not knowing the nature and scope of the new job and not sure if he had successfully masked his disappointment.

"You will be the county clerk for the entire district, the head of a department that manages the documentation of mortgages and liens and supervises the research of interested parties. You'll have no ceremonial or public obligations."

Frederick repeated, "Thank you, sir."

"And thank you, sir, for your service. You will be hearing from me soon. Thank you for coming."

"Thank you, Mr. President."

Garfield rang a bell, and the secretary came into the room. "Mr. Douglass and I have finished our discussion. See him out, please."

Frederick bowed his head respectfully and said, "Mr. President." He was befuddled because Senator Conkling had told him that the meeting with the president would be a mere formality. Frederick thought his re-appointment as marshal was certain. The Senate confirmed Frederick as recorder of deeds on May 3.

Frederick was glad that the job would have little contact with the political machine in Congress. As the president indicated, there were no social responsibilities. But thanks to Garfield, Frederick still had national recognition and could continue telling the truth in his autobiography, at least the truths about southern history now being made into romantic, nostalgic lies.

He was not happy with the look of *Life and Times* finally published in early April 1881. The paper quality was cheap, and the eighteen illustrations, thirteen of himself, dim and unfocused. Reviews were tepid, and sales slow. Critics said the last part of the book, the post–Civil War chapters, lacked adventure and drama. The tone of the narrative was elegiac and self-congratulatory, like a farewell to a successful and honored life. In its pages, history mattered more than the future, and the absence of struggle made for boring reading. Frederick was defensive about his book, this child of sleepless nights and hours of labor, and he imagined blistering challenges to his critics in newspapers and journals.

But when he allowed himself a cold eye, he could see what *Life and Times* had revealed: he had become self-satisfied, almost smug, ambitious, and unwilling to criticize publicly his benefactors. One man in a private letter told him, "You're just a black bird in a gilded cage singing the white man's song." As he was writing *Life and Times*, he noted a feeling of regret, a sense that his antislavery work was the best part of his life. He had to ask himself, *Now what*?

He could leave the government now that he had been demoted or he could stay earning money to support his family and, hopefully, change from within a system defined by compromise, corruption, cynicism, and patronage. Once confirmed in his new post, Frederick indulged in nepotism by hiring Charles, Lewis, and Frederick, Jr., as clerks and Rosetta as one of the secretaries for the recorder of deeds office. He also hired Helen Pitts, who had recently returned from Indiana.

Frederick Douglass, the agitator, had become Frederick Douglass, the accommodator.

120.

FREDERICK KNEW HE HAD become an accommodator—and he regretted it.

He sensed he could rediscover his better self by returning again to the days of his youth on the Eastern Shore. This time he would go to the Lloyd Plantation, where his life was forever changed. Frederick was eager to see what it had become since 1826. But more importantly, he wanted to face the descendants of Colonel Lloyd as a lesson in historical irony. He was canny enough to know that this trip was another performance. He was going there to show the Lloyds what he had become. Frederick didn't have an invitation, but the collector of the Port of Baltimore had encouraged him to see the Lloyd Plantation during a previous conversation.

On Tuesday morning, June 12, the *Guthrie* cast off from Baltimore at nine o'clock. Frederick was accompanied by the port collector and a descendent of another distinguished Talbot County family. They turned east from the bay toward the Miles River. Above the trees Frederick saw most of the eight high, brick chimneys of the mansion. He remembered that moment when as a boy he saw them for the last time before going off to Baltimore. He was staring when the collector approached him from behind and hesitated before speaking, respecting his private moment. "It's still beautiful, that. Generations of Lloyds have made sure of this. Edward VII has managed things well."

"Edward VII, like a king," said Frederick, amused.

"I'll send a note up to Colonel Lloyd and tell him that we are here to see him and his beautiful home, and I will express the hope that he will receive us, you in particular. I will underline your name," said the port collector.

A messenger hurried up the hill and returned with a handsome young man and a boy about eight or nine years of age. They boarded, and the young man introduced himself as Howard Lloyd, the son of the current Colonel Lloyd. He had the blue eyes of the old colonel. The boy was his brother, DeCourcy. Howard expressed his father's regrets. "Unfortunately, the colonel was called away to Easton on business. I hope he will return before you must leave, but in the meantime, we will be most happy to receive and show you around. My brother will lead the way. He is always excited when we get visitors. We don't get enough, he tells me. We are too far from everything."

Frederick bent down to the boy and asked him, "Have you been to Baltimore?"

The boy's face brightened with the memory. "Oh, yes. It's wonderful. I can't wait to see it again. Have you?"

"Now, now, Dee, that's enough," his brother interjected. "Let's just show them home."

Howard spoke with a dignified gentleness that reminded Frederick of Howard's great-grandfather when he was not provoked by anger. The correlation of familial biology and history moved him.

"What do you want to see first, Mr. Douglass?" asked Howard.

"It was called the Long Quarter, where people worked. Where the *enslaved* worked."

Howard didn't react to the word change, saying only, "There are buildings that are still here from when you were here: the stable, the store house, the shoemaker shop, the blacksmith shop, the barn. But there are not as many people here now as then. Machines and ten men do what was done by seventy."

They continued walking. Frederick stopped when he saw Aaron Anthony's house was still standing, and behind it the kitchen where Aunt Katy tormented him. He found the window where he used to sing for Lucretia Auld and she would drop bread to him now and then. "May I go inside the kitchen house?"

"Yes, of course," Howard said.

Frederick looked for the small closet where he slept, but it was gone, as the wall had been torn down to expand the main room. The dirt floor had been replaced by wood planks. The fireplace had not changed, its stones blackened by the smoke of recent use.

The stable and the barn were battered but still standing, but the store house and the carriage house were gone. The Lombardy poplars were gone too, but the elms and the oaks, where he would sit with Daniel Lloyd and divide cake and biscuits and talk for hours, stood as tall and grand as he remembered them. "We trapped rabbits here, me and Daniel, the colonel's youngest son," Frederick said.

Frederick then asked, "May I see the family burial ground?"

"Certainly," replied Howard.

"Is Daniel gone?"

"Yes. All the Lloyds are buried here." Howard told DeCourcy, "Run back to the house and tell Miss Olivia to get things ready for us. We'll need refreshment."

"Miss Olivia?" exclaimed Frederick, taken aback. The woman he encountered in the kitchen at Wye House was named Olivia. Daniel adored her.

"Yes, Olivia," said Howard. "That's not her real name, but this family has this tradition, that the women in charge of the kitchen be called Miss Olivia or Miss Livy, like when my great-grandfather had her. That is a vestige of the past that has to stop. When I inherit this place, people should be called by the name they want to be called by, or by the name they were given by their parents. Rules can change. We make them, we change them."

In the family burial grounds, Howard took Frederick to the oldest headstone, dated 1684. As he contemplated that headstone and the long history of enslavement it symbolized, Howard gathered flowers and evergreens. *We made this possible*. Frederick's insight came from the deep fissures of his own body, the culmination of a lifetime of reflection. *My people made all this possible. We built Wye. We sustained the Lloyds' wealth through the toil of mechanics, artisans, gardeners. Through our blood, our muscle, our grief, the Lloyd Plantation was born and survived. There should be no shame in being here, or shame in saying we came from here. This place made us, and we made it. This land is ours, too.*

"Sir, take this back to your home, to Cedar Hill," said Howard, startling Frederick, who turned around to face him.

"You know about Cedar Hill?" he asked.

"Of course, sir. You're the most famous man from Maryland, or at the very least, the most famous from the Eastern Shore."

"Thank you, sir, for the flowers. I will dry them to keep as a memory of this most memorable day."

"Now, let's relax on the veranda before we have some Madeira in the dining room and tour the rest of the house."

Frederick and the others were given chairs that gave them views of the gardens and the broad walks hedged by boxes of flowers and fruit trees. "This is beautiful," whispered Frederick, taking in the moment. Here he was, a former slave, who once hid behind bushes to overhear Colonel Lloyd and his neighbors talk, sitting on this same veranda as a distinguished guest. He felt the hot prickling of guilt, for he had been seduced by the beauty before him, made to forget the agonies and terrors of this place. He saw himself in the crowd watching Bill Wilkes taken away after Colonel Lloyd's family demanded his sale and hearing the lament of Bill's mother and the slaves witnessing his departure. *Should beauty, or can beauty, be denied in such a place? Should such beauty be destroyed to remove any reminder of the cruelties of the past?*

"Come," Howard said. He rose from his chair and led the way into the house and the large dining room adorned with elegant, antique furniture, a mahogany sideboard, cut-glass chandeliers, and the finest decanters, tumblers, and wineglasses. The wine was excellent, and, though not a drinker, Frederick spontaneously offered a toast, "May the children and descendants of this great family maintain the fame and characteristics of their ancestors."

"Most of them," said Howard, a twinkle in his eye as he raised his goblet. "But no more Miss Olivias." He then escorted them to the library, the music room, a sitting room, and the large parlor used for receptions and parties. The Lloyds had maintained Wye House well. The grand staircase was still grand, the sheen of the polished wood sparkling in the filtered light. Flowers filled vases throughout the rooms, and the portraits by Robert Peel and other early American artists still looked down upon them, including all the Edward Lloyds.

It was time to go and see Ann Catherine Lloyd. One of two surviving daughters of Colonel Lloyd. She was eighteen when Frederick came to Wye. Now she was Mrs. Franklin Buchanan, the widow of a Confederate general buried at Wye House. After shaking hands, Frederick departed through the front door that faced the sweeping lawn and returned to the wharf. Waiting for him was a delighted group of Black men and women, most of them young. There were a few excited elderly men and women who said that they remembered him as a child.

He didn't challenge their recollection, but he did ask about Uncle Cooper, who taught all the children the Lord's Prayer with a hickory stick. Cooper was gone now, but they remembered him or remembered the stories passed down. Frederick didn't ask about their current work conditions but thanked them for seeing him. He boarded the *Guthrie* for the trip up the Miles River to the estate called The Rest. The vessel moved slowly, and Frederick watched the waving hands on the wharf and became reflective again.

He imagined future visitors to the Lloyd Plantation and guides who would honor the contributions of the enslaved workers. Their names would be listed on walls with the work they did, gleaned from the records Thomas Auld said existed. Their graves, now in segregated plots that could not be moved, would become hallowed ground, a silent tribute to the Black builders of Maryland, watered with their tears, enriched with their blood, tilled with their calloused hands.

His Talbot homecoming continued. Like her great nephew, Mrs. Buchanan was the epitome of Lloyd graciousness and hospitality. She had only vague memories of Frederick, telling him she was a young woman too preoccupied by the next ball and the search for a future husband to see slaves, especially little boys. She had ignored her brother Daniel, too.

Mrs. Buchanan invited Frederick to sit beside her, and they talked for about an hour, recounting their lives, avoiding unpleasantries but speaking as equals. Again, Frederick was taken by the moment, another example of historical significance in both of their lives. She was eager for him to meet her six grandchildren, who were lined up as if to meet royalty. One young blond girl, who was quite pretty, came forward with a bouquet of various flowers, a profusion that suggested haste and abundance. The girl curtsied and presented the bouquet, her smile radiant as she looked down.

"Thank you so much, young lady. I will not forget your gift," Frederick said. And he did not forget, saying later that her gift and his acceptance of it marked the dawning of a new era of justice, kindness, and human brotherhood. He offered hope to a new generation with a fresh ability to see equality beyond color as exemplified by those children who saw their grandmother and him conversing as equals that fine day on the Eastern Shore of Maryland. If this could happen, anything was possible. This was his religion without the intervention of an Almighty.

121.

HOPE STAYED ALIVE WHEN the president invited Frederick in June 1881 to the Executive Mansion for a discussion regarding future appointments of Black Americans. The president leaned forward. "I think it is time when more steps should be taken to recognize the achievements of colored people. I intend to do this by sending colored ambassadors abroad to other than colored nations, to nations in Europe, especially. Sir, how do you think such representation shall be received?"

Frederick replied, "Sir, in this country, your nominations will be challenged, for they are an affront to the assumption of Negro inferiority. Even so, I remain convinced that respect will not come to us as long as we are systematically ignored by the government and denied participation in its honors and salaried positions. The more of us that can be seen as important and, yes, even powerful, the more others will accept us in the natural order of things."

The president smiled. "I most heartedly agree, and you would honor the nation greatly if you represented us abroad. We are a land of many people, not just white people, and you would make that statement loud and clear. So, what do you think?"

Frederick was speechless. An ambassadorship would be the culmination of a lifetime of struggle, the validation of all he had labored to achieve. This appointment would be proof that he, and all Blacks, were equal to whites. He didn't think the current Senate, a reactionary bastion of mendacity and evasion, would confirm the president's appointment, but the mere nomination would send a clarion message to the nation and the world. A new day was at hand. "I am honored, sir," he said.

"I know, sir, that would mean moving to another country, leaving some of your family behind, and resigning your post as recorder of deeds."

"Thank you, again, sir, but I must decline this opportunity. I need to remain at home. My wife is not doing well." Anna's illnesses were becoming more protracted, already making his trips away from Washington less frequent. He also wanted to spend more time enjoying his grandchildren, many of whom lived or stayed at Cedar Hill for long periods of time.

"Oh, I understand, sir. My wife and children mean the world to me. It would be very difficult to part from them," the president said.

"I have the chance to work with my children at the Deeds Office and . . ." As soon as Frederick revealed this fact, he regretted it. More and more private citizens, public figures, and newspapers were denouncing the patronage system and calling for reforms that would reward merit over personal connections. Garfield had not yet come out in support of these reforms.

"Well, sir, enjoy this moment as long as you can, because some feel the victor should have none of the spoils," Garfield sighed. "In a civil-service system, I will certainly have fewer friends and family members pressing me. I never realized I had so many friends needing jobs. I believe that the current system damages the reputation of the presidency. It certainly is a distraction."

"Thank you for the position you offered me already, sir. I will do my best with it as I continue to live here and not go abroad," Frederick said.

"You are declining my offer, then?"

"Yes, sir. I mean no disrespect."

"None taken. I just wanted to make sure. Would you be willing to submit some other names for my consideration?"

"Yes, sir. May I have a few days to reflect on this matter and submit those names then?"

"Yes, and one day, not too far in the distant future, a president will be asking for names of men and women, as it should be the case. The female vote is long overdue. I know you agree with me, yes?"

"I have never been able to find one argument or suggestion in favor of man's right to participate in civil government that does not equally apply to women," Frederick said.

"The vote for women may come in the next century. That's not too far off, only nineteen years. So much can happen in nineteen years. Look what has happened since the war ended." Garfield became somber. "You know, Mr. Douglass, I didn't want or seek this job. And now that I have this burden, sir, I will make the most of it. I have plans, so don't forget those names." The president stood, marking the end of the interview.

"Thank you for your consideration, sir. I will provide those names as quickly as possible," Frederick said.

"Take your time contemplating this weighty matter. The Senate is not in session anyway. And we will need to prepare for the outcry when colored names go before southern Democrats. Fortunately, I have the support of the majority. Good day, Mr. Douglass."

Less than three weeks later, the president was shot in the back in a train station by a man who blamed Garfield for his not receiving a position in the federal government.

★

Frederick was home in the library when he heard the loud pounding of the door. "Frederick, Frederick," his neighbor Hiram Pitts yelled. "The president's been shot!"

Frederick hurried to the door and found a stricken Pitts, his face as bloodless as marble. "What happened? Is he dead?"

"No, he's still alive, with doctors, ten of them." Pitts had stayed in town to get as much information as possible before he returned to Anacostia.

The president was at the crowded Baltimore and Potomac railroad station waiting for the train to join his wife in Ohio. Unguarded, he was in the waiting room, when Charles Guiteau, a job applicant, shot him twice, first in the arm, and then in the back. "My God, Frederick, the man had a letter in his pocket addressed to General Sherman. It said he had just shot the president, and his death was a political necessity. My God, the man planned it. How could this happen? How could anyone want to hurt so good a man?"

"Where is he now?"

"They took him back to the mansion. People are saying he might not last the night. He fell to the floor and vomited. There was so much blood. He didn't talk but was calm, I heard. Just like him, always calm." Pitts erupted, "They should have shot that man on the spot!"

"Maybe it would be best that we go back to town and get as much information as we can. Knowing as much as we can, we'll feel better. There will be reports coming out of the White House. Let's see what we can learn," Frederick said.

Pitts had heard that the president wanted to stay at the White House. "We are so fortunate to live across the river, away from this swamp. They need to get him away," he said.

"His wounds may be too severe for him to be moved. We'll just have to wait. Thank you for coming and telling me," Frederick said.

Garfield survived the night, and the next night, and the next night. By the end of the following week, there was growing belief that the president would recover fully. Life returned to some semblance of normality. No longer distracted by the horror of attempted assassination, the press resumed its war against the patronage system.

Frederick was attacked in Black newspapers for hiring his sons and daughter at the recorder of deeds office. The *New South* called him "the veteran place hunter, the indefatigable and obsequious Fred. Douglass." The *People's Advocate* came to his defense: "Frederick Douglass is our most illustrious American Negro. He stands pre-eminently our foremost man, towering over all others, his character as fixed as the Alleghenies or the Rocky Mountains. Of better educated men we have scores. Of men more cultured there may have been, but there can be but ONE Frederick Douglass."

At the same time, the nation received news about the president's condition. His doctor allowed almost no visitors, but Doctor D. Willard Bliss issued medical bulletins to be posted at telegraph offices and on billboards outside newspaper buildings. The president was suffering, and that suffering united the nation in the anguish of waiting and hope for his recovery.

President Garfield insisted that he be moved out of the White House, having been offered a summer home by a wealthy New Yorker. To get a railroad car there two thousand men had to lay new track, but the engine was not powerful enough to breach the hill. Hundreds of men rolled the three coaches up the hill. This news report brought tears to Frederick's eyes. Did the mere title of president earn such devotion? He doubted it. Here was a man who had endured unbelievable agonies and made it clear in brief announcements that he needed to survive so he could serve his country. Even southern Democrats and former Confederates were rooting for his recovery.

122.

LUDMILLA DIED, AND SHE had left Ottilie completely out of her will. Through letters and telegrams, Ottilie had spent a year trying to settle her dispute over her sister Ludmilla's will, but she realized she would have to go to Italy if she had any chance of success. She was scheduled to embark for Hamburg on August 12, when Frederick arrived in Hoboken on August 8.

Frederick's decision to visit Ottilie before her departure was an act of sympathy. They would revisit familiar sights in and around New York. They would see old friends. Ottilie would leave the country with good memories of their time together. *What harm was there in patronizing her?* He could have stayed away or arrived just before her ship's departure. She deserved more, he decided. Their friendship of twenty-five years deserved decency and kindness. He hadn't come to dislike her, but he was afraid that if they continued to spend time together, he would.

Ottilie continued to hope that Frederick would join her in Europe. Frederick saw no reason to crush this hope and said, "A grand tour of Europe has always been a dream of mine. It will happen one day." They talked about politics and about Ottilie's claims to Ludmilla's estate. But they no longer shared intimacies. At the end, they sat together on a bench when the ship whistle blew warning visitors they had only one hour until departure. The time had come to say goodbye. Frederick wondered, what should be said in that last hour?

Ottilie answered for him, speaking with an unaccustomed serenity: "It's almost time, and I need to say this before you go. I'm asking you to not interrupt, and if you have questions or need to comment, leave it for your letters, as I manage to always provoke objections and more questions. But today will be my chance to speak from my heart.

"Frederick, you are the love of my life, and I have no regret in holding that love in my heart for twenty-five years. I fancied that ours was the perfect love and hoped that one day, after you witnessed my devotion, you would realize it, too. I am a romantic, after all, German at my core, believing that an ideal can and would sweep all before it, removing impediments like an overwhelming flood. But Anna's love for you, and your love for your family, was stronger than my feelings, our feelings, and I had to settle for summers with you and visits to Hoboken now and then. These accommodations made me resentful and angry, and I lashed out in ways that make me ashamed, and for those lapses I am truly sorry. I know now that demanding you choose me over the rest of your family was unacceptable to you, and eventually changed our friendship.

"I should have learned from Anna. She was willing to share you and did for twenty-five years. Some will object to her decision, but she didn't want to risk losing what mattered most to both of you, a family, a family of imperfect children and wonderful grandchildren with a husband who provided a life that otherwise was not possible. Now I am the one who is alone with no family at all, no children, no sister, my parents long gone. But today I don't want pity. I have indulged in that far too often, and I suspect I will lapse into it again, when loneliness strikes me again on the open sea, or when I face hostile lawyers in Italy. But today I need to acknowledge my gratitude. You didn't reject me years ago when you could have. I was indeed presumptuous and arrogant and critical and dismissive and willfully blind. Now I see.

"My life was and is enriched by you, and Anna, allowing me to be a part of it. I betrayed her by coming to you, breaking vows you both made. I justified it to myself. I justify it still, but in this world, changing so fast with breathtaking speed, I can now accept imperfect love, as I can accept an imperfect man who still manages to stir my heart. Like my favorite romantics, I believed in the clarity of love. Now I know better: it will forever be confusing, contradictory, messy. As I leave you today, I accept this reality, knowing full well that I will continue to bewilder and challenge you and myself. But never doubt this: in my own fashion, I loved you, and will love you always."

Frederick listened intently, hearing a raw vulnerability from Ottilie that made him uncomfortable, but he waited until he was certain that she was done. "Ottilie, I . . ."

"Please, Frederick, no questions, nothing, please. No more." Tears were in her eyes. Ottilie stood. "Goodbye, Frederick."

"Don't you want me to wait until the last call?"

"No. Knowing me, I could spoil what I have now if we continue."

Ottilie embraced him, her head on his chest. She whispered, "Goodbye, my love." Then she turned and hurried away.

Frederick whispered, "Goodbye."

★

The news Frederick feared reached Cedar Hill. On September 19, 1881, President Garfield died.

His body was returned to Washington by the same train, now draped in black, that carried him to New York. Garfield lay in state in the Capitol rotunda for two days and nights. The line for the Capitol stretched for almost half a mile, the rich and the poor, Black and white, standing side by side under a hot sun in absolute silence.

Frederick approached the open casket and gazed for only a second at the face made thin by months of pain, as there were so many waiting behind him in line. He shed a tear as he saw the serenity in that handsome face, a peace found after months of agony that seemed to unite the entire nation as it confronted unfulfilled political promises. Americans continued to learn more details about their dead president. Frederick read that Garfield had said, "If a man murders you without provocation, your soul bears no burden of the wrong; but all the angels of the universe will weep for the misguided man who committed the murder." Frederick could not weep for Garfield's assassin. When he learned that one of his jailers tried to shoot him, missing his head by inches, Frederick regretted the poor marksmanship.

He attended Charles Guiteau's trial. Half of the seats were reserved for journalists, lawyers, and distinguished guests, a group that included Frederick. The federal prosecutor urged conviction, presenting evidence of Guiteau's rage and thwarted ambition. The defense insisted that his client was insane and therefore should be acquitted. When he was not attacking his own lawyer, Guiteau proved his insanity through frequent outbursts, interruptions of witnesses, and his own rambling testimony about childhood, life at a commune, years as a traveling evangelist, and his reasons for shooting the president. Frederick described him as "demon possessed," but he agreed with the jury's verdict, "Guilty as indicted." Guiteau was sentenced to hang.

But there was no comfort in revenge. Frederick could only find consolation in memories of a decent man. He wrote to his readers, "I not only shared the general sorrow of the woe-smitten nation but lamented the loss of a great benefactor. Nothing could be sadder and more pathetic than the death of this lovable man. There is no true man in the land who does not share in the pain of the illustrious sufferer while he lingered in life, or who could refuse a tear when the final hour came when his life and suffering ended."

Ottilie's silence about Garfield's assassination disappointed him. Since her departure, they corresponded, but her letters were infrequent. She was constantly on the move, visiting art museums and galleries while fighting officials who defended Ludmilla's right to disinherit her. Delighted by ruins and museums, rolling hills and lush foliage, Ottilie remained the enthusiastic observer, filling pages with details about Florence, Rome, and Pompeii. She assured Frederick that she intended to return to America, but now she had little to say about her adopted country.

Frederick's letters were cordial and superficial, offering details about work and American politics, but he withheld information about his family and avoided personal reflection. However, he revealed his deep anguish about Garfield, repeating rumors and details about the doctors' treatment, while hoping for the best. When Garfield died, Frederick wrote a eulogy praising his character and the nation's response to his passing and sent it to Ottilie. She said not a word about the eulogy or anything else about the president, even though she had once lauded him for appointing Frederick as recorder of deeds. Now it seemed as if Garfield never mattered to her.

Frederick's alienation deepened.

Then death came to Cedar Hill.

123.

IT SEEMED THAT DEATH was marching slowly that summer, a discordant note here and there as Anna's body declined. She stayed in her room more and more, resting for hours at a time. Even when her pain made her grimace, she continued to give orders, summoning Louisa, Rosetta, or Rosetta's two oldest girls to her bedside. On weekends she called for Frederick occasionally. She apologized to him for the interruptions, saying she called him because she needed a dependable man to get the job done. As far as she was concerned, Nathan was useless.

On some days, Anna was up and about, as if the bed days had never happened. She had stopped trying to understand why the good days came. She had her tea and herbs and plenty of rest. And then, like Lazarus rising up, she felt just fine, and did as much as she could until the next attack of pain and exhaustion. "This old body's goin' to give out in due time, but I gotta do what I gotta do," she told Frederick on one of her good days.

Anna was excited about the upcoming holiday season because she had big plans. For Christmas Eve she wanted the entire family at Cedar Hill for a light dinner after church, to be followed by an evening of singing, with Rosetta playing the piano, Frederick playing his violin, and young Joseph, now showing great promise, playing the violin, too. She wanted everyone to bring gifts for the children to place under the tree. When it was time to open them, the entire family would witness their bounty. One definite rule: Rosetta, Charles, Lewis, and Junior would not give gifts to each other.

"I don't know, Anna, this sounds like too much. You have enough to do with preparing for the party, and then dinner the next night," Frederick said.

"I have help. I always have help. This is what I want. This may be my last Christmas," she replied.

"No, you're doing so much better. You'll have other Christmases. You need to keep your strength."

"I need your strength to get our boys and tell them I want nothing ugly during those days. I don't want some argument breakin' out between the boys and Nathan. For two days, everybody gets to act right. Tell them to do it for me, their sick mother."

"Anna!" Frederick said, in mock condemnation of her manipulation.

"We all act, Fred. You, me, we all act. How else do we make it do through the day? We can't do everything we want or feel, or else nothing works. That's why they're rules, commandments. We need to be actors or we become animals. So, tell them I don't want them actin' like animals on my Christmas. I'm too old for my children showin' off about being right about whatever it is they're mad about. I don't have time for this nonsense. No more time."

"We'll do whatever you want, Anna. I promise."

The family trip to the Fifteenth Street Presbyterian Church was Anna's gentle reminder that Christmas was about more than family and gifts. It was also about Jesus and being good people, as Jesus wanted. She also liked the church's young minister, Reverend Francis J. Grimke, who was from South Carolina, born in 1850 to a white planter and a biracial slave mother. Grimke was so fair he could have passed for white. When Anna first saw him, she said with delicate mockery, "Now what is so fine a man doing in a church? Is the Lord testing the reverend's female flock?"

As Anna aged, she became less prudish and more playful. Francis Grimke was indeed a very handsome man. Thankfully, he had other praiseworthy qualities. He was a religious liberal and activist promoting racial justice and equality. Many whites, including congressmen, came to church to hear his sermons. On Christmas Eve, Grimke's message was clear: the secret of the spiritual life was to keep in close touch with Jesus, who demanded good deeds.

Christmas tested the domestic peace in the Douglass household because for the first time in three years, Charles, Lewis, Frederick, Jr., and Rosetta, along with their children, were together in the same house, on the same day. Living in separate Washington homes provided almost rent free by Frederick, who had invested in Washington real estate, they rarely socialized together after work.

On Christmas Eve, they had a light meal prepared by Louisa, who asked Anna for permission to stay in the kitchen and clean up instead of joining everyone afterward. Frederick insisted that Louisa come out of the kitchen, delay the cleanup, sing carols with the family, and listen to Joseph, Frederick, and Rosetta play their instruments. Since Anna's first collapse, Louisa had become her most loyal companion. She was like a second daughter, on whom she relied for everything. Childless, Louisa was also the grandchildren's favorite aunt. Anna usually agreed to Louisa's requests, but this time Frederick prevailed.

Nathan, as always, was the greatest threat to Anna's plan. At one point, she said to Frederick, "Maybe I should just ask him to stay away." But she knew she couldn't do that. He was Rosetta's husband and the father of six of their grandchildren. He had to be present for their sake.

The holiday went as well as Anna had hoped. There was no arguing, no slighting, no bickering, no backstabbing. Everyone seemed to enjoy themselves, eating and singing and treating each other with warmth and sincere compliments. The children were delirious with joy. They were the center of all the gifts, and the bounty made them giddy with delight. No one appeared disappointed.

Toasts were offered by the men of the house, starting with Frederick, who praised Anna for making the day possible. Charles, Lewis, and Frederick, Jr., said essentially the same, lifting glasses of water, since Anna didn't want alcohol ruining her plans. Then Nathan stood with his glass. Frederick and his sons braced themselves. What was he going to say? He was not a Douglass. He was just a son-in-law.

"Thank you, Mother, for being the mother I never had. Merry Christmas," Nathan toasted.

It was clear that his tribute moved Anna most of all.

124.

FREDERICK CONTINUED WORKING IN town, but he was more reluctant to leave Cedar Hill for lectures because Anna's health was not improving. She continued to remain in bed for days, and when she could get up it was for short periods before returning to bed for more days of suffering. The grandchildren were told to play quietly or go outside during Grammy's "peaceful time." The doctors said there was nothing more they could do. When Frederick told Anna about the doctor's latest evaluation, she said, "And what have they ever done? They couldn't save Annie. They can't save me."

Months passed, a period of anxious uncertainty. On the morning of July 7, 1882, between six and seven o'clock, Anna had a stroke. Rosetta always rose early to check on her mother. Her cry was visceral, "Mama, oh Mama!" Frederick was at home in his bedroom across the hall when he heard Rosetta. He found Anna on her back, her mouth open, her body rigid. "Is she alive? Is she still alive?" he asked.

Rosetta was bent over her mother's heart. "Yes, Papa. Yes, she's still alive. Her heart's beating, but her breath is so soft, I can barely hear it."

"Send for the doctor. Hurry, but don't let the children know. Not yet."

"They're still asleep," Rosetta whispered.

"Good."

Rosetta rushed from the room. Frederick reached for Anna's hand under the cover. It was summer, but now Anna always complained about the cold weather. He fell to his knees and pressed her hand to his cheek, feeling her soft skin over the knotty, rheumatoid bones. "Oh, Anna. Don't leave us. Please don't leave us." She mumbled in response and opened her eyes. Anna looked at Frederick with a calm familiarity. She had been through this before. She squeezed his hand, comforting him.

"Oh, Anna, the doctor's coming. We will all make it better. You'll come back. Keep on talking," Frederick said. The doctor came and gave the usual prescription. Bed rest, liquids, massage of arms, legs, and feet, and talking to her, even if she isn't responding.

Respond she did. Within three days, Anna uttered her first word. Then, on the fourth day, she said three words. And by the end of the week, she spoke a sentence. That sentence opened the flood gate to orders, directions, assignments for the household. She was the commander of Cedar Hill again. Rosetta and Louisa, who had shed many tears, fearing the worst, cheerfully accepted Anna's orders. "Yes, Mama" was the constant refrain, an affirmation of Anna's survival and endurance. "Mama's back," said Rosetta.

One afternoon, Anna summoned Frederick to her bedside. He lightly tapped on her door and entered the room, where she sat up on pillows, both hands resting on top of the blanket. "Pull up a chair, Frederick. I have some things to say. Well, the Lord's given me some extra time, I guess, Frederick, and so I better make the best of what time I got to give you a piece of my mind. To tell you some things I should have said long ago, and may not be able to say again and . . ."

Frederick protested gently, "Anna, you need to keep your strength, and talking will sap—"

"No, you can't keep me quiet, so don't try. This is my time, so just sit still and listen."

"Yes, Anna."

"Now, now, don't you fret about me goin'. I want to live longer. Don't we all? And the good Lord might surprise me and all of you and give me many more years, but that's not up to me, and I don't want to take His time for granted. This stroke business happened before, and now it's happened again. I think I'm being told, now don't miss yo' chance' 'cause there might not be a third time. Fred, life has been good to me when I think about it. My life is so much better than I ever thought. Me, big, Black, and ugly. "

"Don't say that, Anna."

"Me! Of all them ladies in Baltimore, you picked me! No, that's not right. I picked you, yes, 'cause nobody else would have you. What fools! I wish I could see them now. See what I attached myself to. I wasn't sure what was going to happen, but it was goin' to be *something*, that's for sure. I never doubted for a moment the decision I made, to help you escape, marry you, and stay with you all these years. Not once, not even when you brought other people in our house. I could not be them. I didn't want to be them. But I knew they gave you what I couldn't. You wanted me to read, but I never learned. I said I was too busy, but that's not true. I didn't want to be a part of your world. I wanted to stay in my part, my special part, as your wife, and as the mother of your children, and be special like nobody else could be. I didn't want to be one of your friends. Now, mind you, I wanted our children to learn, get a good education. But you know education ain't everything. Lots of people have education and are mean and stupid, can't do nothing but take, take, take. Not me. I wanted a family, and I got one, and I worked hard to keep it going. And look at us now. I succeeded. We succeeded. I kept this family together when everything, war, disease, people dyin', people tryin' to take you from me, didn't succeed. You wanted a family. I wanted a family that didn't leave us, hurt us. Now, there has been some bumps, some disappointments. But love, there was no doubt in me, or in you. Our children love us, Frederick, they love us. How many people can say that as a sure thing?" Anna shifted her weight in the bed and reached for a glass of water. She moved slowly but didn't falter, as if she needed to prove she wasn't as weak as many feared.

She continued: "It's because I love you so, Frederick Bailey, that I let you go. I let you be with them others 'cause they gave you things I couldn't give, or didn't want to give. I'm not saying it didn't hurt, what I decided. But look at what happened? They're gone, and I'm still here. I waited, not so you could love me as you loved them. I waited 'cause I knew I was your rock, your steady hand. You *needed* me. You needed me after all the others let you go or were forced to leave you. I was goin' to never let you go, never leave you, no matter what. I am proud of my stubbornness. Maybe it's pride. Maybe it's meanness, too. But you like us strong, all the women 'round you. Maybe you want us all to be like Betsey. And thank goodness for her, 'cause you don't like weak women, and I don't like them, either. We have too much to do in the world, especially keepin' you men from completely makin' a mess of things. It's bad enough when you're not grateful and don't respect us and think we know nothing, and some of you—not you—want to always keep us down. We work our way, and some of you are so afraid of us. Why? 'Cause they know we know how to run things. You men couldn't do half of what we have to do. Have babies, raise em', teach em', cook, clean, everything. Well, you'll need someone after I'm gone. Yes, you'll need someone, and you should marry again, if someone will have you."

Anna chuckled, enjoying her joke. "I'm sure there are many out there who will want you, but you need someone who wants you but don't need you. Please, Frederick, get married again. You need a wife, a good wife. I was a good wife. Oh, Fred, I want you to be happy. I'm not going to ask you to remember me, 'cause I know you will not forget me. I was a part of your life for a long, long time. It's been a good, long time to be Mrs. Frederick Douglass. So, I'm going to stop now. I will miss seein' all my grandchildren growin' up. But we're not promised everything, but I am going into glory with love in my heart, hearing in my heart, 'Good job, Anna Murray Douglass, good job.' Isn't that what we all should have in the end? Knowing we tried our best? You can say somethin' now."

"I don't know what to say," Frederick said.

"Now that's a first." Her laughter was delicate, and she reached for Frederick's hand. "I love you, Frederick. And I hope you realize your good fortune that so many do."

He looked at their clasped hands and said, "I do, Anna, I do, and I love you, too."

"I know you do, in your own way. And one more thing." She closed her eyes for a moment, stirring a second of panic.

"Anna? What is it?"

"Yes, one more thing. Don't let them white folks, some of them Black folks, too, keep you from sayin' what you need to say. You do go on, I hear, but keep on talkin'. They need to hear what you has to say. Say it, Frederick, keep on saying it. Promise me."

"I promise."

"Good. I'm going to miss you . . ."

"Anna . . ."

"Just look at you. You are still so fine, so big, so strong, so smart. You are my star."

"You're too kind, too generous. I've not been my best."

"Hush, now. You are not goin' to have the last word, not today. Just be quiet. Let's sit. Let's just hold hands. Let's just be."

He squeezed her hand, agreeing to her terms, at last.

On July 25, Anna Murray Douglass lapsed into unconsciousness and remained unresponsive until she died on the morning of August 2, 1882. She was sixty-eight years old.

Frederick pulled his daughter close and sighed, "Ah! Rosa. If she could have only lived a few years longer."

"We'll take care of everything, Papa. Louisa and me," Rosetta replied. They prepared Anna's body for burial, washing it and setting Anna's hair for the viewing in the parlor before final internment. They sent notes and telegrams to other family members, friends, and the press. Frederick wanted a floral arrangement that spelled out "Mother," and Rosetta quickly found a florist in town who could deliver it for the funeral in the west parlor.

Rosetta made sure all her children were scrubbed and well-dressed on the day of Anna's funeral. The three youngest, Estelle, Fredericka, and Herbert, arrived from the Washington, D.C., house still owned by Frederick, and found their grandfather alone down the hill weeping. Stunned by the sight, they started to weep, too. "Mother's dead," Frederick moaned. "Your grandma has gone away, and you have no grandma now. Please remember her." He then regretted his emotional display, as he didn't mean to upset them. He stood, wiping his tears. "It's time. We need to get back to the house."

Herbert cried, "There are so many up there! I can't believe so many came today."

Almost three thousand people, Black and white, came to pay their respects. The invited guests waited in the east parlor. There were senators and congressmen, including Senator Bruce, who was one of the pallbearers. The others gathered outside the house.

The eulogy was given by Bishop T. M. D. Ward, who spoke more about Frederick and his career, honoring him far more than he honored Anna, about whom he knew little. Ward invoked a host of luminaries, Benjamin Lundy, Elijah Lovejoy, Nat Turner, Denmark Vesey, William Lloyd Garrison, John Brown, Gerrit Smith, Charles Sumner, and presidents Lincoln and Garfield, unintentionally reducing Anna to a footnote, the companion of her "illustrious husband in his glorious career."

Rosetta was peeved. "This is her funeral, Papa, not yours. She will not be forgotten if I have anything to say about it. Before she lost consciousness, I went to see her and asked about her life, where she came from. I thought it was time I knew. I'll give it to the children, if I ever find the time to write it all down. We can't forget her, Papa. But she knew she would only be remembered because of you. She accepted that. She was proud of that, being Mrs. Frederick Douglass."

"I know, Rosetta, I know," said Frederick.

"It's time to go, Papa. We need to take Mama to the cemetery."

Hundreds of carriages and hundreds more on foot followed the mahogany casket. The family still had a plot of land at Mount Hope Cemetery in Rochester, where Annie and Alice were buried, but the family decided to keep Anna's remains at Graceland Cemetery in Washington, where they all lived near each other, as she had always wanted.

125.

A WEEK AFTER THE burial, Frederick, Rosetta, and Annie, his oldest grandchild, boarded the train for Rochester. Frederick had returned to Rochester since the house fire, but only for occasional lectures. Rochester had grown, but South Avenue was still in the countryside. South Avenue, more than Cedar Hill, would always be Anna's home, where she raised five children, hosted guests, and sheltered runaways. South Avenue was Anna's legacy. Silently, they stood looking at the land, Frederick, Rosetta, and Hattie side by side, the Posts behind them, everyone deep in their own private thoughts. Frederick said to Amy and Isaac. "Thank you for bringing us. Anna loved Rochester and never wanted to leave. 'No,' she said, 'this is home over Jordan. Here, not even Maryland, here.'" His voice cracked, and Rosetta took his hand as they walked back to the carriage.

Frederick, Rosetta, and Hattie returned to Washington, where mountains of condolence replies had to be written, bills had to be paid, and visitors had to be received. Frederick heard from almost everyone he knew, except Ottilie.

Anna's death; the indifference of President Chester Arthur; and the Republican Party's abandonment of any vestige of idealism and its full embrace of the gold standard, monopolies, Chinese exclusion, and xenophobia, combined with the celebration of Rockefeller, Carnegie, Frick, and Vanderbilt as true American heroes, stirred the return of Frederick's fog for the first time in years. But this latest fog was different. Frederick had returned from Rochester and stayed in bed for days. Each morning, Rosetta knocked on his door with food, but she couldn't enter because it was locked. He told her to leave the food on a tray outside and he would retrieve it when he was ready to eat. But it didn't matter. Food repulsed him. He ate only to keep himself alive, the strange paradox of depression that he had to live to feel almost dead.

Frederick's greatest fear was self-knowledge, the screaming reproach of guilt from a demon waiting for release the moment he lowered his guard. His only protection now was the fog and inaction. One step would stir the demon within, so he had to lie still, hoping his brain was too dull to proclaim that he was a terrible human being who had mistreated his wife for decades. Anna forgave him, but he could not forgive himself, the fog's most ruthless judge, the judge who could strip away every shred of evasion, rationalization, and obfuscation to expose every lie and excuse in the hypocrite's arsenal. He was stripped naked and heard the voices of everyone he betrayed or abandoned, from Henry and Gus to Garrison, Ottilie, and Anna. *Traitor! You are nothing but a sack of shit!*

He knew these feelings would pass, but within the maelstrom of illness it seemed interminable with no relief. He bargained with the storm, arguing, *If I can survive this minute, I can live to see the next minute.*

Frederick liked to believe this process was a rational one, that his mental faculties were in control, but he knew this was another lie he told himself to reduce his pain. He prayed for endless, painless sleep. He was not strong enough to kill himself; falling asleep and never waking up was the best alternative. Then on another ordinary morning, Frederick's depression was gone, and he wanted to eat a big meal, take a long walk, read a book.

Frederick was alive again and called out, "Rosetta! Rosetta!"

Rosetta pounded against the locked door. "Papa, Papa, are you alright? Let me in!"

He rushed to cover his nakedness with a light robe. Before, he had not been able to tolerate anything on his skin, he burned so much. Now the robe felt luxurious, comforting. "I'm coming, Rosetta." He opened the door and hugged her. "Rosetta, I'm ready for some scrambled eggs with bacon and biscuits. Tell Louisa I remember her good cooking."

Frederick couldn't say he was happy. He was sure that nothing in the world had changed, but he had vitality, and that was enough. "How long have I been this way? Is Mr. Arthur still president?"

"Papa, it's only been three weeks. And, yes, Mr. Arthur is still president," Rosetta said.

"Do I have any invitations to speak?"

"Of course, Papa, piles of them. You have your pick."

"Good."

The most exciting invitation was from Senator Bruce, who was organizing a banquet on January 1, 1883, to commemorate the twentieth anniversary of the Emancipation Proclamation. "We intend to honor you and your service to freedom, sir. This is a fitting day to that end," wrote Bruce. Frederick had to wait four months, but when the evening finally came, the months seemed to have passed as quickly as the flash of a falling star. The long banquet table was covered with flowers and candles, and on the far side of the table on the wall hung a huge American flag. Only Black men were invited, and the guests were prominent men in their fields, doctors, teachers, ministers, writers, civil servants, scholars, soldiers, and politicians.

Forty-one toasts were offered for a variety of causes and to a variety of people. After dinner, Senator Bruce introduced Frederick, "I now, gentlemen, have the honor to present to you Frederick Douglass, the distinguished guest of the occasion, whose fame as an orator and as an earnest and effective worker in the cause of liberty is not confined to one continent but known throughout the civilized world, and whose name is a household word, cherished and loved by millions."

Frederick spoke and claimed again that he had no talent for after-dinner speeches and that with him brevity was not possible. His prepared speech, "Freedom Has Brought Duties," had the passion of the old abolitionist days and ended with the technique long ago learned from *The Columbian Orator,* the repeated refrain that in the best hands becomes an incantation:

"Until this day the man of sable hue had no country and no glory. Until this day he was not permitted to lift a sword, to carry a gun, or wear the United States uniform. Until this day we fought with only one hand, while we chained and pinioned the other behind us. On this day, twenty years ago, thanks to Abraham Lincoln and the great statemen by whom he was supported, this spell of blasted hopes and despair, this spell of inconsistency and weakness, was broken, and our government became consistent. Logical and strong, for from this hour slavery was doomed, and liberty made certain, and the union established. We do well to commemorate this day. It was the first gray streak of morning after a long and troubled night."

The men rose as one. Frederick was thrilled to hear the cheers and applause, but he was especially thrilled to receive appreciation from a new generation of men, for he was considered by some to be out of the step with the time, a relic of a bygone era. In this speech, Frederick embodied the spirit of all warriors in moral battles who triumph through the power of a dream. He nodded his head and acknowledged the toast and the cheering. He deeply wanted to build a bridge between the generations.

But the fog returned.

126.

THE FOG ROARED BACK like a crazed hound, its force so overwhelming and frightening that Frederick retreated to silence, dread, and hours and hours of sleep. This time he feared that if he didn't seek help he would go mad, forever trapped in his depression, with suicide as the inevitable end. Frederick turned to a doctor for treatment of his emotional and physical collapse. The doctor said he was having "a breakdown" and needed complete rest. That summer of 1883, he went alone to the quiet and beautiful island resort of Poland Spring, Maine, and boarded at a lodge there for a month, waiting for the fog to lift.

What was happening?

Frederick hoped that with peace and quiet he would find answers. He needed to get back to work in Washington to support his family and continue his campaign to maintain relevance with a new generation of activists. Grief over Anna's death still weighed heavily on him. It came in intermittent waves, sometimes taking him by surprise. A smell, a word, a brief recollection of something said or done would trigger deep sadness and an occasional tear. One time, Rosetta casually referred to Anna as "Mother" rather than "Mama," her usual title, and Frederick started to sob uncontrollably. Convulsions racked his body, shocking and embarrassing him. Shaking his head, he apologized. "I don't know what happened. That just happened. I can't explain it."

Alone in Maine, he recognized that grief was not the only emotion that brought him to his knees. There was his blinding rage, too, his noonday demon, described in Psalm 91 as "the terror by night, the arrow that flieth by day, the pestilence that walked in darkness, the destruction that wasted at noonday." It was the ever-present beast ready to pounce. It was always ready. Until now, his worst episode was in 1851–1852, when the break between Frederick and Garrison became vitriolic and public. He was so debilitated that he started falling down and could not bathe himself. He submitted to hired help. Julia was frightened. He was frightened, too. Then his depression passed and didn't return until he was in England after Harpers Ferry.

On a beautiful island with views of the White Mountains, surrounded by the natural order of color, light, soft wind, and the constant, vibrant calls of birds and other life forms, silence allowed for reflection. Frederick saw intimations of a life pattern, not as clearly as he wanted, but there were clues. He recognized that his emotional reactions were not rational. He also understood that one event preceding the other did not equal causation. But there was a through line, a constant, burning thread.

He was angry.

He was always angry, but he thought he had it under control. He thought he had his life under control. But Anna's death, after a decade of deaths, shattered the control he had constructed over the years: speaking engagements almost every day; countless editorials, essays, and letters; constant criticism from the young Black radicals; meetings with leaders too vain or stupid to realize he was manipulating them for his own ends.

He was in control, he insisted.

Back in April, Frederick told his audience at the First Congregational Church, "There is no modern Joshua who can command this resplendent orb of popular discussion to stand still."

He ostensibly welcomed the ardent debate about what activists should do in the current climate, but deep down he wanted to be that modern Joshua demanding agreement. Opposition had become a personal affront, and the intransigence of the younger Black radicals to his appeals was intolerable, unbearable, almost unforgivable.

He said he was hopeful about where the country was going. But that was a lie.

A big lie.

As far as he was concerned, the country had reached a nadir in its racial history, and young radicals like Richard Greener and John Merce Langston were calling him out like children revealing the nakedness of the emperor. The triumphs of the past were no longer relevant, they said, and he needed to be more honest about the Republican Party and the state of the nation. Frederick was embittered by such effrontery, but he was also ashamed by his complicity in reinforcing a false image of the current times. Amid this deepening fog, Frederick thought his depression would never end, and then it suddenly lifted.

As in the past, he couldn't identify the exact moment or the precise antecedent for the lifting of his depression. But Frederick no longer denied his fog. Painful as it was, it was a part of him. It shaped him, defined him, even as it humbled him. He had to learn to live with it, expect its return, and know that, like living with a medical condition, he could endure it and survive, even if he could not destroy it. Frederick was ready to leave Maine by mid-August, prepared for future battles with a renewed sense of himself and his mission.

His family, especially Rosetta, had sent letters filled with domestic news and work gossip at the recorder of deeds office. Rosetta was especially concerned about the way the office manager was treating the newest clerk, Helen Pitts. He thought often about Helen that summer, wondering why she continued to intrigue him. Her letters, always a response to his inquiries, deepened his interest. They were candid and humorous at times. She was serious but not presumptuous like most ardent believers, and Helen's curiosity was an open invitation to engage her mind and heart. Frederick wrote a poem called "What Am I to You?" and answered his question by comparing desire to eating the forbidden fruit of the Tree of Knowledge:

> An apple swinging light and free
> High pendant on a brave old tree
> Flung a sweet fragrance down to me
> That thrilled all my senses.
> In size and form and hue divine,
> Perfect in beauty every line
> Locked frame to pierce a soul like mine
> Though fortified by reason.
> Amazed I stood in wonder sound
> Till then such fruit I'd never found
> I needed help and look around
> For means to gain possession.
> But none was there to give a hand
> And I could scarcely understand
> Why I such treasure should command
> As that so far above me.
> But there it was and there was I
> With face upturned to tree and sky
> With will to do, but not to try
> Held to the spot enchanted.

Frederick never sent the poem to Helen, but when he returned to Cedar Hill he walked the five miles to the recorder of deeds office, as part of his daily routine, greeted all the employees, and asked Helen to come to his office.

★

Frederick saw Helen approaching and rose from his chair behind his desk to open the door. When she entered, he towered over her. He closed the door for privacy. The large interior window made it possible for everyone to see them, and clusters of office gossipers, except for Rosetta, who left for home earlier, had already formed. Frederick pointed his hand to the chair. "Please take a seat, Miss Pitts."

"Thank you, sir," she said.

"By all accounts, I understand you are doing an excellent job, even if you are not universally appreciated," Frederick said.

"If you are referring to the unpleasantries of Mrs. Shelby, I can assure you they have ceased. She has apologized."

"That pleases me to hear."

There was a moment's pause. Frederick looked down and then up again, as if finding his nerve with the rise of his head. "I was wondering if you would join me at the next meeting of the Shakespeare Club. I have no one at home to go with me, and I often fancy that I am losing out on the happiness of such occasions because in all such matters I am alone. I will be reading the part of Shylock in *The Merchant of Venice*, and you could rehearse with me for my reading if you came to Cedar Hill, with your aunt and uncle."

"Why with my aunt and uncle, Mr. Douglass? I am a grown woman, and don't need a chaperone."

"People will talk."

"Which people? My aunt and uncle will not cast aspersions, having been your guests before. And you have your daughter and her sister-in-law, who care for you, and they certainly will not contribute to any kind of rumor mill. Besides, Mr. Douglass, the talk, if there is talk, will be against me, not you. It is always the woman who receives criticism or blame. It is so tiresome, and yet so predictable. It certainly would be worse if you came to my apartment."

"Then I should not visit your home, Miss Pitts."

"That is up to you. Since I no longer live with my aunt and uncle, they might assume that you are courting."

"I will be doing no such thing!"

"Your aversion to the possibility, sir, could be interpreted as an insult, or faint criticism at best."

"Oh, no, I didn't mean to suggest . . ."

"Then it could happen, within the realm of philosophical possibility?"

"Of course, it could. I am surprised you are not married already."

"I am particular."

"May I ask, how?"

"Yes." Helen waited, still smiling.

"What are your particular requirements?" pressed Frederick.

"Very well. Most men see marriage as an institution of control, and I will not be controlled by a husband or anyone else. Most men see women as property, and their bodies to use as they wish."

He did not expect to hear such sentiments face to face in a conversation with an unmarried woman. But Helen was not embarrassed or reluctant to say what she thought and believed. "I see."

"Mr. Douglass, shall we bring this conversation to an end?"

"Perhaps we shall."

"Then I shall return to work, if that's acceptable to you," Helen replied, standing.

"I hope I didn't offend you, Miss Pitts."

"Oh, Mr. Douglass, you did not offend me. I may have offended you, but I meant no offense. I prize honesty, and in marriage especially there should be honesty, and the issues that could potentially divide couples should be discussed before the wedding vows, not after them. No matter what happens, my husband will not be surprised he married a radical feminist and then spend years trying to make me into something else. That would be a lost cause. Better to prevent such a waste of time before the ceremony, don't you think?"

"Yes."

"It's always good to not have any misunderstanding or false expectations. Thank you for your time, sir."

"And thank you for yours. Would you be willing to call me Frederick?"

"Sir, no," Helen replied, still smiling. "Not yet."

"Miss Pitts," he said, standing, too.

"Mr. Douglass."

And she was gone, leaving Frederick to ponder the effect that Helen Pitts had on him. There were surprises, but no tensions. There was disagreement, but no underlying resentments. He felt relaxed even when he resorted to convention or routine. And he was suddenly aware of Helen's essential character. Comfortable in her own skin, she was kind, highly intelligent, with no axes to grind, no emotional battles to wage in offices or drawing rooms. He imagined the serenity of domestic life with her, but he was not willing to court her to see if they had a future.

★

Helen had not returned to Cedar Hill since Anna's funeral, and she worried the house would be shrouded in black as a reminder of Frederick's loss and memories of the long life he had shared with her—his refusal to forget her or allow anyone else to forget her. She understood grief and the need to honor the dead, but the American way of death seemed excessive, the four-hour funerals filled with eulogies and laments, houses draped in black for months, sometimes years, even during the heat of summer, widows wearing black gowns for decades as fierce devotion. It didn't help that the most famous widows in the world, Mary Todd Lincoln, who had just died in July of 1882, a few months after Anna, and Queen Victoria wore only black after their husbands' deaths. Cedar Hill was a pleasant surprise, the house filled with activity, laughter, and the sound of grandchildren enjoying themselves. Rosetta and her children stayed for months.

Helen prepared herself for *The Merchant of Venice* reading rehearsal as if preparing for the balls she rarely attended during her Mount Holyoke days, when boys from the local colleges gathered on neutral territory, under adult supervision, to ogle and court. Although disdainful about these events, and preferring to study over dance, she had worried about how she looked and what she wore for hours, guilt about her vanity racking her soul. That was long ago, but those anxious, ambivalent feelings returned. She again worried about her dress, her hair, her skin tone. Should she wear black? Should she still offer condolences? Would flowers in her bonnet be attention seeking or inappropriate? She fretted for hours, but in the end, after spending Friday with Uncle Hiram and Aunt Frances, she wore a dark blue, bustled dress with minimal ruffles at the neck and wrists. Hiram drove her in his carriage but did not stay, agreeing to return within three hours. It was one in the afternoon.

When Helen and Frederick entered the west parlor, Rosetta and her two oldest daughters were waiting. They stood immediately and, all smiles, greeted Helen warmly, repeating "Miss Pitts." Helen and Rosetta were coworkers who saw each other daily but were not friends. At the office, they were still "Miss Pitts" and "Mrs. Sprague." However, Helen asked Rosetta politely, "May I call you Rosetta here? And if you are comfortable, please call me Helen."

"Helen," replied Rosetta, "I am Rosetta here, but only here." She turned to her daughters. "Girls, it is still Miss Pitts."

"Yes, mother," they both agreed simultaneously.

"Good," said Rosetta, "and now let's have some cake and tea before they get cold."

Helen sat down and noticed the huge, framed print that dominated the space above the black mantle. How had she missed this stunning depiction in hues of brown, black, and creamed white depicting the courtship of Othello and Desdemona from Act 1 of Shakespeare's tragedy? The print was set in a double matting of muted gold and burgundy in an ornately carved dark brown frame, its scrolled curves suggestive of ancient, exotic wealth. As if reading her mind, Frederick explained, "A recent purchase. I saw Edwin Booth play *Othello* in New York. It was a great performance, but I long to see Ira Aldridge or another great Black actor do the part."

"It's your favorite, obviously," observed Helen.

"It's about a great Black man, a great love despite difference, the loss of love and friendship, betrayal, everything. It's all there in language of astonishing beauty," Frederick said.

They talked as if Rosetta and her daughters were not in the room. Rosetta acknowledged the awkwardness of the moment by clearing her throat and saying to her daughters, "Girls, we need to leave Papa and Miss Pitts to their work. For the night of your reading, I assume you will not be reading the entire play. That would take hours."

"No, just scenes," replied Frederick, who also stood. "I want to get my chosen scenes just right, the scene in Act 3 when Shylock asserts his common humanity, asking, 'Hath not a Jew eyes? Hath not a Jew hands, organs, dimensions, senses, affections, fed with the same food, hurt with the same weapons; subject to the same diseases, healed by the same means . . .'"

"Grandpa, you know the lines already, like an actor," Harriet exclaimed. "This will not be just a reading, but like a performance on stage."

"If the reading is good, that's how it should be," Frederick said.

"It will be wonderful seeing it. May we come?"

"You can surely come to our own final rehearsal here before Helen—Miss Pitts—and I attend the reading at the Society. How about that?"

"Thank you, Grandpa."

Rosetta insisted, "Now, girls, Papa and Miss Pitts have limited time, so let's leave them to themselves. I look forward to that final rehearsal as well."

"The pressure is on," said Frederick, good-naturedly. "Families can be stronger critics than professionals. But I will strive to do my best for you, especially my reading of the great trial scene in Act Four."

"You will do splendidly," said Annie, breaking her usual silence. "You always do."

"Thank you, dear."

Rosetta, Annie, and Harriet left, and when the door closed, Helen noted, "They all adore you."

"A blessing and a curse, the promise of inevitable disappointment," Frederick replied.

"And the promise of inevitable forgiveness, too."

"But is there forgiveness of Shylock in the hands of Portia, despite her words about the quality of mercy? At the end of the act, he is a broken man, and she seems to be the instrument of his downfall."

"Is he not the instrument of his own downfall? Are we assigning blame to Portia for speaking her mind, as is done so often with strong-minded women?"

Frederick clapped his hand, delighted. "Oh, I am so glad we are friends. This work is going to be so enjoyable."

"I will do my best."

"And thank you for including Rosetta and the girls in the discussion. Sometimes I can be so forgetful of the social niceties."

"I will always help."

"Always?"

"If you allow me."

"Consider it done."

Instinctively, Helen knew. She wanted to live with Frederick for the rest of her life, defending him, protecting him through the power of her own voice. Today, she had fallen in love. She needed to be his wife, for his sake and her own.

A month later, the reading of excerpts from *The Merchant of Venice* was a triumph. As the main reader for the night, Frederick was allowed to bring a guest as his prompter and reader of other roles. And he was also allowed, as a special dispensation to the most renowned member of the Society, to bring also, for one night only, his daughter and granddaughters. As the applause resounded, he whispered to Helen, "Maybe next year, readings from *Othello.*"

"Maybe," was all she said.

The following morning, Frederick and Helen were back at work at the recorder of deeds office, and he again summoned her to his office. He waited until she sat in the chair across from his desk. "Miss Pitts, please excuse me for my boldness. But I have a question to ask you. May I?"

"Yes."

"Are you looking for a husband?"

"No," she answered, unfazed by the question or her answer. She had already found him, and so was telling the truth.

"When you do, I wish you good luck."

"It won't be a matter of luck. The man will have to be as remarkable as you are, sir, and there are not that many in this world."

"Oh, Miss Pitts, you honor me far too greatly."

"I do not exaggerate, sir. I never exaggerate."

"Thank you. And thank you for the superb assistance with *The Merchant of Venice.*"

"I look forward to receiving your instructions for other readings."

"I think our friendship is developing nicely, if I might say so myself."

"You may, sir."

"I appreciate your time and your candor."

"Thank you, sir, Good day."

"Good afternoon."

127.

HELEN LEFT FREDERICK'S OFFICE astounded. Forty-six years old, she had not anticipated having such a conversation with Frederick Douglass, a man she had known of and admired most of her life. This moment felt inevitable, like the culmination of her proud ancestry running from the Mayflower pilgrims to the American Revolution and the migration to western New York. Politically, her family were dedicated abolitionists, and Helen was devoted to duty and service with a strong commitment to Christian values. The details of her journey all made sense now. They were all part of a divine plan. Her life had prepared her to be the wife of Frederick Douglass. Helen and Frederick came from different parts of the country, from diverse families, races, and cultures, and together they would exemplify racial equality and reunion across boundaries and divides. They would represent the future, and they would create it as well.

Born on October 14, 1837, Helen was the first child of Gideon and Jane Pitts's four daughters and two sons. Gideon was a successful farmer on land he had inherited. He and his two brothers were considered well-to-do by western–New York standards. They were not the wealthiest family in the village of Honeoye but carried prestige as descendants of the founder of the town's Richmond Union Church, which was committed to antislavery when other local churches refused to condemn it.

By the time Helen was an adolescent she espoused antislavery. She grew up listening to her father's pronouncements and tirades, reading newspapers, and helping her mother host countless traveling abolitionists, including Frederick, who came to Honeoye in April 1852 after his move to Rochester, thirty-three miles north. He came frequently to Honeoye during the 1850s, but Helen could not remember any overnights. But she remembered that first visit.

She was fourteen, and what impressed her most was his size. Frederick was tall and big and handsome and well dressed. By comparison, he had made her father, whom she adored, look small and inconsequential. Gideon Pitts reinforced her impression by extolling Frederick's virtues and accomplishments, as if he were Douglass's disciple. She had never seen her father respond to anyone in this way. Intrigued, she asked about Frederick's book, *The Narrative*, and Gideon presented her with a copy and said with gravity, "He is a man for the ages."

Frederick was too remote to matter much to Helen then. She had more pressing concerns with her father, who determined that his daughters become highly educated, independent, Christian women dedicated to serving others. Gideon's first son had died in infancy, and his namesake, born in 1852, was still young. The time required immediate action, and his daughters would lead the way. Gideon made sure Helen attended secondary school, where she took courses in English, Latin, Greek, German, French, mathematics, geography, philosophy, penmanship, drawing, and educational pedagogy, which prepared her well for college and a career as a teacher. She then attended Mount Holyoke College in Massachusetts, one of the few schools for women in the country, where her sister had enrolled the year before. The sisters loved the pursuit of knowledge. They were also attracted to Mount Holyoke's mission, the promotion of young missionaries and teachers in service as evangelical Christians committed to moral perfection and a just society.

Helen graduated in 1859 and returned home to the routine of family life, anxiously waiting to see what role she would play in a nation falling apart. Gideon did not push her to find a job or a husband, saying at one point, "Be patient. You will find your place in the coming storm." When war finally came in 1861, Helen saw it as a war against slavery, even though Lincoln insisted the fight was for the preservation of the Union. She applied to be a teacher with the American Missionary Association, the largest organization dedicated to helping the freed slaves who swarmed federal encampments after Union soldiers seized Confederate lands. She applied for what she deemed a healthy location. Helen was assigned to an army camp in Norfolk, Virginia, and realized her ignorance about the South and Black people, who were rare in western New York.

Helen became comfortable with Black people through teaching hundreds of youths and adolescents in day classes and tutoring adults at night. They were eager to learn, and she empathized with their struggles for justice and equal treatment as they were mistreated by local whites and Union soldiers. She expected local white hostility. Outsiders were repeatedly jeered on the streets of Norfolk and called "nigger lovers." But she didn't anticipate the bigotry of her fellow missionaries. Black teachers were expected to room with whites, but immediately, some of the white teachers and even ministers disparaged them and all freedmen as crude, ignorant, undisciplined, and lewd.

Helen was more than disappointed. She was appalled. She challenged a white coworker who casually referred to an absent Black teacher as "that nigger."

"You should not use that word," said Helen softly but firmly.

"Who are you to tell me what to say?" asked the offended older woman, her disdain meant to shut Helen up.

"A Christian reminding you of your Christian duty. Our Lord would never say something so cruel," Helen replied.

"How would you know what the Lord would say?"

"He said, "Love thy neighbor as thyself.""

Her colleague stood. "I do not have to listen to you."

"And I will not allow you to believe that I will go along with your cruelty. You misjudged me, casually using a word that you assumed I would not object to. You don't know me, but you assumed my complicity. If you ever say that word in my presence, I will challenge you again. Expect it. Do you understand?" Helen said.

"Well! Of all the nerve. Our supervisor will hear from me."

"And what will be your accusation, that I had the audacity to remind you of kindness and Christian charity?"

The woman left the room and lodged a complaint with Mr. Greene. He smiled at Helen and said, "Good work."

Malaria and Helen's demanding teaching schedule almost killed her, and her father came to Virginia to take her home. She intended to return but never did, remaining in bed for months, tired and depressed, fearing she would never again be engaged in work as transformative and socially redemptive. Helen prized honesty and abhorred self-deception. She knew she didn't like teaching, and even with her eager learners she didn't want to face the drills, monotonous recitations, and exams while she maintained order through threats, intimidations, and punishment. Her students said they liked and appreciated her, and she didn't doubt their sincerity. Nor did she dismiss the praise of Mr. Green, who told her, "We need more teachers like you, Miss Pitts." But the chaos in students' lives outside the classroom rumbled like a nearby storm, and the storm often broke, making her feel helpless and incompetent as she tried and failed to fulfill her role.

What else could she do?

Helen didn't want to marry and be burdened by endless childbearing. She prized her autonomy too much. Fortunately, her father never pressed her to marry and produce heirs. That role was satisfied by her sister, Lorinda, who married and produced children year after year. Helen became the maiden aunt who helped raise her sister's children, created schedules, and set boundaries with the blessings of Lorinda, who appreciated all the help she could get. Ten years passed.

By 1876, Helen was restless. She moved to Washington, failed to find work there, and then went to Indiana to serve as a substitute teacher for her sister, Eva, who was going on maternity leave. She didn't like her temporary job. The students were not eager, enthusiastic, or passionate about learning. Indiana was drudgery that was only relieved by occasional letters from Frederick, some of them asking questions about women's issues and discussing current politics. He even visited her while on a speaking tour. They went to the County Fair, where his presence stirred interest.

"Your fame precedes you, Mr. Douglass," said Helen, when she noticed people pointing.

"It's not my fame, Miss Pitts. It's my presence. They assume we are together, and that is unacceptable."

"But we are not, Mr. Douglass," she protested.

"Mere appearance is enough. But at least we know the truth. We can't be a couple, since I'm a married man. Unfortunately, we can't control what people assume or think." Hard frowns, staring, and pointing of fingers continued, but Frederick behaved as if oblivious, his dignity deepening her respect for him.

Now, after her meeting with Frederick in the recorder of deeds office, she realized that before being hired as a clerk there she had seen him only three times: once in Honeoye, when she was fourteen; once at Cedar Hill, when she encountered that termagant Ottilie Assing; and once at the County Fair in Indiana. Her sense of him was primarily based on a few letters, reprinted speeches, and press reports. In fact, after Helen returned to Washington, she was more excited about meeting Doctor Caroline Brown Winslow, the president of the Moral Education Society of America and the publisher of its journal, the *Alpha*.

Unlike Helen's mother, Hiram's wife, Frances, was a radical feminist who supported women's suffrage. She had even attempted to register to vote. Frances was an ardent member of the Moral Education Society, whose mission was the strengthening of the influence of women in professions, business, and culture, and she urged Helen to join. Helen was hungry for a renewed sense of mission and joined the Moral Education Society soon after arriving in Washington and meeting Dr. Winslow. She read the *Alpha* assiduously, inspired by its respect for women and their choices. Helen still believed that women, as dedicated Christians, should be moral guardians of the nation. She had found a leader, an organization, and other women who appreciated her intelligence and skills. She was elected corresponding secretary and taught classes about reproduction to women eager to replace their ignorance with information.

Helen then applied for work as a copyist at Frederick's office, anticipating that her connection to him, however casual and brief, would help her application. Connections always mattered in Washington, the capital of patronage. He accepted her application, and she worked hard to please her employer. She didn't anticipate a deep personal relationship with the most famous and respected Negro in America. But on reflection it seemed both miraculous and inevitable.

128.

FREDERICK WAS CERTAIN THAT nothing in his and Helen's public behavior warranted assumptions of courtship. When they were together riding, walking, or sitting side by side, he didn't offer his arm for support, and he avoided even the slightest touch of her hand except when he helped her out of his carriage. They avoided telling side glances and broad smiles, and when they talked they made sure not to whisper.

Nonetheless, Frances Pitts was suspicious and told Frederick so in a note laced with what he characterized as "hints, innuendoes, implications, rumor and mean suspicions." Writing a response, he demanded a meeting to address "anything you may think it well to say." Frances could meet with him alone or with Helen too, but for the sake of Helen's reputation, all talk about courtship or worse had to be squelched.

However, Frances did not accept his challenge. There was no meeting and Frederick was relieved because he was bluffing. He didn't want to explain his feelings to Frances Pitts or anyone else, for that matter, and create complications for Helen. And he would lie to protect her if he had to.

He and Helen were becoming close friends, but technically he was not courting her. He had not declared that intention, as Helen required. It was time. They were sitting on the divan in the office side by side behind closed doors but within the sight of everyone through the door windows. Frederick began, "Miss Pitts, I . . ."

"Helen, please. It's time to call me Helen."

"Helen, I will be honored if you gave me permission to court you."

Blunt but soft as usual, she asked, "Do you want to marry me?"

Frederick started but considered his next words carefully. "That is what courting is all about, finding out if we want to marry. You've made that clear."

"It's already clear to me, if it's not yet clear to you. You should know now I am ready to marry you," Helen said.

"You want to marry me?"

"Of course, and if you are not ready, I can wait. This is a big step. Take your time."

"Will you marry me?"

"You already know the answer. Will you marry me?"

"Yes, you have my answer. Yes," said Frederick. He wanted to embrace her but held back, ever careful.

"Do you love me?" Helen asked.

"Yes," Frederick replied.

"You will need to love me because all the hounds of hell will come our way."

"I'm ready."

"So am I."

★

Following Frederick and Helen's secret engagement that fall of 1883, the U.S. Supreme Court, in an 8–1 ruling, declared in *United States v. Stanley* that the prohibition against acts of discrimination applied to states and not to individuals or individual businesses. The people of a state were allowed by the court to do what the court prohibited states from doing. The court also declared the Civil Rights Act of 1875, Sumner's bill, unconstitutional. Private citizens and institutions could now discriminate at any time. Once again, as in the past, Frederick attended a mass gathering to express his outrage. Before a standing-room-only crowd, he denounced an American institution for inflicting a grievous wound to Black pride and hope: "No man can put a chain about the ankle of his fellow man, without at last finding the other end of it fastened about his own neck. The lesson of all the ages on this point is, that a wrong done to one man, is a wrong done to all men. It may not be felt at the moment and the evil day may be long delayed, but so sure as there is a moral government of the universe, so sure will the harvest of evil come."

That harvest was not only a political and cultural one, it was a psychological harvest of devastating power. Frederick said that the Supreme Court had "given joy to the heart of every man in the land who wishes to deny to others what he claims for himself. It is a concession to race pride, selfishness, and meanness, and will be received with joy by every upholder of caste in the land." This was the worst consequence, leading Frederick to conclude, "and for this I deplore and denounce that decision."

After *United States v. Stanley*, Frederick and Helen understood what they would have to face. They loved each other, but their love would be questioned, challenged, and scorned. In 1883, interracial marriage was rare and not accepted. Called "criminal intimacy" in one state, it was illegal in most. The District of Columbia was one of the few exceptions. They decided to marry secretly so as not to give their families the opportunity to object and create impediments or delays. They didn't want or need permission, but if not their blessing, they hoped for support for their union from family members. Frederick believed a fait accompli would gently force their hands.

That calculation was a mistake.

Frederick was sitting at his desk eating lunch, and Helen was sitting beside him when Frederick got a surprise visit from Reverend Grimke. "The Reverend," Frederick whispered.

"I'll leave the two of you alone," Helen said, immediately standing. She departed and nodded her head at Frederick but said nothing. Grimke only nodded, as well.

The young bespectacled minister entered Frederick's office smiling and said, "Frederick, I was in the neighborhood, and I thought I would drop in and pay my respects."

"Please take a seat, Reverend. Sir, you are just the man I want to see. I was just thinking about calling on you."

"Well, Frederick, what's up?"

"I'm thinking about getting married, and I want you to perform the ceremony."

"I will be delighted to do so, and who is the fortunate lady?"

"Did you see the lady who was sitting by me when you came into the room?"

"Yes."

"She's the one."

Grimke signaled neither shock nor surprise. "There were rumors that you might be interested in getting married again, and I was curious, since the names of two prominent women of color were mentioned."

Frederick was not interested in knowing the names of these women, and said, "Her name is Helen, Helen Pitts. And I have known her family for years. Her father, Gideon Pitts is a well-to-do farmer in western New York, near Rochester, and was a staunch abolitionist. I often went to her father's house and remembered her because she was so intelligent and direct, even as a young girl. Of course, I never dreamed that in the years to come she would become my wife. But here we are, ready to wed."

"When do you want the wedding?"

"Will January 24 around seven in the evening work?"

"Yes. Come to my home at 1608 R Street Northwest, and I will perform the ceremony. Who will be your witnesses?"

"Senator Bruce and his wife."

"Will there be anyone else, from her family or yours?"

"No."

"Do they know?"

"No."

"Then such a distinguished and prominent couple will be a strong defense when the storm breaks."

"I don't wish to bring trouble upon you, sir."

"Some will say I should refuse your request. But on what basis can I as a Christian minister refuse? Refuse because you are Black, and she is white? Racial prejudice is incompatible with Christian values. Love is love, and loving thy neighbor is the directive of our Lord. He didn't make exceptions."

"Thank you, sir. That sentiment is not as common as it should be, and you will be challenged," Frederick said.

"I anticipate the challenge, and I am ready. Are you?" Grimke asked.

"Yes, sir. We are ready to go into this next phase of our lives with our eyes fully open."

Grimke stood. "I neglected to offer my congratulations, Frederick." He put out his hand. "Congratulations. You will begin the new year dramatically, and

I will most certainly not regret the expansion of my notoriety. Many will come to my Sunday sermons just to hear the man who dared to marry Frederick Douglass and Helen Pitts. But once there, I will have my chance to persuade them about the power of love. Good day, sir, and thank you for receiving me without an invitation."

Frederick was pleased to have chosen Grimke for his wedding. He would be an invaluable, articulate ally in the future. However, a deeper, more powerful emotion resonated within Frederick. He felt blessed to know a young saintly reverend of thirty-four years for whom he felt neither jealousy nor envy. Grimke was no competitor. He was a model of hope, a reflection of what a man could be at his best. The son of a white planter father and a biracial enslaved mother, Grimke represented the union of white and Black that Frederick wanted his own union to represent and foster.

Two months later, on Thursday, January 24, Frederick, dressed in a simple, dark day suit, drove his carriage to the marriage clerk's office at City Hall. It was filled with workers. He bowed his head, smiling at them and courteously acknowledging his fame. Frederick found the clerk and whispered his intention. The clerk took the marriage ledger out of a drawer. The clerk and his assistant filled in their sections, as did Frederick, who was then to deliver the sheet to "any minister of the gospel authorized to celebrate marriages in the District of Columbia." The minister needed to complete the card by writing his name at the bottom, his church, and the day and year of the ceremony. Frederick paid the $1 fee and hurried home to freshen up before leaving Cedar Hill for Helen's residence. He arrived around six o'clock.

Helen was not dressed for a special occasion, wearing what she had worn for work earlier in the day. It was cold, but she did not wear a shawl. She told him that a reporter from the *National Republican* had come earlier.

"Oh, no," Frederick said.

"He was quite persistent. I didn't say much, but I did finally confirm that I would soon be a bride."

"Did you tell him where?"

"Oh, Frederick, ours will be a private ceremony. Now let's go. It's almost time."

Frederick drove his carriage to the house of Senator Bruce and his wife, Josephine. He knocked at their door, and they quickly gathered up hat, cane, and shawl to follow in their own carriage to the house of the Reverend Grimke and his famous wife, the author Charlotte Forten.

At the Grimke house, in a fashionable but segregated part of Washington, they all exchanged greetings, and the Grimkes offered their congratulations as Frederick introduced Helen. They listened politely as Helen briefly told them how she met Frederick long ago. "Let us begin," the reverend finally said without fanfare. The brief ceremony involved only six people: the Grimkes, the Bruces, and Frederick and Helen. No music, no flowers.

Frederick and Helen had requested brevity without stipulating the ceremony's content. Grimke obliged by reading the Lord's Prayer, a portion of Paul's letter about love to the Corinthians, and then the traditional exchange of vows, "Do you, Frederick take . . ." and "Do you, Helen Pitts . . ."

The reverend declared them, "Mr. and Mrs. Frederick and Helen Douglass."

"You may kiss your bride," said Grimke. Frederick held Helen's hands for the first time during the ceremony and kissed her on both cheeks.

The wedding party had tea and cake, and afterward Frederick and Helen excused themselves. They needed to retrieve some of Helen's belongings to take to Cedar Hill before dark. A reporter awaited them at Helen's place. Frederick helped her out of the carriage, and the reporter tipped his hat and offered his hand. He said, "Mr. Douglass, may I congratulate you on your marriage to the new Mrs. Douglass. Congratulations, sir. I have some questions for your consideration."

Frederick stopped. "And what do you need to know?"

"Were you married today, sir?"

"Yes."

"When and where?"

"That will be your job to discover."

"I don't have time, sir."

"And I don't need to endure your impudence, sir. Good night. Come, Helen."

They went inside, and Frederick held her close. "Mrs. Douglass, I love you."

Smiling, she stepped back and said, "Mr. Douglass, I love you, too."

After retrieving Helen's things, they returned to the carriage and said nothing until they came to the entrance of the Navy Yard Bridge. Frederick turned to Helen. "Ready?"

"Ready."

Rosetta and Louisa awaited them in the west parlor like domestic guardians of stone. They did not rise when Frederick and Helen entered the room. "Papa, I should not have heard . . ." Rosetta began.

Frederick cut her short. "Congratulations are in order for Mr. and Mrs. Frederick Douglass."

Rosetta stood, her hands in a tight grip below her waist. "Why did I, your daughter, need to endure the indignity of finding out about your nuptials from a reporter, a *reporter*? I had to hire a driver to get here as soon as possible."

"A reporter? How?" asked Frederick, curious to know about the speed at which news now traveled.

"Your marriage certificate was posted, and a reporter, obviously informed by the staff, immediately came to the office. I was leaving for the day, and . . ."

"Rosetta, I am sorry you had to hear about it that way."

"You are sorry? You didn't trust me, trust any of us to know about this? Did you tell Lewis or Junior or Charles?"

"No," he replied, noticing the fury in Louisa's face. "Louisa, you have something to say?"

Louisa remained seated. "How could you do this to Anna. How could you?"

"This has nothing to do with Anna."

"Yes, it does. It has everything to do with her, with this slap in the face to her and to all colored women," Louisa said.

"Enough!" Frederick shouted. "It was foolish of me to ask. I don't need your approval, and this is my house."

"I will not stay here," announced Louisa, standing. "I will no longer stay here and work to keep this house going. I stayed after Anna's passing to help you, and this is what you do! How could you?"

"You can pack your things as soon as possible. I will not keep you here a minute longer."

Louisa rushed away, her mouth covered with her fist to prevent another anguished outburst.

Rosetta softened her tone. "She was Mamma's closest friend. Her shock and dismay are understandable. I am even more upset. Yes, *more*, because you are trying to replace my mother."

"I am doing no such thing," Frederick replied.

"Miss Pitts will never be my mother."

"I don't expect her to, nor does she want to, replace your mother. And you will, in my house, stop acting as if my wife is not in the room."

"She is half your age."

"That is irrelevant."

Rosetta turned to Helen and said, "Miss Pitts, some would love to make this affair all about race, but I have been raised far too successfully by my father to oppose this marriage because of your race. If you were as black as coal, I would still oppose what happened today." She started to leave.

"Rosa," pleaded Frederick, anguished now because he saw tears in his daughter's eyes.

"No, I will return when the boys arrive. Yes, you will have to face all four of us, the children you didn't trust enough to tell us about your wedding. I couldn't hide my shock before that reporter, it took me so aback. That will be the story I will have to live with in the papers. The great Frederick Douglass did not care enough to tell his children before he married again. You have disgraced the family."

"Don't say another word."

"I won't. Unlike my brothers, I learned to stop talking when you demand it." Rosetta left the room, and Frederick turned to Helen. "I'm sorry that you had to see and hear this."

"The storm has only begun. I will leave you alone with them. You need to talk to them," Helen said.

"This is our marriage."

"Yes, but tonight you need to see them without me."

"My room, our room, is upstairs to the right of the stairs."

"I will wait for you there."

Later that evening Lewis sat with his brothers and sister in the west parlor. Always the diplomat, he told Frederick, "Father, you have the right to marry whoever pleases you. But you should have consulted us, not for approval, of course. We are in no position to demand it. But you could have demonstrated your faith in us by telling us first, before the entire world finds out."

"I agree, Father," said Charles, whose second marriage had mellowed him.

Junior, the most taciturn, now said, "With all the pain and drama surrounding this family, my first reaction was, now this? But then, I thought, we all deserve as many chances at happiness as we can get. The world has enough misery."

Rosetta jumped up and faced them all. "You are all alike. You men close ranks, fathers and sons, to justify your outrageous behavior. What about *Mamma*? What about her? Doesn't she count for something after all is said and done? This marriage is an insult to your mother and to your Black wives, to all Black wives. Don't you see that? Of all the people, he could have chosen, and there are many who would want to be Mrs. Frederick Douglass, he chose his secretary, his white secretary, who is half his age. And you defend and excuse as if none of this matters. How will I be able to explain and excuse this with my own daughters?" Frederick and his sons looked to each other, the irony of her comments escaping none of them. Rosetta had spent her life at odds with her mother before and during her marriage, making excuses for Nathan Sprague.

"Your mother wanted me to marry again," said Frederick. "Before she died, when she was giving us all orders—remember? She wanted me to be happy. She said, 'Find a good woman.'"

Incredulous, Rosetta cried, "*She* said that? She told you *that*?"

"Your mama wanted me to be happy. She wanted all of us to be happy."

"Well, you managed to break that promise, Papa. Now we are all caught in the mess you've made."

Charles, once her bitter enemy, was shocked by her imprudence. "Rosetta, please. You go too far."

"I have not gone far enough! I will not allow Annie to stay here. None of my daughters will be required to endure Helen."

"Then bring her down, Rosetta. Ask her if she wants to stay," Frederick said.

"Why put her in the middle of this, Papa?"

"You did, Rosetta. Are you afraid of her answer?"

Rosetta stared for a moment and hurried out of the room. Waiting, the rest of them remained silent. She reappeared with her second-oldest daughter, Annie, now twenty, who frequently visited Cedar Hill to help her Aunt Louisa run the house. Conscientious and always pleasant, Annie had a grace and poise that everyone admired. Frederick was sure that when she was ready for courtship, she would have a host of suitors if she wanted them. She also had ambitions, having told him she wanted to be a teacher or a nurse. Her education was important.

"I suppose your mother and Aunt Louisa have told you about what has happened, about my getting married again?" His voice was as even as he could make it. He loved Annie dearly.

"Yes, grandfather."

"I have another question, Annie. Would you be able to respect the new Mrs. Douglass, Miss Helen, as you respected your grandmother?"

Annie considered his question for a moment. "I can't do that."

"Then you had better go," said Frederick.

Rosetta gasped. "You are throwing her out? How can you do that? Why would you require a granddaughter to give equal treatment, equal respect to your *second* wife. Why did you make this a choice?"

"Helen deserves respect," Frederick said.

"Not equal respect."

"I believe in equality, in equal treatment."

"Your equality is cruel. Look at what you are doing?"

Standing still, arms to her side, Annie shed a tear. "I will leave with Aunt Louisa in the morning."

Rosetta said to her daughter, "I will spend the night with you, and Uncle Lewis will return tomorrow morning and take us and Louisa to town. Come, Annie. I have heard enough for one day." Rosetta took her by the arm and left the room. She behaved as she so often did, as the second mistress of Cedar Hill after her mother.

"We need to leave, too," said Lewis, who had driven his carriage with his brothers out to the house. "Good night, Papa."

"Good night, Papa," repeated Junior.

"Good night, Father," said Charles.

Unsmiling, they passed their father without looking at him, shaking his hand, or offering an embrace. Frederick watched them leave without following them to the front door. He waited until he was sure the carriage had descended out of sight, locked the door, and walked slowly up to his bedroom.

There was no consummation of marriage that night.

129.

BY THE TIME A reporter from the *Washington Post* arrived at Cedar Hill at eight o'clock, Rosetta, Louisa, and Annie were gone. He was a young man thrilled by his audacity, knocking at the door of an important man so early in the morning to get his scoop. "Sir, my ambition has no bounds. I had to be here first to get your version of the story before the other hounds arrive, my position will be assured. Your marriage is the marriage of the year!"

Frederick stood at the open door and replied, "Young man, my marriage is not an event of public moment. My decision is a family matter, and I owe no explanation, let alone an apology. I am astonished that a city so large as I considered Washington to be should become at once so small."

"You can control the narrative of this story, sir. I will listen carefully and tell your side of it. There will be other versions, considering that your marriage can never be private, since you are who you are."

Frederick scanned the reporter from head to boot, wondering about the benefits and liabilities of talking with him. He could slam the door in his face and be done with him and any other reporter. Or he could give him an exclusive interview and tell future inquirers that all he needed to say was said to the *Post*. That would enhance this young man's journalism career for certain. Frederick asked, "What's your name?"

"Barrett Sinclair."

Frederick stepped back. "Well, Mr. Sinclair, join me in my parlor, and I will tell you what I need to tell you, not what you want to know." He was determined to use the moment to explain racial bigotry and its poisonous influence on the thinking of others. They sat down in opposite chairs in the formal east parlor. Frederick resumed. "You realize your story only has significance because of my race, and the race of my wife. The mere fact of my second marriage would generate little interest."

"That is true, sir. The opinion has been expressed that the colored people, who look to you as a leader, will consider your position in the light of your present action, as equivocal."

"Equivocal?"

"But surely her race had some baring on your choice, did it not?"

"There are many colored ladies of my acquaintance who are as good as I am, and who are great deal better educated, yet in affairs of this nature who is to decide the why and wherefore? I have been associated with the lady who became my wife for some time past. I came to know her well, and was pleased with her, and she, I hope, with me. I chose with my heart, and she is only a few shades lighter than myself anyway. But this obsession with color is absurd, for as scripture tells us, 'God Almighty made but one race.'"

"And where is that passage, sir?"

"In Acts 17 verse 24, Paul says, 'He hath made of one blood all nations of men to dwell on all faces of the earth.' One blood. I adopt the theory that in time the variety of races will be blended into one. You may say that Frederick Douglass considers himself a member of the one race that exists, and I have the natural right, as you have the natural right, to marry whomever I please to marry."

Sinclair was writing quickly, using a symbol system to transcribe what he heard. He looked up and asked, "Do you think your position on interracial marriage compromises your position as a leader of your race?"

"I am a leader because I am a man who will jump into the water to save a white child from drowning, and I will do whatever I can for the downtrodden, Black and white, male and female." Curious, Frederick then asked, "How am I able to know that what you are writing is what I said?"

"I will rewrite it so you can check it. I don't do this for most people, but since I told you I would, I will rewrite it. My other sources trust me."

"I trust you and will not require more of your time."

"Thank you, sir, and now I have some questions about Miss Pitts."

"You mean Mrs. Douglass."

"Yes."

"I will not answer any of those questions. She can speak for herself."

"Then may I speak to her?"

"No."

Sinclair's face fell. "This, sir, is not what I expected."

"This is more than you would have if I had not answered the door at all. Consider yourself fortunate to get any of my time."

Sinclair quickly restored his air of affability. "Sir, do you have any more statements for the record that I may share with my readers?"

Frederick paused, staring. Sinclair shifted in his chair, as if realizing he was a student before an imposing teacher.

"Are you ready?" Frederick asked.

"Yes, sir."

"Tell them that Frederick Douglass believes Mrs. Douglass is a courageous woman, for in choosing me she publicly rejects the racial assumptions of our time. The color line does not exist for her, or for me."

Frederick stood. "That is all."

Sinclair stood as well. "Thank you for your time, sir."

"I look forward to your piece in the *Post*."

"My editor may want more details, and because I don't have them, he might reject my piece."

"I will speak to no other reporters, so this will be an exclusive. He should applaud you. Good day, young man, and good luck."

130.

HELEN HAD BEEN RELUCTANT to imagine herself as the wife of a handsome, brilliant, and famous man, indeed, one of the most renowned men in the land. She now understood why Frederick was the object of her father's adoration. His magnetism was unmistakable, and his mind was like a bright inexhaustible light that brightened every room, every conversation. She wanted to do everything in her power to please and satisfy him, without sacrificing herself. She knew he wanted no less.

They were sitting up in bed on the second night of their marriage, dressed for a winter's night in loose-fitting but warm clothes, waiting for the delayed consummation to begin.

"I want to please you," Helen said softly, beginning the exchange, looking straight ahead.

"I want to please you. It's been a while. I am getting old, and my walks have not yet reduced my weight. I'm still carrying two hundred and thirty pounds of flesh." He laughed lightly.

"We'll discuss what you're eating. Food makes a difference. More vegetables, less meat."

"I'm a product of Maryland."

"In all parts of the country, we eat poorly, but we can change our habits, step by step. It won't be easy. But we can begin by taking the fullest measure of our bodies. We should stand before each other in our nakedness. See and accept what we have become and start from there. But not tonight; it's too cold."

"I've never done that," Frederick said.

"Neither have I with someone else. But taking a long, hard look in the mirror is bracing and instructive," Helen replied. Frederick shifted slightly and covered his lap with both hands. She said, "I've never been with a man because I didn't want to give control of my body to a man raised to believe I was his property."

"You are not my property."

She turned to him and placed her hand on his cheek, and said warmly, "Domestic slavery is not dead, but I know I am free to be myself with you."

"What do you need? Tell me what to do for you."

"Tell me what pleases you."

His hands trembled. "I want to touch your breasts."

Frederick looked down and Helen untied a bow that revealed her breasts. "Now, see? Was that too difficult to say?"

"Yes."

"Well, let's begin," she said, untying her gown at the top. She opened it widely, taking it off her shoulders.

Frederick placed his full palm over the mound of her breast.

Helen closed her eyes at his touch, and then said, "For you . . . what . . . may I feel?"

Frederick pushed away the blanket. "I'm ready."

"I'm not ready," she said. "There is a spot. It takes women longer. We're different, remember?"

She tossed her gown on the floor beside her and fell back against the pillow.

Frederick lowered his body to hers and his face was against her ear and cheek. He whispered, "I love you, Helen."

"I love you, Frederick."

Afterward, looking at the ceiling Frederick whispered, "That was . . . "

"See what a woman can learn from lectures and books, especially books," Helen said, amused and satisfied all at once. "You know, Frederick, there are some novels that are especially provocative. Do you want to read one?"

"You have some?"

"You disapprove?"

"No, I was just surprised."

"Men are always surprised."

He reached for her hand and kissed it. "You were a teacher once. I had no idea that--- . ."

"We will all the pleasures prove . . ."

"Poetry? Is it Shakespeare? Or Byron?"

"Another controversial poet, John Donne."

"Shall we read him together?"

She laughed delicately. "Some readings can be disruptive. We may not finish, being interrupted by their power."

"So be it," said Frederick.

"Promise me you will always tell me what you need or want. Our marriage will be more meaningful, more exciting because we know what to expect. Too many women who speak with me tell me about disappointing honeymoons."

"I'm sure it's the men who make it so."

"We can pretend, you know, but men can't, especially when they insist their wives be almost bodiless saints. We'll get the vote long before we get sexual equality."

"I think you might be right."

"I know I'm right. In the meantime, let's get some rest, and be ready for tomorrow night and more fun."

"Tomorrow?" cracked Frederick, astonished again.

"Yes, and why not?"

"And why not?"

131.

THE SOUTHERN WHITE PRESS was predictably apoplectic about Frederick and Helen's marriage, but Frederick paid more attention to denunciations in the Negro press. The *Washington Grit* proclaimed, "We are opposed to colored men marrying second rate white women. There has been as much fuss and noise about Helen Pitts as if she were the daughter of the Secretary of State or some other dignitary. Barnum could make a mint out of this couple if they would consent to go on exhibition. We do not believe that it adds anything to the character or good sense of either of the two races to intermarry with each other, and when it is done it will generally be found that moral depravity is at the bottom of them." Frederick read this aloud to Helen and said, "If I were younger, and this was the age of dueling, I would have to shoot the man."

"Your dying for my honor would not comfort me. That editor is free to be mean-spirited. The First Amendment is a double-edged sword," she replied.

"We should do something."

"How about ignoring him? Let's focus on those who are happy for us. Your friend Julia Griffith congratulated us, remember?"

"Yes, and I hope you will her meet someday, if we ever get the chance to go to Britain."

"I've never been abroad. Going to Britain and to Europe would be wonderful."

"Yes, someday. And in the meantime, I heard from Elizabeth Stanton. She is happy for us."

"Have you reconciled over the Fifteenth Amendment, then?"

"Yes. But Susan B. Anthony is unrepentant," Frederick said.

"Time heals," Helen said.

"Time heals, and sometimes it does not."

Frederick wrote Elizabeth, "You have made Mrs. Douglass and myself very glad and happy by your letter, and we both give you our warmest thanks for it.

Helen is a braver woman than I am a man and bears the assaults of popular prejudice more serenely than I do. She has sometimes said she would not regret our marriage though the storm of opposition were ten times greater." He concluded his letter by saying that Helen would fold and send it, and remarked in closing, "How good it is to have a wife who can read and write, and who can as Margaret Fuller says cover one in all his range." In his vast correspondence, Frederick had never said so explicitly his disappointment about Anna's illiteracy. Helen said, before posting it, "Frederick, perhaps you should eliminate the line about Anna. It could be read as a criticism, an unnecessary criticism."

"But it is true, Helen."

"But need it be said?"

"It was not meant to be unkind. It's an appreciation of you, my dear. We are partners in every way. That is what I am saying, and for this, I am grateful," Frederick said.

"Very well," she said. In Helen's refusal to make a comparison and thereby honoring Anna in her own way, Frederick's love deepened for her.

"You're a good woman, Mrs. Douglass."

"And a dangerous one, too."

★

Frederick and Helen planned their honeymoon around an extended stay at Niagara Falls before visiting her parents in Honeoye, New York. Helen had heard from one of her sisters, Jennie, that her parents were "very upset" about the marriage. But Helen was sure that Frederick, a longtime acquaintance, would assuage their concerns when they saw him face to face and relieve their years of worry about their oldest unmarried daughter. Their silence was ominous. No notes or letters congratulating them had ever arrived at Cedar Hill, but Helen remained hopeful. Her father was a stern, sometimes rigid, man, but he was principled and spent his life dedicated to racial equality.

They planned to be gone for almost six months, but the death of Wendell Phillips and an attempted extortion from Nathan Sprague derailed their departure. Wendell died on February 2, and Frederick was determined to get to Boston with Helen for the private funeral to be held on February 6. But just before they were to leave, Nathan arrived at Cedar Hill with a list of demands. He said, "I need to speak with you, Mr. Douglass," and entered before Frederick invited him. Nathan turned to the formal east parlor as if to emphasize the importance of his mission.

"What is it?" For years Frederick had barely tolerated Nathan, and only because he was the father of his grandchildren.

"I have a bill for you."

"Excuse me?"

"You owe my sister for all the years she worked for you free after she moved in with you on Capitol Hill in October of 1872," Nathan said.

"You can't be serious. Your sister came on her own free will, and Anna very much appreciated all she did for her."

"Appreciation is not payment, and she deserved to be paid for the services she rendered. I went to see a lawyer, who agreed, and recommended you pay Louisa. Or we will sue for payment in court."

"Sue! You can't be serious! And you saw a lawyer who agreed with this non-sense? Which lawyer?"

"Thomas J. Mackey, the former judge."

"That former Confederate from Carolina, him? He only became a Republican to get a job, and he has said things about race that prove he remains the enemy of us all."

"He is not my enemy, and I don't care what he has said about color. We need a recognized lawyer who is willing to take you on if you do not cooperate."

"Nathan, he's a bastard for thinking I can be extorted."

Nathan shouted, "You threw her out, and she left without her earned wages!"

Frederick shouted back, "I did no such thing! She left because she would not work under Helen. She never once said she expected money."

"She was not your slave."

"She was a member of our family."

"She was family to Mrs. Douglass but never to you!"

"You don't know what you are talking about, and . . ."

Helen entered the room. "What's going on? I heard shouting. This is not . . ." She inserted herself between the tall men, who were about to come to blows, their fists balled up for immediate use. "Stop this! Stop this now!" They backed away but continued shouting.

"I'm defending my sister's honor," Nathan said.

"You wouldn't know honor if it slapped you down, you ungrateful bastard," Frederick replied.

"I'm not the bastard in this house."

"Get out, and never come back here. You are never to come here again, for any reason. Anna is gone, and so now I'm rid of you."

Helen turned to Frederick. "Frederick, enough! Please. You don't need this kind of agitation." She turned to Nathan. "You need to leave."

"I'm not leaving until Frederick pays my sister," Nathan said.

"What are you talking about?" Helen asked.

Now calm, Frederick said coldly, "Louisa wants money for all the years she worked here."

"Was there a contract?"

"Of course not. She never mentioned one."

Nathan was calm now, too, but the chill in his voice matched the ice of February. "You pay her or she was your slave, and that will not look good in court, a refusal coming from the great antislavery man."

Frederick took a step toward him again, but Helen pressed her hand against his chest. "No, Frederick, please." She turned to Nathan. "Draw up an invoice for the expected amount, and we will see to it after the funeral in Boston."

"Helen," Frederick pleaded. "This is a matter of business between Nathan and me."

"This is our business, and it is taking time away from us. We can afford whatever the amount is," said Helen.

Unrepentant, Nathan said, "And Louisa was not cheap labor."

"Draw up that invoice, and we will take care of it when we return," said Frederick. "And you will not step into this house when you come. I will meet you at the door."

"I will not need to face another insult from you. You can give the payment to Rosetta."

"Get out."

Frederick waited until Nathan was out of the house, then he sat down in the parlor he rarely used and said, "You know, I don't believe in hell, but if there is one, may he burn in it, the ingrate. The damnable ingrate!"

Helen leaned over and gently touched him on the shoulder, "Frederick, Frederick, you will pay this, and you will do more for his children. He knows this. I know this. Family matters to you, no matter what. And your family will matter more to me now that I fear I might lose my family because of us."

"You can't be sure of this," Frederick replied.

"I want to be wrong, but I have to be prepared for the reality that the only family I will have will be yours."

"What about your sisters?"

"They usually go along with Father."

"That will be unfortunate, truly sad."

"But I will accept it only because I have no regrets about us. Not one."

"Neither do I."

"Let's get to Boston."

★

It had been years since Frederick had seen or corresponded with Wendell, but he remained one of his heroes, and it pleased Frederick to see the honors bestowed upon him at his death. The city was draped in black, and thousands of people lined the streets when Wendell's casket passed through on the way to the funeral at Hollis Street Church. After the service, the casket was taken to Faneuil Hall accompanied by two companies of colored militia, who served as honor guards and marched to the roll of muffled drums. Inside, the casket was flanked by the flag of the Shaw Veterans of the 54th Massachusetts and by the regimental flag of the colored militia. It seemed that the entire Black population of Boston came to pay final respects to their white champion, and by the time the doors were closed at four in the afternoon, thousands were still waiting in the bitter cold.

Nathan managed to intrude while Frederick and Helen were in Boston. The *Philadelphia Press* ran a story telling its readers that Louisa Sprague planned to sue Frederick for an unspecified amount if he did not pay her. "Damn him, he went to the press to pressure me," Frederick growled when he learned about the news item by telegram. "He is a scoundrel."

"Please remain calm, Frederick. This conflict is not good for your health, let alone your peace of mind. Was there mention of a price?"

"No."

"Let's wait and see."

When they returned to Washington, Frederick received an invoice delivered by a messenger to his door. Louisa and Nathan wanted $2,640, from which they were willing to subtract $675 for money received for clothing since 1872. "How did they arrive at this total?" Frederick asked, as he and Helen sat in the west parlor. "Did they keep receipts for the money given for clothes? This is ridiculous nonsense."

Helen didn't respond.

The Spragues were not done with manipulating the press to achieve their ends. One story said Louisa had entered a contract with the Douglasses for $25 a month but was never paid more than an average of $40 a year for clothing. Another newspaper claimed that Frederick could easily afford to pay the Spragues, since he earned "well over $200,000 a year." Louisa and Nathan also made sure readers knew that their suit had nothing to do with Helen, having planned to demand payment months before the wedding. "It was not a personal matter at all," Nathan insisted to the *Washington Star*, "only a matter of dollars and cents."

"What a lie. There was no such contract. Never. It's their revenge against you. Louisa was never going to work for a white Mrs. Douglass," Frederick said.

"Will you pay anyway?" asked Helen.

"If the amount is reasonable."

"Then how will the amount be settled?"

"I don't know. If the affair goes to court, then a judge will determine the amount or throw the case out, as he should."

"Perhaps you can settle out of court."

"With Louisa, maybe. With Nathan, never."

Nathan showed his hand publicly. He meant to humiliate Frederick, telling the *Washington Star*, as if speaking to Frederick directly, "According to your well-known habit, you place yourself on a lofty pedestal and flaunt your assumed dignity before the public." After reading this, Helen observed, "He hates you. He hates you because he needed you, still needs you. You make him feel dependent, and so he must hate you."

"He has a strange way of showing his dependence. Isn't gratitude easier?" asked Frederick.

"Not when he hates himself even more. He can't admit to himself that he's responsible for who he has become. He needs someone to blame."

"This is irrational."

"Hatred is irrational. And love is also irrational. And that brings me to Rosetta."

"What about her?"

"She loves him, by all accounts, and she has not spoken out about what he's doing. Has she said anything to you?" Helen asked.

"No. We have not spoken since Annie left. And now after what Nathan has said and done, she has greater reason for not speaking to me. She has always supported him even when she was miserable because of what he was doing," Frederick said.

When Frederick and Helen finally arrived at Honeoye, her sister confirmed her worst fears. Jennie met them on the porch, reached for Helen's hand, and embraced her. She said, "They won't see you. He's adamant. Father said he will not come to Washington if he knows you and Mr. Douglass are in town. Uncle Hiram and Aunt Frances won't see you, either, even though you're neighbors. Everyone is on Father's side except me. I have no problem with your marriage and wish you nothing but happiness. I hope my future husband is as distinguished and handsome as Mr. Douglass. Congratulations, Mr. Douglass." Jennie was striking, more beautiful than her sister, and like Helen she was kind and intelligent.

"Frederick, please, Frederick."

"Congratulations, Frederick, and may I commend you for your excellent taste in selecting my sister."

"My judgment is not always right, but in this case . . ."

Helen interjected, "I hope your position doesn't harm your relationship with Father."

Jennie giggled. "Oh, that won't happen. I'm his youngest and favorite daughter, remember?"

She hugged Helen again. Frederick heard sadness behind her nervous laughter.

"We look forward to you coming to Cedar Hill," said Frederick.

"So do I, and I hope, if you will allow me, to have an extended visit."

"Absolutely," said Frederick.

"Absolutely," confirmed Helen.

By late August, Frederick and Helen returned to Cedar Hill. Both of them noted that the days in Niagara Falls were especially delightful because Frederick and Helen had not yet received confirmation of the Pittses' hostility to their marriage. It seemed that the roar of the waters and the rising mists, combined with the giddiness of countless couples, most of them young, and the warm hotel receptionists and restauranteurs, who were happy to receive hundreds of honeymooners, granted everyone permission to relax, enjoy the scenery, and wish one another only the brightest of futures. Hope made everyone smile.

Memories of sex and the anticipation of more sex made everyone smile, too. Of course, no one dared mention what was happening in the morning, afternoon, and night, but legal lust lightened steps, broadened smiles, inspired proximities not allowed in other places. Frederick and Helen tried to make love every day, occasionally twice a day. Their desire seemed inexhaustible, their love bright as if their skin reflected the blazing sun. His body did not always cooperate. He apologized again and again.

"There are other ways to show love," Helen said gently after his first failure.

"You deserve more," Frederick said.

"I have you."

Like most couples, their stay was memorialized in a photograph with the Niagara Bridge and the roiling misty water of the Niagara River as the backdrop. With these fond memories, Frederick shared his feeling about his marriage to his friend Amy Post. "You will be glad to know that my marriage has not diminished the number of the invitations I used to receive for lectures and speeches, and that the momentary breeze of popular disfavor caused by the marriage has paved away. I wish you as an old and dear friend to be entirely satisfied with this: that Helen and I are making life go very happily and neither of us has yet repented of our marriage." He also reported to her and other friends good news about Louisa: they agreed privately that he would pay her $645 and she would drop the case.

Louisa and Nathan never returned to Cedar Hill, but Rosetta, who had brokered the settlement between her father and Louisa, was allowed to return, as were her children, who demonstrated their willingness to not only accept Helen but respect her. Charles, Lewis, and Frederick, Jr,. and their wives graciously accepted Helen as well.

Returning to Cedar Hill, Frederick prepared to campaign on behalf of the Republican candidate, Secretary of State James G. Blaine, who faced the relatively unknown Democrat, the one-term governor of New York, Grover Cleveland. Frederick planned to campaign with Helen at his side as a public statement of support for interracial marriage. She was eager to be with him. He had a true partner: intellectual, emotional, and sexual, and he was content and happy for the first time in a long time. Frederick envisioned another longer honeymoon, a longer one away from the travails of family and American politics.

"I want to see Europe, especially Paris. I've never been to Paris," Frederick said to Helen.

"But what about your job?" she asked.

"We'll see. If Grover Cleveland wins, then he'll replace me, for sure. New presidents do this."

"You have served well. If merit matters, he should keep you."

"He says that he supports merit and civil service, but all politicians say that now. It's an easy, popular position."

"You can't work forever, not because you can't do the work, but because you've earned a rest."

"I don't know if I can rest. But I am a born traveler."

"There will always be Paris," Helen said, smiling.

Then Frederick received a telegram from Dr. Frauenstein about Ottilie.

132.

THIS WAS NOT THE first time Dr. Frauenstein had contacted Frederick about Ottilie since her departure for Europe. In June of 1882 Ottilie had procured 500 Regalia cigars and sent them to Frederick. "Did you get them?" asked Frauenstein.

He did.

Frederick wrote a brief note to Ottilie thanking her for her generosity. He restricted himself to two lines, hiding his feelings. Her gift seemed flamboyant, almost vulgar in its excess. It also seemed inappropriate, coming only two months after Anna's death.

For almost a year, Ottilie stopped writing to almost everyone. She told no one where she was or where she planned to go. One of her German editors printed a plea for information as to her whereabouts. Concerned, a friend from Hoboken begged Frederick, "As I may suppose that you are in frequent correspondence with Miss Assing, please let me know when you heard of her the last time." Frederick was more preoccupied with his own mental health in 1883 and didn't write to Ottilie after his courtship of Helen began, although he was relieved when Frauenstein informed him that Ottilie was not "lost" and described her extended absence as a "venture," adding that she was touched by the concern of her friends.

During the presidential campaign and after the election, information about Ottilie came to Frederick in bits and pieces. On August 21, 1884, her unidentified body had been discovered near the Seine River on a bench with an empty vial of cyanide nearby. The police took the body to the city morgue, where it was displayed for identification before burial. Two weeks after her death, and just before the medical school was set to claim the body, an acquaintance of Ottilie's just happened to be touring the morgue. Recognizing the body, Rinaldo Kientzel arranged for her burial and notified her attorney and other friends.

Ottilie's attorney reported to Frederick that she had received a diagnosis of incurable breast cancer and had left instructions in her will that Frederick receive all her books and the income from a $20,000 trust fund to be paid semi-annually "for and during the terms of his natural life, in recognition of his noble labors in the antislavery cause." Her will also dictated that her lawyer destroy immediately all letters "found in her possession." He complied, burning every letter Frederick wrote to her since they first met. Why did she make such a request? Was she destroying his and her letters to save their reputations? Or was she destroying them to punish him for abandoning her?

Frederick recalled how Ottilie had told him years ago that she would kill herself "if afflicted with an incurable disease and save herself the pain of a lingering death and her friends the trouble of caring for her." Whatever her reasons for suicide, Ottilie didn't deserve animosity, for she was remarkable, bright, inquisitive, fascinating, frustrating, and talented. Frederick had to admit that he had used her. In his desire to have a mistress, he was willing to hurt Anna and confuse his children, who had to suspect what was going on. And yet they didn't turn against her.

Sadly, she turned against them, for they had become impediments to her dreams of a future with him.

Frederick lay in bed thinking about Ottilie. He was saddened by her suicide, but he was not surprised or devastated. He felt loss but not grief. He felt regret but not anguish. He did not want to spend too much energy untangling the complexities of their relationship. She had been a part of his life for a long time, and yet she remained only a part. He kept her compartmentalized in his mind and heart, and it had worked for him.

But not for her.

★

Grover Cleveland won the presidency, returning the White House to the Democrats for the first time since 1856. He won the election by a narrow margin of under 25,000 votes out of ten million cast. Frederick heard that some southern towns celebrated Cleveland's win with Confederate flags and mock slave auctions and was appalled but not surprised. Some Negro editors and commentators now demanded his immediate resignation as recorder of deeds. If he did not, he was, said one, "a renegade who lives solely for himself and not for the race." Frederick refused to resign, waiting for Cleveland to show his hand. He hoped that whatever happened to him would not affect the welfare of his children, who all now, thanks to him, had federal positions.

Cleveland surprised him. The president allowed Frederick to remain in his job for more than a year after his inauguration, and he also invited Frederick and Helen to several White House receptions. Cleveland wrote some of these invitations in his own hand, attended all receptions Frederick and Helen attended, and always spoke congenially to them.

As a Republican, Frederick disagreed with almost every Cleveland policy, but he credited Cleveland's refusal to snub him and Helen as a "manly defiance" against "malignant and time-honored prejudice." The new president won Frederick's respect and admiration.

Frederick and Helen continued to assert their solidarity. They attended sessions of Congress, their mere presence interrupting the business of the hour, as necks craned to see them and opera glasses suddenly appeared for closer inspection. They sat in front pews of major churches in Washington, outraging some congregants. Helen hosted small and large receptions for invited guests, sometimes over a hundred people, at Cedar Hill. The elite of Black Washington, under the kind but firm encouragement of Reverend Grimke, reopened their doors to Frederick and Helen. They spent many afternoons and evenings drinking tea, reading, discussing books, and attending weddings and birthday parties. Frederick stipulated in his will, drawn up that summer of 1884, that Helen would have sole ownership of Cedar Hill, his papers, and his books.

Life was good, but it was far from perfect.

His place in public life was unsettled. The nation was unmoored, and he could not see clearly what role he could play in it. He was old, and aging diminished the body and the spirit. He needed that fire that forced him to rise, do the impossible, make a difference in the world, even at the age of sixty-seven. His body wanted and needed rest. But surely it had to be the rest before upcoming battle.

Frederick found his way when the president finally asked him to resign as recorder of deeds in March of 1886. Frederick graciously accepted Cleveland's decision and told Helen, "Now, we can plan for Europe, and be gone for months. We will go to England and Ireland, London, Rome, and Paris, especially Paris. I need this trip, dear Helen. Truly, I need this trip."

They scheduled their departure from New York to Liverpool for the morning of September 15 on a 560-foot-long steamer, the *City of Rome.* It was one of the largest and most beautiful ships on the high seas, its rooms meant for wealthy Americans traveling on "the grand tour." On the evening before departure, Doctor Frauenstein came to see them off. He talked about Ottilie, giving Frederick and Helen a few more details about her death and will. But the doctor made clear he did not want to darken the joy of his reunion, and when it was time for him to go, he hugged Frederick, threw his arms around his neck, and kissed him before hugging and kissing Helen, too. He then rushed away.

"He loves you, Frederick," observed Helen.

"He is a good man," Frederick replied, marveling at the friendships he had made through Ottilie.

The *City of Rome* arrived in Liverpool on September 22. Frederick and Helen spent a week there, visiting art galleries, churches, and libraries before going to St. Neots, a small town west of Cambridge, to spend a week with Julia Griffiths Crofts, now a widow. She took them to tea every day at different shops and meeting halls, and they all toured what Helen called "the glories of Cambridge." The highlight was attending Evensong at the stunning King's Chapel, a masterpiece of English Tudor architecture. Despite the exquisite choir music of William Byrd and the word of God, Frederick resisted the sacrifice of self and focused his thoughts on Julia and on what could have been.

He was no longer in love with her, but he was grateful that she had remained his friend these many years, writing letters regularly, sharing his triumphs and his disappointments. Now that they were finally reunited, it seemed that in the passing years distance had meant nothing. Passion was fleeting, but love, the love of true friends, conquered time.

If church was a place for the giving of thanks, he gave thanks for Julia, and for Helen, Ottilie, his mother, his grandmother, his sister Eliza, Lucretia and Sophia Auld, Anna, Rosetta, Abby Foster Kelley, Elizabeth Stanton, Susan B. Anthony, all the remarkable women whose character, temperament, principals, and dreams shaped his remarkable life. He had other influences, from Thomas and Hugh Auld to William Lloyd Garrison, Wendell Phillips, John Brown, Abraham Lincoln, and others. But the women shaped him most of all and helped him rise in the world. And when that world shifted, and his star fell, they were there, in their own unique ways, to lift him up again.

After a long journey through London, Paris, Rome, Florence, Naples, Pompeii, Pisa, Port Said, and Cairo, it was time for Frederick to rise again. He climbed to the pinnacle of the Great Pyramid of Cheops in Egypt on February 22, with Helen there at the base encouraging him.

From a distance, as the ancient structure shimmered in the muted sunlight of morning, the surface of the pyramid appeared like walls fused together into a solid triangle by a miracle of Egyptian engineering. Frederick knew slaves had dragged individual limestone blocks for miles and hoisted them up one by one over many years until the summit was reached. Nonetheless, the size of the individual stones surprised him; three to four feet in thickness and height, they were so huge that an ascent seemed impossible. The top seemed to touch the sky.

Because the 400-foot climb was a popular tourist destination, there were others already on the way up, inspiring excitement and awe in those who waited their turn. Frederick heard the chattered doubt and fear. There were some who decided at the last minute to not make the climb. Young Egyptians, all thin with muscular arms, hoisted men twice their size, but Frederick still worried. At 230 pounds, he knew he would require the assistance of more than one man to lift him. He was sure nothing they could do would mitigate the indignity of a heavy six-foot-two man being pushed and pulled hundreds of feet against and over rough, dusty stones. Frederick didn't have a fear of heights, but he had never been at the summit of anything this high. One misstep could mean death.

He hesitated. His wide, skittering eyes betrayed him. Helen touched his arm lightly. "You can do this. I'm sure of it. Don't worry. They won't drop Frederick Douglass. That would be a national embarrassment."

"How do they know who I am?"

"They know. And to memorialize this moment, before you get dirty, let's have a photograph taken for posterity. Proof that we were here in Egypt. Can you believe it, we are here at the base of the Great Pyramid!"

Arrangements with a photographer were quickly made, and Frederick and Helen stood side to side, holding hands in front of the camera box. After the photograph was taken, Helen whispered, "It's time, Frederick. Tell me what it looks like up there."

Frederick sighed. "Here it goes."

One of four men, speaking excitedly in Arabic first, gave instructions in perfect English. Two would push him up, and two would pull. Frederick had to lift his right leg and then his left over the edge of each stone to the top of it and stay there for a few seconds before repeating the process. He inhaled deeply and tightened his muscles. He could feel the strain throughout his body. He began to sweat.

"Ready, sir," said the main guide, smiling.

"Ready." Frederick took another deep breath and stepped forward. He looked back at Helen, put the tips of his right fingers to his lips and kissed his fingers before blowing them away, a gesture he had never done before with anyone. The guide gestured him toward a stone that wasn't as large as most of the others. Apparently, he wanted Frederick's first step to be successful. "And, remember, don't look down, when you go up or when you return."

Frederick followed his instructions, lifting his legs, pressing his hands, allowing the men to push and pull with each block. He tried to ignore the strain in his legs and arms, but that was impossible, and now and then, he thought, *I can't do this. I can't go on.* But Helen's faith and the promise of a spectacular summit view made him press on. At the halfway point, he almost looked down out of curiosity. But he obeyed his instructor and continued, even though he was sure the next step would be his last, that he would admit defeat and turn around for the descent. As if reading his mind, the guide said, "Take your time, sir."

Frederick reached the summit after about an hour. The view of the world below him made the effort worthwhile. He could see the inexplicable Sphinx, other pyramids, the winding Nile in the Valley, the vast desert, ancient Memphis and Heliopolis, and in the far distance the mosques, minarets, and palaces of a great, teeming city.

Frederick saw the ages and events that swept over the country and the millions who lived, worked, and died there. He saw Egypt and Europe as one land, the Pyramids inextricably linked to the cathedrals of Europe, the Great Pyramid connected to King's Chapel, the pride of rulers and the multitudes who made their power possible. He saw the aspirations of creative artists, and the tenacity and grit of laborers, enslaved and free, building monuments to princes and to themselves.

He saw truths.

From out of Africa came the world.

Its people spread far and wide and, reshaped by geography, climate, politics, and religions, they forgot or no longer believed in a shared identity and history. Philosophers, rulers, and citizens touted immutable racial differences and justified conquest in the name of racial and cultural superiority.

The view from the Great Pyramid verified what Frederick had understood since he was a young man.

The Earth was one world.

Everyone was connected by their common humanity. Frederick Augustus Washington Bailey Douglass was the convergence of two families, one white and one Black, representing the past and the future. He had a responsibility to descend the Great Pyramid as a universal reformer, demanding justice and equality for everyone, Black and white, red and brown, men and women, Christian, Hindu, Muslim, Buddhist, and Jew. He could no longer be Frederick

Douglass, the representative Black man for Black people. He was now Frederick Douglass, the representative for all who wanted and needed a better life and future. He would be a champion for everyone, with justice for all. Frederick Douglass would agitate, agitate, agitate with passion, righteous anger, and love until the end.

He was ready to go, and he was not afraid to look down, for he knew what waited for him there: Helen, his family, and a future bright with the promise of tomorrow and a North Star rising again.

EPILOGUE: 1895

Frederick

HE DIED AT HER feet.

On the morning of February 20, Frederick took a carriage to a meeting of the National Council of Women on Pennsylvania Avenue. He was not scheduled to speak but was escorted to the platform by Susan B. Anthony and introduced to the fifty delegates anyway. Susan and Frederick had reconciled a few years before and now sat next to each other occasionally whispering.

During the day, Frederick frequently rubbed his left hand but did not complain of pain.

He arrived back at Cedar Hill around five o'clock for dinner with Helen, during which he described some of the speakers. Still talking, he rose from table and moved toward the front hallway. Helen thought he was going there to have more room to imitate the speakers and emphasize key points.

In the hallway, Frederick continued talking. He dropped slowly to his knees and fell back, spreading out his legs and arms. He didn't move when Helen called his name, and instinctively she knew he was having a heart attack. She ran to the front door and cried for help just as the carriage approached the front porch to take him to his previously scheduled lecture. The driver rushed off, and soon a doctor arrived. He checked Frederick's pulse and solemnly stated, "He's gone. I'm sorry." Immobilized for a moment, Helen asked the doctor to convey messages to Frederick's family.

His distraught children arrived and assumed responsibility for planning the funeral. Within four days, they arranged for a family service at Cedar Hill, the transportation of an oak casket to the Metropolitan AME Church, and a service of prayer, music, and eulogies.

On the day of the funeral, thousands, Black and white, passed his casket between mid-morning and early afternoon. Outside, there were thousands more waiting and milling about. The service lasted four hours. Flowers were abundant, including a display from the Auld family. Frederick's children and grandchildren sat on one side at the front. Helen sat alone on the other.

In the audience were the leaders of Black Washington and distinguished honorary pall bearers, including former Senator Bruce, the hotel owner W. A. Wormley, and Frederick's old friend Charles Purvis. The chief justice of the Supreme Court also attended. After the service, the casket was carried through Washington's packed streets by twelve uniformed men from the city's "Colored

Letter Carriers." It was accompanied by 150 Black veterans of the Grand Army of the Republic to the train station, where it was bound for Grand Central Station in New York City. The body would lie in state at City Hall for two hours before being transported to Rochester, where many schools were closed on the day of Frederick Douglass's burial, February 27.

Helen, Rosetta, her daughters Harriet and Estelle, Lewis, Charles, and his son Joseph went to Rochester. Nathan did not. Rosetta barely spoke to Helen. There were so many eulogies, so many words in Washington, New York, and Rochester that Helen could barely remember them. But the theme was essentially the same: a great man, who was a former slave, had through his gift of speech conquered slavery and made his country and the world freer and more just.

Two tributes Helen remembered.

One was from an unknown, young professor at Wilberforce College who said Frederick was "a builder of state outside traditional power." W. E. B. Du Bois noted his achievements as U.S. marshal, recorder of deeds, minister to Haiti; his recruitment of Black soldiers; his pursuit of suffrage; and his campaign against lynching with the remarkable Ida B. Wells. Perhaps most importantly, Du Bois said, "Our Douglass stood outside mere race lines upon the broad basis of humanity."

Our Douglass. He belonged to the world.

The other memorable tribute came from Reverend Grimke, who reminisced about a night at Cedar Hill three weeks before Frederick died. He recounted: "Standing in the doorway between the sitting room and the hall with violin in hand, he struck up 'In Thy Cleft, O Rock of Ages,' and sang it through to the very end with a pathos that moved us all. It seemed to take hold of him so. I can almost hear now the deep mellow tones of his voice and feel the solemnity that pervaded the room as he sang the words:

In the sight of Jordan's billow,
Let Thy bosom be my pillow;
Hide me, O Thou rock of Ages,
Safe in Thee.

That voice, that incomparable voice, thought Helen. Remembering that night, Helen committed herself to preserving Cedar Hill as Frederick's legacy, a permanent reminder that a great man, a great American, had given his voice to the welfare and dignity of everyone.

Rosetta and Charles opposed Cedar Hill being made a national monument, wanting it instead as their inheritance to be sold for profit. Their opposition only deepened Helen's resolve, even when they contested Frederick's will in court. Helen was not deterred when she found out that they had moved Anna's body from Washington to Rochester. She won the case and preserved Cedar Hill as Frederick left it, keeping a cup of nasturtiums, his favorite, on the dining room table.

Helen died at Cedar Hill in 1903. Her will ensured that Frederick's furniture, books, favorite portraits, and busts go to a foundation that would eventually donate the house and grounds to the U.S. National Park Service, where thousands now visit every year.

Helen is buried beside Frederick in Rochester, with Anna and Annie on the other side, united in their love of a great, complicated, imperfect, magnificent soul, who stood, as Elizabeth Stanton observed on his death, "like an African prince, mighty in his wrath."

SOURCES AND ACKNOWLEDGMENTS

YEARS AGO, WHEN I was a young man, I read my first book about Frederick Douglass, *There Once Was a Slave: The Heroic Story of Frederick Douglass* by Shirley Graham (1947). The subtitle suggests the book's purpose and tone: tell and celebrate the story of a model for the rest of us. I was impressed by the dramatic details, but the reverence made Frederick Douglass a statue, unbelievable, inhuman, almost ludicrous. A great story had been reduced to hagiography, and a remarkable man reduced to a saint. Dissatisfied and arrogant, I decided I could write a better book.

Years later, I discovered James Baldwin's 1947 review for the *Nation* reprinted in the Library of America's *James Baldwin: Collected Essays* (1998). Entitled "Smaller than Life," his essay clarified my trouble with Graham's portrait of Douglass and reinforced my desire to write a more complex, more nuanced portrayal of him. At only twenty-five, Baldwin astutely observed,

> There is a tradition among emancipated whites and progressive Negroes to the effect that no unpleasant truth concerning Negroes is ever to be told, a tradition as crippling and insidious as that other tradition that Negroes are never to be characterized as anything more than amoral, laughing clowns. Frederick Douglass was first of all a man—honest within the limitations of his character and his time, quite frequently misguided, sometimes pompous, gifted but not always a hero, and no saint at all. Miss Graham in her frenzied efforts to make him (a) a Symbol of Freedom, and (b) an example of what the Negro Race Can Produce, has reduced a significant, passionate human being to the obscene level of a Hollywood caricature.

Baldwin's brilliant and eloquent critique suggests why there are few plays, novels, films, or television series about Douglass. In times demanding certainty, simplicity, and unassailable heroes, Douglass is too complicated, too human. And as a handsome, charismatic Black man who insisted on having relationships with white and Black women, within and outside marriage, he generates confusion, embarrassment, and resentment. But this complexity, and the range of reactions to it throughout his lifetime, inspired me to write a novel about this magnificent, gifted, flawed soul and the people, Black and white, who shaped it. After writing three versions of this book, the first completed in 1978, this "Sources and Acknowledgments" afterword reflects an adult lifetime of reading and research. Here is my own literary autobiography.

Thankfully, Douglass wrote millions of words for books, speeches, essay, and letters. These primary sources are essential, and like all such sources, they give invaluable details of his life and times. But there is so much—his speeches often lasted more than two hours—the selection of what to include was frustrating. He was, as the historian David Blight observed, "a prose poet," and the quality of his writing was so consistently high I wanted to quote far more than space allowed, even in a book as long as this one. What I ultimately included was drawn from Yale University Press's *The Frederick Douglass Papers*, the multivolume collection of Douglass's speeches and letters edited by Johns W. Blassingame and others (1999–2022). The chronology for all Douglass's speeches and the notes explaining the references to people and events in those speeches made this series a crucial source for me.

Writing three books about himself throughout the course of his long adult life, Douglass obviously wanted to control his own story, presenting only what he wanted the public to know about his public and private lives. Most of what we know about him, especially about his life as a slave, comes from these three books. All memory is flawed, incomplete, and often inadequate, and Douglass had no documents when he wrote his first book, *Narrative of the Life of Frederick Douglass, an American Slave* (1845), as a denunciation of slavery. Most historians consider it the best antislavery narrative ever written. It is eloquent, passionate, and gripping, but as in all propaganda, people are stock characters, props in a moral drama of good versus evil. Often assigned in high school and college courses, the *Narrative* can be found in multiple editions. One of the best editions is the Barnes & Noble edition with introduction, annotations, and suggestions for further reading by Dale Edwyna Smith (2012).

The two other autobiographies, *My Bondage and My Freedom* (1855) and *Life and Times of Frederick Douglass* (1882; revised edition, 1892), provide additional details about his enslavement and his public career. All three books can be found in the Library of America's *Frederick Douglass: Autobiographies* (1994), with notes written by the great American scholar Henry Louis Gates, Jr. I consulted this edition constantly, underling and scribbling notes in the margins throughout. The chronology alone is essential.

There are mistakes and glaring omissions in the original texts. When *Young Frederick Douglass: The Maryland Years* by Dickson J. Preston (1980) was published, historians and general readers discovered that there was a wealth of documentation about Frederick, the Baileys, the Aulds, and the Lloyds that Douglass did not and could not have known. *Young Frederick Douglass* is an indispensable and well-written book for which many historians and biographers have expressed their indebtedness. I cannot recommend it highly enough.

About the omissions: Douglass was married for forty-four years to Anna Murray, but in three books she received about three sentences, usually referred to as "my wife" or "the mother of my children." He barely mentioned his children. Julia Griffiths and Ottilie Assing, essential women in his story, received passing notice. His daughter Rosetta's troubled relationship with her husband, and the conflict with her brothers were not mentioned at all.

What was this about? Was he protecting his family from public scrutiny? Or were there other issues, like shame, embarrassment, and disappointment? Thanks to indefatigable researchers, scholars, and critics, we know so much more about Douglass and his family. There are full-length biographies of Douglass's life that have been with me throughout the writing process and have deepened my understanding of Douglass's complex personality: Benjamin Quarles, *Frederick Douglass* (1948); Philip S. Foner, *The Life and Writings of Frederick Douglass*, five volumes (1949–1952); William S. McFeely, *Frederick Douglass* (1991); and David W. Blight, *Frederick Douglass: Prophet of Freedom* (2018).

Biographical studies of other figures in Douglass's life were significant, too. I depended on John Stauffer, *Giants: The Parallel Lives of Frederick Douglass and Abraham Lincoln (2008);* Leigh Fought, *Women in the World of Frederick Douglass* (2017); Maria Diedrich, *Love Across Color Lines: Ottilie Assing and Frederick Douglass* (1999); Henry Mayer, *All on Fire: William Lloyd Garrison and the Abolition of Slavery* (1998); Dorothy Sterling, *Ahead of her Time: Abby Kelley and the Politics of Slavery* (1991); and David S. Reynolds, *John Brown, Abolitionist* (2006). Finally, Maria Chapman has recently received overdue recognition in *The Color of Abolition: How a Printer, a Prophet, and a Contessa Moved a Nation* by Linda Hirshman (2022).

Critical studies of different aspects of Douglass's career were also invaluable. See Waldo E. Martin, Junior, *The Mind of Frederick Douglass* (1984); David W. Blight, *Douglass' Civil War* (1989); Paul and Steven Kendrick, *Douglass and Lincoln* (2008); James A. Collaico, *Frederick Douglass and the Fourth of July* (2006); Robert S. Levine, *Martin Delaney, Frederick Douglass, and the Politics of Representative Identity* (1997) and *The Lives of Frederick Douglass*, a wonderful comparative study of the three autobiographies (2016); and John Muller, *Frederick Douglass in Washington, D.C.* (2012). Two works helped me to understand Douglass' bouts with depression: Andrew Solomon, *The Noonday Demon: An Atlas of Depression* (2001); and William Styron, *Darkness Visible: A Memoir of Madness* (1990).

Everyone interested in Douglass should also explore two unusual but invaluable books: *Picturing Frederick Douglass: An Illustrated Biography of the Nineteenth Century's Most Photographed American* by John Stauffer, Zoe Trodd, and Celeste-Marie Bernier includes a range of photographs, posters, and paintings showing how Douglass thought of himself and how others thought of him. The epilogue by Henry Louis Gates, Jr., and an afterword by Kenneth B. Morris, Jr., a direct descendent of Douglass, were informative and inspiring. We know more about the Douglass family because Walter O. Evans of Savannah, Georgia, spent years collecting Douglass family letters, including letters from Frederick's children and their spouses. Now we have the original letters photographed, reprinted in legible print, and annotated by Celeste-Marie Bernier and Andrew Taylor in *If I Survive: Frederick Douglass and Family in the Walter O. Evans Collection* (2018). I came upon this book, which I was fortunate to have found it at the UCLA research library, late in my writing. It broadened my understanding of the Douglass family and humanized the children in several ways.

The American literature of the periods from antebellum through slavery, the abolitionist movement, the Civil War, Reconstruction, and the presidencies of the second half of the nineteenth century is vast. There is a wealth of material to explore, making research endlessly fascinating and potentially dangerous, with all the rabbit holes in which to get lost. Beware!

But there were standout resources: The Library of Congress, *Born in Slavery: Slave Narratives from the Federal Writers' Project* (1936–1938); Julius Lester, *To Be a Slave* (1968); Kenneth M. Stampp, *The Peculiar Institution: Slavery in the Ante-Bellum South* (1956); Richard C. Wade, *Slavery in the Cities* (1964); Leon F. Litwack, *North of Slavery: The Negro in the Free States, 1790–1860*; George M. Frederickson, *The Black Image in the White Mind: The Debate on Afro-American Character and Destiny, 1817–1914* (1971); Herbert G. Gutman, *The Black Family in Slavery and Freedom, 1750–1925* (1977); Elizabeth Fox-Genovese, *Within the Plantation Household: Black and White Women of the Old South* (1988); Gerda Lerner, *Black Women in White America: A Documentary History* (1972); John W. Blassingame, *The Slave Community: Plantation Life in the Antebellum South* (1972); Ira Berlin, *Slaves Without Masters: The Free Negro in the Antebellum South* (1974); James Oakes, *The Ruling Race: A History of American Slaveholders* (1982); John Stauffer, *The Black Hearts of Men: Radical Abolitionists and the Transformation of Race* (2004); Aileen S. Kraditor, *Means and Ends in American Abolitionism* (1969); Peter F. Walker, *Moral Choices: Memory, Desire and Imagination in Nineteenth-Century American Abolition* (1978); James Oakes, *The Radical and the Republican: Frederick Douglass, Abraham Lincoln, and the Triumph of Antislavery Politics* (2007); James M. McPherson, *Battle Cry of Freedom: The Civil War Era* (2003), the best single-volume history of the period I have ever read, *The Struggle for Equality: Abolitionists and the Negro in the Civil War and Reconstruction* (1964), and *The Negro's Civil War: How American Blacks Felt and Acted During the War for the Union* (2003); Martin B. Duberman, *The Antislavery Vanguard: New Essays on the Abolitionists* (1964); Benjamin Quarles, *The Negro in the Civil War* (1989); Ibram X. Kendi, *Stamped from the Beginning: The Definitive History of Racist Ideas in America* (2016); and Elizabeth Cady Stanton, *Eighty Years and More: Reminiscences, 1815–1897* (Schocken Books,1971 edition). About Stanton herself, a short and incisive work by Vivian Gornick, *The Solitude of Self: Thinking about Elizabeth Cady Stanton* (2005), was invaluable. See also Geoffrey C. Ward and Ken Burns, *Not For Ourselves Alone: the Story of Elizabeth Stanton and Susan B. Anthony* (1999).

About the U.S. presidents, I also consulted, Ronald C. White, *A. Lincoln* (2010); Philip B. Kunhardt, III, Peter W. Kunhardt, and Peter W. Kunhardt, Jr., *Looking for Lincoln: The Making of an American Icon* (2008); Jan Morris, *Lincoln: A Foreigner's Quest* (2000), a short, wonderful work; Robert S. Levine, *The Failed Promise: Reconstruction, Frederick Douglass, and the Impeachment of Andrew Johnson* (2021); Brenda Wineapple, *The Impeachers: The Trial of Andrew Johnson and the Dream of a Just Nation* (2019); Ron Chernow, *Grant* (2018); and Candice Millard, *Destiny of the Republic: A Tale of Madness, Medicine, and the Murder of a President* (2011), a brilliant and moving study of James Garfield and his assassination. I cherish *The Speeches and Writings of Abraham Lincoln: A Library of America Boxed Set*. The two volumes prove that a politician can also be a great writer.

About art, architecture, music, literature, medicine, transportation, fashion, food, entertainment, and other aspects of daily life, there are too many sources to identify here. But there is one standout worth mentioning, a literary masterpiece from Edmund Wilson, *Patriotic Gore: Studies in the Literature of the American Civil War* (1962).

But why a novel? Novelists can imagine conversations, thoughts, and family conflicts, explore and dramatize characters in ways biographers, who must depend on documentation, cannot. Take Anna Murray Douglass as an example. She was illiterate. She wrote no letters, left no diary. But who was Anna Murray Douglass, described by Frederick as the pillar of his life? What did she think about her famous husband? How did she cope with Julia Griffiths and Ottilie Assing? We have a short pamphlet, *Anna Murray Douglass, My mother as I Recall Her* (1903), written by her daughter Rosetta and published only after her parents were both dead, a few references to her in the letters of her children, and little else. The novel gave me the freedom to imagine a complex, multidimensional character. As the German poet Novalis once observed, "Novels arise out of the shortcomings of history." I think Anna is my most successful creation.

But this is my story, not *the* story. This novel reflects my own preferences, biases, and mistakes. And surely there should be more novels, plays, and other works about the man who is often considered one of the two greatest Americans of the nineteenth century—the other being Abraham Lincoln, about whom there is no end to the novels, plays, essays, and biographies written. See the recent *And There Was Light: Abraham Lincoln and the American Struggle* (2022) by Jon Meacham. Hopefully, Frederick Douglass's time has come, and there will be more works in all artistic forms, and more exhibitions about this genius who refused to allow others, including his enslavers, to define him. His is truly an American story.

This novel could not have been written without the support, encouragement, and feedback of several readers: my publisher, Rhonda Hughes; her copyeditor, Scott Parker; my first agent, Kimberley Cameron; my current agent, Steven Scholl of Waterstone Agency; and friends who consented to read part or all of the manuscript in early and later versions: David P. Barker, Cheryl Bracco, Cheryl Ernst, William and Clarissa Garlington, Senta Greene, Joyce Hallgren, Glenn Johnson, David and Teresa Langness, Constance Lue, Masud Olufani, Anita Rice, and Robert Ballenger, to whom this book is dedicated. His annotations, comments, questions, and small essays about the characters, always trenchant and often hilarious, could be a book of its own and serve as a window to the collaborative process. Novels begin with the dreams of the individual novelist; they end as a team project. Although he will disagree, my book is as much his as mine.

I thank my wife of fifty years for patiently listening to all my stories about Frederick Douglass. In private conversations and during conversations with family and friends, Karan has heard so much and listened to so many of the passages I have written that she wonders if she needs to read the final version. I always smile when she talks to others about Douglass and the other people in his world. When I get excited and talk too much and too fast, creating confusion with names and pronouns, she gently interrupts me with clarifying questions for the benefit of my listeners. She has never complained about the many hours I have spent in my office reading and writing, away from her and our children. All writers should have such constancy and support.

However, I must take sole and ultimate responsibility for any errors or mistakes here. I hope I have successfully dramatized a remarkable life. But the judgment of success I leave to my readers.